KANY RISING

To
Mavelle and Mateo
Of Kany Generation

ISBN: 978-1-961677-73-9 (Paperback)
ISBN: 978-1-961677-63-0 (E-book)

Printed in the United States of America

Published by

info@thequippyquill.com
(302) 295-2278

Contents

CHAPTER 1
Kentucky Scientists

Kano Wasiri was shaken, confused, and definitely worried. The deliberating panel, about to grant him his PhD degree in mines engineering, was reaching the final stage of a successful review of his thesis. His mentor, Dr. O'Shea, out of blue and in a voice trembling with outrage chose this ominous moment to berate Dr. Larry McKinley, a panel member.

"There is absolutely nothing that you can say or do today that would change the course of things to come. I am sorry to say this, maybe I should have said this the first time I met you, I stand ready to deflate the bubble you live in, the bubble you have been carrying around here a bit far too long. I can assure you, no matter what you said, no matter how long you said it, the air has already gone from that bubble, and the light that you have missed all along would continue to tower so bright and so high to enlighten the likes of yours for years and years to come."

Under any circumstance, the outrage from Dr. O'Shea was untimely. It was being delivered in the midst of the most solemn review of the lifetime work of his beloved protégé, Kano Wasiri. Dr. O'Shea had suddenly lost his composure when his younger colleague, Dr. Larry McKinley piqued his rage by asking what, in any other instance, amounted to a basic and ordinary question.

The heated exchange taking place in the Conference Room M203 was bewildering to Kano. He had just completed all requirements to receive his PhD in mines engineering with the mention of excellence, the highest grade attained by super achieving doctoral students. The advisory panel and the major professor planning and guiding his dissertation were extremely supportive. They have concurred every step of the way with what they convinced him to be an original contribution to knowledge in the field of mines engineering.

He was then mystified by the strange behavior his mentor, Dr. O'Shea, was displaying during his final PhD dissertation review.

Kano Wasiri had every reason to be worried now after the terrible incident that crashed the entire computer network of the University of Kentucky about a week ago.

He was told that his elaborated research has overextended the capacity and the scope of the recently acquired supercomputer. He was using layered upon layered formulas designed to establish the location of the exotic mineral Alpha-M for his PhD thesis. But the formulas created such an infinite dynamic iteration that the supercomputer was overwhelmed and crashed. Furthermore, the supercomputer crash disabled the entire computer network of the university. In other circumstances, the feat was to be commended and lauded for a doctoral student. Unfortunately, this incident became a major problem for Kano Wasiri, a PhD student guided by the famous iconoclast Professor Anthony O'Shea, a gadfly of sort at the Faculty of Mines Engineering at the University of Kentucky.

For all obvious reasons, Kano Wasiri's mentor, Professor O'Shea, took extreme pride in the computer network crash. This was another way to show his colleagues that his lifetime devotion to the research of exotic minerals was not in vain. As a matter of fact, it was being vindicated in the demonstrated limits of the so-called university supercomputer to process his student's elaborate research computation to establish the location of the exotic mineral. He reassured his student, Kano Wasiri, but showed absolutely no concern or remorse about the university properties. While Kano was being seriously reprimanded about the incident at every level of his research contacts throughout the university, Professor O'Shea endlessly bragged, saying, "How we showed them!" This alarmed him greatly at the moment he was preparing to defend his thesis. Now the heated discussion that was taking place during his final examination for the PhD diploma was not reassuring.

His major professor and mentor, Dr. Anthony O'Shea, had convinced him the day before that this final examination session was going to be, as he put it, a breeze. He said that his dissertation had pushed the bounds of mines engineering scholarship to a level where very few students have dared to go. He added that his defense of the dissertation titled "Alpha-M in Mezi Strata" would land him the highest collation in the Dissertation Approval Form.

Dr. O'Shea arrived to that conclusion based on comments he said he had collected from the original members of the advisory committee, including the dean of the Mines Engineering School of the University of Kentucky.

This did not include the opinion of the outside examiner, Dr. Larry McKinley, appointed in last minute in replacement of an original member who had a mild stroke four days before the dissertation review date. Dr. O'Shea had discounted the input of this young and ambitious professor, his nemesis, at the risk now of jeopardizing his protégé's final examination and all that he had worked for his entire academic life in the promotion of exotic minerals study.

The discussion between the old Dr. O'Shea and the young Dr. McKinley got so heated and degenerated to a point where the dean of the Mines Engineering Faculty had to excuse Kano Wasiri and to clear the Conference Room M203 of everybody but the advisory committee members for private consultations.

Kano Wasiri, completely dejected, was now outside the school building in complete fear of failing his final PhD examination. He was reflecting over the exchange that his mentor and this young professor had a while ago.

This happened at the end of his final examination when Kano was going over the conclusions of his dissertation paper. He mentioned that based on the mathematical equations he had resolved in his paper, Alpha-M, an exotic mineral thought to have been released throughout the universe at the beginning of time, was located and can be extracted from the high plateaus of the province of Tongeo in the Republic of Mezi.

Dr. Larry McKinley leaped at that conclusion and challenged Kano to answer the following questions: "How do you know that the mineral to find in those high plateaus has to be Alpha-M? How can you have such a leap of faith and arrive at such a conclusion? Why not gold, tin, copper, or zinc?" What Kano Wasiri thought to be an ordinary academic challenge, and was ready to address, was taken as a major offense by his mentor. Dr. O'Shea stopped his protégé from answering.

He proceeded to tell the younger professor that he did not appreciate his line of questioning with the extremely biased and loaded mention of "leap of faith."

With deliberated anger and without retinue, Dr, O'Shea told the advisory panel members that the young professor was in fact directing his questions not at the PhD student being examined but to him, the dissertation major professor.

The exchange went nowhere but downhill after Dr. McKinley responded by saying, "Dear colleagues, it is my opinion that this distinguished student, I mean Kano Wasiri, has been forced after a first rate and original research to draw a biased, unscientifically proven conclusion that only and only the exotic mineral Alpha-M must be found in that location. That, I am afraid, is an academic perversion of dissertation guidance, a complete abuse of student profile."

Dr. O'Shea was livid when he heard this. He reminded his colleagues that Dr. McKinley had made similar comments in another meeting that took place two days before concerning other topics of similar interest. He also rehashed a number of instances when he had endured similar insults. The exchange became so acrimonious between the two academics that the dean of the Mines Engineering Faculty had to clear the conference room.

Kano Wasiri was still outside two hours later while private consultations continued in the conference room. In light of Dr. McKinley's comments, he now thought that he should have been a little bit concerned and should have requested more clarifications when his mentor kept saying that his dissertation was pushing the limits of established mines engineering science. He was now slowly resigning to the possibility of a failed PhD examination while admiring the greening of the Kentucky blue grass over the field behind the engineering school in the middle of month of May.

Kano reviewed all he went through in this university through date. It had been a rather pleasant journey, everything considered. He had been a successful student throughout his bachelor's and his master's degrees. He sincerely convinced himself that it should not be difficult to modify that PhD dissertation to address valid objections raised by Dr. McKinley. In fact, he thought that this young professor had revealed himself to be as pleasant as most of the academics he had encountered at the university. Dr. McKinley was never devious or malicious in a way his mentor, Dr. O'Shea, had portrayed him to be during the preceding debate. If anything, Dr. McKinley had always been fair and supportive during few contacts he had with him. He believed that Dr. McKinley was not concerned about the computer network crash. As a matter of fact, he told him sometime later that it was the duty of the university to provide efficient supercomputer for any type of research. He was one of the rare academics who were supportive during the incident period. Kano was now terribly confused by his mentor's behavior. He wondered aloud what could have triggered his mentor's outburst and mostly why now in the middle of his most important time of academic life.

While waiting for the advisory-panel resolution, Kano also thought of the time he spent in the high plateaus of Tongeo in Mezi. It was during a summer vacation before his high school senior year, he was dispatched there to work in a church construction site. He remembered the story he heard from two of older bricklayers. They made mention of the time when people of the area had plenty of food and had a lot of gold, thanks to this rock they called Kany. They said that at a particular time of the year, the rock was broken in small pieces by the area highest priest.

The small pieces were thrown in the fields giving a bountiful harvest and in the rivers for magnificent catch and plenty of fishes. The remaining pieces of the rock were sometimes mixed with gold and that produced a large quantity of gold specs.

Now that he was sitting outside the School of Mines Engineering, Kano was wondering about Alpha-M to be found in the same area according to conclusions in his own thesis. He surmised that the younger professor should not dismiss his conclusions so quickly. He asked himself what if Alpha-M turns out to be the fairy "Kany." As quickly as he thought about it, he dismissed the connection. He reverted back to Dr. McKinley's questions, "How do you know that it must be Alpha-M? Why not gold, tin, copper, or zinc?" He was shaken back to reality when someone tapped him on his shoulder. It was his mentor, Dr. O'Shea.

"I am truly sorry for all that has happened there. This was to be a coronation for all that you have done. But that jerk of so-called professor had to ruin it for all of us. Son, this had nothing to do with you. It is all about me and that very ambitious professor. Your dissertation is fine. It has been approved by the entire panel but that outside examiner. It is all clerical now. The panel has decided to remove that professor as outside examiner. The approval form will be brought to the original outside examiner who fell sick. He should sign it in a day or two, and you would be officially a PhD graduate. I cannot imagine what you are going through, and I am truly sorry for that. The bottom line is that you have passed the final examination. Forget this day. I have told you before, and I should repeat it now. We would see setbacks here and there in this long journey and battle for Alpha-M. Today you have crossed a milestone. I sincerely hope that you are not discouraged and are going to stay the course with us in this long battle all the way to Mezi. As a matter of fact, Emily has prepared a nice dinner for us, and she is waiting for us at home."

"Dr. O'Shea, I really appreciate the invitation, but I have to decline this time. After what has happened today, I have to confess I came out of the conference room a bit shaken, perplexed, and worried.

I believe I need time for myself to think things through, to reflect about where I go from here. Please extend my sincere apologies to Emily. Better yet, I would clear my Saturday evening schedule to come and pay you two a visit. Today is just not possible. I really need a time out."

"I understand, son, but remember, Emily is counting on you and hope to see you on Saturday."

The mentor and the protégé left the School of Mines Engineering, both embittered by what had happened. Kano Wasiri felt completely let down by his mentor interrupting his final examination in an unprofessional manner. Dr. O'Shea was remorse for his uncontrolled temper and almost getting his best student protégé fail his defense of the dissertation they worked on so assiduously.

When he reached home, his wife, Emily, found him even more despondent. Dr. O'Shea looked tired and completely defeated.

"Honey," Dr. O'Shea said to his wife, "We are going to lose him if we don't do something fast. The final examination was almost a disaster because of my stupid temper. I would not give that professor wannabe the pleasure of trashing our master plan, our design. The wannabe insulted me again right there during the review. I couldn't stand his innuendo. Would you believe, he said that I forced our precious Kano to reach a scientifically unproven conclusion? Dr. McKinley became obnoxious because of the dissertation conclusions. He could not believe that all the mathematical equations that Kano performed would lead to finding Alpha-M in the high plateaus of Mezi. The ambitious one said in front of my colleagues that I forced that conclusion. Honey, you cannot imagine how mad and uncontrollable I became. The final examination became a brawl between both of us. The dean had to excuse Kano, and the advisory committee discussed the whole conclusions privately to grant Kano his well-deserved PhD degree after Dr. McKinley was removed as an outside examiner. What got me is that he had no respect for the final examination protocol. He was appointed in the last minute. He had no authority to challenge the findings except to bring to table the opinions of the previous outside examiner. It turned out he did not. His intervention was carried out only and only to upset me, and he succeeded. But Kano did not know this and could not understand why I behaved so badly. He would never forgive me for almost getting him to fail his final examination. He must be thinking that I am crazy or worse. You got to intervene very quickly.

After all, we have invested in our Kano; we just cannot afford to lose him. Remember, we selected him to be the next one. Otherwise, all our work would be in vain."

Emily was shocked to hear what her husband was saying and understood why Kano was not around for the dinner she had prepared the whole afternoon to celebrate his successful final examination. She started sweating bullets at the same time she was trying to calm her husband.

"Nonsense, Anthony, we have not lost our precious Kano. You just leave this to me. We need to give him a few days to come down. Of course, he was disappointed by your outburst. Any student would be if his dissertation advisor overreacts during his final examination. Kano never knew what we went through all these years in the hands of the little ones at the university. They would never match your scholarship. I told you before, and I would repeat it again it has always been jealousy or not being able to operate at the level beyond the primal mines engineering concepts. I also told you not to waste your time with these little ones. Do not feel sorry for what happened today. Not for them. You only defended the master plan. We would have plenty of time to repair it with Kano. He would be back into the fold before long. I would take care of that. But you would need to take time out too. Find yourself a conference to attend, somewhere to unwind before the children come back for their summer vacation. You know how important it has been for all of us that they are not engaged. I don't want them to find you home all remorseful and defeated as you look now."

The day after his final examination, Kano Wasiri started making plans to leave Lexington, Kentucky. He wanted to either go home to Mezi to start his academic career or to gain a college or university teaching position in the United States as long as it was not at the University of Kentucky. His first alternative was not appealing. He had not been in touch with folks back home for some time. He was not eager to start his academic career at the time of entrenched military regime at home. He was not about to play the political games, as he was told, in order to secure an academic position in one of six or seven institutions of higher learning in Mezi. Kano preferred the anonymity of US colleges or universities where he can slowly and surely build a stable academic background. After the sad episode over his dissertation, he was also worried to secure a reliable reference for his placement in addition to his mentor, Dr. O'Shea. He started sending résumés to a few universities.

After eight years of enduring extreme unpredictable Kentucky winters, Kano had a strong preference for the southern states' universities. However, he was seriously handicapped in his job search, when about two weeks after he received his PhD, Dr. Larry McKinley, the nemesis of Dr. O'Shea, the professor removed as his dissertation outside examiner, was appointed dean of the School of Mines Engineering at the University of Kentucky.

He was left with only one effective reference: Dr. O'Shea.

He would not dare request a job reference from Dr. McKinley; he did not know that the professor had a distinct superior opinion of his credentials regardless of his dissertation episode. But he would not dare cross his own mentor. That would be a betrayal of shameful proportion

Kano Wasiri would not entertain. When Mrs. Emily O'Shea bumped by accident into Kano in the largest Lexington supermarket, a week and half after the sad final examination episode, he was absolutely ashamed of himself for not keeping the previous Saturday dinner appointment and for avoiding the couple O'Sheas the following days. Mrs. O'Shea had literally spied on his daily routine to seize the right opportunity to meet him. She took full advantage of his excuse. She extended a personal invitation to Kano to join the O'Sheas two weeks later at their favorite steak house restaurant.

The evening of the dinner appointment, Kano was surprised to notice that Mrs. O'Shea was alone waiting for him. He became concerned about his mentor's whereabouts. Emily reassured him that her husband was perfectly fine. She said that he was abruptly requested to attend a conference in Helsinki, Finland, and was very sorry not to attend this reunion. Emily said that she could not cancel the dinner appointment as she was eager to find out what Kano was up to and, if possible, find ways to help him. She also extended her deep apologies for what went on at the final examination.

She said that she had never seen her husband so contrite for a long time because of his behavior. She also added that she strongly recommended to her husband to go to that conference at Helsinki; however, sudden was the request, only to give him a chance to get out of Lexington and to change a little bit of atmosphere. She was confident that it would help him.

"Kano, now that you have received your PhD degree, what are you planning to do, teach, research, or work and where?" she asked. "Mrs. O'Shea, I intend to teach at some college or university in the United States preferably. Mezi, my country, is out of question at this time for political reasons you should know.

I am not particularly crazy about the military regime in place at this time. It is so retrograde that I would need a week to explain. I have been sending my résumé to a lot of southern states' colleges and universities to be interviewed. I guess it would take some time. Will see how it will go."

"What about academic references, you know Dr. O'Shea would love to provide you a lot of references. Kano, do not hesitate to ask him for these references any time, written or oral. You know that he would do anything to get you hired anywhere you want to go. What about here in Lexington, at the University of Kentucky? Have you thought about it? You had already established extraordinary credentials here. They should count for something. Dr. O'Shea and I would really want you to be around as long and as close as you want. You know that we have virtually adopted you as our son. You are and will remain a son to us, remember that.

By the way, talking about references, I have to warn you that you cannot give the current dean as your reference. He would move on very soon. Dr. O'Shea was informed before his trip that his next boss would be, would you believe this, the same Dr. Larry McKinley. The guy who almost torpedoed your final examination. I don't know what the world is coming to. If the message is to force my husband to leave this university, they could not have made it any plainer. But Dr. O'Shea is no quitter. He would continue his battle no matter who is in place. That is why he needs you around. Two is better than one. Kano, do not worry about Dr. O'Shea. He has been at this for more than thirty years, and this one would not match him. He needs you because he has seen your potential, and he does not think other students or colleagues would ever measure up in the field you two work on. He believes that you two are a superb team in this royal battle."

"Mrs. O'Shea, with all due respects, why is it so important that you have to put an academic research in terms of battle with winners and losers? You know I have been asking myself that question since that afternoon of my final examination. Maybe I am missing something about all the research I have done with Dr. O'Shea. For me, it was simply a matter of establishing and confirming an academic curiosity that Dr. O'Shea has instilled on me in the field of mines engineering. I have never looked at it as a battle plan or anything of that sort. I had a proposition to confirm, I did a research about it, and I confirmed it, period. I was surprised by the level of acrimony that was unleashed in that conference room between Dr. O'Shea and Dr. McKinley around Alpha-M.

Every day I reviewed the scene, I have to tell you, I am at loss why it got so heated. I am here now, Mrs. O'Shea, I am hearing the same level of conflict. Why? Am I missing something?"

"Yes, son, you are missing a great deal, indeed. I pray that I am around long enough to see the day when you would at last realize what Dr. O'Shea is fighting for. It goes back to the essence of being. I was doubtful myself for all the years I have been married to that man. I am now coming around to his way, thank God! You know, pursuing knowledge at the exclusion of everything can be perilous. I have seen my husband in moments of despair and hope. He has managed all these years because he was resolute and resolved in his quest for the truth and for the essence of science. Most scientists abandon the quest because they are exhausted and tired of being insulated, insulted, ridiculed, and humiliated. Dr. O'Shea has reached and tested all these levels. Then you came. You raised the bar and pushed his quest to levels he never thought possible. He was, so to speak, born again in his field, thanks to your contribution. That is why he needs you more than you would ever know."

"I appreciate all that you are saying, but my problem is that I do not have the intensity of your belief. I sincerely wish I had it, but I don't. I don't think we are going to resolve that today. After hearing what you said about references and the new dean, I now have a serious concern. I see that I would have a lot of problems if I want to get a teaching job wherever I want now. I doubt that Dr. McKinley would provide me with an outstanding reference after that episode. What am I going to do now? What am I going to do now?"

"Kano, have faith. Dr. McKinley should be considered as a mere accident in our journey. He would never amount to anything, believe me. We would not need him anyway. Dr. O'Shea has been around much longer than that useless wannabe. He would always carry the way. He would find you your teaching position soon. Have faith!"

Born on October 28, in later part of the sixties, in the mountainous Kiwese, fourth arrondissement of the western province of Nyerengi, Dr. Kano Wasiri was from the cattle raising Bleuh Tribe. A brilliant student from young age, excelling in Mathematics, Philosophy, Latin, and Greek studies, Wasiri was quickly recognized for his academic prowess and was encouraged to pursue college studies at the University of Kentucky at Lexington, Kentucky, where he received his bachelor of Science, master's and PhD in mining engineering studies.

At the age of twenty-seven, Mr. Wasiri completed and presented his PhD dissertation paper about the mining and extraction of Alpha-M, a rare exotic mineral that, although never discovered on earth, was believed to have been formed at the beginning of the universe. Some scientists speculated that Alpha-M was part of the family of the first elements or combinations of elements emanating from the big bang event and were dispersed around the universe. No clear finding or usage of Alpha-M has been noted through ages, but speculations about the mythical aspects of the exotic mineral have run extensively from ancient times to present. Studies around Alpha-M were categorized in mining engineering learned circles as a series of wild speculations leaning toward sheer fantasies. However, the young Wasiri, a curious and enterprising student, encouraged and cheered on by Professor Anthony O'Shea, was tempted and attracted by the challenges. His PhD thesis would answer a series of questions and propositions. What if Alpha-M really existed on earth and much good usage could be made of it? What if, after countless computation and calculation using the most powerful supercomputer the University of Kentucky can afford, Alpha-M could be determined to be in the ancient seismic plateaus of Africa located in the Republic of Mezi? And what if, after extracting it in the mines in Mezi, Aplha-M starts living up to all the properties that were attributed to this mineral and the financial bonanza accrued to the Republic of Mezi? Armed with these inspirations and dreams, Wasiri worked hard and presented his dissertation paper plan to the absolute delight of his adviser, Dr. Anthony O'Shea, professor Emeritus of Mining Engineering Sciences.

Dr. O'Shea was an affable man of humbling disposition, given to exotic researches in mineralogy, reaching sometimes far to areas his peers hardly ventured: Astronomy, Philosophy, Anthropology, etc . . . Where Wasiri sought definite empiric connections, Dr. O'Shea encouraged and pushed for further sheer speculations, at times exhausting the young man's imagination.

Nevertheless, when completed, the Alpha-M dissertation paper was lauded for its outstanding originality and sheer size of mathematic speculation and wizardry on top of crashing the university computer network while testing various research computation assumptions. But at the same time, instead of being widely published or quoted, the paper was quickly discarded, buried, and forgotten by other faculty members to the amazement of Dr. O'Shea and total disbelief and shame of its author, Dr. Wasiri. The old mentor struggled to reassure his defeated young protégé.

After many attempts, Dr. O'Shea finally delivered a prophetic sermon to the young scientist, "Son, you should not worry about the reaction of these faculty members, for they are incapable of raising their level of scientific discourse and understanding yours. Theirs is so backward and elementary, I dare compare them to the faculty members at the end of the nineteenth century. They have reacted to your Alpha-M paper the same way university professors would have reacted to "The Theory of Relativity" paper if Einstein presented it in 1890. You see, everything on this earth has its time and its place. Things do not happen by chance, but by orderly fashion. In 1890, theoretical physics knowledge was not advanced, and Einstein could not have surmounted the level of scientific knowledge reached and in place in 1890. He would have been chased out of any university scientific circle listening to what would have been considered as utterly crazy propositions. Son, you cannot fight over what people do not know at a particular time. The trouble with the progression of knowledge has always been abject ignorance. Remember, my dear son, you are far ahead of your time when it comes to the studies of Alpha-M. Your paper will be sought after worldwide in the near future, and you will get recognition you could not have dreamed of."

Dr. Wasiri nodded politely to the compliment but, deep down, still doubted the wisdom of the old man, given to what he heard his peers often said were lunatic speculations. What if Dr. O'Shea has encouraged a useless study of a never seen mineral?

What if Dr. O'Shea was just as crazy as so many people have pretended, he is? Did he waste my time and energy working on an off-the-wall PhD dissertation paper? How is he going to get a teaching job at any mining engineering school with such a terrible reference? So many doubts nagged Dr. Wasiri. He could not get a good night's sleep worried about his potential and his academic future. One day, after noticing how depressed Dr. Wasiri was becoming and feeling extremely responsible for having guided and cheered him to the advanced research of an exotic mineral, Dr. O'Shea summoned him to his office and gave him a lecture about the long battle he had waged against the same faculty members around exotic minerals and reminded him that his great work, his PhD dissertation, will never go to waste.

He referred him for a teaching appointment to a close friend Dr. Jeremy Winston, dean of Mining Engineering Faculty at Kentucky State University in Frankfort, Kentucky, where Dr. Wasiri settled down teaching minerals extracting engineering courses for the next twenty-three years or so.

During those years, Dr. Wasiri took care to stay away from any reference to his own PhD dissertation or exotic mineral studies. He focused on teaching the basic fundamentals of mining engineering. He also befriended and, six years later, married Miss Dorothy Hasbo Winston, a distant cousin to Dr. Jeremy Winston. Dorothy, as she loved to put it, was from the lower side of the Winston clan. Her father, Mr. Harry Sperling Winston, nicknamed Hasbo, wound up literally drunk in one of Kentucky coal mines towns, worked there, and married a hardscrabble hometown girl named Vivian. They had a beautiful girl named Dorothy and gave her the middle name Hasbo. When Dorothy was five, her father succumbed to his hard drinking ways and died, and soon after, her mother was killed in a car accident. Not willing to raise a young girl in a mining town, a surviving aunt, herself a single mother of three, decided to find Dorothy's father's relatives and shipped her to the Winston Clan of Frankfort, Kentucky, the site of Kentucky State University. Dorothy grew up among countless cousins and managed to go to the state university, graduating with a degree in English Literature. Throughout, Dorothy developed a deep resentment of the Winston Clan and tried desperately to escape the Winston Clan cocoon of Frankfort, Kentucky, in spite of all latitudes extended to her by all members of the clan without exception. In the tall, dark, handsome Dr. Wasiri, Dorothy found the ultimate escape she had longed for all her life. She paraded Dr. Wasiri as if he was the prize none of the Winston Clan will ever take from her. Successively Hasbo bore him two boys and a girl with strange authentic African sounding names of Meno, Belo, and Fazi. In time, Irish-sounding Dorothy Winston name was also dropped, and from then on, she insisted to be referred as Mrs. Hasbo Wasiri, completing her full African authenticity at the Wasiri household. Dr. Wasiri labored in his teaching position and stayed away from any research with Alpha-M connotation. He turned out a few perfunctory research papers in fields of very remote interest to his original thesis. He did all he could in the name of satisfying his tenured professorship requirements. He went about quietly with Hasbo in raising their children in the peaceful university town of Frankfort.

Dr. Wasiri packed his family every two or three years to visit his native country of Mezi. Every time he came back from Mezi, he became less and less resolute to neither go back nor settle down in Mandi, the capital of the Republic of Mezi in spite of pleas from relatives and friends. The overall spectacle of political corruption, military repression, and vast economic and management waste left him shaken to the core, praying to see when the whole cycle of destruction would end.

The rapid succession of military coups, from General Falangi to Colonel Wapiyi to Major General Bomileh to a group of captains to a total civil war, foreign interventions, and then finally UNMEZ for United Nations intervention force in Mezi, all that left Dr. Wasiri dizzy and hopeless for Mezi. It also left him more than ever resolved to look forward to a quiet retirement from a tenured teaching position at Frankfort, Kentucky. In fact, there was a deeper and troubling ambivalence that Dr. Wasiri increasingly felt now about Mezi, and he could not muster enough courage to share it with his wife: the degradation of social values he witnessed not only in the Mezi elite class but also among his own peers and inside his own extended family.

He was certain that he could put up with the country's economic mismanagement that the military dictatorship brought about. He reasoned that it was part of the growing pains of the relatively young nation that Mezi represented. But he could not stomach the collateral social anti values that the mismanagement engendered. The most disgusting was the case of corruption of minors of age, male and female. When the military elite was done with abusing girls of a certain age, they did not hesitate to clamp on the next lower age bracket to a point where it became routine for an old retired general of sixty-five to be surrounded during his nightly escapades with fifteen, fourteen, or twelve-year old girls, while their longtime suffering and abandoned spouses were cavorting with younger male lovers of seventeen- or eighteen-year-olds.

In the same revolting ambiance, when not satisfied to maintain one household, the same elite started the expensive display of maintaining two or three households of equal standing with much younger companions, draining without end the ever-depleted country treasury. Unfortunately, the corrupting practices of the military elite were quickly adapted and practiced by Mezi business and social elites at large. If Dr. Wasiri can close his eyes on the trampling's of the nouveaux riches he did not associate with, he was much revolted by the rites of bowing nowadays. This was another aggravation altogether. Dr. Wasiri had nothing against the rites of bowing. He grew up with these rites when he was young. But the rites of bowing were reserved to honor age and wisdom, and in that specific order. He bowed to the chief of the village, to the elders, to the teachers, and to his parents, of course. He was incensed now to see a complete perversion of the rites when monetary power, military armed power, and various forms of power of corruption became the norms for bowing. Age and wisdom were set aside. Anybody with an iota of power over anybody started demanding to be bowed at.

A child of a military general from his chauffeur, a low-level bank manager from his household nanny, a housewife from her servant, a manager from his subordinates, and so on. Whenever he left Mezi to come back to Kentucky, Dr. Wasiri was relieved to escape from the aggravating spectacle of perverted bowing practiced even in his own extended family.

However, as much as Dr. Wasiri distanced himself from Mezi, Mrs. Hasbo Wasiri couldn't be happier every time the family was in Mezi. She was not fazed by all the political agitations going on around them. Mrs. Wasiri, Hasbo as she was delighted to be called by her in-laws, extended her stay in Mezi sometimes way beyond the three months of summer vacation to learn more about the country and people of Mezi. She immersed herself in the Mezi cultural setting; she learned to speak and write Mambele, the local vernacular language spoken in Mandi, the capital of Mezi, and by more than 45 percent of citizens of the country. She also perfected speaking Swahili, the second official language in Mezi, after the English. Dr. Wasiri had already taken care to teaching and tutoring his wife and children to Swahili at home to prepare them for rare visitors from Mezi when they dropped by in Frankfort, Kentucky. Whenever she had a chance, Hasbo said to her husband that she was much happier only when she was in Mezi. She added that with their three kids soon to be attending US colleges, it would be about time for him to try to take a sabbatical leave and settle in Mandi for a time to see if it was possible to live and settle there. Dr. Wasiri thought that his wife had gone crazy. He asked, "What about the endless coups, the civil war, the many rebel armies all over the place?" Mrs. Hasbo Wasiri was not discouraged.

From bits her husband had shared in the past, she came to learn how important and pivotal Dr. O'Shea had been in his formative academic background in addition to the fight over the Alpha-M paper. She enlisted the support of Dr. O'Shea in her campaign to go back to Mezi. Surprisingly she got more than she bargained for and much more. As usual, under the pretext of visiting his old friend, Dr. Jeremy Winston, at Kentucky State University, Dr. O'Shea came to Frankfort and met with Dr. Wasiri. They reminisced over old time but not a word was said about Apha-M until the day Dr. O'Shea was to leave.

He mentioned it by accident in front of Mrs. Hasbo Wasiri. He said that he was more convinced than ever that Alpha-M can be extracted exactly where Dr. Wasiri had predicted in his paper. He had verified this theory with a lot of scientists from the world over in a recent conference he attended in St. Petersburg, the former Leningrad in Russia.

These scientists, unlike his esteemed peers from the University of Kentucky, never raised a finger or an objection when he surreptitiously presented the finding of Dr. Wasiri's paper. He stunned his protégé by saying that his paper was received with a standing ovation at the end of his presentation. When he came back to the United States, he requested and finalized a well-deserved leave from his thirty-two-year teaching position to dedicate his remaining years studying the intriguing Alpha-M mineral. He had extended his collaboration with the scientists he met in Russia, although he cannot help to find that they all looked alike, a bit weird, almost like robots as he put it, in size, manner, and speech pattern. In passing, Dr. O'Shea joked that maybe these scientists were part of a cloning invention of the old Soviet communist system. He also said that his research was now privately funded by a grant set up by a British mining company controlled by one of those new billionaires in Russia's new capitalism system. His name was Nadov Kiriyan.

He begged Dr. Wasiri to think about pursuing his life dream research, now that people who believe in the Alpha-M study can fund this as his own. This is all that Mrs. Hasbo Wasiri needed to hear to realize her life ambition of completely severing ties from the Winston Clan by relocating to the far away country of Mezi. She grabbed the topic, though with much less understanding and appreciation of the past trial that Dr. Wasiri suffered over his PhD dissertation. Day after day, she drummed it into Dr. Wasiri that he ought to pursue his life dream of extracting Alpha-M in the ancient seismic plateaus located in Mezi. After two weeks of incessant assaults by his wife, Dr. Wasiri relented and confided that he will be making plans to go back to Mezi. But before making the final decision, he needed to have a heart-to-heart chat with his old mentor to go over what he had suddenly shared with him and his wife.

But so many things Dr. O'Shea had referred to remained a vast combination of enigma to Dr. Wasiri. The leave from teaching, the conference trip to St. Petersburg, the contacts with faraway Russian scientists, the research funding from a Russian billionaire, all these stories formed a giant puzzle in Dr. Wasiri's mind and needed to be explained by Dr. O'Shea. However, for Dr. Wasiri, the capitulation to Hasbo's incessant assaults was purely tactical. Deep down, he was not convinced of the merits of going back to Mezi on the grounds of continuing researches around Alpha-M or on the account of good old Dr. O'Shea. He was, as he loved to put it, done with the exotic mineral's studies. If he goes back to Mezi and when he will go back to Mezi, it will be on his own time and for his own purposes.

He decided to let time take care of the latest outburst from Dr. O'Shea. As long as Hasbo does not bring it up, he will take his sweet time before visiting with his mentor to check on his latest fantasies.

Unbeknownst to Dr. Wasiri, Dr. O'Shea had continued a merciless fight with his peers and the faculty administration over the funding over various research projects he championed after the Alpha-M paper episode. The contention over his next project around another exotic mineral element grew far worse than Dr. Wasiri's paper when the dean of Mining Engineering Sciences Faculty, Dr. Larry McKinley, threatened Dr. O'Shea of expulsion from the university after a third peer review of the paper and in the face of vehement and obnoxious defense that Dr. O'Shea had put out. The episode was resolved when out of nowhere a substantial funding from the Advanced Weaponry Research Seventh Directorate of the US Defense Department Intelligence Council quietly supported the paper. As a matter of fact, Dr. O'Shea received a call from a Maj. Gen. Richard "Bull" Fadden describing the strong interest the Defense Department was showing over all projects concerning exotic minerals including Alpha-M.

The general shared the excitement of his directorate over potential applications of such exotic minerals to advance the next generation of thermo-nuclear weapons delivery systems. The general could not be any more specific, only to say that his counterpart in the then Soviet Union showed similar interest. Dr. O'Shea did not share any of this exchange or the dissertation paper funding origin with his PhD student, the future Dr. Wasiri. He only provided sustained encouragement to advance and complete the paper.

When Dr. Wasiri moved to Frankfort, Dr. O'Shea continued championing more projects over exotic minerals to the dismay of his peers and faculty administration. Dr. McKinley did not forget the slap he got over the Alpha-M paper. Dr. John Matteson, president of University of

Kentucky, who allowed the secret funding, in fact, overruled him. Dr. Matteson had extensive contacts in the intelligence community where he worked prior to joining the University of Wisconsin as university dean of the School of Engineering Sciences before being selected as president of the University of Kentucky. After a few inquiries and in order to quiet the loud and acrimonious debates going on in the Faculty of Mining Engineering Sciences, he managed to secure funding for the famous and crazy Dr. O'Shea as his well-placed eyes and ears throughout the university revealed to him. He contacted Maj. Gen. Richard "Bull" Fadden who then called Dr. O'Shea with the good news.

Now Dr. McKinley smelled revenge and took advantage of a research funding budget crunch that affected the whole university to eliminate most funding for exotic minerals projects.

With the collapse of Soviet Union and the abating of the cold war, research funding from Intelligence departments started also to dry out. Dr. O'Shea was at the crossroads. Not able to continue his famed research, and with his wife's deteriorating health greatly affected by a brain's tumor, Dr. O'Shea took a year of sabbatical leave to take care of his dear lifetime partner, Emily Thomas O'Shea. His wife passed away less than three months later and two weeks before the Thanksgiving holiday. She was seventy-two years old, and he was seventy-four years old. Dr. O'Shea and Emily had three children, a son Anthony Jr. and twin daughters Danah and Emma. The birth of the twin daughters was extremely trying for Emily, and Dr. O'Shea speculated that it was the cause and the beginning of the brain tumor. The O'Shea children were well raised and well educated and each with solid academic tenures. Anthony Jr. completed his PhD in Molecular Chemistry and was dean of Faculty of Sciences at the University of Arizona. Danah was Doctor of Medicine, specialist in cardiology at the University Hospitals in Philadelphia. Emma became the first woman president of the University of Manitoba in Canada, after securing a PhD in Operations Research at MIT. The O'Shea children were all married raising kids of their own. In spite of their many preoccupations, the O'Shea kids faithfully managed the yearly trek to the famed Emily's Thanksgiving dinners without exception to the immense delight of Dr. O'Shea and his wife, Emily. And every year, at the end of each one of the famous family dinner, Dr. O'Shea invariably pulled his wife aside, and holding her hands, he said, "Emily, we have done good with the kids. And you have given more than a man can ask, and I pray to God that you will see the next year Thanksgiving gathering and the next year after."

The O'Shea rushed back to Lexington, Kentucky, to join their father for the funeral of their mother. The ceremony was moving and well attended by many people Dr. O'Shea and Emily have touched, including Dr. Wasiri in his only second visit to Lexington since the graduation. Dr. Wasiri paid Mrs. Emily O'Shea a visit during one of her numerous stays at the hospital. The entire personnel from the Faculty of Mining Engineering Sciences were also there, including Dean Dr. Larry McKinley who appeared more remorseful than most, convinced that his last budget actions have precipitated the demise of poor Emily. He extended his condolences to Dr. O'Shea with pleas to come back to continue his exotic minerals research with funds that he will reallocate personally to his cherished projects.

Dr. O'Shea thanked him for the considerations and mentioned that he would think about his offer. However, he was most delighted by the presence of Dr. Wasiri and confessed to him that the main reason he defended his paper so assiduously was for poor Emily. With so many people to greet and thank, Dr. O'Shea could not explain nor elaborate much about what he said.

Dr. Wasiri took his statement to mean that Emily and her husband obviously share in the same regard and consideration for him as they have toward many people of different culture and origin, this attitude being much different than the one shown by the other esteemed peers from the university. Dr. Wasiri resolved then that the O'Sheas were blessed people and thanked God that he has met them. He went back to Frankfort with no chance to talk extensively with the good old professor now surrounded and comforted by the grieving extended family.

The same night, Dr. O'Shea gathered his children and revealed to them that he has done everything in his power to stop and cure their mother's brain tumor through his own exotic minerals research. However, his research was not adequately funded and was abolished at the end. He failed their mother miserably at the end and was begging for forgiveness from them now. The children, Anthony Jr., Danah, and Emma were shaken to the core by what their father was saying and collectively concluded that their father was either severely depressed after the ordeal that their mother went through or he was getting well senile. They rushed to their father to calm him down and forbid him to say any more of the nonsense he was putting out.

"Mother," Anthony Jr. said, in a rising and pleading voice, "had a brain tumor which was being treated as best as medical sciences allow. The tumor had progressed far beyond any cure, and all doctors concurred with this diagnosis. There was nothing, absolutely nothing you, Father, could have done to save our mother. We, O'Shea children, thank God for all you, Mom and Pop, have done for us raising us, educating us, and making certain that we reached all the potential we have today and more. We also thank God to have spared our mother this long to be with us and see the birth of her grandchildren. We appreciated all you have done for our mother, and we would like you, Dad, to be the same you have been and continue the same endeavor you have done for the sake of all of us, your grandkids, and above all, for the sake and memory of your wife, our cherished mom, Emily Thomas O'Shea."

Dr. O'Shea's eyes swelled, tears poured on his cheeks, and he understood the plea from the children to live from then on for the sake and memory of Emily, his wife, and all other Emilys out there who were suffering from all kinds of tumors and are waiting for the fruits of his research over exotic minerals. Dr. O'Shea thanked the children for their support and retired to his bedroom for the night. What he did not share with the children or with Dr. Wasiri was the conversation he had with another gentleman that day at Emily's funerals. The gentleman was of middle age, very well dressed, tall with German or Scandinavian accent, he thought. He has never seen him before, and he approached him in the garden in the back of the house while he was alone, taking a break from friends and family members. The gentleman introduced himself as Dr. Neal Hansberger, a nuclear physicist from the University of Koln in Germany, currently a visiting professor at the University of Minnesota. He said that they met at a conference in Chicago two years before.

He was fascinated by Dr. O'Shea's research presentation about exotic minerals and has been following with strong interest all his publications. He added that they had a mutual acquaintance in Gen. Richard "Bull" Fadden who had also supported some of his own research projects and has been instrumental in funding his current visiting teaching assignment. He said that the general has sent his regards and condolences. He added that he came to pay his respects as soon as he heard the news of the passing of Emily. He said that this was the best way for the community to show its support for all he has done in his scientific works. Looking a bit bewildered by the reference to the word "community," Dr. O'Shea tried to pry the gentleman to elaborate more on what he meant. But Dr. Hansberger closed the exchange by adding in an intriguing way, "The community will stand by you if you continue your work. The community will support you always. The community will be in touch one way or another."

Before going to sleep, Dr. O'Shea reminisced the exchange again and pondered what this Dr. Hansberger was talking about, what in the world he meant by the word "community"?

He reread the business card he had given him and saw in the back an urgent instruction to call as soon as possible a number in New York! Dr. O'Shea shook his head and thought that the Gen. Richard "Bull" Fadden and his intelligence services cohort just have a twisted way to communicate to people. He concluded that if it should take the so-called community to see his research on exotic minerals through, so be it.

Now he could not go to sleep. He started reviewing what has preceded this Dr. Hansberger's visit. He has been suspecting all along that he has been working anyway for the community if there was one. He remembered pointedly the fierce debate around Dr. Wasiri's paper about Alpha-M. He remembered how, out of the blue, he got the support to continue the research when the general called. At that time, he never thought much about how this grant came about. He suspected all along as before that the university suffered his well crazy work over exotic minerals, thanks to some intelligence department's grants. He surmised that only the folks in CIA, Defense Intelligence Directorate, and many other similar institutions appreciate the kind of researches he was doing with pay-off in the far distant future. Now that Emily is gone, why not continue the same research? And maybe, he would finally stumble upon a remarkable application or two from his beloved exotic minerals. At this stage, he was really tired and fell deeply in sleep. He was awakened the next day in midmorning by the sounds of his grandchildren who have accompanied their parents to his wife's funerals.

His daughter, Dr. Danah, was in the adjoining room, monitoring from afar her father sleep. Dr. Danah has been delegated by the family to keep a constant vigil on Dr. O'Shea's physical condition after his very strange utterance the night before at the end of the funerals. When he came out of his room, Dr. O'Shea was fussed over by his daughter Danah, who was in fact checking his vital signs at the same time to the bemused delight of the professor. He jokingly requested that his daughter provided him with his chart showing his heart pulse reading from six to ten o'clock that morning. Dr. O'Shea went on to reassure every member of the family in the house that he was all right and was grateful for their presence at this difficult time. He also added that all were welcome to hang around as long as they wished, not for him but if they choose to do so. He told the family again and again that he has reconciled with the Lord about the departure of his beloved Emily, and he was ready after a few days of rest to dedicate himself to what Emily had wanted him to do, continue his research around exotic minerals. By the end of the second week after the funerals, Dr. O'Shea's house was finally empty of the last family visitor, Emily's sister from Kansas, who stayed much longer to sort out some of her departed sister's affairs. Dr. O'Shea took two weeks of additional vacation before paying a visit to his nemesis, Dean D. Larry McKinley. He came, in fact, to collect on what the then distraught Dr. McKinley promised at the funerals.

Dr. O'Shea took the lighter side of the bargain. He requested that Dr. McKinley provide him with an office with no staff and as small as possible research grants to continue his research on exotic minerals. He also wanted to be as much removed as possible from teaching or PhD Students' advisory functions. Dr. McKinley readily agreed to this deal, sensing that the days of contentious, acrimonious debates over exotic projects with his august peer were over. Dean Dr. McKinley can manage the dwindling days of Dr. O'Shea until his full retirement due in about two years. By giving Dr. O'Shea what he requested, Dean Dr. McKinley can now clear his conscience after the terrible ordeal of the dying wife. Dr. O'Shea resumed his research functions virtually behind closed doors and away from most peers. His contacts with faculty personnel were limited to morning and evening salutations as he took to eating his lunch alone by his office. He spent his time cataloguing all his previous research works, including those he advised for PhD degrees. Dr. Wasiri's paper was also catalogued. This took him over six months. Later on, with the funds from the allocated grant, Dr. O'Shea rented time to use the university new supercomputer to retest data from his previous research works to ascertain their empirical value.

Now he was able to quietly support or discard theses he has supported all his forty-year-plus academic career life. The data retest took another three months. To his amazement, he discarded a significant number of them. However, with outstanding exception, Dr. Wasiri's thesis around Alpha-M not only stood up to the rigor of data retest using the university's powerful supercomputer latest models, but remarkably it pointed to Alpha-M's practical applications in the fields of medicine, energy production, supersonic space rocket design and construction, thermonuclear weaponry, to say the least.

Alone in his recently assigned office, cluttered with hundreds of stacks of the supercomputer paper output, and with tears in his eyes, Dr. O'Shea felt finally vindicated at this time for all he has advocated and defended the past forty or so years of his academic career. At last, he can show to his peers, empirical evidences of the practical applications of one of his cherished exotic minerals. At last, he can celebrate and show to the world that he was not as crazier as he was held to be. But should he, he thought!

His agreement to return to the faculty with Dean Dr. Larry McKinley explicitly forbade him to engage his peers in reviewing his research projects findings. The understanding of the agreement was for him to stay locked in his office, conduct whatever research he wanted alone, while counting his days through retirement, and, at the end, simply fade away.

That much he and Dr. McKinley agreed upon. At the threshold of his extraordinary discovery, Dr. O'Shea resolved to reach out to a world beyond the academic. He thought that maybe it was about time to touch base with the "community" that the German-sounding doctor, what is his name, mentioned at Emily's funerals nine months ago.

At about 1 p.m. Dr. O'Shea quietly closed his office and went home to look for the business card the German professor gave him. He found it and called the New York number he was instructed to call. Expecting to hear another German-sounding person at the other end, Dr. O'Shea was pleasantly surprised to listen to an English lady answer the phone. She introduced herself as Lady Rebecca Allistair, managing director in charge of marketing operations for the US branch of Anglo Minerals Exchange or AM.

CHAPTER 2
The Executives

Lady Allistair, as she preferred to be called, said that she has been expecting Dr. O'Shea's call from some time since Dr. Neal Hansberger made contacts. She was delighted to hear from and talk to Dr. O'Shea. She mentioned that she was very much aware of the great scientific works Dr. O'Shea had done on exotic minerals. She had also followed with great interest his published research papers from her university days at Oxford, where she had accumulated the equivalent of three master's degrees in applied mathematics, astrophysics, and mineralogy. She added that she would be delighted if Dr. O'Shea would accept an invitation, she was extending to him to come to New York City to have an extended review of his current and past research projects. She added that Dr. O'Shea could come under the cover of attending a conference on advanced mineralogy studies taking place in about a month at Yale University in nearby New Haven, Connecticut. Listening to Lady Allistair, Dr. O'Shea did not get around talking about his most recent extraordinary findings. He politely accepted the invitation and enrolled in the conference at Yale University.

During the phone conversation with Dr. O'Shea, Lady Allistair did not elaborate on her background. She did not say she was born Helena Rebecca Mendham, a third-generation Russian émigré in London suburbs. Her great-grandfather, Mr. Vassiliev Mendareko, was an industrialist with extensive business interests, including copper, coal, and gold mines in Siberia mainly around the Lake Baikal before the October 1917 Soviet revolution.

After raising funds for the White Russian Army victory in vain, convinced progressively of its eventual defeat, Mr. Mendareko decided to gather his entire family and emigrated to United Kingdom from Vladivostock with other countless aristocratic Russians. Thanks to the elder Mendareko's prior business connections in London, the adjustment to British life was much less painful for the Mendareko family. And before long, the family integration was decidedly accelerated and completed when the family name Mendareko was shortened to Mendham for the second-generation siblings.

However, to honor the elder Mendareko's memory, the family involvement in mining interests continued and expanded with the fortunes of Mendham Minerals & Associates, a family-controlled firm specializing in and controlling mining joint ventures throughout the world.

Lady Allistair did not also say that after her graduation from both Oxford and London School of Business, and thanks to her family connections, she was able to join Anglo Minerals Exchange, AMX, a much larger conglomerate, also with worldwide mining interests. By that time, Mendham Minerals & Associates has already merged with AMX. The merger gave the Mendham family a substantial but not outright controlling percentage of AMX outstanding shares. Lady Allistair joined AMX first as a mineralogy research assistant in AMX joint ventures with Baikal International in the southern part of Siberia in a town called Amovir. Afterward, she started moving up the corporate ladder with short-term corporate assignments in AMX joint ventures in Indonesia, Bahrain, Peru, and the countries in Southern region of Africa, including South Africa, Botswana, Angola, Mezi, and Congo.

In the meantime, she married a powerful London barrister Sir George Allistair. But the marriage ended in divorce after three years of their separate extended work assignments overseas. The marriage was doomed, with Sir Allistair being constantly gone and engaged in international litigations, corporate mergers, and acquisitions on behalf of an oil international consortium and Lady Allistair involved in international operations for AMX. After the severe financials debacles that AMX suffered in Peru mines during the earthquakes of 1998, Mr. Nadov Kiriyan, the main Russian partner in the joint ventures AMX had in Siberia, agreed to provide financial assistance in exchange for 64 percent equity control of AMX.

Another family member, Mr. Robert Mendham, managing director of Mendham Minerals & Associates with substantial direct connections with and backing from Mr. Kiriyan, was appointed CEO of AMX. She owed her current appointment to that family member, her uncle. Despite all the financial resources that her managing director position in AMX afforded her, life in New York City for Lady Allistair was rather boring, limited to work and much work, with no visible social life short of very discreet and sustained company of few lady friends and preferably Russian émigrés.

This was from the same habits she had gained from her first AMX assignment as research assistant in Siberia. The long winter season of Siberia limited her social involvement outside the scientific compounds of AMX Research Center at Amovir. From the first time Lady Allistair saw Miss Ludmilla Borensky, another research assistant assigned to the same unit, she was smitten. Ludmilla was of an incomparable natural blonde beauty, tall, about six feet, svelte, and well proportioned. When Rebecca was informed that she would be sharing the apartment with Ludmilla at the scientific compound, she was seized with panic to be attracted to a woman for the first time in a life. Ludmilla's appearance was overwhelming for her. She covered her fear of strong attraction by telling Ludmilla that the only reason she would agree to share the apartment was if Ludmilla would help her speak perfect Russian while she would help her speak perfect English. Ludmilla and Rebecca were both fluent in English and Russian. They still agree to the deceptive agreement. The pretension was cast aside that evening when after helping Ludmilla to settle in the large two-bedroom apartment, Rebecca was invited by Ludmilla to share the bath tub and massage her back from the painful move. The sight of nude Ludmilla made Rebecca blush. Instead of massaging Ludmilla's back, Rebecca found herself in the midst of kissing and caressing Ludmilla all over. Ludmilla responded likewise. Both wake up naked the next day morning under the same cover, sharing the same bed in the same room. They looked at each other for a brief moment without saying a word and like other lovers understood what both wanted and passionately kissed each other. This went on for the next two years of Rebecca's assignment, interrupted by short vacation stints back in London, UK.

However, faithfully on weekly basis, Miss Ludmilla Borensky reported the progress of this affair to Miss Nadia Kirilenko, sometimes with delicate nude photos she managed to take of both of them. Miss Nadia Kirilenko, a KGB/FSS relic, served as "eyes and ears" liaison for Mr. Nadov Kiriyan throughout the industrial complex he was building and putting in place in Siberia. Nadia specialized in spying on foreign advisors recruited to work in various joint ventures Mr. Kiriyan has set up. Nadia's assignment was not different from what she did before the collapse of Soviet Union when she spied on foreign politicians, businessmen, or students at Patrice Lumumba University in Moscow. Her specialty was getting these people compromised in sordid sexual misconducts. She supplied them with heavily made up minor girls, twelve to sixteen years old. She knew that in the Soviet Union at that time the penalty for sexual deviations with minors was a minimum of fifteen years of jail without parole.

After calling the police on these poor foreigners and getting them caught in the act, she managed to blackmail them and extract all kinds of information from them for a long time. In some cases, when these students or businessmen returned home in higher business or government positions, the blackmail continued unabated. When her services were no longer required at the end of Soviet Union, Nadia bided her services to the new Russian business elite, just as ruthless as her former KGB/FSS patrons.

Mr. Nadov Kiriyan, with similarly obscure background, recruited Mr. Nadia Kirilenko before he set his sight in building his present empire. To present, nobody through the entire eastern Siberia Region, Lake Baikal Area, or Russia could point to Mr. Nadov Kiriyan's origins, family or otherwise. He seemed as tough as he appeared out of nowhere and got a job as a mining engineer in one of many gold mines in the Krasnoyarsk Krai Region and moved to countless mines around Lake Baikal. But with uncanny accuracy and precision, Mr. Kiriyan impressed mines administrators with his ability to precisely pinpoint the next gold, diamond, copper, platinum, or uranium finding location. Slowly and surely, he started moving up the echelons of mines Soviet administration in the resources rich East Siberia economic region. At the time of Soviet Union collapse, Mr. Kiriyan has been assuming the much-coveted position of Director of Fourth Mining Region of USSR for a period of twenty years.

The fourth region comprised of all state mines and oil explorations in the East Siberia economic region, including areas around the Lake Baikal. The East Siberia economic region included the following republics, oblasts, and krais: Irkutsk, Chita Oblasts, Tyva, Khakasia, Agin-Buryat Autonomous Okrug, Taymyr, Evenkia, Krasnoyarsk Krai, and the Ust-Ordynsky Autonomous Oblast.

Mr. Kiriyan has management authority over the extraction and sale of copper, gold, zinc, oil, diamonds, uranium, coal, iron, manganese, graphite, antimony, and gas products from the region. He also managed to place people answering only to him in strategic key positions in mines management and the Fourth Region administration. Mr. Kiriyan's people or K people, as they started to be known and called, were strangely alike in size, demeanor, and appearance, as if they were born of the same mother and father. With these people's connivance Mr. Kiriyan decided to build a whole new city that he named Amovir on the isolated northeastern region of the Lake Baikal, in the current Russian Republic of Buryatia.

Amovir was to serve as the main headquarter for the Fourth Region Directorate and a mining scientific center far from the political control of any one of the state governors or military commanders based around the lake or the East-Siberia economic region. With revenues from various mines, Amovir was built as a huge city for about fifteen thousand employees and scientists, with its four own modern brands of well-stocked supermarkets, a modern theater center sitting two thousand, a huge campus, like with 120 ultramodern buildings for management offices and scientific research, beautiful high-rise apartment buildings around the campus, twenty dachas for executive officers on the outskirt of the city, and a forty-acre villa on the lake for himself, the director of the

Fourth Region Directorate. Amovir was also dotted with well-paved three-lane streets and underground railways connecting basically all Amovir buildings with the exception of the dachas and the main villa. A new port on the lake and a new airport completed the access to Amovir from the outside world.

At the same time, Mr. Kiriyan saw to it that no highways or railways were built to reach the isolated Amovir City. In one form or another, the Fourth Directorate employed the entire population. Amovir did not welcome tourists or wandering vagrants. Only visiting scientists or security-cleared officials and foreign business people were accepted in Amovir. An internal security police force of about five hundred agents sponsored by the Fourth Directorate maintained the peace and secured Amovir from the outside world. The planning and building of the new city were completed about six years before the collapse of Soviet Union. Mr. Nadov Kiriyan's ability to accomplish and pull such a feat earned him the fear, the respect, and the adoration of many, including local Communist Party members in the East Siberia economic region who searched in vain to find out which ones of the powerful Kremlin Politburo members were protecting him and giving him, a mere mining engineer general manager, so much latitude to literally build his own empire above all political control.

The party members were just amazed to find out that, now and then, the secretary of the Communist Party of USSR himself will spend a day or two at the villa that Mr. Kiriyan has built for high-level guest in the mountain surrounding Amovir. The high-level guest will depart as quickly as he came. All of them, Breshnev, Andropov, and Gorbachev paid Mr. Nadov Kiriyan a weekend visit. Strangely enough, Kiriyan never left Amovir to go to Moscow or any other center of power. He was at his villa almost every day of the year.

Instead, he maintained an invisible link all the way to Kremlin through an array of spies and other officials he has managed to place throughout the years and thanks to the Fourth Directorate financial resources in key strategic positions in the Soviet political, military, and security apparatus. He was all ears and eyes throughout the seats of power as he dispatched his people and emissaries all over USSR and the world. It became a matter of consistent debate and gossiping to find out what bribe or scandal stories, if any, comrade Kiriyan kept on each of the successive masters of Kremlin and the overall leadership politic of USSR for years to afford complete freedom of action in the management of the Fourth Region Mining Directorate. To each inquiry about his high standing with the country political leadership, Mr. Kiriyan always responded that his consistent and uncanny ability to pinpoint with precision the next extraction location for gold, diamond, uranium, gas, oil, and other mineral resources has earned him the respect and utmost confidence of the leadership. Mr. Kiriyan claimed to know mineral deposits in the East Siberia economic region and around the Lake Baikal like the back of his hands.

What he did not share was that he had maintained continued super-secret conversations with the political leadership of the Soviet Union always and only at the Communist Party secretary general level. During these conversations and representations, he confided that he was on track to discover the most potent mineral deposits around the Lake Baikal. The decisive argument in swaying successive secretary generals to embrace and bless his full control management of the Fourth Mining Region Directorate always came when Mr. Kiriyan mentioned, in almost inaudible and monotonous terms, that these minerals will at last provide, for the first time in human history, for concrete verification and manipulation of the unified field theory without the help of expansive machines currently used all over the world in the best advanced research academies. He showed to them small samples of the exotic minerals during those impromptu weekend visits at Amovir. He invariably convinced them that these minerals with extraordinary qualities, when mined in industrial quantities would make USSR a military superpower with no match in the world. These minerals will provide USSR, according to Mr. Kiriyan, with unprecedented economic growth, with extraordinary regenerative applications in agricultural, manufacturing, thermonuclear energy and weaponry, and medical fields. Mr. Kiriyan was able to maintain and guard an extreme oath of secrecy around these minerals at the highest echelon of country's political leadership and security. This enabled him to operate as freely as he did year in year out as the general manager of the Four Region Mining Directorate.

In one interview released in Pravda in March 1977, when stories about multiple UFO sightings over Lake Baikal became the most intense and loudest, Mr. Kiriyan jokingly said his success in finding mineral deposits was due to reports that extraterrestrial people have provided him during those UFO events. Quite a few people believed the story and started attributing superior Kiriyan's fortunes to extraterrestrial contacts and without proof.

This view was consolidated by what happened during the confusing times following the end of the Soviet Union. As soon as Boris Yeltsin proclaimed the new republic of Russia, Kiriyan could not wait for the promulgation of the new laws around property ownership or the ownership of various means of production in the new republic. Instead, he called for the board meeting of the Fourth Region Mining Directorate, read new bylaws for the enterprise, and renamed it Baikal Industries or BI. He spent the next few days with his handpicked board, poring over the list of the Fourth Directorate assets and picked the best managed mines and gas and oil exploration sites to become part of the new enterprise. Per the new bylaws, Kiriyan carefully took control of about 85 percent of BI equity with the remaining fifteen divided among his executive officers and a retirement home foundation for BI employees in Irkutst. The same day, to the amazement of the new masters of Kremlin and the new inner circle of Russia power, Kiriyan issued a worldwide press release announcing the birth of BI. Not a word of complaint or objection came out of Kremlin. And overnight, Mr. Nadov Kiriyan became a multibillionaire in control of close to a twenty-billion-dollar industry consortium. At the same time, Amovir's airport traffic became very busy with correspondences from all the main financial centers of the world. In search of lucrative contracts with BI executive, jet planes started touching down from New York, London, Paris, Munich, Berlin, Hong Kong, Shanghai, Tokyo, etc. Modern management consultants descended on Amovir to train people on the intricacies of every aspect of modern corporations. In less than two years, BI became an uncontested stellar corporation in Russia and started matching in style and outstanding performance the best of corporations in Tokyo, London, Paris, Munich, and New York stock exchanges. Before long, BI started joint ventures with companies abroad, including the British company Mendham Minerals & Associates, whose Russian background did not escape Mr. Nadov Kiriyan. When approaching Mr. Robert Mendham, managing director of the family-owned firm, Mr. Kiriyan won him over with stories of the elder Mendareko and the still legally valid substantial shares of the now BI Company.

Mr. Kiriyan said that BI as an enterprise was actually started by the old man per documents in his possession dating back to 1908. Mr. Kiriyan said that all along, he has been putting in place the elder Mendareko's dream of owning a mining consortium around the Lake Baikal. The old man, he said, was ahead of his time.

Unfortunately, the October Revolution of 1917 cut short his dream. Then came the exile to London and the nationalization of the family business for the next seventy years or so and the building of the Fourth Mining Region Directorate. But at the end, Kiriyan was most proud to see that the Mendham/Mendareko family has continued abroad in England, the elder's dream establishing a strong foothold in minerals industry with Mendham Minerals & Associates. Mr. Kiriyan put out the bait to Robert Mendham by stating that if the joint ventures and other business alliances between BI and Mendham Minerals & Associates evolved to mutual substantial benefits, he can see the day when the Mendham/Mendareko family can reclaim their rightful control of BI in

Russia. After this conversation, Mr. Robert Mendham multiplied and deepened the family owned company relationships with BI. In addition, he provided Mr. Kiriyan with an effective entry into London business elite and all over Europe business centers. That was a step Mr. Kiriyan needed to open contacts into the mega business centers of the United States.

Shortly later, Mr. Robert Mendham artfully negotiated the joint ventures between AMX and BI. At the same time, he convinced his niece, Rebecca Mendham, armed with multiple advanced degrees from Oxford University, to take a research assistant position with the joint venture's operations at Amovir. This was to provide him with an on-site view of BI operations. Later, Mr. Robert Mendham negotiated the takeover of AMX by BI, resulting in his appointment by Kiriyan as the new CEO of AMX. Robert saw this as the gradual fulfillment of his family ambition of regaining the rightful control of his grandfather's dream company. At the same time, Mr. Kiriyan talked him into promoting Rebecca Mendham, now Lady Allistair, as managing director in charge of marketing operations for AMX-US branch in New York City. It was in that capacity that Rebecca was to touch base with Dr. O'Shea regarding the advanced research projects around exotic minerals.

CHAPTER 3
First City Meeting

The nature and essence of all these transactions completely escaped Dr. O'Shea when he decided to come to New York City to review the progress of his research projects with Lay Allistair. Dr. O'Shea was still thinking that he was indirectly being financed by the US intelligence "community" as Dr. Neal Hansberger has put it during Emily's funerals. Dr. Hansberger has mentioned Gen. Richard "Bull" Fadden by name for God's sake. And the general was, for all he knows, still in the intelligence services. Dr. O'Shea did not realize that the general has since retired from military services when Intelligence Services budget was drastically reduced throughout the government after the Soviet Union collapse. The general has also found a well-paid seven-figure consultant job in Washington, DC, lobbying in support of minerals exploration worldwide. That lobby was almost entirely funded by a mining consortium representing, among others, AMX. As far as Dr. O'Shea was concerned, he was about to share his research projects reports with US Intelligence folks, including this Lady Allistair with British-sounding accent. Dr. O'Shea's arrival into New York City was a nonevent except for the limousine ride provided to him from Kennedy Airport and the sumptuous suite at the Hilton Hotel in Manhattan, all paid for by AMX corporation! Dr. O'Shea, a very modest man, was a bit unease during the ride to Manhattan from the airport. He was reflecting over the turn of events which have occurred during the past year, first the passing of Emily, followed by the Alpha-M data retest results, and now the limousine ride. This was a bit too much for about-to-retire professor from the University of Kentucky. He was then startled by the limousine driver, he could not see, asking him through the limousine intercom to pick the telephone next to the limousine bar. The telephone has been ringing for the past two minutes, and from what the driver can tell, the call was from Lady Allistair herself. She greeted the professor by welcoming him in New York City and looking forward to a productive meeting the next day around six in the evening. The appointment was scheduled so late in the day to allow him to attend the Yale University conference on minerals during the day and come back to Manhattan. She hoped he would enjoy his stay at the Hilton Hotel. And the limousine would be available for any ride anytime during his stay in the area.

Lady Allistair congratulated herself in taking good care of the professor in style in Manhattan. She was now accustomed in providing similar hospitality to the bigwigs she deals with in other business matters.

However, Dr. O'Shea protested the exorbitant treatment he was costing the intelligence community for a short stay in New York area. He could have provided the same presentation by phone from Lexington, Kentucky. He said that he came to New York City for the sake of keeping his latest findings secret and sharing them in strict confidence. He could not possibly go along with so much luxury spent for a trifle stay. On the other end of the line, Lady Allistair could not believe what she was hearing. She has used her own company expenses account to spoil the ungrateful professor, and this is how she was being thanked for. But she resolved to remain calm for the sake of Uncle Robert Mendham and Uncle Kiri, as Nadov Kiriyan has become to be known around in the Mendham family. She remained calm in order to find out why and where there was a misunderstanding. She proceeded to calm Dr. O'Shea down but still remained puzzled why he was making references to the intelligence community. She went along with this intelligence community line by stressing that all the spending for his stay was intended to thank him for his lifetime commitment to the research on exotic minerals. She wished him good night and hoped to see him in better spirits the next day. From her contacts from Amovir, she has heard that she needed to treat the good professor with the utmost courtesy and care and, above all, to convince him to attend an upcoming international conference in Amovir in about two months, in the month of July. Dr. O'Shea needed also to be convinced to make a presentation of his research projects findings over exotic minerals at the same conference. The professor is becoming a tall order of challenge she was not used to handle. She was instructed to treat the professor during his New York visit as if he was more than the precious diamond carats that adorned the expensive gold ring and gold necklace that she was wearing on her way to a dinner party at the Park Avenue duplex residence of an AMX wealthy customer.

Sir Allistair gave these pieces of jewelry to her on their second wedding anniversary when for all practical purposes, their matrimonial union was barely holding before the final split. She loved to wear them whenever she wanted to show off her British upper gentry's style in middle of what she always considered American Park Avenue nouveau riches. The jewelry was also a weapon to scare off any potential male suitor who might think of making passes at her. The jewelry was a statement of how much this male suitor will need to spend to match such an expensive piece.

That strategy worked most of the times as she always managed to return alone to her large Fifth Avenue apartment, not far from Washington Square. She always managed to return alone to the comfort of naked Ludmilla Borensky look alike waiting for her in her oversized king bed.

The following day, Dr. O'Shea went to Yale University to attend the conference on advanced mineralogy studies. After reviewing the list of guest speakers and the topics of workshops, he was disappointed beyond despair. He could not recognize any of the prominent researchers he used to meet at such conferences. In addition, the quality and depth of workshops left a lot to be desired and were, in his view, mediocre. By lunchtime, he decided to leave and was on his way back to Manhattan to wait for the six o'clock appointment with the British lady. He debated whether it was appropriate for him to start sharing with her his most recent findings about Dr. Wasiri's paper. He had the impression that Lady Allistair would not be able to appreciate the importance of these findings anyway. He resolved to keep his presentation as general as possible.

He also decided that the first person to hear about his most recent findings should be nobody else but the main author of the paper, Dr. Wasiri. But he knew that Dr. Wasiri has left Lexington, Kentucky, with the bitter memory of the fierce debates that Dr. O'Shea waged for his paper. He was convinced that Dr. Wasiri was more than happy to forget about his own paper and started anew wherever he went to teach. He came to the same realization every time they met, including their last exchange during the funerals of his beloved Emily. He started going over what has happened at Emily's funerals. Dr. O'Shea thought, "I was not even able to hold him to stay for one day after the burial. Dr. Wasiri left without saying good-bye. Or did he? It is true that the house was crowded with the whole assembled family from Emily's and his side. Maybe Dr. Wasiri did not feel at ease hanging around me. He came from Frankfort, paid his respect to Emily's passing, and that was generous of him. He did not come to talk about a paper. He never mentioned it for their friendship's sake since he left Lexington. It was up to me now to bring Dr. Wasiri the good news of definite verification of Alpha-M practical applications specifically the regenerative processes that Alpha-M has shown to provide when combined with any other element known on earth. The good news for Dr. Wasiri will have to wait for the right time. But when will the right time come? I am now seventy-four and not getting younger. In fact, Emily might call me 'home' anytime the way I have seen it happen many times in my dreams lately."

Prior to the much-awaited appointment with Dr. O'Shea, Lady Allistair made inquiries first with her contacts in Amovir, then with Dr. Neal Hansberger, still acting as visiting professor at the University of Minnesota. Lady Allistair wanted to know and get clarification about what the professor was alluding to when he talked about the "community," the intelligence "community" to be precise. Dr. Hansberger told her that she needed to keep the same appearances that he has entertained with the professor at his wife Emily's funerals. That is, let the good professor continue to think that his research projects were continued to be funded by US intelligence "community." Dropping the name of Gen. Richard "Bull" Fadden as a general reference now and then will reinforce this. The professor does not know and has not met the general but by reference. He was and is only glad to have the "community" pickup his research tabs. Dr. Hansberger also informed Lady Allistair that, by the way, the General Fadden is currently working as a paid lobbyist for AMX interests in Washington, DC. But that needs not to be shared with the professor anyway.

Lady Allistair greeted Dr. O'Shea at her spacious Park Avenue thirty-second floor window office of managing director—marketing operations. Dr. O'Shea was much impressed by the welcoming solicitations extended by this stunning beautiful woman he talked to on phone before. He was struck by her apparent young age and wondered at the selection process the intelligence community had to go through to get such a charming British lady subject. Lady Allistair did not waste time and jumped in requesting a summary of his research projects. Dr. O'Shea gave her a folder of about twenty-five pages. This folder contains various most important research projects he has led for the past forty years, including PhD dissertations he has advised on. He has categorized them by order of practical impact. He has deceptively ranked Alpha-M research project by Dr. Wasiri as seventeenth. As he went over the entire twenty-five-page summary, he was impressed by the inquiries, questions, and comments that Lady Allistair made. She was very much on top of the mineralogy field. Most interestingly, she could easily connect the practical applications of various so-called exotic minerals that Dr. O'Shea was talking about. The open-ended presentation that started at six o'clock went on for four hours without interruption. Dr. O'Shea was elated by the interest and depth of knowledge that Lady Allistair has shown. For a moment, he was back at his most prized element when he used to lead animated debates around advanced mineralogy studies with PhD students he was advising. He was so happy that he invited Lady Allistair to a late dinner in an expensive Manhattan French restaurant to continue the animated conversation. She reluctantly accepted.

Before the meal was served, Dr. O'Shea apologized profusely about his intemperate remarks the day before about the exorbitant cost of his stay in Manhattan. He said, aided by the expensive aged Scotch that he has ordered and they were sharing, that, after all, he could see now that the spending for his stay in New York City was appropriate, especially now that they had the lively exchange. During the meal, Lady Allistair expertly raised the issue for the professor to attend a conference on advanced mineralogy studies scheduled in two months the coming July at Amovir in Russia.

She impressed upon him. This will almost be an all-expense-paid trip to a premier site of advanced mineralogy research in the former Soviet Union. The professor needs to bear witness, for himself, of what advances have been made in his cherished field in Russia since the collapse of Soviet Union. True, the research spending in the United States and other Western countries has declined significantly since the end of Cold War. But the intelligence community is not definitively sure if it has been the same in the new Russia despite the many problems and issues besetting the new republic. The "community" was not confidant, nor satisfied, that the new Russia has definitely abandoned his quest for super power hegemony through the acquisition of extraordinary means of destruction, including advanced applications of super exotic minerals. That is why it was important for the professor, after attending a high-level conference meeting such as this one at Amovir and through an exchange of prior and current research projects, to make an evaluation of where the new Russia republic was at as far advanced mineralogy research was concerned. The third millennium super power hegemony will fall on that nation which will master advanced applications of super exotic minerals.

Listening attentively to Lady Allistair, Dr. O'Shea remained quiet for a long time, reflecting. He was beyond amazement that the intelligence community has reached the same conclusions he has reached thirty-seven years ago when he dedicated himself to the research of exotic minerals about the same time Emily, his wife, had painfully bore the twin daughters and suffered intermittent migraines for a long time. Although different, he thought the conclusions reached by the intelligence community were pointing to the same direction as his. He could not care much about military hegemony and all that super-power nonsense.

As far as he was concerned, the advances in practical applications from exotic minerals will bring about untold miracles in medicine, agriculture, manufacturing, energy, etc . . . These advances will push what is known as civilization today at a much higher level, bringing about many cures to countless problems plaguing the world all over and probably stopping the endless crazy search for the so-called super-power hegemony among nations. The reason was that with so much progress being made resolving mankind problems, thanks to the exotic minerals, no time would be spent in searching to achieve super-power military hegemony. So thought the good old Dr. O'Shea! He said to Lady Allistair, after deep reflection, he will attend the conference only if he was reassured that he will not be treated like a spy while he is at Amovir. He wanted to have a complete freedom of movement while there if that could be arranged. At that point, Lady Allistair told him that things have changed and are not the same in Russia as in the time of Soviet Union. There were no longer KGB/FSS agents crawling all over the country and following foreigners around. The main problems at present were crime and a lot of civil insecurity occasioned by the so-called Russian Mafia or underworld. This was typically more of an urban problem in places like Moscow and other big cities of Russia. Again, if the professor goes, he will be far far away from these crime-infested urban centers. Amovir is a well-managed, secured, and protected research center. Lady Allistair went on to reveal to him that she has spent two years at Amovir, after Oxford graduation, as research assistant. She knew exactly what she was talking about Amovir, skipping unnecessary details about her liaisons with Ludmilla Borensky. She described Amovir as an isolated and self-contained city of about sixteen thousand people. She assured Dr. O'Shea that his trip to Amovir, if he decided to go, would be memorable. Dr. O'Shea accepted the invitation and went back to Lexington the next day.

CHAPTER 4
His Honorable Jeremy Massay

The contact with Dr. O'Shea was one of the most important assignments Lady Allistair was entrusted to carry very confidentially by Uncle Kiri in the United States. Another one consisted of identifying a prominent African American to head a nonprofit organization that Mr. Nadov Kiriyan wanted to establish in the United States, preferably and obviously from the African American elite, to support aggressively the economic development of the new independent countries in Africa, specifically those countries with substantial mineral deposits. She has lined up a few candidates that she had interviewed surreptitiously during countless conferences she has attended relative to African economic development. The most impressive candidate was Jeremy Owen Massay, state senator in Georgia for more than six years, representing a county in the eastern coastal region of Georgia. She met the State Senator Massay for the first time at Athens, the site of the University of Georgia, and where a weeklong conference was held about how Sub-Sahara African countries could meet the mounting debt incurred as a result of increasing oil prices. The secretary general of the UN called this meeting urgently. In addition to African government delegates, delegates from UN, IMF, World Bank, and US government's various development agencies, Economic Development professors from prominent universities, private industry specialists, such as Lady Allistair and legislators came to the conference. She was most impressed by Mr. Massay's presentation, where he urged the African government delegates to improve their economic bargaining and purchasing power by setting up an alliance of African buyer countries in order to meet multiple oil points of sale. Mr. Massay, in a passionate eloquence and flourish, urged the African delegates to unite their voices in every economic forum in order to maximize their economic bargaining clout. Although, at time demagogic and, at other time, very pragmatic and sincere, Mr. Massay's thesis could not be dismissed lightly. As a matter of fact, the African government delegates adopted his proposition as one of their no-so-distant goals. That evening, Lady Allistair mustered every ounce of her abilities in order to talk to Mr. Massay. She went further in insisting on a private meeting with the state senator before he was to leave for Atlanta, Georgia, where the Georgia State Senate was in plenary session. Mr. Massay was a bit taken aback by the aggressive stance of Lady Allistair.

He thought of a trap another African American state senator, Willy Ogden III, fell for two years ago in similar circumstances and had to resign his seat after being caught in compromising positions with two white minor girls who have seduced him into joining them for a long weekend of sexual escapade at a remote retreat of expansive bungalows no far from the Shawnee State Park Reserve. His future as a rising political star in Georgia Democratic Party was squashed, and he was never to be heard of again. He was obviously even more vulnerable now, going through a painful separation from his wife of twenty years, separation formulated by what he came to know as Vanessa's rules. He could not figure out what this strikingly beautiful white woman wanted from him or had in store for him. He was skeptical of the requested private meeting beyond reproach but needed to keep the appearances and be polite. He suggested to Lady Allistair that he was urgently due back to Atlanta that night, and an appropriate meeting could and should be arranged for her in the future if she called his state senator office the next day. He handed her his state senator card and left for Atlanta. Lady Allistair accepted the offer and apologized for her aggressive posture as she realized the level of faux pas she had committed. She noted that she needed to pay the state senator a business visit as soon as possible.

Jeremy Owen Massay was born on the island of Sapelo in the coastal eastern region of Georgia. Sapelo is one of the sea islands that extend from the coast of South Carolina to the northern coastal region of Georgia. What was remarkable about these islands was the strong presence and imprint of the Gullah or Geechee culture and population living in the region. Gullah or Geechee identifies both the African American natives of sea islands and the language they speak, a Creole mix of African dialects and nineteenth-century Elizabethan English. These African Americans are direct descendant of former slaves generally from West-African countries of Sierra Leone and Ghana. Gullah people have lived in those islands, and their unique culture has remained largely intact. Their ancestors were picked for their knowledge of rice cultivation. They came with their own traditions, skills, and beliefs that they were able to maintain to date. The isolation of living on the islands made this possible. At a very young age of five, Jeremy Owen Massay was brought to his grandmother in Savannah, the next biggest town in the area. First, he lost his father, Blackbird Otis Massay, when he was one year old. His father, a fisherman, did not survive when the fishing boat where he worked capsized against a 130-mile wind from an approaching hurricane along the Cumberland Island. Four years later, his mother, Mrs. Maxine Massay, more and more despondent over the loss of her husband, started to show signs of acute mental illness and was committed to a home of invalids. Jeremy was the only and firstborn. Grandma, Odella Massay, living alone in Savannah took in her grandson. Grandma Odella worked as a nursing assistant at a Catholic nursing home and was nearing her retirement.

In the meantime, and by habit of being daily next to Catholic nuns and priests, Grandma Odella converted to the Catholic Church and became a devout servant, never missing her daily mass. When Jeremy Owen Massay joined his grandmother's household, the Roman Catholic religion became the norm. Grandma Odella routinely woke young Jeremy at five in morning to say the rosary before she attended her daily mass at the nursing home chapel. Sunday masses were attended at St. Mary of Perpetual Salvation Church. And Jeremy was successively enrolled in various Savannah Catholic elementary, middle, and high schools with tuition and books payment being waived, thanks to Grandma Odella's church connections. Though most of the times lonely for being the only African American in most classes, Jeremy afforded himself the best education Catholic schools could offer. Jeremy excelled in his studies. As time progressed, Jeremy thought and Grandma Odella reinforced the notion that he was destined to become a Roman Catholic priest. He was enrolled in a program to become deacon in the Savannah diocese and was accepted and sent to study at the University of Notre Dame in Ohio. His college years went by without incident, with his faith reinforced into becoming a priest. After his graduation, with a degree in economics and philosophy, Jeremy was accepted at the Theology School of Divinity at the American Catholic University, Washington, DC. This is where he met by accident an African American novice student. The brief encounter turned into a major crush and forbidden love affair for a future priest and a future nun. Jeremy Owen Massay had to tell his disappointed mentor at the Savannah diocese that he was no longer fit for priesthood. The novice did the same to her mentor back in the diocese of Birmingham, Alabama. Her name was Vanessa Lafontant. The two birds cut short their Theological graduate studies and decided to take up law studies at Duke University in North Carolina. They lived together for a while in the campus and married while successfully completing their law degrees at the top of their class. Both were quickly snatched by top corporate law firms from Atlanta, and with substantial double high income they decided to settle in the life of upper mobile African American middle class in the growing metropolitan area of Atlanta. Their only daughter was born shortly after. She was named Maxine Debaly Massay after Jeremy's mother. In the meantime, Jeremy's mother and Grandma Odella's health started deteriorating. This required Jeremy to make frequent extended trips to Savannah and his birthplace of Sapelo Island. While there, he started to reconnect with the great and rich Gullah culture. Finally, when his mother succumbed to her long mental illness and Grandma Odella passed away of old age, Jeremy told Vanessa that he has made a promise to his Grandma Odella, still disappointed that he did not become a priest and worse, corrupting and marrying Vanessa, a future Catholic nun.

The promise was about saving the soul of Gullah culture by stopping what she perceived as the economic and moral erosion that was sapping the Gullah culture and population. During Jeremy's frequent visits, Grandma Odella lamented over the growing migration of Gullah people from the sea islands to new life in the rapidly growing metropolitan centers of Georgia and South Carolina. Something got to be done, according to Grandma Odella, to stop the decline of Gullah culture, and Jeremy, having failed her to save Gullah folks soul as a priest, needed to take up the cause of Gullah people somehow. Besides, Jeremy and Vanessa, powerful lawyers down there in Atlanta, with many powerful contacts should be able to do something. After much soul searching following the funerals of his beloved Grandma Odella, Jeremy decided that he ought to do something about the Gullah people and culture. He was going to do that by getting into politics, representing and defending the interests of whole Gullah people in Georgia State Senate. Vanessa supported his decision. The reality was much simple and straightforward. The southern region of the United States has known the biggest migration of people and economic resources from the late seventy through the 2000s. That migration has continued unabated through present. Unprecedented economic expansion followed and was visible in Atlanta, the crossroad of more than five major east/west and north/south super highways in addition to the biggest airport and a major hub in the entire southeast of the country. As far as the sea islands and the Gullah people were concerned, the same economic expansion that was significantly changing and renovating most of Southern states, finally reached the eastern coasts of South Carolina and Georgia. The low-lying grounds that gathered to fishing and sparse rice plantations were becoming very attractive as major centers for retirement and recreation. Real estate values of these lands started to increase. Sea islands now offer better alternatives to those who did not want to leave southern states all together for sunny Florida. It did take long for the long-suffering Gullah people to take advantage of the skyrocketing real estate values of their farms and lands. One after another, families gave up their lots to huge corporations willing to invest in entirely new retirement or recreation centers. In some instances, these companies bought entire islands. This is the time Jeremy Massay entered the political fray of sea islands. His objective was to stamp the outflow of Gullah people from sea islands. He was not against the newfound riches for Gullah people. As a matter of fact, he delighted in this. He was simply calling on his people not to rush to the first offer of real estate price, rather to unite their resources and to insure that for every five or four acres sold to real estate outsider companies, one acre will be permanently kept in a Gullah family, community, or association. This will ensure that Gullah culture and people will not disappear on the face of sea islands. After much contacts and debates within the Gullah community, the "One for Gullah" slogan as it became to be known, started to take hold against powerful economic interests bent on takeover Gullah lands.

It also became obvious that without a strong legislation and support from the Georgia legislature and State government, the "One for Gullah" strategy was not going to survive. Jeremy Massay was selected by the Democratic Party to run for the Georgia senator seat from sea islands region. The seat has been left vacant for some time after the passing of an old retired banker from the Cumberland Island. The banker was more interested in keeping sea islands as pristine as ever and was decidedly against any real estate development in the area. He was left alone to keep the seat as long as sea islands economic interests were limited, and the islands were viewed as a series of swamps inhabited by backward fishing people, including Black Gullah people. The new reality called for an entirely different approach. Jeremy Massay "One for Gullah" slogan, strangely enough, united both the Gullah community and the business community vying to invest in islands. The two communities saw quickly how they can benefit from the concept and overwhelmingly supported Jeremy Massay in his first political bid. He won by 74 percent. He was also able to garner support and passage in Georgia State Senate for his "One for Gullah" legislation. His push for the legislation centered on the emotional need to preserve the African American Gullah culture. The emotional bond of Gullah people runs deep in Georgia African American community. The economic merits of "One for Gullah" were not even debated. The legislation was rushed in the State Senate in a record time with the support of the governor and every political luminary on both sides of political spectrum. The powerful business community of Atlanta lent its lobbying arm to the same legislation, and Jeremy Massay became one of the outstanding political sensations overnight in Georgia.

For the next six years, Jeremy divided his time being a prominent state senator on top of being a top corporate lawyer in Atlanta. He commuted frequently to the sea islands while maintaining a year-around office on Sapelo Island.

His wife also continued her climb in legal circles of Atlanta. Through the couple's powerful political connections, she was appointed judge in the Federal Ninth Court of Appeals in Atlanta. However, for the couple, the diverging career pursuits began to take its toll on their marriage. Vanessa Massay concentrated on tuning her new function of judge and raising their daughter while the frequent visits to sea islands area caused Jeremy Massay to distance himself emotionally from his wife. The void started to be filled by his Sapelo office executive assistant, the very beautiful Ms. Dianah Willforce, a recent divorcee, mother of two young girls. Ms. Willforce recently left Atlanta's fast pace after divorcing another African American prominent lawyer, a good friend of Massay's household. Vanessa had urged Dianah to leave the tumultuous Atlanta and, if possible, settle in the calm region of sea islands and invest in the booming real estate of the area. She took Vanessa's advice and came to Sapelo Island.

She also volunteered to run Jeremy Massay's office while he was in session or business in Atlanta. Vanessa did not count on her literally filling her shoes when her husband was in the area. This betrayal was kept from Vanessa for a time. However, when Vanessa asked her husband to hire her niece, the twenty-year-old Emory University student Stacy Lafontant, as summer intern at the Sapelo office, the damn broke. Vanessa thought that this was a chance for Stacy to stay away from Atlanta during the summer, to bounce back from the recent breakup with a longtime boyfriend, to get a bit of working experience, and to enjoy the restful areas of sea islands. Instead, Stacy started falling under the spell of State Senator Jeremy Massay. While visiting various communities of sea islands, Stacy cannot help but glow over Uncle Massay's aura. In one of overnight trips to Cumberland Island community, while they stayed in a single hotel room with two separate beds, Stacy, pretending an emergency to relieve herself, insisted in coming into the bathroom while State Senator Massay was taking his shower. After she was done with her quick emergency, she undressed and joined him naked in the shower. Startled, Jeremy started to leave the shower, but Stacy reached to his now raised member and pleaded with him to stay and make a woman out of her. Her young and beautiful body got the best of Uncle Massay. They continued the forbidden encounter the entire night. Afterward, they started communicating in the worst tradition of secret lovers while in the office. It did not take long before Ms. Dianah Willforce sensed this new office dynamic and became upset by Jeremy's supposed letdown. Two weeks later, in a violent pique of jealousy, she threatened Jeremy with telling his wife of the tryst with the tender and younger niece. Jeremy denied the encounter categorically. He forbade Dianah to compare him to her former husband whom she separated from after she caught him in similar conditions. Her ex was involved with both her twenty-year-old niece and her friend when they came to Atlanta for a summer vacation. This unfortunate affair started when Dianah's husband discovered that the two young girls were in fact lesbian lovers, only four days after they were in his household. The husband, a very prominent lawyer, blackmailed Dianah's niece and her friend into submitting to his sexual advances the whole summer. He pushed the envelope a bit too far when he insisted that the niece's friend traveled with him on a business trip to New Orleans. That was the start of the breakup with Dianah. She could not bear the sight of her ex's involvement with younger girls developing right there in front of her eyes. The betrayal was way too much to suffer for Dianah in spite of her own sexual escapade with her friend's husband. She will excuse her own depravity but not Jeremy's, nor her ex's. She will never excuse any man's depravity when a much younger girl is involved. She called it an economic rape as to say that a younger woman or man will get involved with an older man or woman for one and one reason only, money. What she did not realize was that all along her ex-husband had shared the sordid details of his folly with Jeremy Massay, his very close friend.

As a matter of fact, her ex-husband had continued the affair with the niece and her friend when Dianah left Atlanta, visiting with them in their North Carolina State University campus or inviting them back for weekend romps at the posh bungalow he had purchased after his divorce and deep in a Georgia State Park Forest recreation center. Many times, he had invited Jeremy to partake with the younger ones but to no avail. Jeremy was ambivalent about his friend's behavior. Part envious, part very much scared of what will happen in his own household if caught in similar affronts. Jeremy responded to Dianah's high mindedness by telling her not to forget to mention to his wife about their own steady sexual escapades every time he came back to Sapelo. Ms. Willforce resigned her position on the spot and retreated to her beach villa. When Jeremy shared this turn of event with Stacy, she went to confront Ms. Willforce and told her that she knew all along about the affair she had with the state senator. She added and lied that her aunt and Dinah's good friend, Judge Vanessa Lafontant Massay, had suspected the affair all along, and she had sent her to Sapelo to take the internship and to verify what was really going on between Uncle Massay and the very beautiful Dianah. She, Stacy, came to rescue Uncle Massay from this sordid affair. As far as she was concerned, she categorically denied having anything to do with Uncle Massay. And besides, Dianah had absolutely no proof of any sexual involvement between herself and Uncle Massay. Dianah replied that as a woman, she has seen plenty to reach her own conclusion that Uncle Massay was sexually involved with her. On top of their many overnight trips throughout sea islands spots, there were just many instances of their forbidden affair. For one, there were the deliveries to the office of packs of condoms, other feminine and male sexual enhancers; these deliveries always took place before their overnight trips. And for some insane and immature reasons, she left the detailed invoices of these deliveries all over the office for anybody to see. In addition, there were the explicit sexual e-mail messages that she had started sending to the state senator after their first tryst. Dianah said she read these messages to confirm her own suspicions of their affair and added that she had the master password to read all e-mail messages coming in and going from the office while they were away at their philandering ways. She thought but did not add that since Stacy came to Sapelo, Jeremy has stopped paying her mind nor attention. She told Stacy that she had no choice but to tell Judge Vanessa what was happening in Sapelo and beg for forgiveness for her own mistakes and anything she had done to her. She will not let Judge Vanessa suffer the same humiliation she had suffered because of some young chicks. She told Stacy that she was very stupid to destroy the trust of the only person who stood by her and her mother every step of the way and was paying for her college education. Finally, she asked a panicked Stacy to leave her house immediately and to start packing, as she was just about to call the judge and spill all the beans. Stacy left Sapelo the same night and went back to Atlanta to stay with a friend while waiting for the school to start.

She did not talk to the state senator or her aunt, the judge. She decided to stay away from them, her own mother, and her own family.

For she did not know how to explain all the discrepancies that Dinah Willforce will share with Aunt Vanessa and the scandal that was about to burst open. When Judge Vanessa Lafontant Massay received the call from Dianah Willforce, she was at home alone, reading her Bible late in the evening. She listened intently as a very excited and crying Dianah told her story. She did not contradict her nor request proofs or details of her husband's betrayal with Dianah and her niece. After she got the gist of her call, she thanked her calmly and told her she did not want to hear anything or any more from her ever, and she was not forgiven for having an affair with her husband. She hung up the phone. After that, she tried in vain to get in touch and talk to her niece, Stacy, who was unreachable then. She waited until the return of her husband on the weekend. She calmly again shared with him what Dianah said. He confirmed his sexual escapade with Dianah but categorically denied any involvement with Stacy. She told him that they would have to be separated while she started divorce procedures. She then laid down what will be known as Vanessa's rules. The separation will amount to having different quarters in the big house they have in one of Atlanta suburbs. There will be no question for him to leave the house.

For the sake of Maxine, their daughter, they will maintain appearances and pretend some medical conditions to validate their separate quarters. This will go on until Maxine leaves the house for college. She will then make their divorce final. The separate quarters will mean no more sexual contact or other forms of intimacy. They will not be free to find intimacy outside the household. As a matter of fact, they will impose upon themselves the life of celibacy they were supposed to lead when they wanted to become Catholic priest and nun. They were to look at this time of their life as a long phase to atone for their pursuit of carnal from the time of their first sexual encounter against their initial vocation through the ultimate betrayal Jeremy has shown with her friend Dianah.

As far as her niece Stacy Lafontant was concerned, she will see to it that no scandal will ever be aired in her own family. She will have a long conversation with her niece and make her an offer she would not refuse to prevent any airing of their transgression, whether true or false. She will get Stacy transferred far away to a west-coast college and ensure that their paths never crossed. She will do all she can to spare her sister, Stacy Lafontant's mother, another tragedy after the recent passing of her husband following a long bout of colon cancer. She will do all that to keep the peace within her own family even if she had to bear all the humiliation that Jeremy has brought on their household.

Judge Vanessa Massay was, in fact, blaming herself to have facilitated the betrayal from Jeremy. First with Dianah, by encouraging her to go live in Sapelo after her painful divorce, knowing very well the dispositions a vulnerable and hurt woman can take in company of close acquaintances. She also was very aware that she had not been making herself available lately to any sexual intimacy with her husband for some strange reasons. Placing a recently divorced woman however as well intentioned as Dianah so close to her husband away from home on extended trips was literally begging for trouble. Dianah, a few years younger than herself, was very beautiful and sexy. From their own mutual gossips, she was very aware that Dianah had been aggressively pursued by a lot of very successful single and married men in the African American high society of Atlanta but to no avail. She also knew that Dianah was all along faithful to her ex-husband. But she could not realize what hurt and humiliation have done to Dianah after the breakup. Was Dianah simply validating her womanhood after her divorce with somebody she knew before? She was now wondering if she had not placed Dianah in Jeremy's path and bed as a way to gratify his sexual needs when she was not forthcoming. As far as Stacy was concerned, if anything has happened, she has suggested the internship. Of course, she did not expect any deviation from her husband. Judge Vanessa Lafontant Massay has been on this cathartic journey for some time since the day she had her first intercourse with Jeremy in Washington, DC, while still under Catholic novice vows of chastity. Although overwhelmed by all woman carnal feeling in case of her first sexual intimacy, Vanessa had a very deep sense of guilt for what had happened. She felt that she had betrayed all that she stood for as a Catholic novice for which she had prepared herself all her life. She had wanted so much to dedicate her life to glorify God, Jesus Christ, and all the Catholic saints in a congregation of religious sisters that she did not quite drop her novice clothes in spirit after the sexual encounter with Jeremy. She believed in secret that somehow their transgression that snowy day of January will come to pass and that they will find their way back to priesthood and sisterhood. Even after they had resigned their vocation to study law at Duke University, Vanessa still maintained hope to go back to a dedicated religious life. She did not share her misgivings with Jeremy.

Instead, she supported him in their amorous journey all the way to the Catholic marriage ceremony. She extended and displayed all signs of matrimonial love a loving wife is expected to show to her husband. But now and then, for no apparent reasons, she also exhibited signs of deep sorrow and anxiety, which turned at times to acute depression. Luckily for her and Jeremy, these bouts never lasted but for a day or two. Vanessa covered these bouts every time by plunging excessively into whatever work at hand. At law school, this was translated into producing the most brilliant papers written by a student, earning her multiple academic citations and the election to Distinguished Law School Students Advisory Board president.

At the law firms, extraordinary filing papers, supported by originally researched references and writing, made her professional contribution to shine above peers, making it possible for her rise to law partnership in a record time of two years, three years before Jeremy. Jeremy could not understand the reasons for these bouts. He had completely removed any reservation he had about himself and priesthood. It was a closed chapter in his life. He attributed these bouts of depression sometime to typical female mood swings and, after his own unscientific consultation with a noted psychologist friend, to some awkwardness and guilt feeling that Vanessa might have for being the only one in her family to have succeeded so far and so high. Jeremy never, for a second, thought that Vanessa regretted seriously and sincerely the turn that their life took after that first tryst while they were destined to be priest and nun. He could not imagine that what he has welcomed as a liberating event from the binds of priesthood was for Vanessa a sacrilegious breach of her solemn vows of chastity.

This did not make Vanessa frigid or anything like that. When she was not in her mood swings, as Jeremy called them, Vanessa was very sensual and sexual as a wife can expect to be. But the mood swings could also make her very distant. After listening to Vanessa's rules, Jeremy understood that his wife was giving him a chance to repair their marriage bonds. He was certainly ready to abide by the rules if their union was to be saved. He did not believe that divorce would ensue after their daughter has gone to college. He did not argue the temptations Vanessa had placed upon him lately in his frequent trips to sea islands nor the fact that Vanessa has been sexually distant from him at the same time. He resolved to make the best of the bad situation and follow the dictates of celibacy that Vanessa imposed on their matrimony. By the way, he has practiced it before meeting and falling in love with Vanessa. This will be a small price to pay to win back his wife. Dianah and Stacy will be unfortunate turned pages in his life.

Lady Allistair met the state senator in his office in Atlanta during those conditions. Lady Allistair had called before this appointment to suggest a more cordial meeting at his home to engage his wife at the same time she was to make her proposal. Not knowing the state of their matrimony, Lady Allistair thought that her appeal to Jeremy's wife would close the deal. Jeremy declined, for obvious reasons, and insisted in a formal meeting at his office at the State Legislature. Lady Allistair obliged. She started the meeting by inquiring about Jeremy's political ambitions. She asked, "What political office you would like to advance to in the next five years?" Jeremy laughed at the question and replied that he would like to represent Georgia as senator in Washington, DC, and broke into a long laugh again. At the end, he excused himself and told Lady Allistair that this political aspiration is a bit unrealistic, given the nature of southern politics of Georgia.

At the end of the day, it will always be a matter of race in Georgia, black minority versus white majority. This is as simple as it can get. Jeremy also added that if Lady Allistair had any idea to promote him politically and God knows for what reasons, she was wasting her and his time. He had done pretty well, thank you, and had all the support he needed to get reelected as sea islands' state senator and where he could rightly count on an overwhelming African American population of Gullah extraction in addition to a sympathetic white business establishment. Lady Allistair said that she needed to confess that she did not know much about the state of Georgia politics. But one thing she was very much aware of was that financial interests, especially big financial interests, have a way to sway political favors in anybody's side in the United States, irrespective of race. She said that she came to propose to the state senator to align himself in the path of big financial interests that will make his political ambition possible in five years. Jeremy responded by saying that he was all ears. Lady Allistair continued by asking Jeremy what he thought will be the next biggest economic challenge that the world will face. Before Jeremy answered, Lady Allistair said that the challenge would be in replacing oil as the affordable source of energy worldwide. Lady Allistair continued by saying that Jeremy's intervention in the conference in Athens, Georgia, was an illustration of what the future holds as far as the alternative economic, affordable source of energy besides oil. That future, she said, lies in the very countries of Africa Jeremy was urging to unite and face the current exorbitant oil prices together. The new sources of energy, other than oil, will definitely be found in Africa. Lady Allistair concluded by saying that she came to propose to Jeremy to lead a nonprofit organization that will aggressively promote the economic development of African countries with substantial mineral deposits among which the new sources of energy, replacing oil, are located. This nonprofit organization is bound to attract big financial interests in the United States and will become a powerful tract for Jeremy to realize whatever political ambitions he has, including becoming the senator from the State of Georgia. The state senator got up from his chair and went near the large windows of the office. The office was dead silent for two or three minutes while he gazed at the sky and noticed a gathering of cloudy storms from the south. He looked at Lady Allistair and said, "You must be on something here, there are gathering storms coming from the Southern Hemisphere. I pray to God Almighty that that these storms will bring a long-awaited salvation. I am flattered by your proposal. On principle, I will be delighted to lead this nonprofit organization. God only knows what these African nations have endured and continue to endure after the so-called political independence. I will be honored to lead such an organization. But I need first to run it by my wife, my life partner.

CHAPTER 5
Amovir Trip

The first surprise Dr. O'Shea had, preparing for the trip to Amovir was the long itinerary. First came the one-hour flight from Lexington, Kentucky, to Chicago, where he was to take a seven-hour transatlantic flight to London, UK. Then another five-hour flight was to carry him to Ankara, Turkey, where he was to be whisked into a private business executive jet belonging to a company named BI that was to fly him to Amovir for another eight-hour flight. Altogether the trip accounted for about twenty hours of flying from Lexington to reach Amovir. The second surprise was that there was no lay away over Moscow he was looking forward to sightsee. He thought that there was no way to get to Russia without going through Moscow.

"Was Lady Allistair a bit too overprotective, not wanting to expose him to the crime- and mafia-infested big city of Moscow as she had described it during their last dinner in New York City. What can Moscow-based criminal people get from the modest old professor from Lexington, Kentucky?" he wondered. At the same time, he concluded that maybe he should stick to the proposed itinerary. The "community" knew better. A day before his trip, he contacted and provided his three children with his itinerary, as a measure of precaution and just in case the other sides had dire intentions about his whereabouts. He also talked to Lady Allistair, who reassured him about all the safety and comforts arranged for him in Amovir. He told the staff secretary at the university that he was going to Europe and more precisely to Madrid, Spain, where he was to start a two weeks' vacation that will take him almost all over Europe. He thought that the less he shared with the staff, the better off he will be. Besides, his reclusion from all faculty activities was not to raise a concern one way or another about his condition, whether he was there or not, whether he came to his office or not.

For all practical purposes, he had resolved that he was a nonentity in the faculty, punching his time until retirement scheduled in about a year or two and not soon enough according to Dean Larry McKinley. The trip to Amovir went on schedule without a problem from Lexington to Amovir. He was a bit overwhelmed when he found that he was a lone passenger in the executive business jet flight from Ankara, Turkey, to Amovir.

He was greeted by the BI private jet crew when his flight from London arrived at Ankara. He was then whisked into the private jet as if he was the head of a state. Beautiful flight attendants and a regimented military-like flight crew fussed over him in perfect English on their way to plane. When he boarded the jet, he was shown a large leather seat all the way in back of the plane with a mounted desk and telephone set. He was told that he could contact anyone in the world if he wished to talk. As soon as the plane was airborne, he was served an exquisite meal that was advertised by one of the flight attendants as the ultimate French dish of côte de veaux. He washed the delicious meal with an aged red French wine he could not quite make out the complicated long name. That was enough to put him to sleep but not long enough as the executive jet was already descending over the Lake Baikal region to land at Amovir.

Mr. Andropov Baliev, who introduced himself as Dr. Baliev, director of scientific operations for BI, greeted him at his arrival. Dr. Baliev spoke perfect English without a trace of an accent. He confided to Dr. O'Shea that he has spent more than fifteen years in the United States as a son of a Soviet diplomat at the United Nations. While in the United States, he has studied at Princeton and Cornell Universities, majoring in Mathematics and doing further graduate work in Operations Research. He completed his PhD in "Chaos Theory" at Harvard University. Dr. Baliev was going to be his main contact during his stay at Amovir. He took the visiting professor to one of the plush VIP bungalows in the headquarters compound. He informed Dr. O'Shea that he was to be attended at all time by a middle-aged couple in the bungalow. Although it was only about three o'clock in the afternoon when Dr. O'Shea arrived at the bungalow, he decided to excuse himself from Dr. Baliev and retire to sleep after twenty or so hours of voyage. He was tired. The VIP bungalow was ostentatiously furnished and well kept. Most furnishings were imported from Sweden and Denmark. There were no Russian motifs around. And the middle-aged couple expected to care for the Dr. O'Shea made themselves as invisible and circumspect as possible. Dr. O'Shea did not even see them when he arrived although all was in place and order as if they knew every slight detail of his wants and desires. He woke up the next day around six thirty in the morning and readied himself for the first day of the conference. He was pleased to notice that he was not scheduled to give his presentation until the next day in the afternoon. This scheduling will give him enough time to regain his full stamina from the unbelievable long jet lag. He thanked Dr. Baliev, who came to join him for breakfast at the guesthouse, for the convenient schedule.

Dr. O'Shea took notice that the breakfast was ready the minute he came out of the bedroom, prepared by still invisible middle-aged couple. Dr. Baliev advised him that he did not have to push himself attending all the presentations scheduled the first day of the conference. As a matter of fact, most of eminent speakers like himself were scheduled to start talking on the second day. The first day is usually reserved for the young ambitious minds that compete to make their marks and impressions. Dismissively, Dr. Baliev said that the younger ones always come up with the weirdest theses that are easily forgotten after the first day of the conference. At this point, Dr. O'Shea rebuked him and said that he would love to attend the first-day sessions and listen to those weird theses as he has missed and always enjoyed these lively exchanges from his teaching days. He told Dr. Baliev that he sorely missed the interactions with the younger minds in his present occupation, which he deceptively described as more administrative than teaching, leaving aside his complete seclusion status from the faculty staff back in Lexington. His main concern being that he might not be able to follow presentations made in Russian or any other language that may be spoken. Dr. Baliev reassured him and said that the conference being international, all presentations were made, translated, and debated in English. In case where the presenter spoke another language, a contingent of translators stood ready to provide perfect English translation of all proceedings. The conference was carried, according to Dr. Baliev, like a UN assembly general. He added that BI could afford it. He also informed him that if it was all right with him, he was invited that evening to attend a dinner given by the CEO of BI, Mr. Nadov Kiriyan. The dinner was given to thank the eminent foreign and Russian guests who have accepted to attend the conference and share the latest in the field of advanced mineralogy studies.

Dr. O'Shea accepted the invitation without much inquiry. Besides, he thought, if the big man was footing the bill and going to so much length and trouble to entertain them, here at Amovir, what a splendid opportunity to thank him back just the same for all he has done. This will be a simple courtesy call. Also at this point, and against his own advice, Dr. Baliev changed his mind about attending the presentations by younger scientists and decided to join Dr. O'Shea at the first-day sessions. He was surprised by the first presentation given by a beautiful Scottish lady, a PhD student at the University of Glasgow, Scotland. Her name was Stacy Northbridge. Her talk centered on the properties of a particular rock found along the coast of the desert of Namibia. Her thesis was that this rock has all the properties of matter at the time of the big bang, the beginning of the universe, as we know it.

Stacy Northbridge held forth against a barrage of questions from the audience, including Dr. O'Shea who alternated from supporting to denigrating questions shot at her. After about fifty-five minutes of lively exchanges, Dr. O'Shea left his chair and walked down to the podium to congratulate Stacy Northbridge for the brilliant defense of her paper.

Stacy Northbridge was elated and thanked him for his support. She also reminded him that peers and professors back in Glasgow warned her about his incisive and probing intervention. Now as far as she was concerned, getting a congratulation note from his eminent Dr. O'Shea meant only one thing: her PhD thesis was completed. Dr. O'Shea made only one request: he will be happy to get a specimen of the rock she talked about. She promised that this would be done the minute she gets back to her laboratory at Glasgow. During the next break, Dr. O'Shea talked with Dr. Baliev who had reluctantly joined him at the first day conferences. He said the following to Dr. Baliev: "Nothing warms my heart and mind more than the so-called weird theses that the younger ones come up with in these conferences and many other forums around the world. Without them, no advance in technology or science is possible, in my opinion. You hardly learn something new from established scientists who, in fact, spend the rest of their productive time repeating and embellishing thesis that made them famous back then. I have fought all my life against the closed mind of my peers at various institutions of higher learning. It has always been the same condescending attitude and arrogance toward the younger brilliant minds. What is the most amazing fact is that many of my peers tend to completely forget when and how they gained their expertise, when and how somebody notices them: it was precisely when they were young PhD students.

Youth has always brought with it irreverence to established ways of thinking. Breakthroughs in every known science come from the challenges to what is known today. Only youthful zeal is sorely and precisely needed to accomplish this. As you have noticed, I was challenging and enticing Stacy Northbridge to rise to the level of that irreverence. I pray to God I have succeeded." As he was addressing Dr. Baliev and making the point around breakthroughs in sciences by young scientists, an elegantly dressed young lady approached Dr. O'Shea with an urgent note to meet with the CEO of BI, Mr. Nadov Kiriyan himself in one of his residences high in the mountain overlooking Amovir. Dr. Baliev recognized the lady as one of the five executive assistants attached to Mr. Kiriyan's office. Dr. Baliev confided to Dr. O'Shea that this request was the most unusual coming from Mr. Kiriyan as he was a very methodical and disciplined manager, not given to abrupt changes of schedule.

He urged him to honor the request to find out what on earth was the big man up to, given that Mr. Kiriyan was scheduled to meet with all distinguished foreign scientists that evening. Certainly, Mr. Kiriyan had decided to have a talk with Dr. O'Shea before the scheduled evening gathering. Dr. O'Shea left the morning conference sessions with the executive assistant. Outside the conference auditorium, a big Mercedes limousine was expecting him to be whisked to the big villa high in the mountain. As the limousine arrived at the destination, Dr. O'Shea noticed a tall six feet three nicely dressed gentleman nervously pacing the second-floor balcony of the sumptuous villa. The executive assistant, who answered curiously by an Italian name of Dalila Chiotti, identified the gentleman as Mr. Nadov Kiriyan. She also added that she had never seen Mr. Kiriyan so excited to meet a distinguished guest as he was to meet Dr. O'Shea. She said that Dr. O'Shea must be the bearer of a very important message to Mr. Kiriyan. Dr. O'Shea was obviously surprised by these comments. He was quickly brought to meet the CEO of BI, who was still pacing the balcony. The first thing the good professor noticed was how Mr. Kiriyan looked, as immaculate as any man Dr. O'Shea had ever seen. His very expansive suit testified to an upper-class British taste uncommon to most workers and managers in Amovir. His face was almost sculpted Olympian-like, splendidly tanned with no beard nor mustache contrasting to a pair of deep but shining green eyes. His hair was dark brown, cut short in front, growing with a shade of light gray in the back. He looked more like a retired movie star from Hollywood who never grows older than the powerful CEO of BI. Another most noticeable thing about Mr. Kiriyan was the huge ring that he was wearing in the right-hand middle finger. This ring was ablaze with a shining diamond-like relief adorned with a capital letter K in the middle.

Mr. Kiriyan greeted the professor profusely as if he was a long-lost member of family. He invited Dr. O'Shea to stay on the balcony, as their meeting will be held as informally as possible among trusted friends. He inquired about his health and his long journey to Amovir and extended his deep but belated condolence for the passing of his wife. He inquired about every member of his family of whom he mentioned correctly names and places of stay. He sounded like a distant cousin very knowledgeable with every tiny detail of the family. For about thirty minutes, Dr. O'Shea thought that he was attending a family reunion in the United States, instead of being in presence of the CEO of the most gigantic business enterprises in the world. Mr. Kiriyan sensed his discomfort and reassured him by saying that they have known each other for a long long time for reasons he will share with him shortly.

He apologized for cutting short his attendance to the first-day-conference sessions. He said that their meeting was the most urgent he could not imagine.

He told his guest, "Time is running out and short for what I have been set all along in my career and wanted to accomplish. Dr. O'Shea, you are absolutely the right person I sorely needed to accomplish my goals." He went right to the point. "Alpha-M project needs to be accelerated in its execution. Now is the time to bring about all promises that Alpha-M entails to fruition. You have been and are an important link in the Alpha-M chain of evolution. Your considerable work over Alpha-M is witness to the victory of mind over matter." Mr. Kiriyan added that whatever was needed would be made available to insure that Alpha-M project moves forward.

Dr. O'Shea did not hesitate to set the record straight. "Mr. Kiriyan, sir, as far as I am concerned, the promises that Alpha-M holds would be rightfully fulfilled only where Alpha-M is buried in the seismic plateaus of Mezi. I have done and pushed the Alpha-M project as far and as much as I could. With my advanced age and very soon declining health, I am ready to hand the next steps of the project to the right person who has invested as much energy and time as myself in the project."

To Dr. O'Shea's amazing surprise, Mr. Kiriyan jumped in and concurred, "I am totally in accord with you that Dr. Kano Wasiri is and must be the next person to faithfully carry out the Alpha-M project's next steps. Dr. Kano Wasiri is the next logical link in the Alpha-M project. To insure and to effect the rapid engagement of Dr. Kano Wasiri by all means necessary, I called this urgent meeting. I am counting on you to accelerate Dr. Kano Wasiri's engagement."

Dr. O'Shea took time to reply, wondering by what turn of logic or deduction Mr. Kiriyan mentioned his protégé by his name. So far, the only remote reference to his protégé he made was Mezi. How and why did Mr. Kiriyan jump the gun mentioning Dr. Kano Wasiri? He realized that he was dealing with a determined and powerful executive who has carefully studied the Alpha-M project and its major protagonists. Dr. O'Shea decided not to dwell on identification issues. He would check to find out how much Mr. Kiriyan knew about the project. "To date, Dr. Kano Wasiri has been extremely reluctant to talk about or be involved in Alpha-M projects after the terrible episode of his defense of his paper at the University of Kentucky. I do not know how you are going to change his mind. You should know that I have tremendous respect for him and his family.

I have to tell you right now that I would not be part of anything that will bear any harm to Dr. Kano Wasiri and his lovely family."

Mr. Kiriyan smiled at the mention of harm to Dr. Wasiri.

"I am very much aware of what went on at the University of Kentucky, the defense of the paper, and what Dr. Wasiri endured. I know exactly where Dr. Wasiri stood and stands now, and I can assure I have the utmost respect for him and his family. I also believe that time should have taken care of Dr. Wasiri's posture. Now is the time to bring him back to the fold of Alpha-M. And all will be made possible to accomplish that without bearing any harm to him or his family. Believe me; Dr. Wasiri will come out of this project much fulfilled than anything he has imagined to date. The stakes for Alpha-M project are way too big and too important for an entire generation of people to be left undone. In addition, I want to take this opportunity to dispel any misgiving or apprehension you might have, working with us at this time. I want to assure you that BI, Baikal International, is and would remain international in every sense of the word. I would go even further to say that BI is supranational. It answers to no state or regional economic entity but to itself. It is not an American or Russian business company.

It is an international concern with no ideological or hegemony inclination but its own purpose and pursuits to make profit, to make money, buying and selling minerals worldwide. It is by accident that it has its headquarters in Amovir in Russia. But its operations are substantially international, in New York, where you met Lady Allistair; in London, where AMX is based; in Dubai, where we are a major player in oil business or in Thailand, where we have extensive real estate properties. I want to excuse myself now. I believe that I have shared with you my most urgent message. We will have more occasions to talk about the urgency of this project while you are still with us here in Amovir."

As abruptly as Dr. O'Shea was summoned to see Mr. Kiriyan, he was brought back to the conference hall. But while the limousine got nearer the hall, Dr. O'Shea changed his mind and decided that he needed time to be alone in the VIP guesthouse to think over and absorb the surprised exchange he just had and what Mr. Kiriyan instructed him to do as if he was already part of BI's empire and needed to execute his marching orders. He has never met the man but for the first time and already he was receiving instructions relative to his own protégé, Dr. Kano Wasiri. That disturbed him greatly.

At the same time, the unequivocal statement that Mr. Kiriyan made, clarifying the nonideological bent and the international and strictly for profit purpose of BI, removed all of the "community" ambiguity and nonsense that Dr. O'Shea has carried on this trip. The limousine carried him back to the guesthouse. When he arrived at the house, he saw for the first time and asked the middle-aged couple charged to look after him not to disturb him until the scheduled evening reception. However, while he was instructing the couple not to disturb him, Dr. O'Shea noticed that both were wearing rings at the right hand middle finger. The rings were exact replica of the one that Mr. Kiriyan was wearing, although much smaller with the capital letter K in the middle of a shining relief. Dr. O'Shea became a bit alarmed and curious. He turned around and could not resist but ask the couple where they got such beautiful rings and what kind of jewel was adorning the rings. The couple said they went by the name of Mr. and Mrs. Jolen Dudarev and were delighted to hear such a compliment and became eager to talk about the rings if the eminent professor had time to hear their story. All the same, the professor obliged them.

They all went to the living room and sat down. Mr. Dudarev brought a bottle of a fine Glenfiddich eighteen-year-aged Scotch and served the professor, his wife, and himself. He raised his glass as to make a toast and said, "To the second tiers," his wife responded, "To the second tiers." Dr. O'Shea, without realizing it, also said, "To the second tiers" while raising his glass. Then Dr. O'Shea said to Mr. Dudarev, "This 'to the second tiers' toast should mean something, and please, indulge me." Mrs. Dudarev laughed at the comment and said, "Yes, indeed, we will indulge you. We have been expecting to indulge you in our ways since you came here. Mr. Kiriyan himself before you set foot here instructed this. Let me explain. We are the second tiers people in our universe domain. While Mr. Nadov Kiriyan is part of the first tiers people. From the order established from more than four hundred thousand years ago, our universe has been set with a clear and disciplined hierarchy in our society which is divided into about five tiers. This hierarchy is not based on race, merit, or other criteria, but mainly upon an order of succession. Succession in our universe is determined by the length of time your primary instincts are regenerated. If the primary instincts are regenerated by more than hundred thousand a cycle, your existence will tend to move from a lower tier to an upper tier. If the regeneration process declines, you will move downward from an upper tier to a lower tier. Every unit or individual is endowed with the same regeneration process that is basically random. The randomness of the process allows for a permanent equilibrium among all units, removing all senses of friction among them.

In other words, the randomness of the process has helped to instill a permanent unbroken peace pact among all units in our universe for a long, long time. This makes it so that all units work for and strive for the maintenance of that equilibrium. The position or hierarchy of a unit in the universe is determined at any time by the regeneration level. The regeneration process for a unit can last sometime for an infinite time by human standard, three or four thousand human years. It goes without saying that units at first tier level have a regeneration process set at a much higher level than other tiers below, and therefore, these units are trusted with significantly higher tasks while their regeneration level is high or peaking.

Their contribution to the overall universe is expected to be high too. As their regeneration process changes or progresses to a lower level, so does the level of tasks they will take on. The monitor of the regeneration is the ring you see us wearing. The bigger the ring, the higher the regeneration process. Does all this make any sense to you?"

Dr. O'Shea responded categorically and sarcastically, "No, but a very interesting story you got there, but essentially rubbish all the same. I have asked you to tell me what kind of jewel, mineral you have on your ring, and you gave a lecture about your universe and a regeneration process of primary instincts lasting thousands of years. Are you alien? Is Mr. Nadov Kiriyan an alien? Why on earth are you telling me, revealing to me these things? I am very tired at this time and definitely need time to be alone. These are two successive mind-blowing conversations I have in one day, and I believe I have my fill of fantastic stories for a day."

Mr. Dudarev replied, "We are sorry if we have troubled your sense of logic with our story. We thought that you were ready to understand our ways. Obviously, you are not. To answer your questions, first the mineral on our rings you wanted to know has countless names: cuba, petiius, jarew, danisla, and so on, but we call it kabislovoskry, a rare mineral you should be aware of. Second, you will be in the better position to attest if we are aliens soon, the same for Mr. Kiriyan, and third, we were mistaken in thinking that your appreciation of things to come needed to be accelerated by the revelations we are sharing with you now.

However, it looks like we have overestimated your condition. We will let you take rest, and we hope to continue this conversation some other time."

At that instant, Dr. O'Shea went to his bedroom to sleep, and the Dudarev couple left the VIP guesthouse for good. When Dr. O'Shea woke up at around 4:45 p.m., his clothes for the evening reception were ironed and readied, but there was no sign of Dudarev couple. Instead, another young lady was in the house, telling the good professor now that she was attending to his house chores. When asked whether Mr. and Mrs. Dudarev were gone, she replied in a broken English that she has been the only help residing in the VIP guesthouse since the good professor arrived, and she had no idea of what Dudarev couple Dr. O'Shea was talking about. The young lady named Fedora Barov did not wear the famous K ring. Dr. O'Shea started wondering whether he had dreamed the encounter with the Dudarev couple. Just to be on the knowing side. He sat down and keyed in his PC the whole encounter with the so-called Dudarev couple. Dr. O'Shea thought for a moment that he was losing his mind or was having a major senior moment. He resolved to run the encounter through Dr.

Baliev who, he remembered, has introduced him to the Dudarev couple when he arrived at the VIP guesthouse. Better yet, he went to look for the bottle of Glenfiddich he shared with the couple. He found the bottle, but it was uncorked and unopened. It was time to head down to the evening reception and perhaps to clear his foggy mind.

As soon as Dr. O'Shea arrived at the reception, Dr. Baliev was excitedly intent in finding out how the urgent and unscheduled meeting with the big boss of BI, Mr. Kiriyan himself. He came in a hurry to greet him at the door. He wanted to know all that was discussed. Dr. O'Shea was more circumspect. He mentioned vaguely that Mr. Kiriyan simply inquired about his health, how long he intended to continue his research around advanced mineralogy studies at the University of Kentucky, whether he needed additional funding to carry out his research, and other general inquiries. Dr. Baliev was not impressed by his vagueness and pursued his line of inquiry. But Dr. O'Shea persisted and turned the table on Dr. Baliev and related the unbelievable conversation he had with the Dudarev couple. He shared his apprehension about the whole context of the universe of "first tiers" and "second tiers" in addition to the theory of randomness of the first instincts generation as related by the couple. He mentioned the sight of the K ring capped with what looked like a diamond relief, the same but much smaller than Mr. Kiriyan's. He also noticed that Dr. Baliev did not wear the K ring. At that instant, Dr. Baliev stopped him cold. He assured him that he believed that Dr. O'Shea had a very long trip and was very tired. He doubted that the Dudarev couple had the conversation he was relating. He said that this couple was hired two months ago as temporary housekeepers for the international conference taking place.

They were ambulatory workers from one of the Siberian provinces of Russia. As a matter fact, their performance has been less than satisfactory in many regards he would not share. So much so that they were let go sometime this very day and were on their way back to their town or village of origin. Dr. Baliev advised Dr. O'Shea, "In Russia today, as in time of Soviet Union before or the prior Russian Empire under the Czar, you can find thousands upon thousands of people ready to tell unbelievable stories bearing on fantastic, spiritual, demoniac, or whatever.

Some of these people carry on to a point of being addressed as revered holy men, far seers, and all the same for men no more than con men. These people can sometimes rise to the top of political echelon, remember Rasputin? The harsh and long Russian winter has rendered a lot of people completely deranged and devious. As long as you are here, just stay clear of these people and stick to the rational and scientific endeavors you are used to."

Dr. O'Shea was still not satisfied and asked about the K ring and the likeness of shape found with the Dudarev couple and Mr. Kiriyan. Here again, Dr. Baliev said, "In my humble opinion, the Dudarev couple must be a set of deceitful people who certainly have seen many of Mr. Kiriyan's pictures adorned in countless magazines, TV programs, and on the Internet. As a CEO of BI, with far-flung interests in Russia and around the world, Mr. Kiriyan is featured almost on daily basis somewhere and somehow in Russia. The Dudarev couple must have studied his appearance and why not copied his habits down to wearing a likeness of his ring. In this period of difficult economic transition in Russia, with countless of con artists about the land, this happened all the time, and I bet that likeness of K ring and concocted stories the couple has shared may have opened few doors for them in the past.

Now that you have mentioned it, I was also struck by the likeness of Mr. Dudarev with Mr. Kiriyan. I can assure you that the couple must have been playing a very dangerous part in a con game. Thank God, our management and security people here in Amovir were rapidly awakened to their sordid deed and fired them. I did not realize that this couple has troubled you so much with unbelievable stories, and I am relieved that they were fired before they were to cause you further harm and now I have to tell you that I am personally sorry to have exposed you to such people. Please accept my apology and let's get on with the reception at hand and enjoy what BI is reserving for us this evening."

Dr. Baliev's explanation left Dr. O'Shea even more perplexed than before. He wanted to continue the inquiry further to connect all the dots which started to pop-up in his mind when Mr. Nadov Kiriyan, the CEO of BI, was making his entrance under sustained applause from the gathered assembly of Russian and foreign guests and various high-level management of BI present at Amovir.

Mr. Kiriyan was led to the lectern emblazoned with BI and Russian flags. Above the lectern, there was a screen, as big as one found in a big movie theater, flashing BI logo, which was confounded into a K ring capped also with a multicolored diamond. Before long, Mr. Kiriyan addressed the assembly:

"Good evening, ladies and gentlemen. It is for me a great honor to welcome all of you here at Amovir for the international conference on advanced mineralogy studies. I do not have to remind you of the great expectations that BI entertains around the studies each one of you is conducting in advancing the frontiers of mineralogy. BI goals are not just to commercialize every known mineral in this world but also, above all, to insure that uses of every mineral found in this world benefit the all known universe. We do not limit ourselves to use what is found on earth. I believe that when perfected, BI's advanced technology will bring about the exploration and extraction of multiusage and extremely sophisticate minerals in distant planets. But before we get to that not distant stage, BI will do all it can, and I have to emphasize as urgently as possible as it can to dig out the most promising and scientifically advanced minerals known to man. I can assure you, that has been my goal all along when BI was established, and I am happy to tell you that thanks to significant and advanced mineralogy studies conducted throughout the world by all you assembled here, it is now a matter of time when this goal is reached.

To that effect, I am very happy to welcome among us the very august Professor Emeritus Dr. O'Shea from the University of Kentucky, who, single handedly, has more than anybody else I know, advanced the mineralogy studies in so many directions. It gives me a great pleasure to bestow upon Dr. O'Shea the highest honor that BI has reserved for the scientists who have contributed most significantly to mineralogy studies to date. Two things represent that honor: the highest medal of BI's enterprise and the K ring. Dr. O'Shea, could you please do us the honor to join me and receive these presents." At that very instant, Dr. O'Shea was surrounded by two stunning ladies and was guided to the podium where he was provided with BI's highest honor presents.

As if in daze, Dr. O'Shea, still in shock from the encounters with the Dudarev couple, the previous and unscheduled meeting with Mr. Kiriyan and the tortuous conversation with Dr. Baliev, accepted both the medal and the K ring from Mr. Kiriyan.

Dr. O'Shea managed to say, "I thank you, Mr. Kiriyan, and BI for the warm reception I have received here in Amovir. I am of course surprised by the regards and honor you have extended to me at this time. I pray that I have merited all this. I know that the mineralogy studies have advanced a great deal these last twenty or so years, no thanks to me but thanks to, as I have said it and will continue to say, the irreverence of many young scientists who never ceased to question established theories and bodies of knowledge in mineralogy.

My humble role in this field has been and will continue to be to nurture and cheer these young scientists in their irreverent pursuit of scientific research and knowledge even when I have to endure the label of scientist fool from my esteemed colleagues. If these presents honor this role, then I am in the solemn obligation to accept them graciously. Thank you." The assembly guests were at their feet and responded with laughter and sustained applause as Dr. O'Shea wore the K ring and draped himself with BI medal.

It was a very hectic day for the good professor. It suddenly occurred to him the paradox or the contrast between the honors this august assembly of scientists from around the world in Amovir was bestowing upon him for all he has contributed in the field and the complete neglect and humiliation he has been enduring the past thirty or so years in the Mining Engineering Sciences Faculty at the University of Kentucky, where he has been, for all practical purposes, shown the door and relegated to a nonperson among the teaching and research faculty.

He resolved that things would definitely change when he will be back in the United States. The good old scientist also resolved that he would cast his lot over whatever Mr. Kiriyan wants as long as there is a definitive benefit for the advanced mineralogy studies.

Dr. O'Shea spent the remaining three days of the conference in the eminent and august role of moderator of various paper presentations, reviews, and debates. However, the main purpose of his visit to Amovir's conference, his own presentation of the latest findings around Alpha-M never materialized.

Dr. Baliev told him that his presentation has been canceled after his meeting with Mr. Kiriyan, who insisted not to put him and his paper findings under peer reviews scrutiny, which in international conferences such as these can be at times brutal and demeaning. Mr. Kiriyan who has already conferred the highest honor from BI to the good professor will not allow any embarrassment of the eminent Professor Emeritus Dr. O'Shea during any peer review meeting. Although Dr. O'Shea was looking forward to such scrutiny, Mr. Kiriyan's posture suited him just fine. As far as he was concerned, too many encounters since his arrival in Amovir have left his mind a bit foggy and perplexed. He seriously admitted to himself that he was not in all mental standing to sustain the barrages of questions which may have come about challenging the far-reaching findings, conclusions, and recommendations embedded in his paper. If he can make his case in places other than this godforsaken Amovir Bourg, he was all for it.

He will play along his host wishes for the remaining days until he is out of the place and back home. But unbeknownst to him, the copy of his entire paper had already found its way to Mr. Kiriyan's private personal computer and safe the very next hour of his arrival to Amovir when he was being entertained and attended to by the Dudarev couple. As soon Dr. O'Shea arrived and requested time to rest and sleep after the twenty or so hours of his long trip from the United States to Amovir, the Dudarev couple accommodated him with all the VIP help, including a good glass of Johnny Walker Black blended with some mild soporific ingredient, which kept Dr. O'Shea sleeping for the next seven hours, enough time for the couple to go over every scientific documentation he had brought along including the latest paper.

The unscheduled meeting with Mr. Kiriyan was simply a testimony from Mr. Kiriyan to let Dr. O'Shea know that his latest findings were very important to him and should remain secret, and the priority at this stage was to engage Dr. Wasiri as soon as possible to advance the next phase of the Alpha-M project: its extraction. Dr. O'Shea did not fully appreciate the chain of events from his arrival and the various encounters he had. He hardly recovered from the long tiring twenty hours or so trip, four days after arriving Amovir. As the conference was reaching its end, he can only think of going back home to the United States as slowly as he could with stops over Rome, Paris, and London for sightseeing. The day before his scheduled return to the United States, he decided to get another appointment with Mr. Kiriyan to request that his return trip includes these stops over. His request was quickly granted with VIP accommodations at every turn.

Mr. Kiriyan told him the accommodation was all-natural and came about as a result of the honors, which were bestowed upon him by BI at the international conference. By the way, as a matter of even greater shock to Dr. O'Shea, he also learned that a funding of five million dollars to be used as wished by the honoree came along with the honors from BI. During their last conversation, Mr. Kiriyan made a last plea to Dr. O'Shea to seriously engage Dr. Wasiri to the next phase of the Alpha-M project. Mr. Kiriyan intimated that all the work that Dr. O'Shea had done all his life would amount to nothing if Alpha-M is not found and tested to verify all the extraordinary properties that the professor claimed are proper to Alpha-M. And the only logical link to this next stage remains Dr. Wasiri who must be trusted to carry this task in location in the Republic of Mezi. Mr. Kiriyan also added that all necessary means would be made at the disposal of Dr. O'Shea and Dr. Wasiri to accomplish this.

Dr. O'Shea thanked Mr. Kiriyan for the wonderful and extraordinary hospitality he had enjoyed since coming to Amovir, and he was certainly to look forward to be fully engaged in the next phase of the Alpha-M project and to do all he can to convince Dr. Wasiri to join him in this endeavor. The next day, after having said good-bye to Dr. Baliev and other conference participants, Dr. O'Shea was led this time to another remote and private airstrip about twenty miles from Amovir, where he boarded a huge luxurious private jet with the latest VIP accommodations with private bedroom, salon, and entertainment center. Besides the jet crew he never saw, Dr. O'Shea was a lone passenger surrounded by three airline hostesses who fussed over him at every request he made. After a restful six- or seven-hours' flight, the plane landed in Rome where he was limousine driven to a five-star hotel in Rome for a three-day sightseeing stay. He was flown in the same fashion to Paris and London, and he availed himself of the same accommodations in these towns.

The only exception was the call he made from Rome to Dr. Wasiri's residence at Frankfort, Kentucky, and where he was lucky to reach Mrs. Wasiri. After exchanging long greetings, he told Mrs. Wasiri that he was calling from Rome, on a business trip, and would like to meet with Dr. Wasiri urgently in New York City upon his return as they have talked about before. He wanted to share with Dr. Wasiri outstanding developments around some researches he had been involved in, and above all, he wanted to introduce Dr. Wasiri to some prominent international researchers from Japan, Australia, and China, who will be in New York City for a brief stay and who are eager to hear about Dr. Wasiri's latest research. Dr. O'Shea added that he was sending the round-trip airfare by FEDEX promptly and the hotel stay and all other accommodations in New York City are being taken care by the same scientific organization in care of the foreign scientists. He begged Mrs. Wasiri not only to transmit the urgent message but also to persuade Dr. Wasiri to accept to come to New York City to check this great opportunity. Dr. O'Shea remembered that Dr. Wasiri was to meet with him back at the University of Kentucky as planned after his first visit to Russia. He had already convinced both Hasbo and Dr. Wasiri to start taking steps to return to Mezi, a decision that Dr. Wasiri had taken but with strong reservations. The second meeting with Dr. Wasiri, he needed to clarify a few things he had shared like, his imminent retirement from teaching, the first conference trip to Siberia, the contacts with faraway Siberian scientists, the research funding from a Russian billionaire, etc.

These stories have created more puzzles for Dr. Wasiri. Now he was calling from Rome, adding even more confusion with references to foreign scientists from Japan, China, and Australia. He insisted to Mrs. Wasiri to allow her husband no excuse as this meeting in New York City will occur around the school spring break. After paying for Dr. Wasiri's airfare and hotel stay and forwarding all by FEDEX, Dr. O'Shea made sure not to give Dr. Wasiri any chance to reach him until he will get and meet with him in New York City. As he conversed with Mrs. Wasiri, Dr. Wasiri was also listening at the other end. When Dr. O'Shea hung up, Dr. Wasiri was laughing loud to his wife's surprise.

Dr. Wasiri told his wife, "My old mentor is certainly at the end of his long academic rope. From what I have learned, he has been all but kicked out of the faculty. He was now without any particular assignment, counting days, punching cards, waiting for his forty-year retirement from faculty to take effect, and his stay has been prolonged, thanks to his old buddy or nemesis Dr. McKinley, who has managed to keep him more out of pity, if any, essentially since the passing of Ms. Emily, his wife. All that because he will not give up on his weird research, and I tell you, including the Alpha-M project he got me involved in for a PhD thesis. Believe me, there is nobody, I mean nobody I have more respect for than Dr. O'Shea. However, things are what they are, what he has always championed seems not to be appreciated in the scientific environment at large. Is he far a seer than anybody else out there? Is he better than all his colleagues? Or is he just plain crazy? I do not know. All I know is that he was the only one to go to bat for me with that Alpha-M thesis and almost wreck my tenure as a professor. You know I do not want to relive all these dramas back then, but every time I hear from him, all that come back. It is at times very painful both for him and for me.

Don't get me wrong, I love the man, but given all that have happened, I am very skeptical of any research being reviewed by professors from Japan, Australia, or China. I do not know what the hell he is doing in Rome. Did you get his reach number in Rome? Never mind, I will make some inquiries with his family. But you bet that I am going to New York City as requested by my good old professor first to visit with some countrymen stationed at the UN and get the most current news about the forgotten country of Mezi and, second, to bring Dr. O'Shea safely back home to Kentucky from whatever adventures he has been found himself in lately. As far as Mezi is concerned, I believe that the good professor has already convinced you first, then I, to go back. I need a little bit of new stories about the country as we prepare to go back. My dear Hasbo, believe me, if anything I owe him to go to New York City for his entire family's sake and, above all, for the sake of his wife, Miss Emily, whom I adored and who has always treated me like a son. There is no need for you, my dear Hasbo, to persuade me. I will go to New York City."

"I am glad you do not need persuasion," Hasbo responded approvingly, "and that you are going to New York City anyway. As far as I am concerned, I will remain forever grateful to Dr. O'Shea, who has always given you extraordinary regards not just as an academic but also, for me, as a simple human being, a father. And you are right, that nobody, yes nobody, has stood by you, your thesis, and your research as much as Dr. O'Shea did as well as Ms. Emily. And for that, and as long as I live, I will remain the most grateful. Please take time out and go to New York City to meet with Dr. O'Shea.

CHAPTER 6
Second City Meeting

While Dr. O'Shea was talking from Rome with Mrs. Wasiri, Lady Allistair received the full report of Dr. O'Shea's stay in Amovir with urgent instructions to accelerate the establishment of the nonprofit organization talked to and arranged with the Georgia state senator, His Honorable Jeremy Massay. Lady Allistair was not convinced whether the Honorable Massay was the man to undertake the next phase of whatever BI had in mind. She argued with Amovir Station the merits and shortcomings of the state senator from Georgia with emphasis over the matrimonial issues he was currently facing, issues she learned through various paid sources in the Georgia State Legislature. She argued that the Honorable Jeremy Massay had not shown to be a politician with the stature to become a senator representing the State of Georgia in Washington, DC, and ready to advance the interests of BI as defined by Amovir station. She based her conviction on the combination of Massay's matrimonial problems with the long, complicated and tumultuous history of Southern politics aggravated by race relations in the state. Amovir Station sent a terse advice to Lady Allistair saying that the Honorable State Senator Jeremy Massay remains the man to carry out the mission defined by BI as sanctioned by the CEO, Mr. Kiriyan, with a noticeable caption: "The business of USA and the state of Georgia is business, and whoever carries the levers of business, i.e. money, will carry the business of the state. Let the levers of business carry the day."

This was another fundamental opportunity that Lady Allistair missed to learn from Mr. Kiriyan, her boss; how he operates, specifically how he selects people to work for him. An astute management student would have noticed a pattern in Mr. Kiriyan, established as long as he had appeared on this earth. Mr. Kiriyan is always going after the most determinant individual human factors to select people. These factors do not have to be humanly favorable. But as soon Mr. Kiriyan is satisfied that he has found that determinant factor, he decides whether the factor would enhance or diminish the task at hand. Everything else becomes irrelevant. In the case of Lady Allistair, Mr. Kiriyan knew that she was distrustful of the Mendham family and wanted to show that she can, as a woman, assert herself professionally. In addition, she had a social life she rather keeps in a closet.

The humiliation that Dr. O'Shea has suffered his entire professional life was also a determinant factor and would endear him to Mr. Kiriyan for life as long as he is helped along in his quest and he would drag his protégé, Dr. Wasiri at all cost. Vanessa's rules were a major determinant factor for His Honorable Jeremy Massay on top of his limitless political ambition; working over those two factors would keep His Honorable very motivated. It was on that basis, to Lady Allistair's surprise, that Mr. Kiriyan decided to maintain His Honorable as the potential ABDI chairman of the board and the future senator from Georgia.

In addition, Lady Allistair was also instructed by Amovir Station to assist Dr. O'Shea in every way possible when he will get back to New York City very shortly, especially if he is to meet with Dr. Wasiri. The latter instructions made it plainly clear to Lady Allistair that in the hierarchy of priorities, Dr. Wasiri was a superior target for BI's overall long-term plan. Whatever needs to be done to bring Dr. Wasiri to BI's circle should be done with the utmost care. Nothing, absolutely nothing, needs to be spared to that end. These latter instructions added more puzzle in Lady Allistair's mind. But as a dedicated officer of BI, she will carry Amovir Station instructions without reservations. She placed a call to the Honorable State Senator Jeremy Massay inquiring about whether he was ready to lead the nonprofit organization they talked about the last time at his State Legislature office in Atlanta, and above all, whether Massay's wife, Vanessa, has given him the green light to lead this nonprofit organization. To both questions, the Honorable State Senator Jeremy Massay responded affirmatively with one caveat, he insisted that the nonprofit organization be attached with the African Studies Institute of the University of Georgia in Athens. This will lend an academic credibility to the objectives of the organization without mentioning that the dean of the institute was his longtime friend Dr. James F. Stringer, an economist also from Duke University, in dire need of notoriety.

Lady Allistair and the honorable state senator settled on the name of the organization: "African Breakthrough Development Institute, ABDI" and its location in Atlanta. They also agreed on ABDI's first main officers: the Honorable State Senator Jeremy Massay, chairman of the board of directors, and Dr. James F. Stringer, vice chairman and director of operations. Lastly, Lady Allistair and Mr. Massay set an appointment within three weeks to meet again in Atlanta to review the legal papers establishing ABDI, its initial board of directors, its initial funding, and start preparing for the launching of its activities in various parts of Africa.

At the end of the phone exchange, Mr. Massay wondered whether all he just heard was just hot air from that beautiful lady he met first at the University of Georgia in Athens and latter at the office a while ago. He started suspecting that Lady Allistair must have ulterior motives in the setup of another African development research organization.

He surmised that Lady Allistair was either in some sexual jungle fever journey, or she was bound to ruin him politically or both. Besides, he reflected there were so many of these organizations throughout US universities and most erected simply to appease radical Africanist elements of these universities rather than to actually bring about concrete acts of development in the dark continent.

Mr. Massay determined that if Lady Allistair were intent to have an affair with him, she would be sadly mistaken. The last six months have brought havoc in his life, and he was extremely grateful that it was not expunged in the public arena as in cases of many of his peers in the legislature when the public display of their escapades ended most of their political career. That much he has learned about these silly, misguided, and unfortunate sexual pursuits, and he has resolved not to fall into any of these traps, Lady Allistair notwithstanding.

He intended to live by Vanessa's rules until their marriage is saved. Besides, he has gradually adjusted to the rules, and above all, for the sake of their unique child, their daughter. He wondered what version of his duplicity his daughter has been made aware of. He asked himself many times what Vanessa has shared with his daughter to explain the separate living quarters arrangement that has been instituted in the household after his confession. He tried in vain to pry from Vanessa how their daughter was dealing with their marital problems.

He would not dare have a frank talk with his daughter. This was plainly forbidden by Vanessa, who insisted on sparing their daughter their own drama. As Vanessa loved to put it, "Better two than three wallowing in this drama." And for one salutary observation made by Mr. Massay, his daughter never gave a hint of being distraught or unhappy about the tense moments between her parents, at least, during the first three weeks after the famous confession and confrontation. At the end, Mr. Massay was relieved, trusting his wife to have somehow managed to keep the relative peace in their house.

He faithfully availed himself to prayer sessions that Vanessa engaged the family every weekend. These sessions were divided into two sequences: the first forty-five minutes were intended for the entire family in the living room after dinner. Then their daughter was excused and the Massay couple retired for one to two hours of additional prayer sessions in Vanessa living quarters. These latter sessions addressed various marital and human issues as reviewed mainly in various St. Paul letters, Vanessa's favorites, and other Roman Catholic publications. They touched upon the failings of adultery, pride, prejudice, fairness, and equality in marriage.

They also addressed the purpose of marriage in Roman Catholic religion, the presence of God in the marriage, etc . . . These latter sessions always started with a loud reading of a passage followed by a thorough and honest discussion of what transpired from the passage and the definitive conclusion and recommendations for both of them. A deeper invocation to God closed the session. For some strange reasons, and as Vanessa intended these sessions to be, they brought the couple back to their seminarian days when they were preparing themselves for the life of devotion to God with chastity. During these sessions, there was no sexual inclination from any of them. They became more a conduit to salvage their life as a married couple. These sessions went a long way to reconcile their daughter to the separate living quarters' arrangement.

From this perspective, His Honorable Georgia State Senator Jeremy Massay decided that in case where Lady Allistair insisted on having any fling, he will slowly and resolutely steer her to his much-accommodating Dr. James F. Stringer, still a single in spite of his advanced fifty-two years of age with a long list of broken relations, mainly with his own students, as he loves to repeat, from nineteen through ninety-one-year-olds, not discriminating and from all races. Brother Stringer already appointed vice chairman of the board would not wait for Massay's indication. At the first sight of the beautiful Lady Allistair, Brother Stringer will be on his typical behavior and on the chase. This will spare His Honorable any additional headaches during this precarious time of his life.

As soon as the plane bringing Dr. O'Shea back to the United States landed at JFK Airport, he called Lady Allistair to let her know that he had a wonderful trip to Amovir, including the international conference. He thanked her for all the wonderful accommodation and hospitality he enjoyed in Amovir, including the meeting with the august chairman of BI, Mr. Kiriyan himself.

He proceeded to explain that he wanted to make strong impressions on a longtime friend and peer from Kentucky State University to convince him to join in his work on behalf of BI. He wanted Lady Allistair to make arrangements for outstanding and impressive VIP accommodations for their stay in New York for no more than three days. Lady Allistair understood right away what Dr. O'Shea was asking, given the last instructions and report she received from Amovir Station. She also guessed that the friend or peer must be Dr. Wasiri but did not mention it.

She told Dr. O'Shea to come by taxi straight to the office, where he met her before this last Amovir trip. She would use the time to start putting together the New York City VIP accommodations Dr. O'Shea needed for his friend and peer from Kentucky State University. When Dr. O'Shea reached the office, Lady Allistair was waiting for him on the lobby with a large envelope inside which there was an all-paid-for five days reservation of a suite at the Pierre Hotel on Fifth Avenue and Sixty-First street, an all-paid twenty-four-hour chauffeur-driven stretch limousine service, four dinner reservations at plush five-star restaurants around town from China Town to Upper East Side, reservations to outstanding spa locations of Manhattan. The only question Lady Allistair asked Dr. O'Shea was whether it was a bit overdone.

Dr. O'Shea answered that it was OK by him and added that he thought he was going to pay for all these expenses without mentioning what was already known to Lady Allistair that he left Amovir five million dollar richer. Lady Allistair said that was not the case, all was being paid for by BI, and she wished Dr. O'Shea and his guest a wonderful stay in New York City.

However, before departing, Dr. O'Shea dropped his guard and asked Lady Allistair to handle a small financial matter regarding the five-million-dollar-prize-money check he received in Amovir and that he has been carrying around. He wanted the check to be deposited in some London discreet investment bank company for the time being while he makes up his mind for the final disposition of the money. Dr. O'Shea insisted on the character discreet of the deposit. Lady Allistair replied that she knew exactly where he was coming from, and she would take care of the deposit and that Dr. O'Shea should not worry about any tax liability consequence for the time being. She added this would happen as if the check never entered the States. Dr. O'Shea had no idea what she was talking about and muttered, "I trust you would do the right thing."

In his ride to the Pierre Hotel, Dr. O'Shea was further surprised to find inside the same large envelope another envelope containing five thousand dollars in hundred-dollar clips and a set of shining credit cards made out to his name, one from Citi Bank, another from Bank of America, and a third from American Express, and each had a twenty-thousand-dollar limit with the instruction to just sign his name in the back. By the time Dr. O'Shea reached the hotel, he was literally rushed to a private elevator like a celebrity and taken to the twenty-seventh floor to a private suite of three bedrooms and all sort of unbelievable amenities. The most impressive of all came about when he entered the suite. Waiting for him, there were two gentlemen with a series of suits, shirts, ties, and shoes. They asked him to try and choose three suits, seven shirts, seventies, and three pairs of shoes of his liking. They asked him when he expected other guests. They said that they will return the next day with the nicely fitted suits and also to make available to the new guest the same service being provided at the time, all compliment of the House of Lord So 'Onley from London, couturier for VIPs and kings. Then they left him alone in the big suite. Dr. O'Shea shook his head and wondered whether he was getting a bit accustomed to this grand train of life after his stay in Amovir and the stopover in Rome, Paris, and London. And through all this, he has even not withdrawn a cent from his new five-million-dollar-trip bonanza. He resolved that if there were anybody who should share in this VIP accommodation, it got to be Dr. Wasiri.

He was just a bit concerned how he was going to explain this new grand living to his favored student. He decided he needed to get back his clear head after the hectic Amovir trip and the three European stopovers. As it was only three thirty in the afternoon, he needed a good evening and night's rest before going the next day to LaGuardia Airport to fetch his longtime student, friend, and now peer arriving from Louisville at about one in the afternoon. Before retiring for the day, he noticed the long table adorning the suite living room with all kinds of first-quality food and beverage to feed more than fifty people. He thought, What a waste, what a life! Dr. O'Shea was awakened at about nine that night. A courtesy call came from the desk inquiring about his long sleep and whether he needed anything at the time: a massage, a dinner, or whatever. He agreed to a massage before a light dinner. Shortly after, he was being serviced by a staff of five people, three of those in charge of massage and equipment while the other two busied themselves to cook on the spot a light pasta dinner with generous cutlets of Domenico steak. When he was done with the massage service and a quick shower, a delicious dinner was served with the best red imported wine, a Merlot from France.

The entire accommodation prepared Dr. O'Shea for a full night of rest until the next morning when he was awakened at about nine thirty by a call from Lady Allistair inquiring about the general state of the suite at the Pierre Hotel and how much he enjoyed the stay. He responded affirmatively and thanked Lady Allistair for the VIP treat. He assured her that it would be very effective on his guest due to arrive sometime the same day in the afternoon. When he hung up the phone, he realized then that he had already made, from Rome, the arrangement to stay with Dr. Wasiri at a different hotel at a much cheaper rate, and Dr. Wasiri was likely to join him at that hotel from LaGuardia Airport.

He knew from Dr. Wasiri's previous stays in New York City that he spent most of his time meeting with many of the Republic of Mezi countrymen working either at the UN various offices midtown or at the Republic of Mezi UN diplomatic mission. Dr. Wasiri has always mentioned one of them, a Mr. Beni Mbow, working for PNUD for more than fifteen years and fully established somewhere in the New York metropolitan. Dr. Wasiri said that both of them came from the same region of Mezi and attended the same missionary school back then but did not know each other. Dr. Wasiri was a generation four or five years younger. When Dr. Wasiri came to the United States to pursue his college studies, Mr. Mbow had already gone to England, where he received a master's degree in international economics from the London School of Business.

Mr. Mbow returned and worked back home in various economic ministries. But he left the country and joined the PNUD staff first in Vienna, Austria, then after in New York City. The reason he left the country was that he seriously antagonized one of many military junta leaders, General Pogato, in charge of the country internal affairs over the issue of resettlement of nomadic tribes from the southern border desert area to the high plateaus' agricultural provinces of Mezi. The resettlement issue was politically delicate including disparate tribal interests. It also required funding that Mezi central government could not afford. Completely fed up by what he was witnessing, Mr. Mbow wrote an article in one of Mandi leading newspapers denouncing the resettlement process and claimed that it was becoming a trust fund designed to enrich few generals and colonels with no accountability whatsoever to the country treasury. This was happening during the long military regimes of 1980s through 1990s, the time of generals and colonels. Mr. Mbow literally took a great risk to challenge General Pogato, the deputy leader of the military junta at the time, the power that be.

During the same period, he was the main highest civilian manager of the resettlement process and built a strong and close relationship with PNUD representatives dedicated to the resettlement issue. The bras de fer with the general became untenable; he was quickly selected to join PNUD when it became obvious that his life was in danger. After a short stint in Vienna, he was transferred to PNUD New York offices. He established himself and his family in New York City, rising through PNUD management ranks with no intention of returning home. These two countrymen met by chance at a PNUD conference held in Chicago. Dr. Wasiri was invited to talk about mining extraction economics in Southern Africa, and Mr. Mbow was the PNUD conference moderator. They hit it off right then and exchanged various contact numbers. Dr. Wasiri and Mr. Mbow shared so many sad events and stories from the Republic of Mezi. Mr. Mbow had more contacts back home to garner news from the home front and will share them with Dr. Wasiri every weekend. Their weekly Saturday morning phone calls were legend in their respective households in New York City and Frankfort. These calls usually brought the two households at standstill. Nothing else filtered out of the house during these sacred hours. Mrs. Wasiri had a joke about these calls and said that cellular phones were made to bypass these spirited calls. As a matter of fact, unbeknownst to Dr. Wasiri and Mr. Mbow, she conspired with Mrs. Mbow to purchase the first cellular phones as gifts to their husbands just to free the Saturday morning calls.

Dr. O'Shea was aware of these New York City contacts of Dr. Wasiri but forgot that it will be the same this time around. He knew it would be very unlikely for Dr. Wasiri to come to New York City without spending a lot of time with Mr. Mbow. The VIP accommodation at the Pierre Hotel looked extremely out of place. But he wanted to have the complete and full attention of Dr. Wasiri for at least the next two days. At about four hours before Dr. Wasiri's arrival, the list of conflicting appointments for Dr. Wasiri became a crisis. He reached again to Lady Allistair who suggested keeping the first reservation for the extended stay of Dr. Wasiri while insuring that he makes himself available for an important meeting for two days at the Pierre Hotel. She will come up with an urgency to keep Mr. Mbow very busy at the PNUD office in New York City or for an urgent PNUD presentation in Washington, DC, for the World Bank. His only reservation was to find out if Dr. Wasiri and Mr. Mbow have made their own plans from the time Dr. Wasiri was to reach New York City. But he trusted Lady Allistair's abilities to come up with appropriate solutions in short times.

She proved that the day before with the Pierre Hotel suite and the whole VIP treat, and within forty-five minutes. It was already about eleven in the morning, the time to head on to the airport to beat the endless traffic snarling the city. By the time he came down by the private elevator, the limousine driver met him on the lobby and led him to the gleaming dark black Cadillac limousine much different than the previous day. He settled in the back and spelled Dr. Wasiri's name for the driver who printed on the spot a good-size flier with Dr. Wasiri in large capital letters enough to catch anybody's eyes from three hundred feet. At the airport, Dr. O'Shea took a seat opposite the arriving crowd while the driver held the flier sign with Dr. Wasiri's name about the exit post. There was already an indication on the "Arrival" big board that the flight from Louisville has landed on time, and the passengers have already disembarked.

At that very instance, while Dr. O'Shea was reading the magazine he found in the limo, Dr. Wasiri was stunned his name was written on a sign held very high by a limousine driver. He went straight to the man and asked where was Mr. Mbow, who was expected to pick him up. The driver said that he had no idea who was or where was Mr. Mbow. Dr. O'Shea, seating about ten feet from them, got up and rushed to meet with him. The driver asked for his luggage and took him to Dr. O'Shea, who was delighted to both surprise and greet him.

The first thing Dr. Wasiri noticed was the expensive suit, shirt, ties, and shoes that Dr. O'Shea was wearing and which were brought back to him that very morning from the House of Lord So'onley. He also noticed a ring adorned by a multicolor jewel glow on his left finger just above his perennial wedding ring. This was not typical of the academic mentor he used to know. This was a completely changed man, not the same man he tried to console at the passing of Mrs. Emily, his beloved wife, the last time he saw him.

"What are you up to, dear Dr. O'Shea" he asked. "Before you say anything, what are you trying to pull on me? And while you are at it, where is my friend, Mr. Mbow? In fact, what is going on here?" He let out in crescendo.

"My beloved son," Dr. O'Shea responded in the same manner he did when he had a grave communication to part with him, "listen to me very carefully, the winds of change are upon us, and we should not miss the call, not this time. The winds of change are calling for your station. Please do not miss the call. I will not say anymore until we are set in our proper midst.

Let's go back where I will have so much to share with you. Follow me." Dr. Wasiri, deep in thought, followed Dr. O'Shea to the limousine while the driver mounted his luggage in the trunk of the car. When they were settled in the back seat, Dr. O'Shea summoned him not to say a word until they reached their destination.

This was the longest ride Dr. Wasiri has taken in his life, not being able to say a word all along. He was now perplexed and confused. He could not make out what station, if any, he was in. Was Dr. O'Shea in danger but then why all this VIP accommodation? The expansive suits, the luxurious limousine transportation, the sumptuous bar, and TV monitoring set inside the car. After five minutes of deafening silence, Dr. Wasiri, to calm his nerves and senses, reached out to the bar empty glass, put in two or three ice cubes and filled it with the first bottle of Johnny Walker Black he found. He took two rapid sips. Dr. O'Shea left out a big laughter and requested a similar glass for himself, saying to Dr. Wasiri, "You will get used to this grand life very quickly." They continued laughing together at their nonsense until they reached the Pierre Hotel.

While Dr. Wasiri was protesting that this was not the hotel he was supposed to stay in, his luggage was already being taken to the suite through an elevator different than the one Dr. O'Shea was opening with his own key. When they entered the suite, the couturiers from the House of Lord So'onley were already there, and this time with the same proposals for Dr. Wasiri, who was now beyond amazement. He duly and fully picked the shirts, ties, and shoes. His choice of suits fit nicely and did not need any retrofit. The couturiers were out of the suite in less than thirty minutes, and the big suite was now available for Dr. O'Shea and his longtime student, Dr. Wasiri. He was quickly shown his unbelievable spacious bedroom. He excused himself with the urgent need to collect his own thought, freshen up, and take a shower before confronting his mentor. While in his room, he was tempted to call his wife and share the first impression of Dr. O'Shea. But he decided against making the call as long as he has not gotten to the bottom of what the good doctor was up to, without mentioning the new four expansive suits he has just bought for him. Very confusing indeed! He took a quick shower and got in one of the new set of dresses, compliment of the House of Lord So'onley. He came out and could not see Dr. O'Shea, who at the time was at the other end of the suite's huge living room, peering out of large windows, giving into a splendid view of Central Park from the twentieth floor. Dr. O'Shea was deep in thought, collecting every bit of his remaining wisdom to set the stage and to make the case for what Dr. Wasiri needs to do in the near future.

As he came to notice Dr. Wasiri advancing toward him, he directed him toward one of the deep sofa to seat while he sat right in front of him for dramatic effects.

"Son," he started, "let me first dispel all that you are ruminating in your head about your friend Mr. Mbow. He sent his regards and was very happy that I was there to pick you up at LaGuardia Airport. Mr. Mbow will be detained in Washington, DC, for the next two days. He was delegated by PNUD to make an important presentation to the folks of World Bank for a project of the utmost priority for the eastern region of Africa. If I remember correctly, all this is related to the funding of resettlement of about three million people displaced by both the acute drought, which has drained that region, and the war between Somalia and Kenya. He tried in vain to reach you at home while you were getting ready for your trip. He finally reached your wife, who managed to get in touch with me this morning while you were already airborne.

He was the most grateful that I will keep you company before he comes back by the end of the week. The outcome of his trip could be career impacting in PNUD. Let us pray that he reached a very successful outcome from this exchange and for all these suffering people. You will see your dear friend in no time, in about two days. I can only guess how important your get-together is, and believe me, by the time you and I have concluded our meeting, you will be able to extend your stay in the city as long as you want. By the way, I have already taken care of extending your stay at the hotel where I originally planned our meeting. Which, in your mind, I guess, leads to the next question, why the planned meeting has been changed from that original hotel to here, why here in this luxurious suite of the most expansive hotel in New York City, the Pierre Hotel, and why now. All fair questions indeed, which need to be answered."

"Before I do, let me recount for you the long journey, I should say the long friendship you and I have shared since I met you that cold September day you came to my office awkwardly looking for guidance for your PhD studies. I was taken, above all, by your humility. Maybe because I was not used to African culture, especially how all people revere elders. You particularly radiated in the unconditional respect that is commonly extended to old folks in your society. What I never told you and what you did not know is that our first encounter came right after a terrible faculty meeting, I attended, where I was vilipended and derided by new upcoming young and, yes, brilliant faculty member in front of the entire staff.

"He went as far as to say that my days in the Faculty were numbered and that he will see to it that, I quote, 'the rubbish' that I dare call science will be expunged from the curriculum if he can help it. This happened, I recall, about twenty-seven years ago, counting your PhD studies, the defense of your thesis, and the twenty-three years you have spent teaching at Kentucky State University.

"From that day, I have waged a constant battle to defend my 'rubbish' science. This went on through the painful and long period of my beloved Emily's sickness. This went on through her passing. What you also did not know is that only three people, or I should say four people, including your wife, you, Emily, and myself were registered to wage that battle. You and your wife were reluctant warriors as always.

I have seen Emily eaten away by that battle because she always stood by me. Believe me, the cancer that doctors pretended to have killed her was just a by-product. I know that the primary driver of her demise was the fact that she cannot bear the sight of her husband being ridiculed day in, day out at the Faculty. Another thing, after our first encounter, I called Emily and shared with her the morning faculty meeting diatribe and the next meeting I had with you. Emily admonished me to go all over the university, looking for you and to bring you home for the dinner the same evening."

At that moment Dr. Wasiri smiled, "Yes, I remember, and I found it very awkward all the attention and kindness your family extended to me that evening."

Dr. O'Shea waved at him to continue listening and resumed in a solemn tone, "Emily had, at that time, already decided to recruit you for the battle to come. Since she was most apt at raising my kids, she knew that none of my children was interested in the studies of mineralogy. I believed she managed to steer them away from that field after she had witnessed the mental ravage that afflicted her own husband.

Deep down, I also agreed with her. But the question was always who will continue waging the battle if I was to pass away. That scared the hell of us daily and more so for Emily. She spared nothing to welcome you at home and to gradually adopt you as her own son. During her long illness, she was never tired of asking about your status in the battle. I lied to her saying that you were more than engaged. Remember when you came to visit her at the hospital during one of her many lapse periods.

That morning, when I announced that you were coming to pay her a visit, she asked the attending nurse if she can let her get out of the bed so that she can go down to the clinic kitchen an cook your favorite meal veal shin. Of course, that was not possible. But the nurse was so moved that she left early and cooked that meal you ate with us that evening. The nurse was also surprised that you were the recipient of all that commotion. Emily rejoiced immensely about your visit and started to walk the next day. The entire family thought that it was a miracle. But that was not to be, and Emily passed away three weeks later. And it was the same with Dorothy Hasbo, your wife. As soon as you introduced Dorothy to the family, Emily took over. I have to confess she invested more time in insuring that your relationship with Dorothy went a long way than she will over her own children's relationships.

Dorothy was readily coadapted. They spent an unbelievable amount of phone calls every day. Sometimes, more than ten times a day. If you did not know, you would think that Dorothy Hasbo was her daughter. It just worked out for Dorothy because when you started dating her, the household was slowly emptying out. Anthony, my son, Danah, and Emma went about their ways very fast. Emily took in Dorothy as a long-distance daughter when Emma started her graduate studies. To all my kids she came up with a rule: it was always 'I raised you, I will not indulge in your happiness.' This was true for both the twin girls and the boy.

At the end, I came to realize that Emily did not want to spread herself too thin when she had to attend to the big battle. She made an exception with Dorothy Hasbo because she was one of the warriors. I must confess when Emily passed away, and given all that was happening in the Faculty, as you well know, I thought that the battle was lost to the

McKinleys of this world. I really thought that with my retirement coming up next year, I will just hang it up in a beach in South Carolina, where I have planned to buy one of those fully equipped retirement town houses and to spend the rest of my life jetting all over the country, visiting with my many grandchildren six months of the year and staying put the other six months of the year fishing, picking up and playing golf along South Carolina beaches. I was prepared for that life with all that Emily and I have put away, her life insurance, my forty years' retirement income of full professorship at the university. As we speak, my kids have had already two meetings to finalize the retirement set deal. Now you remember my daughter Emma, the University of Manitoba president. She is also fully engaged.

They have yet to report to me about the whole deal. But I have learned through one of the real estate lawyers they have hired that they are making sure that they will provide me with the townhouse and yearly retirement facilities fee as a present when I retire. They want me to keep all the money I wanted to use to get the townhouse for myself. I am all grateful to these kids, but I still have to confess, the one thing Emily and I knew about our children and having spared them the awareness of it all, they have no idea about the battle we have waged all along and how to win it. And all along, Emily and I always counted on you to continue waging the battle.

"I know very well that you were a reluctant warrior. Whatever you have done to date was either for my sake, Emily's sake, and your academic sake. But yet, every time you were engaged, we came closer to victory. For instance, your thesis discredited every notion that Alpha-M did not exist. You proved not only that it existed but also where to find it in the high plateaus of Mezi. Let me tell you, when you left the University of Kentucky, I continued your research over Alpha-M. But the graduate students who assisted me were not the same, they were less dedicated, as you can suspect, than yourself. I wound up doing all the work by myself with the support from Emily. After Emily's passing, I deliberately reduced all involvements outside Alpha-M. I swore to discover all the known properties of Alpha-M for the sake of Emily and before my own demise. And I certainly did find all of them. The day I completed the scientific verification of these properties was the happiest of my life. I simply noted all the findings and locked them into a safe in my home. I would not dare publicize without your consent or permission. Now that I have shared them with you, they are all yours. I took some observations to my second trip to Amovir International Conference. But I never had time to present them. And deep down, I was not sure if I should divulge all these findings to those Russians out there even if they have been funding all of my research since. I have decided that I will turn all to the real scientific leader of Alpha-M, and you would do whatever you want with them. But I have to tell you right now that holding these findings in secret will be the worst thing you can do. This is the time to make use of all the properties in Alpha-M for you, your family, your country, and possibly the world. I have also to tell you that there is only one way to achieve all the potentials that Alpha-M keeps. You have to go back to Mezi, find Alpha-M, and make use of its properties.

"There are people and companies ready to spare no resources to help you achieve this. And that will be the case only and only if you take steps to go back to Mezi. Dr. Wasiri, this is trust of my message in inviting to join me here now.

This is the trust of the battle victory that you will win for Emily and me. Now you can ask me whatever you want, and I will try to answer you to the best of my ability."

Dr. Wasiri remained quiet for a while and then said, "I have already decided to go back home at your urging and that of Hasbo's. She has been quite a pain for some time to get the family to go back to Mezi. Frankly, I am reconciled with the idea to go back. However, I did not reach that decision with all that you shared today in mind. I am going back because I want to go back. I have to tell you right now that I am not certain that I would look into Alpha-M findings or continue some forms of research around Alpha-M by the time I will reach Mezi.

I am actually, for your information, working or negotiating to gain a tenure professorship in the Polytechnic University in Mezi's capital, in the town of Mandi. I intend to quietly, and I insist quietly, continue teaching mineralogy studies in the same manner as I have done the past twenty-three years. I have absolutely no desire to verify the existence of Alpha-M in the high plateaus of Mezi. I am not about to be involved in mining development as you are proposing. Nor would I be involved in any way shape or form in the Mezi politics, which would be the logical next step when one starts being involved in mining development in Mezi. No and no. I am to reach a peaceful accommodation with Hasbo by going home. She deserves that much. The rest, including Alpha-M, will not be part of any plan. Dr. O'Shea, I am saying all this for you to remove any consideration from your mind about me being some kind of reluctant warrior in your famous battle. I do not consider myself being part of the battle, and I will not wage it. I am sorry. I will always cherish your support, guidance, love, and the gracious support from your wife, Emily. I will always love you two and your family for all the considerations you have extended to Hasbo, my family, and me. I will always be grateful, and I will appreciate that you and I limit us to those considerations and nothing more. Let us forget the famous battle."

At that sound, Dr. O'Shea retorted, "What about the prize I have received for both of us in Amovir in recognition of the lifetime work involving Alpha-M? We certainly have to share it. I cannot keep all the prize for myself. My conscience will not allow it.

Besides, the prize had a five-million-dollar stipend associated with it. That works out to two and a half million for you and me. Now even if you do not want to be involved in Alpha-M researches in the future, you got to keep what is due to you for your past researches.

That will only be fair. By the way, since you want to remain as politically independent as possible when you reach Mezi, that much fund will allow you to stay clear of any political involvement back home. And for your information, I have used my part of the prize to amaze you with the VIP treatment we are enjoying at this time. With my advanced age and my children relatively settled in their life, I have nothing else to do with that money but leave it to my grandchildren. But their parents are also rightly providing them. Here again, I have nobody to run to but you, Hasbo, and your children. What else can I possibly do with the rest of my prize part fund? It is also for you. I respect very much all that you say. I have already mentioned that you will remain a reluctant warrior. But do not refuse your own share of the prize for your own family's sake. I was not expecting to change your mind here and now about Mezi's prospects. I want you to keep your options open. Please think about it."

Dr. O'Shea, by those statements, was steering his protégé toward the main instruction he received in Amovir from Mr. Kiriyan himself to convince Dr. Wasiri to go back to Mezi to complete the great researches over Alpha-M. Although he was ambivalent about all that he saw and heard during his stay in Amovir, including the encounter with the Dudarev couple, Dr. O'Shea decided that the way to finish his long battle around exotic minerals was to engage his protégé to go back to Mezi. He was the only one he trusted to bring his lifetime devotion to fruition. He judged it to be mere coincidence the fact that Mr. Kiriyan of BI Corporation was also interested. Lady Allistair and all these other strange characters he had met since have all had a great interest in seeing Dr. Wasiri go to Mezi. Theirs was dictated by basic commercial or other specific business purposes, and he understood that. But his was of much higher purposes, an academic goal of far-reaching importance destined to set the final score for the battle he had waged all his life in academic circles. He was not to let go this chance. He had the best advantages of all the protagonists. Dr. Wasiri was his protégé. He was going to use every influence over him to achieve his goal. This was the reason he bent the story of the monetary prize, leaving aside the K ring he was wearing. The mention of the five-million fund got Dr. Wasiri in a state of mind bordering lunacy. He had no additional question or retort for his mentor. He suddenly realized the depth of the lifetime commitment he reluctantly signed up when he conducted his doctoral thesis with the guidance of Dr. O'Shea. The good professor will never let him go until he died. The good professor had taken steps to insure their forever-lasting relationship in the temple of Alpha-M by securing a five-million-dollar prize. There was absolutely no point in arguing otherwise.

He decided to go along with the stay in New York City and to enjoy the stay until such time he will be with Mr. Mbow in the latter part of the week when he will part company with Dr. O'Shea.

At least, his mentor was in good health enjoying the VIP accommodation in New York City, thanks to a five-million-dollar prize from the Russian company of BI. Finding out the health standing of Dr. O'Shea was the main reason he came to the Big Apple. There was no point to find out about this from his children who were not even aware that he had traveled to Russia and Europe. Dr. O'Shea hardly discussed his work with his children, and Dr. Wasiri was very much aware of this since the time of Emily, his beloved wife. He was now reassured of his health standing all right.

But as far as the entire story about Alpha-M went, including his half share of the five-million-dollar prize, he convinced himself that he needed more time to sort it all and leave it out when he will talk to Hasbo, his wife. Maybe, just maybe, by the time he will meet Mr. Mbow, he will have made sense of the entire story. At the same time, Dr. O'Shea, who has known his protégé for more than sixteen years now, had a better reading of his mind. He also decided not to press his query. He started to talk about family matters and the like. He proposed that both of them go out in search of the most expansive late afternoon lunch in town. A telephone call at the hotel lobby indicated a very pricey French restaurant at East Fifty-Fifth Street. They were led there by limousine in about twenty minutes and talked through the sumptuous meals about pleasant past things, families, and all mutual colleagues and acquaintances.

It was amazing to see the two academics carrying on with their endless conversations. Any stranger will have concluded of the deep bond emanating between both of them. Lady Allistair who had followed them from afar from the hotel and managed to sit a few feet unnoticed from their dining table also observed this. She was to render a personal report to Amovir Station about her first observation about Dr. Wasiri and the observed relationship between Dr. Wasiri and his mentor. The station had already taken steps to record the entire conversation that had taken place that afternoon in the suite. The sarcastic tone that Dr. Wasiri had displayed alarmed the Amovir Station. Dispatching Lady Allistair to the restaurant was decided to reassure the station that there was no breaking point in the relationship; little did the station know that the rapport between the professor and his protégé was at times tense and at times, very cordial. The question to Lady Allistair was to find out whether their disagreement was by design or just plain natural.

After about three hours of the late lunch, the two academics decided to pay visit to a natural location of their predilection, the New York Library on Forty-Second Street and Fifth Avenue, where they devoted the rest of the evening through about 10:00 p.m. browsing over archive papers of mineralogical studies dating back to year 1200.

When they got out, Dr. O'Shea invited his protégé to a jazz nightclub in the Village section of the city to wallow the night over some beer and other hard liquor of which he had been taking strong interest from this last European trip. There was no jazz band playing there that night, but a selection of classic tunes from Miles Davis enchanted the club just the same. It was around two o'clock in the morning when the academics retired in the suite of the Pierre Hotel very, very tired.

When Dr. Wasiri reached his bedroom, he called his wife. He reported how he found his mentor in good health, leaving out the VIP treatment he has been subjected since he landed in New York, including the extraordinary accommodation at the Pierre Hotel and the chauffeur-driven limousine.

He also left out the four sets of costumes, shirts, ties, and shoes—compliments of the House of Lord So'onley. He left out the extraordinary accommodations, knowing very well that Mrs. Wasiri will seek out proofs, probably from her friend, Mrs. Mbow. But since he will be visiting with his friend Mr. Mbow only on the latter part of the week, when he will be moved back to the first location of hotel rental, there was no point to mention the VIP treat. He also decided not to talk about the new Dr. O'Shea he has met. Otherwise, he told his wife about the long plea that Dr. O'Shea made about him going back to Mezi.

This was the same plea he has made before. But the difference this time was to be in a context, as Dr. O'Shea put it, of mentor to protégé, of academic father to academic son. This was the main reason Dr. O'Shea had invited him to New York City. And for all these instances, he told his wife, he responded that he had already agreed to go back, thanks both to her constant insistence and Dr. O'Shea's and now that their children were moving out and about to start college studies. He also left out the sore Alpha-M subject. He got this close to mention the prize money of five million dollar but left it out also as this would have enlivened the Alpha-M subject. He kept the whole phone conversation as banal as possible, hoping to fill pertinent blanks when appropriate. It was close to four o'clock in the morning when he felt asleep.

When he woke at about eleven o'clock, the suite was very quiet, and there was no sign of Dr. O'Shea. Before Dr. Wasiri started making inquiries at the front office, he got a call from the good professor. He said that he did not want to trouble him but needed to go out and make a few errands and shopping before going back to Lexington the next day. He should be back in about two hours or so, and they should be ready to go for another late lunch as the day before. His call did not ring convincing to Dr. Wasiri. So far, they got anything they wanted by simply calling the Pierre Hotel. Front desk, thanks to the VIP accommodation.

Why the good professor needed to bother with some personal errands and shopping? He thought that he was getting to understand the good old mentor less and less. And this was for a good reason. When Dr. O'Shea called, he was reaching the office of Lady Allistair. The turn of the conversation he had with his protégé required him to request a few services from Lady Allistair. He related to Lady Allistair the need to set up an account of two million and half from his prize money on behalf of Dr. Wasiri for the primary reasons to facilitate his return to Mezi to settle down there.

The account will be set in a bank in London, of course with ease of withdrawal and usage at any time from Mandi, the capital of Mezi. The second request centers on the need to provide financial and technical support to the Polytechnic University of Mezi in Mandi, specifically the Mining Engineering Faculty, with special mention to set up an advanced postgraduate chair of Mineral Extraction Sciences. This should start as soon as possible and will be a surprise gift for Dr. Wasiri when he will get there.

The last request, for the time being, will involve Mr. Mbow to reinforce his plea to get Dr. Wasiri to return to Mezi. At this stage, there is no one he will listen to as readily as he listens to Mr. Mbow when it comes to his country of Mezi. Before Lady Allistair was to respond, he placed a call to the chauffeur of the limousine and gave him a long list of personal items he was to bring back from his supposed errands and shopping.

At that instant, Lady Allistair said that all of his requests were granted, including the incentive to get Mr. Mbow on board. In return, she said, she also had her own request. Lady Allistair wanted to know if Dr. O'Shea and Dr. Wasiri were willing to become board members of a new organization called ABDI for "African Breakthrough Development Institute" attached to the African Studies Institute from the University of Georgia.

She explained the main purpose of the organization, which will be headquartered in Atlanta, Georgia. She also added that ABDI was still in its infancy and will become a major driver of economic development in many parts of Africa. She said that if both agree, the new chairman of the board, the Honorable State Senator Jeremy Massay, would be calling on them very shortly. Dr. O'Shea responded that he had no problem joining this board, but he will need more convincing for his good protégé. He will need more information from this Georgia state senator to line up Dr. Wasiri. And he said, "Dr. Wasiri is not a joiner." Dr. O'Shea added that he would have another frank conversation to bring Dr. Wasiri along. He thanked Lady Allistair for accepting to handle all his requests and at the same time refrained himself, as he was becoming to get used to when dealing with Lady Allistair, to ask how she was going about to fulfill these requests. He also thanked her for all the VIP accommodations she pulled for him and his guest so effortlessly. He said good-bye and left, as the two hours allocated for the sortie was getting close. His only reservation was the incentive request he made for Mr. Mbow. He was a bit apprehensive as he realized that this last request started crossing a few paths. He did not mind when all was done in the name of the great battle, and it always involved the major protagonists: Emily, Mrs. Wasiri, and Dr. Wasiri. Whether they like it or not, they have signed up to the great battle. And they were supposed to be engaged. Now he had started to enlarge the circle of engagement including people not primarily connected or sold to the cause of the battle, people like Mr. Mbow, a friend of his protégé. Dr. O'Shea did not feel a bit good about this and wondered how he should make amend.

When Dr. O'Shea was questioning the merits of involving Mr. Mbow in convincing his protégé to return to Mezi, Lady Allistair was already taking steps to accelerate the process by engaging the old soldier in the person of the same Maj. Gen. Richard "Bull" Fadden, now in charge of AMX, lobbying activities in Washington, DC. The major general, through his endless list of contacts in the community and by extension in the World Bank, managed to attend Mr. Mbow's presentations regarding the worrisome impacts of the drought and the war in the Horn of Africa. He approached Mr. Mbow after his first presentation and invited him to lunch along with the Africa Eastern Region World Bank coordinator by the name of Clas Hassen. During the lunch in an average-looking restaurant not far from the World Bank headquarters, the general lamented over the plight of the three million people displaced by both the acute drought and the war between Somalia and Kenya. He went on to suggest that only rapid economic development of the region would spare the indigenous population of the calamity visiting upon them.

To this, Mr. Mbow replied that the region in dispute is completely barren and a desert with no resources, mineral or agricultural, to speak of. That, he insisted, was the real tragedy of this calamity that two countries will wage war over absolutely nothing. The World Bank manager agreed completely with Mr. Mbow. This did not disturb the general who had introduced himself to Mr. Mbow as a minerals extraction executive consultant attached with the worldwide well-known consulting management company of Mattley & Barr. This being one of the many obscure titles, he prefers to exhibit when he wanted to impress new recruits. The general went on to say to the surprise of his guests that "what appears to be desert today may hold underneath bounty of minerals nobody knows of at this time" "Now," he continued, "when you look closely at the map, you see the whole peninsula of Saudi Arabia next door with unknown quantity of oil and gas from the same sediment going from the Hazan Region of Iran, crossing down the United Arab Emirates through Saudi Arabia and Yemen. Tell me why that sediment of oil and gas will not extend itself to the Horn of Africa through Somalia, Ogaden Region of Ethiopia, and to precisely the region in dispute between Somalia and Kenya. I will not say that the dispute is about oil and gas. But what if one of those murky oil companies has whispered to the war lords of Somalia and the government authorities of Kenya that the potential of finding oil and gas is there, and it was about time to reassert territorial claim over this or that portion of that forsaken barren territory? Now tell me, gentlemen, will that not lead to war?"

To this observation the World Bank manager chuckled and said that the observation was as far as he was concerned pure speculation with no basis on facts. From every political, economic and scientific input he had gathered to date, the whole calamity in the region was as a result of lack of resources. "If Mr. Fadden adds any other factual input, he is welcome to include it in his current analysis," he added. All along, Mr. Mbow remained very quiet listening intently to Mr. Fadden. Mr. Mbow was very sensitive to the implication of the talk carried out. Throughout his PNUD functions, Mr. Mbow came, many times, across stories of buried or hidden analyses pointing to the findings of minerals in many parts of underdeveloped regions of the world. These minerals remained buried unexploited until either the prevailing stage of economics made them relevant to be extracted or, and worse, when the political leadership in place changed through wars or brutal changes of political regime or in very few cases, through peaceful political changes brought about by elections. In his mind, Mr. Fadden had an interesting point that was not to be easily dismissed.

At the same time, he was not about to openly contradict his host, Mr. Clas Hassen of the World Bank, especially now that he was in the middle of a very sensitive negotiation with the World Bank on behalf of PNUD, in fact, begging for funds to address the dire needs of the three million war-and-drought displaced people.

He offered a neutral saving-face observation for both and said in a typical UN diplomat jargon: "Although nothing to this date and to PNUD's knowledge supports any sinister design from the belligerents to gain territorial and mineral control through militarily conquests, we at the UN always keep in mind, analyze, and sometimes anticipate the underlying and deep causes of these types of conflicts. This analysis will necessarily include facts, speculations, and all available discourses from both sides from the ridiculous to the most logical. And believe me, we have seen all kinds of discourses as usual, and I can spend days sharing them, and you will be amazed to hear some of them, and I seriously mean some of them are just plain insane. In all instances, the analysis always helps, when the belligerents start enunciating their grievances to table what appropriate solutions to the crisis at the end should be advanced. As you can appreciate, our role at the UN is not to start crisis but to resolve them."

It was also time to attend to the afternoon session with other luminaries of the World Bank. Sometime later during a break from the afternoon session and when Mr. Clas Hassen was not around, the general managed to extend another invitation for a dinner with Mr. Mbow to continue their conversation. He knew that Mr. Mbow was much interested in the bait he has laid during the lunch. He knew that he was not going to decline his request. This time the general raised the selection of the restaurant a bit, insuring that it will be way above the like of Clas Hassen. This restaurant gathers to "five million dollar or more a year" lobbyists like he, the cream of the cream of K Street. The restaurant had a general quarters area at the middle, surrounded by multiple discreet private rooms where the political business of America is decided most of the times. The general had made a reservation for one of those private dining rooms, and this time for two only. Mr. Mbow was well impressed. He surmised that this meeting will involve more than the business he came to Washington, DC, on behalf of PNUD. In his case, he came to request funds from World Bank and not to give funds. Lobbyists or consultants or people of Mr. Fadden's ilk, from his knowledge, are in business to request funds from this unit on behalf of that unit. What this gentleman can possibly expect to get from PNUD was a bit confusing. And in all honesty, if it is about some minerals, oil, or gas in the war zone, this gentleman will be wasting his time.

PNUD was not in the business of granting licenses to exploit minerals, oil, or gas in war zones. Besides that, he will be all ears and certainly enjoy the expansive meals. At that time, the general and Mr. Mbow were being seated in one of the private rooms with all-dark-brown leather chairs surrounding an ebony shining table covered with what looked like a satin beige sheet and assorted gleamed covers. They will be attended by a maître d' very discreetly standing outside the private room, holding a silent small cellular look-like set which vibrates at the guest instigation. The maître d' will communicate with the main guest in whispered tones as not to disturb adjoining conversations in the main area or other private rooms. To push the discretion to an even higher level and for those in need of that feature, all communication could also be done in writing using the cellular screen and a discreet desktop in the room.

The general went for the discreet conversation, ordering the menu du jour after inquiring and agreeing with Mr. Mbow. It was time to get on with the subject at end. To his surprise, Mr. Mbow noticed that instead of making any request regarding the business he came to the World Bank, the general started asking questions about Mr. Mbow's whereabouts, where he was born, where he was from, what he had done his whole life, including his academic background, and his professional background. Mr. Fadden asked questions about his family, his life back home in Mezi and in New York, his functions in PNUD, his likes and dislikes in PNUD, etc. It was as if he was being interviewed for a job. Somewhere he asked the general whether he was conducting an interview and for what purpose.

The general answered affirmatively and added, "I am looking for someone with an extraordinary background on behalf of Mattley & Barr to direct consulting management functions in relation to multiple business interests that Mattley & Barr needs to supervise in eastern part of Africa. As matter of fact," the general added, "I am also extremely delighted to hear that Mr. Mbow is from Mezi because in addition to this regional consulting function that Mattley & Barr is interested in filling for the East Africa Region, Mr. Mbow must be well placed in identifying country men from Mezi with strong background in mines engineering consulting.

Both functions will pay in above 150,000s range a year with all kinds of benefits. There are also tremendous incentives to fill each one of these positions. For the eastern region job, that is for yourself, Mr. Mbow, there is a forty-thousand-dollar hiring fee that will be available to you six months after you have accepted the job and are on the job.

Now as far as the Mezi job went, if you are able to identify such a candidate and the candidate is able to work in place in Mezi, you will be paid thirty thousand dollars of finding fee first for identifying such a person and another thirty thousand dollars six months after the candidate has taken up the job in Mezi."

The general continued, "I will be very lucky to resolve the filling of these two positions, thanks to your involvement. At this time, I need only to know if you will be considering the offer for the eastern region function and if you are willing to assist me to identify the candidate for the Mezi consulting job. If that is the case, I am ready to sign a check of ten thousand dollar for that simple consideration, and you will walk out of this restaurant ten thousand richer and no string attached. This will testify to my good faith and to the extremely urgent necessity that Mattley & Barr attached to these two functions.

"To circle back to our conversation this afternoon, this will attest to the importance that my organization attaches to the correct analysis of resources in place in many parts of this world and especially in Africa. It comes down to the right analysis of all that can be seen or is hidden. In the final analysis, soon or later, these resources need to be unearthed, exploited for the benefits of the mankind. But one has to know where they are and what it will cost to extract these resources. What is the point of not knowing how and when to extract these resources?

"This is where I come in. This is where you and the fellow in Mezi would come in. At this point, you, Mr. Mbow, have the most thankless job in the world. You have, in fact, to repair situations with limited or no resources. You come in to address a problem with no resources. You come to the World Bank, yes, to beg for resources. You come, in fact, one step behind. Think about it: if the Kenyans and the Somalis had enough food to eat on both sides on the border, jobs to provide for their children and families, and means to satisfy their basic and other needs, would they be fighting this useless war? The answer is no. Human beings will wage war when their needs are not met or not satisfied or not readily available. This is as old as the humanity, and it comes down to finding resources first to address the humanity problems. I will be the last person on this earth to diminish the importance of what you are doing at PNUD. It is a noble cause. But as I said before, it is one step behind. Now it is up to you to come one step before the crisis. Join us in this endeavor. I believe I have run my mouth quite more than I should, Mr. Mbow, what do you think?"

"Mr. Fadden, I want to thank you for this sumptuous dinner. As I said, I was surprised by the turn of our conversation. It started this noon over the calamity we are confronting in the Horn of Africa to wind up to this, like interview you have conducted this evening. I have to tell you that I am honored for the consideration you have extended to me all this evening. I wish you had requested my curriculum vitae or résumé this afternoon. I would have brought it without hesitation. Not that I need or I am looking for a new job. But I learned longtime ago to stand ready to accept or reject any new job opportunity when it comes. Believe me, I appreciate your forthrightness and the ability to call a spade, a spade. You were completely correct when you said that in my functions, and where my organization stands, we have to come one step behind. I know that, but then, that is the role of UN to come after disaster or crisis and clean it up. It will be more effective to be in the front of crisis and disaster and prevent them. That will be the right thing to do and that is also in the goal of the UN; unfortunately, we are not there yet. We are hoping to get there, and I believe we are getting there slowly, member nations helping. While we are striving to get to that goal, we will still be putting out fire here and there. I can also tell you that we have come a long way. We are evolving and growing. We are not today, as a world community, what we were twenty or ten years ago. And thanks to rapid and growing communication around the globe, what people thought to get away with twenty or ten years, they will think twice to do. That has become a more potent prevention of evil doing around the world. I trust that this evolution will only grow as the world becomes more connected, and what is happening in Karachi, Pakistan, at nine o'clock in the morning is broadcast at the same time in Quito, Ecuador. I am proud to be part of that evolution, I am proud to be in a position to enable it. The question from you is whether I want to be one step ahead. The answer is yes. And I am making it happen now in my job. Should I consider making it happen in any other capacity? Yes, sir, I should consider the option only to find out if it fits my future goals. In the same veins also I will look into assisting you to identify a citizen from Mezi in taking up the mines engineering consulting position. As a matter of fact, I have a few very strong candidates for such a position I may recommend. I will only ask you to give me enough time to conduct my own research and get back to you primarily within a week or so. Is that fair?"

The general was delighted by his response, especially as far as the mines engineering position. He sensed that Mr. Mbow was not keen to leave the PNUD as yet. But he was open to provide a strong reference for the engineering function. Deep down, he concluded that it was the so-called Dr. Wasiri.

The general felt that he had closed the deal as requested by Lady Allistair, and he was ready to tackle the menu du jour. He pulled his checkbook and signed a check of fifteen thousand dollars payable to Mr. Mbow, no string attached. He pulled another blank envelope and inserted the check there in and handed the envelope to Mr. Mbow, who was nibbling the assorted hors d'oeuvres.

The general ordered a red French wine to toast Mr. Mbow's consideration of his twin job proposals. The remaining dinner time was spent over general review of the politics around the current UN debate to stop the war in the Horn of Africa and other UN crisis. It was around one o'clock in the morning when Mr. Mbow reached his hotel room. He was also most delighted when he opened the envelope to find out that he was, not ten but fifteen thousand dollars richer after less than four hours of a dinner conversation. He resolved that he needed to change the tone of conversation when he will meet his old friend Dr. Wasiri. No more unpleasant stories about Mezi as he did in the past. Forget about the political violence, the coups, the endless labor, and student strikes besetting the country.

Forget about the current political leadership under the barely elected President Badegou, his prime minister, Sonjedi, and his cohort of useless ministers. No more sorry tales of the do-nothing Parliament and senate where tribal dealing had been taking overtly precedent over national goals leading to a total legislative paralysis when addressing any challenge of national interest. Maybe a night out with both Dr. Wasiri and his dear friend, the first counselor at the Mezi Diplomatic Mission at UN, His Honorable "Sir" William Ewas, will do.

It will not be bad to collect within the next four or five months another sixty thousand dollars on top of this bundle of fifteen thousand dollars if he can convince Dr. Wasiri that it is about time for him to go home and put into practice his brilliant background in mines engineering. By the way, Dr. Wasiri had mentioned all that beating he keeps getting from his wife, Mrs. Hasbo Wasiri, to go back. It looks like he is making up his mind about the trip home. The 150,000 dollars or more gig as mines engineering consultant for Mattley & Barr should be a great incentive to go back compared to the tenured professorship, he had kept the past twenty-three years. He will be getting maybe four times what he is earning in the godforsaken Kentucky State University. And if all goes well, it will amount to sixty thousand dollars for poor Mr. Mbow. Therefore, no more stupid stories about Mezi. Mention only growth and development prospects when talking about Mezi.

Now as far as this eastern African region job that this Mr. Fadden was dangling in the restaurant; he needed to think about it very carefully, keeping in mind that he may move up two or three rungs if this DC trip soliciting World Bank funds was successful so said his departmental director. That will change everything, does it! If the trip is successful, he will move up the management rank and will get as much as what Mr. Fadden was proposing. He will remain in New York, safe with his family, away from that uncertain eastern African posting that was being discussed. He had invested already more than twenty years of international management experience at the UN. He will not blow it now for a vague position for Mattley & Barr. He needs to consider it very carefully. Of course, there will be no word to the wife or anybody about this proposition from Mr. Fadden. Time will tell what it will really amount to. He should be able to explain his newfound riche of fifteen thousand on the account of some management retainer fee or hardship incentive from PNUD secret funds. At this stage, he needs to be mentally prepared and alert to meet his old friend, Dr. Wasiri. The first deposit of thirty thousand will depend on it.

That Thursday morning, while Mr. Mbow was ruminating how he was going to approach his old friend, Dr. Wasiri, in matter of returning to Mezi, Dr. O'Shea was also surmising how the two days meeting with his protégé went. In the middle of packing his suitcase, he made a mental note and concluded that he had faithfully passed the baton to Dr. Wasiri. He was leaving New York City with no doubt in his mind that the next phase of his lifetime battle will be waged in its next logical station, which is Mezi, where Dr. Wasiri, the rightful heir in waging that war, will be very soon presiding over the mighty army he, Dr. O'Shea, had put in place since he joined the Faculty of Mines Engineering Studies at the University of Kentucky more than forty years ago. In a matter of time and with the resources the unsuspecting BI management will make available to Dr. Wasiri in Mezi, victory will be finally ours in the long-fought academic battle of the preeminence of exotic minerals. It had always been Dr. O'Shea's belief that from the time of the first big bang, exotic minerals were released in the universe with powerful properties which, when properly harnessed, will bring the humanity closer to the design of his creator, the design of plentiful bounty of goods, endless life, endless happiness, and the Adam-and-Eve paradise on earth that ancient books talk about, the ultimate God's design. That belief when expounded in academic circles was met with a lot of skepticism and sometimes ridicule. That had hurt Dr. O'Shea a lot all his life. No matter how he had tried to push it, even to the most God-believing scientists, his theory fell on deaf ears.

Very few scientists were ready to make that leap of faith as he did. That was the case when he rightfully demonstrated throughout the history of the humanity when the discovery of every new mineral was thought to be a gift from God to bring about a better mankind. He asserted that the discovery of each one of the minerals, iron, copper, gold, diamond, oil, and aluminum was exclaimed all over the world to be the beginning of a new mankind era. However, each time, when that discovery became only a small link in the long chain of minerals discovery, the hope generated by the mineral evaporated quickly and was again dashed. Dr. O'Shea maintained that in addition to those minerals, there must be the exotic minerals with extraordinary properties to have maintained the lesser-known expanding stability of the universe as intended by the creator. Dr. O'Shea concluded that without those exotic minerals, there would be no universe and only chaos. This is where Dr. O'Shea expanded his theory to include astrophysics, philosophy, and yes, theology. This is also where he radically parts company with his peers. This is where Dr. O'Shea found less and less common ground in the design of his so-called unified theory. His appeals fell on deaf ears for most of his teaching career. There were very few graduate students who took up his thesis and were quick to abandon it as soon as they advanced to safe teaching or mining positions. Dr. Wasiri was an exception, in that he literally adopted him in his own household. Out of loyalty, this student protégé had no choice but to write a thesis of his liking. That thesis was also controversial crossing academic limits as not done before, even when it was anchored in scientifically demonstrable facts.

It was unfortunately in the same realm of Dr. O'Shea's theories and almost cost a promised career to Dr. Wasiri. Now Dr. O'Shea was thinking that maybe Dr. Wasiri was godsent. Coming from a region of earth where the probability of extracting one of those minerals was the greatest only reinforced his faith. He knew that Dr. Wasiri was a very reluctant warrior in the battle since the time he had met him. But slowly and surely, Dr. Wasiri was moving toward the same goal. He was now more determined to assist his protégé after his trip to Amovir when he had witnessed with his own eyes what he had not been able to prove to date. The sight of and conversations with Mr. Kiriyan and the Dudarev couple had convinced him that there are people or civilizations in this universe in quest of the same exotic minerals he has promoted all his life and for the same properties. For the first time in his life, he had met with people who have the same common understanding of these exotic minerals. He rather works with these people to advance the academic understanding of these minerals. Whatever they are, aliens or not, they have the means and resources to do honor to his theories.

From then on, he will not burden his protégé with lengthy exhortations or explanations. He knows now that he had strong partners with the same designs as himself, and with extraordinary means and ways to accomplish the same goal. He decided that he will do all he can to get these people to assist his protégé in the next phase of the battle. At that very instant, Dr. Wasiri was knocking at the door to inquire about his mentor he had not seen since that morning. He was relieved to find him ready, all suitcases packed and about to leave the Pierre Hotel and to go back to Lexington. He said, "It is so nice to see you so fresh and so well disposed this morning. I was waiting for you to have our last breakfast, and you were taking forever to come out. You have worried me a bit there after the long night out."

"Well, son, I am no longer as young as I have been. The night out was very relaxing, and I have enjoyed very much. I am about to return to Lexington. I want to let you know that it was a great pleasure for me that you came to New York City to share these two days. That meant quite a lot to me. I am leaving very satisfied that you are going to undertake what I have always wished for you. You must be wondering why we did not meet in Lexington, Kentucky. Why New York City. The simple explanation is that this city gives and shows opportunities like no other city in the world. Forget about the VIP accommodation we have enjoyed the past two days. I know that you have never shown much attraction to any of that. On the other hand, you have always been the most humble person I have known in my professional life. That is what I have always been drawn to you. Humility in thought and talk, humility in discourse even when you knew that you were hundred percent right, humility in social setting, humility in your faith in God, humility in your family life, how blessed are Mrs. Hasbo and your children to have you as husband and father, that humility is also what Emily had discovered before me as usual, she being a better reader of people than myself. If anything, my son, never lose that precious humility that has carried you to date and to this place. That humility I have lacked and that has prevented me to promote what should have been so easy to advance. I wanted you to share that brand of humility. I leave very satisfied that you will carry it to the next level when you will become ready to affect the fruits of our shared goals and destiny. I will no longer bother you to undertake this or that for the field of sciences that is very dear to me.

Rest assured; I leave with only one thought: I have carried my mission very well. Before I leave, I have one last request that came from one of your colleagues from the University of Georgia, Institute of African Studies. The request came to me before my trip to Amovir.

The institute was looking for faculty members like you, with strong commitment and interest in Africa's economic and industrial development, who would like to participate in setting up a new think tank named African Breakthrough Development Institute or ABDI. The objectives of ABDI appear to be specific hands on approach in push for development projects in Africa. I thought about you joining the ABDI board at its inception. Now that you are thinking about going back home, I am convinced that this kind of connection will come handy to maintain back here in the States in addition to your current network within Kentucky State University. You never know where these kinds of connection back home and in the States can lead in the future. I want you to promise that you will follow up and accept the invite to become a board member when you will hear from the new chairman of ABDI board, a Georgia state senator by the name of Jeremy Massay. I really hope that you join this new think tank."

CHAPTER 7
Geffadi Soul-Searching

Dr. O'Shea finally said, "Now that I have shared all that I needed to share, I think it is time to keep company with me to the airport before you transferred to the other hotel as it was arranged."

Dr. Wasiri was again perplexed by all that he heard from his mentor and did not know how to respond, except to joke one more time, "I thought that we were going to reminisce about Miles and Coltrane tunes we heard last night. I was not prepared for a lecture on humility and African development. But, believe me, I appreciate the thought and everything you said in between. And I will follow up with the folks from the University of Georgia. Now let us get ready to bring you to the airport."

When they were seated in the limousine, Dr. Wasiri noticed again the huge K ring and asked his mentor when he started wearing rings like movie stars. His mentor was silent for a moment, not willing to reveal how he came to receive the K ring and the five million dollars.

After a while he opened up, "My trip to Amovir was a life-changing moment. The standing committee that has organized the conference gave me this ring for what they said was my lifetime contribution to the study of exotic minerals. These people are very high on these minerals as opposed to the folks you knew back at the University of Kentucky. They are more open to the proposition I have made for so long. They have pursued similar studies I have done. They are most grateful that some of us here in the United States are doing the same work. I have to tell you that I am honored to wear this K ring all the time for that reason. But this gift was separate from the five-million-dollar prize, which was specific to Alpha-M research and which I told them I was honored to share with you. Talking about the prize money, I have to let you know that I am taking every step to get that money to you with the minimum of tax penalty or liability from IRS. It is currently parked in one of London's investment bank accounts until such time when the tax issue is resolved. I will certainly keep you informed. I trust you will not share this with your wife or anybody until the final disposition.

If you ask me, that amount will come handy to ease your initial steps to settle back home since you have not been home for so long. Buying a nice home upfront, having affordable means of transportation, providing living expenses the first few months of getting back home, and other expenses that you may face. I am just giving you all types of suggestions. What do you think?"

Dr. Wasiri responded vaguely that he would address the prize issue when it will be made available. He thanked his mentor for dealing with the tax angle. He assured him that he would not mention it to his wife or anyone until it is made available. He also thanked the professor for the wonderful time they shared when dropping him off at the airport. It was then time to go back to the original hotel, which turns out to be Embassy Suites on the East Side River.

As he was taking leave of the twenty-four-hour-a-day limousine service, Dr. Wasiri was told that the service had been paid for until his departure. Surprised, Dr. Wasiri thanked the driver and insisted that this was the last time he will avail himself of the service. He will use common transportation for the rest of his stay in New York City. He added, joking, that he might have to go places where limousine service does not venture in Brooklyn and Bronx. He then disappeared in the lobby of the hotel. When he finished registering for the hotel room, he was given a large envelope, compliments of Prof. Anthony P. O'Shea. He chuckled at the sight of the large envelope and the name of his mentor on it. He went up to his sixth-floor room. With the envelope on hand, he was not surprised that the room rented by the professor turned out to be another large suite. The envelope had two small envelopes and a small note from the professor. The note mentioned the need to rent a suite with three bed rooms and something about Dr. Wasiri being able to receive, with the least of inconvenience, whomever he wanted and to accommodate as many people as possible to spend the night in the suite after a long night in the city. One of the small envelopes contained ten thousand dollars in hundred bills. The other one had a Citi credit card issued to Dr. Kano Wasiri with a five-thousand-dollar limit. There was also a large file of papers inside the envelope. Dr. Wasiri decided that he was not ready to read the papers and filed them in one of the suitcases. He was also puzzled by the fifteen-thousand-dollar total amount that the professor left to his disposal for the next four days remaining until his return plane trip that he had pushed to the following Tuesday when he came to realize that he will see his friend Mr. Mbow starting the week Friday when he will be back from the sudden trip to DC.

The last time he came to pay a visit to the Mbow family, he came with his wife and the three kids for a whole week; the total expenditure was no more than three thousand dollars, including their plane fares. This time when all has been paid for, including his hotel stay, the expansive garment sets he had received, various hotels and meals, he was at loss figuring out what he will be funding with the fifteen thousand dollars. He concluded that his mentor was really flushed with money from his last trip in Russia, and his mentor had no idea how to spend it. Dr. Wasiri concluded that he was simply a logical conduit for that money in the name of the so-called battle that he has been waging with his unsolicited assistance. That must be the only reason why Dr. O'Shea, in his very twisted crazy way, has been showering him with so much money and all the VIP accommodation. He cannot decline it now. He had to get along. But how will he explain this sudden-found fortune to his friend Mr. Mbow and his wife? The thought of Mrs. Mbow got his mind awakened. He did not call her since he came to New York City. He wondered whether she had talked to Hasbo, his wife, since he had been in the city with Dr. O'Shea. He rushed to the phone and got Mrs. Mbow right away.

"Good day, Mrs. Mbow, I am very sorry to reach you so late since I arrived here in your very exciting city, so many conferences to attend, all of them squeezed in such a short time. How are you and the kids? And what about Mr. Mbow, is he still due back tomorrow as I learned from Hasbo? Do not trouble yourself. I will go fetch him at the airport myself and find out if he has secured the secretary of secretary of secretary of deputy secretary of UN immigrant affairs, he has been applying for all these years."

Mrs. Mbow was laughing so loud she could not bring herself to stop, but at the end, she said, "Yes, your friend is due back tomorrow. I talked to Hasbo, your wife, when I did not hear from you. Both Hasbo and my husband said that you would be much occupied in the conference you were attending and that I should expect to hear from you today. So, everything worked out as planned. I thank you for saving me for the trip to LaGuardia Airport. I tell you, driving from our home in Hudson-Township to LaGuardia Airport always upsets me. The multiple byways and noways you need to negotiate to that airport will never endear an above-fifty mature lady like myself. The most troubling fact for me now, Dr. Wasiri, is the short and long sight that my eyeglasses need to adapt to. Some times what is far seems so close, what is close seems so far. It is getting a bit complicated. I said to Mr. Mbow that I need a new set of glasses. But I just cannot find time to schedule myself for a new eye exam. Oh dear, enough for me, I cannot wait to see you tomorrow.

I have already started cooking that home meal you love, and I will not reveal it at this time. Just bring my honey home, and you will see how you will be treated. By the way, I am also assuming that you are going to spend the rest of your stay with us here in Hudson-Township. Now that I am reassured that you are coming, I need to go out for more shopping for food and booze. Thank you for the call, and I will see you soon tomorrow."

Although he suggested it at the beginning of the call, Dr. Wasiri was a bit troubled by the fact that both Hasbo and Mr. Mbow have both suggested that he was attending a conference in New York City. He had not mentioned this to Hasbo or Mbow. He was certain that his mentor had worked overtime to insure the utmost privacy for these two days he shared with him. Was he underestimating all that the good professor had done and had intended to share with him during these two days? It was about three o'clock, and he needed to take a bit of fresh air out and take a tour of few shops in the city. These shops, he had visited every time he came to New York City and gathered the needs of many of his countrymen. His friend Mr. Mbow had always made references to these shops for home country foods, newspapers, magazines, music CDs, DVD documentaries, and movies and short stories, and authentic garments. With the money that Dr. O'Shea has provided, he was able to buy as much as he wanted. For home country fresh foods, he requested to get them nicely wrapped and shipped home to Frankfort, Kentucky; they should arrive by the time he would get there. This was also the case for the pack of CD and DVD, newspapers and magazines he did not want to carry on the plane. He kept only a few political magazines with very good articles and new sets of authentic home garments he will wear to impress the Mbow couple during the Friday evening dinner. He also made a stop at a wine and liquor store nearby the hotel to buy the most expansive wine, champagne, and liquor bottles he could find. He bought about twenty various bottles at about eight hundred dollars with a strict stipulation that they were to be gift wrapped, and he will pick them up on his way to LaGuardia Airport to pick up his friend Mr. Mbow. The shopping took most of the day and evening by the time he was back to his suite. The only surprise he noticed from the hotel staff was how neatly cleaned and ironed were all the clothes he had hung in the closet.

The new expensive garments were now shining. Dr. Wasiri ordered a light menu for the night ate and went to sleep.

He was awakened the next Friday morning at around nine o'clock by a call from his mentor, Dr. O'Shea, to advise him that he got home safe and sound and to inquire about his stay in the city.

He also reminded him not to forget about the call to the Georgia Senator Mr. Massay about becoming a board member of ABDI. Dr. Wasiri assured him that he would attend to this the first thing when he will get back home in Frankfort, Kentucky. He also added that he was enjoying his stay in the city, thanks to the large sum of money he left for him in the large envelope. He also added that he was about to go meet with his friend Mr. Mbow and probably spend the weekend with the Mbow family in Hudson-Township. Dr. Wasiri again thanked his mentor for everything. At the other end, Dr. O'Shea was surprised to hear that he left a large envelope for Dr. Wasiri with a large sum of money. Then he remembered his own ordeal with the large envelope from Lady Allistair. He knew now that she was also working on Dr. Wasiri through him and hopefully for the same design. He was happy that he was getting a lot of assistance from the beautiful Lady Allistair.

When he finished his breakfast, Dr. Wasiri called the front desk and made inquiry about a car transportation service that can be made available from noon until such time he will bring his friend back home from LaGuardia Airport to his home in Hudson-Township. Ten minutes later, he was told that there was a limousine available for him twenty-four hours a day until his day of departure. He called back and said he did not want a limousine service but a simple basic car transportation service for business people. When he came down with a weekend luggage, he was met by a tall nice-looking African American of middle age. He guided him toward a four-door large sumptuous shining black Cadillac much to his liking. The man said that he would be at his disposal from that precise time until his departure. Dr. Wasiri asked him if a professor O'Shea had hired him. He responded that in his business he is never told who had paid for what service. He added that he had learned longtime ago that in order to keep his job, he had to stay clear of knowing anything about people he was transporting. The name of the game is and has always been privacy and he got to abide by it one thousand percent if it was no problem to him. Dr. Wasiri said that he understood, but he still needed to insure that the driver would stand ready to resolve a possible embarrassment when they would pick a very old friend at the airport. This old friend may be making inquiries regarding the special transportation. He was hoping that the driver would back him up when he would say that the car transportation service was paid for, all compliments from a professor Anthony O'Shea. That is the only breach of privacy rule the driver should allow, if there was such a rule. That is the only rule that he wanted him to break, and this breach will remain secret between both of them until his departure.

In addition, the breach will be compensated with an extra incentive that will be generous to the driver just the same. The driver said that he will be happy to help Dr. Wasiri as long as that will involve nobody else but both of them. The deal was then struck. The driver made a stop at the nearby wine and liquor store to pick up the twenty bottles nicely wrapped in paper gift. They were then on their way to the airport to pick up Mr. Mbow at about two in the afternoon. The driver agreed to be stationed at the general limousine waiting area and will be advised to drive to the arrival gates with the help of an alarm system kit appropriate for the occasion. Dr. Wasiri did not want to use the elaborate greeting scheme that Dr. O'Shea had reserved for him at the beginning of the week. He had found it a bit ostentatious. For his friend Mr. Mbow, he wanted the greeting to be a bit modest with full of friendly surprises.

While he was checking the arrival and departure board, Mr. Mbow slapped him in the back. "Already at the gates, sir," he said, "and my luggage is right here with me. Do you care to carry it, sir?"

They embraced African style with bobbing heads and loud laughter. They greeted each other like long-lost brothers which, in fact, they have become these last five years.

"How were you treated at the seat of world power, Washington, DC, were they respectful of the high luminary from the PNUD, Sir Mbow? Did you get everything you wanted for the godforsaken people of the Gantwani Region at the border of Somalia and Kenya? How many lives are you going to save now? What about the interview for the position of the secretary of secretary of secretary of deputy secretary of UN Immigrant Affairs, was it successful?"

To each of the question, Mr. Mbow did not answer but released a pitched laughter. At the same time, Dr. Wasiri pressed the alarm kit as they approached the huge revolving door to vehicle transportation. Mr. Mbow then asked how far was parked his rental car. Before Dr. Wasiri could answer, the shining Cadillac stopped before them, and the middle-aged driver was opening the trunk and retrieving the only luggage that Mr. Mbow was carrying. That left the PNUD manager to utter simply "Whoa." The driver was at the same time opening the back door for both of them. It was at that moment that Dr. Wasiri was able to say loud that it was all compliments from his old mentor, the professor Anthony O'Shea.

And the driver seconded the lie by adding, "Yes, sir, good old Professor O'Shea, a good man, indeed."

Mr. Mbow would not let the remark about Dr. O'Shea's newfound largesse go by without a comment. "When I was there begging for funds from the irascible folks from the World Bank, you were having VIP accommodation, thanks to your mentor, Dr. O'Shea. How was he? What does he want from you now? Don't tell me he wants you to replace him and take his funky chair at the University of Kentucky? I hope you say hell no to that. I mean, from everything you told me, he has always meant well, but now I believe he is going too far. Bribing my poor lowly paid professor brother with a limousine chauffeur-driven car in New York City. Is it on twenty-four-hour call? Now where did you stay, was it Waldorf Astoria? That is not right. The last two days I was begging for money for our poor displaced people in Somalia and Kenya because of the drought and that stupid war. My mental stage was, well, all the time much somber. Only to go back to the riches of Dr. O'Shea, chauffeur-driven home in the company of His Excellency Dr. Wasiri. Well, I am very happy you came to see us here in the Big Apple. I hope you will tell me all that your mentor was trying to pull on you. Now first you called telling me you were coming on Tuesday. I was ready and prepared to romp. Then I got a call from Dr. O'Shea that you two will be very busy attending a conference somewhere in midtown. That sucks. And while I was sitting there, minding my business, one of our high directors walked in and started talking about how important and career-impacting this trip to DC was going to be. I was selected because of my background as Mezi countryman and my last involvement in the Mozambique resettlement efforts. I tell you I never met this guy before, and there he was telling me how he has been monitoring my career and the results of this trip will be extremely important for my career. That left me no room to maneuver. I went home and packed for the trip. I have to tell you right now that it went very well. PNUD is getting all the funds requested and much more resources. I do not know if I should thank you for messing up my schedule. You see all that happened well in spite of you. I mean, here I was getting prepared to welcome you. Instead, I was yanked out to go represent PNUD at this important meeting and voila. When I could not see you these last two days, a lot of things just happened. Just fantastic and mind-blowing! You should come more often to New York City to bring good luck. Now what about you?"

"Well, my trip has been rather smooth so far. In all sincerity, I did not attend the conference in midtown as planned. I spent most of my time listening to exhortations and harangues from my dear mentor over the ominous battle I have already explained to you about. This time he wanted really to impress me about various contacts and support he has made around the world, especially at the conference he attended in Amovir, somewhere in Russia.

He went on about prizes he won at that conference and how much he wanted me to continue sharing in his work and researches around exotic minerals. He came back really loaded. When I was with him, it was VIP accommodation twenty-four hours around. I mean the class of it. First, there is the suite at Embassy Suites that I am still occupying until next week Tuesday. Then the stretch limousine he had on call twenty-four hours. I had to downsize it for my personal usage now. My friend, rich folks know how to live. That limousine had everything comfortable anybody needs. Anyway, he also took me somewhere around East Fifty-Third Street to French restaurants you have never heard since you lived and worked here in the great apple. Was I spoiled? Would you believe that Dr. O'Shea now dresses like a British barrister? He managed also to get me dressed up the same. From the hotel suite, he ordered for me four garment sets from the House of Lord So'onley from London. Each set included a suit with matching shirt and ties and shoes. I needed to buy a new suitcase for all these garments. It was just unbelievable what the good old professor did. Finally, I came to realize his true motive for inviting me to New York City and entertaining me so lavishly. Believe me or not. He does not want me to replace him at the University of Kentucky. No, he is done with these folks there he considers until now as enemies. He wants me to go home to Mezi to ascertain what I have deducted in my PhD thesis around Alpha-M mineral. Remember that thesis that almost stopped my college teaching career? Yes, my mentor would not give up. He wants me to continue his great battle back home in Mezi. Well, I listened to him as politely as a protégé got to do in front of his mentor. I did not answer affirmatively or negatively. But I tell you, at this point in our relationship, it does not really matter. Hasbo, my wife, has been coming hard on me on the same subject. She said that with the kids nearing college studies, we should strongly consider going home. And you know with Hasbo, there is no let up. She fell in love with the country since the first time she got there. She does not see any future here in the States. As she repeated so many times, she would rather grow old and die in no other place but Mezi. At this stage, I start believing that I owe her that journey. So, before this trip to New York City, to calm Hasbo, I have already taken steps to contact the Polytechnic University faculty staff right there in Mandi to check out teaching positions. We are in heavy discussion process, and I hope it will be successful. So that will get me off Dr. O'Shea's bug once for all. I am not sure if I will pursue any of Dr. O'Shea's work around exotic minerals, but I will be far away finally from his emprise and focus. To tell you the truth, I hope to get there the next year summer before the academic year. In fact, twenty-three or so years in Kentucky State University are long enough for me.

So, you see, my trip was not that bad. By the way, I will spend tonight at your place, but I want to invite you and your wife to share a bit in my VIP accommodation, compliments of my esteemed mentor, Professor Anthony O'Shea. A long weekend will not be that bad in that suite with three large bedrooms at the Embassy Suites. What do you say, brother?"

Listening attentively to the happy turn of events after the talk or interview with the General Mc Fadden, Mr. Mbow wanted to probe further, but at the same time, he did not want to appear to be joining Hasbo and Dr. O'Shea in the same design of goading his friend to go home. He also wanted to be extra careful as not to jeopardize his future retainer fee of sixty thousand dollars.

"Brother Wasiri, I don't have to tell you, but you know very well how many traps and disappointments await many of us that the country people called "Diaspora." I want you not to take that decision lightly and when in your case, you have an American born Caucasian wife and kids who have been growing in a completely different environment. It would not be an easy adjustment, if you want my input. Frankly, we will have plenty of time to talk about that this weekend. And now that you are talking about going home, I believe that a view from someone who recently resettled here from Mezi may be helpful. I am talking about the first counselor of the Mezi Diplomatic Mission at UN, His Honorable "Sir" William Ewas. If you don't mind, I want to invite him to join us sometime this weekend at home or at your new expansive digs in Manhattan."

At that point, Dr. Wasiri told Mr. Mbow that the name William Ewas seemed very familiar to him. He knew of an Ewas family from back then in his village. And he remembered growing with Ewas boys: Joseph and William. Joseph or Joe, as they loved to call him, was the most brilliant soccer player in the village. He remembered that he was in his Episcopalian school most of the time. He was always the soccer hero when it came time to play against the team from the St. Paul Roman Catholic School that resided a few miles from his village.

"When I was growing, the soccer game between the two schools was the biggest social event of the year. Joe whom we all baptized 'The Magician' always came up with the most magical display of soccer artistry in the game. He was the author of two or three goals in each one of those games. And as handsome as he was, he was the darling of most of the girls. We all envied Joe. William, on the other hand, was just as modest as Joe was a showman and very preoccupied with his studies.

I was closer to William, and we studied together a lot and formed the first debating society in the school. We were called the bookworms in the school. It is very funny how things in life sometimes evolve. But sometime before I came to the United States, the Ewas family migrated to the capital of Mandi, and I lost all contact with the Ewas boys. If this first counselor at Mezi UN Diplomatic Mission was the same William Ewas I knew, it will be wonderful to renew our long-lost contacts."

They were getting closer to Mr. Mbow's house in Hudson-Township, and Dr. Wasiri gave a few instructions to the driver. He let him know that he was spending the Friday night at his friend's house. He told the driver that he might need him to come back to Hudson-Township to pick him, his friend, and his wife in order to be in the city sometime on Saturday. The driver gave him a reach number for that request. It was about four o'clock when they reached Mr. Mbow's house. Silani, Mr. Mbow's wife, was already outside to greet the man from Kentucky. She led the guest inside the house, while Mr. Mbow struggled with the driver to retrieve from the car trunk the twenty wine and liquor gift bottles, his own luggage, and Dr. Wasiri's weekend luggage. Silani had already put out Mezi country's preliminary dishes on their long dining room table. Two of the Mbow children of high-school age were also available, assisting their mother in setting the table. After a brief grace prayer to greet Dr. Wasiri, the Mbow's couple retired to their bedroom, leaving the guest to exchange a few words with the children. As soon as they were alone in the bedroom, and while he was freshening up in the adjoining bathroom, Mr. Mbow told his wife of the new mission he has set for himself as long as Dr. Wasiri will be their guest. He was going to limit any bad reference to things back home in Mezi. He wants to reinforce Dr. Wasiri's decision to go back home and avoid saying or alluding to anything that may raise objections to his plan to return. He added that he had to help his friend to open his mind to all the benefits and possibilities that his presence in Mezi would bring. He noticed that his wife looked at him with an incredulous face, knowing how he, Mr. Mbow, can go on mercilessly for days criticizing anything he heard coming from the latest political dramas from Mezi without mentioning the Saturday morning endless diatribes he shared with Dr. Wasiri. To stop any argument from Silani, Mr. Mbow said that this time, he was rising above the petty observations about Mezi he had been guilty of many times and that he needed to concentrate on helping a dear friend make a tough decision of his life, and that was a serious matter. It will be selfish and of a very bad taste if his friend who needs his counsel now bases his decision on his distractions.

Mr. Mbow added that he did not realize how serious Dr. Wasiri was about that decision until he took the ride with him from the airport to back home. He finished his talk by begging his wife, "Darling, please help me on this as we need to help Kano and Hasbo to make the right decision."

When they came down to the living room, their guest was alone, reading one of the Mezi political magazines he bought the day before. The article that he was reading related to multiple conflicts of interest that five ministers in the current government have been allegedly involved in their administrative decrees. The story involved management consultancy firms conducting various studies on behalf of ministries while the same ministry titular heads maintained majority equity of shares in those firms.

Putting the article aside, Dr. Wasiri allowed another comment about Mezi politics,   "Well, Mr. Mbow, just another one of the endless soap operas going on back home in Mezi. Can you imagine five ministers caught in similar conflict of interest scandal at the same time? How far will this go on? Even if the whole government is dismissed, the next ministers will do the same with the exception that they would have learned how to hide their misdeeds from probing journalists. This has happened just like you have said to me time and again."

Filling their glasses from one of the French wine bottles that Dr. Wasiri brought, Mr. Mbow made his first move, "You know what, I have to confess that I have been guilty all these years of rambling every Saturday about what has gone wrong back home when we talked on phone, you and I here in the United States. Hear me right. While I was in one of the meetings in DC, an African American manager at the World Bank took me aside and asked me a question that until now I have not been able to answer. You see, I was there, providing all kinds of statistics to those who came to the meeting. I believe there were about thirty-five to forty people in the room. As I said, I was very good, providing the statistics of the calamity of drought and war visiting upon the people in the Gantwany border region of Somalia and Kenya.

I was very good at describing the horrific horror of war and famine. Mind you, that was why I was selected to take the trip and present. In other words, my role was reduced to shell shock the hell out of the attendees to act. As I told you, I was very successful. The response from the World Bank will be forthcoming and above the initial request. All that was all right.

But the question from that young African American brother who came out of the meeting shaken and emotional wreck was, "Why was the calamity not prevented? And if you are from that region, how you could let it happen with all your knowledge, contacts, and resources?" I listened to the young man and could not muster any response because I knew right then and there that it would be another excuse. It will be the same excuse that will come from the World Bank in the forms of whatever relief efforts that are being mustered now. My dear Kano, acting before the calamity is better than after it, which becomes again another excuse. I said to the young man that I hope to get back to him sometime soon with the right answer as I was not able to answer him right then and there. He appreciated my honest answer, and we exchanged e-mail addresses and phone numbers. I saw the young man again the next day. He came to me apologizing for what he considered harsh inquiries. I advised him that his inquiries were not harsh enough, especially for someone like me. At this time, I am still struggling with these two questions. That leads me back to the scandals you were reading. It is all very fascinating but the question at the end, like the young man, should be, why were those scandals not prevented? And if we are from Mezi, how could we let those scandals happen? You know, each one of us at this time has a ready-made answer to that question, and most likely, it will be a fatally flawed excuse. The answer will be given unfortunately in the context of our environment, which is now the United States, Hudson-Township, Kentucky, nice living room, nice dining table, nice kids, and before I forget, chauffeur-driven limousine, etc. My dear Dr. Wasiri, no matter how we color it, it will be an excuse. The sad fact is that those in Mezi, those in the Gantwany region, those in Somalia, those in Kenya, and in fact, those in Africa have no use for the excuse. They only have use for peace, and things working better with no cheating, stealing, and no silly breakdown. As I sat in the car from the airport listening to you struggling about your decision to go home, I was very relieved, and I said to myself, At last, there is someone who will not give another excuse. He will show us the way of no more excuses. Dr. Wasiri, I will not prevent you from reading those articles. In fact, they are very good in the sense that they will show time and again what you will not do once you are home. Yes, I confess I have been guilty of merely criticizing all those scandals and dramas evolving back home. Granted the political actors are of last known mediocrity. But hold it, they are of our generation, and we have seen them and lived with them here in New York City, there in London, Paris, Berlin, and Moscow as students and like. They are not much different from us who have remained behind in New York, Toronto, Paris, or London, struggling day by day to make a living and abiding by the rules of the game of these countries.

What I never understand is that why we are ready to abide by the foreign country rules of game but abandon them very quickly when we get home even when we know and have seen that these rules make things work relatively well in those foreign lands. Why not use them or use the ones we strongly believe are the most efficient and appropriate? I am confident that after struggling to make the decision to get home, you will do us honor to abide by the rules you have learned that will work for all. Forgive me if I am talking like this, that young man in the DC is still in my mind, and I am also struggling to give him a decent response which will not be an excuse."

Mr. Mbow left his wife completely bewildered. Silani excused herself and retreated to the kitchen with her two daughters. She told them that their father came back from his trip to DC as a completely changed man, and she is trying to put her fingers in what could have changed her husband. The elder daughter suggested that maybe her father had an affair in Washington, DC, according to stories she had read in many African American novels, recounting DC as a sin city, not to trust one's husband for three days. Silani dismissed her husband's alleged change on the account of any silly tryst in DC. The couple had gone way past these silly adventures. If he was to engage in any tryst, why not right here in New

York City with all available single women he comes across in Manhattan at work and the countless easily available women from Mezi who have been showing up lately in the Big Apple in quest of commerce or other sordid business according to her cousin who lives in Brooklyn. She told her daughters that their father being involved in a tryst at this time of their life would be the last of her worries. She was more afraid that there must be something much deeper that her husband came across while in DC. His speech had completely changed. She needed to find out quickly what had affected her husband and why. She retired to her bedroom and, using her cell phone, called Hasbo, Dr. Wasiri's wife. She reassured her that her husband was at the moment in their care in Hudson-Township. She deftly asked about their preparation to go back to Mezi. Hasbo said that she was still struggling to convince her husband that it was about time to go back. But she also added Dr. Wasiri is inching toward that final decision very slowly, and she was more or else hopeful now and will appreciate any additional pressure points from both Mrs. and Mr. Mbow while Kano was their guest. As she was completing her call, she noticed an envelope protruding from the large work planner book that her husband carries with him all the time and never leaves aside. When she opened the envelope, she saw the check with the amount of fifteen thousand made to Mr. Mbow and signed by a Mr. Fadden. The envelope and the check bore a business name of Mattley & Barr.

She was now completely afraid that her husband might be involved in some sordid affairs, including some kickbacks from PNUD contractors. She remembered that this was what had happened to one of her friends from Malaysia two years ago. Her husband was managing large PNUD contracts with various American and European companies. These contracts amounted to five hundred thousand dollars or more a year on the average. Then he started taking kickbacks from some of those firms and was dismissed summarily, and the family had to go back to Malaysia. She asked herself if this was the source of the new attitude that her husband had been showing. She will need to confront him very delicately. She was completely confused and started perspiring profusely and needed to take a quick shower. Her husband heard all the commotion going on upstairs and excused himself and came up and saw the fifteen thousand dollars check on their night table. He knew that he needed to rapidly explain the meaning of the check from Mattley & Barr.

He entered the bathroom while his wife was drying up with a towel. He sat on the stool, "Darling, I was going to explain the check you saw. It has nothing to do with my job, but everything to do with Dr. Wasiri. It is an advance retainer fee for me to convince anybody to take up a job with Mattley & Barr subsidiary in Mezi. But since the only mines engineer, I know who fits every requirement for the job is my friend Kano, he will be my prime candidate. Rest assured that Dr. Wasiri does not know anything about the job or that mining company. I repeat, the fifteen thousand dollars is an incentive for me to convince anybody to take a job with Mattley & Barr in Mezi. You got to realize how difficult to hire anybody to go back to Mezi.

These companies are paying a lot to get engineers like Dr. Wasiri to go back and take up the appointment. My charge during this whole weekend will be to bring my friend along and to convince him first to go back and, second, to consider the job. And I hope you will support me along and stop making long faces as you did just recently when I started talking about the need for our friend to be back home to face the challenges of the country. Trust me, I know exactly what I am doing. By the way, that retainer comes handy for our household and will help us on few expanses coming up during the holiday. Silani, I am not doing anything sinister about a close and trusted friend. If you are not comfortable about me being paid to convince Kano to return to Mezi, let me know, and I will find a way to return the retainer. By the way, this Mister Fadden told me that the retainer was paid to me to consider talking to anybody. I repeat, 'To consider to talk.' No more no less. It was what they called a shake-hand agreement.

Are you with me? Are you following what I am telling you, Silani? The heart of matter is that I could have said to Mr. Fadden, 'Thank you, I will not assist you in identifying or talking to anybody about the hiring,' and that would have stopped the process right then and there. But all I said to him was, 'Yes, I would consider.' I did not mention any name. I did not mention Dr. Wasiri that Mr. Fadden does not know. By saying that 'Yes, I would consider,' I was handed this envelope. My commitment for all I know was a simple consideration. Is that OK with you, darling?"

Silani had been listening to her husband's plea, wrapped with a towel and sitting in front of the small bathroom cabinet mirror, her hands sadly clapping her head. She was no longer tormented as before. She was certainly mesmerized by what her husband was telling her. She did not like the idea of her husband entrapping his best friend into whatever schemes Mattley & Barr had in mind back in Mezi. She did not like the fact that there was a substantial monetary interest being accrued to her husband to entrap Dr. Wasiri.

"Darling, sincerely, I was first shocked to see that envelope. I could not help but think of what happened to the Mohktari Belem family, you remember, the one that was expelled to Malaysia. That check made me extremely uncomfortable and dizzy. I had to take a quick shower for that reason. Now I am a bit relieved that it was not the case. But I have to tell you, I am not happy about this retainer fee. I would very much appreciate that you share it with whomever you are going to talk about the hiring. If it is Dr. Wasiri, then please, tell him up front that you have received a retainer to talk with him and would be glad to share the retainer with him. That will be the right thing to do and will go a long way to calm my conscience. After all, Mrs. and Dr. Wasiri have been and remain here in the States what I consider family. We have grown to become very close, and I will say, more than family. I would hate to think that some monetary considerations would start tearing us apart. My dear, I would not accept it. And that is all I want to say at this time. Just follow up your conscience and do what I have told you and everything will be all right. Now please go back downstairs and keep our guest company before he becomes alarmed and starts worrying about us or something happening up here."

By the time Mr. Mbow reached the living room, Dr. Wasiri looked like he was taking an afternoon nap. Mr. Mbow shook him up, "Kano, if you need to, you can go lie down in the guest room. It was readied since yesterday, I am told."

Dr. Wasiri woke up brusquely and responded, "My, my, how long have I been asleep, my man? Must be old age or senior moment steadily gaining on us like this. I cannot even hold on my own after that half glass of the French red wine you served. What, is it a Merlot? Wonderful. No, I do not want to lie down now. No way. No way after all that Silani has prepared for us. My good man, I think you will need to get more company to attack that table full of all these dishes. How about this William Ewas! How far does he live to join us and share the latest gossips of Mezi? From the Diplomatic Mission he should know. Besides, I really want to find if he is the same guy I used to know."

Mr. Mbow was now bowing in front of his guest. "Your wish is granted, Sir Wasiri. I would call Sir Ewas. Now I would have two sirs to entertain as guests. Sir Ewas lives also in Hudson-Township with his small family, in the western section of town, along the river. It is five o'clock now, Friday afternoon. Sir Ewas leaves the office at three o'clock to start his weekend if there is no high delegation from Mezi to entertain in the city. He must be already home or close to get home. Hello, there, he is on the phone. Yes, sir. Where are you now? Home, good. Would you like to join me and one of your longtime friends at my house? No, I would not say who he is. You would find out only if you come and join us. In about twenty minutes? That will be fine and splendid. Will see you later."

Dr. Wasiri was almost on the floor laughing while Mr. Mbow was carrying on the British butler session. He told his host that he needed to freshen before the arrival of Sir Ewas and retired to the guest room. When he came down in thirty minutes, he saw a nicely draped middle-aged man speaking in an English Oxford accent. The man kept a typical diplomat pose while seated. But as soon as Sir Ewas saw Dr. Wasiri, he lost his British composure and yelled Dr. Wasiri's youth surname "Geffadi." At that moment, Dr. Wasiri knew that he was back with his longtime youth friend and whose contacts he had lost for more than twenty years. It had been a long time since he was addressed by the surname of "Geffadi," which meant in his native language the learned bookish one. Sir Ewas and Dr. Wasiri embraced for a long time. Their eyes were now wet with joy, and Mrs. Mbow could not hold her own tears. The two men looked at each other and admired how age and fortune have not ravaged their bearing but preserved their friendship. Mr. Mbow opened a bottle of champagne that his wife had cooled since the day before for their guest. They toasted the reunion of their two guests. Sir Ewas extended an invitation to Dr. Wasiri to visit his family the next day on Sunday. They spent the next six hours reminiscing about the village, the old friends, and acquaintances.

After Sir Ewas migrated to Mandi and graduated from now a Roman Catholic secondary school, he went to study in England first at Leeds University and went on to read law at Oxford University. He practiced law in London for a while as a fully vetted barrister. When his Joe brother, the great soccer player, was assassinated during one the many military coups, he decided to come home and help a bit with family business, which had grown substantially large then. Through numerous political contacts, he was asked to come and join the Mezi UN Diplomatic Mission as first counselor. This is to get groomed to full ambassador position in a year or two.

Sir Ewas reminisced the following:

"After we migrated to Mandi, Joe was also registered in a Roman Catholic school. He became a big soccer star in the capital. I thought that he was going to pursue professionally. But as soon as he started mechanical engineering degree in the Polytechnic University, he lost all interest in playing soccer, and before long, he was married. After graduation, he worked with the Water Commission and started hanging out with various military commanders of the time. He left the commission and started his own business doing car dealership. He started with Peugeot, then Volkswagen, then Honda, and finally, Mercedes. He had the largest Mercedes dealership north of South Africa. He was really loaded then. Remember that was the time of generals. He befriended quite a few of them. I am sure he was in a way the bagman for some of them. He set up a few partnerships with them. Unfortunately, he must have also made a few enemies among these generals. So much so during one of the multiple military coups, the government official version stated that he was caught in the crossfire along with the four-star General Baktaki who was trying to put down a rebellion of disgruntled petty officers in Sawele barracks, which are located just outside Mandi along the Highway No. Four leading to Batwatown in the direction of the town of FortLake. Our family never understood why in the middle of a military coup, our brother Joe found himself along a four-star general leading a military expedition to put down a rebellion of armed petty officers. What in the hell a civilian like my brother was doing there in the military barracks during a military coup? My most likely version is that he was doing some kind of business with General Baktaki when their meeting was interrupted, and they were arrested and brought to the Sawele barracks, where they were assassinated. General Baktaki was one of the two highest-ranking military men at the time. He was buried with largest military honor I had ever seen in Mezi. My brother also received full state honor at his burial. That is when I started building my own political contacts when I came back. In fact, I had no choice but to come back home and run, in addition to the car dealership, the multiple partnerships my brother had built in farming, gas stations, and real estates. I reorganized those partnerships I found profitable and sold that were a bit cumbersome. But to tell the truth, I never really like to run the main part of the family business, which was the car dealership business. I was most uncomfortable with the like of people I came in contact while running the company. They were basically what you can call Mezi's corrupt political leadership. This is where I was able to observe the corruptible and corrupting intersection of the political and business leadership of the country. As you know, Mercedes cars have always had that distinction of excellence, a lot of money, upper reaches of society, nouveau riches, etc. So, I could always tell when a new leader, political or business, is coming to stage in Mandi. The first thing to acquire was a Mercedes car. For those who wanted to distinguish themselves as quickly as possible, only a fleet of cars will do, and I mean three or four cars. That is the limousine for himself, another one for the wife, a third one for children's transportation, and, oh yes, the fourth one for the second wife. We are talking in less than three months the spending of about four to five hundred thousand dollars in a poor country like Mezi. The Mercedes car cost zoomed when you included the overall cost of importing and the multiple cross border tariffs to Mezi. Mind you, it was extremely profitable for my family business. But deep down, I knew that I was in middle of the worst corruption and corrupting cycle in my country and the whole traffic, the unbelievable display of ill-gotten riches, the unbelievable waste troubled my conscience to no end. So, I invested my time in preparing our younger brother to run that company. After three years, I believed I have groomed him enough to let him run the business. I decided to join the diplomatic corps through the multiple political contacts I have gained. Believe me, no matter what anybody tells you, Mezi will always remain under the bottes of generals. Yes, we have a multiparty system; yes, we have a president, a prime minister, a parliament, and a senate. But when you look very closely behind each one of the so-called civilian leaders, there is a general or two, a powerful colonel or two. These military people are the real power behind the civilians. They have continued their old arbitrary ways until now, and there is nothing the civilian authorities can do in face of these abuses of power. I cannot hide to let you know that I owe my diplomatic delegation function to UN to one of those generals who had prosperous cattle raising partnership with my brother in the northern state of Chelow. His son is running that farm up there. The general met me one day in one of those fancy digs of the capital of Mandi. He was reminiscing the time when the military was running Mezi and how much he appreciated my brother's services then and how the family was managing the same services now, including that partnership.

He wanted to know what my diplomatic aspirations were, as soon as he had learned that I had joined the diplomatic corps. I told him. The next day, I was called in by the deputy minister of Foreign Affairs who asked me how soon and where did I want to start a diplomatic delegation? He suggested that UN was the best place that carried a lot of clout if I wanted to climb to the level of ambassador as quickly as possible. Three weeks later, I was in New York City with the family. It is sad, but that is the way if you need to manage your life in Mezi. The motto there is "Corruption and More Corruption." I have elected to join the diplomatic corps because I got tired of seeing the overt display of that motto every day and everywhere. I pray for my country every day, wondering how that insidious cycle can be broken. I don't know, and I don't think it will ever be broken. Never. If it did, then I could very well be wrong, but time will tell."

Noticing that he had held the attention of Dr. Wasiri and the Mbow couple for a long time, Sir Ewas interrupted himself, "I am sorry intruding the politics in the midst of our wonderful reunion. I was very happy to see you "Geffadi" and, as always, Mrs. and Mr. Mbow. We will have plenty of time to reconnect and now let us not keep Mrs. Mbow waiting on all these wonderful home dishes she has made for us. I am sorry that I have not alerted Mrs. Ewas about this gathering. She will kill me when I will tell her about all these dishes. I hope it will not be much trouble if you pack a few of these on the side so I will be spared at home."

Now Silani was at the helm and directing her guests to partake her various dishes. She said, "Mrs. Ewas will have her share, of course. Do not worry, I will personally see to that. Please, brother Ewas, do not apologize for the talk you gave us a while ago. I get those talks every day from Mr. Mbow. But our guest, Dr. Wasiri, needs to come all the way from his place out there in Kentucky to New York to hear these stories. He is so far out there in the country. Sometimes I think he is spared of hearing all these political drama going on back home on a steady pace. After all, it gets a bit discouraging to hear those stories every day as you do, Mr. Ewas at the Diplomatic Mission. I don't know what is worst, staying away from the stories forever or getting a daily dosage of the same. But I say, you cannot leave home forever. Sooner or later, you are back there physically or in your mind, and the process will start all over. I guess each one of us needs to decide how we need to deal with this up close or from afar. I tell you no matter what, the hurt is always there. In all honesty, I am very glad that you two have reconnected after so long and that this has happened in our household. Now Dr. Wasiri will need to set up a large telephone fund for his Saturday routine.

Let me see, four hours to talk to my husband and four hours later to talk to Sir Ewas. Well, that will leave Hasbo busy talking to your own Silani for a whole day. I am so glad. Before we attacked this dinner, I will ask Dr. Wasiri to lead us in a thanksgiving prayer. Amen."

It was after about an hour after midnight that the great reunion lasted. By then Dr. Wasiri had extended an invitation to the Mbow couple and the Ewas couple for a night out about town the next Saturday and to stay and spend the night at his suite at the hotel. But Silani, remembering what her husband had shared in the afternoon, suggested that maybe it will better for the three of them, her husband, Mr. Mbow, Dr. Wasiri, and Sir Ewas to continue their big reunion at the hotel without the company of the wives. Besides, if Hasbo were around, the night out would come handy for all of us. Without Hasbo, it will be awkward. She will talk to Mrs. Ewas very soon to convince her of the same. The men readily agreed to the Saturday appointment. They will leave Hudson-Township at about four in the afternoon and spend the night at the Embassy Suites and will return home sometime on Sunday. Sir Ewas then left. Dr. Wasiri retired to the guest room after another full glass of the French red wine. He was a bit mellow then. He managed to talk briefly with Hasbo to wish her sweet dream and went to sleep. The Mbow couple stayed behind and cleaned the dining room and the kitchen and retired to their room. Before sleeping, Mr. Mbow thanked his wife for the suggestion she had made about the three men continuing their conversation the next day without the company of the wives. This will be important. This will give him the time and the big chance to make his case. But Silani repeated what she had said before and requested that Mr. Mbow states openly what he expected Dr. Wasiri to do and shares the retainer fee with him. Silani also added that now with Sir Ewas in the picture, his mission to convince Kano to go back to Mezi would not be that easy. She remarked that Sir Ewas came with totally opposite perspectives, which may influence Dr. Wasiri differently. By the way, she added that their relationship dated from way back, and they treated each other almost like brothers. Silani warned her husband to be very careful in his talk and, above all, to respect her wishes not to disrupt or destroy the longstanding almost family-like relationship they have built with the Wasiri family. No amount of money was large enough as far as she was concerned to change her mind about what she had said. She was still very uncomfortable about all that her husband had shared and was now afraid of what else her husband might do now that he was so focused on this retainer fee, regardless of all that they have shared with Dr. Wasiri and his wife.

After dozing for a few minutes, Silani woke up and startled her husband by asking him if he had not made some other commitment to entrap his very dear friend. Mr. Mbow was now indignant and denied having made any other commitment to Mr. Fadden regarding the hiring process. Silani was hardly convinced and fell back to sleep. Mr. Mbow stayed awake an hour or two deeply troubled by the suspicion raised by the last question his wife asked. He was convinced that his deal with Mr. Fadden was so banal that he did not expect his wife to raise so many questions about it. Worse, Silani was putting him in a rather precarious position by her definitive request to share all that conversation he had with Mr. Fadden and also to divide the retainer fee, which had literally fallen from the sky and should help with a few years' expenses. He got to find a way to do otherwise. Next thing he knew he was awakened at about nine thirty on Saturday morning by a call from Sir Ewas who was still undecided to go with them to the city as long as his wife had not been called by Mrs. Mbow to advise her why the trip to the city with a great possibility of staying over was to be partaken only by men as it was decided the night before. Sir Ewas also requested that Mr. Mbow comes to pick him up as soon as possible to guide him to a nearby shopping mall, where he can buy an appropriate weekend luggage and other weekend garments and toilet needs. Mr. Mbow relayed the first request to Silani who had been up early and was cooking a special breakfast for the guest. She proceeded to call Mrs. Ewas right away and was effective in convincing her of the need to stay behind when the three men went to the city. She insisted that she would come and keep her company that evening. Mr. Mbow then went to pick Sir Ewas to buy whatever he needed for the weekend in the city. While they were on their way to the shopping mall, Mr. Mbow casually advised his diplomat friend that both of them, during this weekend in the city, needed to be a bit circumspect about news from Mezi. He continued, "William, our friend Kano is in the midst of a very difficult decision. At the end of this academic, he needs to determine whether he will go back home to Mezi to teach at the Polytechnic University, or he should take up a new teaching assignment now at the University of Kentucky. We two should not be the ones to sway him one way or another. But to tell you the truth, and for our country's sake, I will be very happy to see our country gains a great deal of benefit from the contribution of somebody like Dr. Wasiri if he was teaching back home.

Now we are talking of an eminent professor of mines engineering. How many of PhDs in mines engineering do you know of from our country?

"Not one besides Kano. He is a jewel for our country. If our country had a positive outlook, I will be begging him to go back. But as you were so clear and so convincing about it last night, Mezi leaves a lot to be desired at this time. Yet, Kano has to make a difficult decision of his life. He is visibly struggling about it. I am sure that this trip to New York City is part of his way to find good answers and reasons to go back. You know me. I am a full-throat-Mezi-bad-news babbler. But since he has shared with me his decision, I am trying everything in my power to refrain from giving him anymore bad news from Mezi if I can help. I want you to do the same for our friend's sake. He trusts both of us and will base his final decision on our input. Please, I am not asking you to lie or sugarcoat anything. I am asking to guide him in the way of being supportive in making the right and honest decision. That is what friends are for."

Sir Ewas reflected a while and said, "I wished I knew about this before, and I would not have spit out last night all that story of corruption back home and why I wanted to leave. I hope he did not register it in the wrong way. I trust "Geffadi" can tell that the story was a personal one, not general. Frankly, I will do everything from now on to guide him in the way of what they call back home, KMC or 'Kwendae Mpya' Cell in Swahili, or Cell for New Directions. This is a new movement taking hold slowly and surely back home. He might find it interesting, and it will assist him in finalizing his decision to return back home. I will share it amply when we will be in New York City. By the way, thank you for warning me. I really appreciate. You are right. 'Geffadi' has always been and is still a jewel for our country even after all these years. You have no idea what he represents for many of us who grew up in that village with him. He was our teacher in any subject after school hours. There was no problem, no test, or no subject that 'Geffadi' could not help you on. I am talking of mathematics, sciences, literature, religion, Latin, Greek, etc. He was always above and ahead of all students. He probably told you in his modest ways that we studied together. Well, nobody studies with 'Geffadi'; people came to be tested by him before taking any exam. He always showed the way.

But he was never cocky, always respectful of every teacher, even the most ignorant. I tell you, one year, when school funding was cut so low as a result of government budget problems and we could not get nice imported books from South Africa and England, 'Geffadi' was invited by the school principal to review syllabus that teachers were asked to assemble during the summer recess for Mathematics, Biology, English Literature, and History subjects. He was paid for that review like a consultant all summer.

Now tell me, would a syllabus reviewer sit in the class as a student? Well, 'Geffadi' did, as if nothing had happened and always ready to help. I heard when I was already gone to Mandi that his last day of school was feted as if they were losing a big teacher. He was given all kinds of prizes and citations from every teacher in the school. That was something. You have no idea how much I share your wish to see him renew his mission of teaching and helping all back home. I will venture to say that it is not a struggle he is going through. Absolutely not! He has probably decided to go back and needs only confirmation and reaffirmation from his trusted friends. That will be easy to be done. God, I was a bit reluctant to join you in the city on the account of my wife not willing to spend the end of week by herself, but now I realize that we have a serious mission for the nation. You can count on me, sir."

Mr. Mbow was relieved to hear that he had an ally in his not-so-secret mission now but for totally different reasons. Although he always had much respect for his friend for his distinguished academic achievement, he never heard of the other side of his academic achievement prior to coming to the States. And Dr. Wasiri always as modest and humble as no other person he knows will never talk about himself or about academic eminence. It is true that he brought up the topic of Professor O'Shea quite often, but more to express his annoyance about what he endured under his mentorship, the lack of respect that the old man suffered from his peers, and above all the fear that the same disdain might extend to his own academic standing. His friend had never mentioned that he was an erudite back home commanding so much awe and respect from the like of Sir Ewas. If what Sir Ewas said was true, Mr. Mbow resolved that his friend Kano must have had an impressive following from his generation. That must have been the case when Sir Ewas said that even when he left the village school to go to Mandi, he kept following the scholarship that his friend named "Geffadi" was leading only to lose his contacts until yesterday. That was very impressive. He also decided that he would pursue his mission in spite of his wife's misgivings. After dropping Sir Ewas and reconfirming the time they will pick him up for the city trip, he placed a call to his wife using his cell phone. He wondered whether their guest was up by now and told her that he was on his way back. When he got home, he found Dr. Wasiri eating a late breakfast with the family. He excused himself for not being available when his friend Kano woke up around eleven as he went out to help Sir Ewas shopping. He added that this had become a weekend routine since the Ewas family settled in Hudson-Township. He had been helping them a lot to adjust to the suburban life of Hudson-Township.

He confessed it could be daunting for anybody not quite familiar with the greater metropolitan area of New York City. His friend responded sarcastically that he would never leave the peaceful rhythm of Frankfort, Kentucky, to settle in the Big Apple. To everybody's laughter he said that he would be lost every day in the area until he would decide to pack and leave. Still, he added that he was grateful to have friends like the Mbow family so he can visit the city with the proper guidance and then quickly depart without getting lost. It was about the time to go to the city. He called the limousine driver who was already entering the city of Hudson-Township and advised his two friends to get ready to leave. As they were settling in the limousine car and he was thanking Mbow family for another wonderful reception, he heard Silani telling her husband not to forget her request to talk to him and to share you know what. He did not say anything until they left the house; then he asked his friend what was it that he was supposed to talk about and share with him. Mr. Mbow replied that it was nothing of importance.

"My friend, you know the ladies with their inclination to drag matters to no end. Silani was insisting that we take back to the hotel suite the remaining bottles of wine and liquor that you brought as gifts. She wanted that we use these bottles before you go and buy new bottles. I was telling her that you were generous enough to bring them as gifts. I was not going to let you take them back. No way. She got furious about that; you know. She started telling me that we needed to share this or that expense. Here again, I said that you have extended the invite and will play the JP Morgan of Kentucky this weekend in Manhattan for your two friends, all I have to do is to enjoy the ride. That was another side of contention. As you always advise me in this wife business, you cannot win. Forget it . . ."

The limousine car stopped in front of the Ewas house. And Sir Ewas was already out with his wife and their two very young daughters. Dr. Wasiri and Mr. Mbow got off the car and Dr. Wasiri was introduced to the Ewas family. Mrs. Ewas said that she heard so much about Dr. Wasiri since she started dating Sir Ewas at the University of Leeds in England and was honored to meet him in person. She added that she would be happy to receive Dr. Wasiri and his entire family as their guests from

Kentucky anytime he wanted to come to New York City area. They extended contact numbers, and it was time to go back to the city.

The weekly long bumper-to-bumper ride to the city had disappeared on Saturday, and they reached the Embassy Suites hotel in about forty-five minutes.

During the ride, the three friends could not agree on the right night-out itinerary. The driver, an old hand of the best spots of town, suggested a China Town exclusive dining restaurant, followed by two all-night Jazz joints in the Village area, and finally, a Third World hangout place to close the night. Unbeknownst to the three amigos, each of the spots was selected by Lady Allistair and transmitted to the driver. Lady Allistair was going to place in each spot her many eyes and ears to simply follow their conversations and to observe their interactions throughout the night out. They went up to the suite to get rid of their weekend luggage and descended to the hotel bar for another cocktail before the night out. When they were seated, and after receiving their first cocktail glasses, Dr. Wasiri raised his glass for a toast and proclaimed that from then on all was on his account.

"Friends, drink as much as you want and eat as much you want, all is on me, but as long as you talk. Why talk, well, for a very good reason. I trust you two, my very dear friends, to guide me in a momentous decision. I want to leave this city with my mind made up about whether I should go back to Mezi or not next academic year. I do not have to tell you that I left the country long time ago counting four years of bachelor's degree, two years of master's, about four years of PhD Studies, and thirteen years of teaching, that makes for a total of about twenty-three or so years of being away from home. During that time, I have managed to go home twice on vacation. But you know how fast and how short are those vacation periods. Because while you are there, you know that you are coming back to the States, you are not really home in Mezi. You are in fact in transit, home away from home. Instinctively, you spend your time comparing your country with what you are going back to in terms of almost everything. I remember, twice when I took the family to Mezi, it was more to find out how the family members were getting by in the difficult economic environment of Mezi, and in some cases, I helped them financially. I have told Mr. Beni Mbow here that my wife, Hasbo, took more advantage of these trips than I did. She traveled with the kids from one end of Mezi to another, while I stayed behind in Mandi and you know what for: to prepare for the fall semester mines engineering courses at Kentucky State University. Whatever political drama taking place while I was there did not really concern me. All was very distant to me, and I acted accordingly. I was not interested in engaging anybody in a discussion or a political discourse about the future of the country. For me it was all so hopeless, it did not matter to talk about it. As more talk, discussion, or exchange led to the same final point, an endless vicious circle with no end. In short, during these trips you are not home.

It is totally different when you are making a decision to go back and settle down there with all the differences and yes, the privations that will come about. I want you to help me in that journey from now on. On one hand, I am struggling with the idea of going back, not very much for myself, but for my family, and on the other hand, I am quite resolute to make my return and my settling down as natural as what used to be like coming from a village and going to settle in Mandi. Am I making myself clear? In other words, I do not want to be a "Diaspora" settling back in Mezi with personal requirements far exceeding what Mezi can give or afford. I want to be like any other citizen of Mezi who has lived anywhere but, in the capital, and has now decided to settle in the capital of Mandi or any other big city of Mezi. I want to settle in Mezi for what Mezi needs, not for what I need. Can you two helps in this, Mr. Beni Mbow and Sir William Ewas?"

This was a challenge much larger than either Mr. Mbow or Sir Ewas had imagined. Dr. Wasiri was challenging his friends in a level much higher than they had estimated.

Sir Ewas took the gauntlet. "I don't know anybody more prepared and ready to make the trip and settlement back home as much as you are. You see most of us will decide on the basis of what is in for us. And that is a fact and the truth. I have to tell you that I went back for an obvious family reason, a death in the family. When this had happened, I was doing quite all right, earning a decent living as a barrister in London. The truth was that I was very comfortable there and did not want to leave. So, when my brother passed away, I went home duty bound. But I spent the next five or six years there, trying desperately to leave because of what I did not like and could not change. The first chance I got I used it to get out of there. Remember, I got a much younger brother in charge of a very prosperous enterprise. But for some reasons it was not for me. And I left. My wife always suspected that this whole diplomatic delegation was a way for me to be home away from home. And I should say that she is right. But in your case, it is totally different. You have achieved academic and scholarship way behind what most of us can think or dream of. I must say on that basis alone, your place is not with cowards like us unable to separate home and away from home. Your place is home in Mezi. I will go further. Many of us have seen you back then in the missionary school where you have displayed a level of intellect unsurpassed in the annals of that school until today. Many of us have always wished to see you continue the same zeal of teaching and helping Mezi students. I was overwhelmed and not surprised when I was told that you were an eminent professor at Kentucky State University.

I said to myself why Kentucky State University, why not the Polytechnic University at Mandi. "Geffadi," I can sit here and make a long speech about why you need to go home. It could be on the account of this second glass of this nice French wine. But in all seriousness, at the end, it is your personal decision involving yourself and your family. If you ask my opinion, I would say, you are not half way, but you are already there in spirit, you got to get there now in flesh, because so many of us have wished this to happen. One last thing, I have told you last night about the motto in our country: Corruption and More Corruption. I said that I did not see any end in that vicious circle. I want to stand corrected at this time. I say this because, the three of us are forming a circle of trust I hope enduring. I will not say this in any other circle of people I could not trust. During the time I was in Mezi, I saw a movement that I sincerely believe may break that vicious circle and upon which you need to lean on when you get to Mezi. If anything, to maintain a certain level of sanity. The movement is named Kwendae Mpya Cell, which in Swahili means cell for new direction. There are many of these cells all over Mezi now. They are growing in face of the abject corruption that is sapping and demoralizing the nation. Funny thing, the movement started in St. Ignatius Roman Catholic School I attended in Mandi. Two Jesuit priests, members of the school faculty, were clearly upset over the high tuition that the school was charging and which literally eliminated children of low economic means. The two priests accused the school principal, another high Jesuit priest, of insuring that the school became the enclave of children of generals, colonels, and the elite who were raping the country. The two Jesuit priests were expelled from the school and were sent back to Ireland, where they were from. A year later, the same Jesuit priests, now defrocked, managed to come back to Mezi under assumed names and managed to set up what is now called the New Academy of Sciences, a boarding school. The academic was built and managed, thanks to funds that these priests raised through endless fundraising in Ireland, UK, and Germany. The academy was generally staffed by various people of high academic or professional standing from all over the world willing to devote a year or two of voluntary work in Mezi.

This formula really worked. The school stood not far from St. Ignatius and started to attract very bright children recruited around the country on the basis of exams. The notion was that these bright students were to attend the academy free of tuition and free of room and board as long as they maintained high grades. From the beginning, there were about three hundred students from the seven through the twelve grades. The academy became the breeding ground for KMC, as we love to call it in Mezi.

What set the academy apart was that each student must excel in one particular course called Society and Ethics before graduation with an attending internship as volunteer in a hospital, auspices, remote village school, etc. That course was loaded with comparative studies of ethics in various world societies. It went without saying that these students exceeded all parameters in college recruitment from all over Mezi, and after college graduation, they are now starting to flood every level of public and private management levels. Their impact is growing underneath all that garbage we see every day in Mezi. Today the academy has completely displaced St. Ignatius as the top private school of higher academic excellence. The academy is now charging a modest tuition but has generally kept the same goals that the two defrocked priests had established.

By the way, the priests were expelled again three years after it was learned that they had entered the country under assumed name. But with the growing political acceptance of their realization, they were received back in Mezi by the previous president. They are now retired and still on the board of the academy. I want to tell you that KMC is the future of Mezi. At this time, another native Jesuit priest, Father Albert Zolani, has taken up the national coordination of KMC. He goes around every village, city, and area of Mezi, preaching the merits of KMC. I personally have attended few of his conferences. He is a dynamo and keeps his audience spellbound.

He is not there just screaming about the shortcoming of the current political process. No, he goes further and suggests concrete solutions in taking charge of every sector of the country: economic, political, and judicial institutions and insuring that the delivery of service is accomplished with the highest ethics without corruption, in the small and in the large. I come to believe that this is our only solution. And for your information, there are about four of us members of KMC right there in the Diplomatic Mission of Mezi at UN, of course unbeknownst to the ambassador and other staff members.

This is how we believe that we will break the vicious cycle. We are not naive to believe that we will win this battle overnight. It is a long-term war. It is generational. I have invested in this for my little young daughters so that they can find their place in a decent society. This is to let you know, 'Geffadi,' that going home at this time may portend great change to come for all. Do not hesitate because of the apparent state of affairs. The undercurrent promises great things for Mezi."

Sir Ewas's monologue got both Kano and Beni very excited, especially the references to KMC that they were not aware of. Change was coming to Mezi and fast in spite of all the stupid daily display of political incompetence. Change, real change was on its way.

Kano was looking at his friend Beni, who could not contain himself.

"Good Gracious Lord in heaven, this could not come fast enough. When I was running away from Mezi for my life because of that General Pogato who almost got me killed, I said to myself never again. For the past twenty or so years, I witnessed from afar one general after another, one colonel after another, one corrupted president after another, and one incompetent prime minister after another. I have witnessed from afar one political assassination after another. I moved from desperation to another to political abyss. And here you are telling me that the whole cabal is being expunged. Good Lord the Redeemer in heaven. This cannot come fast enough. William, tell me how and where do I need to sign up? I do not want to put you on the spot. Am I missing the message you are sharing with us? Certainly, you have seen the movement from the start and have witnessed its growth, but what has convinced you that this is it? I am certainly coming to realize that all reactionary regimes have been swept in the similar fashion. Name it and you can see the similarities: the French Revolution, the American Revolution, the Bolshevism Revolution, the Mao Revolution, and the Castro Revolution. Each one of those revolutions started with a deep undercurrent of slow but unshakable belief that what was there could no longer be sustained, what was so corrupt and for better or worse it needed to be replaced. Are you witnessing a revolution back home or is it a simple evolution to clean the slate for brighter future for Mezi? One way or another, will KMC be enduring with deep tentacles to sustain a new political era? William, as I said before, I do not want to put you on the spot. Please do not feel that I am directing all these questions to you alone. They are in fact rhetorical questions for each of us, whether we believe in the KMC concept or not. I am certain that Kano here is asking the same questions as we are helping him to decide. Still, I see a lot of merits in everything you have told us now, and I appreciate very much to have come here and hear what you have said. At this time, I am more than curious to hear what Kano thinks about what you have said."

"I heard what William told us, and I need to reflect upon it a long time. But I will not lie to both of you at this time, the sound of what William's monologue delivered was extremely edifying.

Listening to Sir Ewas, I say to myself that the long night Mezi plunged into since acquiring its political independence, that long night was coming to an end. There seems a shining gleaming light at the end of that long political tunnel in Mezi. I was always of the opinion that the awakening of the people of Mezi will come from within. I am more than relieved that it is happening, and there are very great reasons for hope. I do not know if that light will shine much brighter during my lifetime, but I am with William that it should be there when my three children reach their age of maturity. So, I hope. I am not saying that I need the movement of political awakening to make my decision to go back. These things take a long time in gestation and only to burst out when least expected. Many times some of us had our hope and dream dashed when we thought that a particular political event would hasten that awakening. But it will be nice to be there and witness it. At this time and place, I cannot deny that all I have heard today will be enabling to my decision. I am glad that I have both of you as friends, and you have been extremely helpful today. Now I think we need to go back up in the suite and get ready for the first stop of the night at Chinatown."

On their way to the lower Manhattan area, Mr. Mbow saw the opening after their exchange at the hotel bar and decided to raise the ante and carefully started talking about Mr. Fadden's proposal in a form of a simple casual suggestion, "Kano, I heard and sympathized with what you said about going back to Mezi for Mezi and not going back with a bunch of requirements over the meager resources of Mezi. You were right to say that this has been the main problem of Diaspora people not realizing how burdensome they become over the poor country they have left behind. This, I agree, and if anything, else, it has put a brake in developing many of African countries. As one friend has put to me one time back in Mezi; "Those intellectual people who have left Mezi, some with mere sandals, are coming back and want to be bombarded overnight into ministerial position here, directorship there, CEO here, special counselor there and more; they are no longer satisfied with the shacks where they were raised, now only a large mansion with swimming pools and all year around seventy-two degrees temperature air-conditioned rooms will do." However, and unfortunately, the reality is often an equalizer. You, personally, may not want to burden the national treasury as you say it. But remember, you have a family very much used to a minimum of American standards which can easily be translated to a very nice house, a very nice transportation, in short, a very nice and high standing in Mezi. Your decision to go back must involve the answer to how you will provide for that standing and those amenities.

I have to tell you right now and as long we are talking frankly to one another; it will not be fair to your family if you start proposing to them a standing much lower than they are used to here in the States. Believe me, I know Hasbo, your wife, and I have observed how much she loves our country. As I was saying, I know Hasbo will go along with whatever program and hardship you will propose and bring along once in Mezi. One, because she loves you, and two, because she hates her own country and will do anything to leave the United States. That much she has said and expressed it in many occasions. That is Hasbo, and there is no other way about it. But I am more concerned about your children. They may not adjust as readily as Hasbo with the consequences of going to Mezi, consequences I know you may not want consider. So, we are left with a matter of choice. As far as I can tell, you have three choices: The first one where you stay in United States and continue your teaching profession in American institutions of higher learning and safeguarding your family American way of life, the second one where you go back in Mezi to pursue teaching profession in Polytechnic University with uncertain compensation to provide for your family and the temptation to impose undue requirements on the country resources, and the third choice where you still go back to Mezi to pursue teaching profession at the Polytechnic University as all of us are praying you would do for the greater benefit of Mezi students, while at the same you are working as a highly paid consultant for major foreign mining companies getting enough compensation to provide for your family while avoiding to impose any resource requirements on your country. You will agree that the third choice is ideal for you. This third choice will resolve the great dilemma you have and which we share. In your case, the resolution is clear and evident, thanks to your high academic scholarship. You cannot help but be engaged in the mines engineering at both the academic and professional levels. It will certainly be a waste to concentrate in one area only at the exclusion of the other. Maybe ten or twenty years from today and when you have formed enough PhDs in your area, you can relax your participation in that key development field. But at this time, you are sorely needed in both academic and professional fields. You need to be compensated accordingly, and you will do this for Hasbo and the kids."

This was a clear suggestion that Dr. Wasiri did not expect from his longtime friend and thought that the suggestion was probably the reason of the background noise he had observed between Mr. Mbow and his wife when he was visiting with them from Friday through Saturday afternoon. Maybe his friend and his wife had a long discussion about this topic before he came from Kentucky, and they were going to be kind enough to share it the first chance they had.

Now that he was expressly seeking advice, Mr. Mbow took the chance to deliver the suggestion. He felt very indebted to Mrs. and Mr. Mbow's kindness. They were now seated at the Chinese restaurant.

"My very dear Beni, I am in debt to you and Silani, your wife, for thinking about this suggestion. You have to realize that when you are cocooned as I am, in my little corner of Frankfort, Kentucky, you do not go around thinking about maintaining your family in their standing in faraway places like Mezi. You just go about preparing your courses, delivering them, coaching, and advising PhD students, day in, day out. That is all. In all fairness, it is only when I venture out of my cocoon and come to visit with you, and now with William here with us, then I can really confront various realities of Mezi. I am thankful for that specific suggestion. I am convinced, you thought about it long and hard. I will look into this, and I know my dear mentor, Professor O'Shea, had already made multiple references in that area for me. I will ask and talk to him about this adjustment process when I will go back. Knowing him, the minute I have told him during the reunion this week that I was negotiating a tenured professorship, he must have started talking to the management and staff of the Polytechnic University to insure that I get the chair of faculty of mines engineering that he probably want to fund right away. In a way, I am blessed to be surrounded by people like my mentor, both of you here, your wife, and Hasbo and the kids. I am all very blessed and, of course, grateful."

Mentioning Dr. O'Shea was a way for him to advise his two friends that when it comes to professional references or consultancies in his field, they need not bother as his mentor was working overtime on this subject. In addition, he knew and did not reveal that Dr. O'Shea will also insure that his transfer to Mezi will go with no financial or other difficulties of resources as he was sharing his prize share from the Amovir trip to the amount of two million dollar and a half. That will be his security blanket that will come handy during his adjustment process. The frank discourse from his trusted friend, Mr. Mbow, helped to effectively put this security blanket in its right perspective. While he was mentally evaluating the direction of the exchange he was having, Sir Ewas saw the need to relax the atmosphere and started to share in a comical fashion the latest political drama in the Mezi body political.

"My dear friends, I need to tell you about the latest political melodrama in Mezi. This one has reached the top leadership of both chambers, the Senate and the Parliament. It has resulted in a very popular and funny tune back home.

I don't know if you heard of 'Miss Two Chambers' song. This tune is relating the story of Miss Monica Kello Ngoma, the national delegate to the Parliament from the Ngazima District in the lower plateaus of the province of Kiesse. Miss Ngoma is about thirty-two, mother of a five-year-old son, previously married to a high school sweetheart named Adrian Ngoma. Adrian and Monica met and dated when they were going to school together at the University of Zurich in Switzerland, both majoring in Mathematics. Mr. Ngoma pursued his studies further to get a PhD in Applied Mathematics while Mrs. Ngoma at that time stopped her education at the master of Mathematics education level while raising the new infant baby. Both of them came back home about six years ago. At their return, Mr. Ngoma joined the faculty of Applied Sciences at the Polytechnic University, while Mrs. Ngoma preferred to work at the Mezi Institute of Economic Research. One thing that was evident, Mrs. Ngoma was a very attractive tall lady as well as very successful in her professional job. She moved up very rapidly in the Institute of Economic Research to the level of associate director. She was also extremely solicited in the economic policy circles of the country. Unfortunately, her professional progression coupled with incessant rumors and innuendos started to put a lot of strains in her marriage to Mr. Ngoma. The catalyst was the last trip she took to the FMI-World Bank fall-season meeting that happened in Kuala Lumpur in Malaysia. It was supposed to be a week and a half journey, but she was not back home until four weeks later. The Mezi delegation chief was the previous finance minister, but the Speaker of Parliament came along and was the behind-the-scene real patron. He was the one who selected Mrs. Ngoma to come along. When the entire delegation returned home on schedule, Mrs. Ngoma and the Speaker took another trip to London for some obscure noneconomic policy meeting, which lasted another two weeks. From their London escapade, they were welcomed back home on a midnight flight by the Speaker's wife and Mr. Ngoma at Mandi's International Airport. It was a big scandal for all onlookers to see at the airport the confrontation between the Speaker's wife and Mrs. Ngoma. They fought in the presence of their husbands. Mr. Ngoma left the airport without his wife and that was the beginning of their separation. But the Speaker would not relent and continued an increasing public display of their relationship, pushing it further to insure that after her divorce, the now Miss Monica Kello Ngoma would stand for election in the Ngazima District. Well, she was elected national delegate at the Parliament and was quickly placed, thanks to the Speaker's influence, as chairperson of two Parliament committees, economic policy and foreign affairs, a splendid cover for their overseas escapades.

It was no longer denying about their relationship and that Miss Ngoma was in fact the number-two wife as far as the Speaker was concerned. But unfortunately for the Speaker, the chair of two committees went to Miss Ngoma's head. She wanted to gain a certain aura of respectability about her function as chair of the two most powerful committees of the Parliament. Miss Ngoma started slowly to take a bit of distance from the Speaker while increasing further association with the honorable president of the senate, no friend of the Speaker. Miss Ngoma effectively played these two leaders against each other for about two years, pretending to be intimate with both while trying in vain to regain her former husband. As Mandi lives on rumors, the scandal news spread very fast, and Miss Ngoma took on the title of 'Miss Two Chambers.' It was not long before she entered the musical tune as 'Miss Two Chambers.' The most funny line I like in the tune is the refrain that goes like this: 'Dear Monka (short for Monica) when are you going to unite the two chambers to deliver Mezi from Kello-Kello-Kello.' You should see the younger ones when they are dancing the tune and repeat Kello-Kello-Kello while bobbing their head in and out, back and forth like birds in the morning in the imitation of the tall Miss Ngoma when she walks. It is just plain hilarious. I wish to show you the tune video next time you come to my place. Miss Ngoma is still running the two committees. The Speaker came down with a mild stroke and is now out in disability after his wife came to the Parliament and confronted Miss Ngoma rather violently for the second time. I doubt that the Speaker will run for any election again in his condition and as long his wife is around. There is an interim Speaker until the next election. The president of senate is still in place and has denied any involvement with Miss Ngoma. Her ex-husband has sued Miss Ngoma for child abandonment on the account of her multiple overseas trips and is rumored to remarry very soon with a very close friend of Miss Ngoma. I don't think we have heard the last piece of Miss Monica Kello Ngoma."

When William related the "Miss Two Chambers" story, the laughter from Kano and Beni was so loud and irrepressible that the Chinese restaurant manager had to come twice to their table to request that they tone it down. The manager most likely would have shown them the door, if their fare plus the tip did not exceed five hundred dollars. They left the restaurant and embarked in the limousine for the Amazone Jazz joint in the Village. They were still reeling over Miss Ngoma story when they arrived at the joint. Luckily for them, the place was a bit noisy waiting for the close-to-midnight production of the latest Jazz Quartet in vogue in New York City. The place was packed for the usual Saturday gang.

They were not disappointed when the group delivered their four main tunes each lasting more than twenty minutes. The piano cut was exquisite while the trumpet and horn players reminded the audience of some great players of time past. It was past two thirty in the morning when the trio convened to try the Third World Club on the East side. However, the packed club entrance signaled to them that they were not going to be comfortable among the younger and numerous fanatics of the Brazilian Mocambo Jazz Ensemble. They decided to return back to the hotel around three thirty and went straight to the bar that was now empty. The bartender recognized them as top tippers and kept the bar open for another hour and a half. After a few funny stories from back home, the three men from Mezi were ready to retire to the suite after a long merry day. It was past five thirty when the celebrated night out was over, and they were all sound asleep. The three amigos were awake at around three in the afternoon, and it was already time to bid each other farewell. They still agreed to meet again for lunch the next day, Monday, at a restaurant not far from the UN building. As Beni and William were boarding the limousine for the trip back to Hudson-Township, Beni said again that he might run by Dr. Wasiri a high consultancy reference as they talked about and that he had in mind. He just needed to consult again his many PNUD contacts to come up with these references. Dr. Wasiri thanked him just the same and while still very tired after the long night out, he returned for another afternoon sleep rest in the suite. Before taking another long nap, he called his wife and gave an abbreviated and respectful version of the night out with Sir Ewas and Mr. Mbow before excusing himself to rest. At the same time, his two friends were arriving at their respective homes and equally expressed the need to continue their afternoon nap. But in case of Mr. Mbow, it was another matter altogether, he found his wife Silani in the same mood he left her the day before. She asked the same questions in five different ways; whether her husband had delivered the message to Dr. Wasiri as both have agreed upon and whether he offered to share the fifteen thousand retainer fee. Mr. Mbow responded affirmatively to both questions and requested a little bit of peace and quiet so that he can take another long afternoon nap because he did not get much sleep from the marathon discussion, they had about so many things from Saturday through Sunday morning. When he was awake at about nine at night, his wife was lying next to him and reading a women's magazine as if waiting for a final explanation of his deeds in New York City. Then Mr. Mbow said, "You will not give a break for nothing, woman. Let me tell you now, Dr. Wasiri was already far gone in the process of getting a position similar to what I discussed with you. He has already discussed it with his mentor, that Professor O'Shea.

Both of them have already agreed that when he will get to Mezi, he will need to supplement his college professor salary with a highly paid consultancy job with a mining company. At this stage, he has not selected which company he wants to work for. He told me that Professor O'Shea has thousands of references in that field, and he is working full time to get him something concrete and highly decent. He repeated many times that we did not have to worry about it. He gave me the impression as if he has already something lined up. You can ask Sir Ewas about this if you do not believe me. He was there and heard the same conversation. As I said, he did not mention a specific company. Who know what could that be, may be Mattley & Barr. Believe me, all along I was there with him, I was feeling ashamed of what you have accused me of doing. Only to find out that he had already taken steps to do the same. In those circumstances, it was highly not appropriate for me to mention the conversation with Mr. Fadden as you requested. I am going to see him tomorrow and will obliquely suggest that he gives a call to Mr. Fadden of Mattley & Barr, a foreign company with mining interests in Mezi looking for somebody with his credentials for a highly paid consultancy job in Mezi. You see, my dear Silani, in serious matters as such, you need to be a little bit patient. You also need to listen, observe, and strike at the opportune time. This is what I was aiming to do in spite of all you have deliberately accused me. Now given those conditions, I could not suggest to Dr. Wasiri to share the retainer fee. That will be tacky obviously. I will save his share until such time when I will be in a position to remit it to him for a reason totally different than what we are discussing. Don't you agree, my dear?" Noticing that Silani was entirely buying his new version of the conversation around the hiring process, he accelerated the rubbing motion about her lower thigh. Mrs. Mbow was moaning at that instant; she did not give an answer to his question but submitted to the now warming rubbing motion. Both of them fell asleep.

Mr. Mbow was even more delighted to learn the next day that Sir Ewas was not going to join them at lunch. He will have Dr. Wasiri for himself and make a forceful representation of the Mattley & Barr proposal. His friend had already taken a lunch table at the designated restaurant when Mr. Mbow arrived. Kano was disappointed to learn that Sir Ewas was not going to come.

Mr. Mbow informed him that that was the way of Diplomatic Mission business. The ambassador had asked him to keep him company to greet the deputy foreign minister who was coming sometime that afternoon at JFK International Airport.

The ambassador said that he was surprised of the arrival of the deputy, and he was not clear of his sudden arrival. The ambassador needed Sir Ewas to be an unintended witness for any misplaced conversation they may have. The ambassador was no fan of the deputy and the feeling was mutual. Sir Ewas sent his regards and said he was looking forward to Kano's calls and wanted to know when he would come back. Kano and Beni selected a light lunch and reminisced about the night out. Beni then asked Kano if he had firmed up his decision to go back to Mezi after the long weekend.

Kano answered in the affirmative. Beni then said that his friend Sir William Ewas was going to be delighted to have assisted him to firm up his decision. Beni added he was also very happy for Kano, Hasbo, and the children. He asked him to forgive him for being up front and a bit rude in his talk the night before, especially in presenting stark choices. Beni indicated that he believed in laying out all that needs to be said and presented when helping friends to make difficult choices. He felt that he would have let him down if he had not been as direct as up front as he was. Thank God all worked all right, and he was happy with the outcome.

Then he asked him, "Do you know a company named Mattley & Barr? It is a mining company with considerable interests in Mezi. I spent the whole morning looking for this card that I exchanged with this Mr. Fadden, the company representative in Washington, DC. I met him last year when I went to Kenya at the beginning of this protracted conflict. When we talked this weekend, I thought about the guy. He mentioned back then that he wishes that Mattley & Barr had somebody like you not to mind the mines but to provide a great deal of consultancy from Mandi in many aspects of their operations in Mezi. You owe to give him a call. I know that you mentioned that your mentor working overtime finding something for you. I have great respect for Dr. O'Shea. But look into this for me. As a token of my help, that is all. I will appreciate if you follow up on this. Better yet, ask Dr. O'Shea if he knows of this company. Too bad Sir Ewas is not here. He could have found out about this company right away too."

Dr. Wasiri took the card, and to show the seriousness that his friend was expecting of him, he pulled his large address book and immediately placed the card inside the book.

"I assure you I will talk to the man when I am back home tomorrow. I thank you again for your help. You are a friend's friend. Now that you need to go back to work, I want to thank you for the wonderful time with you, Silani, the kids, and Sir Ewas.

My special thanks to Silani for all that food preparation. I appreciated a lot. Rest assured that you and Sir Ewas have educated me enough over this weekend to solidify my decision. Most likely the next time I will see you, you will be taking me to the airport for the beginning of my return home. It has been a great joy to have been with you all these years."

They embraced again African style, and Dr. Wasiri took the limousine back to what he calls now the Mezi store for last-minute shopping as he came to realize he had barely put any dent to the fifteen thousand Dr. O'Shea left for him to spend in less than four days. He still had twelve thousand to spend before his eleven o'clock flight back to Lexington, then to Frankfort, Kentucky. It was also definitely too late now to go back to give, say, five thousand dollars to Mr. Mbow. His old friend would not accept it if he did not offer a good explanation to make use of it. He didn't see any reason to bother him now that they have already said good-bye. He decided to just give what will remain to Hasbo, who would find plenty of use for the remaining change. While he was visiting the store, it occurred to him that he had already bought and sent home what he was about to buy. He changed course and went to various huge book stores, searching for recent books covering mining engineering. He also realized those stores were the same book stores he had visited with Dr. O'Shea when he was sharing the Pierre Hotel suite. He definitely had a serious burden of riches. He decided to go back to the hotel to start packing and rest. The flight from New York to Frankfort, Kentucky, with a stopover at Lexington was fine. Hasbo picked him at the airport in company of their daughter Fazi, the last child, who was sleeping when Daddy arrived. Dr. Wasiri mentioned to his wife that he had so much to talk about. Hasbo responded that if what he was about to say was not related to going back to Mezi; Dr. Wasiri was going to waste his breath. Jokingly, Dr. Wasiri said that he had wasted a lot of breath during his stay in New York City, and he will work hard the next two weeks to gain back both his health and his sanity, both polluted by the foul air and the impossible noise of New York City. He added that he would do this only if Mrs. Wasiri will be kind enough to listen to what he was going to say regarding the possible return to Mezi. When he uttered the last word of Mezi, Mrs. Wasiri literally abandoned the wheel of the car she was driving to embrace her husband, realizing in the nick of time what she was doing and rapidly seized and straightened the wheel and moved the car off the road and parked it. She looked at her husband to verify if he was truthful about what he was saying. Dr. Wasiri nodded. Hasbo jumped from the driver seat to the passenger seat where her husband was and gave him the noisiest and tender kiss.

Their daughter Fazi was then awakened and wanted also to kiss her dad. Hasbo took hold of herself and said lovingly to her husband, "Let's us go home, I am not done with you yet."

She put the car on drive, and they proceeded home. When they arrived at home, their now teenage boys, Meno and Belo, had already finished their dinner and were busy finishing their homework in order to catch a very popular evening episode on TV. They quickly greeted their father and disappeared in their room. Fazi was still battling her sleep and was also excused to go to sleep. Hasbo informed her husband that she received around noon that day the entire set of goods he had sent from New York City. She was overwhelmed by the variety of food staples from Mezi. She added that every weekend from then on, she would get appropriate cooking instructions from her friend Silani in order to entertain the entire family with Mezi home cooking. She also let her husband know that the stack of Mezi newspapers and magazines that he sent did not particularly please her. She read a few of the articles and was not pleased by the tone of endless criticism she found in the papers of anything related to Mezi politics. She found them very discouraging and would prefer that her husband stopped reading them if he had decided to return to Mezi. Her husband responded that he was not swayed one way or another by these articles, which, in fact, gave the current political temperature of the country. He said that it was true that the current direction of the country was generally not good. But that will not be the reason for him to decide whether to go or not to go. He added that he was a man solely driven by the future of Mezi, which had not been decided yet. At that point, Hasbo asked him, "Then what have you decided at this time and place? Are you going back to Mezi and when?"

Dr. Wasiri responded, "I have decided to go and live in Mezi starting the end of this academic year. We should be back in Mezi in June and that will give us enough time for the entire family to prepare the kids and for me to adjust to the next year academic year. I believe that I have put as much preparation for my next assignment here in Frankfort. I think I am ready for the next step in my teaching profession, which will be in Mezi. I already mentioned that I have sent my application to join the Polytechnic University in Mandi. I am now negotiating terms of my tenured professorship with that university. As a matter of fact, this was one of the major topics of conversation that I had with Dr. O'Shea in New York City. You should know that he was extremely pleased to hear this. I bet that he is working at this time to make sure that this transition to Mezi is as smooth as possible for our entire family.

Did you two coconspirators talk while I was in NewYork City? Remember, you have ganged up on me all these years to go home. Well, I have succumbed to the pressure at last."

Hasbo was now completely transfigured and was trembling of joy.

"Yes, Dr. O'Shea and I talked and when he came back from New York City, he begged me not to disturb you much and to leave you alone in New York while you were about to make your decision. He said that you have already taken steps to do that, and your friend Mr. Mbow convinced him that by the time you will be back, you would have firmed your decision most likely after running it ten thousand times in your mushy brain of yours. Have you noticed that I did not call you all that time you were in New York? I followed Dr. O'Shea's instruction, and he was right. I prayed that you will bring me this decision, and you know that I am very grateful for that. I am grateful for our entire family. Do not worry about the children. We have enough time to prepare them for the transition. For all I know, they have also been looking forward to this move. I am sorry that I am trembling. My whole body needs to be generously soothed, and I hope you will be up to the task tonight, Dr. Wasiri."

After barely and quietly eating the dinner, Mrs. and Dr. Wasiri retired very quickly to their bedroom.

The next day, Dr. Wasiri made two important calls. The first was to the Honorable Georgia State Senator Jeremy Owen Massay to tell him that he was returning his call from two weeks while he was visiting with friends in New York City, and he will be honored to join the board of ABDI. He requested the board yearly calendar in order to accommodate it to his own schedule. The honorable senator was pleased to hear that he had accepted the invitation to join the board. He also told him that he was highly recommended by Dr. O'Shea, who was already a board member. As far as the honorable senator was concerned, his selection was a matter of forgone conclusion, given the combined status that Dr. Wasiri carries: a native African and a scientist with impeccable academic credential in the field of mines engineering, a field at the top of the economic development of Africa. With a lot of politician flourish, the Georgia state senator stated that he was looking forward, and with a great deal of impatience, to talk and to meet him. The honorable state senator said finally that a complete calendar of ABDI events was being expeditiously mailed to Dr. Wasiri and indicated the first board meeting was scheduled to take place around the fifteenth of the month of November.

After saying good-bye to the honorable Georgia state senator, Kano called his mentor, Professor O'Shea, and said, "I am calling to let you, Professor O'Shea, know that I am back home and the rest of the trip in New York City went just fine, thanks to all that money you left for me in that big envelope. I have struggled to spend it, but I was not able to get rid of it. Let me know how you want me to forward the remaining balance of 11,325 dollars and 42 cents."

There was almost thirty seconds of silent moment before Kano heard his mentor's voice saying, "Is that all you have to say so early in the morning, disturbing my morning nap? I don't know what I have to do with you, son. I was trying to figure out what money you were talking about. Please tell me something of value, something of interest, instead of telling me that you want to return eleven or so thousand dollars from last week. Now what makes you think that I will take it back? What makes you think that I left that so-called big envelope? I have no idea what you are talking about. Could it be that the bank I am dealing with in London has decided to start advancing you the share of your prize money? Remember, I have told that I was making arrangements to lower or to eliminate any tax liability you may incur from your share of the prize money. The bank had advanced me a little bit of money that I used in New York City as you have witnessed. Maybe the same bank wanted to do the same for you when I told them that you were to stay at the Embassy Suites until Tuesday and you may need some change. Surprise, surprise, you have used your own money, my good man. You can therefore keep the balance from that money too. All right. Now tell me any news that will make me proud of you. Did you call the Georgia State Senator as I have asked you? It looks like we have to be in Atlanta the weekend of November fifteenth for the board meeting of ABDI. What else you have in mind so?"

The thought of already starting to use the share of the so-called prize money was a bit disturbing to Kano, and worse, the fact that he had not told Hasbo about the money made it plainly unbearable. He was not in the habit of hiding financial matters to Hasbo. When he woke up that morning, he dismissed completely the whole idea of keeping the balance of that money. And, in his opinion, eleven thousand dollars were still a lot of money. He did not want to put himself in the situation of explaining to Hasbo what he had not fully grasped from his conversation with Dr. O'Shea the week before. His story of receiving the prize money was far-fetched. He accepted to spend the money only to please the good old man who always tries so hard to indulge him in all kinds of deeds.

He thought that by sending back the balance of the money to Dr. O'Shea, he was going to remit it to its rightful owner. Now that table was being turned on him and that he was really the owner of the share of the prize money, exactly as Dr. explained it in New York City, left him speechless.

"Are you there, son?" Dr. O'Shea was shouting on the phone. After regaining his composure, Dr. Wasiri said, "Surprise, surprise, indeed, Dr. O'Shea. Now you know I was not paying attention when you mentioned that I was to share in that prize money. Now I have to explain all this to Hasbo. That will not be easy. I should have done this yesterday when I came back. My good man, you have put me in a difficult position indeed. Well, I will manage. Yes, I have also something in mind to tell you. This has already made Hasbo extremely happy last night. I think by the time I will bring up this money business, it will come to her as a closed full circle. Well, my dear Dr. O'Shea, I am going back to Mezi to take up a tenured professorship at the Polytechnic University starting next academic year. I know that you have been waiting for this decision for some time. Well, I have decided to go back to Mezi. Now please advise me how I need to approach Hasbo regarding this prize money."

Elated, Dr. O'Shea responded, "You should not worry much.

Hasbo knows that your work cannot have gone without compensation. She has been your partner all these years. She has seen your struggle and pain. She should not be surprised if you are rightfully compensated and if you and I are sharing the same prize. Tell her that one of the reasons I have invited you to come to New York City was precisely to sign certain papers with the investment bank trusted to administer the prize money. The reason you did not share the news with your wife yesterday was precisely you need to get a certain confirmation from me the co-prize winner. After this call you were able to get the same confirmation from the investment bank. Now you feel that you can share the information and insist that the money will come handy to smooth the transfer to Mezi, just like I told you. Hasbo will be happy and grateful just the same.

Son, I have to tell you that you have made me a very happy man today. I will talk to you soon about the Atlanta trip. May God protect you and your family!

CHAPTER 8
Emily Thomas O'Shea Foundation

Dr. O'Shea hung up the phone and made a sign of cross. His eyes were swelling with tears of joy. At last, he thought, the true valiant warrior has joined the battle. His task now was to make the road to Mezi as expeditious as possible. He needed to prepare a successful battle plan. He remembered what that man from BI said in Amovir to the effect that if Dr. Wasiri is not in Mezi, the battle is lost. He was on the verge of delivering Dr. Wasiri. He needed to put everything in motion to make the move a reality. He reached his phone and called Lady Allistair, but she was not available in New York City. She had gone on a business trip. Less than ten minutes later, she was calling actually from a vacation spot in Cayman Islands. She did not mention that she was vacationing in company of a Brazilian bombshell.

Apparently, the New York City lesbian scene had graduated from the tall Scandinavian blondes to the multiethnic mezzo nymph mulattoes converging from the Caribbean nudist beaches down to coastal lanes of private Brazilian bungalows deep in the Amazon jungle. Her lover, named Nettina, was a mulatto of Caucasian, black, native Amazon Indian and Japanese mixed ancestry. Lady Allistair acknowledged to Professor O'Shea that she left instructions back in New York City offices to forward his calls as urgently and at any time.

Dr. O'Shea told her that Dr. Wasiri had agreed to go back to Mezi. Therefore, they needed to meet as soon as possible in order to plan various steps to be undertaken in order to insure an orderly return of Dr. Wasiri back to Mezi. The news hit Lady Allistair like a ton of brick. The sight of the naked Brazilian bombshell in the Jacuzzi Pond they were sharing became a distant memory. She left the Jacuzzi and got herself inside a large towel and went straight to the bedroom. While she was drying up, she set an appointment with Dr. O'Shea to meet in Chicago within forty-eight hours.

When her bewildered lover entered the room, she looked a bit annoyed by her sudden change of mood and departure while they were in the middle of a once-in-a-lifetime orgasmic medley; Lady Allistair feigned a deep sorrow and said that she had just received sad news from Chicago. There was death in the family, and she got to leave. They needed to schedule another vacation together. Her lover can remain for the rest of the weeks' vacation if she chooses to or leave to go back to her hometown of Belem in Brazil the next day. She was going definitely to get paid as planned the going rate of twenty thousand dollars as promised. Lady Allistair hoped to see Nettina after the funerals the following week Saturday night in New York City at the Petite Lydia Very Exclusive Club where each member, and without exception, had to use a digital card key to gain entrance to the club located on the twentieth floor of an upper east side regular condominium. She then made a flight reservation with the next plane leaving the island for the States within the next hour. She was in Miami within three hours and transferred into a LaGuardia-bound plane in no time. Lady Allistair was back at her desk in midtown Manhattan by eight in evening. She fired an urgent message to Amovir Station advising the big man's return home and the Chicago trip; she then waited for further instructions. The response came back very quick, and it was also ecstatic from Uncle Kiri himself.

His instructions were concise: "No bounds, No Retreat!" In other words, nothing should be spared in accommodating whatever Dr. O'Shea had in mind. Lady Allistair made all the travel arrangements for Dr. O'Shea and herself. They will meet at the new North Shore Lake Plaza Hotel, the latest five-star hotel built along the lake from Thursday morning at ten until such time that Dr. O'Shea had shared what he had in mind and received guarantees that he would get full satisfaction over his requests. She called the good professor at home, and they agreed on the appointment on Thursday that week. As soon as Dr. O'Shea hung the phone, he received another call from his protégé, Dr. Wasiri, who wanted to let his mentor know that Hasbo was so caught up with the idea of going back to Mezi, she was in full agreement with the story of the shared prize money. At least, the story that Dr. O'Shea asked his protégé to share with his wife. She was even more than delighted to learn that it will be primarily used to make their transition as smooth as possible. The only request she made was to deposit the remaining advance money in their shared bank account for the usual household expenses. Dr. Wasiri told his mentor that he was most surprised by the matter-of-fact attitude that Hasbo showed when he told her about the shared prize money. She did not blush about the 'two million and half dollar' size of it.

She was very cool about the whole story as if the amount of two million and half dollars was an ordinary amount among their assets. Dr. Wasiri asked his mentor if he did not already tell his wife about his Amovir trip and the circumstances of the prize money. Dr. O'Shea assured him that he did not on the account that he was not about to put his protégé under unnecessary matrimonial test that will put all his future plans in jeopardy. He would never allow it. A bit reassured, Dr. Wasiri changed the subject and started raising the issue that his friend Mr. Mbow raised in New York City about getting an additional high-paid consulting position with a foreign mining company while still teaching at the Polytechnic

University. He also volunteered the name of Mr. Mbow's contact, a certain Mr. Fadden working for a company named Mattley & Barr, which had extensive mining interests in Mezi. He mentioned that this gentleman was looking for a candidate of his credentials.

Dr. Wasiri asked his mentor to advise him about these kinds of opportunity and to check about this Mr. Fadden and the Mattley & Barr firm. Surprised to hear the name of Mr. Fadden, who, when described, sounded no other but his longtime contact, the Maj. Gen. Richard "Bull" Fadden, Dr. O'Shea feigned not to recognize the name and convinced his protégé not to worry as he should be able to provide him ample details about consulting positions in Mezi and whatever he will learn through his contacts about Mattley & Barr and this Mr. Fadden. When the phone call with his protégé was over, Dr. O'Shea did not know what to make of the involvement of Mr. Mbow with his old contact from the "community" as the major general used to put it.

He was not aware that the major general was now in charge of government relations for AMX in DC, in other words, its main lobbyist. He resolved that only Lady Allistair should be able to sort this out since he was the one who requested for Mr. Mbow's sudden trip to DC. He made this request to Lady Allistair. But there was no reference then to the fact that Mr. Mbow was to become an additional pressure point over Dr. Wasiri in order to get him a job in Mezi, which job somehow now involves the famous major general. Things were getting very intriguing to the old professor. As long as they were not jeopardizing his battle plans, there should be no problem. Just the same, the presence of too many pressure points on his protégé was annoying Dr. O'Shea. He would tell the Lady Allistair that he would prefer to be the sole contact to deal with his protégé when it comes to his definite return to Mezi. The next day, Wednesday morning, he called the major general; "It has been a century since we talked, General.

Have you abandoned me at the University of Kentucky? What are you up to? Have you left the 'community'?" The Maj. Gen. Richard "Bull" Fadden was at his first morning martini at his office when he took the call. He reminisced with Dr. O'Shea about various research works they have done back then when he was a Defense Department coordinator of advanced weapons research from thermonuclear sources to exotic minerals. That was way back during the Cold War era. The general was the main contact with various universities researchers for various advanced researches supporting the United States' weapons. Dr. O'Shea was his main contact at the University of Kentucky for researching the application of exotic minerals over these weapons. The general was one of the few people who appreciated his line of work and told him in confidence that at that time similar research works were being undertaken in the Soviet Union. There was no way for the States to lag behind in such crucial area. More than once, he would call to tell him not to be distracted by the other faculty members who had a rather narrow defeatist view of the Pentagon Advanced Weapons Research Program. He encouraged him to continue his researches and funded them with obscure Defense Intelligence resources when the faculty at the University of Kentucky removed them from government grant requests. At the end of Cold War, the general informed him that the Advanced Weapons Research program was being dismantled and shifted to other agencies, and he was going to retire. That was about the time of his first trip to St. Petersburg in Russia.

The general then said, "Soon after my retirement, I got a call from this lady in New York City who asked me if I wanted to represent her company AMX here in the capital doing a lot of government relations, in other words, lobbying. The offer was so generous, I could not refuse and here I am, working as little as possible and pulling seven-figure salary while literally parking my monthly pension pay. Not bad indeed. Well, how in the world have you found me? By the way, I heard all that went on with your projects at the university after we closed the funding window. I tell you that was pitiful. I was always amazed by the short sight of your faculty about your researches when out there in the Soviet Union. They were killing each other to harness those exotic minerals. Well, now that all is put on ice, including yours truly, what are you doing now? I bet close to retirement; you don't say?"

Dr. O'Shea responded, "Yes, close to retirement after all these years and all those researches. I tried to dabble in here and there, but there were no takers. Forget it. It is now down to retirement. But tell me if you may.

Since you are dealing with mining with AMX, do you know of a company named Mattley & Barr? You know how those companies are using so many different names in different locations of the world. Is Mattley & Barr a legal entity for AMX? I need to know this for one of many references I need to give to a graduate student here at the University of Kentucky."

The general said, "You are right. Mattley & Barr is the legal entity name that AMX uses in many countries: Bolivia, Equator, Paraguay, Zambia, Uganda, Mezi, and Vietnam. This is to allay a lot of obvious political sensitivities in those Third World countries. It is much easy to deal with Mattley & Barr than the huge AMX. It is as simple as that. You can always pass on the name of that graduate student if he is interested in employment in one of our overseas posts. It was a great pleasure to hear from you, Professor O'Shea. Let me know anytime if I can be of some help."

Dr. O'Shea learned that the general was on Lady Allistair's payroll too. He also closed the loop around the consulting position story full circle, from himself to Lady Allistair to the general to Mr. Mbow to Dr. Wasiri back to himself. The same day in the afternoon, Mr. Mbow was also closing his deal proposal with Mr. Fadden. He told him that he had identified a close friend as a main candidate for the highly paid consultancy position in Mezi. His name was Dr. Kano Wasiri, currently a professor of Mining Engineering Studies in Kentucky State University. This citizen of Mezi has been expressing interest to return home and to continue his teaching assignment at one of the Mezi Universities. He would be very glad to secure a consultancy position as they have discussed. He would have to complete this academic year by next year June and then return home. Mr. Fadden was very happy to hear the news and assured Mr. Mbow that he would get the full hiring retainer of sixty thousand dollars as soon as this Dr. Wasiri gets to Mezi. He also made inquiry about the other eastern African regional manager that he had proposed to Mr. Mbow himself. He said that he was getting a lot of resistance from his wife on that job proposal. He needed more time to work on his wife. But he insisted that from the conversation he had with his friend from Mezi, he will be happy to get such a position in Mezi in addition to his academic job. Mr. Fadden thanked Mr. Mbow and urged him to stay in touch for both proposals in the future. At the same time, he sent to Lady Allistair a report over the highly paid consultancy position that Dr. Wasiri was disposed to take in about eight months in Mezi. Lady Allistair was extremely pleased with the speed of the resolution all pressure points directed over Dr. Wasiri were taking. She knew that Uncle Kiri also was going to be extremely pleased.

She was a bit bothered and still not clear about what Dr. O'Shea needed to do to accelerate the process. But she also remembered the instructions from Uncle Kiri as "No bounds, No Retreat." She had no choice here but to execute. It also occurred to her at that instant that there was also another larger pressure point that needed to be closed, the installation of the African Breakthrough Development Institute, ABDI. This institute should remain a US internal initiative with direct tentacles to Africa of course. This initiative was under her supervision and control. However, she was not convinced at this time of the complete commitment to the initiative from His Honorable Georgia State Senator Jeremy Owen Massay. She had noticed that he was a bit reluctant to the project despite the clear financial bait to advance his political career to the Senate of the United States. She was wondering if the price to finalize the initiative would be an intimate engagement with the senator, the like she had not indulged since the time she was married to Lord Allistair. That was the time of never-stayed-at-home Lord Allistair. That was the time when she, tired of waiting for the distant Lord Allistair, also played the field, sexually entertaining a long series of high-class London bachelors, including the well-endowed high commissioner of the Republic of Zambezi. She stopped these escapades after one of the bachelors started sending her nude pictures to Lord Allistair, who then requested the end of their unfulfilled marriage. Afterward, she resumed her discreet love affair with the lovely Ludmilla, who moved to London from Amovir. She had not returned to a heterosexual involvement since then. Now if she had to consider that possibility with His Honorable Jeremy Massay, it would be a price she was prepared to pay. In addition to the ABDI initiative, Lady Allistair had been thinking about a much bigger initiative that she needed to carefully run by Uncle Kiri. The initiative consists of getting a clear path to the White House inner sanctum. To date, the Maj. Gen. Richard Fadden had operated as far from the White House as any single business issue lobbyist operates in DC. The general had already shown the extent of his reach. He could not go beyond what was being considered. Lady Allistair was seriously thinking of a super lobbyist with close links with the White House executive offices.

Not necessarily a buddy or a friend to the sitting president, but somebody with multiple accesses to the decision makers in both the legislative and executive branches. With all the powers that Uncle Kiri seems to carry, maybe there is somebody in place playing such roles and who is directly accountable to Uncle Kiri and whom she does not know or has not been made aware of. Uncle Kiri more than once has shown his ability to operate below every radar, more like a submarine. And he has been effective in that way.

She just needs to close that loop next time she will communicate with Uncle Kiri. She took the late flight to Chicago to prepare for a meeting with Dr. O'Shea the next day. The good old professor took the early morning flight from Lexington to Chicago and was at the hotel on time. The conference room reserved by Lady Allistair was at the thirty-ninth floor and gave a splendid view to the lake. Dr. O'Shea started his lecture with a deep appreciation for all that Lady Allistair has done to date to facilitate the execution of the instructions that Mr. Kiriyan gave him at Amovir. He was also pleased to announce that Dr. Wasiri has expressed his definitive desire to go back and work in Mezi. He requested the meeting to lay down specifics steps to make this return as productive as possible.

He went, "My dear lady, the return of Dr. Wasiri to Mezi must be put in a totally different context. And I am certain that Mr. Kiriyan will agree with me if I said so. We are dealing here not just with the return of my protégé, Dr. Wasiri, and his family but with the beginning of an era in the definitive extraction and business applications of the Alpha-M. You should know by now that all the resources you have expanded and are going to expand would return to BI and Mr. Kiriyan billions, if not trillions, of dollars of revenue for a long time if this return is properly and rightly managed. I understand that it is all business, and I have no issue about that. My immediate concern is to determine what is in for Dr. Wasiri. I am for all practical purposes done with my time, my energy, and my contributions. My only remaining role in this endeavor is to see that Dr. Wasiri carries forward the new phases of Alpha-M, because he has worked on it and is the sole inheritor of the fruits of the Alpha-M researches I know of. This is what I want to urgently communicate to you.

As far as I am concerned, his return must be preceded by certain steps BI needs to undertake, and they include: building a new Faculty of Applied Sciences associated with the Polytechnic University, building a large dormitory for about six hundred students taking classes in the new faculty, providing scholarship, room, and board to all students in the last three years of engineering studies at the Faculty, setting up a foundation with enough financial resources to support and guide the first three initiatives right there in Mezi. These steps will be the first ones to insure that Dr. Wasiri will return to Mezi in an environment geared to him continuing the research works around Alpha-M. I would be ready, and as soon as possible, to take the trip to Mezi and negotiate with the Polytechnic University Board the initiatives I have laid out. We are now pressed for the time to realize all these initiatives before the beginning of next academic year.

What do you think, Lady Allistair?" Gazing the endless realm of water dancing on the lake, Lady Allistair was absorbing all that the old man was saying and told him, "Thank you so much, Dr. O'Shea, I really appreciate that you have thought about these initiatives. Let me also tell you, money should not be an object as far as BI and Mr. Kiriyan are concerned. I will only suggest that the foundation carries the name of your beloved wife, if you don't mind. I have wondered a lot about your closeness with Dr. Wasiri. I have learned from many people that you and your wife have welcomed Dr. Wasiri as more than a passing graduate student, but as an adopted son. I also learned that your wife was your ultimate support in your research works and that she certainly enrolled Dr. Wasiri, then student, to take up the research about Alpha-M. I could be wrong, but there will be no better honor to your wife than to give her name to the foundation. Of course, you will be the main driver of the foundation as a chairperson. Dr. O'Shea, please rest assured that these initiatives will be done and on time. Is there anything else you want to add?"

Dr. O'Shea was all tears and trying to wipe his eyes with the mention of his wife, and he said, "My Emily would be delighted to hear that a foundation will be set up with her name to continue, as she used to say it, the great battle of minds for Alpha-M. I must agree and so would Dr. Wasiri that it will be the greatest honor to bestow to my Emily if the foundation carries her name. Emily Thomas O'Shea Foundation would sound excellent. Really. I do not want to bother now with the members of the board of that foundation. But I cannot help but suggest at this time a key future board member in the person of Hasbo Dorothy Wasiri, Mrs. Wasiri. That position will come handy when she would land in Mezi. Just fantastic. Before we break, and talking about a position, Dr. Wasiri run by me a high consultancy position with Mattley & Barr in Mezi that my old friend the General Fadden floated to Dr. Wasiri's friend, Mr. Mbow when he went to DC. Dr. Wasiri asked me to look into this, as he trusts me to find out about it through my academic contacts. But I knew that it came from you. What should I tell him? Is it real or would it come about when he will reach Mezi? How should we position this offer now?"

Lady Allistair responded very quickly, "I must confess that I rushed my inquiry to the general, and he went all the way with the offer in his conversation with that Mr. Mbow. I am terribly sorry it came back full circle to you. Dr. O'Shea, I will assure again from then on, you have full management of what you call your protégé, Dr. Wasiri. As a matter of fact, I believe that the suggested foundation should be the proper channel to carry out discreetly all the support we would want to provide to Dr. Wasiri.

This way, we will not run into the unfortunate oversight that you have witnessed. I am fully aware of your privileged relationship with Dr. Wasiri, and I would do nothing to jeopardize it. Thinking of jeopardy, how did Dr. Wasiri manage with the fifteen thousand I included in the big envelope for him? That was also an unfortunate oversight I should not have pulled. No more. Let us all agree that you have full management of your protégé from then on."

Dr. O'Shea listened attentively. "Agreed. I was going to raise the matter of fifteen thousand dollars that you provided him in one of your big envelopes. I managed to tell him a story about shared prize money and that I felt compelled to give him that much money to cover his expenses while in New York City. He told me that fifteen thousand dollars for less than four days was rather excessive and tried to return to me the balance of eleven thousand dollars. I asked him to keep the balance for the sake of his family. To tell the truth, I was a bit embarrassed by the whole episode. We never had in the past discussions around money. We have tried to deal with each other in our humble and modest ways. The sight of me hanging out in VIP fashion in New York City was the last thing Dr. Wasiri expected of me. I had to come up with all kinds of lies and stratagems to convince him that I was still his old mentor he used to know and who was trying to guide him in new paths. In all honesty, I was not convincing. But knowing my protégé, I believe he came around to his decision after a long and deliberate thought while alone in New York City. At the end, it was still a successful trip after all but for different reasons and definitely not as a result of the VIP treat, not at all. Just the same, I am glad that you have anticipated my reaction, and I certainly appreciate the understanding we have reached. Believe me, as we were talking, it occurred to me that we are both adjusting to an endeavor, or should I say a major plan, that had no guidance or rules.

We may trip all over each other now and then but with common understanding, and if we keep our eyes on the final objective, we should overcome our differences and reach our common goal. Now there is another matter I will need clarification about. I just shared with you what I believe to be a long-term view of how to support the next phases of Alpha-M project. We have agreed that all should be done to insure that the next phases of the project center around and include the return of Dr. Wasiri to Mezi. Our common objective, we have agreed, is that these phases should be managed successfully. Now at the same time, you have asked me to join the board of ABDI and to convince Dr. Wasiri to do the same. So much so, we are invited to the November fifteenth first board meeting in Atlanta.

My point and question is this, since ABDI, at least from what I read in the flier, is being set up to promote breakthrough development in Africa, would it be involved in the initiatives I have laid here? What relationship you have in mind between ABDI and the Emily Thomas O'Shea Foundation?"

Lady Allistair got up and, with strong emphasis, declared, "Absolutely none. I believe today we have come to a mutual understanding that you will be managing all that would fall under the preview of yes, the Emily Thomas O'Shea Foundation. Dr. Wasiri's return to Mezi falls under the foundation's support. You may be wondering why ABDI. It is very easy. Our goal in putting together ABDI is to garner strong support for various business projects BI will be involved in the future in Africa. That support was determined to be more effective if it is nurtured from both sides of Atlantic Ocean within the African elite community in Africa and African American elite community in the States.

The growing affinity between these two communities is becoming self-evident given the recent migration of African to the United States.

By the way, we have recruited the Honorable Jeremy Massay for that very reason. Most of projects we have in mind for ABDI will be country specific and generally providing strong support for the country strategic natural resources. These projects are divided generally between intensive agricultural projects and minerals extraction projects at the beginning. The emphasis for us is on insuring a significant impact on the development of specific country strategic resources. We will insist on that impact, otherwise there will be no project implementation.

This is the same strategy we are applying for Mezi with the difference we have already been engaged in executing this long-term initiative and that Alpha-M is the strategic resource we will build on. As far Mezi is concerned, you have also been engaged in the project along with Dr. Wasiri. Our Mezi involvement is completely outside ABDI. That is the reason why I have suggested that Dr. Wasiri and you become board members. Your involvement and Dr. Wasiri's will be to act as consultants supplying as much guidance and to insure that there is no duplication of effort when Mezi topics are raised by the board of ABDI. Of course, as ABDI expands, we will expect that various other experts will join the institute. It goes without saying that the recruiting of those experts will concentrate as much as possible among people of African descent."

What Lady Allistair did not say alludes to the fact that BI had realized it must literally buy the goodwill from both sides of Atlantic Ocean in various issues it was about to confront. The reality is that BI had no Western governments that it can call on to assist in its business initiatives in Africa. BI is a holding international company started in Russia. It has a strong international presence, thanks to multiple mergers accomplished all over Europe, the United States, and Canada. The mergers included companies specialized in energy exploration and minerals extraction all over the world. However, and in fact, because of its Russian background, BI is still regarded as an odd entity in international business. The Western governments for better or worse have their client states all over Africa. They are very good at advancing their company's business agendas because of their past and postcolonial relationships with these states. And they never stop from indulging the elite community within those states by various ways and means including outright bribes. BI has shied away from those cross-continental forays. It has been very profitable in its own right. Companies from emerging developing nations, including China, India, and other countries from Asia Pacific region can rely on the old nonaligned mythical pacts with African states dating back to the fifties and sixties. In spite of the past frightening collapse of the unmitigated capitalism in the Western world and the rise of the emerging economies in China and India, there was still no clear path guiding their involvement in the slow economic development of nations in Africa. It was not obvious that China to a great extent and India to a lesser extent were effectively taking advantage of their newfound economic leverage in that part of the world. The reality was that, in order to counter deep-seated suspicions held by African people against any foreign business agency after so many instances of deliberate economic exploitation, the new Chinese or Indian enterprises were still lining up behind the old colonial power companies to effect their African design or strategy. These initiatives were at best extremely tentative. They worked sometime but not all the time, and they are not as effective as the old alliances. Western companies can count on, thanks to African states' continuous reliance on the French, the British, the Portuguese, the Spanish, the German, and the American governments. Now that BI is about to implement extensive projects in Africa, it cannot rely on or line up behind such government support. BI has no choice but to build all its support from ground up. It was obvious that ABDI would become a major vehicle to do this. With Dr. O'Shea nodding his head while listening to Lady Allistair, she concluded that her explanation was satisfactory and started to close their meeting by saying, "I am very happy that we had this meeting today.

It looks like we have a lot on our plate for the next six to eight months. I just want to propose something to you. I know you have your own involvement with your school.

I do not know when you are going to retire from your tenured professorship. BI would like to hire you as a consultant. You have already done so much for us on voluntary basis. The conferences you have attended and now the Dr. Wasiri's return to Mezi and more, I believe you should be compensated somehow. I heard about the prize money you received in Amovir. That does not apply even for anybody out there, winning the Nobel Prize. Look for instance, you took time to come here to Chicago to attend a long business meeting from ten in the morning, and it is about three in the afternoon. Don't you think you should be paid for this participation? I do. Just think about it and let me know what you think sometime soon. Also remember you are priceless. Now as I go back to New York City, I will provide you with the definitive answer regarding the initiatives you have proposed and how much funding you would get to start the foundation. That will be the key. Do not trouble yourself with the legal aspects of the foundation. BI will take care of that. What you will need to think about now is how soon you have to get to Mezi to negotiate your suggested initiatives. I should also have answers about your departure by next week. Again, think about the consultant position proposal. By the way, I meant to ask you something for some time since the last time we met briefly in New York City. It was about the ring you have on your finger. It looks very much like the one that Uncle Kiri wears but a bit smaller. Tell me have you joined a secret business society along with Uncle Kiri that I should be aware of."

`Dr. O'Shea demurred and said that the ring was a personal gift from Mr. Kiriyan in Amovir along with the money prize. He received both presents during the ceremony to honor his lifetime work in exotic minerals. He added that he did not join any secret society with Mr. Kiriyan, and at his advanced age, he would never dream reaching the business pinnacle where Mr. Kiriyan and, for that matter, Lady Allistair sit.

To the last caustic comment from Dr. O'Shea, Lady Allistair replied, "Oh well, I am being checkmated by the senior professor Dr. O'Shea, and this is well put indeed. Then I can assure, Dr. O'Shea, that BI can certainly use a lot of business acumen demonstrated by the like of yours, and this in spite of your advanced age, as you like to put it. Just the same, still I thank you for coming to this very productive business meeting, and I hope to see you soon on your way to Mezi."

Lady Allistair proposed to Dr. O'Shea to stay overnight at the hotel and return to Lexington the next day. Dr. O'Shea declined on the account that he got to go back quickly home and prepare for his trip to Mezi by expanding on paper what his suggested initiatives should look. He promised to send the complete documentation of his initiatives in the middle of next week at least while the foundation legal papers were being developed. He took a ride back to the airport with Lady Allistair on her way to New York City.

Dr. O'Shea was home at about eight in the evening. After a short nap, he called his protégé and talked about the initiatives he had shared with a BI representative who came to see him to request to work for BI as a senior consultant. He described the initiatives around the new Faculty of Applied Sciences at the Polytechnic University, the new dormitory and the distribution of scholarship. He left aside the Emily Thomas O'Shea Foundation. He told his protégé that BI had agreed to all of these initiatives in order to hire him as senior consultant. He added that he needed to go over the documentation of the initiatives as soon as it is completed to get his feedback. He informed Dr. Wasiri that soon after BI approves the final version of his suggested initiatives with adequate funding, he would have to go to Mezi to negotiate the suggested initiatives with the board of Polytechnic University.

Dr. Wasiri responded, "I am not surprised by all that you are saying. I expected that you were going to do something as soon as I mentioned that I was going back home. But I must say you have exceeded my last expectations. I have no choice but accept and agree with your initiatives as they are the ultimate initiatives anyone in Mezi can pray for. Of course, I will give you my feedback regarding the documentation of these initiatives. At this very moment, I would like to jump on the plane and come to Lexington to help you draft the documentation of these initiatives. Dr. O'Shea, you have to forgive me when sometime I appear to be doubtful, and I am afraid, ungrateful for all that you have done, are doing, and want to do for me. I hope that from then on, I appreciate your disposition for all that it is, a disposition for the good. I have no words to thank you for these initiatives. Send me the documentation as soon as you are done with them. As far as going to Mezi, I would put you in contact with very good people who would support your initiatives without reserves. Let me know when you will go. For myself, I would start touching base with some board members of the Polytechnic University to sound them up about these projects. I can tell you that they would be grateful to no end."

Dr. O'Shea was also grateful for the kind words he heard and said to his protégé that he was doing all he can for his adopted son, no more and no less. He also added that in his remaining years, he had resolved to do as much as he could, and as instructed by his beloved Emily, sometime before her passing. That was always the code word to Dr. Wasiri to discount all he was doing but to thank the memory of his adopted mother, Emily Thomas O'Shea. That always worked. As usual, during such time, their phone conversation ended with muffled voices. They ended their talk with tears and calmly retired to their respective quiet rooms to reminisce. It was that bond that had united them for this long in spite of all the doubt Dr. Wasiri felt about his mentor now and then. When he gained his composure, Dr. Wasiri called his friend, Sir William Ewas, at home. His wife received the call and reiterated her invitation to host the Wasiri family the next time they were in the New York area. When William came on the phone, he was also delighted to hear from his friend.

He shared a few jokes going around the UN Diplomatic Mission about the various political dramas evolving back home in Mezi. After exchanging a few more laughter, Dr. Wasiri asked him how he could get the list of board members of the Polytechnic University with their current contact telephone numbers. To his surprise, his friend told him that he should be able to send the list by next day by e-mail. As a matter of fact, he had employed himself to gather as much information about the university since their last weekend in New York City after his friend "Geffadi" had expressed his desire to go back to Mezi to teach at the

Polytechnic University. He did not know how far "Geffadi" had negotiated his tenured professorship position with the university. But he stood ready to provide as much information as he needed. If needed, all that he gathered to date, he was prepared to ship them by FEDEX the next day first thing early in the morning and to guarantee a Saturday super-express delivery. He added that he would do anything to ease his friend return to Mezi. He had a lot of contacts, very good contacts with extraordinary good disposition to help Mezi out of the present morass. Anytime he needs to get in touch with them, he should let him know. Dr. Wasiri thanked his friend and said that he will appreciate to receive all that he had gathered relative to Polytechnic University and especially, all kinds of maps of the university locations. Dr. Wasiri was elated by the ready support he was receiving from his longtime friend, Sir Ewas. All along the next day, Friday, he received through e-mail; the progressive draft reports that Dr. O'Shea sent to get his feedback regarding the initiatives. On Saturday, he was really overwhelmed when he received a large package from Sir Ewas.

The package contained various documentations concerning the Polytechnic University. Descriptions of various faculties making up the university, faculty members' names and credentials, residence halls for students, scholarship sponsors, past and present board members, minutes of board members meetings for the past seven years, political connections, students' body composition, rate of graduation, maps and tons of maps, and more. These documentations came handy when he was providing precise feedback to the progressive draft reports that his mentor was sending. Most of the times, he was able to expand each draft page sent to three or four more pages, and Dr. O'Shea was extremely delighted by the shape and depth the documentation was taking. He was glad that he had gotten his protégé involved up front. He was much impressed by the precision Dr. Wasiri provided regarding the exact locations where the new Faculty of Applied Sciences and the dormitory should be built. He thought that Dr. Wasiri must have consulted with people back home regarding the initiatives, but he did not ask him. After all, the more he was involved the better. The initiatives were as much Dr. Wasiri's as his.

Dr. O'Shea had no reservation to include his protégé's feedback, which now had made the initial five-page draft to grow almost to a sixty pages draft report. It was now reading as an elegant professionally made proposition with charts and maps far beyond Dr. O'Shea had in mind. He thought that by the time the Emily Thomas O'Shea legal brief will be added, the full final documentation would probably exceed one hundred pages. That will make for a decent professional presentation to the university board members. That will validate also the excuse he made to Lady Allistair to come back home on Thursday after the Chicago meeting.

He was really earning his keep of senior consultant for how much he had no idea. Before coming to terms with the proposed job, he would need to send his resignation from the University of Kentucky and request his retirement papers. That will need to take some time. By Sunday, he told his protégé that they have worked so hard and the draft report of eighty-four pages was now final, and he was going to send it to BI for review. He insisted that Dr. Wasiri's name would be inserted as a significant contributor to the final documentation. His protégé did not protest. He was rather proud of his contribution for having significantly enhanced the report. Lady Allistair was surprised to receive the final documentation so well documented that early Monday morning. She was expecting it sometime in the middle of the week. She was beyond herself when she read that Dr. Wasiri was a significant contributor to the documentation.

This left her with no doubt and a definitive indication that his decision to go back to Mezi was final and irreversible. She forwarded the documentation to Amovir Station along with her extensive report of the Thursday-meeting in Chicago. It did not take long for Amovir to react with a positive answer from Uncle Kiri himself who suggested that a preliminary funding of 150 million dollars should be allocated to the Emily Thomas O'Shea Foundation right away. Lady Allistair could not restrain herself to call Dr. O'Shea to announce the news. She announced that she was expediting the legal papers for the foundation that was being set up in New York City, with funding coming from London and Cayman Islands and works execution in Mezi. She was also gratified that Dr. O'Shea was able to engage Dr. Wasiri so early in the process. She advised the professor to get his shots and other papers ready for the eventual trip to Mezi. At the same time, she took up again the job proposal to Dr. O'Shea who this time assured her that he had already made up his mind to join in as a senior consultant for BI after he had sent his letter of resignation from the University of Kentucky and signed his retirement papers very shortly.

The good news prompted Lady Allistair to say that she was signing a check of 2,00,000 dollar hiring acceptance fee made to Dr. O'Shea, and she was sending right away before he changed his mind and hung up the phone. Dr. O'Shea was relieved that the final documentation was so well received and all seem to go the way he wanted. He wrote his letter of resignation from the University of Kentucky and was going to request to sign his retirement papers after almost forty-two years of academic teaching and research in the Faculty of Mines Engineering. At about two in the afternoon, he personally delivered the letter to the faculty human resources desk. When the Faculty dean came out, looking surprised by the unexpected letter of resignation, he invited Dr. O'Shea to come in and explain the surprise. Dr. O'Shea took a seat on the sofa in the dean's office and mentioned that it had been close to four months he had not been at the university premises. He knew that he was marking his time to increase his retirement pay with no particular involvement with the university. He just got tired of pretending to be a professor at the august university.

He came to submit his resignation, terminate his employment with the university, and sign his retirement papers. This way, he can calmly go on with enjoying his retirement life with his grandkids when he can or to take up that place that is waiting for him at the seashore of South Carolina, the place that was bought by his children. He intended to learn playing golf and fishing all year around.

He added that he was also really tired of fighting with colleagues at the Faculty if the dean wants to know. It was as simple as this. Dr. O'Shea added, "My last request is for you not to hold any retirement party for me." He finished signing the last retirement papers, got up, said good-bye to the dean and walked off the Faculty office. While driving home, he felt like a prisoner who was jailed for forty-two years and had just been released and was on his way out. But he could not help stopping in front of the huge park adjacent to the university football stadium and where he took his wife and kids to spend free time and have outside barbecues. He was saddened that the only good memory he kept from the university was this huge park.

When he left the university compound, he decided to pay a visit to Emily's plot at the cemetery. After placing the flowers, he had bought, he held his hands together as in a prayer, "We are finally done with them, Emily, those pitiful short brains of the university. Too bad they will never learn. There is nothing we can any longer do for them. We are embarking on the long phase of our battle. I am happy to announce that we got strong and steady allies now. And mind you, our adopted son, Dr. Wasiri, has definitely joined the battle. The enemies do not know what vengeance our adopted son will wage against them. Emily, time is on our side. Yours truly is about to put the final touch of our engagement for the next phase of the battle. We shall not fail. The rise of Man should come from the East. Amen!"

By the time he reached home, he called each of his children and broke the news of his resignation and retirement. He caught them a bit by surprise, as they had not finalized the purchase of the town house in South Carolina. They thought that they were going to give it as a present when he was going to retire as promised by the end of academic year. They were still arguing among themselves about the final architecture the town house will have. Construction was to start in March and finish around June when he was to retire. They had no idea that their father had stopped going to teach or work at the university since last July. From the time their mother was alive, they were instructed never to disturb him during class hours. They always called him at home. He gave no hint of his problems with other faculty members. As their mother had decided, the children were not signed up to join the battle. So, the least they knew the better. As he listened to them, he agreed that he was going to remain in Lexington, Kentucky, until such time when the South Carolina town house will be completed. By the way, he told them that he would take trips here and there with friends to relax. He will keep them informed, of course. As soon as the weather would allow, he will pay each of his children a visit.

He also added that they needed to check with Dr. Wasiri now and then if they cannot get in touch with him, as he would be in constant contact with Dr. Wasiri.

As soon as he finished talking to his children, they arranged a conference call with Dr. Wasiri and asked him about the state of mind and health of their father. Protecting his mentor, Dr. Wasiri said to the children, "Your father is in excellent health as far as I can tell. We just completed a draft report of a paper these last four days. We went back and forth about it until this past Sunday. He mentioned that this was going to be a last paper for him, and I needed to carry on alone from now on. He also said that he wanted to sign up for his retirement very soon. Maybe he made up his mind to do it after forty-two years. I would hang it up after thirty-two years, I like that number, thirty-two. And you know why, well, it will be ten years less than your father's. Seriously, your father has contributed enough in that university. I think he deserved his full retirement and after raising crazy kids like all of you. My God, he should have retired after thirty years in my view. Do not worry about him, he is fine, and I will call him right away to congratulate on the job well done. Regards from Hasbo, the kids, and me to all your families. Please stay in touch."

When he was hanging up, he received a call from his mentor, "Well, I would have known they were calling you, my kids, weren't they? I am sorry, I caught you by surprise. So much has happened today, and I am just getting around to talk to you. First the final documentation was well received by BI, and they are ready to disburse a large sum of money to make it happen. I will be going to Mezi very shortly, and you should prepare all these contacts you told me about. Second, I have accepted a position of senior consultant for BI effective today. This led to my resignation from the University of Kentucky and signing up for my retirement papers. You should have been there. I delivered my resignation letter personally to that Faculty dean, and I told him that I was tired of fighting with my colleagues. I told him please let me go. Well, he complied. I went home, and I told the kids that I was retiring from my teaching job after forty-two years. They were a bit upset and thought that their father was at his deep end.

You see, they were not aware that I have been a zombie of professor since July. I did not want to aggravate them. The retirement news probably hit them unprepared, and they assumed that I was not well. I knew that they would call you sometime tonight after they have spoken among themselves. That would have given time to share with you what has happened this hectic day. Well, they went ahead of me and talked to you.

I am certain that you have put them at ease and relieved their unnecessary anxiety. From then on, I trust that you will do your part and share with them only the good news. I also trust that you will make absolutely no references to BI or Mezi to these kids. If they cannot get in touch with me from then on, give them a good story until I will resurface. You will be my cover from then on. This is probably the way Emily would have wanted it."

Dr. Wasiri said with deep sarcasm, "Indeed, the way Emily would have wanted it. But I don't think that Emily would have wanted her kids to be so worried about your health. Come on, Dr. O'Shea, you seem to carry your so-called rules of battle a bit too far. You can play them with me as long as you want but not with your own flesh and blood. I certainly don't like to be put in a position where your kids have to rely on me to relieve their anxiety when I don't know what I am talking about. I love your kids very much, and I don't like these hide-and-seek games you are playing with them. They are, after all, grown up. What is the need to protect them from your most prized and innermost battle, as you love to put it? I tell you, no matter how it will hurt, I will never put my kids under such painful inquiries. It is just not fair to them. And please leave Emily's name out every time you want to pull your stunt. Now I have to draw the line and tell you that you have started calling her name in vain then. That is not right. Why would Emily put her kids asunder? I just don't believe it. Well, for your information, I told them you were fine, and we have worked on a scientific paper the last four days and that you told me that this was the last paper you wanted to get involved in and let me know that you were going to sign up for your retirement very soon. I told them that I did not know what you meant by very soon. I added that I was not surprised that they were informing me that you just did it. Well, as you can see, it was all lies that I made up to protect Daddy Dear. But why?

Can you imagine if Hasbo had answered the phone first and heard the alarm from your kids?

She would not have hesitated to drag me then and there to Lexington to your place to attend to your bad health and only to find out that you were fine. Do you know why she would have done that? Well, because she cares, because we care so much about you. Dr. O'Shea, please do not put us again under these silly positions. Level all with your kids. That is all Hasbo and I are asking you to do." With great remorse and behind pale, Dr. O'Shea replied, "I will, I will, just give me time, and I will level with the children. But just remember that Hasbo and you are my children too. I know you care about me, otherwise we would not be having this conversation.

Remember that you two mean a lot to me too. You are right about Emily; maybe I have started using her name in vain. But God help me for what I will say. My lovely Emily definitely wanted to spare the kids all the pains we both suffered at the hands of the mean ones at the university. It is true that I have not shared these indignities with them. As a parent, you will grow to understand these rules one day. Dr. Wasiri, I am telling you all this because I want to burden you with the charge of telling them one day. Not today, nor tomorrow but when the time will be right if ever, I miss my chance to tell them. And I was not lying when I said that those were Emily's rules."

With sadness and disgust Dr. Wasiri responded, "I understand. But I also needed to tell you what I had in my mind. I am sorry if I came out a bit harsh. Now let me congratulate you on your well-deserved retirement and the start of a new important career. In spite of all, I should say that I am blessed to have known you all these years and will remain forever thankful for your help. Now let us concentrate on getting you ready for your first trip to Mezi. You should know that I feel so excited about your trip as if I was the one going. That is so amazing."

CHAPTER 9
ABDI in DC

While the mentor and his protégé were sorting out their relationship, Lady Allistair was completing the legal framework for ABDI and advised the Honorable Georgia State Senator Jeremy Owen Massay that they should meet in Washington, DC, to go over ABDI papers. His honorable felt a bit uncomfortable to take the trip to DC, fearing the bait and the trap he was concerned about since he met this fine-looking lady the first time. At the same time, he could not continue meeting Lady Allistair in the safe and open environment of the state capitol now that it was clear that ABDI was becoming relevant to his functions as state senator. Worse, any open meeting in one of the conference rooms of the Atlanta major hotels would start unnecessary gossips from so many intrusive eyes of the African American elite community. These gossips would find their way back to his wife, Vanessa, at the moment when he was slowly inching his way back to her bedroom quarters. The last two prayer sessions have ended with the relative suspension of Vanessa's rules when the holding of hands led to deep-eye soul-searching then to the tender kisses and to a progressive submission by Vanessa. The next morning, Jeremy was awakened by another one of Vanessa's crying sessions; she was upset and disappointed that she had broken her own rules by submitting to her own bent-up carnal desires and asked her husband to leave her bedroom very quietly so not to alert their daughter, and she started another prayer session to last the whole Saturday morning. She usually spent the rest of the weekend as silent as in penitence for those unforgiving sins. As far as Jeremy was concerned, it was all a matter of time, and twice in a row there was a pattern that could lead to a permanent suspension of the rules. He was not about to jeopardize his chances. He reluctantly accepted to go to Washington, DC, and agreed to meet at the Watergate Plaza Hotel while insisting on no overnight stay. He pretended having so much work related to the current state senate heavy calendar. When they met in the reserved conference room from ten in the morning, his Honorable's fear of being alone with Lady Allistair became all the more justified. She was seated alone in the conference room with a stack of papers in front of her. When his honorable came in, she stood up to greet him warmly and started to remove her raincoat. Lady Allistair was wearing under her raincoat a relatively see-through long black dress that left no parts of her sexy body hidden from head to toes.

Not only she was not wearing bras, it was also obvious that she was wearing a Chinese red G-thong slip that gave away a sensuous profile to her voluminous derriere. She was looking straight in his Honorable's eyes as to find out what he thought of her appearance.

His honorable let out the expected observation, "Ms. Allistair, I don't know how folks at your New York City office manage with such fine looking lady like yourself. You must be breaking a lot of vows there. Thank God for some of us, we got to hold tight to what we got. I am not saying that it is easy, but we are trying. Thank God we are not in New York City. I pity those folks in New York City."

That was the break they needed to start the meeting as both were laughing now, and Lady Allistair added, "That is why they call me Lady Allistair. I am glad you like the dress. I thought that I have overdone it, but I am relieved you are OK with it. I picked it up in the rush so early this morning to catch the early commuter flight, to tell you the truth, I was shocked when I realized that the dress was a see-through, and I had forgotten to put the bras. I kept my raincoat throughout the flight until now. Well, I hope I am not embarrassing you."

"I am charmed but not embarrassed, if you want to know. But times have changed, indeed. Way back, I would have followed the sign and probably indulged you in what you have in mind. But now, fate and time have brought me wisdom and discernment, only my eyes have been left to wander, but the mind is holding the flesh in its place at all the time."

He broke out in a deep laugh. Lady Allistair was relieved and understood that she did not have to press the charm button any longer with his honorable, and it was about time to move on with the business at hand. She pulled a big folder with a black leather cover and handed it to his honorable. On top of the folder was the meeting agenda that they were to follow. They started with the short version of the legal briefing describing the purpose of ABDI, its objectives and goals, its legal status, its preliminary location and address, its initial board members. His honorable was surprised to find out that ABDI was to be located in the finest new building in Atlanta at the recently rebuilt Peachtree Circle Plaza. ABDI will occupy three floors in the building. ABDI will also have another building in the campus of the University of Georgia in Athens next to his buddy's Institute of African Studies. He will be delighted. The list of initial board members included people he had been already in touch. He expected to meet all of them by the fifteenth of November.

He was fully satisfied with what he read relative to objectives, goals, and strategies. They were completely in line with what he had in mind all along. He can now visualize how much political sway ABDI will have, what impact this initiative will have in Atlanta. His honorable already saw himself receiving visiting African heads of states in the Peachtree Circle Plaza and waving at the glares of TV cameras. ABDI will force those visiting African heads of states to add Atlanta to their regular itinerary stops of New York City-UN and Washington, DC-White House. And guess who will be acting as their host while they are in Atlanta, not the Georgia state governor, not the Atlanta mayor, not the business big shots, or other dignitaries but your humble and lowly Honorable Georgia State Senator Jeremy Owens Massay, from Sapelo Island, son of the Gullah people. This is one in a lifetime political opportunity he cannot screw up, not for the sake of this almost-naked lady parading shamelessly her beautiful full breasts every time she raised her hand for emphasis or when she was bringing in full-naked view her bulging inner thigh when she got up incessantly to take a cup of tea or a glass of water.

Her raised profile left no doubt what she did not realize was showing a dangling thread of her G-thong slip. His honorable was now fixated on the slip frontal left thread which seemed either broken or loosened and revealing Lady Allistair's wholesome shaved inner thigh. No, sir, thought his honorable, not this time, Vanessa's rules should not be broken. His honorable was brought back to the meeting when Lady Allistair started talking about ABDI funding. She mentioned an initial funding of 150 million dollars. She explained that this funding was the balance of that initial funding after accounting and paying for the annual lease and maintenance of ABDI facilities in Atlanta and Athens, Georgia, the office equipment, the staff salaries in both locations, the board members' retainer annual fees. The fees were extremely generous in a seven-figure range. The chair, that is his honorable, was going to be compensated in the half million range along with various performance bonuses. His honorable was now beyond ecstatic. However, he also noticed that his lower member started stiffening and rising uncontrollably and for absolutely no reason. At the same time, Lady Allistair moved her chair around the corner closer to him to review the financials making up the total funding.

Lady Allistair said something to the effect, "Not bad for the chair's retainer fee, a whole half million, not bad." When she moved closer to his honorable, he chose that instant to call for a break in order to get a drink of orange jus.

Unfortunately, when he got up, his growing raised member was in plain sight of Lady Allistair and almost broached her face. His honorable was now embarrassed and went to the large window to take a bird's-eye view of the capital. Lady Allistair, who had been burning up below with the endless rubbing of the loosened broken G-thong slip's back thread against her crotch, asked to also be excused to the bathroom.

When she was alone in the private conference-room bathroom, she realized what had happened with her now loosened G-thong slip. She removed it, and while she was searching her handbag for her emergency reserve slip, she noticed she was getting wetter every passing second while reprising the effect her revealing dress and the now loosened slip were having on the poor honorable next door. His member had stiffened beyond control and had certainly embarrassed him to a point of asking for this break. In spite of herself and while seated on the stool, she was now reminiscing the huge lower member of the now forgotten high commissioner from the Republic of Zambezi during those crazy times in London, and worse, she also visualized now his Honorable's raised member growing bigger inside her. She was surprised that she could still invite herself mentally to indulge in men after all these years. But she could not help, so unbuttoned the lower part of the see-through dress, reclined herself wide, and started touching herself to relieve the orgasm that has been building all throughout this morning meeting and since she intentionally put the Chinese red G-thong that early morning. All of a sudden, she squirted uncontrollably and let out a loud moaning scream.

His honorable, thinking that Lady Allistair needed help, came rushing in the bathroom only to find her partially undressed, naked from her navel down, and crouched on a small sofa close to stool with her hand wrapped around her crotch trying to stop an already voluminous discharge. Lady Allistair was shaking as in trance. Before she noticed that his honorable was in the room, she let out another moaning scream and another quick discharge below. Then she reached for the small towel in the room, wiped her hands and crotch, straightened herself on the small sofa, faced his honorable who was helplessly very confused now, looking at the wholesome sexy display while she said in hushed tone, "I am all right, I am right. You got to excuse me, I never had it so bad as today, it started since this morning and when I saw your stiffness, I could not hold any longer, and I had to let it go. Don't you want to help this poor girl? I am begging you."

She reclined further down in the small sofa with her legs now wide open, her whole lower part glistening, she looked up and motioned his honorable to finish her pain. It did not take his honorable long to lower his pants and body and charge Lady Allistair who was again shaking now at her third orgasmic irruption. They lay next to each other on the small sofa for about six minutes, saying nothing. Then Lady Allistair got up and cleaned herself. His honorable sat contrite; he was now terribly sorry that he broke Vanessa's rules after all the mental gyrations he went through not to succumb to this lady's temptation. He also cleaned himself and joined Lady Allistair back in the conference room.

Lady Allistair was the first to say, "This was bound to happen between you and me since our first meeting. There was just too much sexual electricity between us to prevent this. And as far as I am concerned, it has been years since I have had intercourse with a man. I do not know why you have this effect on me. But before you get carried away, I have to tell you that I have a very strong preference for women, if you can understand. I also would appreciate if we can leave what happened here as a wonderful incident and leave it at that for pleasant memories. Hopefully, it won't happen again for our own sake."

"I couldn't agree more. I really mean it when I say that the mind is holding the flesh in its place all the time. I failed this time, but I expect not to in the future for my own sake. For your information, I am repairing some grave errors of judgment in my marriage at this time, and what has happened here will not help it a bit. I completely agree with you not to let this happen again. Maybe we needed to get over what you called sexual electricity between us. We have done it, and let us move on."

They renewed the meeting, where they left it off, with the financials of the ABDI initial funding. Lady Allistair did most of the talking now while his honorable did most of the attentive listening. After expanding on the voluminous funding financials, Lady Allistair started covering the probable schedule of ABDI projects for the next year. Twenty projects in twelve African countries were tabled. They ranged from intensive agricultural projects to building extensive fish farms and investing in light minerals extraction, such as bauxite and tin, and extensive water irrigations on a wide regional basis. Each project was carefully documented with financials, cost and benefit, risk factors, environmental impacts, political impacts, population impacts, country impacts, etc.

They reviewed the first five projects and the process that the board members needed to adopt to do project review. That was a delicate point that needed to be thoroughly examined with considerable feedback from both donor and recipient inputs. Lady Allistair ended the meeting with the review of the first board meeting agenda. She informed the honorable that this initial board meeting would be his show. In addition, from then on, all matters concerning ABDI's board members will be his own concern and of course, the entire sitting board. He is the chairman, and he will guide ABDI as he sees fit. Lady Allistair emphasized that she is not a board member and will never attend ABDI board meetings. She might show up at other functions such as large conferences, head of states' visits, and, in-country project celebrations. She will be available a telephone away for counseling and projects funding. She urged him to fill ABDI staff member positions as quickly as possible before that first board meeting. She told him not to hesitate to avail himself of the support of the board members as soon as possible, including in hiring staff members. Such requests will only increase the goodwill that the board members will show in the future to readily assist him in many other issues. Lady Allistair was the first to leave the conference room while his honorable was gathering all the materials she brought into a large suitcase. Lady Allistair thanked his honorable for his cooperation and wished him a lot of luck as the ABDI chairperson.

Before leaving, she pulled him and gave him a wet kiss while whispering, "Thank you for the memory and the wonderful relief. I would never forget." Lady Allistair was gone. It was still two thirty in the afternoon and his Honorable's flight back to Atlanta was scheduled to leave very late in the evening at around eight o'clock. He had nothing else to do but review the pile of ABDI materials in front of him. He ordered a light lunch. He thought about what happened between him and Lady Allistair. He was a bit late to realize that there was really a lot of what the lady called sexual electricity between them during the two previous times they met. But it looks like he either missed it or denied it. He was so confident not to fall under her spell, and he even thought of steering the lady to his friend, Dr. James F. Stringer. He tried to reconstruct what led to the unfortunate tryst. He remembered that his lower member started getting very hard after the mention of the chair fee of half million dollar. Why was he to become sexually aroused by the mention of half million dollar? That would be very bizarre of him. Or was he being built up all along first by the sight of her wholesome body under that see-through dress? The full breasts hanging out and yes, her naked shaved inner thigh in full frontal view when that stupid slip thread broke.

Did the lady set the whole stage? Why was she mentioning that she was a lesbian and would rather not do this again? What would any man do in front of a naked vixen like Lady Allistair, already in deep orgasmic trance and inviting you to partake, to indulge her? What would a man do? He was so relieved that what had happened took place in this anonymous conference room in DC, far from the prying eyes of Atlanta gossips mongers. If this had happened in Atlanta, one of the many hangers on and spies in the African American elite would have paid their ways to tape the noises or to videotape the whole commotion that had happened. He would have returned home to find his stuffs on the street, this time around to pay for the last assault on Vanessa's rules. Thank God for DC, where he can walk around unnoticed, where he is not well known, as yet. After finishing the review of the first board meeting agenda, his honorable called his buddy Dr. Stringer in Athens, Georgia. He impressed on him the need to attend the first board meeting of ABDI as the vice chair of the board. He broke the news of his current meeting in DC and gave him a summary of the meeting he attended. He highlighted the funding that was going to be made available and board members' retainer fees. His friend's fee as vice chair amounted close to three hundred thousand, or four times his current salary, in addition to various incentives and benefits unheard-of when compared to countless boards he had been associated with as director of African Studies Institute of the University of Georgia. That perked Dr. Stringer's interest beyond the usual. Remarking the seriousness of the endeavor the two friends were embarking on, Dr. Stringer asked his friend what else he should do.

His Honorable's response was direct, "Get married as quickly as possible. You cannot afford any longer to pursuit your player life. The risk is just too great. To tell you the truth, I will be the one and the first to cut you off from this unexpected wagon train at the occurrence of the first impropriety. And I mean it. My very dear brother Jimmy, we hit what we can call the jackpot. And we cannot blow it, if I can help it. Remember, I did not hesitate to call on you to be my backup when I was asked to give a close reference. You and I come a long long way. We should always remember that and count on each other. So let us do the right thing. It is up to us. Don't forget, get married soon! I know you usually entertain five or more at the same time. I know you. It is about time to seriously examine which one would make the best wife for you. I can help choose. No, I won't. Too risky. But seriously think about it and decide soon. I am saying this because before long, you know, ABDI would be holding major conferences, parties, and galas in Atlanta, and it would look very bad and in poor taste if you parade a different lady at every other major gathering.

Gossips will fly, the staff will talk, and you just don't want to be in such dire straits. Not when all other board members display the usual boring married-type profile like mine and, in some cases, with children. I know this because I am reviewing these profiles as we speak. And especially for you when you are pulling three hundred grand. It is obvious that it is not worthwhile. Buddy, I am giving you this quick feedback because I want you and I to succeed in this endeavor and to be the best African American board members for ABDI."

The fact of getting so indignant about his player friend and saying all this right after breaking Vanessa's rules through his own sexual escapade with Lady Allistair no less than four hours ago surprised and shocked his honorable. But the stakes were too big and too high for both of them this time around. He just could not help and in spite of his own transgression he felt he needed to say this anyway.

Dr. Stringer told his friend, "You are completely correct. I personally did not realize that ABDI was so huge. I initially agreed to your reference out of friendship's sake. I know in your political body, the Senate, you come across various projects to help this or encourage that overseas. But the funding of these projects is usually a drop in the bucket, to tell you the truth. When you called and started talking about ABDI, I was not surprised about your proposition. Remember the conference that took place here where you made your eloquent presentation? It was indeed well received. But you got to realize in my lines of work, I attend many of these conferences where lofty presentations about enhancing the development in Africa are always made. The lofty presentations usually died down right after the end of those conferences. But the funny thing is that I have met the same people making the same lofty presentations time and again. Well, I have become a bit discouraged and chose to go with the motion after a while. Maybe that has led me to other pursuits you are warning me about now and which cannot be justified under any circumstance. Forgive me if I am stretching the facts here. Again, back to lofty presentations, when you called me and started talking about ABDI, my inclination was to lower the expectations of your intention. I thought that your well-received presentation probably went over your head, and you managed to garner from the Georgia State Senate body few hundred thousand bucks to fund relatively low-budget projects around said water irrigation needs of some sub-Saharan countries. I was inclined to support you in the feasibility studies and all kinds of development-support processes anyway. But to hear you today and listening to all the funding commitments that are being made on behalf of ABDI surprise me of course.

It is an all totally different ball game altogether. My dear Jeremy, you may not believe it, but I should say it anyway, it is not the vice chair retainer fee that will motivate me to support you. I would support you, first because of your confidence in me; second, because of the necessary achievement of the lofty goals ABDI assigned itself for Africa. I was honored that you have chosen me as your vice chair. And you are right; the stakes are too high to allow any letdown. As far as my other pursuits go, I want to let you know that I am getting a bit tired of the running around. At the end, it is always the same. It is definitely about high time for me to settle down. My poor mother has been saying the same for the past ten years. Lately, she has told my sisters that she would not take my calls and would not allow any more visitations in her farmhouse outside Baton Rouge, Louisiana, until I get engaged. That has been the last straw. Can you imagine, the farm is the only place I run to take refuge when I have to break from these girls? I can never be reached when I am there under Ma's protection. Now she is cutting me off from her protection. Don't you worry! I have already settled down on a lady for my life. You probably don't remember her. I confused you with some other introductions as well. Seriously, she visited with me during the last conference you attended. She is completing her postgraduate degree in tropical diseases medicine at Emory University in Atlanta. Her name is Suzette Beaulieu from Lake Charles in Louisiana, like myself. I am confident that Ma would approve. Believe me, you have just tipped me over the other side of matrimonial line. Give me time to tie this around. I would not disappoint you, Jeremy.

I wish to see as soon as possible in Atlanta to assist you in setting up ABDI office in Atlanta and Athens. Forget it. I want to come over to Atlanta this weekend to review with all these documents. I cannot wait to contribute on this one in the lifetime endeavor. We will get it right, I am confident."

His honorable was pleased to hear what his friend said and agreed to the important meeting over the weekend. His honorable was not completely sold on this Beaulieu lady becoming the next Mrs. Stringer. He remembered seeing her in Athens last time around. She was also a knock out, as only his friend Jimmy knows how to pick them. He met her over a lunch that he was sharing with his friend the first day of the conference. She came over and stayed the length of lunch and excused herself to go back to Atlanta to attend a seminar that evening. He also noticed that his friend was in his best behavior around this lady. It was not clear if she was the chosen one because that very evening Dr. Stringer invited another flaming lady to join them for a dinner at an exclusive restaurant of Athens.

When they dropped his honorable at his hotel, you can tell that the two lovers were not going their separate ways for the rest of the evening but were up to a long night of cavorting. On that account alone, his honorable dismissed further involvement of this Beaulieu involvement with his friend who never brought her up the next two days of the conferences. Instead, he managed to introduce his honorable to two more different ladies before the end of the conference. Taken aback by his friend's player style, his honorable remembered telling him before returning to Atlanta to Vanessa's rules to settle down and all that running around does not amount to anything at the end but trouble. He never explained to his friend why he did not mention what the hell he was going through lately in his own marriage. He was certainly happy that he reached out to a friend at this time. If he is to change his way, it will make their involvement in ABDI so much better and easier. It was about time to go back home. His honorable gathered the extensive documentation that Lady Allistair had brought and put them in the large suitcase she left behind and called for a cab to the airport. When he came down to the lobby of the Watergate Plaza Hotel, he was met by a debonair gentleman by the name of Mr. Fadden, who introduced himself as a representative of AMX in Washington, DC. Mr. Fadden apologized for not being able to meet him that morning to give him a lift from the airport to the hotel. He said that Lady Allistair seriously reprimanded him for not providing the timely transportation service that morning. This apparently had caused their meeting to start a bit late. He insisted that this would never happen again. He gave his honorable his business card and told him that from then on, anytime he wants to schedule a trip, any trip to DC to let him know. He directed his honorable to a waiting limousine at the same time the cab was pulling in. He handed to him a medium-size envelope containing a thank-you note from Lady Allistair for the successful meeting, so he said. He also assured him that he was going to take care of the cab driver. When the limousine driver finished loading the luggage in the limousine trunk, his honorable saw Mr. Fadden giving a couple of bank notes to the cab driver for showing up unnecessarily and rushing back to the limousine to wish him safe return home. His honorable was so surprised by all that had taken place; he simply waved at him.

When the limousine pulled from the drive, he reviewed the business card again and noticed Mr. Fadden's full title of AMX Government Affairs Executive Director, or a paid lobbyist. Further he opened the envelope and found two checks made to Jeremy Owen Massay each for twenty thousand dollars, paying for a successful conclusion of the meeting, a red tread and a large thank-you card where Lady Allistair scribbled what she had whispered before leaving, "Thank you for the memory and the wonderful relief.

I would never forget." His honorable placed the two checks in his huge calendar notebook and back in his attached case and started tearing the card in pieces. He thought that Lady Allistair was not keeping her end of bargain to let bygones be bygone. He definitely will not be back to Atlanta with the red tread and the card near him. That red tread smelled the musk that Lady Allistair gave away in that bathroom. His honorable shook his head. Too many evidence pieces to carry around. What was Lady Allistair thinking? He would throw the reaped card and the red tread at the first trashcan he would find at the airport. He was still a bit perturbed by what this Mr. Fadden he never met before said. He was on time for the ten o'clock meeting. Then why Lady Allistair had to reprimand Mr. Fadden for not providing a limousine to fetch him from the airport to the hotel? He did not mind taking a cab to the hotel. He certainly did not notice his name on the held-up signs that limousine drivers present at the airport. Maybe Lady Allistair had a beef to pick with this Mr. Fadden. Well, he would not find out, would he? What about the forty-thousand-dollar checks she left for the honorable? Why not give them at the conference room? These kinds of check donation through different hands have a way to leave indices and traces to cause a lot of trouble to politicians like him.

Cash donations would have been preferable. He made a mental note to share with the lady next time around they would talk. The card and the tread were all another story apart. He would ignore it and never bring it up. When the limousine pulled along the departure gate, his honorable gathered the reaped card inside the envelope along with the tread, got out, and dumped the dangerous pieces of evidence in the first garbage dumpster he could find. He then returned back to collect his attached case and the remaining luggage to board his return flight.

CHAPTER 10
O'Shea to Mezi

At the time when his honorable reached home in Atlanta, Lady Allistair, already back in New York City and still in her office, received another call from Dr. O'Shea.

"From my estimation," the professor started saying with obvious urgency, "it would be preferable that the construction of the new Faculty of Applied Sciences and the dormitory starts before the rainy season reaches its full swing in Mezi. That is the reason I am calling you now, that is the reason I need to get to Mezi as soon as possible. Contacts with the university board members have been made regarding the initiatives and preliminary feedbacks are all positive. Board members are suggesting the earliest meeting if possible. In their view, if all is agreed at the board meeting, the construction should start right away, including the considerable excavation in the location, the laying of foundation, sewer system, and electrical main architecture. In that case, the full swing of rainy season would not deter the next steps of the construction from ground up. By the time the longer dry season would come, the construction will be so far advanced as to guarantee completion of both buildings around the end of May and the start of installation of equipment to render these buildings adequate for the teaching and boarding functions we have proposed in the initiatives for the start of the next academic year by the end of September. I concurred with the board's assessment, and I am ready to go as soon as you allow it."

"I expected this request any time after our last conversation. From BI perspectives, all is practically ready. I need simply to coordinate your departure with one of our lawyers and another academic, both from England, who will travel with you to Mezi when all is set and coordinated. The lawyer would be there to answer any legal-issue question that may arise. The academic is an old hand
of the Polytechnic University. A British fellow, he retired after teaching for more than twenty-five years at that university. He was there at the beginning when the university was being built. He has a considerable wealth of knowledge about that university. I believe he was the first provost of the university. He was much impressed by the presentation you have prepared with Dr. Wasiri.

He said that your presentation must win the case. His name is Dr. John McMillan. The lawyer's name is Barry Newcomb. So, as you can see, things are moving very rapidly from our hand too. What I would eagerly suggest to you is to pack your bags and get to London as soon as possible in order to acquaint yourself with your fellow travelers. My strong wish would have been to have Dr. Wasiri travel with you, but this would be a bit too early, and I understand that. Dr. O'Shea, hopefully you have already taken your shots and your visa to Mezi."

Everything that Lady Allistair said pleased Dr. O'Shea so much. "My good lady, I see that you have not left anything hanging. I admired your management style. Everything always in place, from head to toe. Lady Allistair, allow me to say that you are a shining pearl inside out. For your information, I already had my shots, and Dr. Wasiri had done wonder to secure for me a multiple entry visa for three years. He already seems to have strong connections at the embassy and back home. He introduced me to more than half of the board members of the university. We had lengthy conference calls with some of them. The initiatives have created a big splash there, and I have no doubt it would be a go. The meeting is becoming, at this time, a mere formality according to Dr. Wasiri. By the way, I want to thank you for the last checks you sent for the documentation preparation including the 110,000 dollars for Dr. Wasiri. I am struggling to find ways to give it to him. I understand my compensation; I am your employee now. What about Dr. Wasiri? I am sure I would find a way to deliver the check when I will meet him in two days before I leave for London. By the way, talking of checks, I need to see these folks in the investment bank in London where you deposited the five-million-dollar prize money. We have not talked about it since. What is the name of the company, and where is located? I now have a definite view of how I need to dispose of that prize. I would share this with the bank while I am in London."

"The investment bank name slipped my mind every time we talked lately. I am very sorry for that. The name is Childs and Coventry LLC. I will send you an e-mail right now with the complete address, phones, and contact's name. The company is super-discreet in any financial matter disposition worldwide. I use them all the time. You will not be disappointed. Go on now and get ready for your trip, Dr. O'Shea."

"Now as instructed, I am going to finish packing and should be in London in about three days. Of course, I will keep you fully informed of my travel plan."

Dr. O'Shea then called his protégé to announce that he was on his way to London and Mezi in about three days. He also insisted in coming to pay his family a visit in Frankfort before leaving for the much-anticipated trip. Dr. Wasiri accepted. The professor busied himself to buy whatever he thought he needed for a trip to Africa. He certainly bought much more than he needed, but you never know what you may confront. Besides, this was the first time he ventured in that part of the world. He was reluctant to ask his protégé for tips and alike. Maybe by the time he will visit with the Wasiri family, his adopted daughter, Hasbo, who had been to Mezi more than twice, will have concrete suggestions.

Following the advice of Dr. Wasiri, the professor sent a message to his kids that he was going to London for a much-postponed vacation trip. He said that he would be there for three or four weeks. Again, all messages needed to go through Dr. Wasiri who would be in touch with him most of the times. No mention of Mezi was made in his message. No mention of his new job for BI was made. The children were delighted that their father was really enjoying his retirement the way they expected. All the children and grandchildren responded with good wishes in his trip to London.

Dr. O'Shea was not happy with his concealing the main purpose of his trip, especially to his grandchildren. But he resolved that Emily's instructions were clear. None of children and grandchildren need to be involved, and he will abide by the instructions. A day later, he came to spend an overnight with the Wasiri family. The visit was turned into a send-off of an old family member to a magnificent journey. Dr. Wasiri was beyond himself inquiring about one thousand things the professor might have forgotten. He also volunteered so many contacts back home willing and able to make his trip as successful as it can be.

The children suggested many places to visit where they spent wonderful moments during their stay in Mezi. Hasbo took most of his time, explaining little details of preparation she made for a first trip and dispelling all crazy notions that her adopted father may have about a stay in Mezi. They talked till around three or four in the morning. The old professor was extremely delighted by the reception he received in his protégé's home. He was definitely the adopted father and grandfather in Wasiri's household. He could not have any better send-off than what he was getting now. The next day morning, the children insisted on waking him up to wish a wonderful trip.

The parents and the professor obliged the kids before going back to sleep. It was around eleven in the morning that Mr. Wasiri offered to give him a ride to Louisville International Airport for a more convenient flight than from Lexington.

He bade farewell to Hasbo, and they were on their way to Louisville. Dr. Wasiri was never so agitated and could not stop talking about the dos and don'ts in his country. His mentor mentioned the names of people who were going to travel with him. Dr. Wasiri remembered Dr. John McMillan's name from way back. He heard about the man when he actually became the chancellor of the Polytechnic University about five years after he left Mezi to come to the United States. He never met the man. He saw his name in many references that he received from his friend William Ewas of the UN Diplomatic Mission. Dr. Wasiri said his mentor was very lucky to be surrounded in this trip by someone like Dr. John McMillan who had been in Mezi for a long time in various academic functions in that university. As they approached Louisville, the old professor pulled a closed envelope containing the check payable to Dr. Wasiri and gave it his protégé. He said, "Before I forget, I got a check here for your extensive contribution in developing the documentation that we are going to present in front of the university board.

BI was very grateful for your work and insisted on paying for your very effective collaboration and contribution. Please accept the payment for my wonderful adoptive family. And I do not want to hear any excuse or argument from you this beautiful sunny and merry day of my departure to Mezi and especially after the graceful send-off from my beloved family."

Dr. Wasiri smiled, took the envelope, and put it in his inside jacket pocket. He was also in no mood to spoil such an extraordinary event, his mentor going for the first time to his homeland. He had wished to fund this trip from the time he met the O'Shea couple. He had said to Hasbo many times how much it would have meant to him to be the host to Mrs. and Mr. O'Shea somewhere in Mezi. He had not been able to fund such a trip after all these years for one reason or another. Then Emily passed away. And at this very moment, he would not stand on the way of seeing his mentor take that trip, no matter the purpose of it. For Dr. Wasiri, the essential thing was that Dr. O'Shea was going to Mezi and would come back and talk about his homeland. That was joyful enough for him. Whatever is inside the envelope can wait. The main thing was to get his adopted father to the airport to start the long trip. They were already at the departure gate of the airport.

Dr. O'Shea was quickly registered for his Chicago flight, the first leg of his long trip to London, then Mezi. He warmly embraced his protégé as father to son and advised to stay closely in touch with him throughout. He disappeared in the airport labyrinth. Dr. Wasiri pulled his car and took the direction to Frankfort.

Along the way, he pulled the envelope that his mentor had given him and opened and was shocked to find the110,000 check made to him for his contribution to the development of the documentation. The only thing he can think of was that he needed again to explain to Hasbo the meaning of this large payment from BI.

Then his worry subsided and alone in the car, he burst into a loud laughter. "Jolly, jolly, Dr. O'Shea, what am I going to do with you, Dr. O'Shea! You must be taking me to places I don't probably want to go. I pray that this journey you may be tracing for me would be safe for both us and for the sake of our families. Yet I still trust you."

When he reached home, he told his wife about the check. Hasbo maintained the same posture as before when he mentioned the shared prize money. She said that the new check was all for their smooth transfer to Mezi and that is all she cared about. As far as she was concerned, the return to Mezi was a done deal. All the money they have received lately, thanks to the good old professor O'Shea, reinforced her determination to finally leave Frankfort, leave Kentucky and the United States and build an entirely new life with her family far.

She will go far away from people who have looked down on her all her young life when she lost her mother and her father, starting with the so-called different adoptive families from back then, the various made-believe sisters, brothers, aunts, and uncles who have abused her sometime physically, in some unforgettable moments sexually, and all the time mentally. And when she married Dr. Wasiri, they would not give her the satisfaction of honoring her family, not a single day. She became even more ostracized on the account of marrying that black man from the jungles of Africa. She was convinced that she was wholly accepted in only two sets of places, first and foremost, in the O'Shea family and, second, in the various families of her husband's friends. In both cases, the reception was always without reservation. What has Emily O'Shea not shared with her to keep her steady in the right course? She counseled her day and night.

She advised her not to waste her energy on fighting people fixed on the past prejudices. She admonished her and insisted on looking only toward the future of her family, the only base she needs to defend at all cost and to forget in the dumpster of the past all that would keep her back. Hasbo was mortified when Emily passed away. She felt abandoned for a long time and became depressed.

Noticing how much the passing of their cherished and beloved Emily was wreaking havoc over his wife, he decided a change of venue. He consulted with his mentor for a long time.

Knowing better Hasbo's circumstances from bits that Emily shared, Dr. O'Shea suggested a trip to Mezi. Hasbo's mood did not change until when the family went to Mezi, where she felt extraordinarily renewed and vibrant. She was alive and happy. She busied herself over one thousand ways and places and did not want to come back to the States. She relented when her husband insisted and pretended that he needed to put in more time to gain a tenured professorship. The same thing happened the second time the family went back to Mezi. Hasbo did not insist. She enjoyed the vacation with her children just the same. She bid her time while secretly being encouraged by the old professor not to be discouraged, that he was working on a major plan to enjoin her husband to a return to Mezi, and that her time would come.

Now all of a sudden, things started happening from the time her husband came back from New York City. She noticed that he started showing an entirely new dynamism. Her husband was finally and sincerely committed to go back. And now without any confirmation from the old man, she decided that the time had come, the cap was directed definitely to Mezi by next year May or June. Anything that would happen in between was only happenstance. So far, there was mention of more than two million and six hundred thousand dollars to smooth their way back to Mezi. She knew that was four or five times more amount than they needed to live decently in Mezi for about ten years. Whereas she would be concerned about their first or second year of adjusting to life without adequate funding, she was relieved that Dr. O'Shea had done all he could to come up with the initial funding and to open their way back to Mezi, back home. Hasbo was also reassured without a current knowledge of details that even this trip that Dr. O'Shea was taking to Mezi had only one purpose: to prepare his protégé and family for a complete and safe return to Mezi. In fact, she did not need the details from the two scientists. She thought that all that talk about building the new Faculty of Applied Sciences was all smoke screen.

She was told back then by Emily a week before her passing that the return to Mezi would happen on its time, and Dr. O'Shea would see to it as long as Hasbo keeps her end of bargain in maintaining a good household for the Wasiri family. She had not only kept her faith all these years but also her bargain.

She was now about to reap the benefits of her lifetime engagement in the sacred battle Emily had told her about. In time, she did not quite understand what the battle was all about. She was some time lost in the intrigues of researches over the exotic minerals when Emily tried to explain that her husband and Dr. O'Shea were joined in a lifetime battle over the exotic minerals studies at the university. When all that went over her head, she always asked the same question to Emily what was her role in the battle, how can she help her husband? The response was simple from Emily, "Stand by your husband as I am standing by Dr. O'Shea." She thought that this was easy and sparred nothing to accomplish this and maintain a stable household for the Wasiri family. Now that her dream was being realized, she attributed the benefits of winning parts of Emily's battle to simply maintaining a good household. In her mind, it was just as much the whole battle was won. Hasbo took the check from her husband and went to deposit into their account at the nearby bank. Dr. Wasiri was a bit disappointed. He was expecting a drone-out discussion about where all that easy money was coming from and for what purposes. He surmised that maybe the good old professor had already explained everything to his wife, and this was the reason she did not show any interest or curiosity in finding out what was going on.

When she came back from the bank, she noticed the sullen face her husband was giving, and he asked her whether she had talked about the check with Dr. O'Shea. She answered, "I did not talk with Dr. O'Shea about this check nor the shared prize money. You have shared all that with me as you should and as my husband. And as far as I am concerned, my dear Kano, I said to myself, it was about time, it was about time, indeed, after all that you have invested in that field. I will not make any excuse or feel guilty at this time and place to use every penny of that money coming your way. My dear Kano, you earn it fair and square and let me repeat it again for you, it was about time. That is what I feel. And you know where my mind is, and where my heart is. In Mezi, with you and the kids. Anything that will make our return to Mezi smooth and easy, I am all for it. And that money is just accomplishing what you know I wanted all the time we have been married, to go back to Mezi.

I would have argued with you if you had stolen it. But, my dear Kano, you earned it, and why should I feel sad about it? You have no idea how happy I am to get the hell out of this place, city, state, and country. I would never look back. Mark my word. I would never look back to those people who have abused me day and night back then, all that because I was motherless and fatherless. Kano, you have no idea."

Hasbo started crying and Kano rushed to hold her and wiped her tears. "Darling," he said, "I thought that we have gone beyond all that past recrimination. I thought that we have left all that past, as you loved to say, in the dumpster of things past. Why are you still going there, Hasbo? Look at where we are today, beautiful kids, stable home, and still bright future ahead. And you are still worried about these people. We have agreed and decided all along in our marriage not to pay mind to negative people who do not bring anything of value to our welfare. We have lived decently without these people, thank God. Then, Hasbo, why now, why now? I am sorry that I troubled you with my silly questions. It was all playful. There was nothing there to upset you or bring about all these sorry stories. My dear, I have always told you as long as you stand by our family and me, we will be all right. You have done so time and again. All that stands here in this household is proof enough to see. What else do you need? Please leave all that sorry past in the past. Come with me to the bathroom, and I will make up your stunning beautiful face before the kids come back from school. Come closer and closer to me. Give me the love I need and crave." Dr. Wasiri kissed his wife so tenderly and initiated another tender pass by kissing her long neck while caressing her breast. Hasbo had already stopped crying and felt the urge to respond to her husband when from the home side entrance, they heard the commotion of their kids coming from school and entering the house noisily. Hasbo straightened herself and whispered to her husband, "Later." Before her husband regained his composure, Mrs. Wasiri was already downstairs, directing her children to their different tasks while starting the evening dinner.

She was relieved to witness in front of her what her husband was talking about a stable and happy household just like the beloved Emily had predicted. Hasbo shed a warm and tender tear in Emily's memory. When her younger daughter Fazi asked her why she was crying, Hasbo responded loud and clearly that she was crying of joy seeing her children growing so fast. This did not quite make sense to the younger one who expected a sad story. She then said to her mother, "Mom, you are funny."

The next day when Dr. O'Shea landed in London, his two future traveling companions met him: Dr. John McMillan and the lawyer Barry Newcomb. They took a ride back to the city using the barrister's very big and roomy Bentley. The lawyer was driving. In order to prepare for their trip, they agreed to drop off Dr. O'Shea at the Drake five-star hotel, let him rest from the transatlantic flight for the balance of the day, pick him up at nine in the morning the next day, and hold an all-day meeting in a private conference room in an exclusive inn outside London. Depending on the progress they would make, decide if they needed an extra day of meeting before finalizing their presentation and flight to Mezi afterward. All along their exchange, Dr. McMillan kept asking who was this fellow, Dr. Wasiri, who contributed to the early documentation. He said that the name sounded so familiar but could not place it at that moment. He was certain that he was not a member of faculties when he was in Mezi. But somehow that name keeps coming back to him for some reasons. At the end, he said, he would find out anyway from his countless sources from Mezi and would be able to reveal what he knows about this Dr. Wasiri the next day they will meet. He begged his colleague Dr. O'Shea not to tip him off until then. The old professor obliged. Dr. McMillan although closing in to the age of seventy, did not look his age at all. He was tall, very svelte, extremely tanned from the longtime exposure and easy life of expatriate in Africa. He could be mistaken for a retired four-star general. He had a steady and confident walk about him only given to people who either commanded large troops in the armed forces or, as in his case, led great learning institutions managing and leading people of considerable intellectual and academic background. Dr. O'Shea had met his kind all along his academic career and the interaction had always left a lot to be desired. He recognized Dr. McMillan from far and prayed that his involvement would not jeopardize his delicate mission. Just as much as McMillan was tall and svelte, Mr. Barry Newcomb was short and extremely jovial, joking nonstop British style from the airport to the hotel. Dr. O'Shea readily enjoyed his companionship and felt that he will be a constant referee between the two scientists if needed. When he arrived in his room, Dr. O'Shea decided to spend the rest of the day rereading the documentation he had prepared with Dr. Wasiri. He did not want to give his new traveling mates any opportunity to shoot down the merits of his own initiatives. He even took new notes over many aspects of the initiatives. At around ten thirty that evening, he completed his own review and was comforted by the depth of the documentation. After another light dinner, he went to sleep. He was ready and waiting for his London hosts at the lobby when they came to pick him up.

Again the lawyer was driving his Bentley, with Dr. McMillan next to him up front. As soon as the big car was in the highway in direction to the inn, Dr. McMillan made the most startling revelation about Dr. Wasiri, his protégé. "Dr. O'Shea, do you know that your friend or colleague there, this Dr. Wasiri, was a certified wonder child or boy in Mezi when I was there climbing the professional ladder of the Polytechnic University. I got it last night from very reliable sources that he used to review and grade various teachers' syllabus before publication.

This happened when Mezi government got into this terrific budget mess, and schools could not afford to import books from South Africa or England. The decision was made that every school was going to request his teachers to work in the summer, writing their class own materials, which were to be reviewed by a board which in turn was to decide which of the best selected syllabus was to be publicized and printed using whatever printing facilities available to the government. The syllabus was to cover mainly Mathematics, Biology, Latin, Physics, Chemistry, English Literature, and Greek subjects from the nine through the twelve grades. During that summer, your colleague, Dr. Wasiri and only about sixteen or seventeen years old, was asked to start reviewing those syllabus in each of the subject and grade them. He was thorough and effective, he not only graded but corrected the best syllabus. The minister of education hired him at the time as a consultant. The kid took it all in stride and, from what I heard, was very modest about the whole affair. When the school resumed the following September, he calmly took his seat back in the same classes where he had failed some of his teachers' syllabus. He never confronted these teachers, nor spoke ill of them when some of them started to harass him. I heard that when he graduated, each one of his teachers from seven to twelve grades presented him with a citation. It was a whole-day event to honor this kid at his school. Never heard of him since then. We, at Polytechnic University tried in vain to recruit him, but it was too late. He had already gone to the United States to study at your University of Kentucky, I learned later. I believed that is where you must have met him. I also learned that he is now a full professor at Kansas State University. What a waste! He should be teaching at Polytechnic University if I can help it."

Dr. O'Shea felt a burst of pride he never experienced for anybody, not even when he held his firstborn son. It was that burst of pride that leaves one's heart aching with such a pain of joy that if Dr. O'Shea was observed from afar, he could have been mistaken as having a heart attack. Dr. O'Shea's face was completely transfigured and blemished.

He absorbed calmly all that Dr. McMillan was saying and kept repeating silently "Ecce Homo" to himself. When Dr. McMillan was done with the story, Dr. O'Shea recovered from his near-trance and said, "Indeed, I recognized my dear student then and now my protégé, Dr. Wasiri. Funny, he never mentioned any of this. Again it has never been detected in his last bone to brag about himself. As a matter of fact, I have known him to be modest like a saint. I have been honored to work with him all these years. I have always thought that he was a very bright fellow with an intellect level to celebrate. I have also told him that I have wished that I had just 1 percent of his humility; then I will move mountains.

Dr. McMillan, I appreciate your concern about him still teaching in one of our bright American universities. I am working as hard as I can to change that and to bring him home."

Dr. McMillan jumped on the suggestion, "The sooner the better. Now that you are embarking on this wonderful initiative to build that new Faculty of Applied Sciences, I personally hope that this Faculty would open with Dr. Wasiri right there on the premises the next academic year, educating a new generation of scientists for Mezi. I want you to know that Dr. Wasiri has already a large following within the academic circle in Mezi. People who have known him back then in that village school literally swear by him as the next one as they love to put it. I never understood that term, the next one. Do they mean the next Einstein or the next great political leader or both? Dr. Wasiri must be the only one to answer that question. From what I have seen and heard prior to my retirement, Dr. Wasiri has the ability to be both. Only time would tell. But he must be right there on the spot in Mezi to realize all these dreams. Dr. O'Shea, I am not sharing any pipedream here. Just be prepared to answer any question relative to Dr. Wasiri when we arrive in Mezi. I prayed that only a few people are aware of this documentation among those board members. In that documentation on page three, the line reading 'Contributors: Dr. Kano Wasiri and Dr. Anthony O'Shea' will raise a lot of commentaries during the board meeting, I can assure you. I am sorry, putting you so early on the spot before we have begun the meeting. It looks like His Honorable Barry Newcomb, barrister at the Queen Court, has brought us safely to the inn."

The three mates chuckled profusely as they got off the Bentley with large cartons of documentations for review. They were guided to a large private conference room. The room had a large table with all kinds of morning breakfast amenities.

They all helped themselves at the same table and after about twenty minutes, the review started. Barry, the lawyer, suggested to start the meeting with his legal brief review as not to bore them to death later on with arcane terms around Polytechnic University and the newly formed Emily Thomas O'Shea Foundation mutual legal obligations in Mezi, England, and US legal institutions or courts of law. Barry also went on to cover various funding obligations that the foundation had decided to engage in these explicit initiatives around the building of the facilities, the purchase of equipment for these facilities, their installation, the mechanism to grant scholarships to selected students, etc. Unexpectedly, Barry's presentation took almost the entire morning period. It was close to lunch period break that Barry shortened his legal presentation.

The three traveling mates struggled to decide how long the legal brief needed to be. Every part of the legal brief that they wanted to remove became pivotal to subsequent presentation. They tabled the motion to revisit the length of the legal brief and broke for lunch. When they came back from lunch at the huge dining hall of the inn, it was Dr. O'Shea to go over his well-prepared remarks.

After less than thirty minutes of talk, Dr. McMillan intervened and said, "Dr. O'Shea, I believe Barry here would agree with me when I say that you don't need to rehearse your excellent presentation with us. The documentation is so well written; it does not need any more enhancements. You can give your summary to be typed up by the AMX folks by the end of this meeting. They are waiting for this to complete the whole presentation package.

They will print out about twenty sets, each for the thirteen board members and about seven other copies for us. Your charge would be making the whole presentation, and mine would be to literally cheerlead you and keep the board members from endless and boring questioning. Barry's task should be the easiest. Nobody, during those board presentations, likes to hear legal briefings. But Barry would stand ready to answer any legal inquiry, and yes, as briefly as possible.

Dr. O'Shea, I say this because I know most of these board members, and I was instrumental before retiring, inviting eleven of the thirteen members. By the way, BI sought my involvement when you came up with these initiatives. I was very impressed with them, as I have already said.

My only concern at this time, and I am not sure if I should say that it is a concern, is the listing of the foundation board members. It is empty at this time. That can give some pointed inquiries. Barry, how we will deal with this?"

Before Barry answered, Dr. O'Shea intervened, "I am currently the chairman and sole board member if you want to know. By the way, the foundation was put together in memory of my beloved wife, Emily Thomas O'Shea, and for my lifetime contribution in the studies of minerals studies. BI is funding the foundation, as we all know. The initial funding is enough to satisfy the initiatives I have proposed. To date, I was not told by my BI contacts that there would be a problem about the composition of the foundation board members. I am prepared to say so if asked at the meeting. I am also prepared to say that the foundation would be recruiting board members within the academic community of Mezi as the implementation of the initiatives progresses. Would that be satisfactory, Barry?"

Barry rose to say, "Of course, Dr. O'Shea, you have to excuse Dr. McMillan who has not been privy to the establishment of the foundation and who is raising obvious questions as far as the nationalistic sensitivity of the funding of the initiatives would go in Mezi. Remember that you are talking about Africa here. Remember, Dr. McMillan has been there for a long time, building institutions of higher learning. He knows what he is talking about. By the way, as a chancellor of Polytechnic University, he chaired the board members we are going to meet. It is not far-fetched if the questions in their minds during the meeting could very well be, why, why Polytechnic University, why now? The answer could not be that easy to simply say, well, we are all so dedicated to Mezi development; therefore, we have decided to invest in building this Faculty of Applied Sciences.

Remember your expertise is minerals, and Mezi is noted to be producing and selling huge quantities of copper, gold, tin, and uranium worldwide. Mattley & Barr, a subsidiary of AMX that consolidates into BI, is heavily involved in the extraction, marketing, and selling of each one of those minerals. The question from the board members could be around the relationship between your foundation and Mattley & Barr. And let me tell you, Mattley & Barr did not distinguish itself for a long time in their business dealing in Mezi. It was not, shall we say, a paramount corporate citizen in Mezi. This is what Dr. McMillan is alluding to obliquely.

This has nothing to do with all your good intentions, Dr. O'Shea. Well, in our small way, within the legal staff of AMX, we have debated this issue at length in support of your initiatives. And that is the reason I was requested to join you to Mezi. I think leaving the foundation listing blank was deliberate, Dr. McMillan. If the question about the listing arises during the meeting, it will be a good opportunity to do exactly what Dr. O'Shea has proposed. We have already concurred with the legal staff, to invite names from the university academic circle to join the foundation if the question is posed. And if it is not, while we are still there in Mezi, we will take upon ourselves to solicit those names anyway. This would go, I believe, a long to alleviate a diplomatic and sensitive issue. As you have just observed, Dr. O'Shea, I would appreciate that you refer to Dr. McMillan, an old hand of Mezi, or to me any question that you would find a bit too political during the meeting. By the way, from what I understand, you have never been in Africa, Dr. O'Shea. A lot of things are not as obvious there as in Lexington, Kentucky. To put it straight and without joking, it could be another planet there altogether. Believe me, Dr. McMillan and I will be there to help you succeed. That is our charge, and we would not take this trip to fail."

Though partially relieved by Barry's answer, Dr. O'Shea was still not happy that Dr. McMillan was going to be part of the trip. He already sized him to be the enemy. He represented all these deans he fought back at the University of Kentucky. He thought that he left them back in the dean's office that last day he went there delivering his letter of resignation and signing up for his retirement. Why does he have to put up with another dean now, and for God's sake, when they'll be talking about his beloved Emily's foundation?

Dr. O'Shea gazed outside, searching for Emily's mythical guidance when Dr. McMillan started speaking, "I hope that I have not upset you, Dr. O'Shea, by raising this matter of the foundation. I am only acting on my capacity, as I say, of cheerleader. I want to make sure that you are aware of various political realities in many parts of Africa. Seriously, I want to temper your zeal in this endeavor. Mind you, there is no way that your initiatives could be rejected. No way. But in those parts of the world, the way things are accepted is more important than the actual gifts, however important. That is the way it is there. And funny thing is you would not be aware of this until it is very late when you start noticing that every conceivable expected cooperation started drying up and you, the donor, are left with all the good intentions intact but also undone. I have seen this happen not only in Mezi but also in many parts of the continent.

I have to be frank with you. Americans, Russians, and lately, the Chinese have encountered that behavior time and again the last fifty years or so after these African countries have become independent. However despised, the colonial past has prepared the British, Portuguese, and French to know these circumstances and deal with them more effectively. While the others have encountered countless fiascos in their programs with admirable good intentions, I do not want you to fail. BI in calling for my engagement wanted also to ensure that nothing is left to chance. Besides, let's face it. Your initiatives are for a long haul, a longtime involvement. It is not just the building of these two buildings and their equipment that should be of interest to you, but you also mentioned the grating of scholarship to six hundred students the first year, and the second year, and so on. All this suggests a lasting cooperation with various segments of Mezi's society for a whole generation. Now I am convinced you see where I am going. And by that time, Barry and I are already back to our comfortable British semi-upper-class life and would be reading from afar how your initiatives are faring. Hopefully, very well, indeed, very well, indeed. In fact, to my understanding, the all-purpose of this meeting was not to review the documentation. I have already said that it is well done indeed. The purpose of this meeting was to educate you in things African.

I do not know how much your protégé, as you call him, Dr. Wasiri, has done in that regard. I would guess not much, if you have not asked or probed him. And that is all normal. My experience has been that the African would not volunteer intricate information about their country, their society, and culture unless asked time and again. Answers would vary depending on the level of interest on the part of the one asking questions. If you are not pertinent, you will receive vague and generally unsatisfactory answers. I have observed and seen the level of frustration to those not used to that what is known as mind games that are played there. An answer is never obvious unless the context is evaluated, determined, and reassured. Of course, you learned as you go, as you stay there for a long time as I did. But those with the so-called European or Western mind-set, used to quick in-and-out search trips, are usually frustrated and disappointed. The reason of their deception is invariably that they missed in gaining the confidence of the other party. Confidence is a rare commodity in Africa. The mistake made nowadays in many Western circles is in thinking that confidence can be bought through bribes and other stupid entreaties. Yes, it could be bought, but for how long? That is the question. We all know that the economic condition of many of these countries is precarious.

Financial resources are highly concentrated in very few hands leaving the majority of population in dire straits. And what is worse, those with financial resources are not in the business of building wealth from one generation to another as it usually happens in Western societies. Rather, they are the gatekeepers of the highly concentrated financial resources to faithfully share these resources to benefit the large extended family. So much so, when they are no longer in the privileged positions or God forbid, when they pass away, their own immediate family starts teetering in the brink of abject poverty. In that case, confidence that had been bought dissipates quickly and needs to be bought again at a higher premium from the new set of the privileged few controlling the limited financial resources. In those circumstances, you ask yourselves how the elite is faring, how is it dedicated to both, furthering academic teaching and research in the midst of endless economic penury. Well, this is where my disposition was seriously tested as an academic and manager of Polytechnic University. The faculty members with skills in constant commercial demand, such as medicine, pharmacy, dentistry, construction engineering, mechanical engineering, electrical engineering, mines engineering, financial and commercial management find themselves in various highly paying contractual works while still engaged in teaching at the university. I was never happy with that arrangement. I knew it was always tilted toward the contractual works at the expense of the academic teaching function even for the most dedicated of our tenured professors.

Faculty members dedicated to soft sciences fared far worse when they could not parlay their skills beyond the university classrooms. Most left for university teaching positions in Europe, the Unit States, Canada, China, or anywhere they thought they can earn a decent salary and living while helping out their extended family. In general, there was nothing that could be done given the relatively modest pay scale of the faculty members who stay in Mezi and have to really struggle to balance the professional expectations of this dual function they provide daily against the ever-expanding financial expectations of their typically large extended family. It was not an exception to see in front of some faculty member offices long lines of people waiting, very old and very young, and none of them actual university students. The very old and very young were there to request money for food, clothes, school tuition, medical doctor visits, rent, or anything you name it. In time, it got so bad that some students joined in to request the same. And this led in case of some enterprising and desperate female students to exchange sex for the same. Before long, scandals erupted all over the campus. Compromised professors and students were expelled.

The university board decided to seal off the whole campus with high walls to stop the abuse. Specific digital cards were issued to the entire university population with different sets for the administrative staff, the teaching body, and the students. Access to the campus was seriously restricted, but everybody knew that outside the university walls, the problem persisted. The sight of poverty, the display of abuse and corruption, which were banished or no longer taking place on the campus, flourished unabated outside the campus high walls. It became, I am afraid to say, terribly hopeless. And this is the environment I left behind when my retirement came about, and I departed from Mezi to this silly British petit bourgeois life. I have kept regular contacts with my successor, the new chancellor, my very dear friend, Dr. Henry Umzigwe, a very special man, in the same caliber as your protégé, Dr. Wasiri, if I may say so. You will meet him soon and would be impressed just the same."

The long expose that Dr. McMillan made improved his standing with Dr. O'Shea. After all, he thought, Dr. McMillan was not the enemy. He was not one of the deans from the University of Kentucky. He was genuine in his outlook. He wanted to help the cause. Maybe he has this quirky British way of going about it. Well, he said he was a former colonialist still dedicated in the cause of helping Mezi find its own place. Still Dr. O'Shea was not ready to share the main purpose of his going to Mezi, to pursue the long battle around Alpha-M. Dr. McMillan will be used as a facilitator in the battle. The same way BI, Mr. Kiriyan, and Lady Allistair, and all others were being used as facilitators in the battle about to be won.

He will not join it. At this stage, there were only four true warriors to be counted on: himself, Hasbo, Dr. Wasiri, and his beloved Emily, guiding him from above.

He was now ready to let the meeting charged atmosphere come down. "Dr. McMillan, I am sorry if I gave the impression that I was upset because of your inquiry around the foundation board listing. Listening to

Barry and now to you, I believe that the question was extremely relevant and valid. I am also happy with the disposition Barry gave to the question. I can assure both of you that I will be very circumspect around anything political when we are in Mezi. Thank you for the advice. I wish we had this meeting and conversation long time ago. But things are what they are and time seems to precede our action and in such terrible speed that it is not allowing us to catch our breath. I am therefore very thankful for this session that turned out extremely educative for me.

By the way, Dr. McMillan, you were right when you said that Dr. Wasiri had not given me as much background about Mezi as I need now.

You are also correct that I did not insist, and I was not pertinent. I realize now that I have to do a lot of catching up. One thing is clear now, and I have to repeat what Dr. Wasiri said when I mentioned your name, Dr. McMillan. He said that I should be extremely lucky to take this trip to Mezi in company of Dr. McMillan. I did not appreciate the meaning of what he said then. I am now fully aware what he meant. Maybe that was his way of saying to open my eyes and ears as widely as possible when you will talk and guide me along. And by God, he was right. As you well know, and I don't know about you, Dr. McMillan, people with advanced age and learning like myself, we tend to get a bit restive and closed to new thinking or suggestion. We certainly believe that we can swim through any adverse current and river, small or wide until we come against the reality of it, and we are deeply humbled as I am now. So, with sincere apology, Dr. McMillan, I am now at your disposition."

Before Dr. McMillan would say anything, the lawyer Barry, desperate to enlighten the meeting, jumped in, "Well, I am not going to be left out of this trip completely by you two old timers except for finding out this very cold bottle of Chardonnay wine that we desperately need now to toast for our successful trip to Mezi. While you were exchanging your thoughts, I was informed through this Blackberry alert e-mail message that the trip is all set for the day after tomorrow, departing at eleven in the morning and arriving about nine in the evening at Mandi.

Let me see, it is almost six in the evening, we have less than thirty-six hours to get ready for the trip. I don't know about you, but I need to bring back to the office all the updates to the final package waiting to be color printed and bound. I would be glad to drop Dr. O'Shea at the hotel before heading back to the office, and Dr. McMillan will continue his return with me."

The three traveling mates toasted the success of their trip and closed the meeting. On their way back to the hotel, Dr. O'Shea asked for direction to Childs & Coventry Investment banking location. It turned out to be less than two blocks from the Drake Hotel. The lawyer suggested giving him a ride to the place anytime tomorrow. Dr. O'Shea replied that he would call him if the bank happens to be too far. Otherwise, he will walk to the location, as he needs a bit of walking exercises anyway.

By the way, he added, teasing the lawyer, he was out of place riding in the back of his huge luxurious Bentley.

Their laughter grew louder when Dr. O'Shea suggested that the Bentley ride was way above his regular American Buick vintage 1987 with different color on every side of the car with no phone, no radio, and the lawyer added, "No toilet seat." They separated on that jolly note. When he reached his room, and still troubled by the question around the foundation listing, Dr. O'Shea called Lady Allistair in New York City. Lady Allistair proceeded to calm him down by suggesting that a decision about including five names on the list was made. The list will include his name on the top as the chair and below recently proposed four other names including a Dr. Henry Umzigwe, the university chancellor, a Dr. John Awassa, an up-and-coming dynamic young economics professor at the university, and two AMX executive officers in New York he does not know.

The proposed names would simply mean that the board of the foundation is being put in place and the indicated persons are being asked to join the board. This would go a long way to resolve this issue according to Barry and the AMX legal staff team. Lady Allistair said that she concurred with the step. And in the legal staff view, absolutely no question should be raised the minute the board members would see the name of Dr. Umzigwe as board member. Lady Allistair also suggested for his information that Dr. Umzigwe and Dr. Awassa were already contacted, and they agreed to be board members of the foundation with a definitive substantial yearly retainer fee of course. Further, Lady Allistair added, as they have already discussed, Hasbo Wasiri's name would not appear on the list at this time. She would be made board member only when the Wasiri family reaches Mezi and will set a foundation office on the spot in Mandi.

She reassured Dr. O'Shea that the lawyer Barry Newcomb was keeping her apprised of the meeting that took place that day, and she felt that much progress was made. She reminded him to make plans the next day to go see the investment banker in charge of his account. The banker was eager to accommodate all that he had in mind to dispose of his prize money.

Dr. O'Shea was relieved that the foundation-listing question that could have been a game changer was resolved so quickly. He shared his relief with Lady Allistair. He then called his protégé, Dr. Wasiri. He shared the minutes of the day meeting less his concern about the foundation listing.

He teased his protégé for not telling him about his wonder boy episode in his high school day and that he needed to come to London to learn about it from nobody else but Dr. McMillan himself. He told him how proud he felt about him after listening to the story and how much stokes Dr. McMillan placed on him for the future of Polytechnic University. He also added that Dr. McMillan seemed to know so much about Dr. Wasiri than he is letting out, especially about the large following that he had at home in various academic circles. That was a surprise to Dr. Wasiri, who dismissed the wonder-boy incident as a youth show off back then.

Dr. Wasiri stated that since he left Mezi, he had not talked to any large gathering of academics or people. Twice when he went back on vacation, he spent most of his time attending to his extended family needs and did not even have time to visit with longtime friends right there in Mandi. He was definitely surprised by Dr. McMillan's assertion that he had a following back home. Since Dr. O'Shea remained unconvinced in face of his denial, he suggested to him to check the so-called following among those academic circles in Mandi while in company with Dr. McMillan. Dr. O'Shea told him that he would follow up on that.

Dr. O'Shea also added that he did not realize how much he needed to bone up on Mezi's background all that time they were together talking. Now he had to depend on Dr. McMillan to play catch up. He hoped that he would do his best. Before hanging up, Dr. O'Shea asked his protégé if he knew Dr. Henry Umzigwe, the university chancellor and Dr. John Awassa, an eminent young professor of economics.

Dr. Wasiri said that he did not know Dr. Awassa, and he only learned of Dr. Umzigwe through various university documentations that he received from William Ewas. He added that if Dr. O'Shea needed additional background material on these two academics, he should be able to get it soon enough. Dr. O'Shea said that it was not that urgent, but he can share whatever he can get when he will be back to the States. Later, he went down to have his dinner alone and went back up to sleep. He was awakened the next morning by Barry Newcomb, the lawyer who told him about the updates that Lady Allistair already shared with him the night before, the ones regarding the foundation listing. He also wanted to give him a ride to the bank if he wanted to. Dr. O'Shea thanked him but declined, and after a quick shower and a light breakfast, he went to the bank that was located less than five minutes by foot from the Drake Hotel.

When he arrived at the lobby of what looked more like a private lawyer cabinet than a bank, a gentleman who introduced himself as Louis Whitesand III, the Private Investment Banker that Lady Allistair had mentioned in her e-mail, quickly whisked him into a large room. Mr. Whitesand said right away that he was honored to be of his service and of Lady Allistair's, her longtime client. He suggested that he went to school with Lady Allistair at London Business School, and they knew each other since that time. He asked Dr. O'Shea what he wanted to do with the five-million-dollar prize money.

Dr. O'Shea waved at the young banker and requested a cup of tea before answering. After taking two or three sips of tea, he said with a grave voice, "Son, first of all, I want to stand you corrected, what you just called prize money should be rather called shared prize money. I received the check for two people, including Dr. Kano Wasiri and myself. Have you noted that name correctly? Dr. Kano Wasiri who was the other recipient of the shared prize money for the scientific work we have conducted together and were duly compensated at a conference I had the pleasure to attend alone recently.

I was given the prize while my colleague was still in the United States, completing some urgent work. Fair is fair, I want to make sure that this colleague of mine shared fifty-fifty this prize, that is, he will get two million five hundred thousand dollars. Can you set up not one but two different accounts each with the equal amount of two million five hundred thousand dollars? Can you also divide equally into each of the accounts whatever income the original five million dollar has accrued since the prize money has been deposited? Now what do you need to set up the accounts?"

The young banker was furtively writing Dr. O'Shea's instructions and looked up and said, "I would need the complete name of the owner of the account, town of residence, country, the name or names of beneficiaries in case of death of the owner of the account. That will be about all for now.

Please, Dr. O'Shea, if it is no much trouble, can you write all these pieces of information in these application forms and sign them both? I would provide you with another form that you ask Dr. Kano Wasiri to sign for proper identification and mail back to us when appropriate. Are there any other account dispositions that you want from us?"

Dr. O'Shea reviewed the new form requirements and said, "Yes, how difficultwould it be for your bank to disburse on monthly basis a payment to an account in, for instance, Mandi, the capital of the Republic of Mezi"

"It would not be difficult at all, we have bank correspondences all over the world, including in Mandi where we disburse regular payments for many individuals.

That should not be a problem at all. Would that be the case for you, sir, or Dr. Kano Wasiri?"

Dr. O'Shea answered quickly, "It would be for Dr. Kano Wasiri, but I am asking just for information purpose that he wanted to know at this time. When appropriate, he will make his own personal banking arrangements. I hope in addition to the form you mentioned for Dr. Kano Wasiri, you would provide me with some kind of bank card to allow me to provide you with investment directions or instructions and to track balances in the account privately on the Internet anywhere in the world."

Mr. Whitesand III continued to take notes and added, "I am glad that you asked. By the time I would complete registering these two accounts, you will receive two VISA cards for each of your accounts and all kinds of instructions over how to access your bank account information using our web site. You can also use the VISA to make purchase or withdraw cash from ATM machines anywhere in the world. Now if you want, I can mail all these documentations and the card to Dr. Kano Wasiri in total confidence, or I can give you a FEDEX envelope already paid by the bank and you would include your own private note to Dr. Kano Wasiri along with the card and bank access instructions. I would do whatever you require."

Dr. O'Shea was almost done filing the requested information for himself and Dr. Kano Wasiri. He handed the forms to the banker and told him that he would prefer to handle privately the confidential correspondence to his protégé. The banker excused himself for about fifteen minutes, and when he came, he had two sets of packages of bank information, one for him, a brown envelope with his new VISA card and bank access information, the other was a FEDEX large envelope containing his protégé's VISA card nicely embedded in another hard envelope, bank access information, the usual Childs & Coventry new customer booklet, another form requesting his signature with envelope to return the form.

The FEDEX envelope was not yet sealed and had the form where to ascribe the sender and receiver addresses. Mr. Whitesand added that he can drop the FEDEX envelope at any FEDEX mail drop in the city, including the one within the lobby of the hotel after he had included his own note and signed the addressees form. He also gave a hard copy of Childs & Coventry investment services he can avail himself and the copies of the current balances for the two accounts and thanked him for allowing Childs & Coventry to provide its private investment banking services to both of them. He told Dr. O'Shea to never hesitate to call him directly from anywhere in the world if he needs any particular private investment banking advice or service. Dr. O'Shea left the bank premises, went back to his already cleaned room, and wrote a note to Dr. Wasiri, advising about the new account he set up for him in the London private investment bank and accessible anywhere in the world. He left with him the surprise of checking the account balance on the Internet using the included VISA card. He advised him to read the bank-welcoming brochure and various ways to rebalance his account investment. He asked him to review his account owner profile he submitted and correct it wherever possible. He insisted that he fills the form requesting his signature and mails it back promptly. He sealed the FEDEX envelope, completed the addressee's form, and dropped the envelope at the FEDEX cart he found in the hotel lobby. Unbeknownst to Dr. O'Shea, as soon as he left the Childs & Coventry bank building, Mr. Whitesand III, as instructed, was on phone with Lady Allistair in New York City and told her what Dr. O'Shea did with the prize money check. To Mr. Whitesand III's amazement, Lady Allistair gave another instruction to his banker friend to transfer an additional five hundred thousand dollars amount to Dr. Kano Wasiri's account from her own account at the bank. He complied forthwith at the same time that Dr. O'Shea was dropping the sealed FEDEX envelope with his protégé as the receiver. When Dr. O'Shea came back up in his room, he received another call from Barry Newcomb inquiring about him and whether he needed to complete his shopping before the next day flight to Mezi. Dr. O'Shea declined the offer but accepted to join the lawyer to a dinner in the evening at about six.

They were joined to the dinner by another AMX lawyer at a nearby fancy restaurant. The dinner lasted until about nine thirty. Dr. McMillan was not available as he was also preparing for the next day's trip. Since this was the first time, he was going back to Mezi after about six years, he was getting ready to bring back as many presents as possible to longtime acquaintances of the last thirty year or so he spent in what he loved to call his second native country.

But the dinner became a bit uncomfortable for Dr. O'Shea when Barry Newcomb spent the rest of dinner asking a lot of background questions about his family, his teaching assignments, his research assignments, and mainly his relationship with his protégé, Dr. Wasiri. It was obvious that in arranging this dinner, Barry intended to learn as much as he could about this Dr. Wasiri. It had become apparent to him from what he learned from Dr. McMillan and from bits of information he gleaned from Lady Allistair that Dr. Wasiri was the main reason they were taking this trip to Mezi. He wanted to know why so much was being expended over this Dr. Wasiri who had not even dared to take the trip. Why so much focus over this man? Was he being prepared for something big in Mezi? In addition, every time Dr. Wasiri's name was mentioned, it was always in heightened hush tones and with much reverence even from these two highly considered academics, Dr. McMillan and Dr. O'Shea, who were obviously his senior. He wanted to be prepared to answer whatever inquiries about Dr. Wasiri that may arise when they will set foot in Mezi. Unfortunately, the more Barry tried to learn about Dr. Wasiri the less Dr. O'Shea gave away. He ventured to say that he did not know the fellow as much as he wished, and he used the wonder boy story that McMillan related to excuse himself for limited knowledge of his background from back then. In fact, Dr. O'Shea was not about to get anybody into the sacred pact that unites the foursome, including himself, Emily, Hasbo, and Dr. Wasiri. This was a nonstarter for Dr. O'Shea. He bid his time until Barry was tired of inquiring, and they separated for the night. Barry suggested an early rise to the airport for the late morning flight. The eight-hour flight from London to Mandi, Mezi, with a British Airways wide body jet, was smooth. The three traveling mates were in the first class. Dr. O'Shea kept to himself and slept most of the flight, while Barry and Dr. McMillan exchanged jokes and drank heavily the length of the flight.

Their arrival was another story. It was about nine twenty in the night when the plane landed in Mandi. They were quickly whisked to the airport VIP section where the Polytechnic University delegation was waiting for them. The delegation included Dr. Henry Umzigwe, the chancellor, Dr. John Awassa, a bright young economist and new member of the university board, and Mr. Baptist Sangeno, a high functionary at the Ministry of Education in charge of higher learning. The three dignitaries rushed to greet Dr. McMillan who seemed to know each of them. Dr. McMillan in turn introduced Dr. O'Shea and Barry Newcomb. After brief entry procedures, their luggage was quickly retrieved, and they were divided up in two Polytechnic University big SUVs.

Dr. McMillan joined Dr. Umzigwe and Mr. Sangeno in the first car while Dr. O'Shea, the lawyer, and Dr. Awassa shared the second car. It took about two hours for the escorts to arrive to the exclusive and secluded Tanzire Hilton Hotel that was next to the Polytechnic

University's huge campus and was located right there on the banks of the largest lake in Africa, the Lake Nyerengi. This lake was as big as Lakes Erie and Ontario combined. Mandi, the capital of Mezi, sat on the northeast border of the lake where it smacks against the slowly rising mountain of Kansi.

As soon as they arrived at the hotel and got settled into their respective rooms, Dr. McMillan was nowhere to be found. He left with Dr. Umzigwe for some longtime catching up together around the university campus. Dr. O'Shea and Barry stayed behind and were joined for a late dinner by the young economist Dr. John Awassa, who dazzled them with stories of major projects of economic development all over Mezi. Dr. Awassa was very eloquent, and to listen to him, you got the impression that more was expected from this young man of about thirty-seven years old with advanced degrees from Harvard University, Imperial College London, School of Business, and the University of Paris-Sorbonne. One other indication about the young man was that everything started and ended with Dr. John Awassa, displaying tremendous flouting of knowledge and endless references equally to well-known and obscure papers and authors.

Dr. Awassa's guests grew tired of his monolog at about one in the morning and retired to sleep. They were up at about ten in the morning and joined Dr. McMillan for a breakfast. Dr. McMillan shared with them the board-meeting agenda that will start at 1:00 p.m. for Dr. O'Shea's two hours presentation. The board members will adjourn for two hours to deliberate their response. At about four o'clock, the board will state its answer and elicit a final concurrence, and the meeting should adjourn no later than 5:00 p.m. This schedule was about what Dr. O'Shea expected. At about noon, they were collected to go to the main administrative building of the campus, a ten-minutes ride. They were greeted by the chancellor and led to the sumptuous board-meeting room on the third floor of the administrative building. The board meeting was two doors away from the chancellor's office. The entire board was attending.

There was an elevated large viewing LCD board above the guests' honor table where the entire presentation from the laptop was going to be piped. The honor table had also a range of three microphones.

The chancellor and board chair solemnly started the meeting and introduced the august guests from London and the States. Dr. McMillan was warmly applauded for a first-time visit.

Dr. O'Shea gave his two-hour presentation. He was surprised that he was not interrupted for a question or a clarification from the board members. As a matter fact, he was also applauded and congratulated at the end of his presentation. Then the three traveling mates were excused into an adjacent room to wait for the board members' deliberations. While in the room, Dr. McMillan said that the presentation went smoothly because the board had already discussed at length all the initiatives and have already concurred to its implementation. He learned about this yesterday after the arrival. Dr. McMillan thought that the deliberations would not last long, and all things should be done by four o'clock. However, two hours later, they were still not called back to the boardroom to hear the board's response. An hour more lapsed before the chancellor came back in the room and presented his excuses for the long deliberations. Dr. O'Shea thought that his initiatives were being rejected.

When they were seated back in the boardroom, the chancellor presented the response. He said that the board had concurred unanimously to the initiatives and was extremely grateful for the foundation to have been gracious enough to put its resources in enacting what was being proposed. However, the board was also aware of two main issues that were plaguing the university at this very moment. The board thought that resolving these issues takes priority at this time to expanding the Faculty of Applied Sciences. The issues have to do with the retention of faculty members in the soft sciences and the retirement environment of the faculty members. In the first case, faculty members were leaving the university and Mezi because of the tremendous cost of living in Mandi, the capital of Mezi. The most important cost they faced is housing. If the problem of decent housing facilities were resolved within the university campus, the faculty members in soft sciences would consider, in majority, keeping their positions with the university. The retirement environment of faculty members also turns to housing shortage in addition to various problems associated with advanced age accommodation for our retired academic members. The board realized that the initiatives as proposed would enhance the prospects of the university. The board is calling on the Emily Thomas O'Shea Foundation to seriously consider means and resources to assist Polytechnic University in resolving these issues. There was a period of silence in the room when all eyes were directed to the august guests.

Dr. McMillan jumped in and said, "Dear board members, we are grateful that you have concurred to the initiatives presented herein. I am certain that the Emily Thomas O'Shea Foundation should be given enough time to consider this totally new request from the board. I would not put my friend present here, Dr. O'Shea, on the spot to answer one way or another. I believe, given time, he should be able to evaluate the feasibility of considering this request. By the way, what funding the chancellor and the board had in mind?" A board member, who was seated at the center left table and who probably was the champion of the request, raised his hand and said, "Dr. McMillan, we are talking of between twenty-five- to forty-million project, give and take two million dollars."

Dr. McMillan responded, "Please, give us another thirty minutes to table this with our States staff and get back to you." As soon as they were in the adjoining room, Dr. O'Shea erupted, "Dr. McMillan, you had told me in London if the foundation board membership was in place, it was still in a proposal stage. Now you are asking me to answer to a financial request well beyond my limited and evolving scope of foundation board chair, what do you think I should do?" The lawyer intervened and said, "Funny thing how time zones can assist in resolving matters. I believe your main contact is Lady Allistair in New York City. It is still morning there, and she should be able to assist at this time. Give her a call and ask her what she thinks." Dr. O'Shea calmed himself and requested to make the call in private. He was shown another room where he called and reached Lady Allistair. He presented the case that the university board was advancing.

Lady Allistair responded that the initial funding of the foundation should accommodate this additional request. Lady Allistair added that she was not surprised by the need to resolve these two issues. In her view, the foundation should be expected to deal with these kinds of issues when in place in Mezi. She calmed the excited Dr. O'Shea further. When he rejoined his traveling buddies, he said that there was concurrence to the request, and they needed to tell the board the same. They went back and Dr. McMillan shared the happy news to the board members. They concurred by acclamation to the initiatives and included the building of about hundred apartments for the soft sciences tenured professors and the retirement home for retired tenured professors. It was about seven in the evening when the board meeting adjourned to the delight of Dr. Umzigwe, the university chancellor who now invited the three guests to a dining room not far from the chancellor's office along with the board members, and where local dishes were being warmed.

When finally seated, the chancellor proposed a toast to the successful implementation of the initiatives. An unassuming oldest board member, who invited Dr. O'Shea to say a few words about his protégé, Dr. Wasiri, seconded this toast, the long lost wonder boy of Mezi, as he put it.

Dr. O'Shea rose to the occasion, "In less than a week, I heard about the story of the wonder boy from Mezi in two different and separate occasions. First, from your own, Dr. McMillan, my current fellow traveler, and now from this august member of this board. I would hate to disappoint you all, dear board members, Dr. Wasiri, I am fortunate enough to call my protégé, never, and I repeat never, mentioned that story to me. That, as I will always testify, shows to all of us the strength of character, the highest level of humility and modesty that Dr. Wasiri continues to show in every aspect of his work, behavior, and life. I have already said that I am fortunate to call him my protégé. But I believe in saying so I am very much out of character. Let me explain. If you asked him, he would probably say that he had studied under my guidance and tutelage. True, I was his PhD Advisor, reviewing his thesis. But believe me, his entire thesis was his in its originality, in its elegance, and in its definitive findings. My job was made much easier. My job was simply to concur. And I went on to concur time and again until today, until the present days. Now tell me in this case, who is the protégé and who is the mentor? I never cease to learn from this gentleman every day in my current advanced age. At the end, I should say and I should toast to that honor of the wonder boy from Mezi, Dr. Wasiri. Thank you."

All board members and guests stood up and raised their glasses to Dr. Wasiri to the amazement of the lawyer Barry Newcomb who did the same. He decided to get more information from the oldest member and joined his table. When Barry asked this board member to talk about Dr. Wasiri, he managed to say that he heard that he is what they call in Swahili, the next one. That confused Barry even more. He finished the evening, wallowing in even heavier drinking. The next day, Dr. O'Shea met with the university chief planning engineer who was going to be in charge of the whole construction as proposed in the final and complete initiatives. He reassured him about meeting the deadline before the raining season. He expected the excavation to start as soon as in a week when already heavy moving equipment will arrive from South Africa. He took the three guests around the locations of the new Faculty of Applied Sciences, the new student hall for the six hundred students, the retirement home, and the hundred or so apartment buildings. The locations were vast and outside the current walls of the campus.

The overall construction was going to increase the campus complex by two-fifths. When they completed the survey, the three fellow travelers went to see first Dr. John Awassa to request officially his becoming a foundation board member. He readily agreed with flourish. Afterward, they visited with Dr. Henry Umzigwe, the university chancellor, to request the same. He also concurred. The new board members were left with the foundation prospectus, which, on page seventy-one, stipulates that each board member was to be compensated annually with a minimum basic retainer fee of eighty-seven thousand dollars. They were also advised that the next board meeting was scheduled in London on January fifteenth of the next year, all traveling expenses paid.

On the third day of their stay, Dr. O'Shea called Dr. Umzigwe, the university chancellor, privately and decided to pay him another visit, this time he wanted to do it alone. He left a message for his traveling mates at the hotel lobby that he went to see a doctor. The chancellor decided to receive him at his other office of Advanced Studies of Architecture School, where he still maintained a light teaching schedule and mainly to post-graduate students. He knew that this meeting needed to be far from many prying eyes around the campus administrative building as word already went out that Dr. O'Shea was a bearer of great gifts to the university, every one of visits to any university place would amount to another major financial giveaway. When Dr. O'Shea arrived, Dr. Umzigwe was wearing an undistinguished white robe of a teaching assistant and whisked the professor in his small office.

"My good professor O'Shea," the chancellor started saying, "I really appreciate that you have decided to have this private talk with me. I knew perfectly well that you would not leave our campus without getting the status of the hiring process of Dr. Wasiri. Since he made an inquiry in getting a tenured professorship with the Applied Sciences Faculty, I have been personally handling all the process. Actually, the request landed with that other old board member, the professor who asked you questions about Dr. Wasiri's whereabouts at our board meeting the day before, and you gave us that eloquent testimony of his humility and modesty. He is the current dean of Applied Sciences and about to be retired by the end of this academic year. Because of the notoriety of Dr. Wasiri, he has asked me to handle it personally. So at this time, there are only two people in the know that Dr. Wasiri will be joining us next year. I cannot tell how excited and extremely delighted we are of the news.

I was also very happy to see how extremely circumspect and protective you were about your protégé. Well tell him that all is going well, very well indeed, I would say. We are very happy about the prospects of having the wonder boy teach in this university. Let me tell you, this will be a big shot in the prestige of Polytechnic University to receive Dr. Wasiri. My only request to you at this time will be to find out how Dr. Wasiri would react if in addition of becoming a tenured professor of mines engineering, he is requested to become the dean of the new Applied Sciences Faculty. That will be, in my estimation, a logical step irrespective of the extraordinary donations Polytechnic University is receiving from you his mentor. How would Dr. Wasiri react to these double appointments? The current dean, Dr. Wutugrase, pushing seventy-five well beyond tenured professor retirement age, will swear only by Dr. Wasiri. Dr. Wutugrase is well respected and adored by students and faculty members alike. His tenure contract has been unanimously renewed every year since he had tried to retire. At this rate, there is a joke going around that he will carry his tenure to his coffin. Yet he told me that he would retire under no circumstances but to be succeeded by Dr. Wasiri. He claimed to have seen Dr. Wasiri in action and was much impressed. I do not quite know when and where, but I would not doubt his conviction. So I leave you with that charge to convince your protégé not only to take a tenured professorship but also to lead the new Applied Sciences Faculty as its dean. Would you do this for this university and communicate privately to me as soon as possible when you get back home? I am giving you my business card with all the private contact information to reach me through letter, e-mail, or phone."

Excited and at the same time surprised by another unexpected accolade being bestowed over his protégé, Dr. O'Shea was a bit at loss of words. "Well done, Dr. Umzigwe, for the good news. I am sure that Dr. Wasiri will be happy to learn that the hiring process is going well. However, I have to tell you that I am not certain that he would accept becoming the new dean of the new Applied Sciences Faculty. For all I know, he would say that he would need time to absorb his teaching assignments first before taking on administrative duties of a dean. I know him enough to think that this is probably what he would say. Then again, my evaluation could be completely wrong here, but then, I don't know until I would talk to him. I would certainly encourage him to do both for the sake of this university. Dr. Umzigwe, you have been kind enough to handle this matter in a very private manner all along. I owe you the utmost regard to report it duly to our friend Dr. Wasiri, and I expect him to honor your request and Dr. Wutugrase's with the highest diligence."

Dr. Umzigwe responded, "That is all we want you to do. Transmit the request, let him think about and collect and give us his response. We did not know how we should have made the request. We knew that it would have been very awkward to respond to his letter with another request letter. You can imagine how happy we were when we learned that you, his PhD advisor, were coming and most likely would make inquiries about his hiring process. This is a prized channel to Dr. Wasiri that was missing then. We are happy to use it. And we trust that all we have said here remains as private and delicate as it can be. With that, Dr. O'Shea, I can tell you in the name of the university board and the university entire body how delighted and happy we have been to meet with you and to thank you for all you are planning for this university. If I don't see you again before you leave, I wish you a safe return and I am looking forward to your next visit with us here in Mezi."

The two scientists bade farewell. Dr. O'Shea took another ride around the campus and returned to the hotel. His meeting with Dr.

Umzigwe lasted about three hours, much longer than that quick, urgent doctor's visit he said to his fellow travelers he needed to make nearby because of some unspecified stomach aches. His fellow travelers were worried that the medical visit took that long and wondered if he had an extensive medical condition need. He reassured them that all was all right and showed a medicine that the doctor prescribed—an ff-the-shelf medicine very popular in the States. He also said that he was ready to start his trip back to the States now that they have basically and successfully accomplished all the objectives of their trip. At his surprise and Barry's, the lawyer, Dr. McMillan, said that he needed to spend another week in Mezi if that was not a problem. He needed to sort out some family issues that he had left unresolved when he left Mezi. He was also hoping that AMX would cover his extended stay in the beautiful Tanzire Hilton Hotel. Barry the lawyer had no objection with his stay at the hotel and told Dr. O'Shea that both of them were going back to London with the earliest flight that night if he did not have any other dealing in Mezi. Dr. O'Shea assured him that he was ready to go back. They both confirmed their flight back to London at 10:00 p.m. that night, and the professor also decided to stay in London for a day before continuing his last leg of flight back to Louisville, Kentucky. When the old professor reached his room to start packing, he received an excited call from his protégé, Dr. Wasiri, who told him that he just received excellent feedback from the board meeting and that all initiatives were well received and concurred in addition to some new requests from the board.

He mentioned that a Dr. John Awassa was delegated by the board to give him the wonderful news. That was a surprise to Dr. O'Shea, who was not made aware of the need of sharing anything with his protégé. He just hoped that the confidence that was just shared with him about the hiring process was not part of the excellent news his protégé received. So he listened attentively but nothing filtered from his immediate conversation with the chancellor. Relieved, he thanked his protégé and assured him that all went wonderfully well, and he will give him a thorough and complete feedback when he will reach Lexington in about three days. Before terminating the call, he teased him again about countless wonder boy stories he had collected while in Mezi. After finishing packing, he went to see Dr. McMillan who was already in conversation with Barry the lawyer. He thanked him for all he had done during the trip and wished that they would see each other either in London or Mezi. The university SUV limousine took them to the airport afterward.

It was only when they were airborne that the lawyer mentioned to Dr. O'Shea that Dr. McMillan was very disappointed that he had not made him a board member of the Emily Thomas O'Shea Foundation. Dr. McMillan's main objective in joining them on this trip was to explore personally the eventuality of becoming a member of that board for many reasons: the first one was to give him opportunities of affording to come back to his so-called native home as often as the board work will permit and the second one was to visit with his old buddies at the Polytechnic University that much often. Barry said that Dr. McMillan missed his beat in Mezi a lot. His retirement life in England did not turn out to be what he had hoped. Dr. McMillan said that in spite of all, he left his heart in Mezi. He had wished to be able to go back as often as he could. Barry added that Dr. McMillan could not bring this matter up to Dr. O'Shea after their first encounter around the foundation board membership. Dr. McMillan realized that it would have been awkward to raise the issue and only to come back and request to join the same board. Barry remarked that after the encounter, Dr. McMillan literally avoided to talk to Dr. O'Shea altogether until the board meeting. Dr. O'Shea said that he noticed the same and felt very much the same way. He said that the encounter in London was misplaced. He was just a bit sensitive about a subject he had no control over. His motivation was simply to protect his wife's name. Besides, Dr. O'Shea added that he did not control that board membership; it is all New York's function. He did not wish to elaborate that New York meant Lady Allistair, hoping that Barry understood. But as a chair, Dr. O'Shea said that he wanted to be comfortable to work with members who will be selected.

Now that he knows Dr. McMillan's intention, he will bring it up to New York's attention, and he was certain that Dr. McMillan, with his considerable background in Mezi, should be of considerable value.

Dr. O'Shea asked Barry if there was more than he needed to know to steer this selection about Dr. McMillan. Dr. O'Shea said that he did not buy what Barry mentioned about Dr. McMillan avoiding him during the trip. He said that he had noticed that he was not much around when they were at the hotel. He was practically off to somewhere during the trip except for the board meeting. Afterward, Dr. McMillan had to be begged to come with them to see the chief planning engineer. He did not last long during the excavation survey that was given to them. Dr. O'Shea said that he did not want to probe further, but when he requested to stay to attend to some family issues, he finally realized that this was what preoccupied him during the trip and left it at that.

Barry then opened up, "Yes, that was it. Just as Dr. McMillan himself said before we came to Mezi, and if you remember, 'An answer is never obvious unless the context is evaluated, determined, and reassured,' when he was talking about Africans. I strongly believe he was talking about himself. Because, African he became, African he is. Let me explain, Dr. McMillan graduated from the University of Kent with a PhD in construction engineering around the time most African states were acceding to political independence. He had a maternal uncle who was teaching electrical engineering at the newly established Polytechnic University in Mandi, Mezi. The uncle made a strong impression on Dr. McMillan to join him at the Polytechnic University, which showed much promises and opportunities for a young nontenured professor. Dr. McMillan came to Mezi with a new bride, Mrs. Colette McMillan. The young couple established themselves quietly into, at the time, a basically all-white semi-colonial community of teaching faculty members. This was the time of great upheavals throughout the continent of Africa. As time went on, there was a substantial turnover of the teaching faculty members with an increasing number of young African faculty members graduating from American and European universities, taking over. And that was only normal. Thankfully, Mezi was relatively stable politically with no ethnic or civil wars to speak of. Then came the time of generals and colonels to Mezi and the degradation of political discourse that ensued. This only accelerated the exodus of remaining white teaching faculty members. The McMillan couple still gave the appearance of a stable marital life, but they remained childless.

The exodus and the lack of child started to affect their household. Mrs. Colette McMillan was now set to go back to England. But Dr. McMillan, who had been climbing the Polytechnic University administrative ladder, and at the time already the youngest university provost, thought otherwise. The real reason was also that all along, Dr. McMillan had substituted his matrimonial commitment to a lasting love affair with a graduate student from Angola by the name of Anna Lourenco De Olivera. University gossips had it that the good Dr. McMillan was spending night and day with Miss De Oliveira who graduated with a master's in Economics and was now hired as administrative assistant in the provost offices. Colette McMillan retaliated by giving a warning, delaying to come back to Mezi after her summer vacation in England through about Christmas. That did not work. She came back and lasted only four more months and departed to England again for good. Dr. McMillan did not join his wife in England. It turned out that Miss De Oliveira, in the meantime, had borne him a son by the name of Alberto McMillan, and they continued to live in common law marriage while Dr. McMillan tried in vain to finalize his divorce from his wife. Not long after, Colette entered Her Majesty's foreign services and started working in various Eastern Block UK embassies and hoped against hope to be reunited with her husband. Anna Lourenco De Olivera was a product of what was called a Métis relationship between a Portuguese Merchant banker and a fifth-generation daughter of a prominent mixed-race family in Luanda, Angola. Anna's father decided to send his daughter, his only child, to study English and Architecture at the Polytechnic University of

Mandi in Mezi. After getting a bachelor's in Mathematics, Anna decided to do graduate studies in Economics with concentration in Econometrics. When civil war broke out in Angola, Anna lost complete contacts with her family. She decided to remain in Mandi. That was the time she came in contact with Dr. McMillan who took more than an academic interest in this beautiful young lady when she came in to express her desolation and complete despair about her inability to reach her parents in the offices of the provost. Dr. McMillan's inclination to help slowly developed into a forbidden intimate relationship. It was the time when increasingly he went home to an empty bed where his almost depressed wife endlessly lamented her barren womb. Sometime in the middle of the night, frustrated, he will leave Colette and run up to the guest bedroom to have some sleep and rest. The change of venue with Anna was a welcome distraction at first. But the attraction grew deeper and heavier with this warm blooded 'Métis,' whose bed customs left the poor Dr. McMillan begging for more. When Anna became pregnant, Dr. McMillan felt his manhood finally vindicated and resigned himself to pursue the forbidden affair.

A second child, now a daughter named Filia McMillan, sealed the common-law relationship two years later and forced Dr. McMillan to move the de facto separation from his first wife to a legal divorce which Colette would not grant. This situation lasted for more than twenty-five years until Colette passed away in a bout of lung cancer while in assignment in Budapest, Hungary. The situation lasted into the majority of both kids, Alberto and Filia McMillan, when both went to college in England, the son as oil engineering student at the University of Kent and the daughter as law student at Cambridge University. Alberto went on to work for ARAMCO in Saudi Arabia first and is now working as oil engineer managing director in Abu Dhabi. Filia joined a law firm in Brussels, Belgium, specialized in European Union Trade laws. McMillan kids are both doing quite well. The issue is with their mother, Anna Lourenco De Olivera, who felt left out and had never taken McMillan's name and was never legally married to Dr. McMillan after all these years. Of course, the children never forgave their father and have not reconciled with him since. And when he decided to retire, Dr. McMillan was still reluctant to take Anna back to England. I think he was afraid of any legal claims from the estate of his first wife since their divorce never took place until she passed away. And he never took legal steps to find out of guilt or being superstitious or both. And he claims to still be in the limbo and does not want to share it with Anna. He is now Lourenco De Olivera still works at the university as director of admissions office now. She is all right and is quite well settled and connected in Mandi upper echelon community. She sees her kids every summer when they all gather in a huge family house that the son has bought somewhere in the South of France. But poor

Dr. McMillan is still not welcome there as long as he does not take steps to marry Anna, their mother. Mind you, Dr. McMillan seems to get along quite well with his common-law wife Anna. You probably did not notice. She was there at the airport when we came in. She was already seated in the other university SUV limousine when we came out of the VIP section and went to the hotel. Dr. McMillan went to spend the night with her for old time sake when we settled in our hotel rooms. That is why he did not join us with this Dr. John Awassa. He came in the morning only to join us for the board meeting. After the meeting, he was less and less available. Now you can understand why he wants to be a board member of your foundation. Maybe that will probably seal his long-awaited marriage to Anna and allow him to settle in Mandi for good. That is what he wants I believe. I have learned all this through various talks, calls, and conferences we had since AMX traced him back in England to support this trip. In my opinion, Dr. McMillan will be a strong asset in the running of the foundation on the spot in Mezi.

Unless you have anybody in mind, I do not see anyone with the depth of his background who can support the foundation as much. Just think of it."

Dr. O'Shea was a bit tired now. "I can't agree more. He should be our man in Mezi irrespective of his family issues. I will share the extent of your support with our folks in New York City. I am convinced that they would concur to our conclusion. Now, Mr. Barrister, give me a chance to catch some sleep and rest. You see you will calmly and freshly disembark when we reach London while I would have to continue this long trip to the States after only one day to relax. I am now working on my long-term rest. You can have a full glass of Johnny Walker Blue on me. I would talk to you later." Dr. O'Shea went to sleep.

CHAPTER 11
New York Foundation Visit

After about three hours of sleep, Dr. O'Shea woke up and did a mental note of things that did not connect during the trip. He took a paper out of his attached case and wrote down: "First issue was that foundation goals, short-term and long-term scopes, structure, and management were still not clear to him though he was the chairperson. Second issue concerned himself: how is he going to determine that the foundation is properly managed when he is so far in Lexington, Kentucky, should he move to the foundation's headquarters in New York? The third issue concerned the communication he owed to make to his own kids regarding this foundation bearing the name of their own mother. The fourth was relative to Dr. McMillan's association with the foundation: should he be made a board member or should he oversee projects and a decision would be made later whether he should join the board."

Dr. O'Shea tried to enunciate steps and means to resolve these issues. It was obvious he was the only one person to resolve it by calling a family meeting sometime soon. He also remembered what his protégé, Dr. Wasiri, had said about engaging more his own kids about family matters. He felt guilty then for not having mentioned even to his own children that this foundation was carrying their mother's name. That was definitely a family matter. God forbid, they have to learn it by accident somewhere in a magazine, a newspaper or an isolated conversation. Emily's rules need not to be carried this far. The children will learn very soon how he was honoring their mother's name and memory. He would come up with an urgent occasion to gather them around in Lexington along with Dr. Wasiri's family. They will be thrilled. However, no matter how he looked at the other three issues, he realized that he needed another face-to-face meeting with Lady Allistair. He decided then to change his itinerary. He will go home by way of another stopover in New York City. He will contact Lady Allistair during his one-day stay in London. He won't mention this to Barry who was not at his adjoining seat, probably at the first class bar, drinking heavily as he did on the London-Mandi flight. Dr. O'Shea put his notes back in his attached case and went back to sleep. When they reached London, he declined a ride to his hotel in Barry's Bentley now driven by his wife who came to pick him up.

He also insisted that Barry did not need to give him a ride to the airport a day later. He would manage. As soon he was alone, he cancelled his reservation at the Drake Hotel and requested a taxi to a regular hotel closer to Heathrow Airport. As soon as he reached the hotel, he called Lady Allistair and told her about the change of itinerary and requested to see her as soon as he would get to New York City. Lady Allistair was happy that he had decided so.

She was expecting to talk to him anyway the minute he was in the States. She was elated to learn that he was coming straight to New York City. Dr. O'Shea changed his travel plan and got into the same day all-night flight to JFK Airport.

He was leaving London at about eleven at night. That gave him almost a full day's rest at the airport hotel. By the time he was back at the airport, he was erected with no hangover from the flight from Mandi. Dr. O'Shea slept during the entire transatlantic flight, and when the plane landed at about seven in the morning, he felt ready to go straight to AMX's office. However, the limousine chauffeur who picked him up told him that he was told to bring him first to the Pierre Hotel and pick him about one in the afternoon for a meeting with Lady Allistair. He did not have a suite this time at the Pierre Hotel, but the room was just as huge as a suite in other hotels. He was settled in as comfortably as before. But before he knew, he fell deep in sleep till about eleven in the morning when he received a call from Lady Allistair to confirm their one o'clock appointment. He took his lunch in the room and was down in the limousine around twelve thirty. His ride to the office took less than ten minutes. When he was dropped, Lady Allistair greeted him at the sidewalk. He looked around and was convinced that the address was not the same as where they usually met. Dr. O'Shea did not realize that he was now on Park Avenue about three blocks north of Waldorf Astoria Hotel. Lady Allistair took him inside the marbled lobby building and then to the twenty-seventh-floor. They came out in front of a large double wooden door with a shining copper sign on the top reading, "Emily Thomas O'Shea Foundation." Dr. O'Shea got goose bumps at the sight of his wife's name. He almost fainted. When the door opened, he was greeted by sustained applauses and greetings from foundation staff members who lined up the length of the office to the huge office of the foundation's board chairperson. He responded kindly to the greetings. Lady Allistair and two other executive-looking gentlemen escorted him to the office. They directed him to the big-leathered chair of the chairperson behind and equally huge wooden desk. Lady Allistair and the two executives took their seat on three other leathered chairs on the other side of the desk.

Dr. O'Shea slumped into his chair and requested a glass of cold water to calm his nerves. He also requested to have a private conversation with Lady Allistair and excused the two other executives. Lady Allistair stood up and escorted the two executives out the office and closed the door behind. She also realized that the good old professor needed to catch his breath a little. She waited outside for about five minutes while chatting with the other two executives. She told them to stand ready to join them inside when needed. She went back inside and found Dr. O'Shea looking outside the big window behind his desk.

Lady Allistair started to apologize, "Dr. O'Shea, I sincerely want to extend my apologies. I now realize how overwhelming the reception that I have planned today could have disturbed you. I should have been more sensitive to your feeling . . ."

While Lady Allistair was talking, Dr. O'Shea stood up, went on the other side of the desk, sat next to Lady Allistair, took her two soft hands, and said very loud, "Nonsense, Lady Allistair, the reception was appropriate. Please do not make any excuse. Apologies not accepted. It was all me. I was just overwhelmed seeing my beloved Emily's name on top of the door. That did it for me. You should forgive these old tired bones and senses. I should have controlled my emotions a little bit better. I hope you and Emily would forgive me now. Lady Allistair, you have done Emily honors that I did not expect in my lifetime. I am sincerely the most grateful. I wish you would tell the staff outside that I would extend my whole heartfelt gratitude for all they are doing on behalf of the foundation sometime before I leave for Lexington. Now that we have dealt with our emotions, let me go over what I wanted to talk about. I have noted them on this paper. There are about three issues I wanted to run by you. I don't know when you would feel obligated to get the other two executives engaged in responding to my inquiries or you would prefer to answer them all by your selves."

He handed a scratch paper where he restated the three issues he came to review with Lady Allistair, who read them quickly and said, "Dr. O'Shea, I am relieved that I did not cause your discomfort. I will be glad to go over the last two topics concerning Dr. McMillan, you, and the foundation. The first issue, related to the foundation's management, would be expounded and presented by the two executives I wanted to introduce you to previously. But before I start, can you give me your own feedback about the trip and the support you got?"

Dr. O'Shea obliged the lady, "In my opinion, the trip was very successful from the beginning to the end. The reception by the board of Polytechnic University was excellent. They treated the three of us very well. Dr. McMillan, being their former chairperson, made our reception the better. Although, I was not clear at times if he was pushing the board agendas or the foundation's agendas. Then again, you cannot help when you have worked with an institution like Polytechnic University for as long as Dr. McMillan did. In his position, I think, I would have acted likewise anyway. But overall, he was well balanced in his delivery. The lawyer, Barry Newcomb, got the easiest part. He did not have to say much however well prepared he was for the trip. To tell the truth, I was a bit taken aback by the additional requests the board raised during the meeting. You see, I have never sat on any board meeting in my entire professional career. I was not quite familiar with the usual give-and-take process that goes on in those meetings. But as the meeting went on, I realized that it was only fair for the board of Polytechnic University to bring about their current priorities and to find out if the foundation could help. The board did this not to reject our initiatives but to present to us the urgent need to address their current issues. The board acted like a head of any family. It was no different as in the case where somebody approaches this family to help it with, say, outstanding medical bills when the family was being fed every three days. Now it will not be surprising if the head of family goes on and raises with the benevolent person the urgent need to feed the family on daily basis and postpone the payment of the outstanding medical bills. If the benevolent person can attend to both needs so much the better. I was entirely relieved and thanks to your intervention that the foundation would address both the proposed initiatives and the additional requests. It was a major lesson I took back from the trip and that drove me to come straight here to have this meeting. I suddenly realized that to be successful and effective, the foundation would never be so narrow in its objectives and goals. These goals should evolve and change depending on the needs of the recipients. I decided that I, personally, needed to get a thorough rounding, a thorough appreciation about this foundation. When I arrived here today it dawned on me that you have already taken steps to lead the foundation in that direction. I am ready for further education."

Lady Allistair beamed and responded, "So you will, so you will, Chairperson Dr. O'Shea. Now let us not beat ourselves over the process. I believe that we are not off track on this Foundation endeavor. Remember, it has taken us less than three months from the time you came up with the initiatives to the time you went to Mezi to present the initiatives along with the Foundation superstructure.

All these events happened so fast that they looked as if they were tripping over one another; the setting up of the Foundation and the trip to Mezi to present initiatives backed by the same Foundation. Back here, we worked very fast and very hard to make the trip a success. It was a very high risk we took. I am glad that it paid off, especially considering our very tight timeline basically leading to the next year academic year opening. I am saying this to get you on the same plane where we are here. The essential thing is that the Foundation has made some commitments and would deliver on these commitments in a proposed timeframe. This is where we need to keep our focus, energy, and eyes on. When you arrived here today, I wanted to show you that the Foundation infrastructure was in place to deliver in its commitments. I can assure you that we have a location and a superb staff to do the job. Now I will turn to the discussion of the last two issues. You already said that you were not clear with the role of Dr. McMillan. He was selected for the reason and the role you saw him play in Mezi. He knows Mezi inside out as no other person you can think of. He had lived there for more than thirty years and has risen to the chairperson of the board within the same institution where we want Dr. Wasiri to play a major scientific role. He is an invaluable asset to our endeavor. I am happy that you came around understanding his role. If you ask me what he should do for us in the future, I would say that we give him as much incentives to stay in Mezi. I understand that you are not ready to make him a board member, and I agree with you there. But he does not have to exercise a board membership at all cost. In order to keep him in Mezi, we need to find a permanent, extremely lucrative executive position for him within the Foundation so he can continue to assist us in many directions. We can also provide him with a bait of a future board membership depending on the performance of his execution within, say, a year. We can make him understand that board memberships are closed for now. But by the time Dr. Wasiri will be in place in Mezi, he would be elevated to the board along with Mrs. Wasiri, as you have already proposed. I believe that should work for him as long as he can stay and earn a decent living in Mezi. In addition, I am fully aware of his family issues. He would have no choice but to buy into the incentives I mention if properly proposed. Do not worry. If you agree with this proposal, Barry would run it by Dr. McMillan very soon, and I would let you know if he has come on board. Now the Foundation's whole board membership positions will be discussed later. Now as far as you are concerned, let me tell you up front that you do not need to be physically present here in New York City. We can retrofit your house anywhere you choose in the United States to have a fully functioning office of the Foundation board chairperson. I am saying this because your role is also to be as close to Dr. Wasiri as possible to smooth his transfer to Mezi.

You would not be able to do this from New York City. You would be a plane flight away from this office, and you would have access to any information you need at any time. When Dr. Wasiri would be in Mezi, you would be able to decide whether to move here or any other place you want to continue acting as chairperson of the foundation. I hope I have provided answers to your two issues and to your satisfaction, Chairman Dr. O'Shea." With a slight chuckle, Dr. O'Shea said, "To my satisfaction, yes indeed. But Lady Allistair, you are killing me with this chairman business. I am not used to this."

But Lady Allistair demurred, "I am sorry but you need to get used to the title. The next two executives will be addressing you accordingly when they would join us after a ten minutes break, Chairman Dr. O'Shea."

She got up and went to locate the two AMX executives. She was back after about twenty minutes with the two executives. They introduced themselves to Dr. O'Shea. The first was Derek Anderssen, AMX vice president for northeast region; the second was Patrick Berger, AMX vice president—US Marketing Strategy. The executives were both middle-aged and have been lent by AMX to the Foundation for about a year. Their charge was to get the Foundation up and running before a permanent management structure was put in place. They were both very happy to meet with the much talked about Dr. O'Shea, chairman of the foundation board.

They advised Dr. O'Shea that they were also made temporary board members to expedite current foundation business until their assignment will end and they will transfer their current duties. Then Mr. Patrick Berger mounted a board where he projected to the start of his presentation from a PC; then he said, "Chairman Dr. O'Shea, it is with great pleasure that I want to provide you with the current management structure of the foundation. I would start with this display showing the foundation leadership overview. At the top, we have the board of directors/members who will oversee all the foundation efforts. A schedule of board meetings is being prepared at this time to ensure that it is performing efficiently. The board members currently include yourself as chairman of the board, Dr. Henry Umzigwe, Polytechnic University chancellor and chairman of the board, Dr. John Awassa, Polytechnic University board member and professor, and my colleague Mr. Derek Anderssen and myself, both from AMX management team. The board members' function is to shape and approve the foundation strategies, review results, advocate the foundation's issues and set the general direction of the foundation.

Below the board is a management committee led by a managing executive director to lead the foundation mission, that is, to promote higher applied sciences education in Mezi. That position is vacant at this time. The managing executive director leads a management team comprised of five managing directors: a managing administrative director to oversee the foundation's human resources, information technology and security; a general counsel and secretary managing director to lead the foundation's legal team; a managing financial director to oversee finance, financial planning, and analysis and strategic planning; a managing operations director to oversee site operations teams; and a managing communications director to protect and advance the foundation's reputation and increase awareness of foundation issues. All these positions are currently vacant while Mr. Anderssen and I are pitching in to fill the administrative, financial, and operations managing directorship positions to the best of our abilities with the assistance of the staff you have seen when you came in. It is our conviction that this foundation structure as designed will effectively serve the goals and objectives of the foundation. It goes without saying that a lot of issues around the implementation of the Foundation have been resolved on ad hoc basis since we started, and that will be the case as the foundation takes shape. However, I should share two observations I made during the time I have worked on the implementation of the foundation. The first concerns the process of grant making. It is obvious and evident that there is a need for a quality grant making and grant improvement directorship. Since the purpose of any foundation is to make grants or other forms of resources donation, I am convinced that quality grant making process should be elevated to a management leadership component. Another observation alludes to the ability or a process to analyze the impact of the grant. Most of time the inclination to analyze the grant impact would be to limit the analysis to financial or economic impacts. You would agree with me that, for instance, the support provided by the foundation in the case of a new Applied Sciences Faculty construction goes well beyond the mere short-term financial or economic impacts we can readily assess. What about the overall impact of the education accrued to the all-new generation of students who would benefit of this new Faculty, that benefit needs also to be assessed? I am probably venturing well beyond the sphere of my competence or authority. But it occurred to me that it is also important."

Dr. O'Shea clapped his hands and said, "You are right, Mr. Berger, and that level of impacts is what we expect the Polytechnic University body and the population of Mezi would appreciate to its full extent. Otherwise why bother to go there? You are providing very insightful comments over this foundation endeavors.

And if I may, your presentation of the leadership structure of the foundation is excellent and is also giving me a lot to think about. One suggestion that came to my mind at the board level would be to make the managing executive director a board member. I understand that the position is vacant now, but adding dual responsibilities over this function would make it an effective link between the board and the management team. I am already thinking of a person capable of filling this position, and I would share this with Lady Allistair later. For the time being, I want you to know that I very much appreciate your presentation . . ."

There was a sharp knock at the door at that instant, and a young sharply dressed lady entered the office with an urgent note for Lady

Allistair who proceeded to read it quickly and announced that she needed to be excused to take up an important call.

In the meantime, Dr. O'Shea and the two executives continued their exchange over the structure of the foundation. About ten minutes later, Lady Allistair came back with a somber look that Dr. O'Shea had never seen on her gleaming face. He then asked her what was going. Lady Allistair said that she received an urgent call from Uncle Kiri, the chairman of BI who was holding an urgent management meeting at Amovir in about a week and insisted that Lady Allistair makes herself available for that meeting. Uncle Kiri said that important decisions regarding the future management of BI would be discussed and taken at this meeting. Lady Allistair added that she had never heard Uncle Kiri talk with such grave tone before. She was afraid that this might portend to a management succession at BI. She also said that she was more worried about Uncle Kiri, whose health has been reported to be declining lately. She hoped that he was not reaching the end of his tenure. While she was talking, Dr. O'Shea was brought back to his impression of his last Amovir trip, Mr. Kiriyan, the strange couple Dudarev, and the unbelievable alien people theory they pretended to share with Mr. Kiriyan. Dr. O'Shea then asked Lady Allistair how old was Mr. Kiriyan; she did not know but said that Uncle Kiri must be about eighty-five or more.

Then she requested that the meeting be brought back to the subject at end and said, "Mr. Berger was correct to say that the managing executive director position was vacant at this time. I would venture to say that I have been filling that position on an ad hoc basis so to speak, expediting the resolution of various business needs which came about in order to meet the self-imposed deadline of the next year October academic opening. I must also have to agree with you about the suggestion you made.

The Foundation bylaws will be change to incorporate that change. As you can see, Chairman Dr. O'Shea, the Foundation is still a work-in-process at this stage, and by the time our two executives would be gone, I am convinced, they would have left a Foundation in solid standing grounds. Then the task would be to fill their board memberships. From our prior discussions, I believe, the fore-mentioned candidates should fit nicely in these positions. It is also getting very late. And if Dr. O'Shea does not have any more questions, I would like to excuse Mr. Berger and Mr. Anderssen at this time." Dr. O'Shea indicated that he did not have any more questions for the two gentlemen.

They were excused, and Lady Allistair continued her monolog, "Dr. O'Shea, I believe you wanted to raise Dr. McMillan's name for the managing executive director's position. I would agree with you except at this time, the most important position and very convenient for Dr. McMillan would be the managing operations directorship. He should be interested in managing all Mezi sites operations from now until next year academic opening period, at which time he would be elevated to the managing executive directorship and would gain the foundation board membership that he wants. He may continue to exercise the managing operations directorship if he wants to do so until a new director would be selected. This way, he would have been tested along and would have earned the top spot. I had a long discussion with Barry Newcomb, the AMX lawyer, around this topic. Barry has also reported your ambivalence about Dr. McMillan. He concluded that Dr. McMillan ought to be our man in Mezi but brought up gradually. Listen, Barry has already gained enough confidence with Dr. McMillan. He should be the one to bring him along and to signify to Dr. McMillan how much the foundation needs him in Mezi with appropriate compensation with a shot to board membership as soon as it will become opened. I believe this would be feasible for Dr. McMillan, and I hope for you too, Chairman Dr. O'Shea."

Dr. O'Shea got up from his chair and walked to the large office window. "I agree, Lady Allistair, I knew that you would have thought of every detail of any management issue I would raise. I should say that AMX is lucky to have a management expert like you in its midst. Barry was correct. I was a bit ambivalent about Dr. McMillan for other reasons than the expertise I know he would bring for us in the foundation business, nor for his family issues which are, well, none of my business. We all have our own private social cross we carry now and then. The important thing is not to let it impact our professional tasks. I am completely reconciled now to the fact of bringing him into the foundation.

I have absolutely no reservation about that. If you want, I would personally sign the letter of job offer to Dr. McMillan to remove any doubt about my intention. I would come back here tomorrow to sign it and hold a short meeting with the staff to thank everyone for the wonderful job accomplished to date. My very dear Lady Allistair, I want to end this meeting at this time as you have already said it is getting very late, and I want to grab a late dinner."

Lady Allistair suggested two fancy restaurants, but Dr. O'Shea declined and said that he had not dined to date in the Pierre Hotel fancy restaurant. He would prefer to eat there. Lady Allistair led him downstairs to his limousine, and they separated for the night. The next day, Dr. O'Shea signed the letter offering Dr. McMillan the position of managing operations director in Mezi with an annual compensation of about 375,000 dollars. The letter was promptly sent to Barry Newcomb, who was expecting to talk to Dr. McMillan on his way back from Mezi in about two weeks later. Instead, Barry called Dr. McMillan still in Mezi with the news and faxed the signed letter of offer. Dr. McMillan accepted the position on the spot and made plans to come back to London much sooner to wrap some outstanding legal issues he was facing from his first wife's estate and to go back to his native Mezi second country and also to the still warm embraces of Anna Lourenco De Olivera, his common-law wife. Dr. McMillan thought that the new foundation position and its compensation, in addition to his chancellor's retirement income, would allow him to provide for a matrimonial standing that Anna had been asking for a long time, even though he knew that Anna did not care much about whatever income he was bringing home.

But for a very selfish and strange reason, Dr. McMillan was always very uncomfortable to live with Anna as a married couple using what he considered a meager retirement income which ranged in 120,000 dollars annually. When his first wife, Colette, would not grant him a legal divorce, he conveniently found plenty of excuses not to marry Anna, his two children's mother. When Colette passed away, he became frightful of any legal liability toward Colette's estate. So much so, when he retired as chancellor of Polytechnic University, he purposefully left Anna in Mezi and moved to London to address the estate's liabilities. After five or six years of wasteful legal research, there was still no material legal liability from Colette's estate to address. By the time, Barry Newcomb, the AMX lawyer, found him, he was very lonely and sorry that he had left behind in Mezi the love of his life. He was even more remorse that his children, now highly professional managers, would not forgive him for abandoning their mother in Mezi.

The faxed letter Dr. McMillan received was a saving grace to return to Mezi for good and finally to propose the long-lasting marriage to Anna. Hopefully, this would reconcile him with his children. Dr. McMillan mentioned to Anna that he was going back to London to wrap up some unfinished business and would come back to her for good. Anna, as always as serene, kissed her common-law husband and said that she had waited before for six years, and she was ready to wait for him for six times six times six years more until death does them apart. But she added, "Please do right by your children." Dr. O'Shea held the meeting to thank the Foundation staff for the excellent work accomplishments delivered in such short time.

Before leaving for the airport, he took Lady Allistair back to his office and asked her point blank if the whole Foundation project was in jeopardy in case of Mr. Kiriyan's departure or any other management changes projected in the just announced Amovir big meeting. Lady

Allistair protested the assertion. She apologized to the old professor if she gave such erroneous impression the day before. She explained that her family had long time and deep business relationship and connection with BI and Uncle Kiri. She saw any eventual departure of Uncle Kiri from BI management from that personal perspective. Besides, the talk of any management change was pure speculation on her part. She got a bit carried away with her own thoughts. She was sorry that she had led him to believe that the Foundation project was in jeopardy. She added that the Foundation was being funded for a long term at this time, for about twenty years at least. Dr. O'Shea was a bit reassured and took leave of the staff and Lady Allistair and flew to back to Louisville, Kentucky. When he reached Lexington later that night, he called Dr. Wasiri and gave him a detailed report of his trip.

He emphasized the overall eagerness his country people have shown to have him back home. He described the tremendous spirit of respect and regards the board members reserved toward his name and memory. He added that Dr. Wasiri should not wait until next year May or June before going back to Mezi. He suggested to his protégé to plan for a short visit of a week or two sometime around January before the beginning of spring semester. The trip would provide the university with a solid proof of his impending return. The trip would also give him a preliminary view of how he would settle his family in Mandi, which part of the city they would reside, the likely house they would rent or purchase, and which schools the children would attend. He would have also the opportunity to have a discussion around the tenured professorship he would apply for and any other professional occupations of interest which may come his way.

Dr. O'Shea also managed deftly to raise the prospect of Dr. Wasiri becoming the dean of the new Applied Sciences Faculty, but he left the prospect as part of the discussion Dr. Wasiri would have with the university chancellor when he would go there in January. This January trip would help cement a lot of things he did not feel ready to share with Dr. Wasiri at this time. At the end, Dr. O'Shea mentioned that he would be more than pleased to go along with him to Mezi in January. In his case, it will be simply to get a close look of the progress around the construction of the new buildings they have talked about. Dr. Wasiri did not hesitate a second and told him that he would be very happy to go to Mezi with him in January. After he hung up, he sent an urgent e-mail to Dr. Henry Umzigwe, the Polytechnic University chancellor of the January trip he would undertake with their native son, Dr. Wasiri. He also shared the positive response that Dr. Wasiri gave regarding the tenured professorship in the new Faculty and made it clear that the offer of the dean position was also raised but needs to be thoroughly discussed with Dr. Wasiri when he would come to Mezi. Dr. Umzigwe responded quickly and said that he was extremely delighted about the news and would be in good standing to prepare Dr. Wasiri's reception thoroughly to convince him to take both the dean and the tenured professorship positions. The next e-mail Dr. O'Shea sent to Lady Allistair was to share the results of his conversation with Dr. Wasiri. She also responded quickly and mentioned that this will be the best news to bring personally back to the Amovir meeting. She added that Uncle Kiri would be extremely pleased.

Lady Allistair also added that construction contractors would be visiting him next to start the setup of the remote office of the foundation chairman of the board in his present house. Whatever it would take would be paid for by the foundation. The construction or extension should take about three to four days. When he checked his calendar, it was about the fifteenth of November when he should be attending the ABDI board meeting in Atlanta. He should be fine away from the construction noises. He called Dr. Wasiri again to remind him about the Atlanta trip. He was up-to-date with this trip.

CHAPTER 12
ABDI First Board Meeting

Dr. O'Shea and Dr. Wasiri coordinated their flight to come and to stay in Atlanta where two weeks ago the Honorable Jeremy Massay, ABDI board chairman, and Dr. Stringer, ABDI board vice chairman had an excellent exchange around the top five projects to be reviewed at the first ABDI board meeting. After his honorable's trip to Washington and the memorable encounter with Lady Allistair, Dr. Stringer came to Atlanta to review the huge packet of documentation that his friend brought back.

They were inside one of the unfinished office room of the ABDI office in downtown Atlanta surrounded by the incredible construction noise around them. After extensive reading of the top twenty projects to present, Dr. Stringer was focusing over three water irrigation projects in the Sahel Region of the Republic of Mali, Republic of Senegal, and the Republic of Niger. These projects brought him back to his own PhD thesis around Development Economic in the Sahel Region presented at Duke University. The thesis proposed a cross-country water irrigation process. Although well received, the thesis never gained substantial advocacy in many economic development circles at FAO, FMI, or World Bank. The reason was that it underestimated the political, ethnic, regional, and country sensitivities around the Sahel Region. Dr. Stringer begged his friend to aggregate the three projects into one major regional project.

He requested to take over the overall design of the project for presentation to the board. His honorable, impressed by his friend's dedication, delightfully obliged. Three days later, they met again. This time Dr. Stringer had two sets of water irrigation projects: one in the West Africa, another in the East Africa. The project will consist of first desalinating water from Atlantic Ocean and Indian Ocean and using extensive elevated pipelines to bring water from the coast to most arid and semi-desert areas of the region, the Sahel in the west, the Ogaden in the east. In the West Africa, the logistics of the project start with a huge desalinating combine south of the town of St. Louis in Senegal, the water would then travel east in the elevated pipelines across the St. Louis Province then into Mali in the northern parts of the provinces of Kayes, Koulikoro, and Segou.

Then the water will go north through the provinces of Toumbouctoo, Kidal, and Gao crossing into Niger in the province of Tahoua and the southern part of Agadez toward the provinces of Zinder,

Diffa, and Kanem at the last stop in the town of Agadem. In each of the mentioned provinces, a decision will be made with local authorities about how much of the water distribution would take place to which towns, villages, or water irrigation areas. The St. Louis-Agadem project was a regional project crossing three countries within three time zones. The East Africa project will start also with a huge desalinating combine in the golf of Atara in Djibouti then the water will be carried south into Ethiopia through the valley of Rift across the lower eastern part of Ahmar Mountains to reach the Ogaden Region around K'ebri Dehar, continuing south toward Somalia all the way to the town of Sinadhago.

The West Africa project was more expensive than the East Africa project, yet much more feasible, given the relatively integrated economies of the three West African countries from the French colonial time. The East Africa project was similarly urgent, but country political conflicts were major obstacles to trump the project. Dr. Stringer decided to push the West Africa project as effectively as he can. The remaining projects were relatively small compared to the huge water irrigation project. They consist of a cooperative of five vast fish farms in Cameroon, an agriculture marketing support in Ouganda in charge of buying high plateau tea harvest from about hundred villages, a rice extensive agricultural project in Burkina Fasso, a recently found copper mines development in Zambia, and a micro-finance bank to support about three hundred agricultural cooperative farms already using micro-credit facilities in large plains of central Tanzania. Dr. Stringer delved into each project with additional extensive documentation covering every aspect of the project impacts as to spare no details and to raise no doubt to future successful implementation of each project. His honorable was very proud of his friend's overall dedication. He felt lucky to have brought him along into ABDI. Together with the staff they have hired, they prepared for the first board members' meeting. They had about seventeen additional board members, four coming from the United States, two from England, two from France, and seven from Africa. They were a good mix and all specialized in their respective fields and highly recommended. Most of the members have attended various African Economic Development conferences Dr. Stringer had attended. The only two exceptions were Dr. O'Shea and Dr. Wasiri. His Honorable Jeremy Massay knew that Lady Allistair, who had bankrolled this whole institute, selected these two scientists.

There was no point to question their selection. As a matter of fact, his honorable decided, a special attention should be paid to these two honorable guest board members who could have been especially delegated to the meeting to spy on his management of the meeting. His honorable suggested to his friend Dr. Stringer to be extra careful with the two professors from Kentucky. Dr. Stringer reassured his honorable that he would go toe to toe with the special guests from Kentucky. They went over the agenda of the board meeting and other arrangements. They were ready to receive their distinguished guests the next day, November fifteenth.

Dr. Wasiri picked up his mentor in Lexington and drove to Louisville to catch the flight to Atlanta. They arrived at about seven o'clock and literally sat in the traffic for an hour in the limousine before getting to the North Plaza Hilton Hotel on Peachtree Circle Plaza almost next to the ABDI building. His Honorable State Senator Jeremy Massay met them at the hotel lobby, ABDI board chairman followed by a Dr. Stringer introduced as board vice chairman. They exchanged pleasant greetings, and the Kentucky scientists were invited to join other board members who have arrived before in the private dining room on the fifth floor of the hotel after they had a chance to freshen up from the flight and the long ride from the airport to the hotel. When Dr. O'Shea and Dr. Wasiri came down to the fifth floor, the other board members, having predinner cocktails, were already engaged in spirited conversation and debate about the various projects proposed for review at the board meeting. Dr. Wasiri had a chance to read the summaries of the proposed projects that were included in the board-meeting package sent a week ago. Dr. O'Shea did not see the package which was in the pile of mails he found when he came back from the Mezi trip. He was completely lost in the topics of conversation that was taking place. Noticing how much out of place his mentor was among the board members, Dr. Wasiri summoned him to stay as close to him as possible and to remain as vague as possible. He also noticed that Dr. Stringer was staying very close to them every time they moved about the private room before they were asked to take their seats at the dining table. As by coincidence, Dr. Stringer was seated next to Dr. Wasiri. Dr. Stringer inquired about his background and wondered why he had never met him in various African Economic Development conferences he had attended since he became the director of African Studies Institute. Every year, he usually attends a minimum of three of these conferences, Dr. Stringer confided. Dr. Wasiri explained that the last time he attended one of these conferences was about eight years ago in Chicago. He made a presentation around mining extraction economics in southern region of Africa.

Dr. Wasiri added that he had not been invited back to these conferences. Then he joked that maybe his presentation was full of too many precise engineering technical terms well beyond the abstruse logic of economists given to five or more views of the same condition. They laughed at the comparison between economists and engineers and were joined by Dr. O'Shea seated also next to Dr. Wasiri. Dr. Stringer managed to add that no condition in this world of sciences is completely explained, as soon or later an improvement is made to the last explanation of the condition. And according to this theory of permanent change, Dr. Stringer said that economic theory will always trump over engineering concepts at all the time.

It was already time for His Honorable State Senator Jeremy Massay, ABDI board chairman to greet the seventeen board members in Atlanta to attend the board meeting starting at ten o'clock the next day. He invited each one of them to read carefully the updated summaries of the proposed projects they would review at the meeting. He then toasted the attendees for a successful first board meeting. Afterward, during the dinner, Dr. Stringer continued probing deftly Dr. Wasiri's background while Dr. O'Shea followed carefully their exchange. Dr. Wasiri responded as superficially, generally, and politely as he could.

`But when he asked Dr. Wasiri if he knew a Lady Allistair, Dr. O'Shea jumped in furtively and said that Dr. Wasiri had joined the board under his strong recommendation to those who have funded ABDI. Dr. O'Shea mentioned that he did so because Dr. Wasiri, from Mezi and by the way one of the best students he had the honor to mentor at the University of Kentucky and currently a full-tenured professor teaching Mining Sciences at the Kentucky State University, would make an excellent advocate of economic development endeavors in Africa. He also added that Dr. Wasiri does not know Lady Allistair who approved his recommendation to have Dr. Wasiri to join ABDI board.

Looking Dr. Stringer straight in the eyes, Dr. O'Shea said, "If you want to know anything else regarding myself or Dr. Wasiri's attendance or participation to this meeting, I would appreciate that you direct your questions to me." Dr. Wasiri was surprised by the grave tone that his mentor had taken. He tried to calm him down and turned toward Dr. Stringer to inquire about the meaning of the lines of questioning he was subjecting him to a point to get his colleague all riled up.

At the sight of a commotion that was burgeoning where his friend was seated, his honorable came quickly to join his side of the long dining table and asked Dr. Stringer to get up and join him on the side. After a few minutes, the two friends came back to the Kentucky guests and apologized for the unfortunate lines of questioning and begged Dr. O'Shea, already standing up, to stay and finish his dinner. His honorable took the seat next Dr. O'Shea and continued to apologize for his friend, Dr. Stringer, who disappeared from the private dining table.

When the dinner was over, His Honorable Jeremy Massay took Dr. O'Shea on the side for another conversation, while Dr. Wasiri was engaged in animated conversation with other board members about the merits of using oil pricing as a development weapon. Dr. O'Shea explained to his honorable that he was surprised to see Dr. Stringer ganging up on Dr. Wasiri as if he was unwelcome to the board meeting. He added that he reacted so violently because he was keenly responsible of the presence and the attendance of Dr. Wasiri in ABDI board meeting in Atlanta. He said that he was the one who communicated to Dr. Wasiri the need to join the board of an institution he thought highly of after many conversations with various contacts in the academic and business circles, including Lady Allistair whom he had been in constant contacts after providing various consultancy works over AMX mining projects around the world. He said throughout many of the conversations he had with Lady Allistair, he was convinced that it was obvious to him that AMX was lacking in building a lot of goodwill in many places where it conducts business. As a matter of fact, he had insisted to Lady Allistair to start a major goodwill effort for Africa, a continent where AMX had been last to invest and where, as you know, economic development was seriously lagging.

Professor O'Shea continued, "This was the reason why Lady Allistair came to that conference in Athens, Georgia, and sought after the most prominent African American attending the conference. She was lucky to run into your presentation which was well received by all participants, especially those who came from Africa. After convincing you, Honorable Jeremy Massay, to take the helm of ABDI, Lady Allistair asked me to join the board, and I saw to it to engage Dr. Wasiri to join as well for obvious reasons. And here we are. Honorable Jeremy Massay, you can see now how disappointed I was to hear Dr. Stringer, who identified himself as your deputy, asking Dr. Wasiri a lot of questions over confidential matters, which have made this association possible and of which he has no knowledge.

I don't know what relationship you have with the fellow, I would trust that you share with him the background I have just provided you in order to prevent further embarrassment. Otherwise, I would be compelled to report my total disappointment about this board meeting to Lady Allistair, and I don't need to tell you what will ensue."

His honorable seized the full extent of the threat and assured Dr. O'Shea that he would do everything in his power that such incident would never repeat. But what struck his honorable more than this threat was the sight of a ring on one of the fingers of the old professor's left hand. His honorable had never seen such a ring in his life with a multicolored shining motif on top in a shape of capital letter K. The shape of the ring fascinated him greatly when Dr. O'Shea was talking, shaking his finger with the ring for emphasis. At one point, his honorable was tempted to change the subject and ask the professor where he got such an obviously powerful ring. He thought better and did not venture there, given the circumstances. Instead, he came back to the matter at hand. He would instruct Dr. Stringer to use an appropriate conduct for the remaining of the board meeting. His honorable also wondered deep down if his DC encounter with Lady Allistair would not provide a cover for him in case things went bad. He thought that he should have kept the red tread that he discarded so quickly at the airport so not to upset Vanessa's rules. At the end, his honorable resolved that ABDI was too important a gig to jeopardy it over this old professor's outburst. He would call his buddy Dr. Stringer back in order. Then thinking back how they got to this mess, he was the one who had triggered Dr. Stringer's suspicion and was almost paying for it now.

When all the board members retired to their rooms, his honorable went straight to his friend's room, which was next to his, and found him contrite. His honorable gave his friend the same background that Dr. O'Shea had provided and told him that they almost blew the gold gig they dreamed of all their lives before even it started. His honorable instructed his friend to wake up early and find out when Dr. O'Shea and Dr. Wasiri would be down for their breakfast and join them while expressing the most heartfelt apology, mentioning no name nor Lady Allistair. Dr. Stringer should limit his conversation to the presentation he was going to make around the West Africa Water Irrigation Project. At the same time, Dr. Wasiri was leading Dr. O'Shea to his room and asking about the reason of his outburst and who the hell was Lady Allistair. Dr. O'Shea finessed his reply saying that he was disappointed with this Dr. Stringer asking him questions he could not answer.

Knowing that Dr. Wasiri was not going to verify what he was about to say, Dr. O'Shea embellished Lady Allistair's background, he said that she was an English businesswoman in charge of AMX marketing in the United States as well as a US Chamber of Commerce executive officer. He added that under the umbrella of the US Chamber of Commerce, Lady Allistair had been prominent in raising funds from many American companies with extensive African operations to establish ABDI. Dr. O'Shea stated that Lady Allistair was engaged into this endeavor on benevolent basis, and the fact that Dr. Stringer raised her name when he knew that she was loath to take any credit for raising funds for ABDI was an act of betrayal he could not tolerate. He concluded that Dr. Stringer made matters worse when he asked Dr. Wasiri if he knew her. Dr. O'Shea was deeply incensed and offended that the name of this good lady be brought up so publicly. That was the only reason of his reaction. He also told his protégé to forget the incident. He had a long talk with His Honorable Jeremy Massay and that all had been patched up. Dr. Wasiri shook his head in disbelief and walked back to his room. While in his room, he thought about the whole story and decided that Dr. O'Shea was not telling him the whole story and as usual trying to protect him for some strange reasons. He had been getting used to his behavior by now. If Dr. O'Shea insists on keeping this Lady Allistair in the dark, it was all right and fine with him. But why the secret? He could not answer the last question and went to sleep.

At the same instance, before going to sleep, Dr. O'Shea rehashed the same story. He hated himself for having overreacted to Dr. Stringer's inquiries. There was a better way to handle the situation. But sometime Emily's rules take over, and he can become the worse of the mission protector. When the name of Lady Allistair was brought up, Dr. O'Shea saw only the unwinding of all that he had built to date to further Emily's rules in these last segments of the battle. What if the pivotal role of Lady Allistair in getting Dr. Wasiri to Mezi was revealed? How was Dr. Wasiri going to react? He reflected that he had no choice but to nip it in the bud as the football fans love to say. It did not matter whether his honorable and his friend were shaken to the core, especially with the threat he laid on them. Emily's rules must prevail. Dr. O'Shea went to sleep. He was awake at about eight the next morning and called his protégé to join him downstairs for a breakfast. While he was in the hotel main dining area in the lobby, he was surprised to see Dr. Stringer joining him and apologizing profusely for the incident the night before and assuring him that it would not happen again. While he was about to leave, Dr. Wasiri showed up and Dr. Stringer repeated the same apology.

The Kentucky scientists thanked DR. Stringer politely and assured him that they understood. When he was gone, Dr. O'Shea waved his hand as to tell his protégé to forget about the silly affair. He changed the story completely and asked Dr. Wasiri how Hasbo had reacted in learning that both of them were going to Mezi in January. Dr. Wasiri laughed and said that it had been better than honeymoon for Hasbo since. He joked that his wife would not leave him alone a minute from the time he had mentioned the trip. Any time they were alone in the house, Hasbo found herself in her birth clothing and in heat. Hasbo was acting as if her husband was going to Mezi for a long long time, and she needed to make sure that her scent was forever left on all his most intimate parts. Twice the last week, they were almost caught by the children returning from school if she had not locked all doors. The children had to call them from the neighbor's house to come in. Twice they were very busy in the basement and could not hear the main door ring. It had become a bit embarrassing with the kids around. He was now wondering if the kids suspected something weird with their parents. Dr. Wasiri concluded that he was very relieved to go on this Atlanta trip to take some rest. His mentor then raised the laughter by saying that at this rate, it is not her scent Dr. Wasiri needs to worry about, rather Mrs. Wasiri will be expecting a triplet by the time they will reach Mezi in May and June of next year. He added that Dr. Wasiri should enjoy the attention as much as he can, youth and happiness allowing. The conversation made for a merry breakfast morning before the board meeting.

When they reached the ABDI office conference room, all members were already seated, and the meeting started at ten o'clock sharp. His Honorable Jeremy Massay delivered a relatively short welcoming speech. Then he asked each board member starting with himself to introduce himself/herself to the assembly by giving their full name, title, qualification, country of origin and residence, current occupation, and main area of interest to assist ABDI. The introduction took a good part of the morning session. The introduction offered overall a board with an impressive array of expertise, leaning more on economics but with solid background in medicine, engineering, law, basic and social sciences. The board gender and race composition was also well balanced including six women and thirteen men—seven Caucasians, two Arabs from the Maghreb Region, six black Africans, and four African Americans. Before the lunch break, each board member was given a huge ABDI board member package leather bound which included the institute objectives, goals, and bylaws, board members' functions, responsibilities, and compensation schedules.

In addition, the members received another package with the detailed documentation of each of the proposed projects to be reviewed later in the afternoon.

A motion electing the board secretary was read and a sixty-year-old African American lady by the name of Marcy Jones-Bytone, an econometrician from the University of California, Berkeley, was unanimously selected. She was promptly seated as board secretary. Her first duty was to propose to the board members a ranking of the proposed projects by order of discussion priority. The ranking was quickly disposed of with the largest funding project closing the review time. The new board secretary's second duty was to call for a lunch break, which was promptly approved to the entire board's relief. It was almost one o'clock. The meeting resumed at three in the afternoon. Dr. Stringer led the proposed projects' review discussion. The proposed projects in Cameroon, Burkina Fasso, Ouganda, and Tanzania with initial investments of less than thirty-million dollars were discussed in less than two hours and half. They were lauded as specific endeavors responding to respective country priorities. The general expectation was that in order to advance the agreement of these projects from local populations and authorities, a shared responsibility in the funding of these projects should be the first order of priority. ABDI would not start implementing these projects unless the respective country government was ready to afford and pay between 10 to 15 percent of the initial investment cost. That condition was viewed as necessary to increase local commitment to the eventual success of the project. The general concurrence was that the results of these initial investments would need to be carefully monitored to allow for future investments being internally generated by these projects.

Dr. Stringer turned out to be an eloquent proponent of these criteria, and he navigated seamlessly from each aspect of the project to another. His general and accurate preparation for guiding the review of these projects showed. So much so that he was applauded when he requested a time out for the entire board before moving to the review of the last two projects. During the break, Dr. Wasiri, willing to give the due where it was rightly deserved, approached Dr. Stringer and congratulated him for the excellent presentation he made of the intricate project proposals and for guiding the board on a swift approval of these proposals. Dr. Wasiri added that he wanted to commend him for reinforcing the criteria to trigger the projects' initial investments. He said that he had always wished that those at FMI, World Bank, and UN used the same criteria in order to raise the level of local commitment to these projects.

He insisted that many of projects promoted by these well-meaning development organizations have floundered for lack of support and commitment by local government or authority. The only way to gain such commitment was to engage local government to pay for a certain percentage of the initial investments, however small. Then the local government priority would become, like any other investor's, to recoup the initial investment by providing a sustained engagement to the overall project-management process. Dr. Wasiri asked Dr. Stringer what prompted him to include such interesting criteria in these projects' proposals.

Dr. Stringer happily obliged by saying that he was only practicing what he had preached for a long time in his own Economic Development classes at the University of Georgia in Athens, and he was only applying the central tenet of his own PhD thesis around Development Economics in the Republic of Ghana from independence time through the year he was completing his post-graduate studies at Duke University. Dr. Wasiri was much impressed by the depth of his involvement and commitment and said that there was a serious need of his approach in many economic development circles. Dr. Stringer was delighted to get all this consideration from a colleague scientist who was thoroughly displeased by his unflattering behavior the night before. This meant a lot for him more than anything that day. He thought that maybe, just maybe, in this ABDI business, he should stick to what he knows best, Development Economics, then he would do all right.

Dr. Stringer guided the next two proposed projects with the same virtuoso as the one exhibited from one in the afternoon. He laid all the economic benefits and constraints for the mining project in Zambia. This project required a higher initial investment of about 160 million dollars and calling for a larger initial monetary commitment from the government. Both Kentucky scientists, Dr. O'Shea and Dr. Wasiri, experts in mining technologies provided eloquent support to the technical feasibility of the project to the delight of His Honorable Jeremy Massay and Dr. Stringer. The general concurrence was gained from the board member to advance the project to a preliminary review of the project with government officials to be invited to Atlanta in about a month. The results of this preliminary review would help assess how far the Zambia government would be committed to the project. The final review covered the West African Water Irrigation Project, the brainchild of Dr. Stringer who did not spare anything to argue the propriety of the project.

He covered the financials, economics, technical logistics, political concerns at regional and country levels, the various tribal and ethnic allegiances, the daunting extreme climatic environment of the Sahel Region, various partners needed to fund the project, including the governments and international development agencies, the seven-year timeline to complete the project and the ability of the project to earn its keeps at every stage of its implementation and before the final delivery, and laying of pipeline at the Agadem town in the Niger. Dr. Stringer spoke for about two hours and half in support of this project. Board members realized at the end that in this project, they faced a monumental undertaking of grave economic and political implications. They wisely tabled the motion to continue to fully digest different aspects of the project during the evening break. This will allow them to come back the next day fully charged to thoroughly review the project and to decide how to insure to advance the project evaluated at more than a billion and a half dollars. The board members divided themselves in working groups for the evening reviews of various aspects of the project: financials, economics, logistics, politics, water pipelines engineering, and so on. They took their dinner in their respective groups and retired to their rooms accordingly.

Afterward, when they were alone and left behind, His Honorable Jeremy Massay could not contain himself; he gave his friend Dr. Stringer a double high-five salute and shouted his name, "Jimmy, my man, what a show you pulled out there! I am very proud of you. This was a top-notch presentation you gave out there. You left every board member and me speechless. You left no doubt in the board members' mind that we mean business, and they also got to earn their part with homework to boot. Man, oh man! That was a class act with a big C. I owe you the largest glass of twenty-years Scotch you need right now. Let's go down to the hotel bar and unwind a bit. Jimmy, my man."

When they reached the hotel bar, they could see not a single board member in sight. They were all upstairs in groups, reviewing the project and gathering questions to ask tomorrow morning. His honorable and Dr. Stringer quietly sipped the twenty-years Scotch, watching a basketball game on the TV, fully aware and convinced that for all practical purposes they have earned the ABDI board chair and vice chair. The gold gig was now definitely theirs. They were now so focused on their keeps for ABDI agenda that the sight of two bodacious and out-of-sight ladies prancing around the hotel bar did not remotely interest them as they continued to analyze and evaluate the progress of the basketball game.

They were absolutely not interested in wasting any time in less than intellectual or sports pursuit. Strangely and with a lot of convinction, his honorable noticed that Dr. Stringer ladies player's mind was completely absent. The presence of the two bodacious ladies in the bar did not register a bit for Dr. Stringer. His honorable did not hesitate to share his observation for his friend as loudly as he could. But Dr. Stringer remained focused on the the day major endeavors. Besides, he added his time to tie the knots was approaching very fast, as he had told his honorable previously. He had already made the longtime expected presentation of that lady from Emory to his sisters and mother. And nuptials are being planned sometime around the coming Christmas holiday when Suzette Beaulieu would become Mrs. Stringer. He insisted to see his honorable and his wife come to the small wedding ceremony in his mother's farm as soon as the wedding day is finalized. Dr. Stringer laughed and said that he can still look at the temptation evolving around him and that will be the extent of it. Besides, he added, why bother with the loose ones and loose changes when the Billion Dollar West African Water Irrigation Project is gathering steam upstairs. His honorable Jeremy Massey, Chairman of ABDI, did not need anymore justification from his learned friend from that time on.

It was time to go to sleep and take some well-deserved rest. The next day, board members fired a lot of questions to Dr. Stringer about the project. Fully prepared, Dr. Stringer answered them all and removed every doubt around the huge project undertaking. He said, "I would not pretend that this project would go on without any problem. As you have already appreciated, it requires a tremendous organization and management to bring it to its successful end. The fact that it crosses three countries makes it all the more ambitious. But after analyzing it and weighing all the benefits accrued to this project, especially the ones related to stopping the slow encroaching expansion of the desert in the Sahel Region over the three countries, I am seriously hopeful of the future success of the project if not now but in the very near future." The board definitely concurred and gave a lengthy timeline, including first, the review of the project with concerned country governments, then the review with international development agencies, followed by the review with the French government with solid, not to underestimate, political and economic interests in the region. The board suggested that the results of these multiple reviews should throw the basis and constraints around the progress of the project. The board also added the need to appoint as urgently as possible a project manager for the West African Water Irrigation undertaking. It was about noon when the review of the last project was completed to every board's satisfaction.

It was time to close the first board meeting and set the agenda for the next board meeting in February of next year. Board members had their lunch and took leave of each other.

When all visitors departed, his honorable went back to his huge office along with Dr. Stringer and thanked their luck for a wonderful first board meeting of ABDI. The next day, his honorable gave a call to Lady Allistair to report the wonderful first board meeting. Lady Allistair said that she had already received tremendous feedback from the attendees who were very impressed about the meeting's organization and presentation. Lady Allistair also added that the West African Water Irrigation Project was extremely well received, and AMX with its extensive business contacts should be of immense assistance to the project. She suggested having a review of this project with AMX management in the near future in New York City. She was also looking forward to meet Dr. Stringer who had done an excellent presentation of the proposed projects. At the end, Lady Allistair said that she was lucky to have selected his honorable to be ABDI board chairman. His honorable then reached his friend Dr. Stringer, already back in Athens and transmitted the good news and considerations from Lady Allistair. Dr. Stringer thanked his friend and invited him and his wife to his wedding now scheduled at the end of the Christmas week on Friday. Wedding invitation cards would be forthcoming.

CHAPTER 13
New AMX CEO

The ABDI successful first board meeting will turn out to be the second batch of good news Lady Allistair was ready to deliver to Uncle Kiri at the urgent management meeting that was called and for which she was getting ready for when His Honorable Jeremy Massay called. The first batch included the long expected news that Dr. Wasiri was going to Mezi to prepare for his definitive return. Dr. O'Shea had delivered as requested by Uncle Kiri at the last international conference held in Amovir. It should be noted, Lady Allistair thought, that all engagement steps that Uncle Kiri wanted were being faithfully executed. Dr. Wasiri was on his way to Mezi, and ABDI, as an arm of BI's goodwill display throughout Africa, was beautifully engaged under the leadership of His Honorable Jeremy Massay. Although there was a lingering intimate price, she was struggling to get rid of in the latter ABDI case, Dr. Wasiri's case was being handled above reproach by the good old professor who had taken hold of every lever to advance this goal. She had sometimes questioned the professor's zeal in this endeavor and wondered whether he had a personal agenda to get Dr. Wasiri home in Mezi. But now after the emotional outburst that the old professor gave at the sight of his wife's name adorning the Foundation entrance on Park Avenue, Lady Allistair understood the zeal to be a personal commitment to accomplish whatever his beloved wife had set for him before her passing and before he joined her on the other side. Whatever Emily O'Shea had set had moved Dr. O'Shea unconditionally. There was no point trying to find out what it was as long as it was bringing tangible results.

Lady Allistair called up the company limousine service to pick her up at six in the evening for the long trip to Amovir by way of New York to Frankfort, Germany, exchanging into a BI private jet to Amovir. Altogether, it was a tiring sixteen hours flight from New York Kennedy Airport. Lady Allistair took care to arrive at least a day before any business meeting to give her time to unwind and reconnect with longtime contacts, including Ludmilla Borensky, her first same-sex lover who came back to Amovir from the London AMX office assignment that Lady Allistair secured for her after she claimed to be terribly homesick. But the real reason was on the account of Lady Allistair.

She was not coming back to London as frequently as promised when she discovered the unbelievable lesbian scene of New York City with an array of ever-young and ever-mixed blood vixens well beyond the

Nordic blonde bombs of years past. But while she was visiting with different BI contacts that day, she received an express call from Uncle Kiri who wanted to talk to her in private over dinner that evening before the next day's scheduled management meeting. She was shocked by the invitation and went back to her visitor's bungalow to collect her thoughts. She did not even attempt to call Ludmilla who had left numerous messages on her phone and sent her a huge bouquet of flowers with a note saying, "A tread for longtime memories," their usual code to anticipate a long night of extreme sexual cavorting. Lady Allistair did not notice the flowers on the bungalow living room and did not read the message. She went straight to the bathroom and took a shower and gave herself a large glass of vodka before hitting the sack to calm her nerves.

She woke up around six when she received a call from one of Uncle Kiri's attendants advising that he will be by her bungalow in about forty-five minutes to pick her up for the dinner with Mr. Kiriyan. She was ready in no time but still a ball of fired-up nerves waiting for the car transportation. She was led to Mr. Kiriyan's villa outside the corporate compound and was extremely relieved when Uncle Kiri himself came out to greet her and took her to the room where he had already started having his soup. Uncle Kiri did not change a bit since the last time she saw him about three years ago, and there was no sign of the terrible illness rumored affecting him.

He still carried the same complexion of "rich aristocrat on top of the world" about him. He did not look the eighty-six years old people and the corporate rumor mill gave him. He was erect and svelte. He held Lady Allistair's hand firmly and guided her to the appointed chair directly opposite to his. He started by excusing himself for having his soup ahead of the arrival of his guest. Doctors who look after him dictated this. He had to take his soup at a certain appointed time of the day, no later or sooner. The main course would be arriving soon after he had finished sharing what he wanted to do.

He went on, "Lady Allistair, there is a time for everything. I wanted to brief you on a few management changes I would announce tomorrow. Since you would be the centerpiece of those changes, I wanted to provide you at this time with an advance notice of these changes. First of all, your family and I have worked for a long time before and after the merger of AMX with BI.

Our business working collaboration has been year after year very successful, and we have made tons of money along the way. It was not by accident that you came over to us for training and rapid management progress. I have watched you with a great source of pride rising along our management ladder to the current position of AMX-US executive marketing chief, and you have delivered successfully and consistently. To tell you the truth, your family has waited to see you evolve similarly in a longtime matrimonial set before moving you up further the ladder. But that was not to be, and I understand that. With the declining health of your uncle, I have decided to trust the whole management of AMX into your hands. You would be appointed CEO of AMX effective tomorrow. You would have to come to London when you have closed on the Mezi assignment, if you know what I mean. Actually, closing the Mezi assignment would be a misnomer. The Mezi assignment, thanks to your invaluable efforts, would become central to both BI and AMX so much so that BI headquarters would need to move closer to the action. BI would move its headquarters to a French island along African coast named Varonne-Sur-Baie. Remember that name. Our stay in Amovir is overstated. I have convinced the power structure in Moscow that in order to advance Russia's interests in high multinational business environment, BI needs to have a multinational headquarters in less conspicuous location outside Russia. Varonne-Sur-Baie, a small French island would do the trick. Amovir will remain as the Russian headquarters for our considerable Russian operations that at this stage are contributing below 20 percent of our total revenues on yearly basis. For that reason it was, as you like to put it, a piece of cake to make the case to Moscow Center for our move that should be completed in about three years.

"The French are very excited to have us in Varonne-Sur-Baie. They have given BI a long-term lease of a large section of undeveloped land on the southern part of Varonne-Sur-Baie to build our corporate compound, which will be as big as almost what we have here in Amovir, the difference being that this new compound will be very high tech and ultramodern. We are still negotiating with the French to have our own private jet landing strip. That should be granted eventually. I realize the concern about French government's so-called unfriendly relationship with corporate world in general with high taxes and much regulation. That has been thoroughly evaluated. And believe me, BI is getting a lot of latitude in both areas that I am not ready to share at this time. Besides, any time a company is ready to invest in excess of five billions of dollars anywhere in the world, some dispensation should come along the way. You would probably see the unbelievable design of the compound tomorrow.

These are the news that I wanted to share with you before tomorrow meeting. There will be some other management changes in BI of no concern to you. Now tell me, Lady Allistair, how does it feel to be the CEO of AMX?"

Lady Allistair was motionless for about ten seconds, digesting what Uncle Kiri was telling her. She only managed to get up and give a kiss on the brow of her cherished Uncle Kiri. After she regained her composure, Lady Allistair said, "AMX CEO, I never thought about it, to tell you the truth. Frankly, after the matrimonial fiasco with that jerk, Sir Georges Allistair, I knew that I would be working the rest of my life for an uncle or a cousin in AMX. And that was going to be the case according to my side of the family AMX ownership. I don't know what you did to change my family minds, but I certainly appreciate the confidence and the honor to lead AMX. I would do everything in my power to merit this mark of confidence. I thank you very much, Uncle Kiri. Talking of Mezi engagement, I brought good news. First, Dr. Wasiri is going in January to Mezi to put the final touches and to prepare his return to Mezi as professor to the Polytechnic University. He would go there with his mentor, you remember, the good old professor O'Shea, who has consistently delivered in this mission. The second good news concern the ABDI that you requested to put in place in order to enhance BI goodwill all over Africa. Well, ABDI had a very successful first board meeting under the leadership of His Honorable Georgia Senator Jeremy Massay seconded by a very able Dr. Stringer. One of ABDI's proposed projects is the West African Water Irrigation Project that will bring water to many regions of the Sahel in three former French colonies, Senegal, Mali, and Niger. You need to look very closely into this project. After what you would announce tomorrow, this project would buy a tremendous goodwill from both the French government and these former French colonies. Talking of coincidence, it does not get any better than this. I understand very well when you say to close the Mezi assignment. As far as I know, this means Dr. Wasiri is back in Mezi working on Alpha-M issues.

The motion to get to this condition is far gone, and I am convinced that there is no point of return. Uncle Kiri, again I want to thank you for the confidence you have shown to me to lead AMX."

While they talked, a couple by the name of Dudarev brought the main course of dinner consisting of salmon with rice pilaf. Lady Allistair quickly devoured her dinner while Uncle Kiri went back eating the same soup he had before. In the middle of the dinner, the male Dudarev came back with an urgent note for Uncle Kiri, who excused himself for the rest of the dinner.

Very excited, Lady Allistair took a ride back to the bungalow where she noticed the bedroom already lighted. She opened the front door with caution and tiptoed inside to catch whoever was in the bedroom. Before she could put the light on in the living room, a tall naked sensuous lady was embracing her. She recognized right away Ludmilla's scent. She was about to protest her ways when Ludmilla took her hand and guided it to her wet and moist lower part, softly repeating their code, "A tread for longtime memories." Lady Allistair continued to tiptoe now to her bedroom discarding each garment along the way. By the time she lay on the bed, Ludmilla was devouring her lower part, and before she knew it, Lady Allistair went in trance and managed a violent jet stream all over her face and her blonde hair and collapsed. Five minutes later, Lady Allistair was in tears repeating uncontrollably, "A tread for longtime memories." Ludmilla consoled her with tender kisses until she fell to sleep.

Lady Allistair woke up the next day as AMX CEO. When she entered the management meeting's huge conference room, she had an appointed seat next to the chairman of BI, Mr. Nadov Kiriyan. It was apparent that she was about to be made an important member of BI management committee. It was an after-thought when Mr. Kiriyan came to announce a series of BI management committee changes and the first being Lady Allistair's appointment to AMX CEO position in replacement of his uncle Robert Mendham, who was retiring effective December 31 of that year. A round of applause greeted the announcement, Lady Allistair, rose and bowed to the lengthy applause. When she sat down, Mr. Kiriyan continued his speech with a series of announcements affecting both the Russian, Middle East, and AsiaPac BI operations. The Russian BI operations remained firmly in hands of newly appointed young Russian managers, most recently graduated from the best Russian and Western best universities and highly specialized post-graduate schools. A good portion of these managers also graduated from current KGB/FSS operations to continue the same BI reliance on and influence over the Russian political and security leadership. Karlov Yelgin, a twenty-eight-year veteran of BI and contacts with Kremlin, supervised this younger crew as managing director of the Russian operations. The Middle East and AsiaPac BI business was thrust upon either locally grown managers or AMX British and American expatriates and highly sought-after managers. One major exception among those newly appointed managers in BI Middle East headquarters in Dubai turned out to be no other but the son of Dr. McMillan, the oil engineer Alberto McMillan, who had been making a name for himself since leaving ARAMCO in Jeddah, Saudi Arabia, and working as a highly paid oil consultant for various oil companies operating in the Emirates.

After Barry Newcomb, the AMX British lawyer learned about Alberto from his father, an intense recruiting effort followed to bring him to BI Middle East operations. He was finally hired and appointed BI deputy managing executive director for oil operations in Dubai. Dr. McMillan was happily surprised to learn about this appointment. So was his mother Anna in Mezi. For Barry Newcomb and Mr. Kiriyan, the

Alberto's appointment had a definitive Mezi undertone. What surprised Lady Allistair, listening to the series of management changes, was the fact that Mr. Kiriyan did not mention the real reasons of the changes with the exception of the perfunctory search for BI growth. There was also no mention of the eventual move of BI headquarters from Amovir to the French island of Varonne-Sur-Baie. Maybe, Lady Allistair thought, Uncle Kiri was sparing Russian sensibilities about their declining contribution to the overall profitability of the giant company and the need to mute the real multinational business inclination of BI. In fact, what was apparent, BI had never been managed as a true multinational company with worldwide business operations around a centralized management lead. BI was looked upon as a Russian company because its main visible business operations were based all over the Russian territory. It was never clear what international business operations fell under BI controls. With the exception of AMX, where there was a direct controlling interest, BI acted more in the mode of an investment house with substantial but noncontrolling percentage of shares of thousands of mining and oil companies throughout the world. BI was most satisfied with a percentage of shares below controlling interest. Even with AMX, there was no strong management imprint from BI or Mr. Kiriyan. AMX had a management structure with no apparent links to BI's management structure except to Mr. Kiriyan himself. This management suited Mr. Kiriyan in the past for obvious reasons. However, the meeting that he called this time was the beginning of management changes Mr. Kiriyan wanted to impose over BI for the first time. He wanted to manage BI now as a worldwide conglomerate with unique, consistent, and transparent business strategy and business goals equivalent to those of multinational companies.

It was therefore apparent that Amovir was not an appropriate location to conduct such a business. French island of Varonne-Sur-Baie, somewhere in Indian Ocean, was ideal. Then why announce it to this Russian audience? When Lady Allistair was mentally reviewing what was taking place, she received another note from Uncle Kiriyan inviting her back to conclude their dinner meeting that was interrupted the night before. At the end of Mr. Kiriyan's two-hour presentation, the management committee members present in Amovir were invited to a lunch.

However, the lining of BI management committee members had produced a definite negative mental impact on the Russian managing director. This completely escaped both Uncle Kiriyan and Lady Allistair. Karlov Yelgin, a confirmed communist, was still partial to the past reading of Kremlin leadership apparatus lining game. To be seated about ten seats away from the chairman of BI revealed to Yelgin how far down his operations management ranked in the current BI scheme of things. And worse, there was not a single true blood Russian at the chairman sides. Lady Allistair, an English lady from AMX, was at his left side and an Arab managing director of Middle East Operations was at his right side followed by more French, English, Indian, and other managing directors. Yelgin, the only invited Russian, was seated tenth on the right side. A complete humiliation right there on the Russian city of Amovir. Although he had no basis on facts to validate this feeling, the Russian manager came out of this meeting, holding a strong suspicion that BI was no longer a Russian company at its core. He felt that the Chairman Kiriyan was betraying BI Russian origins on the invisible international capitalist table. This was probably not a condition that was cleared or agreed to by the BI mysterious Kremlin contacts. Yelgin decided to bring the matter to the attention of Kremlin contacts during his next trip to Moscow. Chairman Kiriyan needed to clarify as soon as possible the direction he was now taking to lead this Russian company. It was about time to eliminate the freewheeling that Chairman Kiriyan had enjoyed these many years running BI, answering to nobody but himself and the two funny Dudarev couple who live with him. Maybe that would be his definite and final opportunity to replace Nadov Kiriyan as BI chairman.

On her way to the lunch that the chairman was giving, Lady Allistair met Ludmilla, who left her desk to come and congratulate her friend and lover on her new assignment. Lady Allistair proposed to her on the spot to move back to London with her for an elevated position very close to the new CEO if she wanted to. Ludmilla did not answer. What she had not told her lover was that she had replaced Nadia Kirilenko, the old KGB/FSS liaison with BI, when she came back from London. Mr. Kiriyan personally entrusted Ludmilla with this job when Nadia Kirilenko resigned and retired for old age and poor health. She passed away sometime later. With the new Russian political structure, the liaison job with what passes for KGB/FSS was a bit different. There were softer intelligence engagement to deal with, compared to rough and hard intelligence activities from Nadia Kirilenko's past and which included sexual trappings, moral corruption, bribes, and sometimes outright murders.

The old engagement goal was to create traitors and eliminate them when they have served their purpose. The new engagement goal was to create true believers in BI causes and sustain them in their operations forever at all cost. If the engagement involved anything of sexual nature, it was a favor given freely rather than an entrapment. There were no bribes but financial enhancement to most entrepreneurial types. Moral corruption was never tolerated. Physical harm and murder were effectively prohibited. Ludmilla busied herself around young impressionable KGB/FSS recruits into BI middle management. This is what Mr. Kiriyan was instilling in Ludmilla Borensky in her new job. She reported directly to Mr. Kiriyan. Ludmilla thought that Lady Allistair's proposition to go back to London was not going to be well received by Mr. Kiriyan unless he had a special assignment for her in London next to the new CEO. Besides, now Ludmilla was doing pretty good for herself with powerful, although murky, access to the top man. She always loved Lady Allistair since their time together as research assistants. But Lady Allistair had moved on to better and young things in New York City. She waited for her in vain in London and was hurt. Does she want to go back to the same? She thought that maybe the supreme orgasmic session she had prepared for Lady Allistair, for old time sake, had gone over her head. Lady Allistair had no idea of the Pradiga potion she had poured in her drink to enhance her libido to trance like was the same potion she had used on her the first time they met in Amovir. Ludmilla was surprised that the Pradiga worked intensely this time around. At least, she still had the power over Lady Allistair's lower parts. She would not be able to give an answer to her proposal until Mr. Kiriyan decides.

That evening when Lady Allistair returned back to Uncle Kiri's villa, she was met again by the couple Dudarev, who, this time, took her almost three floors down in the basement into what looked like a futuristic church with thousands of neo lamps and huge molecule like gravitating balls. The Dudarev couple proceeded to strap Lady Allistair into a huge leather sofa and announced that Mr. Kiriyan wanted her to experiment with his latest toy of galactic jump. The couple disappeared now in the thick of cloud, which was forming, from the basement floor and up. Lady Allistair felt like being transported into a void where there was no beginning nor ending. She was literally floating inside a spaceship passing by thousands of silent gleaming stars some close by but most by far. On reflex, Lady Allistair rested her eyes on her hand-watch that remained motionless with the second arm sitting still. After what appeared like an eternity of time, she noticed a form developing ahead of her. The form slowly took the growing profile of Uncle Kiri.

The form grew bigger but never got closer. Suddenly there was a mythical place that appears with thousands of colorful lights and at times blurring. Whatever Lady Allistair was riding was now passing by very closely a humongous planet with endless shining points of light, which extended for as long as a continent on earth. The endless points of light were enclosed in incredibly large shining glasses. Lady Allistair can now distinguish inside the glasses an astounding variety of millions of very tall skyscrapers, thousands and more stories high. Long, bright glass tunnels and bridges with constant chains of rapidly evolving traffic back and forth linked the huge glasses. Just as suddenly it appeared, the huge planet started receding and became distant bathing in a light that revealed ten or twelve planets orbiting around the humongous planet and traces of bluish light indicating heavy traffic between the orbiting planets and the main very big planet. The mythical place disappeared and was replaced by an array of thousands of forms coming and going. Lady Allistair saw the forms transformed into chariots of huge balls of fire over thousands of fleeing human soldiers. The balls of fire literally pulverized the fleeing soldiers. The chariots of fire then went in the direction of what looked like a river, then a sign reading Saratov came by and disappeared. And very quickly, the chariots became formlike shadows. These shadows kept zipping by so fast, they made Lady Allistair dizzy and she fainted. When she woke up, she was seated across from Uncle Kiri, who was eating the same soup at the same table where they met the night before. She was served a huge size of filet mignon with Brussels sprout, her favorite. She looked across and checked her watch and pulse. She was still alive. She noticed that she was now wearing the same K ring as Mr. Kiriyan but a size smaller.

She was a bit in daze, did not talk for about two minutes, and then asked the obvious, "I am sorry, Uncle Kiri, what the hell happened to me a while ago. Your attendants, the couple Dudarev brought me downstairs a while ago, and I had this incredible space trip they said you wanted me to experiment. I saw an incredible planet and remembered you in this strange form leading a charge or a caravan of chariots of balls of fire literally pulverizing thousands of fleeing soldiers in a place called Saratov. Was I dreaming or did I get such an experiment? And what about this ring? Am I anointed into something I should know?"

Uncle Kiriyan was now smiling and said, "I believe you saw the ways of the light, as it should be viewed, the ways where there is no beginning nor ending. Of course, you were dreaming. The experiment is intended to induce dreams to allow you to go where you have never been as if you are traveling in space.

Just imagine what it would take to go from one part of space to another. Every time I elevate people I trust to positions of considerable power, I want to make sure that they experiment the galactic jump the way some of us should have experimented it. The experiment, of course, is more psychic, if any. But just the same, the goal is for each of my top managers to realize the potential that is there. I don't know about you but take for instance that mythical place you saw with thousands of points of light. What if I would tell you that it exists, and it is Striton-7, the largest planet in the galaxy of Upsala? This galaxy, for all known computation, is about twenty-four million light years from this solar galaxy. And in a glimpse of time, you saw the level of technology in that planet, and you would agree with me that this level of technology speaks of a civilization so advanced that it makes everything you see on earth pitiful and elementary.

Yes, I also realize that is an unfair comparison for the common mortal people out there, but for my top managers, the comparison ceases to be unreal; it becomes a matter of distinction between the past and the future, the probable and the tangible, only and only if we raise all our sights as high as the possible can be as in the galaxy of Upsala. Now we all know that all started with the big bang. I am not going to argue or discuss why the big bang happened or what made it to happen. Let's just say that it happened and a lot of things took place at that time. The amount of energy that must have been released at that time was something we cannot think of. That energy must have produced stuff or elements that are all over the universe. That stuff or these elements are what everything lives off in the universe. If you can harness that stuff or these elements, you would get closer to the first energy that was released. Here on earth, people say that if you get to that first energy, then you will get to the hand of God. I would not dispute that. It is what it is. My charge has been and remains to get not to that first energy, which is quite beyond me, but the next stuff, the elements that were produced at that time. Believe me, where the ways of light have been set, these elements are more than gold, oil, and diamonds combined. They are life.

These elements are terribly abundant and dispersed all over the universe. Happy are those who harness these elements! The glimpse of technology or civilization that you saw on planet Striton-7 was made possible by the harnessing of those elements. Of course, Striton-7 and the galaxy of Upsala had a far advanced start to harness those elements than earth and the solar galaxy, maybe in the range of six billions of years or more. That is a lot of time.

"But, my lady, in my estimation, every time people on this earth had the real chance to harness those elements, given the state of their limited knowledge of the universe, they went about wasting their efforts in stupid wars or unproductive search of new but always perishable and limited sources of energy or futile metals. Human history has been an endless sad testimony of these two events. In one way or another, and sadly, the search had never been enough, and sooner or later, the fighting goes on over limited sources of the energy or limited capacity to produce the latest precious metals.

Whereas, the pursuit of the big bang elements would have, in my humble opinion again, resolved most of these earthly conflicts and settled once for all, as in the galaxy of Upsala, the fundamental issue and satisfaction of wants. But in all humility and sincerity, it should be said that the pursuit of the big bang elements has been made possible only by raising the level of technology and scientific knowledge to a station unknown on earth. In addition, it certainly took a long time, billions of years since the advent of the galaxy of Upsala. It was also made possible by a refined and growing evolution of a structure of our society units based on a random regeneration process that allows for a permanent equilibrium among all units removing all senses of friction among them. I would be glad to elaborate on this structure some other time. Yet, the pursuit of the big bang elements should logically explain the difference in the approach to satisfying wants on earth compared to Striton-7 or the galaxy of Upsala. The former being essentially primitive as you can appreciate at this time, while the latter, very advanced.

Now, I am certain you are debating in your own mind whether this Striton-7 or the galaxy of Upsala are a reality or simply some terms of motivational exercise I am using over you. Lady Allistair, I cannot prove this one way or another according to your level of understanding of things past or things to come. But I am calling on you to trust me on this as I am elevating you to the position of CEO of AMX. Time, and only time, would prove me right. In the same order of ideas, I am also certain that you would discard the forms or shadows you saw as chariots of ball of fire pulverizing soldiers in Saratov. By the way, Saratov actually exists in the Saratov Oblast state or province of Russia today. But the story of I leading chariots with balls of fire should remain well pure a fantasy.

Finally, I also trust that all this conversation will forever remain confidential between you and me, and as far as the K ring on your finger goes, I personally placed it there while you were sleeping, as a token of my regards for all you have done for us all these years and as you are taking on bigger charges for BI. I am sorry that Uncle Kiri took certain liberties by doing this. I did not mean to embarrass you, it was a real token of affection and deep regards I have for you, Lady Allistair."

Mr. Kiriyan was getting up when Lady Allistair waved her hand and said, "Please, Uncle Kiri, remain a while and hear me say this. It was absolutely no embarrassment for me that you have taken time to place this ring on my finger while I was asleep or in daze. By the way, this reminds me of the same touch of affection you have shown me when I was about twelve and was introduced to you by my uncle Georges Mendhan and he called you Uncle Kiri. Remember that you operated a little magic then by pulling this huge bouquet of white flower out of the back of my left ear. I never forgot that moment. I was enchanted then, I am enchanted now. I have since called you Uncle Kiri. I told you that I fully appreciated the appointment or elevation to the position of AMX CEO. But that position means less to me than your touch of affection then and now and especially as Uncle Kiri. And please, let me say it that you have earned my trust all these years not as BI CEO, but always as the same Uncle Kiri I have known back then and now. I hope that I will continue to earn your trust as well in the future."

"Indeed, you have earned my trust and would continue to earn it. By the time you would leave tomorrow, you should get my long- and short-term objectives and goals regarding AMX. Of course, they will be all entirely confidential for the new AMX CEO's eyes only."

CHAPTER 14
Lady Allistair's Doubt

Uncle Kiri was definitely up and guided Lady Allistair toward the large exit door. A limousine pulled up and took her to her appointed new villa. Her head was still full of interrogations after the impressive conversation with Uncle Kiri and the famous galactic jump experiment. The evening of her momentous elevation to the much-coveted seat of AMX CEO was turning out to be a nightmare of untold proportion after spending the time at Uncle Kiri's villa. She kept asking whether all that she went through was real or surreal. She could not really make sense of anything that had happened except the last part of the conversation. When she entered the new villa, Ludmilla Borensky was already there with a small team of close acquaintances. They all stood up clapping their hands for the new AMX CEO. Lady Allistair quickly regained her composure and started thanking the small gathering and chatted about the new position. The party continued until past one in the morning at which time only Ludmilla stayed behind. Ludmilla questioned her mood directly. She said that she had observed she was not as cheerful as she should have been after the evening with Mr. Kiriyan. She asked her what was wrong, or if Mr. Kiriyan had dumped more management load on her as a result of the AMX appointment. Lady Allistair quickly responded that she was simply reflective about the enormity of the change that would affect her life from now on. Lady Allistair was also alert of her new surroundings in this new villa. She would not let any feeling about her new position or the last encounter at Uncle Kiri's villa to come out even to her trusted friend and lover not knowing of her latest supreme BI spy assignments. On the impulse, Lady Allistair asked Ludmilla whether she had thought about her request to come to London to work with her. That was a tip that there had been no discussion of her reassignment with Mr. Kiriyan.

She answered her in a lover fashion. "Lady Allistair, I don't want to wait for you forever as it has happened the last time in London. I know that you were attached in New York. But I have also learned that you were attached more than professionally in New York. You were deeply attached to all those new wave young things, as you loved to call them. I knew I could not compete. I was hurt, and I came home. I am now about forty-one and in need of emotional stability.

Would you be able to give it to me in London when you would be way too busy, my dear? Think about it. I am ready and willing to do anything you want me to do, but I know you are not and would not be. So let us not spoil the moment and enjoy it to the fullest. You will always know where I am, and anytime you want to commit I would be there."

This was a typical lovers quarrel, there was not a no or a yes, but always a lot of maybes. Lady Allistair got the gist of her answer and did not say anything, but they went to sleep. In the morning, Ludmilla bade her a long tearful good-bye and went to work. As soon as she departed, Lady Allistair started looking for an article that Ludmilla gave her in one of her let-downs moments of spy. They were spending a rare weekend together in an inn outside London when Lady Allistair came over from New York City to join Ludmilla. After emptying together a bottle of Vodka, Ludmilla started talking about her boss Nadia Kirilenko KGB/FSS's role in BI. In order to bolster Nadia Kirilenko's KGB/FSS background and warn Lady Allistair to be careful of her, she produced an article that circulated in 1920 about a Mr. Nadov Kiriyan. The article was posted in one of no-so secret KGB/FSS Internet web sites. Intelligence services use these sites for two purposes to misinform people or to let their former agents know that they have goods on them and could at any time reveal damaging information about them if they do not tow their lines. Ludmilla said that Nadia Kirilenko provided the article to her to show how much sway and pull she had over Mr. Kiriyan. She implied that this was an old KGB/FSS trick. It was always difficult to ascertain whether the article was authentic or false. But Lady Allistair, after the evening at Uncle Kiri's villa, wanted to ascertain something she thought she remembered from the article.

She searched her portable PC and found the article written by an Oleg Shvestov in July 14, 1920, in a "Tver Veche" periodical with the appropriate title of "Balls Of Fire." She changed the article title into "The Reckoning" and saved it. She decided to start reading the old pamphlet only by the time she will be out of Russia and in a Western commercial airplane. She then started packing to go to London. She made calls to old contacts in the Amovir Station and managed to reach Uncle Kiri in his daily morning very busy schedule. By the time she stepped out the villa, a brand-new limousine was waiting for her, and she was taken to the Amovir BI private airport, where a shining white and much bigger private jet was waiting for her. This plane did not have a BI logo. Rather, it was blazoned with an AMX logo on both sides of the plane. There was also a young lady from Uncle Kiri's staff waiting on her when she got off the limousine.

She handed to her a large leathered envelope with BI golden motives. The envelope had a seal with the inscription "FOR YOUR EYES ONLY." Lady Allistair recognized the envelope to contain Uncle Kiri's long- and short-term goals and objectives for AMX. When she boarded,

Lady Allistair was greeted by an all-AMX English crew and two passengers, her main connections in London in the persons of Barry Newcomb, the lawyer, and Evelyn Bottown, AMX CFO, the money lady and Lady Allistair's longtime friend. Lady Allistair was warmly greeted by Evelyn and Barry and was promptly congratulated for becoming the new CEO. When the private jet was finally airborne, Lady Allistair was finally relieved to get out of Amovir. She got the strange feeling that this was the last time she would set foot in this far removed and strange place called Amovir. She excused herself to the privacy of her private cabin and started reading the notes in the leathered envelope. They were in the typical Uncle Kiri's style, crisp and to the point. They were presented in matrix-table like from most urgent priority to minor priority and across for every goals or objectives, the expected short-term and long-term impacts on BI. She was not surprised to notice that the most urgent was the move to Varonne-Sur-Baie. Uncle Kiri stated that although the move had no visible impact on AMX per se, it will come with more management autonomy for Lady Allistair in the running of AMX when Uncle Kiri will be solely engaged in managing the move in the next two or three years. He insisted on the complete secrecy of the move. He expected Lady Allistair never to talk about it one way or another. In the longer term, when the move will be completed, AMX will be effectively folded into BI management structure. The second most urgent priority was new to Lady Allistair. It involves the transfer under her direct management, the same as before for Uncle Kiri's, the supervision of the very obscure investment banking company located in the tax-safe haven of Liechtenstein with an unassuming name of "Central Investment Bank" or CIB. Uncle Kiriyan had over the years used this investment bank as the clearing-house for all BI treasury functions outside Russia and with the exception of AMX. With the tremendous growth of BI operations outside Russia, CIB was becoming a large financial center in its own right handling at this time more than 550 billion dollars annually from hundreds of BI investments worldwide. Again, Uncle Kiri's focus on the move to Varonne-Sur-Baie would not allow him the same close supervision of CIB as before. The short- and long-term implications were obvious; there should be no slip up in the management of this jewel during the next three years. The last most urgent priority was already in Lady Allistair's lap, the Alpha-M or Mezi engagement, including, in short term, the return of Dr. Wasiri in Mezi and the acceleration of goodwill engagement in Mezi and in Africa.

In the long-term column, Uncle Kiri also added a new variant in the Mezi engagement, the active promotion of Dr. Wasiri's political leadership. The next category included only one urgent priority. Uncle Kiri stated that with the advent of BI as a worldwide multinational conglomerate, there was an urgent need to raise the profile of BI political connections in major political centers in the world. BI's political connections with Kremlin are already solid. But they are not so strong in Washington, Beijing, Paris, London, Berlin, Brussels, and Tokyo. Given the strong British background of AMX, Lady Allistair would lead this effort on worldwide basis starting with Washington. The last category included also a simple priority also. It alluded to an acceleration of the integration of various AMX owned entities around the world at the same speed as BI own integration. Lady Allistair scribbled notes next to each of these goals and objectives and summarized them for her own presentation that was expected sometime soon in London. Being the first female to become AMX CEO from the long line of Mendham family, she knew that she had to make a very strong first impression with the AMX board; she had to show that she can hit the ground literally running. After about six hours of flight, the private jet stopped at Dubai airport for refueling. It was only then that Lady Allistair remembered to read, again in the privacy of her private cabin, the famous article she was looking for that morning.

She accessed the article, and it read as follows: 'The Balls of Fire' by Oleg Shvestov, Tver Veche, July 14, 1920. The nights of November 11, 1919, will be remembered in the annals of Russian Empire as the beginning of the end in the fight waged by the forces of the White Army of Russia led by General Wrangel to gain back grounds and territories lost to Bolsheviks in the southern regions of Russia. What distinguished this defeat from the routing of the White Army in the eastern front was the scale and speed of the Bolshevik war machine at the time. Everyone knows that the Communist Party governing now the walls of Kremlin loves to attribute every victory of its forces over the White Army to the extraordinary zeal and the righteousness of the winning strategy entrusted to the People Liberation Army exclusively. But I must venture to say at this time that more was at play in the victory of Bolshevik forces in the city of Saratov in the province of Saratov Oblast than was honestly reported. From every living eyewitness I was able to gather information from, the victory was exclusively attributed to the convoy of chariots with balls of fire. These chariots came out of nowhere and, overnight, pulverized the forces of the White Army by spitting out large balls of fire over the soldiers and their equipment. The balls of fire were seventy feet high and hundred feet wide.

They came out at the rate of thirty or more from these metallic chariots. They left nothing but dust wherever they landed—buildings, war equipment, horses, or soldiers, all were gone as pulverized in a matter of seconds. The balls of fire obliterated the first two battalions under General Wrangel's command progressing north of Saratov while the entire Bolshevik forces sat back in the hills observing the carnage around the Saratov's extended valley. The only people who were spared from the massacre were those lucky enough to secure boats or anything to stay afloat over the Volga River going south to the Caspian Sea. The sight of obliteration was convincing enough to start the rout of the remaining White Army forces led by General Wrangel retreating south. In the White Army circles and until today, questions have always revolved around where these chariots came from, who has manufactured them and brought them to the battle scenes, and who led these chariots. I have worked very hard to find answers to these four questions.

The Bolsheviks were numb and treated any answer to these questions as state secrets. Speculations swerving all over the White Army forces were of no use to me as an objective journalist. Through luck and cunning, I have managed to work my way through the closed very suspicious commanding circles of the Bolshevik forces in charge of consolidating the victory won in Saratov. I was able to do this with manufactured titles that appointed me as deputy internal security officer in charge of propaganda for Saratov Oblast War Theater. I was able then to locate a very remote commanding officer of the mechanized infantry tank elite division, the so-called chariots with balls of fire. He was Colonel Dimitri Nadov Kiriyan, who kept to himself most of time with his own chosen elite officers. He did not mix with the boisterous officers from other Bolshevik armies. He was taught to take his orders directly from Kremlin or Lenin himself. When I entered his headquarters, the level of cleanliness permeating his chambers and all other offices around him struck me. Next, the type of office equipment the staff officers were using also struck me; the speaking machines, the glass machines they were looking at and hitting at—these equipment were not of this world at all. When I reached the inner chamber of Colonel Kiriyan, he was barking orders to what looked like a large looking glass with moving objects. The sight amazed me. Colonel Kiriyan did not address nor look at me for ten minutes. When he did, he screamed, "Rank." I was so petrified to respond, so captivated by the large glass board the colonel was talking to, I forgot my title of deputy internal security officer. Instead, I mumbled something about "Sergeant Shvestov, First Cavalry, sir." I was promptly ejected from the premises.

Fearing worse, now that I have discovered the secret of the war machines that the Bolshevik government has gained from whatever demoniac entity, I managed to quickly disappear from my fraudulent title before I was to be found. I ran for my life, going south with the retreating White Army. I knew that the Bolshevik government and the Russian Communist Party would mark me for death the minute I started revealing the secret of the chariots with balls of fire. So I ran as far south as Iran among the White Army and Russian monarchist communities where I have communicated this unfortunate secret. As far as I can tell, the defeat of the White Army was exclusively due to an intervention satanic from these strange people in the chariots with balls of fire. God helps us when demonic people, like this Colonel Kiriyan with a war machine so powerful and so potent and ready to pulverize people, machines, and building as if they were ants, are overtaking Russia. And this should not pass. Before long, our Russian people will be made slaves in service of the machine like this Colonel Kiriyan with no soul or faith, There was an epilogue below the article which said that the journalist, Oleg Shvestov, was tracked by communist agents mercilessly all over the world after he wrote the article. He was finally gunned down in May 17, 1949, in a small village south of Belem in Brazil, where he thought he was safe and has taken refuge under an assumed Portuguese name of Francisco Salma. This happened after the great patriotic war that consolidated Stalin power in USSR. It was said in Russian émigrés' circles in Europe that Oleg Shvestov was the first in a long list of people to pay for their life for revealing the deeds of the powerful and mysterious Colonel Dimitri Nadov Kiriyan. The epilogue concluded that Colonel Kiriyan was later duly compensated for winning many other Bolshevik campaigns from 1919 through 1922 for the Great Liberation War and Soviet campaigns against the Nazi during the Second World War. He gained the supreme management control over the vast industrial and mining complex expanding the entire Baikal Lake Region. He managed the complex with iron fists with no local government oversight, reporting directly to Kremlin, one USSR general secretary after another. That has continued to present days.

Lady Allistair was sweating uncontrollably when reading both the article and the epilogue. She could not help to be brought back to the episodes of the galactic jump of the day before and the half answer Uncle Kiri gave regarding the chariots with balls of fire. For all practical purposes, Lady Allistair thought that Uncle Kiri was not convincing enough when he dismissed the story as if he knew that sooner or later, her curiosity was going to be picked to search more references at least to verify if the story was true.

Now that she reread the article, she was not entirely convinced that the story relating chariots with balls of fire from this Oleg Shvestov was authentic. There was a bit too much of propaganda and anecdotes back and forth from both Bolshevik and Russian émigrés to allow for a definitive way to establish the facts. She also remembered that the whole story came out of KGB/FSS files. Maybe Nadia Kirilenko concocted the whole mysterious article with her KGB/FSS patrons in Kremlin to blackmail Uncle Kiri during the time of the Soviet Republic through the current Russia Republic. But then again, the epilogue sounded so plausible. Pushing the imagination further, Lady Allistair reasoned, the simple historical question that will beg to be answered will be how old is

Uncle Kiri? The historic facts from Oleg Shvestov and the epilogue would be making Uncle Kiri to be more than 130 years old. That would not be logically possible if Uncle Kiri is human. If Uncle Kiri is not human, then he must be an alien on earth for a precise mission to find those big bang precious elements like Alpha-M. At this stage, Lady Allistair realized how absurd and wilder her imagination was running; she started laughing loud uncontrollably. Her friend Evelyn burst in her cabin and found her holding the Oleg Shvestov pamphlet and laughing. She stopped her friend's inquiry on her track by reassuring that she was all right, just taken aback by some funny memos she got from a friend from Amovir. Evelyn retreated and closed the door of the cabin.

Lady Allistair resolved then that she couldn't afford to let her imagination run wild again, especially now in her present AMX CEO position. Besides, she had worked so long and had been far too long engaged in executing various objectives and goals Uncle Kiri had put forth in the past that it did not make sense to back out or question his motives now. If she was literally engaged in some nefarious endeavors all along, she must be up to her head in some criminal activities at this stage, and there were no redeeming factors to extract her from them. It was well too late now. She will have to trust the good old Uncle Kiri no matter what.

She tore the pamphlet and erased the Oleg Shvestov's article file from her PC. Instead, she printed the summary of AMX goals and objectives she intended to share with the board and got out of her cabin toward where Barry and Evelyn, her London connections, were seated. She engaged them with the summary, and they were quite amazed by Lady Allistair's delivery. She was so commanding in her facts and logic that she left no doubt that she was ready to take the command of AMX. Not quite aware of the background of these new goals and objectives, Barry and Evelyn quickly agreed to their imperatives.

Lady Allistair also indicated that after the presentation to the board, she counts on them to shoulder added assignments to carry these new goals and objectives to a successful completion. She said that she was a bit tired and went to sleep in her CEO's private cabin. She was awakened when the private plane started making its descent toward London's Gatewick Airport. Evelyn Bottown came in the cabin and sat across her new boss. She reminded her that she had a full busy day the next day starting with the full board meeting where she needed to share and to gain the approval over the composition of the new AMX management committee. She would then hold her first management committee meeting where she must provide the first outlines of her own objectives and goals for AMX. She would finish her first day as CEO by calling on CEOs of the top ten corporate clients around the world. She then left; it was Barry's turn to brief Lady Allistair. Barry was left as a remote stand-in manager for her from London. He reported that all was running smoothly and in place from New York. On the Mezi front, he received an inquiry from the good old professor Dr. O'Shea who left a message with her New York office. Dr. O'Shea wanted to be reassured if Lady Allistair's appointment to AMX CEO did not jeopardize the Mezi's engagement.

Barry continued, "I sent him an e-mail response stating that that was not the case, and all was 'GO' as far as I was concerned. He was not pleased and would prefer to hear it from you. Of course, this would present a bit of a problem when you would be stationed in London on permanent basis as AMX CEO."

Lady Allistair corrected Barry, "Mezi engagement is so important that I am expected to make myself available between London and New York City as needed. I would give him a call as soon as we reach London. Dr. O'Shea is an interesting man. I tell you, I have always enjoyed dealing with him. You noticed that I have not said working with him. I am sure from your last trip in Mezi, you have come to the realization that you don't work with somebody like Dr. O'Shea, you deal with him. He is not like some of us in this endeavor for what AMX would pay. His call is much higher, Barry, that is why you got to deal with him. In addition, I seem to have this sort of softer side with him. He has always made me extremely comfortable. I got to confess, every time I talk to him, I tend to compensate for the father figure I did not know at all. You know, a long chain of uncles and aunts in the Mendham family raised me. I lost my mother when I was two and my father, a mining engineer, disappeared in a tin mine in Peru two years later. Uncles and aunts on both sides of Mendham family pitched in. They also made sure that I got involved in a family business, and here I am. Barry, please keep this as a precious advice for yourself.

I would not have been elevated to this CEO position if I had screwed up the Mezi engagement or, and especially, the management of likes of Dr. O'Shea. There were a lot of males in the Mendham family more capable than me, and I know that. But where I made the difference in the eyes of Mr. Kiriyan was in the chance I took in handling very sensitive dossiers like the Mezi engagement. I am saying this because I want you to stay as close as possible to this engagement and the Africa goodwill deployment I mentioned in the summary. I want you to be my eyes and ears when it comes to these two endeavors in Mezi or in the United States when I am not available. And please get to know the big players in these dossiers. Talking of players in the Mezi engagement, how is Dr. McMillan coming along in joining the management of the foundation down in Mezi? I believe you mentioned that he was still considering whether to accept that management position to support the sites operations in Mezi. Has he accepted it finally? Is he still in London at this time? By the way, if he is in London at this time, I would like to have a private conversation with him. I may have another assignment for him down there in Mezi."

Barry quickly responded, "Yes, Lady Allistair, Dr. McMillan has accepted the management position with the foundation. We are very lucky to have him with the extensive background he has regarding Mezi. He is still in London wrapping up the outstanding legal matters he had in UK. I believe all is being resolved to his complete satisfaction. He is preparing to go back to reside in Mezi for good in about a week or so. I must be able to arrange the meeting with Dr. McMillan whenever you want it. I want also you to know that I would work as assiduously as possible to live up to your expectations regarding both the Mezi engagement and the African goodwill deployment."

When Barry left the new AMX CEO's cabin, the private jet was landing. Later when the border legal formalities were taken care, Evelyn and Barry rode with Lady Allistair the company limousine to her new corporate-paid residence in the exclusive borough of Kensington and Chelsea. It was a huge mansion with about six bedrooms each with a private bathroom and a large master bedroom the length of the combined living and dining room below. For a single person like Lady Allistair, the mansion was beyond excessive. However, it was part of the perks which came along with the position of CEO of AMX despite the fact that Lady Allistair had always kept a very large and expansive apartment in the same area of Kensington and Chelsea. She bought the apartment when she was appointed America Marketing Executive in order to have a London pied-a-terre. When in London, she managed to stay there.

Now and alone, she had to adjust to the trappings of living in a huge corporate mansion. However, Lady Allistair thought that one of the disturbing trapping of living in this mansion was being attended by a middle-aged butler couple living in the mansion and in AMX's payroll. Lady Allistair was not about to make a public display of her cherished very private social life in front of this middle-aged butler couple. As a new CEO, she would bring about a different accommodation as quietly as possible to suit her lifestyle. Just the same, the butler couple greeted her warmly while her traveling companions departed a few minutes later. She was then shown her private quarters in the mansion, including the huge master bedroom. As soon as she was settled, she went in her home office, which was adequately equipped for the position of a worldwide corporate CEO. She called Dr. O'Shea at home.

It was only ten o'clock in the morning in Lexington, Kentucky. Dr. O'Shea was very pleased to hear from Lady Allistair. He congratulated her on becoming the CEO of AMX. He did not hesitate to go to the point in sharing his concern regarding whoever would be replacing her in fulfilling the corporate support of the Emily Thomas O'Shea Foundation and all that they have planned to do.

Lady Allistair responded tersely by saying, "Dr. O'Shea, listen to me very carefully, nobody, I repeat nobody, is replacing me in fulfilling the corporate support of the Emily Thomas O'Shea Foundation and all that we have planned to do. Absolutely nothing will change in the future as in the past. I am making sure that I will be and remain available to you in New York or London whenever you want. I know that I have come into large and extended responsibilities in my new functions. However, the foundation is an endeavor I am not prepared to let go, and believe me, one of the conditions to take this new function includes continual personal involvement in the support of the foundation. So rest assured that you have and will continue to have my complete attention and support for the foundation. I am sending to you all my new contacts in London in addition to those in New York City. Please, go on with your foundation business as if nothing has happened and keep me posted regarding your next trip to Mezi in company with Dr. Wasiri. Now is there anything I still need to clarify or that you need to tell me?"

Dr. O'Shea, very much relieved, responded, "Lady Allistair, you have clarified all for me. I was certainly taken aback when I read your appointment in the Metals Illustrated magazine two days ago. I was totally devastated. I frankly saw it as one of the many corporate betrayals I have witnessed before.

I sent you an e-mail message right away. My fear was totally confirmed when the lawyer Barry Newcomb responded. I have nothing against the man, but I was so used to deal with you, and I thought that we have built a rapport on a personal level I have found gratifying. I was not prepared to start all over again, especially not at this crucial time when so many steps have been laid down. Understand my inept reaction. I must confess I am not corporately or politically sophisticated when it comes to appreciate management changes. I saw only betrayal.

I am definitely relieved to hear what you just shared a while ago. I would not take too much of your time at this time in the middle of this important transition in your life. Let us keep in touch."

Lady Allistair sensed that she had made her point and had convinced the good Dr. O'Shea of her continual involvement. She did not have to mention that Mezi engagement was one of the top urgent priorities of her new functions as per Uncle Kiri. There will be no let up there. She also thought of His Honorable Georgia State Senator Jeremy Massay. She wanted to know how he had reacted to her new appointment. She searched her old e-mail messages and could not find anything from the honorable.

She thought that maybe he simply was not aware of the changes and decided to send him a note advising of her new appointment. At the same time, she was going to be as categorical as for Dr. O'Shea, stating that she would continue her personal support of ABDI as before and the honorable will continue to have a direct link to her with no need for intermediaries. Lady Allistair then edited the presentations she was going to do the next day for AMX board of directors and AMX management committee. When she completed the editing, she got the butler couple to prepare a light dinner. She ate and retired early for the night after the long trip from Amovir.

However, Lady Allistair forgot a crucial point when she heard about the encounter between Barry Newcomb and Dr. O'Shea. She did not probe enough why Dr. O'Shea distrusted the lawyer so much, and this was the second time he was expressing such distrust. She missed applying one lesson that Uncle Kiri had admonished her to use every time she was assessing people. Oddly enough, Uncle Kiri always insisted on searching and finding "the human factor condition" behind people motivations when they are doing or expediting anything. According to Uncle Kiri, as soon as you seize on the human condition, motivating people, you can get them to do almost anything for you.

Uncle Kiri claimed to have been very successful every time he had applied this dictum. He also added that the moment you miss applying this direction and a crisis arises, a post-mortem review of facts will always point to the delicate time when things started going bad as the human condition reveals itself in an evident way. Now that Lady Allistair had raised the lawyer profile in both the Mezi engagement and the African goodwill deployment, she was putting in motion human condition of regrettable dimension. If she had checked with those who knew, she would have been a bit wary of the lawyer. Barry Newcomb was appointed to his position of AMX deputy chief counsel by Robert Mendham, her uncle and previous AMX CEO.

The main reason Barry was brought in AMX was to be eyes and ears for his uncle, especially in his relationship with BI CEO, Nadov Kiriyan. Robert Mendham was always, as he loved to say it, suspicious of the Russian. In spite of the rightful corporate ownership held by BI and its management over AMX, Robert Mendham was always afraid to be accused by Her Majesty British government of doing the Russian bidding against British interests and, worse, to facilitate some Russian spy activities in UK. To prevent any misunderstanding, Robert Mendham contacted the British Intelligence Services and asked for their advice. To keep AMX clean, Barry Newcomb was the answer. Robert Mendham gave Barry full access to all AMX operations and never asked him any questions about his contacts in M16. As Mr. Kiriyan slowly and deftly increased Lady Allistair's management profile, Barry followed suit and ingratiated himself with Lady Allistair to a point where he became her main contact in AMX headquarters in London. As far as Kiriyan was concerned, Barry Newcomb was already identified as M16 agent by his endless KGB/FSS sources in Kremlin and London. He made certain that Barry was excluded from top secrets dealings he had with Lady Allistair, including Alpha-M. He never alerted Lady Allistair about Barry's status and did not see the need to do this. Alerting her would have raised unnecessary qualms he did not want to indulge in. With the appointment of Lady Allistair to the position of AMX CEO, it was clear that Mr. Kiriyan was going to apply his management concept of human condition motivations to neutralize Barry Newcomb.

CHAPTER 15
Emily's Celebration

When Dr. O'Shea received the news about Lady Allistair's AMX CEO appointment, he had already issued, two days before, the invitation to his children and Dr. Wasiri's family to share with the setting up of the Emily Thomas O'Shea Foundation in about two weeks. He almost went crazy. He was truly devastated, not by the corporate betrayal as he put it, but rather by the probable termination of Emily's dreams that he had kept alive, and he was about to fulfill through the foundation. He was upset to share with his kids the goals of the foundation at a very moment these goals could be curtailed, dismissed, or terminated by a new corporate officer with a completely different reading of the foundation mission. His mind even raced ahead, further suspecting that the foundation would be terminated because of some obscure budgetary constraint. After talking to Lady Allistair, Dr. O'Shea was recovered and at peace with everything now on track and the trip to Mezi with the famous native son well under way. He did not have to worry about the big celebration he had planned in announcing the news about the foundation to his children and grandchildren.

The foundation chair office built inside his house was completed with a huge LCD board for conference calls with the New York City staff. That was the piece of resistance and show-off that he intended to demonstrate to his kids and grandkids. He had also mounted a smaller shining copper sign of Emily Thomas O'Shea Foundation atop the massive ebony double door leading to the foundation chair office. The sign and the double door were covered by shining gold gift paper to be torn-down by his eldest granddaughter during the presentation. Working on the element of great surprise, Dr. O'Shea had locked the door to the hall separating the living quarters of the house and the foundation office. In addition, he would not reveal why he was inviting the family back home except to say that it had everything to do with their beloved mother, knowing very well that the mention of anything related to their beloved would get the children perked up leaving no excuse to skip the event. This guarantees the presence of each child from very busy family and professional schedules. He could not wait to see the amazement on the face of his kids and grandkids at what he had done for the memory of their mother and grandmother.

For the occasion, he had contracted the best and most expansive catering services, by Lexington standards, for food, drink, and entertainment. From the Amovir prize money, he had also managed to completely remodel and extend the house within a short time to accommodate the entire O'Shea family and Dr. Wasiri's family for a long weekend of remembrance and merry doing.

He did not spare anything for the celebration of his beloved wife's memory. By Thursday evening, his daughter Danah, the medical doctor from Philadelphia metropolitan area, came with her family. She was appointed and sent by the other two children to check on their father's condition first. If all was cleared, she was to quickly reassure the other two to come. As usual, she fussed over her aging father and found nothing alarming about her father. While her father went along with the routine and was catching with his grandchildren, Danah reported to the other two that all was fine with the father. The next morning, it was the turn of Emma, the president of the University of Manitoba to show up with her children and husband. Later in the afternoon, Anthony, the elder son, came along with his family from Arizona. Dr. Wasiri showed up Friday evening with his family, but he also mentioned that he had rented a suite not far from Dr. O'Shea's house. That did not please the good old professor. He tried unsuccessfully to get Dr. Wasiri and family to stay in the house. At the end, Hasbo won him over persuading him that they were just two blocks away, and it was most appropriate that this reunion be O'Shea family first. He relented and admonished Dr. Wasiri and Hasbo to be around twenty-four hours a day. The next day, on Saturday, at about one in the afternoon, Dr. O'Shea had his entire extended family in the newly furnished living room. He excused the catering services people as he wanted to talk to his family and Dr. Wasiri's family.

He stood below a large painted portrait of Emily Thomas O'Shea and said, "I am very pleased that you came to join me today on this day of December 17, which is the forty-ninth anniversary of the wedding between your mother and me. Although Emily is not with us to celebrate this occasion, I can assure you that she is with us after you have seen and heard what I am about to share with you. As you know, my wife and I raised you to be all that you wanted to be when we waged our own battle with the power that out there in the university and other institutions. Emily's rules were always strict. She instructed me to leave you my children out of the battle we waged. She had a point. You did not pick the battle, and it would have been unfair to associate you with this.

She insisted to let your flowers bloom wherever you saw it; Anthony went on to molecular chemistry, Danah to medical sciences in cardiology, and Emma to operations research. And you did very well indeed. She forbade me to associate any of you to mines engineering sciences and specifically the exotic mineralogy that was my lifelong expertise. Luckily for us, another child came along, and we were lucky to adopt Kano Wasiri as our own, and that is the reason he is here with his family. For better or worse, Kano, now Dr. Wasiri, along with his lovely wife Hasbo joined the battle and fought along with Emily and me in the trenches of exotic mineralogy. I don't have to tell you that I advised Kano's PhD thesis. I am now proud to report that although we have made a lot of strides in our battle, we have also won prizes in distinguished foreign forums and where it counts. And above all, you would be proud to know that a foundation bearing the name of Emily Thomas O'Shea has been set up to commemorate the memory of your beloved mother to celebrate the long participation and determination she has instilled in me, Hasbo, and Dr. Wasiri to continue the battle. Emily always knew that victory was going to be ours if we persevere. Now I want you all to follow me this way, and I also want my eldest granddaughter, Emily-Lucy to be next to me when we will inaugurate the office of the chair of Emily Thomas O'Shea Foundation in this very house."

By this time, all the three children joined their father in tears while Emily-Lucy was embracing Dr. Wasiri and Hasbo. It was now an orgy of cries from all assembled. It took a while before the elder was to unlock the door leading to the hall toward the covered double door of the office. Emily-Lucy tore the golden paper and the massive double door, with the Emily Thomas O'Shea Foundation sign atop lighted. The assembly then entered the huge office with wall-to-wall dark wooden panels, leathered sofas and chairs, a large office desk, and a seventy-inch diagonally mounted LCD board about thirty feet from the office desk. Dr. O'Shea now took the chair seat behind the desk and pressed a few buttons from below the desk. The LCD board was now alive with fleeting stock market data below and a direct feed from what looks like another office. Dr. O'Shea had arranged to have a few staff members from the New York staff to be at hand to provide for a live conference call for the occasion on Saturday afternoon. He said hello to them and invited them to greet family members in Lexington, Kentucky. The conference call took about fifteen minutes. When it was over, there was a big argument among the grandchildren whether to watch on the big screen a pay-per-view movie or a professional playoff football game. The movie crowd won. Grown-ups left the huge office and went back to the living room.

It was now the turn of amazed children to talk. Emma, the university president, was the first to talk, "Dad, how could you have managed to hide your so-called battle from your own kids for so long? Dr. Wasiri, I do not mean any offense, but don't you think that this was all most unfair to us? We are all academic, and after resisting for so long, even Danah is finally teaching at that Philadelphia Medical College now. We assumed all was all right after I don't know so many years of college teaching. And then you announced that you were retiring. We thought that it was about time. You have worked for so long in your life, you deserved a rest. We were constantly worried about your health, especially after Ma passed away. We have no idea that you were still settling scores with the university. Now all is clear, especially with Ma always sending us as far as possible from Lexington. I wanted to attend that university because I wanted to be close to Ma. But you two were more than adamant that I should go to Harvard, then MIT. All of us thought proudly that you wanted us to go Ivy League and the like and be, quote and unquote, successful. But that was partially true.

Yes, we made it but at what price. I would not deny we have done well, all of us. But I was always suspicious and was thinking that there was something back there in Lexington that my parents were holding on to, and I could never put my finger on. Only today I have to learn that you stayed behind to settle scores. That was never fair. When I was going to college and I came back on vacation, I was always struck by how Hasbo and Ma were close. Ma never gave me as much attention as she gave Hasbo. My dear, Hasbo, you don't know how jealous I became of you. There were days when I was home, I kept to myself in my room, crying for attention while you and my mother talked and talked and talked. And now the truth is out. It was all for this godforsaken battle. You did not have to leave us out of this. We are your own blood, Dad. Can you imagine what people would have thought of me, a university president, not knowing that her own father has won a scientific prize for his lifetime research achievement? Not fair, not fair . . ." Emma was now crying and was being consoled by her father who had his eyes also swelling with tears. The only thing he could manage was to say, "Those were Emily's rules, and I had to live by them. Please don't put any blame on Hasbo and Dr. Wasiri. Emily was very strict."

At that point, Dr. Wasiri rose and said, "I am sorry, Anthony, Emma, and Danah, and I have to speak also for Hasbo. You should blame me for not bringing this whole business of battle with you a long long time ago.

True, I never discussed this with your mother, my beloved Ma Emily. God keep her sainted soul. She always urged me to keep up the good work along with her husband. She was also instrumental to my wedding to Hasbo whom she adopted as her own daughter when Emma and Danah were gone. She counseled Hasbo about a lot of things, especially about standing by me. I will forever be most grateful to your mother on that account. As far as your father goes, I believe I owe nobody on this earth as much as I owe your father. Yes, I signed up for your father's researches from the first time we met. He guided me along, as any faithful mentor would do. But he went further; he adopted me as a son. That is our relationship from then to now. There is nothing I can do to change that. Yet many times I have urged him to share with you trials and tribulations he had back then at the university. He would not do it. When your mother, our beloved Emily, passed away, I told him to do this before each of you left that week. I am now certain he did not. When he informed me that he won this scientific prize, I was very angry with him and repeated the same request to no avail. Lastly, when he asked me to assist him in developing the request to set up the foundation, I told him that I would do it in one condition that he associated you to the memory of your mother. He mentioned what he is saying now, Emily's rules. But I would not hear that anymore and would not help until he assured me that he would call this meeting. Now again, if blame must be placed anywhere, it should be on me. I should have been more forceful and more forthcoming about this a long long time ago. That would have been a decent thing to do. Yet I failed all of you."

Anthony, the elder son, intervened, "Come on, Dr. Wasiri, do not make any more excuse for the old stubborn man that my father is and will always be. Come to think of it. Dad mentioned to me a long long time ago issues he was having with his colleagues at the university. I did not really pay attention to what he was talking about. I thought that he had a bad day at work and left it at that. I was more concerned then about girls, dating, and the colleges I was going to attend. Sometime before my leaving for the University of California at Berkeley, I asked Ma if Dad was having problems at the university. She dismissed it so fast, and Dad never mentioned again. That was probably the beginning of Emily's rules Dad loves to throw around and to talk about. The fact that Dad continued teaching all these years reassured me that all was all right. I should have probed, but I did not. I hear what Dr. Wasiri said, and believe me, we are very proud for all that you have accomplished with Dad and will always regard you as our brother and Hasbo as our sister. You two and your children are part of our family. Ma had decided this a long time ago. We are proud to honor her memory in that respect.

Your presence among us only completes our sense of family. Over the years, during many conversations I had with my father, Emily's rules have come about. Throughout, I have thought a lot about the Emily's rules, and you know, I am a simple man and do not like to make things any more complicated than they appear. I want to ask Emma, Danah, Hasbo, and Dr. Wasiri to take these rules no more than for what they are: a sentimental convenient memory cover for my father. The truth is that they suit his convenient stubborn purpose when all stops." Turning now to his father, Anthony said, "Dad, I want to offer a toast now, this is a joyous event, and I am very happy that we are all here to celebrate it with you. I am speaking for Dr. Wasiri and his family, Emma, Danah, and the entire family to thank you for inviting all of us to celebrate your forty-ninth wedding anniversary, keeping our beloved mother's memory alive in that foundation, letting bygones be bygones, and for finally sharing some notions of past trials and tribulations. Let us raise our glasses high for Ma and Dad."

The old man was moved to tears and could not even respond. Emily-Lucy, who was rubbing his back, eased him down to his easy chair. He remained silent for quite a while reminiscing of time past when Emily was presiding over similar family gatherings. When Emily-Lucy moved on, his protégé approached him and said, "About time! What a lovely family gathering!" That is all he needed to get back to his current sense. He told Dr. Wasiri about Lady Allistair's promotion to AMX CEO and how beneficial this would be for them and the foundation. He asked Dr. Wasiri if he heard anything from home in anticipation for the January trip back to Mezi.

His protégé said that he did not. He was simply in contact with his friend at UN Mezi Mission Office who was taking care of his new passport. To date, he did not hear about the Polytechnic University regarding his application for the tenured professorship. Dr. Wasiri sounded a bit worried about the status of his application. Dr. O'Shea could not help but laugh at the suggestion that his protégé was worried about his application. He said that with his wonder-boy background, he should not be worried. He advised him to continue to get ready for his trip. They quickly changed the conversation when Emma's husband approached his father-in-law to congratulate him on setting up the foundation in Emily's memory. He mentioned also that the Calgary Oil Company, where he works as managing director of operations, had recently been bought by AMX that sponsors the foundation. He added that he would be glad to meet with the new CEO Lady Allistair who had been instrumental in setting up the foundation according to the foundation white paper.

Dr. O'Shea deflected all inquiries by saying that Lady Allistair was so high in the approval process of the foundation that he never had to meet with her. The only contact he had was a congratulation note he received from her when the funding for the foundation was approved. The exchange was terminated when the lead of catering services company announced that it was time for the assembly to gather around for the expected dinner.

CHAPTER 16

KMC

Nothing compared to the excitement the prospective January visit by Dr. Kano Wasiri to Mezi had generated at the Polytechnic University. It was not by accident that Dr. O'Shea laughed when his protégé expressed worry about his application for the tenured professorship at the Polytechnic University. From the latest correspondence he received from Mezi, all was go and more. He knew that during this trip his protégé would be offered the position of dean of the Faculty of Applied Sciences in the buildings being built, thanks to the foundation. What he did not know was the extent to which various Mezi political progressive forces were being marshaled underneath to insure that Dr. Wasiri's visit turns out to be something more than what Dr. O'Shea would have imagined. It was in fact the beginning of political impetus that Mezi had been waiting for a long time. For a start, as soon as Dr. Umzigwe, Polytechnic University chancellor, received the word that Dr. Wasiri was coming to Mezi in January, he called for a private meeting in his own residence with Father Zolani and two other members of the university board; the youngest board member and very dynamic Dr. John Awassa and the most senior board member and current dean of Applied Sciences Faculty, Dr. Wutugrase. These three members of the board were all connected to what was bubbling as a grassroots political movement under the umbrella of KMC.

Besides the loose national coordination given by Father Zolani, KMC was in a desperate search of what could amount to a political leadership. Father Zolani had made it clear that he had zero political aspirations after the various difficulties he had encountered with his Roman Catholic conservative hierarchy when he took over the national coordination of KMC. For all practical purposes, he had been forbidden to conduct any catholic rites, including saying masses. With more than 50 percent Roman Catholic population, that was a tag that could not be easily evaded in Mezi. It did not make for an effective political leadership. In addition, every time a political aspirant came to the scene to claim the mantles of KMC, various groups under its umbrella find a way to torpedo the aspiration through innuendos or simply because the aspirant was at one time or another in the leadership ranks of Mezi various political parties or institutions which were held to be entirely corrupted for one reason or another.

This was the case for the army, the police, the courts, the government, the assembly, the senate or institutions of higher learning.

True political leadership was sorely missing for such an effective and growing grassroots movement. The KMC umbrella included mainly the youth in secondary schools, the college students and professors, the unions, various cultural elite groups, the catholic clergy below bishops, and any other organization that had lost complete confidence in the prevailing country institutions. At this stage, KMC advocated the complete cleansing of these institutions in order to advance the real development of Mezi.

Father Zolani went around enunciating KMC principles of anticorruption, fairness, and justice, proposing concrete steps about how to apply them. He was very impressive, leaving lasting impression over anybody attending his conferences. He always finished his talk urging participants to hold meetings and discuss subjects in a group or cell in order to be vigilant and to identify every failing that they currently confronted, where they lived, and document them. When he came back to talk to the group, he would find an already organized cell with a complete book of grievances to review and to address. He collected the grievances book back to a secret small center in Mandi where they were readily compiled. In fact, that center was right there in Polytechnic University campus and held under the guidance of the three board members; Dr. Umzigwe, Dr. Awassa, and Dr. Wutugrase. The grievances were handed to selected students secretly sworn to KMC principles. These students were charged to analyze and parcel out the grievances into nicely designed categories which in turn were posted into a large university data base deceptively named MFF for Mezi Facts and Fiction. Over time, these board members and Father Zolani formed a growing data bank that, in fact, became a depository of intelligence services unequal in Mezi.

The grievances came from every sector and location in country and gave a sober and extremely sad state of the country. Corruption indicators were alarming in every shape or form. The country's rapid descent into hell can be easily measured by a scant review of MFF. This was the backdrop environment when the three board members and Father Zolani met in the official residence of the university chancellor.

It was the oldest member of the university board, Dr. Wutugrase, who started talking at this meeting, "Thank you, Brother Umzigwe, for calling this meeting so urgently. Father Zolani and Brother Awassa, we all know why this meeting has been called. For me it is becoming beyond urgency.

I don't know if I can hold any longer. The sight that my beloved country is giving every day has dried my eyes for tears. The high and incredible level of moral and material corruption only matches the endless vagary of incompetence at the government's highest circles. The latest being the trading of invectives between two sitting Supreme Court judges over sexual depravations of their respective assistant female clerks, young enough to be their great-grandchildren.

My beloved country's national motto should be changed to B and B or Bed and Bank. It seems to me that, that is where all business of the country is being conducted nowadays between bed to fornicate and bank to steal. Mind you, about six months ago, it was the sad display of the fight between the president of the assembly and the president of Senate over that lady, Monica Kello Ngoma, with the celebrated name of 'Miss Two Chambers.' By the way, she has remained a minister of God knows what. Now the sickness has found its ugly way into the Supreme Court, the last bastion of our fledgling democracy. My God! It is all rubbish. I said enough of that. Brothers, we need to grab the chance that is coming to us in January with Dr. Kano Wasiri's visit. We cannot load on the brother with all we have, but we must make clear to Dr. Kano Wasiri that he represents the clear alternative that Mezi has been waiting for since the time Mezi became independent. We got to convince him to lead KMC in the electoral process within the next two years up to, yes, the presidential elections. Then KMC will file only grassroots candidates at every political slot. Every candidate must be thoroughly vetted for each lot. That should be our clear message to him. My God, we seem to be running out of the time. There is so much to do when Dr. Wasiri comes in Mezi. You know, I have been thinking of something that will be impressed upon him to remove any doubt about our commitment to his selection. Remember, prior to the time of independence and before the first elections by Mezi's citizens, our nation's father, Sir Banfi Bello, had this great imagination to call on every tribal chief in the nation to gather in this village in the northern bank of the Lake Nyerengi. An all-day ceremony was held there in presence of all living tribal chiefs of the nation for two purposes: to cleanse the nation of any foreign power and to vet a native son, Sir Banfi Bello, with the power over the new nation of Mezi, power only the tribal chiefs can give. This ceremony established Sir Banfi Bello as a paramount Mezi leader, irrespective of political parties that came in later. To his retirement from political scene and to his death, Sir Banfi Bello remained highly respected by everybody and was called upon time and again to assist in resolving issues of governing because of his judicial temperament, fairness, modesty, and uncorrupted ways.

"This was the case until his passing and the time of colonels and generals, which completely destroyed that previous order of respect and hierarchy. I am no social or political scientist, but I have always posited that the neglect and destabilizing of our tribal chiefs started the general corruption downward spiral. We can stop it only if we can bring about that sense of order and hierarchy when there is a sense that there will always be someone above us to whom we owe respect and attention. We can start that process by calling on tribal chiefs all over Mezi to come back to that village and to cleanse the present corrupt power gripping the nation and, in the process, to vet under the guidance of KMC, an unnamed native son with the power to restore the nation to its glorious past. The difference this time will be that the native son will remain unnamed until the electoral process, yet KMC will get the blessing of all tribal chiefs to select that unnamed native son. If we can pull that ceremony, we have already won the next electoral process. The rest will be easy. The essential at this stage would be to have Dr. Kano Wasiri attend that ceremony when he would come here in January. He would be presented to the tribal chiefs not as the unnamed native son but only as the shy, humble leader of KMC at this time. To those tribal chiefs who would want to know more about him, he would be introduced, God willing, as the next one. Our cells can start putting out the feel for that ceremony. We should know very quickly if it is possible to hold that meeting in January. I am certain that it is possible. Now what do you think, brothers?"

Father Zolani was first to respond, "What a splendid idea! I did not know that Sir Banfi Bello was instrumental in calling that meeting I heard so much about. Now I understand why he has been called the father of our nation. What wisdom! There could be no other important sign or symbol to give to the nation than that kind of demarcation from the tribal chiefs. It would be even more important if it comes from the tenants of our temporal power, the tribal chiefs. Who in this nation does not hold to a high regard the tribal chief? True, a lot of them have been corrupted by the political process, but time and again, the corrupt ones have been cast aside when problems arise and when their corruption started spitting out its venomous leak and was not able to cast a judicious, fair, even-tempered decision. You see at the end of the village and local level, the anonymous and corrupt decisions we put with in urban centers will not do. It is not only the tribal chief who decides, the village elders weigh in as well. As they say it, it is hard to corrupt all people all the time. That is where the tribal chiefs get their final wisdom. I rather put up with 77 percent of good tribal chiefs at that meeting than none. I must work on this right away, if that is your consensus."

Dr. Umzigwe showed more caution and said, "Brothers, we have gathered today to decide on how we were going to communicate with Dr. Kano Wasiri regarding the proposals of tenured professorship and the deanship at our beloved university. I am suspecting that you have decided that he has already accepted those first two proposals, and you jumped to the ultimate proposal of KMC leadership to guide us out of this despicable dismal where the nation finds itself. Brother Wutugrase, I have already agreed with you regarding that last proposal step. I also agreed with you when you said at the beginning let us not overwhelm our dear Kano with so much on the plate. I believe the tenure professorship, the deanship, the KMC national leadership, and the tribal chief's ceremony as proposed are more than our celebrated native son would be able to chew on his plate for a week of visit. I understand about grabbing the chance being offered with his visit, and I also understand that this nation cannot wait any longer for a new political order. I am the one to do things judiciously. I am for all that have been proposed. But the question that comes in my mind is, how to prepare him for all these introductions. If our man in New York, Sir William Ewas, was closer to Dr. Wasiri all the way in Kentucky, it could not be a problem. But that is not the case, unless Sir Ewas meets him prior to his trip. But then Dr. Wasiri might become a bit suspicious. In my latest call, Sir Ewas told me that he was processing his new passport; he could not initiate a serious meeting with Kano over a matter of passport. Another bigger problem is that Dr. O'Shea would come with Dr. Wasiri. As close as they are, Dr. Wasiri would not tolerate to be separated from his mentor for more than twenty-four hours while in Mezi. The only alternative we have, my dear brothers, is that we will need to be very resourceful and keep him here for another week. That would probably work for Dr. O'Shea who seems to work overtime to get him settled here in Mezi. That would be our only chance to make the last introduction and indoctrination. Now before I close, I want to make sure that we would do this provided that we have all agreed that from now on Dr. Kano Wasiri is the only political aspirant to lead KMC into the next electoral process and Mezi to a bright future. May God help us!"

All attendees repeated after the chancellor, "May God help us!" He turned to Dr. John Awassa and said, "Brother Awassa, my apologies, I closed the meeting before giving you a chance to say something as every body has spoken." Dr. John Awassa said, "There is no need for apologies, Dr. Umzigwe, I am rather grateful I was invited to this momentous meeting when so much was being decided. I am the youngest member of the team and in much need of learning. I would never have thought of the ceremony that Dr. Wutugrase has proposed.

That tells you how much I know about where the real power resides in this country. In none of those major centers of learning in the West, where I have been, I would have learned how important the ascent from the tribal chiefs was for Sir Banfi Bello to affirm his long-lasting sway and power. I am here learning and thankful for the opportunities. We have judiciously settled on the support we have to give to Dr. Kano Wasiri I am dying to meet. Let's do it."

Dr. Wutugrase then rose to recite in Swahili KMC pledges to social justice, fairness, and anticorruption. He also said a closing prayer, and the KMC leadership meeting was adjourned. The prevailing political environment in Mezi also became the major point of discussion when a week later, after her arrival in London, Lady Allistair had a late-afternoon appointment with Dr. McMillan who was still in London working out the final phases of his legal entreaties with his late wife's estate. Dr. McMillan kept a very late-afternoon appointment with the new AMX CEO at the London business center headquarters. It was five thirty in the afternoon when he was whisked in the CEO's wood-paneled conference room. Lady Allistair came in alone five minutes later. She was dressed in a double-breasted businesswoman suit. She took a seat across from Dr. McMillan. She started the meeting thanking Dr. McMillan for accepting to join the foundation effort in Mezi. She said that she was even more grateful after she became aware of the level of his past involvement in academic world in Mezi. She repeated that the organization was extremely lucky to land his services. She also added, to get to the point, that she had an additional assignment for him with a totally different perspective compared to the managing director, sites operations he already had. She wanted him to become the political eyes and ears for the organization in Mezi. With all the philanthropic and economic growing involvement that the organization intends for the country, a definitive political perspective gained from decades of residency and observation would be extremely valuable. She then asked Dr. McMillan for his opinion over the prevailing political situation in Mezi.

Dr. McMillan obliged, "A time bomb to put it mildly. Every known institution in the country is going to hell or about to go to hell. The presidency, the government, the two houses of parliament, the army, the police, the courts were all in varying stages of disgrace, mined by deep corruption. The country, I am afraid, is ripe for a bloodletting revolution of the worst kind if a rapid change or hope of change does not materialize soon. It would take me a long time to share the political status of Mezi.

But all I can say is that for the past thirty years since I got there, I saw a country going from an agricultural food basket for all neighboring countries, including South Africa, to a country that cannot feed 1 percent of its own population. It has become worse than a basket from the time the colonels and generals that we in the West encouraged to take over and by the same token destroy every social and economic fabric of the nation through ever-deepening corruption. The scales of corruption have reached deep in every sector of society. It has gotten so bad that in some urban centers, prostitution is gaining and reaching girls and boys below the age of ten. Worse, it is now becoming a matter of survival for many families that selling daughters to houses of sexual deprivation is no longer a matter of shame or scandal. I would not know where to start when it comes to scandals that are perpetrated every day in the country. People are becoming literally numb with every failing befalling the nation."

Lady Allistair waved her hand to stop the sad litany and asked him why then he had accepted to go back to in that hopeless Mezi.
Dr. McMillan laughed and said, "Better a calamity you know than the one you don't know. I have lived there for a long time and raised a family under those dire circumstances. Just the same, one gets used to things. I run away from the cold corners of north, and I am not about to come back here. I would ride whatever political wave Mezi reserves us when it comes next. I have seen many of those waves. By the way, I am about to rejoin my life partner into a blissful matrimony for a second time. I would give anything to stay in Mezi with her. We all have a price to pay in life. Mezi is mine."

Lady Allistair jumped in the occasion Dr. McMillan opened and asked, "What do you think will be the next political wave, and how can you assist us in mitigating it?"

Dr. McMillan fell for that bait, "I am certain that the next political wave is there already. It is in the air. I saw it building and growing from the start. It is propagating in form of what they call KMC or New Directions Cells in Swahili. That is a grown grassroots movement that is sweeping away the whole country. It would not be changed. It had taken hold in every decent sector of the country and society. The one beautiful thing about this movement is that it cannot be corrupted. It is solidly based on anticorruption pledge. That is one thing that makes it strong. The one who will lead that movement would be able to bring about a new order for Mezi." Lady Allistair then said, "Your charge at Mezi would then be to insure that our interests are not hurt by the rise of KMC. Still I wonder if Dr. O'Shea and Dr. Wasiri are aware of all this change to come."

"Dr. O'Shea and Dr. Wasiri would not be impacted by the change as they are working within the framework of one of the rare institutions which have not been eaten by the corruption virus, the universities and colleges. The institutions of higher learning have been the breeding grounds of KMC. That is why I am so aware of this movement. As long the foundation stayed within the confines of the Polytechnic University, all the efforts it is supporting will be safe. As soon as it will venture outside the campus, that is where problems start. It will definitely get worse anytime a military man becomes part of the enterprise. Dr. Wasiri is another factor all together. From what I have heard and observed, he is a natural born leader among the elite, the university teaching staff. To date, I have never been clear who leads KMC except for a defrocked Jesuit priest named Father Zolani. He acts as a loose coordinator of KMC going lecturing all over the country about KMC principles. He is very eloquent, but he has not shown any desire to take the next step to move KMC to an effective political movement. KMC is rather in desperate need of a leader. Then again, it is proving difficult to lead it, given the many diverse and at times competing orientations which make up KMC. Maybe somebody like Dr. Wasiri can claim that leadership, but it would not be easy to do this. A huge majority of KMC followers have been disappointed by the so-called Diaspora people who come home only to be placed in high positions in the government or private commercial firms and are quickly compromised by the corrupted institutions despised by the KMC. The fact that Dr. Wasiri is Diaspora may mark him as potentially compromised. Then you never know which sectors or organizations will be willing to push his leadership. All I know is that he seems to be highly respected in the university teaching circles. Time would tell if Dr. Wasiri wants to put himself through the rigors of political selection of KMC. These rigors could be sometime brutal. Many politicians have failed to gain KMC political accolade."

Lady Allistair rose to signify that the meeting was ending and thanked Dr. McMillan for accepting the other assignment. She mentioned that Barry Newcomb would advise him soon of the monthly compensation for that assignment. She wished him a lot of success for both assignments and disappeared in her CEO office.

When she reached her desk, she opened one of top security files and annotated "three to five years sequence" in the section called "KW Political Promotion" for Dr. Kano Wasiri's political promotion. She also entered below under a subsection "DrMCM Very effective—$10 MTH," for Dr. McMillan was very effective and should be earning about ten thousand dollars a month for this new assignment.

CHAPTER 17
Father Felix

Concerns expressed at different levels and for diverse motivations over the eventual return of Dr. Wasiri to Mezi were also rubbing over the good old professor O'Shea after the beautiful weekend he spent with his children, grandchildren, and his protégé family, celebrating the memory of his beloved wife. This started with the toast talk given by his elder son Anthony when he said that Emily's rules were a sentimental cover for his family to justify most things he could not explain. That way of interpreting Emily's rules hit him very hard when he was alone. He was reflecting over all was said during the splendid weekend and after all visitors were gone. He thought that if his son was right, then he might have driven his protégé and family in an adventure that Emily may not have approved. He also reflected that he had put in motion so many things that it was a bit too late now to stop the return of his protégé back to Mezi. The best thing he can do now was to engage as many people as possible to give his protégé a complete political perspective and environment of the country where he had not lived for the past twenty-five years or so. He heard him mentioning bits here and there he had collected over the weekends from telephone calls he made with his countrymen living in New York City area. He had mentioned a Mr. Mbow working at the UN, and now this gentleman who works at the Mezi UN Mission and who had helped him to get the multiple entry visas. But he had also observed that when his protégé mentioned these political bits collected here and there, he had a very detached view of news, as if they were from a very distant country, any other country in the world. He did not show any particular outrage usually seen from other foreign students or citizens when they are talking about the failings witnessed in their home country.

Just the same, the good old professor was far to think of himself as a political person. American politics left him very wanting. He was what could be called a typical politically independent person not following the precepts of any political party, Democrat or Republican. He voted, when he voted, his conscience or what he and Emily have determined to be their united conscience. His independent political leaning was strengthened by his long life distrust of authority worsened by his endless battle with the University of Kentucky management at every level.

He expected his protégé, at minimum and at least, to show outrage or revulsion to sad stories from back home that he used to share with him.

But that was never the case. He was rather stoic about it as if whatever problems or failings besetting Mezi at the time will come to pass as long as concrete solutions are brought forth to resolve them. One day his protégé said bluntly that "crocodile tears would not resolve Africa or Mezi problems, concrete well-thought solutions would."

Reviewing these small details started to worry the professor a bit now that he had pushed every button to assure his return back home. He was more so when he remembered that Dr. Wasiri seemed very concerned that his application for tenured professorship at Polytechnic University could be rejected. It was disheartening to see how Dr. Wasiri was disconnected with what was happening. It was as if all that was being done by the Emily Thomas O'Shea foundation was not connected with his return to Mezi. How in the world can the university reject his application? In his humble ways, Dr. Wasiri thought that he was going to be thoroughly interviewed at Polytechnic University to get his tenured professorship the same way he was when he applied for teaching Mines Sciences at Kentucky State University at Frankfort. Though admirable, Dr. O'Shea was determined to insure that his protégé's posture be anchored in harsh political reality of Mezi, where he was bound to live in less than a year.

He was going to find somebody visiting from Mezi who should give his protégé a lengthy long weekend crash course over the current political environment in Mezi. This should happen before their January trip. He searched the phone number of the visa guy at Mezi UN Mission in New York City. He was named Mr. William Ewas. He reached Sir William Ewas at about ten thirty in the morning. He related his concern and requested the assistance to identify a current visitor from Mezi, able to provide Dr. Wasiri a long weekend reading of the current political situation in Mezi.

Dr. O'Shea stated that he was ready to finance the trip of the visitor as long as he or she accepts to stay somewhere close to Dr. Wasiri's residence in Kentucky. Sir Ewas listened attentively and assured Dr. O'Shea that he would do his best to find a solution and would get back to him very soon.

Sir Ewas hung up his phone and said to himself, "God is great." He had a long conversation first with Dr. Umzigwe, the Polytechnic University chancellor the Saturday before and then with Father Zolani the Sunday after.

Both were briefing him about the meeting they had and what they wanted to introduce Dr. Wasiri into. They were upset that there were just too many issues to dump on him on his short week visit. They struggled about how to give Dr. Wasiri an advance notice of things to come. And now his mentor, in the very person of Dr. O'Shea, was requesting that we find somebody to give him a long weekend reading over the political situation in Mezi. This should be used to accomplish what KMC direction wants. Sir Ewas called Father Zolani who was now delighted to hear the request. He said that he had a very good candidate in the person of Father Felix Mulai-Bando, another Jesuit priest who went to the seminary and became priest the same time as Father Zolani. He was among the very few priests who were secret members of KMC and supported their brother Father Zolani against the very conservative hierarchy in the Mezi Roman Catholic Church. Father Felix was the brightest of the bunch next to Father Zolani, who for all practical purposes had been defrocked. Knowing the growing dissatisfaction that the persecution of Father Zolani had brought within the clergy, the hierarchy started the promotion of Father Felix to the rank of Bishop. He was recently named rector of St. Charles Seminary about twenty miles from Mandi. Father Zolani told Sir Ewas that his colleague was in the States invited by the Roman Catholic Bishops Conference to give presentations about Mezi Roman Catholic Standings in Washington, DC. He should be available to Dr. Wasiri if requested. He just asked Sir Ewas to give him the time to talk to Father Felix to state what needs to be communicated. At nine in the evening, Sir Ewas called Dr. O'Shea with the name and contact information of Father Felix Mulai-Bando to pass on to Dr. Wasiri. He suggested that the arrangement takes an all appearance of a fortuitous happening.

The next day, Dr. O'Shea searched in the Internet for the schedules of Roman Catholic conferences in the areas of Frankfort, Lexington, and Louisville. He found one in a diocese outside Frankfort and two in Lexington areas. The conference to be held in a Catholic Church attached to the University of Kentucky was much closer to a visit that Father Felix could be attached to. He would be invited to speak and answer questions for about two hours that Friday evening, and Dr. O'Shea would then convince his protégé to be his host for the rest of the weekend. This would accomplish his goal of providing the much-needed long weekend reading of Mezi politics. He called the pastor of the church at the university. He was delighted to get the participation of an African priest to talk about African issues. He reached Father Felix at DC, who was expecting his call and was entirely agreeable to do what Dr. O'Shea wanted.

He sent to him all references for the round-trip fares to Lexington and considerable traveler checks for pocket money. That evening he called his protégé with the invitation to come join him to a conference being held at the Catholic Church conference room in the University of Kentucky campus the next Friday. He asked him if he knew this Father Felix Mulai-

Bando. He did not, but he had heard about him. He suggested that he should invite him to his home as a guest from Mezi to meet with your family and to get fresh news from home at least less than a month before going back. Dr. Wasiri thought that this was an excellent idea. He asked how he could get in touch with him. Dr. O'Shea gave the contact's name of the pastor at the University Of Kentucky. He had given him the contact information from Father Felix. Dr. Wasiri said that he would call him the next day. Then he called Sir Ewas in New York City to verify Father Felix's whereabouts in the United States. Sir Ewas acted surprised about his inquiry but suggested to reach him at this particular place in DC. Before long, he was on the phone talking with Father Felix, expressing his pleasure to meet him at Lexington and insisting to be his host for the rest of the weekend, if that was not a problem. Father Felix said that it was not a problem and was looking forward to meet a countryman in Lexington, Kentucky. Dr. Wasiri called Sir Ewas later to announce that he will be the host of Father Felix that weekend and was looking forward to get fresh news from home. Sir Ewas, still acting surprised, asked him how he became aware of the presence of Father Felix in the United States. He said that, when reviewing weekend events in the state of Kentucky academic community bulletin web site, he saw Father Felix Mulai-Bando from Mezi giving a lecture in this church at the University of Kentucky. That literally piqued his curiosity, educators from Mezi do not usually come giving lecture in Kentucky, of all places. He verified this, and it was really happening. He felt very much obliged to extend his hospitality to Father Felix who had accepted. He added that he would share with Sir Ewas whatever he will get from the good Father Felix. At the end of their call, Sir Ewas sent an e-mail message to Dr. Umzigwe and Father Zolani, informing them that Dr. Wasiri will be Father Felix's host the following weekend. He ended the message with the caption, "God is Great."

That next Friday evening, the conference room of the Catholic Church became too small for the lecture that Father Felix was to give. The church pastor decided on the spot to move the lecture to the next large auditorium of the School of Religious Studies in the adjoining building. It was very easy to redirect the overflowing crowd ever assembled for a lecture sponsored by the church.

Professor O'Shea and Dr. Kano Wasiri took the honor guest seats next to the pastor and Father Felix. The crowd was not disappointed when Father Felix got up to give his lecture titled, "Mezi Politics and Church Mission."

Father Felix entertained the audience as follows: "Yesterday, when I was attending an engaging debate among Catholic brothers and sisters, clergy and laity at the American University in Washington, DC, where I have been invited as guest lecturer, I was struck by the deep level of debate. To make a long story short, the debate was around a bible passage when our Lord Jesus Christ said to scribes and Pharisees 'To render to Caesar what is due to Caesar and to God what is due to God.' I learned then that is the crux of the debate that goes on in the United States when there is talk of separation of church and state. I listened attentively to the debate and the give and take that went on among the attendees.

The references from the US Constitution, various Supreme Court decrees, legal papers from eminent scientists, precedents from the British laws, and others were made in one hand to bolster the State argument, while theological papers, religious books, including the Bible, were used to uphold the church role. For a Father who is speaking to you now and who is from a country of Mezi, the debate became a bit troubling. It was troubling because in any debate when you are talking of opposite points of view, these points must exist. As the conference debate progressed, I found myself being thrown back to Mezi to the concepts or ideas of state and church. While I can justify the concept and idea of a church, a Roman Catholic Church of which I am a member, I became a bit confused when it came time of talking about the very concept or idea of state for Mezi. Yes, I am a citizen of something called state of Mezi. But can I talk of the state of Mezi in the same sense as those brothers and sisters were talking about in that conference? I doubt it. Dear brothers and sisters assembled in this hall, I would not dare compare what make up the state institutions of the United States with those of Mezi. You have your more than two hundred years of history compared to about seventy of ours. That comparison would not be fair. But I will be comfortably grounded if I decide to take a stock of where the institutions of the state of Mezi should have been as compared to what they are today. This is where the debate of separation of state and church became troubling for me. On one hand, we have the church in Mezi, as we know, struggling day in, day out to fulfill its mission on earth, while the State or all those institutions that make up the entity called State are in varying stages of despair and disappearance.

I am now talking about the presidency, the government, the lower and higher chambers of parliament, the army, the police, and the courts, all these institutions in Mezi are so mired in corruption that they all, and without exception, have become dysfunctional. Three months of lecture would not be enough to give you every detail of corruption eating away at each of these institutions.

"But I can share, for instance, this scheme that three ministers have cooked to share on the barrel of oil price increase. You see one of the Arab Emirates states was willing to sell a six-month supply of oil to the state of Mezi at thirty dollars below the going market price of the barrel of oil. This was directly negotiated between the World Bank, the Arab Emirates state, and the government to assist Mezi in its balance of payments account that was deteriorating at an alarming rate. It did not take long to notice that the ministers of Finances, Energy, and International Trade and the governor of the Central Bank of Mezi banded together to resell that supply of oil to their friends who turned around and resold it in the open market for a total of seventy dollars for one barrel of oil. They were so stupid that they resold their allocated share to some oil interests back in Dubai.

The scandal toppled that government. But the governor of Central Bank remained in his position, and the three ministers, now multimillionaires, recycled themselves as high-level directors in their respective ministries.

"Another scandal involved the current president's elder son. This lad came back from the University of Berlin with a master's degree in bank management. Instead of establishing a legal bank, he convinced his father to set up a Ponzi or pyramid financial scheme where investors were to earn 35 percent of interest for a minimum investment of over hundred thousand dollars for a minimum of three months. Given the references of a president's son, it did not take him long to collect close to forty million dollars in less than three months, mainly from the elite. When he made the 30 percent interest payment to the first time and small number of investors, the popularity of the scheme grew and the pot increased to more than 120 millions of dollars. This also caused a rush of get-rich-quick investment schemes all over the nation. But as it is always the case in any pyramid financial scheme, the expanding competition to get new funds starts drying the availability of these funds. Soon after, the ability to make the exorbitant 35 percent interest payment started to evaporate. Before long, the president's son started pulling all kinds of disappearing acts by taking long vacations abroad, leaving his investment company offices with no money to pay the next batch of investors.

When an irate investor, who happened to be a retired army general, confronted him, he confessed that the financial scheme had already collapsed and the investors had lost all of their money. The president's son was lucky to be shot only at his leg by the general. He was evacuated to South Africa and was not to be heard of again. The president had since pledged to reimburse the investors in various ways, but none of the investors has recovered any money until today. Those were some of many scandals of financial nature to rock the country. If I was not a man of cloth, I could entertain you with devious stories of low moral turpitude, stories that defray the news daily in Mezi, and involve mainly people who manage these corrupted institutions.

"Dear brothers and sisters, I do not believe telling you hundred stories of the same would make any difference at this stage. I rather go back to my initial contention when I said that I have found the debate about the separation of church and state troubling. The debate becomes even more worrisome when the institutions of State become so dysfunctional and nonoperative as it is the case today in Mezi. My question to the audience is this, what do you do when there is no State and you cannot separate church and state?

"That is where we are at in Mezi today as we strive to put back in place those institutions of state. In the meantime, I have to submit to this assembly that we have no other guiding forces in Mezi to lead us to our next social station but the church. That should be the mission of our church. Thank you."

Standing ovations, thunderous and sustained applauses followed Father Felix's presentation for the next ten minutes. It took the church pastor that long to calm the audience in order to move to the next phase of lecture with audience's questions directed to Father Felix.

He was generous enough to entertain about twenty of them. Most revolved around what the church was doing to insure that the institutions do not collapse completely.

Father Felix said, "The church still strongly believes in an alternate political process of political change through electoral process. The overall population has definitely rejected regime change through military overthrow or any kind of so-called revolution. The general consensus that has evolved through time has been that these regime changes always wound up to be a vehicle for one kind of dictatorship or another.

The general population did not have any more stomach for these tragic political comedies. They were even worse compared to what was passing for political democracy nowadays. It was obvious that the general population has now matured enough to recognize the mistake of electing very bad people. At least, the mistake was made deliberately in the process of the electoral process. The result or mistake was not imposed from the outside or a military dictatorship. It was, as it is said, 'vox populi.' Everybody knew that most of time the mistake came from the misguided view people shared in electing politicians on ethnic or regional basis. The process invariably invited the worst vile scoundrels of the world to submit their candidacy trumpeting all kinds of silly promises with no basis of minimum reality except that so and so a native of this village or that region would stand ready to bring untold bounty to the village or region. Once elected, the first order of business of the scoundrel was to drastically revise down the realization of the promises because of unfortunate limitations that some other scoundrels from those distant villages or regions were imposing on the wishes of the elected native son. This comedy repeated all over the nation thousand times while the same scoundrels, in retired dark corners of their chambers, ministries, or other positions of power trade among themselves all kinds of financial favors irrespective of the village or the region they came from. This elite has perfected the process of eating at the pig stall. After being burned so many times and in front of the calamitous display of political corruption, there are obvious signs that the general population is getting tired of this unproductive process and is ready to amend it. Accordingly, the church is preparing and educating the population of Mezi to measure appropriately the failings of those in the political scene now and to insure that they are not returned to any of positions of power after the election.

"To that effect, the church has actively sponsored the campaign called None of Them. The church is also working closely with the grassroots movement called New Directions to reach every segment of the population beyond those of Catholic faith."

At the end, Father Felix added that the progress that this grassroots movement had made in moving the general conscience of the Mezi citizenry had given him much hope that the future of Mezi will return in able and steady political direction after the next election. The questions-and-answers session added more than two hours to the lecture time to the general satisfaction of those who attended. The church pastor was beyond delight for the reception this lecture had generated and tried to get Father Felix to commit to another lecture right after the electoral process had taken place in Mezi.

He took Dr. O'Shea on the side and thanked him profusely for suggesting that Father Felix to come and give this well-received lecture. He also suggested that Dr. O'Shea use his goodwill and contacts to get Father Felix to come back. It was about past ten thirty when Dr. Wasiri pulled his car from the church parking lot in company of Dr. O'Shea and his guest Father Felix. Given about the hour and half or more it would take to reach his home at Frankfort, Dr. Wasiri decided to offer Father Felix a late dinner somewhere in Lexington at a steak joint that Dr. O'Shea knew very well. It took less than twenty minutes to reach what turned out to be a very exclusive restaurant and where Dr. O'Shea was a very familiar guest.

They were given a private VIP room for the dinner. When they were seated, and after being served a fine red wine, it was Dr. O'Shea who spoke first and offered a toast to Father Felix by saying that he had gained in about four hours the education of lifetime about Mezi.

He chided his protégé for not having been forthright about Mezi as much as Father Felix had shared. Dr. Wasiri seconded his mentor's toast and agreed with his rebuke that he had not shared as much as he had wished about Mezi simply on the account of not knowing what was going on in Mezi. Father Felix jumped in to settle the difference. He mentioned that politics in Mezi are a fast moving target.

"What you might believe to be a story at one time can turn out to be a bogus on top of another layer of bogus stories. And that is for us living right there in Mezi, can you imagine what would it be like for people out abroad, reading glimpses of these news? That is not to excuse Dr. Wasiri in any way. But in his position, I would also act on the side of caution."

Dr. O'Shea reclaimed his toast by adding, "Father Felix, I should have first commended you for the extraordinary presentation you gave today. It was very educative for all attendees. But I came out of this lecture even more fearful for my protégé here, Dr. Wasiri, after relentlessly urging him to go back and teach at the Polytechnic University. I am definitely concerned that Dr. Wasiri is returning in to a powder keg with his entire family. What do you suggest that he does now? By the way, he is about to go back to Mezi to finalize his application for a tenured professorship at the university. I am very much confused now. Please help us, Father."

At that point, Father Felix intervened forcefully, "Dr. O'Shea, with all due respect to you and the extraordinary relationship you share with Dr. Kano Wasiri, I believe it is up to Dr. Wasiri, present here, to decide whichever way he wants to lead his life and his family's life in the future. If he has elected to go back to teach, well, that should be his entirely own decision and his wife's, I believe. Besides, where Mezi is at this stage, it needs all that his children can give. And in my humble opinion, Dr. Wasiri has so much to contribute in the next phase where Mezi is headed to; it would be enormously beneficial for him to be there during that transition.

Frankly, it would not help for him to come only when all the dirt has been cleaned. Mezi is a work-in-process. We will be very happy to have the likes of Dr. Wasiri to wash Mezi clean and to establish the new institutions we need. I do not say this in disregard to everything you have done for our countryman. Absolutely not! It would be with the utmost debt of gratitude that some of us down in Mezi would welcome back Dr. Wasiri, knowing that you, Dr. O'Shea, has sown the seeds of greatness and excellence that Mezi is ready to identify in Dr. Wasiri. Dr. O'Shea, you have done your job. It is now time to let go and see the product of your job shine by itself. Talking of shining, why don't we let Dr. Kano Wasiri speak for himself?"

As Dr. Wasiri started to speak, there was a knock at the private room. Two young female servers were carrying their dinner. After they finished serving the three guests, they retired and closed the private room.
Then Dr. Wasiri said, "I have already made up my mind to return to Mezi, and I am not about to change my mind now. For your information, Dr. O'Shea, Hasbo, my wife, is with me one thousand percent in this decision. Father Felix, you have to excuse my mentor here for speaking the way he did. I have been lucky to be associated with Dr. O'Shea, his late wife, Emily, and his family all these years. Dr. O'Shea has been the closest to what I can call father that I ever knew. He is and remains my adopted father. And when he speaks, it is from a fatherly concern that goes way deep to my heart and my wife's. He is coming with me to Mezi in January. We will probably pay you a visit at that seminary when we will be there. I will report to him as often as I can when I and my family are settled in Mezi next year to reassure him about the progress I would be making to adapt to everything Mezi would reserve for us. Again, I repeat, regardless of the current political condition, I am returning to Mezi."

To that last confirmation, Dr. O'Shea raised a wine glass to say, "Father Felix, please join me to respond to what Kano just said, 'Amen.'" Both raised their glasses in unison and said Amen to Dr. Wasiri's bemusement.

Afterward, Dr. Wasiri added, "Now I do not want to get your food and this wonderful steak cold. I am starving. Let us finally have our dinner." But that was not to be without a grace prayer from Father Felix. The rest of dinner was spent listening to Father Felix giving his impression of various areas he visited since he came to the United States, the New York Area, the four-hour bus trip to DC, the Metropolitan Washington, DC, area and now the Lexington town. It was past midnight when they left the restaurant.

Dr. Wasiri took his mentor home and proceeded to drive back to Frankfort with his guest, Father Felix. The ride took about an hour and half. Father Felix was at sleep ten minutes after Dr. O'Shea was dropped and was awakened only when Dr. Wasiri had already parked inside his house and was gathering his luggage. Father Felix apologized for not keeping him company during the ride. Dr. Wasiri dismissed the apology and said that he had a very long day from the flight from DC to the well-received lecture at the church, the late dinner, and finally the long ride back home to Frankfort. Dr. Wasiri added he was the one to apologize for putting the good Father through so much in less than twenty-four hours. He added that he was honored that he had accepted to be his guest this weekend and begged him to come upstairs to his guest room that had already been prepared for him. He also apologized for his family who had gone to bed at this time. They tiptoed in semi darkness in the house and reached an immaculate guest bedroom that Hasbo had so well prepared for Father Felix. He said goodnight to Father Felix and rejoined his own bedroom, where Hasbo was sound asleep. The next Saturday morning, Dr. Wasiri rose at about eleven. He checked the guest room, which was empty and already made up as it was when they came last night. He heard laughter coming from below the kitchen area. He found Father Felix entertaining Hasbo and the children with his imitation of a popular TV African-American bumbling detective who solves his cases by appealing for guidance from his eight-year-old daughter and his eighty-eight-year-old grandmother. The show was the rage of both youth and adult world alike. Father Felix got the actor's voice, walk, and manners down pat to the obvious delight of Hasbo and the kids. It was a big surprise for the family to notice that somebody who had been in the United States for a short time and a priest was able to give such an unmistaken imitation of a current popular TV show.

They were more surprised to learn that the same show was also being shown in Mezi a week or so late. This went on for the rest of the late breakfast. When Hasbo collected her children for what she calls the usual Saturday taxi-cab errands of football, basketball, and cheerleading practices, the house became quiet with Father Felix and Dr. Kano Wasiri seating in his home private office, where Father Felix was guided to access his e-mail messages on his host's PC. He then said that he did not receive a message requiring an urgent response. The two proceeded to another exchange over the political situation in Mezi. It was now a turn for Dr. Wasiri to ask a few questions regarding the topic that Father Felix said at the church's lecture the evening before. Father Felix expected this as he had deliberately opened a lot of avenues during his lecture, expecting that his host was going to question.

"Father Felix, I was surprised yesterday when you said that the Roman Catholic Church was entirely behind the precepts of KMC. For all I know, the main coordinator of KMC at this time, Father Zolani, was kicked out of the Catholic Church and has been fighting the Roman Catholic hierarchy since. My impression was that the church was against KMC, am I wrong over this impression?"

Father Felix smiled, "I am happy that you are keeping yourself informed about what is going on in Mezi. God, was Dr. O'Shea mistaken on this? Well, I understand your reluctance to share everything. Anyway, as you can observe, I say that you were informed about what is going in Mezi. But I have to qualify my statement. I did not say that you were well informed. Brother Wasiri, this is how we address each other in KMC terms, well, Brother Wasiri, I have also to repeat what I said yesterday to be aware of news that you get from Mezi. Many times you get bogus story on top of a layer of bogus stories. That has been the case for the support the Roman Catholic Church is giving to KMC. As far as I know, it is unconditional from the majority of both native priests and nuns. There could be some misgivings about some of KMC precepts here and there in the clergy, and that should and must be expected, as it should be in the general population. Now mind you, I am talking about the ranks and files in the church of the native priests and nuns. We are not much different than our brothers and sisters throughout the general population. We wake up every day and attend to whatever daily tasks assigned to or expected of us under the guidance of the church as dictated by our Lord Jesus Christ. The main difference we have with the general population could be that we live or try to live by the vows that we proclaim when we were made priests or nuns.

Otherwise, we watch with horror and suffer the same indignities that are displayed daily in the political landscape of Mezi. We are not blind, close, or alien to the suffering that our population continues to endure in the current abject mismanagement of public goods. We aspire to the same well-being of our population.

"However, I have to confess, and given the hierarchical structure of our institution, the level of the church expression of outrage may seem muted or not loud enough. I would be the first to tell you that a lot of us within the clergy have not always agreed with that level of expression coming from the current leadership of our beloved church. We have been ambivalent about it. Sometimes we have to defer to the leadership's wisdom as it has happened in countless venues when we are not always privy to the inner workings of our leadership conference or the full political plate they are working with. But we are also taken aback at times by the behavior of the same leadership when scandals erupt and the expression of anger is urgently called for. Nevertheless, let me tell you, the ranks and files in its majority is working days and nights to insure the successful conclusion where KMC is engaging all of us. There is a core group of priests and nuns representing the clergy within KMC. I am part of that core group.

We operate outside the direction of our leadership conference. I am certain that the Catholic leadership conference has already identified this core group, but that is not our concern. Maybe that is the way the conference wants us to continue our engagement that is political any way. That probably gives the conference the cover of not officially sanctioning our support to KMC. That leads me to the coordination that Father Zolani is providing to KMC and the fact that Father Zolani has been, as you put it, kicked out of the church. First of all, our core group stands in total support of Father Zolani and his work on behalf of KMC. By the way, his coordination started as a result of the core group deliberation when it became obvious that, after KMC precepts were announced by a group of graduating Jesuit seminarian students, including your host, there was no guiding person to propagate these precepts around the country.

"Father Zolani, a very close friend and one of these seminarian students, was sent after his priesthood consecration to a remote agglomeration in the southwest part of the country. He started developing and amplifying those precepts in his sermons. He got so good at it that the leadership conference called him back to Mandi to give a more rigorous religious spin of the precepts and develop it into a leadership conference white paper.

He did an excellent job and put out the white paper. He also requested to go around the country to propagate the precepts around the country. As you can see, the original intent was indeed the conference leaderships. However, that is where problems arose. As the audience to KMC precepts started extending beyond the Catholic communities, there was a need to tailor the KMC message to the general population. Unfortunately, this created an unnecessary dilemma within the conference leadership. With no clear guidance from the conference leadership and given the strong urging of the core group, Father Zolani seized the opportunity to extend the message to a more general political reach.

"It did not take long for the political leadership to start attacking Father Zolani for dragging the church into the political arena. With that kind of pressure, that is all the conference leadership needed to withhold all support from Father Zolani's coordination effort. In the process, he was diabolized as an unrepentant zealot in search of political gratification. Father Zolani gave the leadership an opening when he was accused of sexual misconduct with a young very beautiful religious postulant who happened to be a niece of his Excellency Kodeye Henry Nzerima, archbishop of Mandi. The nineteen-year-old postulant was a member of the traveling team of young seminarians and nun postulants that Father Zolani took all over the country. They were about twenty of them alternating in their availability in support of the initial KMC propagation.

She was encouraged by her own uncle to join Father Zolani's team as a way to further her vocation. It was never clear whether the charges of sexual misconduct were true or were invented by one of the seminarians who might have developed an uncontrolled and undue affection for the beautiful postulant. The very sad part of the whole affair was that the young postulant committed suicide when she heard that she was part of a sexual misconduct charge against Father Zolani.

"That left the conference leadership in grave quandary because it had started precipitously the process to defrock Father Zolani with no ability to validate the charges. The process to defrock was being vigorously pushed by Archbishop Nzerima behind the scene. Worse, the Father Zolani traveling team was quickly disbanded and the seminarians and postulants were kicked out of their respective boarding schools for not collaborating with the inquiry or being manipulated by Father Zolani. The whole episode seemed to drag the church further in the same corrupt quagmire as the other political institutions.

The core group, through various channels available to it within the church, drew a loud alarm sound that reached the conference leadership. Overnight, the decision to defrock Father Zolani was held up but not retracted nor cast aside. The lack of a definitive stand was made to mollify Archbishop Nzerima and to save the unity of the conference leadership. Meanwhile, Father Zolani was left with a nondecision and was still forbidden to practice the rites of the church. That situation has continued to date.

"Father Zolani was certain that he would have been completely cleared of the charges if the case were fully aired with the testimonies of all witnesses, including the deceased postulant. However, the passing of the postulant left him with a stain he could not remove no matter how he would have tried. He decided to live with the nondecision of the conference leadership. He was not going to challenge it; instead, he would dedicate whatever the rest of his life would be to fervently work to bring about the change that the young postulant was working on when she joined his team. His life became a mark of endless penitence in search of spiritual redemption for his own soul and the soul of the postulant.

"If you ask me what I think about this story, my personal view runs to something I have witnessed time and again when you have a charismatic person such as Father Zolani surrounded by young assistants who tend to confuse the message with the messenger. They tend to be awestruck by what this charismatic person is saying and start to identify with the person in a way that becomes more and more removed from reality. It is the same phenomena with the so-called stars in movies or singers. I would not be surprised that within that traveling team of young seminarians and postulants there were a lot of conversations and gossips about Father Zolani whose star was growing in leaps and bounds in many quarters around Mezi at the time. It would not be out of range to suspect that this has created a great deal of jealousy or ill-feeling toward the priest on the part of one or two of the young seminarians or worse inside the clergy. In situations like these, it does not take long for stories or pure fairy tales to start being spread to smear Father Zolani. Including the beautiful young postulant in the midst of these stories was probably a way to add credibility to the gossips. The impacts on these gossips may have been far too great to bear on the mind of the young postulant leading to her tragic death. Unfortunately, we would never know who said what to whom. The limbo of the story would stay with us forever. But some of us in the know and from the original core group have maintained our unswerving support of Father Zolani and his coordination effort for KMC.

Thankfully the rapid growth of KMC grassroots movement throughout Mezi has reduced the reliance on the church for financial and technical support of the coordination effort that Father Zolani has maintained. KMC financial and technical support comes now from various walks of life in Mezi, and it is secretly and centrally coordinated effectively where you are going to be, yes sir, within the confines of the campus of Polytechnic University.

"This is a long about the way to answer your question about the church and Father Zolani. It is also my way to warn you about stories you will hear here and there in Mezi. Make sure you check and validate them every time before drawing conclusion."

Dr. Wasiri, who had been listening intently to Father Felix, looked completely astounded by the various turns taken by the explanation Father Felix gave. He caught his breath while reflecting about the unbelievable corrupt sea enveloping Mezi. There was still something that had bothered him a lot about the story. Forget about the different views taken within the conference leadership. At the end, those views could be reconciled to the satisfaction of all parties concerned. Dr. Wasiri was essentially perturbed by the fact that a young postulant could not wait to make her case and defend herself and her sullied name before a probably male-dominated council of the church. She resorted to the ultimate sacrifice. She took her life. That bothered him more than anything.

Dr. Wasiri asked Father Felix whatever happened to the name of the postulant beside the arbitrary position of the grieving archbishop, her uncle, along her family to quickly indict and condemn Father Zolani. Father Felix was taken aback by this unexpected line of questions and said that she committed suicide, a mortal sin in the Catholic Church concept, and died, end of story. However, Dr. Wasiri said that what he had taken from the story was what had been central to the degradation of the mores in Mezi. He submitted that the complete lack of respect for women permeating Mezi society was dooming it. He then asked Father Felix what roles, if any, KMC precepts reserved to women in the society. To be more precise, he asked if KMC had specific directives to promote the general respect for women in Mezi society. Father Felix suggested that the respect for women was not specifically mandated but implied throughout the KMC precepts.

Dr. Wasiri said that for a group that makes up 50 percent or more of the population KMC is trying to disenfranchise, that was absolutely not good enough.

It would not be sufficient for KMC to simply imply such an important fact; respect for women must be specifically spelled out in KMC pronouncements. He added that if KMC does not engage the female population in an effective way, the next electoral process would be just another process designed to elect another male-dominated assembly ready to enable the same endless subjugation of woman and to continue the same cycle of corruption, injustice, unfairness Mezi is ensnared in. It will be a truly missed opportunity to bring about the change that Mezi had been waiting for a long time.

Dr. Wasiri added, "It is about time for us in Mezi to realize that every time we have lacked respect to and for our women, we have lacked respect to our own wives, sisters, mothers, and grandmothers. Every time we have drawn a girl into prostitution or some compromising corrupt position, we have drawn our own wives, sisters, mothers, and grandmothers. We might not know that girl, but eventually, the corruption will come full circle and progressively hit our own wives, sisters, our mothers, and our grandmothers. We might think that it will never come to our family because we are somehow exempted from the diseases growing rampant outside the high walls we have built around our fortress of houses. But guess what, our wives, sisters, mothers, and grandmothers must go out sometime. The minute they are out, the diseases start eating at them. And before we know it, we are shocked to find out that our wives, sisters, mothers, and grandmothers have already joined the other corrupted side. Father Felix, nothing will bring a man down but the sight of a corrupt wife, sister, mother, or grandmother. That man would move mountains to stop that corruption cycle. I am afraid that is where we are at now in Mezi. In KMC, we are lucky to have precepts that have started to stop the cycle. We just need to move and push them a bit further. Therefore, and before it gets too late, I believe what will be effective is for KMC to engage the women by inscribing within its precepts what I will call an 'Edict for Woman,' which will set forth and proclaim that the respect for women is fundamental and that respect must proceed from five distinct values: the equality of woman and man in every organ and precept of the law; the majority of woman from the age of eighteen; the integrity of woman in her body and spirit; the transcending of woman negative values; the valuing of family from woman consideration; and finally, the emancipation of woman in every productive aspect of the society. If such edict is included in KMC precepts, woman will be resolutely engaged in its electoral process victory because KMC will then be fundamentally their cause. By the way, to make it seriously relevant, only women must promote such female engagement.

This finally brings me to the concept of KMC leadership. I hope dedicated women are seriously being recruited for that leadership."

Father Felix clapped his hands for all that Dr. Wasiri was saying while standing up and looking through the windows at the park across the street with trees now devoid of its autumn foliage. He said that he thought that he would be spending the rest of the weekend answering questions from Dr. Wasiri. Now he was on the receiving end of a notion that, from everything he knew, that was not thoroughly debated back in Mezi KMC circles. He suggested that this notion, though obvious, would raise a lot of questions even in female circles. The notion had a lot of merits that needed to be explored, as long it is not advanced as a Western women liberation movement.

Looking at Dr. Wasiri straight in his eyes, Father Felix said, "Only a man with your judicial temperament and fairness can advance such a notion without antagonizing unnecessarily a bunch of people. I would suggest that you write down exactly word for word what you have just said and try delivering it in front of some KMC female leaders. Collect their reactions to the delivery and analyze them. You would be able to modify your delivery accordingly and appropriately until you are ready to bring it out for a much larger audience."

Father Felix's reaction stunned Dr. Wasiri who then said that he was not running for KMC leadership or speech making. He was just giving an opinion over something he thought about long and hard. This did not stop Father Felix who responded that there was no KMC leadership to speak of at this time. He said that he did not suggest that Brother Wasiri was running for KMC leadership. But every time there is a notion so original as the one that he was advancing, it should be widely aired. Preference would be that the one who came with the idea to promote it. That will be only fair.

Father Felix also seized the opportunity to make the point he had been carefully delegated to make, so he added, "What is wrong with this all idea of KMC leadership anyway? Tell me why you should not be considered for that leadership like anybody else? Every organization needs to be led. KMC may be in need for a wise, reluctant, and tempered leadership. What if you are called to exercise that kind of leadership at this time, would you reject it? You do not need to answer me at this time. You would have ample time to reflect on these questions when you are in Mezi, review the dire situation of our beloved country, and come to decide for yourself what contribution you intend to give to the nation.

Let me say that in my opinion, you should know that a lot of us in many walks of Mezi life would support your leadership of KMC for the simple reason that you have a proven track record of the kind of leadership we are looking for. The first consideration is that you have not been tainted by the political pollution that has surrounded us back home for some time. The second consideration is that you have shown a great deal of reluctance to lead KMC. You have made it clear before and right now. The third consideration is that you have shown back then an inane quality of leadership that has so impressed a lot of people that they keep going back to that time to reminisce. To date, they have not found any alternative to compare with or to fall back on. This last consideration could not be denied. Your guest was a much younger student then in the same high school you have attended and has witnessed what took place. So, Dr. Wasiri, your spotless record, your reluctance to lead and your track record are all of the quality of leadership we are desperately searching for. When you will go back to Mezi, you will not tire to hear from many the same plea that your guest is expressing today. I pray, we pray, that you hear it and respond."

The last request literally blew Dr. Wasiri from the comfort zone he had built for himself and his family since he had come to the United States. He went back to the window looking across the street toward the park. The barren winter landscape shot back at him. He stood there for a long time not saying a word, bearing on the weight of the last request the guest he never met nor knew two days ago laid on him. The only thought that kept resounding in his head was to know if this was what he had to go back to in Mezi. He was not certain if he could manage the pressure to come. By the time he looked back at his guest, Father Felix had his rosary on his hand and was praying with his eyes closed. Dr. Wasiri went past him without saying a word. He went down to the kitchen. Hasbo had still not returned from the Saturday taxicab routine. Then he noticed the note she had left for him to start the evening dinner. Hasbo had already seasoned the lamb to be roasted in the oven. He started the oven when

Hasbo walked in with the children. It was five thirty in the evening. Hasbo was disappointed that the dinner would now take place an hour later than anticipated. The only excuse her husband could come up with was to say that he was carried away with a long conversation with Father Felix.

He excused himself back to his office where Father Felix was still waiting for him. The priest was now sorry to have put such a burden and pressure on his host. He said that he was ready to leave his home and stay at a nearby hotel if his presence was no longer appropriate. Dr. Wasiri closed his office door and dismissed Father Felix's request.

"What will I say to my wife and children you have entertained this morning so admirably? 'Well, you know, I had this conversation with the Father. I did not like what he said then, so I asked him to leave.' I am sorry but that is nonsense. Besides, I cannot keep running from Mezi every time somebody mentions KMC leadership. I have made up my mind to go back to Mezi for good. I would not go back on that decision. I have no idea what the future reserves in Mezi for my family and me. I am an academic expert in mines engineering. That has been my calling for the past twenty-five years or so. I am signing up to go back to exercise that same profession. I am a bit amused by the request you made to ask me to sign up for a political odyssey I have no inkling for. Do not get me wrong, I appreciate all the consideration you have mentioned before, but I still say what if your consideration and appreciation of my ability are all off base and wrong, and I am not what you are looking for? What do we do then? You cannot bank the future of KMC movement on the notion that somewhere in the United States you may have found somebody with unblemished past to lead it. I am also concerned that you keep mentioning something that happened twenty-five years ago as my badge of leadership. Father Felix, I was about seventeen years old then, not a reference or mark of leadership to bank on by anybody. I tell you something, if the search of KMC leadership should limit itself to those criteria, then we are in Mezi in a worst position I thought possible. Father Felix, I am not making light of the dire condition our country is in nor the excellent work of education and mobilization KMC has done to date. You may not know this, but one of the factors that seal my decision to go home was the glare of hope that came to me when I heard all the enlightenment work that KMC was doing in Mezi. It was the first time I came across a hopeful sign of bright future for Mezi. I certainly wanted to be part of the movement but was not prepared to hear that, based on my flimsy political background, I should take the lead of KMC. I submit that KMC would do better than that. Irrespective of what you said about Father Zolani, there must be men or women of credible and reliable background right now in Mezi, ready to fill the vacuum of KMC leadership. The advantage these men or women have is that they have been in place in Mezi, they know their way around, and above all, they have paid their price due to Mezi compared to someone like me who has literally been away for so long and will be at best tantalizing when it comes to addressing the challenges confronting Mezi. That is the bottom line reality you and I know and should not pretend otherwise. You may not agree with my assessment today, but with time, you would. Now we have talked quite a long time today, and I want to let you know that I very much appreciated the exchange.

As a matter of fact, you may not know how much you have prepared me for my trip in January. I feel already home. Thank you, Father."

There was a knock at the office door. Hasbo was calling the two men to join the family downstairs for the dinner. As they were sitting and having the preliminary soup, Hasbo could not help but ask what her husband meant when she came up to ask them to come downstairs, she heard him saying "I feel already home." Hasbo did not wait for her husband to respond when she added, "Dr. Wasiri, you are not going to feel already home by yourself, what about us?" Everybody started laughing. Then the eldest son added that his mother would be on the left-wing tip of the plane taking his dad to Mezi in January, if that was possible. Then Father Felix asked the son if he was willing to leave all beyond and stay in Mezi with his parents. The son did not respond but asked the good Father if he had gotten used to the cold weather with the temperature that was plummeting outside. Father Felix responded that he would never get used to such weather. The son then said he also never did though he was born here in Kentucky. He also said that every vacation time he had spent in Mezi had convinced him that he had to come back and live there. So when his dad announced that they were going back to Mezi for good, he had been counting down days to the departure. Father Felix then turned to Hasbo to congratulate her on such an extraordinary preparation she had made for the kids to face the transition to life in Mezi. He added that Kano was very lucky to have a life partner like Hasbo so focused on what lies ahead and could be a very difficult period for the family.

Dr. Wasiri intervened, "Father Felix, please do not mention difficult period for my dear Hasbo. She got our transition to Mezi all mapped out down to diapers, and she assured the entire family that all would be all right. I am convinced that she will make sure that it will go as she said. This is how she runs this household and I cannot foresee any change and I love it that way."

It was Hasbo's turn to speak, "Father Felix, we must be annoying you with our family fairy tale. Of course, it will be a difficult period of transition for life in Mezi. But I am making sure that we do not dwell on the transition per se. That would not be productive. I want to see ourselves past the transition two years later when we are fully settled and enjoying the life Mezi is affording us. That is the focus I hope to keep instilling in my family, and this is the only way I believe we can overcome all the challenges that will come along. Now let me get up and pull out the lamb that my dear husband had forgotten to put in the oven on time."

The dinner proceeded as jovially as it started and when they got to the dessert time, Father Felix asked the children to bring up TV and movie male actors' names and grade how far he was able to imitate their voices and names. It was a riot then. Father Felix was on target about 80 percent of times. When he could not identify the actor, he improvised in the most comical fashion. The whole family enjoyed the spectacle until very late enough to get the kids to bed. When the kids were asleep and the adults remained in the living room, drinking their last cocktails, Hasbo started to bombard Father Felix with all kinds of detailed questions about schools, housing, food supply, basic utilities, tropical diseases and their prevention, the seasons and how they change, etc. By two in the morning, Father Felix was worn out, and her husband had to step in to excuse the priest from further inquiries from Mrs. Wasiri.

It was another long day for Father Felix, so long that the next day, a Sunday, Father Felix woke up late and had trouble locating a Catholic Church in the area. Dr. Wasiri, a protestant, had missed identifying such a church. After a frantic search, they located a church at the outskirt of Frankfort where a one thirty Mass was being said, to the relief of the entire Wasiri family that came along for the search ride, arrived on time, and attended a Catholic Mass for the first time. The Wasiri family took Father Felix for a Sunday brunch afterward. It was already four in the afternoon when the brunch was over. Father Felix then reminded Dr. Wasiri that his flight back to DC was due at eight that night, and he needed to get ready for the trip back to DC from Lexington as soon as possible. Dr. Wasiri, who was busy since that morning, first to get the priest to a Catholic Church Mass and to arrange for the brunch, again forgot that this was the last day his guest was spending with his family. He took the family back home and Father Felix to pack his bag. The priest assured the family that this will be a brief separation as he will be welcoming everybody in Mezi in about five or six months. During the ride to Lexington Airport, Dr. Wasiri told the priest that he wished he had a longer stay to continue his re-education in Mezi mores and politics. He hoped to see him very soon. He added that he was realizing now that he needed more than a week's stay in January to get even more rounded about what was going on in Mezi. He hoped to work it out to get at minimum a two weeks' stay. Father Felix thanked him for his entire wonderful family's gracious hospitality and reminded him to come to Mezi ready to give answers to the questions he had raised the day before. He also added, by the time he arrives in Mezi, he would also realize how desperately the KMC movement is counting on his leadership. They separated on that note.

As soon as Father Felix was seated on the small jet plane taking him back to DC, he pulled his attached PC case and wrote a rambling note that he was going to develop to send to Father Zolani. Father Felix usually does this so as not to forget important features of conversation he wanted to convey.

The note said, "Mission accomplished. Explained your role in KMC standing, expressed need for KW's leadership of same, noted usual reluctance, got a strong animated lecture about respect to/for women in Mezi and the need to include respect for women in KMC precepts, KW said Lack of thereof has doomed Mezi, got a strong extensive feedback on need to include women at every level of KMC leadership, KW Eager to continue dialogue around KMC while in Mezi, Getting Two Weeks' Stay. Entire Family very supportive, set to and very eager to return to Mezi. Will strongly advise listening rather dictating or imposing, as in case of respect for women, let KW expand on ideas and philosophy, Best Way to get him to talk himself into and suck him into KMC Leadership position."

When Dr. Wasiri reached home sometime before ten that night, he went upstairs to his office and called his friend Sir William Ewas to give him the promised feedback over the visit of Father Felix. Sir William Ewas, now a consummate diplomat, remained quiet most of time, trying to determine which way Dr. Wasiri was moving to in the issue of KMC leadership. Dr. Wasiri asked him first how well he knew this Father Felix and if the priest was in any way delegated to sound him of. To both questions, Sir William Ewas was tentative in his answers. He said that he had never met him in person but had heard of him. From his contacts, he had come to realize that Father Felix was destined to advance to a higher leadership position in the Catholic Church, most likely to replace Bishop Nzerima as archbishop of Mandi. He was very popular within the clergy and represents the progressive restless wing of the church that the conference leadership was trying to mollify. He was probably speaking for that very influential progressive wing of the Catholic Church that had started the KMC and continued to more or less control it through the advocacy of Father Zolani. Sir William Ewas also said that his friend should not be so quick to dismiss any request he had made as he spoke for a very broad-based constituency, and he was after all very powerful in the movement. Sir Ewas continued by saying that he did not think that Father Felix was a person to be delegated by anybody within the movement. If he had raised any issue, he was speaking from his own personal point of view about something he felt very strongly. Then he asked Dr. Wasiri why he was asking these questions and what did he learn from Father Felix.

Dr. Wasiri responded by saying that first he learned quite a lot why Father Zolani had not been willing to go beyond his coordination role and take on a political leadership role of KMC. He sincerely sympathized with Father Zolani's tragic situation. Then he was a bit surprised to learn that KMC had not inscribed in its precepts the most pressing issue in Mezi, the respect for women. He said that given a chance he would like to press that issue head-on within the KMC leadership. He added that the lack of respect for women is the fundamental factor dooming Mezi any way you analyze it: corruption, injustice, unfairness, declining mores, all point to the lack of respect for the weak gender.

Finally, Dr. Wasiri touched on the issue Sir Ewas was expecting a lot of feedback.

"I was sincerely taken aback and disappointed when Father Felix came out and requested that I considered taking over the leadership of KMC when I will go back to Mezi. I found it very presumptuous on his part to come out and say it. He advanced some criteria that I found extremely wanting: that I have not lived in Mezi for the past twenty or so years, that I was reluctant to accept the leadership mantle, and he also kept going back to that incident in school that you have also mentioned last time we were in New York. I told him that I appreciated the consideration, but there must be more than those three criteria to move me to consider such an honorable leadership position. I did not also hesitate to tell him that there must be more capable people right there in Mezi who have paid more price and can collect more due than I. These people should be considered for that leadership. But he was still insisting when he was leaving. He claimed that I would understand and come his way when I will be in Mezi. I guess I was not clear enough nor convincing enough in my stand regarding the leadership of KMC if Father Felix still believes that I will go his way as soon as I reach Mezi. Now my good friend, Sir Ewas, as a member of KMC inner circle, please tell me what is waiting for me in Mezi frankly?"

His friend drew a long and loud laugh and protested the cynical attribution that Dr. Wasiri was pulling, "My dear 'Geffadi', I am not part of KMC inner circle of leadership to know what is waiting for you in Mezi. Remember, I ran away from the ship that I thought was sinking. Of course, I support KMC as the last chance to redress our broken institutions. And if you ask me where I stand in this matter of supporting your candidacy to the leadership of KMC, my bias would be clear and without reservation, I would not even hesitate to proclaim it on every mountaintop of Mezi that you should lead KMC.

The reasons or criteria are numerous from the frivolous to the deep serious ones, and among others, you have been and are a close friend, you are greatly admired for your intellect and wisdom, you are a good father and a terrific husband. Yes, you are not touched by the crazy stain-sullying Mezi, your integrity is beyond reproach, you are consistently fair and just in almost all matters, you were a boy wonder, and on and on. Now those are my own biases. Now in all fairness, what Father Felix may be saying is that you will have a serious problem when you go back and find out that those biases are no longer biases but have become serious considerations multiplied many times all over the country in sectors influential enough to count, including those KMC power circles. You and I do not know what is being said about you since the word got out that you are coming back. You can dismiss what happened about thirty years ago in that high school. Remember that for those who have witnessed the event that was the only truly legitimate mark of leadership they could ever remember in their life. And they have become now middle-aged and in position of power or influence or whatever. They have spread or are spreading the word throughout the country and saying the man is coming and maybe, just maybe, he can show the same mark of leadership he had shown back then. Then what will you do? Are you going to fight everybody and say I am not the one, I am not the one, you are all completely mistaken, I am not the one! That would be ridiculous!

"Most likely you would try to temper the requests, but you will be pulled deeper and deeper into that KMC inner circles just as much you will resist. Unless you make a big mistake, there will be a natural broad swell of popular request for you to take the helm. That is the way it usually works for true natural born leader. And if you ask me again, this is how I see it happening for you."

Dr. Wasiri told his friend that he was more eloquent in his promotion effort than Father Felix, and very effective. He said that he brought to bear considerations he did not think about and in a completely different light. But he concluded he was still not convinced of the need to assume KMC leadership. Dr. Wasiri thanked his friend for his comments and hung up. The whole weekend conversations convinced Dr. Wasiri that he definitely needed a two weeks' stay in Mezi during his trip in January. Maybe he would be able to slowly verify for himself what his friend Sir Ewas and Father Felix tried to tell him this weekend. He was a bit too tired at this time. He will collect his thought and propose to his mentor that he will be extending his stay for a week to touch base with family members in Mezi. That should be OK with his mentor.

The next day at about ten thirty in the morning, Dr. Wasiri called his mentor, who had restrained himself to call him all the rest of the weekend after their dinner at the steak joint. Dr. O'Shea was quick to take the call and to sound impatient to get the feedback of Father Felix's weekend at Wasiri's household. Dr. Wasiri first thanked him for being the first to mention the lecture and how much he had benefited from the long weekend of endless of conversations over Mezi with the priest from Friday through Sunday. He joked about the Sunday frantic search of the Catholic Church at Frankfort and the mad rush to bring the priest back to Lexington Airport Sunday night. He also added that the family was happy to exchange so much with Father Felix who happened to be so knowledgeable about almost anything in Mezi. He even entertained the children about American TV and movies actors. Dr. Wasiri was very grateful to his mentor for the invitation extended to Father Felix. At the end, he said that he was calling to let him know that he will extend his stay by a week in Mezi after he had concluded his interviews with the folks of Polytechnic University. After this long weekend of conversations with Father Felix, he came to realize that he seriously needed some time with family members and friends to start his transition or reconnection with Mezi. He apologized that he would not come back with him after the first week in Mezi. Dr. O'Shea, to his protégé, quickly agreed with him.

"If it was up to me, you should spend at least a month there before your family gets to Mezi. But you have your commitments to Kentucky State University that you need to honor. I really want you to be fully prepared mentally with this transition to Mezi. You know how much I care for you, Hasbo, and the kids. I am praying every day that this transition goes without any major problem. So I am very glad you have seen the need to stay a week later. That would be ideal for the time being. The more you are engaged talking and dialoguing with your country people, the easier it will be for Hasbo and the kids. Do not worry about me. I probably will be there for no more than three days. Most likely, I have to go right after to London to prepare the Emily foundation next board meeting that should take place a week or so later. As you can see, all seems to work out better for everybody. I am also happy that the weekend was productive for you and your family. What an engaging fellow this Father Felix was at the lecture! Just brilliant. It should be said that Mezi has so many capable folks with a lot of brainpower. As usual, it is too bad that it does not manifest where it should be in the highest echelons of government. Don't you worry. We got the same problem right here in the States. Come to think of it, it is a general phenomenon in the world.

The best ones tend to shy away from political leadership of many countries. I pray that Mezi becomes an exception very soon, very soon."

Dr. O'Shea's last statement hit his protégé very hard as if he was making a prediction. He did not want to think that he was concerned. Then it does not take much for his mentor to get carried away about people. Father Felix was very eloquent indeed. What else can one expect from the future archbishop of Mandi? Father Felix had shown his colors, he would go far. Then he thought of what Father Felix had said. He needed to put more meat into his conviction in the essay about the edict for woman in Mezi. Every point he wanted to convey should be fully developed with examples and likes so that next time when he delivers a presentation or lecture about the respect for women in Mezi, it comes out as deeply eloquent as possible. Dr. Wasiri decided that he should make time to complete the essay before he leaves for Mezi. He was convinced now that he had to meet two sets of objectives when he reaches Mezi. There was one set of objectives strictly focused on making a convincing case for himself to gain a tenured professorship of mines engineering at Polytechnic University. The other set of objectives centered now around whatever political situation he was going to meet in Mezi. The objectives there were not quite obvious, but Dr. Wasiri was determined to protect whatever he was conceiving to be his own future political engagement in Mezi. He wanted it to be evolving by his own timetable and appreciation, not rushed through by a movement or a set of self-appointed political movers. He also realized that holding to that timetable may not be that easy according to all that was said by Father Felix and his own friend Sir Ewas. He decided to control things in his grasp and let the rest happen as it may.

CHAPTER 18
Barry Newcomb's Betrayal

The ambivalence felt by Dr. Wasiri about his imminent return to Mezi was not matched by the growing confidence that the ABDI leading team of the Honorable Georgia State Senator Jeremy Massay, the institute board of directors chairman, and his friend and vice chairman, Dr. James Stringer was showing. The first board of directors meeting was acknowledged to be a great success, thanks to the three days conference planning and execution directed mainly by Dr. James Stringer. The follow-up meetings with recipient country representatives in Atlanta, New York, and in African locations took so much time from Dr. Stringer and his honorable that they both missed the note from Lady Allistair advising them of the change in AMX management that occurred a month earlier. They caught up with the very important management change when they were staying in a London hotel waiting for an overnight flight to Zambia. His honorable called Barry Newcomb who was designated as a London contact in many instructions that Lady Allistair had provided from the time of the famous Washington, DC, meeting. Barry informed his honorable of the management change and advised him to try to pay his respect to the new AMX CEO on his way back from the Zambia meeting. Barry was surprised to learn that Lady Allistair wanted to see his honorable alone in her residence in Kensington and Chelsea. She made it sound as if it was a personal invitation to his honorable to spend the night at her residence. When he informed her that his honorable was traveling with the ABDI vice chairman, she advised Barry to insure that she meets his honorable alone and to make different accommodations for his vice chairman. Barry faithfully carried the message to his honorable.

He knew exactly what trouble he got himself into. He can deal with Lady Allistair, but since he had never told his friend about the entanglement he was in with the Lady and after consistently urging his friend to cease and desist in his player lifestyle ways, his honorable preferred to mislead his friend, so he came up with a strange excuse to stay in London for two days. He claimed that he was to give a presentation of ABDI activities to selected AMX board members when they would come back from Zambia, and he would do it alone.

That was a blow to Dr. Stringer who had prepared and led every ABDI project dossier and had been conducting most of negotiations with the recipient partners. He did not want to challenge his friend and made his own arrangement to continue his flight back Atlanta with only a two hours plane change in London. It was a grim separation in London Heathrow Airport when they came back from another successful negotiation with Zambia partners over the copper- and tin-mines investment. The only thing his honorable can come up was to say that he would explain everything the minute they see each other in Atlanta. When he came out at the airport, there was a huge limousine waiting for him that carried him stray to a very luxurious inn outside London. When he was in the limousine, he received a call from Lady Allistair who greeted him and asked if he was carrying the red tread she gave him in Washington, DC. He did not. Then she said that he was to be punished for too many strikes out. First, for being the only subordinate who did not extend the obligatory congratulation to her when she became AMX CEO and second, for forgetting a personal symbol of their commitment. His honorable apologized for the first strike out but protested the indictment for the second strike out. He said that she had made it clear that whatever happened was never going to occur again, she had other preferences, and he respected her wishes all along. She responded that he had a lot to learn about women. She added that "never" does not mean never for a woman, and never will "never" be the case when she gives a personal intimate tread. She finally suggested a dinner for the two of them at a very exclusive restaurant not far from the inn where he was staying. His honorable was even more contrite for what will happen and the deceit he had pulled over his friend, Dr. Stringer. He has completely changed his ways in dedication to this gig. He was about to marry for ABDI sake. And now this for Lady Allistair. Maybe it was the price to pay to keep the milk flowing. After all, she is the boss and had given him all latitudes to manage ABDI with absolute no undue oversight as promised. In fact, he was not prepared to share anymore than the lie he had given his friend. His matrimonial situation had not really improved since he got so involved with ABDI. In fact, he had the impression that his wife suspected another affair, no matter how much normal and regular he had maintained his professional and personal life. Hanging out with a well-known ladies player like Dr. James Stringer did not help. Vanessa's rules were unfortunately reinforced now. The Saturday morning breaks completely disappeared. He was getting used to the rules now and leading literally a celibate life. The collection of out-of-sight young female assistants that Dr. Stringer had originally packed the ABDI office in downtown Atlanta left him unimpressed. With no action from higher ups, they started departing one after another.

The ABDI office now reflects the serious and monotonous work atmosphere found in any other corporate office with its share of dedicated female and male nerds along with some remarkable beauties. The ABDI chair and the vice chair measured everything according to bottom line contribution from everybody without exception. Slackers were not welcome.

The atmosphere changed a little bit during dinners or receptions given in the honor of foreign dignitaries who started streaming to the Atlanta ABDI offices on regular basis now. The obligatory invitations extended to local politicians and corporate moguls enlightened the place that at times came alive with packs of sirens that Dr. Stringer still managed to call on. But these affairs became all part of a growing organization flexing its philanthropic muscle in a positive way.

Vanessa enjoyed these gatherings a lot and routinely invited her friends to partake in her husband's newfound power. But at the same time, with a firm and watchful stand, she did not permit any wandering by her husband, who obliged her dutifully. Her good disposition sometimes carried home to a break to Vanessa's rules, especially if the reception took place on Friday nights. His honorable started depending on those dinners and receptions to enjoy rare intimate nights with his wife. Life was getting a bit hard, and he was getting used to it. When the limousine arrived at the exclusive inn, he was shown into a private bungalow completely detached from the main building. When he entered the bungalow, he was completely surprised by the level of luxury the set carried. He had never seen such display of luxury in his life where every surface on the floor, the wall, the ceiling, and in between was covered with either marble or ebony wood panel with distinctive motifs of sixty-four carat gold.

Everything else, be it chair, sofa, even the humongous LCD board TV set was covered in dark brown leather. The bed was a statement in itself he could not even fathom to describe. The bungalow looked like the ultimate deposit of the two hundred years or so the British Empire blunders. This was a parody of luxury probably unmatched in taste and quality. It definitely made one wonder if there exist people who would live in such splendor on daily basis except in make-believe theater or movie sets. But he was there in the bungalow enjoying it and about to spend a night with that Lady, or so he thought. But the question remains why him and why now. After he was settled, he did not even remember that he went to sleep, being very tired from the seven hours flight from Zambia.

He was awakened by a call from Lady Allistair who announced that she was leaving her office to pick him in about forty-five minutes, evening traffic permitting. His honorable freshened up very quickly and dressed for the evening. By the time, there was a knock at the door; it was obvious that Lady Allistair did not come from the office, dressed as she was with almost the same outfit she wore at the troublesome meeting in

DC. The difference was that it was now of shining beige color, matching her constant tanned skin. It was difficult to tell the difference between the see-through dress and her body. When they embraced, Lady Allistair gave the honorable the feel of her naked body in heat below the dress and teased the poor man with the question, "Would you have your intimate dinner right here or parade your lady in this outfit in crazy London?"

The honorable got the message and said that he would go for the first suggestion. Lady Allistair agreed and placed a call to the inn concierge to order an elaborate dinner. She also suggested that the dinner should be ready and served in about two hours, enough time for her to catch up with the honorable, who was now showing the effect of the Lady's appearance with a considerable bulging of the pants' upper side even when he was seated on the large leather sofa. Lady Allistair did not give him a chance. She removed her dress and went straight for the honorable's pants zipper, lowered it, and started feeding on his extended, still bulging lower part while rubbing herself with a strange outsized ring.

The sight of Lady Allistair's glistening shaved lower part prompted his honorable to do the same. She violently climaxed with the same effusion she gave in Washington, DC. His honorable was still holding to give her a chance to recover. Before he knew it, she erupted again and started crying timidly. It was way too much for the honorable, who let it go at the same time as Lady Allistair shook her entire body for a third time as if she was having a heart attack, then she collapsed to a visibly frightened honorable. She woke up a minute or so later with a sly smile, a very distant devious look, and her awesome nakedness in an overwhelming display.

She finally said to a relieved honorable, "Three strikes and you are out." His honorable smiled, "You must be speaking for yourself, lady. You scared me. I am no expert, but I have yet to see someone doing it as much with vengeance as you were. I was convinced that this would not happen again as we had agreed the last time. You must tell me why me and why now."

Lady Allistair did not respond but was now fixing her hair and checking the overnight bag she brought with her. She pulled the slip, bras, and a new dress from the bag and went to take a shower, still parading her naked body throughout the living room. That excited his honorable again even more. He followed her to the bathroom. They had another exhaustive tryst in the shower. Lady Allistair stayed behind to finish her makeup while his honorable changed again into another evening casual ensemble. By the time Lady Allistair came out of the bathroom, there was a complete metamorphosis about her. The sultry nymphomaniac siren was gone; the all business AMAX CEO Lady was back now in complete charge.

She looked at his honorable straight in the eyes. "Why you and why now? It is simple. After a month in this function, I needed to find a good cover to indulge in my preferences. I did not realize the constant watch I would be under twenty-four hours a day as a CEO. At home, I still have a couple of middle-aged butlers I have not been able to find reasons to get rid of. At work, well, forget it, I have to keep appearances I forgot about all these years I was in New York City. I am becoming a virtual prisoner in a golden cocoon. I could not even reach out to my old London flames for fear of starting gossips and you know what. Worse, I get the impression that this Barry Newcomb, the lawyer, my old main contact in London, is working overtime monitoring every one of my moves. Sometimes I want to believe that he is doing everything to protect me, but at times I am not so sure. I am not clear for whom and for what purposes he is doing this. In the meantime, I am refraining myself to ask or to find out. When I heard that you were going to be in London, I thought that this would be a chance for me to renew our friendship, and of course, at the same time to exhale and to regain my bearings after this long, tense month. I am sorry if I used you, but these three strikes were, well, fully appreciated. Seriously, I intended to use your visit to give me the opportunity to verify to what extent our dear Barry will go to monitor my goings and comings. I want to get to the bottom of this comedy. That is why you were initially told that you were going to be my guest tonight at my residence, and I insisted that you get rid of your colleague. I hope I did not cause any problem there between you two. Knowing that Barry was taking care of your transportation through the corporate channels, I have to use a totally reliable different hosting service to bring you here. I also managed to get your look-alike to use his sponsored limousine from the airport all the way to my residence, and I dropped him off when I was coming here. I was very surprised to notice that Barry had a private security service monitoring his sponsored limousine that is still stationed near my residence.

I am beginning to think that Barry is into something way beyond my protection. Believe me, I would find out soon. Maybe he is obsessed in catching me with a female lover, as I am sure he has heard or found out from my not-so secret prior life as an executive with AMX here in London and in New York City. Maybe he is intent to use that to start blackmailing me, I don't know. He was probably confused when I instructed him to make all arrangements to get you to be my guest overnight. A male lover spending the night at the AMX CEO residence. What an affront! And a black man at that! But I needed to push the envelope here, to get him to expose himself.

I would not be surprised if now, in my absence, he has either called the residence to verify if the overnight guest is still there or simply barged in the house to do the same. Luckily for me, I have given the old butler couple a few days off, and I am using a very reliable old butler friend who is very much into this deception. God, I miss my New York City stay with total freedom. To tell the truth, at times, I regret signing up for this CEO golden cocoon. Again, I am sorry for using you in this deception. Wait a minute, why am I being sorry? Did we not enjoy this time, Your Honorable?"

She let out a loud laugh; at the same time, there was a knock at the door announcing that the dinner was ready. His honorable let in an old gentleman with two trays of their elaborate dinner with assorted wine bottles while Lady Allistair managed again to disappear into the bathroom when the old man was busy setting the table. She came out after the man was gone. She whispered that she could not take another chance given the circumstances.

It was the honorable's turn to speak. "I thank you for being honest about this all affair. I would not deny that I have enjoyed all that deception brought my way. I am grateful just the same. But in all seriousness, I would appreciate that our relationship does not turn simply into a lovemaking odyssey. You are a very sensual woman, and I know no man would deny himself the pleasure and time to indulge you. I have been certainly lucky to date. But there must be more than this. ABDI, as you well know, is turning out to be a very special endeavor I would have never dreamed of. It has brought to me and all those who are engaged in it such a satisfaction, I would not destroy if I can help. I want you to know that this kind of entanglement leads to nothing but disaster. We need to refrain ourselves and commit to never put ABDI in jeopardy because of our carnal involvement. Lady Allistair, would that be possible?"

"Yes. Your Honorable, you are taking things way too seriously. I am after all AMX CEO. I did not get here through my crotch, if you want to know. I have been lucky never to use it for business, and you know I could have. I agree with you wholeheartedly that it never works. Why? I am sorry to say as plainly as you would never hear me say this again, my dear. I am under no illusion. I know very well that there would always a better crotch and a bigger and better dick out there to fancy those who run business through lady's or man's bottom parts. And I am old enough to have seen where it usually leads. Rest assured that I would not be stupid to go there. I have only the most respect for everything you and your vice chair have done and continue to do for ABDI. For most management, the real test comes when more or relaxed supervision is called for. And you should have realized by now that you have been left alone to manage ABDI as you saw it fit. If that is not a mark of outstanding management, then I do not know how to congratulate both of you. Just the same, that should not prevent me to enjoy your company and yes, sex when we can, because, well, I fancy you. You mentioned way back that you were working out issues with your wife. I respect you for saying that to me. Few men are as much honest about their own home as you were. I hope things have improved. Your Honorable, I am just stealing a bit of you. I would not dare to claim you all for myself. That is not I. Now tell me how is the ABDI business going, is there any way I can help?"

"ABDI business, I am very happy to report, is going very well indeed. All projects are going full blast and about to reach the implementation phase, thanks to the steady support we are getting from your teams in New York City and London. We are very grateful for that. If there is something you can help us about at this time is to accelerate the review of the Africa-Eastern Region Water Project within your corporate channels.

By the way, you asked me if this detour has caused a problem between my vice chair and me. I am afraid it did when you insisted that I must be a lone overnight guest. I did not want to explain our prior involvement to my colleague, and I came up with a stupid excuse. I told him that I was requested to make a presentation of ABDI activities to an AMX Management team and to do it alone by myself. You can imagine how disappointed my friend, and colleague, was when he heard it. He has worked assiduously in each of these projects. To tell the truth, I defer to him in all matters pertaining to all projects' evaluation. I was very sorry to pull that one on my friend and colleague. I have to bring back something very tangible to prevent any unfortunate friction or tension that is building up between both us as we speak at this time.

Better yet, now that his wedding is coming up this holiday season, if I am able to send him to London to make a presentation of the Africa-Eastern Region Water Project in front of the AMX Management Team that is reviewing it and add all-expenses-paid honeymoon in London and Paris honeymoon, that will go a long way to patch our friendship."

Lady Allistair, sensing where this unfortunate episode was leading to, stopped his honorable, said, "Consider this done for your friend with full VIP accommodations in similar locations in London and Paris, all expenses paid. I am giving myself a note now. Before you leave tomorrow, I would have a follow-up memo to you and the vice chair, first thanking you for making yourself available for the requested review of ABDI activities, however due to unforeseen circumstances the review did not take place and a special request going to both of you to come back on such date in the middle of January to make another presentation of ABDI activities, including a much-anticipated review of the Africa-Eastern Water Project. You, in turn, would decline the request and send the couple to London first for the presentation, and they will be released to their honeymoon in London and Paris all expenses paid by AMX. You will carry the memo signed by myself, and a day later, I will send you the same e-mail message. That should take care of this issue. Again I am deeply sorry for the problem."

The lovers then continued their dinner and talk. At about one in the morning, Lady Allistair bade his honorable farewell, gave another long tender kiss, and took out the beige slip she was wearing, cut the lower bottom, made three holes, and handed it over to his honorable and whispered in his ears, "In memory of three strikes, don't lose it." She went back to her overnight bag and pulled another slip, put it on, and left in the waiting AMX CEO limousine. The next day, when his honorable was leaving for the airport, the limousine driver handed a sealed large envelope containing the signed memo that Lady Allistair promised.

His honorable did not learn about the follow-up story around the deception that almost ruined his friendship with Dr. James Stringer. He was not concerned or did not care about it. But the story took a dangerous turn when Lady Allistair reached home the night before. She learned that Barry called more than three times trying to know the whereabouts of the night guest and the house host. Not satisfied by what the butler was saying, he managed to drive to the CEO's residence as Lady Allistair predicted.

He tried in vain to force his way inside the house despite repeated protests of privacy invasion. It was only when the butler threatened to call the police that he left the house. Lady Allistair called him at once to explain his strange behavior. Barry only said that he was very concerned about her security, and he did all to protect her. Lady Allistair screamed at him telling him that she was old enough to take care of herself and to entertain whomever she wanted when she wanted, and she did not need to be monitored like a teenager. If she needed his protection, she would have requested it. She added that she was not satisfied with his explanation and will get to the bottom of this problem. She slammed the phone so hard it broke. It was about two in the morning. The next day as soon as she reached her desk, she requested to talk to Evelyn Bottown, her friend and the AMX CFO. Evelyn came in at once to her office. She managed to talk about her night issue with Barry, leaving aside the salacious happening with His Honorable Georgia State Senator James Massay except to say that she had a long productive business meeting with the American. She asked her how she thinks she should handle this matter. Evelyn said that she was always very concerned about how Barry managed to get so close to her. She assumed that since Barry came to AMX, thanks to the strong recommendations from her uncle Robert Mendham, the previous AMX CEO, Lady Allistair should have been fully informed of his background, his career profile and path, and any other intention. As a matter of fact, Evelyn's concerns about Barry lessened when he was established as Lady Allistair's main contact in London. But there was still some nagging apprehension about the man. Evelyn added that Barry's HR file was the only executive file kept away from all other executives' HR preview. It was always locked away in her uncle Robert Mendham's office until today. She advised her friend that she needed to talk to her uncle to learn a little bit more about Barry Newcomb and how he came to be where he is in the corporate hierarchy. Evelyn said there could be only one reason why he is behaving as he did, either he is madly in love with Lady Allistair and that is a very remote possibility, or there is a very dark secret that he wants to keep away from you. Talk to your uncle, and you will learn the truth. When Evelyn left, Lady Allistair sat down reflecting about this new challenge and looking a bit defeated.

She circled back to what her mentor, Uncle Kiri, had told her time and again, to check the human factor in every management decision or to forget it at one's peril. When she reviewed how she had managed the AMX CEO function handover from her uncle Robert Mendham, she now remembered she did not want to have a long protracted conversation with her own uncle over AMX's various management issues, even when her uncle was gracious enough to offer the opportunity to do so more than three times.

Her pride took the best of her. She had always suspected that she was never the family choice to succeed her uncle Robert Mendham as AMX CEO. She was convinced that the CEO appointment decision came straight from the majority owner, Uncle Kiri. She based the entire management succession on the guidance that Uncle Kiri gave her. The guidance was forward looking, bearing no input from the past. That suited Lady Allistair very well, and she did not want to concern herself over things that have happened before, missing on very important insights into current AMX management. Now she found herself in the embarrassing situation of going back to her uncle to request information that should have been hers from the beginning. She reached her phone and dialed her uncle's number.

Her uncle now lived in a very wealthy exclusive compound about sixty miles from London. Lady Allistair requested to see him as soon as possible over important AMX management issues. Mr. Mendham said that he would be happy to see and talk to her any time. Lady Allistair said that she was coming that very day. She should reach her uncle's home in about an hour and a half, London's northbound traffic permitting.

When she reached her uncle's house, his wife greeted her and guided her straight to his office where she found him arranging a stack of files. Robert Mendham got up and warmly embraced his niece.

Looking at his wife, the uncle said, "Only the Mendham family can produce such a combination of beauty and brain. Rebecca, we are all very proud of your ascension to AMX CEO's position. I had many conversations with Uncle Kiri about you from the time you went to Amovir for that internship. I knew that he had a strong preference to see you lead AMX and here we are. I knew that you had mixed feeling about this whole succession planning. But I beg you not to listen or believe the gossips that went around about this family favoring a male successor. Nonsense. If that was the case, I want you to answer the question: why was there no male Mendham in the highest executive positions to be in line to succeed me? It did not happen because I knew that Uncle Kiri had already a strong preference, and it was you. I supported and went along his preference. At least, a Mendham is still in control of our cherished jewel of company. Now I have been waiting for you all that time to go over these very confidential files. I did not trust anybody to get these files. It is all there. They are yours as AMX CEO and yours only. I would suggest that you keep them at the official residence and never at your headquarters office.

They are so sensitive to become career impacting to some current high-level managers in AMX. I know that you did not want to deal with some intricate management issues included here, but my dear, when you reach that level, you become the guardian of many good and bad dossiers, and that comes with the territory unfortunately. Enough talk, what is the urgent issue that brought you here?"

Lady Allistair responded, "First of all, my sincere apologies for not requesting these confidential dossiers from you. I should have done so if I have kept the appointment to meet with as you requested. I am very sorry that I have not kept that appointment and now I realize that I missed on very crucial management input every time something comes up. Thank God, it is only a month past, a long, tense month, I may add.

To get to my point and it is probably included herein, it concerns Barry Newcomb who has been behaving strangely lately as if he wants to monitor every step or move I am taking. What is the story about him?"

Robert Mendham got up, "Fire him as soon as you can. Yes, I said fire him as soon as possible before you get any more aggravation from him. He is probably one executive I should have gotten rid of before you came in. I was hoping that you would read through his machinations as soon as you became AMX CEO. He was a mistake I brought to myself for overindulgence. You see, when BI expressed its interests to gain majority stock ownership in AMX, Mendham family was very concerned how the British government was going to react to this proposition. The family was always sensitive to any suspicion that the British government might raise regarding any AMX British interest as a result of this majority ownership; worse, the family wanted to be above reproach regarding any thought of facilitating spying activities to benefit the Russian interests. After many debates and meetings with government officials, the family agreed to hire a government-appointed lawyer who would be monitoring AMX relationship with BI and Uncle Kiri. We had no problem with the first lawyer who was very discreet and did his job as quietly as possible. He was with AMX for about five years, then he went back to the government. Barry Newcomb replaced him. You should know that both these lawyers came straight from the British M16 Intelligence services, as it was agreed. While the first lawyer was extremely discreet, Barry changed the tune, insisted on integrating AMX management rising to the current position of deputy general counsel. As years went by, it became obvious that the monitoring did no longer serve any purposes for the government or AMX.

But Barry claimed that M16 insisted on an expanded legal-monitoring position at the time of the rapid change taking place in Russia. Barry insisted that this was justified because according to M16 best analysis, it was never clear where the Russian political leadership was taking the country; was it on the path of unfettered capitalist social democracy or another variant of the Russian dictatorship? Now with the colossal financial control BI was grabbing around the business world, there was a definite need to consistently check on what BI and its Russian chairman, Nadov Kiriyan, were up to. At first, I took his word as M16's. But when he got greedier, signing on financial matters way beyond his authority, I started checking his claims through some of my back channels in M16 only to find out that he was lying. I made many requests with the government intelligence services to take him back, but there were no equivalent position to bring him back to in M16 according to his contract. I was getting nowhere with these government folks until I retired. Barry, knowing very well the precarious position he was in, started to ingratiate himself with people he knew were in the management fast track, including yourself. He also knew according to AMX and government understanding agreement that nobody could see his file but a new CEO or myself. This issue is a very difficult one that would take an active collaboration of M16 folks. I believe he is acting up to verify if you got hold of his file and you are taking steps to fire him, or he is in big trouble with somebody in M16 bureaucracy who is ready to do away with his farce. I came to realize that this issue would only be resolved through the same hard driving techniques he is used to in M16, a scandal or something very close. We either created one for him or drag him into one if he is not already into one. Rebecca, let me sound off my contacts in the intelligence services to find out why he is acting up so much, and we will map our strategy accordingly. Please do not do anything to raise his suspicions. He is a very devious dangerous man and capable of anything at this time. Please take the pack of these confidential files back home and take time to read them carefully as soon as possible. Call me to discuss anything you need clarification. Good luck to you. Don't worry. We will take care of the bastard."

When Lady Allistair left her uncle's residence, her mind seemed to be spinning so fast that she thought she would faint. She asked the limousine driver to park at the first parking location he would find. Lady Allistair needed to clear her mind to quickly establish ways to protect herself and AMX from this rogue of Barry. When the car was stopped for about twenty minutes, she wrote down a list of priority steps she needed to take. She called her Evelyn Bottown to find out whether Barry showed up at the office.

She learned that he did not; in fact, he took his wife to Milan, Italy, for a precipitously planned vacation. She then called her real estate agent who was directing some improvements at the town house she owned in the Chelsea area. She needed to get her house keys back. She would be using her town house as her third quiet office when she wanted to be away from both her official residence and her headquarters office. She wanted the agent to meet with her within the next forty-five minutes. When she got to the townhouse, the agent told her that the improvements were complete and all that she has requested, including new appliances and furniture, were in place. She went straight to the new office built in the basement and dialed a special satellite number that put her in direct contact with Uncle Kiri. This was the first time she used the number as instructed by his mentor. Uncle Kiri was on line and asked her what was the first crisis she needed help with. She said that Barry Newcomb is becoming a serious problem that needed to be taken care of. Uncle Kiri said that he knew exactly what issue she was referring to. He said that he did not want to alarm her unnecessarily when she was appointed AMX CEO. He wanted to get to Barry's case at some boiling point, and he did not expect to get to it so soon, yet it was probably the time. He also let her know that he was perfectly aware how Barry came to AMX; it was the most unfortunate lack of trust from the uncle, and he never forgave him for that stupidity. And now the mess needed to get cleaned up, and it will be. What needed to be done urgently was to find out first if Barry had not compromised the top priority objectives he had laid down for Lady Allistair by running a complete electronic sweep of all her communication and data contacts. At the same time, conduct a financial audit of everything that Barry was delegated to supervise and fund the past three years. And right away, alert Liechtenstein, CIB, to prevent any contact or financial authorization from Barry. Uncle Kiri advised Lady not to do anything that would get Barry all excited, continue to indulge him as if nothing had happened until the result of all these audits becomes available, and then he will be nailed. Uncle Kiri did not want to share anymore details he was aware about Barry's problems. Uncle Kiri had managed, through many contacts in the British business community, to establish a close relationship with a close friend of the head of Intelligence Commission in the House of Commons. The commission is the watchdog of M16. Whenever the commission head initiated an audit within the M16 bureaucracy, it was very quickly done. Slowly and progressively, Barry's issue found his way to the head of Commission desk. And Barry's immodesty did not help his case. His newfound riches accumulated while rising through AMX corporate ladder created more jealousy within M16 bureaucracy.

It was remarkable that his issue was being escalated, thanks to independent pushes from both Uncle Kiri and Uncle Robert Mendham. When the head of Intelligence Commission got the case, he ordered the M16 chief to appoint an auditor to review Barry Newcomb's activities. In the preliminary report, the one that got Barry so wound up, Barry was accused of diverting important sums of money from AMX in order to feed his Italian wife's insatiable appetite for luxury and dilettante lifestyle. It was learned in the report that his wife had recently bought an out-of-way first-class chalet in the mountains outside Milan, Italy. In the typical M16 switch, the report also revealed that in the worst case, very damaging for people associated with the reputable M16, pornographic videos of scenes from wife-swapping exclusive private clubs circulating in London have revealed frontal sexual exhibitions involving Barry and his wife and their partners. Uncle Kiri had already received a copy of that report and was waiting the right moment to verify these accusations from AMX side. Uncle Robert Mendham was in line to receive the same when he had said to his niece that he was going to check his contacts. Time was really running out for Barry. When Lady Allistair called the general managing director of CIB, Doktor Otto Sweftenwaag, to alert him to prevent any transaction coming from Barry Newcomb until advised otherwise, she learned that Barry had already called that morning from Milan, saying that he was on his way to review financial transactions connected with Mezi initiatives and Africa Goodwill deployment; these were misnomers for money spent on Emily Thomas O'Shea Foundation setup and initiatives in the Polytechnic University and ABDI projects. Lady Allistair instructed the general managing director to be nice and very professional with him and firmly advised him that they were in the middle of major financial re-engineering to redirect CIB financial resources toward Dubai new International Financial Centers, and no analyst could be spared to assist him this week when everybody is working twelve hours a day in order to complete this project within the next two weeks. Tell him that he would do better to come back in about two weeks. Now with the concerns that her uncle raised about Barry, authorizing funding beyond his authority, Lady Allistair could now see what a godsent golden pot of money she had given Barry when she made him her main contact on all matters concerning initiatives for Mezi, the foundation and ABDI. She had delegated Barry to be in charge of funding all these projects from what were appropriately called Center of Excellence Funds originally set up out of CIB in Liechtenstein and cleverly distributed around multiple financial centers in the world. The elaborate financial funding was designed to prevent any relationship or connection with AMX or BI.

Barry must have been in a feeding frenzy, collecting whatever he would determine the difference between the funds he authorized and the funds actually spent for those various initiatives. This is what the financial audit needs to reveal to match what M16 already suspected. There was nobody else in place to review what he was doing except the very busy Lady Allistair, who had authorized this in the first place and who clearly never had the time nor got to asking anything.

Lady Allistair shook her head. What a fool Barry had almost made her to be? Was her uncle Robert somehow connected with this scheme when he allowed this man to get so close to her? Did her uncle Robert allow this in order to sink her promotion? Did Uncle Kiri see through this entire machination and yet prevailed to promote her CEO? What a power play! She felt stupid thinking in the first place that Barry was closely monitoring her in order to blackmail her over her sexual preferences, only to realize now that it was rather strictly a matter of large sums of money or as French love to say, une affaire des gros sous. In her mind, Uncle Kiri's human factors theory came back in full force again.

Thank God, Lady Allistair rationalized that she was into this AMX CEO gig thirty days only; she would have plenty of time to learn, apply, and adjust. Lady Allistair was now very exhausted by the intensity of this crazy episode and fell asleep on the office sofa for an extended time. She was awakened by a call from her friend Evelyn who had been trying in vain to reach her after their last call and after she deliberately switched off all her cell phone numbers. Evelyn, remembering her old townhouse phone number, tried it and woke her up. She reassured her friend that she was all right but just tired from a long night and now a long day of a tumultuous affair.

When Evelyn asked her if she had learned anything from her uncle Robert, Lady Allistair answered that she had indeed learned a lot but she was not at liberty to say much at this time so as not to disturb a lot of things, she was not aware of before, and which were already in motion to clarify Barry's issue.

It will be in a matter of two or three days that she expects this drama to play itself out. She was also happy to report that whatever the consequences of these events, AMX would not be negatively impacted. She instructed her friend to be silent and circumspect at the office about the episode. The normalcy at work will be required to bring the matter to close.

She did not say anything about what Uncle Robert and Uncle Kiri confided about M16 and AMX arrangement concerning the hiring of Barry, nor about the financial audit being conducted at M16 and CIB, nor about the electronic sweep of all her data and communication links, the sweep being conducted at that very moment by a crack team of specialists hired by BI, nor about her own failing in delegating so much authority to Barry about sensitive issues she managed for Uncle Kiri.

Each of these issues and concerns was so far removed from Evelyn's management span of authority that she may be let to doubt her new boss's wisdom for raising so much ado about nothing. But Barry Newcomb, now back in the chalet outside Milan, Italy, had an appropriate appreciation of things to come when he was not able to conduct a review of all financial transactions that he had authorized at CIB in Liechtenstein. He did not believe what Doktor Otto Sweftenwaag told him when he said that there was no staff available to get him the list of transactions he wanted. He knew that with all the powerful and first-rate financial systems CIB had, this could be done in a matter of minutes. Barry sensed that M16 and CIB must have been comparing notes at this time after the appointment of that M16 auditor who had developed his preliminary report based strictly on hearsays and innuendos. That was so characteristic of most audits conducted within intelligence services around the world. Since these services live in the mud, it was not by accident that their preliminary reports are usually full of mud. Barry knew the routine. That will be OK until verification started coming from outside the services, and if CIB shared what it knew, Barry will be toasted. Whatever he had attempted to do to scare off Lady Allistair had now backfired. If her uncle Robert Mendham, the previous CEO, had finally shared his file, it would be a matter of days before he is asked to go back to M16 where so many people are waiting to light up the fire under his feet. And where on world they got those pornographic tapes that the auditor mentioned in the preliminary report? Barry had warned his nymphomaniac wife to temper her excesses. He suspected that M16 enterprising jealous folks would never hesitate to do them in by infiltrating the dozen of wife-swapping clubs they were members of. They have done this before for lesser evils. Barry surmised that as a couple, they can survive a pornographic scandal when he would be forced to retire to preserve the honor and other M16 monkey pretensions. But the mysterious golden corporate egg funding they have enjoyed lately and which allowed them to buy the Italian chalet was what made the real difference between their life and that of other M16 folks That was what worried Barry most of time now.

He decided to extend what could probably be their last rich vacation. But he did not say a word to his wife about all his troubles. Two days later, Lady Allistair received first the report of the electronic sweep that revealed that Barry was accessing most of her AMX e-mail messages and data communications. But most of the communications pertaining to top priority initiatives were safe. Lady Allistair used intricate BI communication systems for that purpose. That was the reason why Barry became so insisting in harassing both Dr. O'Shea and his honorable to get more information about what they were doing every time Lady Allistair requested that he followed up on any tiny issue. These two major players could not understand why they needed to rehash for Barry matters they have already closed with Lady Allistair through different channels. They complained about Barry a lot about these harassments. Lady Allistair, flying too high at the time, dismissed these complaints as normal organization in-fights among team members in different locations. Lady Allistair received new communication accesses and all her data equipment were sanitized. She also managed to communicate her new reach contacts to most of her reliable major players and contacts within AMX and without. She took the financial audit report to read it at her townhouse.

The report revealed that within the time Barry started working as a financial authorizer of various initiatives funds, he had pocketed the difference of fourteen million pounds between what was authorized and what was spent. The funding difference came from the major funding required to build and equip the new facilities at Polytechnic University in Mezi and the total preliminary funding to support the smaller ABDI projects. The funding difference had found its way into corporate accounts Barry had cleverly established in tax-safe havens of Monaco, Dubai, Caiman Islands, and Liechtenstein in the first initial phase. These accounts still held a total balance of about six million pounds. Barry did not have time to liquidate that money into some other personal accounts as he had planned in the second phase of the financial scheme.

The corporate accounts were quickly seized now by respective in-country criminal authorities. In addition, the chalet outside Milan, Italy, the manor house in a London suburb, the expansive Bentley and various items of value found in both residences were also seized. When she finished reading the entire report, Lady Allistair called the M16 contact her uncle Robert had indicated. She set up a meeting to meet the contact the next day in an unpretentious downtown location to share their organizations' audits and map-prosecution strategy. She came along with a private lawyer representing both AMX and BI interests.

At the end of the meeting, it was resolved that M16 and AMX agreement will be abrogated, Barry will be fired from AMX, and he will be returned to M16, where he would be forced to retire at once. CIB and BI will then bring charges in court of law, accusing Barry of stealing fourteen million pounds from CIB funds. Barry Newcomb returned back to London under police guard in chains. His wife, who never asked where the money was coming from but enjoyed spending it, remained in Milan at her parents' house. The gossip around M16 folks was that Barry's wife did not wait to quickly join Milan swinging clubs before long. At AMX London headquarters, the news about Barry was given a subtle twist. A terse official announcement went out saying that "AMX Management has accepted the resignation, effective immediately, of Barry Newcomb Esq. from the position of deputy general counsel." The AMX General Counsel signed the announcement. That was the last time Barry Newcomb was mentioned in AMX archives. His file was classified and remained under the purview of AMX CEO as highly confidential. Barry was found guilty and was sentenced to cope twenty-five years in jail. Out of the fourteen million pounds he pocketed, CIB recovered the six million pounds found in those corporate accounts, the Italian chalet amounting to about a million and half pounds, his London suburb mansion which he bought before, and some valuables not exceeding five hundred thousand pounds. Altogether, it was estimated that Barry had stashed away in some personal accounts between four to five million pounds waiting for him after he had purged his sentence of twenty-five or less years.

The other person to have dearly paid for her standing was Lady Allistair, although it was not widely observed within AMX. But higher ups, including her two uncles, Robert and Kiri, were perfectly aware of the major shortcomings that she had faced during the episode and expected her to quickly correct them. And Lady Allistair did. She abolished the function of deputy general counsel and returned the AMX legal department under the sole management of AMX general counsel responsible of nothing else but AMX legal matters. She appointed Patrick Berger, vice president AMX Marketing Strategy in New York City, with whom she had closely worked for the past five years, as vice president AMX Strategic Initiatives, reporting directly to her. Patrick will oversee the deployment of various key initiatives under the top priorities that Uncle Kiri had put on her plate with the exception of the CIB's initiative. She also set regular timely management and financial reviews of these initiatives with her new subordinate. However, Patrick was going to remain in New York to be in permanent touch with key initiative players like Dr. O'Shea and His Honorable Georgia State Senator Jeremy Massay.

Patrick, a quick learner, will go to spend time in Liechtenstein to learn the intricate financial trails and controls set up by CIB to support these initiatives. Patrick will also go to Amovir to be introduced to BI's chairman, Nadov Kiriyan. The advantage of appointing Patrick to this position was that he was about thirty-two, young, worldly, very smart, ambitious, unattached, extremely mobile, and a corporate team member always willing to learn. He came to AMX straight from Columbia University with a PhD in Strategic Management. He started studying Mathematics for his bachelor of sciences, and then he did a master's in International Economics, which led him to Strategic Management Advanced Studies. Lady Allistair was lucky to hire and train him in many aspects of minerals marketing. But on his own time, Patrick extended his background of minerals marketing from the American market to a comprehensive worldwide perspective of the supply and demand of the most strategic minerals known in the world, including copper, tin, uranium, gold, diamond, cobalt, and other less significant minerals. He even published two authoritative books providing an econometric model covering supply and demand for copper and diamond. He became a go-to guy for minerals information at the New York AMX office. It was not by accident that Lady Allistair brought him to set up the Emily Thomas O'Shea Foundation. As soon as Lady Allistair seconded the notion of setting up the foundation, she again turned to Patrick to develop a comprehensive framework of a corporate funded foundation. In no time, Patrick plunged into learning the management critical steps of a foundation setup, and single-handedly evaluated the proposal that Dr. O'Shea and Dr. Wasiri provided with some inputs from AMX London legal department. Lady Allistair then decided to borrow him from AMX to set up the entire foundation management with his colleague Derek Anderssen reviewing the financial aspects of the foundation. When Dr. O'Shea came to the Park Avenue office in New York, Patrick delighted him with another complete presentation of short- and long-term objectives of the foundation. Dr. O'Shea, a difficult man to please in most occasions, gave a strong commendation and heartfelt compliments for the extraordinary contribution that Patrick was providing. If the past was any indication, Lady Allistair was confident that Patrick's appointment would not give her surprises as the ones she had witnessed recently.

Along the way, in order to prevent any other surprises of financial nature, Lady Allistair decided to appoint her friend Evelyn, AMX CFO, as titular head of CIB. A new function of President of Management Committee was set up combining CIB management with an equivalent financial center, though much smaller that was growing in Dubai.

The general managing directors of CIB and the Dubai Financial Center were going to report to Evelyn Bottown, the new president of the Management Committee of Financial Centers. On paper, there was a logical management authority line from these general managing directors to the President of Management Committee who was also AMX CFO, Evelyn Bottown, to AMX CEO, Lady Allistair. But as Uncle Kiri instructed it in the list of top priorities and given sometime murky processes, it used to fund a lot of worldwide activities privy only to Uncle Kiri, and CIB was to remain very independent of direct supervision from London. Lady Allistair made it plain and clear to her friend Evelyn that her real role in this setup was only to maintain close contacts with Doktor Otto Sweftenwaag, CIB general managing director to avoid and prevent any surprise.

Lady Allistair also took the next steps to reassure her key players in the top priorities initiatives about the management changes she made. She called Dr. O'Shea to talk about Patrick Berger replacing Barry Newcomb. Dr. O'Shea was delighted. He had never liked Barry Newcomb from his first encounter in London while he felt an enormous regard to Patrick Berger. Dr. O'Shea updated Lady Allistair about the January trip to Mezi with Dr. Wasiri.

He expected a lot of positive things to happen during that trip for Dr. Wasiri. He also added that he would not stay long but three to four days in Mezi to return to London in order to prepare for the first board meeting of the Emily Thomas O'Shea Foundation. The meeting was to take place the week or so after the Mezi trip. Patrick Berger should attend this meeting. His Honorable Jeremy Massay was not surprised of the management change after the London encounter. He wished that this Patrick Berger would be less intrusive than Barry was. He assured Lady Allistair that he was able to repair his relationship with his colleague and friend, Dr. James Stringer, who was extremely pleased to come to London to make his presentation in later part of January. He was also very gratified for his next honeymoon in London and Paris, all expenses paid. At the end of the exchange and to liven up the mood, his honorable also added for three strikes sake that the precious tread was not discarded but in a secure place. Lady Allistair replied, "You better for your own sake."

The only person Lady Allistair struggled to call was Dr. McMillan, who was brought in by Barry Newcomb and had been under his direct purview from day one. Dr. McMillan was now finally back to Mezi and had been getting all his marching orders from Barry.

Besides the last and only conversation, she had with Dr. McMillan regarding the political condition in Mezi, she did not know how he should be handled. And it would be awkward to dump on Patrick Berger the Mezi political reporting she had asked him to do, knowing that it was to be channeled through Barry. She decided that Patrick would manage only the financial funding of his activities while she was to be the sole recipient of the Mezi political reporting or spying. She reached Dr. McMillan and shared with him the management change and insisted that Dr. McMillan's service was very much in the same urgent demand despite the management change. She skipped the gory details of the change and Barry's whereabouts. Dr. McMillan appreciated her taking the time to call him. He was saddened that Barry was gone when they were deepening their working rapport. He was looking forward to work under this Patrick Berger's supervision.

What Lady Allistair and Dr. McMillan did not talk about was the background that Barry Newcomb and Dr. McMillan shared. It was obvious that Barry did not dig out Dr. McMillan out of the blue and on his own. Their mutual M16 background was helpful, if any. It was also obvious that Dr. McMillan had rendered a few services to M16 during his thirty years or so stay in Mezi as a British subject whether he liked or not. His rise to the top of the management rank of one of the jewel institutions of higher learning in Mezi, the Polytechnic University, must have included M16 indulgences he was not about to proclaim at the top of the highest building in the university campus. Dr. McMillan had kept contacts with a few M16 handlers from his long stay in Mezi. When he thought that he was retiring back in UK, these handlers discouraged him to do so. They said that the old country would be well too cold for him. So when Barry came in calling on him, he had already decided to go back to Mezi to do the old bidding, the only issue was under what covers. That was the reason why Barry and Dr. McMillan pressed for him to become a board member of the Emily Thomas O'Shea Foundation. When Dr. O'Shea resisted the selection, Dr. McMillan did not mind to work his way up to the same. Dr. McMillan was not blind about Barry's support; he did his due diligence to find out more about the lawyer from his own M16 contacts. What came out spelled a lot of troubles for his next boss. From that time, he did all he could to accelerate his return back to Mezi in order to insulate himself from whatever toxic fallout the demise of his new boss will bring. Luckily for him, the demise came so fast when he was already back in Mezi, and he was being kept to manage the functions Barry had worked hard to set for him. Before the call from Lady Allistair, Dr. McMillan had learned that Barry was in big trouble with both M16 and AMX.

He also got a copy of the M16 preliminary report on Barry and was not surprised about the pornographic tapes. He had been invited by Barry and his wife and declined to attend some weird hot-bath sessions in a London northern suburb private club. Dr. McMillan was most unease with the lavish lifestyle that the lawyer and his Italian wife were leading, starting with the huge Bentley that Barry rode and the frequent weekend round trips to their chalet in Milan, Italy. Dr. McMillan thought that AMX was extremely generous with its executives. As far as Dr. McMillan was concerned, the troubling sign came when Barry started to go every week on overnight trips to Monaco and Liechtenstein. His M16 contacts have informed him of late that Barry was in jail for twenty years for embezzling about fifteen million pounds. This brought Dr. McMillan back to those frequent trips to these tax haven places, always a sign of improper financial dealing.

While Lady Allistair took full advantage of Barry Newcomb's indiscretions, to quickly terminate the agreement between AMX to M16, agreement that came about to great pain, displeasure, and discomfort to Uncle Kiri, she closed her eyes over whatever ties Dr. McMillan must have had with M16 as long as she, along with Uncle Kiri, would be the ultimate beneficiary within the framework of Mezi initiative.

Now with Dr. McMillan in place, the Mezi initiative took an accelerated pace of its own, especially with the January arrival of Dr. Wasiri. Dr. McMillan could not help but notice a tremendous high intensity level of activities around the campus that almost equally matched the vast construction operations which cleared almost the third of the size of the current campus to build the new buildings for the Applied Sciences Faculty, the students gigantic new dormitory for about six hundred students, the extensive chain of townhouse like homes for professors, and finally, the extensive compound for modern large apartments for retired professors. If Dr. McMillan was not in the know to suspect that the level of campus activities was somehow related to Dr. Wasiri's coming home, he would have thought that the students were about to foment and lead some kind of political revolution. There were meetings going on every day from about five in the evening after most classes until late at night in every large faculty auditoriums of the campus. Father Zolani of KMC movement, who had no official duties connected with the university, was literally living in the campus and could be seen moving from each meeting location to another. It was not difficult to tell his presence. Father Zolani tended to keep and to move around with a large retinue of young, very sharp and eloquent male and female assistants.

Most of these assistants came from graduating classes of various university faculties. Dr. McMillan resolved that any astute observer would not have difficulty to conclude that these meetings must portend a launching of a political event or a political career. One evening after dinner, he threw a question to his now legal wife and mother of his grown children, Anna Lourenco De Olivera, now shortened to Anna De Olivera McMillan. He asked whether KMC was preparing Dr. Wasiri for a top political position. Anna, who had been a KMC member for years sworn to many secrets, just said, "Who is Dr. Wasiri?" Dr. McMillan decided from that time to open his wife's political eyes.

CHAPTER 19
Russian Feelings

The Christmas holiday period went on quietly in London for Lady Allistair. She had managed slowly to put the Barry Newcomb episode and aggravation behind her. In the process, she finally retired the couple, providing permanent butler at her official residence. She justified it by saying that as a single, she had no need of such services on permanent basis. She would hire on part-time basis or on need basis house cleaning or entertainment services. She did not mention that for her private and intimate involvement, her own big townhouse in the area was available and sufficient. Her townhouse provided far more discretion she terribly craved in her private life. In addition, she had already completed some remodeling of her basement to set up a third alternative office away from the official office when she had an urgent need to be alone. For some strange reasons, these occurrences increased at each higher professional promotion. Lady Allistair spent a quiet Christmas week.

This was not the same for Chairman Kiriyan. His Russian managing director, Karlov Yelgin, was determined, from the time of BI Management realignment and Lady Allistair's promotion to become AMX CEO, to go on his trip to Moscow to denounce the direction that Chairman Kiriyan was taking BI internationally. But the managing director was now having a lot of trouble establishing contact with previous BI Kremlin handlers. It was as if Chairman Kiriyan had managed to eliminate every trace of BI Kremlin supervision from his secluded office in Amovir. Desperate, he reached out to Ludmilla Borensky, the new supposedly main KGB/FSS liaison with BI. Karlov never trusted Ludmilla as she reported his attempts to have a sexual encounter to Chairman Kiriyan. He thought that he could continue with Ludmilla the same rapport he had maintained for a long time with Nadia Kirilenko, the longtime KGB/FSS liaison. He never understood why this wholesome lady with a reputation to initiate every new young KGB/FSS hired, male and female, to the intricacies of BI spy management routines and also bed routines in Amovir, refused to entertain the idea of sexual relations with the Russian boss. He was suspicious of the closeness Ludmilla enjoyed with the chairman, being part of his inner circle at a level that Nadia had not seen nor contemplated. But he had no choice but to find out for himself whatever happened to those key Kremlin contacts.

When he called Ludmilla for a private lunch conversation, he made it upfront clear that it was going to be very professional. If Karlov knew why Ludmilla had turned down his sexual advances, he would have chosen to have nothing to do with this lady.

Ludmilla hated Karlov from the time she heard rumors he spread about her and Lady Allistair. While Ludmilla was affected to London AMX office, Karlov gave a coarse Russian rendition of Ludmilla relationship with Lady Allistair to a group of new young Russian cadres hired into BI. He literally and figuratively compared Ludmilla to a female German shepherd leaching after Lady Allistair, a female English terrier. The rendition was spread all over Amovir later. When Ludmilla came back to Amovir, she was confronted almost on daily basis with that rumor. For almost three months, Ludmilla spent every night crying herself to sleep until the joke died out. She swore from that episode to take her time until she had a good opportunity to strike back to Karlov and very hard. Now with the strong backing and support of Chairman Kiriyan, Ludmilla was convinced that the opportunity to strike hard at Karlov was at hand. So when Ludmilla showed up at Karlov's lunch appointment, it was with an outfit statement to raise every male lower member on the sight. Karlov Yelgin restrained himself and asked Ludmilla whether she had any knowledge of what was going on in Kremlin as far as BI contacts were concerned. Ludmilla answered without hesitating and dropped the bombshell by saying that Chairman Kiriyan had made a special arrangement with the highest authority of Kremlin to bypass all Kremlin contacts and to deal directly with him from then on. She added that from then on all KGB/FSS related matters including contacts with Kremlin had to go through her for clearing without exception. She was fully briefed and prepared for this meeting by Chairman Kiriyan himself who had lately heard a lot of complaints emanating from the Russian managing director regarding the international composition of BI new Management Membership Committee. Ludmilla then asked Karlov what would be the purpose of his trip to Moscow. Before Karlov was to answer, Ludmilla added that she was fully prepared to go with him to Moscow to have her own first initial review with the appropriate KGB/FSS superiors. Karlov swallowed the bait and saw an opening to advance what had been his longtime ambition to bed the voluptuous Ludmilla.

He thought that the long trip to Moscow far away from Amovir should bring them closer and he must have more than one chance to score on the bi-sexual Ludmilla. Karlov said that the purpose of his trip to Moscow was to give the usual report to Kremlin contacts he used to give every three months.

Ludmilla then asked if Chairman Kiriyan usually got a copy of such report. Karlov said that in the past he had always given Nadia Kirilenko a copy of his report for transmission to the chairman. But that was a lie, for Ludmilla had gone thoroughly over every report copy that Nadia had transmitted to Chairman Kiriyan and already found out that there was no such a report. During the Soviet Union time the Chairman Kiriyan knew that Nadia had her own Kremlin contacts to report on his various BI activities. He suffered that indignity for a long time and made it beneficially to himself too. At the same time that Nadia spied on him, he also used Nadia to provide him with crucial KGB information. The collapse of Soviet Union changed the equation completely. The constant change in Kremlin leadership and economic policy slowly removed the need for Nadia to report on the chairman. Both Nadia and the chairman knew this but maintained the appearance of deceit now that the chairman was using the full KGB/FSS cadres for his own personal needs and purposes inside and outside Russia. When Nadia passed away, Kiriyan managed to get his own contacts installed in Kremlin. These contacts have been receiving monthly retainers from the chairman in twenty to forty thousand dollars a month nicely stashed away in private accounts in a Liechtenstein CIB bank. These Kremlin contacts were strictly passive geared to alert Chairman Kiriyan about mysterious Kremlin twists and changes and were not as useful as the contacts Chairman Kiriyan had cultivated all along in the Duma, the Russian Parliament. The Duma more proactive contacts have infiltrated every Duma commission with financial and economic legislative and oversight impact over BI business. The works of these contacts have made it possible for Chairman Kiriyan to give the international outlook he was implementing over BI on worldwide basis. Karlov Yelgin was not aware of all these contacts perspectives and was up to a serious dreadful challenge in his impossible attempt to check Kiriyan power. Yet Karlov and Ludmilla agreed on the date trip to go to Moscow later in March.

CHAPTER 20
Kano Wasiri Arrival Big Celebration

During the same Christmas season in Kentucky Dr. O'Shea and Dr. Wasiri were facing a different time of anticipation, they were preparing their trip to Mezi. The activities around Polytechnic University redoubled in intensity as the day of Dr. Wasiri return approaches. The various feedbacks received from Sir William Ewas and Father Felix after his weekend at Dr. Wasiri's household have convinced the KMC brain trust of Father Zolani, the University Chancellor Dr. Umzigwe, the dean of Applied Sciences Faculty Dr. Wutugrase and the young professor John Awassa, to push for a tremendous, large and impressive welcome home for Dr. Wasiri. Hopefully this would convince him once for all that KMC had cast its leadership lot on his shoulders. And there was no other way about it but for him but to accept it. That was a big gamble, Father Felix advised, but with each urgent passing day, it became worthwhile. All the meetings and various activities taking place in the campus were as a result of that resolution. Various KMC representations were being called around the country to be present at the airport. The majority of the groups signed up for the home coming welcome. Those groups not in agreement with the proposed welcome were invited for more meetings at the campus. The activities in campus were broken into a set of meetings preparing the arrival of Dr. Wasiri and another set of meetings where the promotion and convincing of Dr. Wasiri KMC leadership were debated and fervently pushed.

Two days before Dr. Wasiri's arrival Father Zolani confided to the brain trust that he had a comfortable 93 percent of known KMC groups around the country signed up for the home welcoming blast, and all was go. It was evident that KMC intended to show for the first time its powerful colors. KMC was out to make a bold political statement to show the world that it had come of age and was a powerful political force to be reckoned with from then on. The logistics for the welcome were divided between the airport and the campus. About three hundred buses were rented to carry people back and forward from the campus and other stations in the capital of Mandi to the airport.

Big signs with KMC motifs and slogans were designed for the purpose. KMC motifs consisted of the three highest mountains of the country banded together in one landscape, starting with the highest mountain of Nyingaro where there was a report of a dormant volcano, and the next two highest Mezi Mountains of Kiese and Kansi. The disposition of the motifs was to show Nyingaro Mountain in the middle saddled by the other mountains of Kiese and Kansi. There was a resplendent eye on the top of the highest Nyingaro mountain with brilliant shining yellow rays splashing all over the landscape. The mountains were drawn in a straight black line while the landscape had a background of the shining yellow color from the rays that were coming from the eye. Thousands upon thousands of colorful KMC T-shirts were also distributed. Through its many staff connections, KMC managed to build a large podium within the airport facilities not far from the arrival gate elongated hall. The podium was completed the afternoon before the arrival of the most famous Mezi native. The night before the arrival, Dr. O'Shea and Dr. Wasiri boarded the all night London to Mandi flight with all other regular passengers bound to Mezi.

There was no indication that there was a passenger of any greater political stature in the plane except that the two scientists were traveling first class. At the same time in Mezi, the KMC brain trust debated for the last time the strategy over the best way to welcome the august native son without causing unnecessary misgiving from Dr. Wasiri who did not hide the fact that he was going to take advantage of the trip to be the best host for his mentor in his own country. The decision was to break the welcoming party in two, one to take care of Dr. O'Shea and would include Dr. Umzigwe, the university chancellor and Dr. John McMillan, the Emily Thomas O'Shea Foundation managing director—sites operations. The other welcoming party, taking care of Dr. Wasiri, will include Father Zolani, Dean Professor Wutugrase and Professor John Awassa. The intent was to divide the two scientists subtly and quickly as soon as they arrive. Dr. Wasiri would then be directed toward the airport VIP section and would be prepared for the tumultuous welcome.

The morning of the arrival of Dr. Wasiri back to Mezi, the brain trust was completely surprised by what it thought it was going to control tightly. It was evident that the brain trust had grossly underestimated the scope of the celebration that the return had generated not only in the campus but also throughout the KMC cells in the capital of Mandi and locations within hundred or so kilometers of the capital. Curiosity over the man KMC wanted to trust to carry its torch spread very quickly all over the capital.

The noise in the capital became so intense that those manning various institutions in the nation find themselves in the obligation to send people or spies to go to the airport to witness what KMC was up to. Mandi various Radio and TV stations joined the fray. They were not deceived. The road to the airport became a logjam of unparalleled proportion that early morning. Buses, minibuses, motorbikes, bikes and cars of all size were all heading toward the airport from six in the morning of the day of the arrival. By the time the plane from London carrying the two scientists landed at Mandi International Airport, there were, by police estimate, close to three hundred thousand people on and around the airport. A strong police force was quickly called to supplement KMC small team of people who were designed to instill discipline in the crowd. The KMC brain trust still managed to line up as many KMC representatives from all over Mezi along the long arrival-welcoming hall. It was a demonstration of unbelievable proportion for the brain trust.

It was even more incredible for the two scientists who could not believe the size of the crowd from the plane bird view and when the jumbo jet was slowly approaching the landing strip. Dr. Wasiri said to his mentor that there must some political event going on the ground and he hoped that he would be able to fight his way through this crowd to take Dr. O'Shea to the hotel where they were to stay. But as soon the plane landed and the plane door opened everything changed. A standing committee of KMC people led by Dean Wutugrase and Father Zolani boarded the plane and went straight to the two scientists. Dr. O'Shea recognized the old professor and greeted him profusely while introducing Dr. Wasiri.

The old dean bowed before Dr. Wasiri and said, "Welcome home, son, we have waited this day for the longest time. This is Father Zolani who needs no introduction, as you will see. Dr. O'Shea, Dr. Wasiri, would you be kind enough to follow me." They did follow the old man outside the plane and to the first stair leading to a parked Polytechnic University minibus with very dark windows.

This was the beginning of the most tumultuous day in Dr. Wasiri's life. The minibus took the two scientists to what looked like a VIP section of the airport where Dr. Umzigwe, Dr. McMillan and Dr. Awassa were awaiting. They were also introduced to the two scientists from Kentucky. At that moment the two scientists still a bit bewildered by the attention were asked to be seated to catch their breath.

It was again Dean Wutugrase who spoke and said that there were quite a lot of people outside the VIP hall who came to extend a rousing welcome to their native son, Dr. Wasiri.

Addressing Dr. O'Shea he said, "We are very grateful that you brought him home as I have requested the last time we met at that board meeting. We thank you so much. In order to fulfill our wishes of bringing Kano home, Dr. O'Shea, our Chancellor Dr. Umzigwe along with your old friend Dr. McMillan would escort you to the waiting area where you would appropriately witness the welcoming party. At the same time I am calling on Brother Kano to indulge us by freshening yourself next door where you would be given a quick haircut and where we have brought your suitcase for you to select the best suit you were going to wear to be interviewed by me tomorrow."

Dr. Wutugrase made a devious look to all assembled and a rousing laughter ensued. Dr. O'Shea was led outside the VIP hall and toward the elaborate podium already jammed with major KMC dignitaries. The scene was overwhelming with people chanting along students from a local high school marching band. Other people were dancing and KMC huge signs and Mezi small and large flags were floating all over. There were small children, young adult and no so young people clapping along the marching band tunes that Dr. O'Shea could barely make. The tunes were sometime in English or Swahili or both but very entertaining to hear the responses that the large and compact audience was giving. Dr. O'Shea was only reflecting over what he had unleashed as Dean Wutugrase suggested a while ago. In the middle of the celebration he made a sign of cross and holding back his tears he murmured to himself, "Emily Rules."

About twenty minutes later, a KMC assistant came to the bank of microphones and said in a chanting mode, "Brother Kano is about to join us now. People of Mandi, people of Mezi, sisters and brothers from KMC, please give a rousing welcome to the native son, Dr. Kano Wasiri, here comes the native son." At that instant, Dr. Wutugrase came out first followed by Dr. Wasiri, now dressed in a sharp dark blue suite with a white shirt and a shining yellow tie with black side bars, the very colors of KMC.

Father Zolani and Dr. John Awassa closed the line. The pandemonium was on and the flicking flashlights of cameras were intense so were the blinding TV cameras lights. Dr. Wasiri walked the firm and decisive leader way behind the old professor who was extending his back to him for support. When they reached the podium, Dr. Wasiri recognized few Mezi family members and Father Felix. He was guided to a chair in front of the microphones and the glaring cameras lights.

Father Zolani became the master of ceremony. For about ten minutes he begged the crowd to settle before the welcoming ceremony started. Father Zolani asked the crowd to remain silent for the next few minutes when a young lady, a KMC representative from the western province of Watu, was about to solemnly read for the first time the KMC hymn composed and sent to the delighted brain trust anonymously by no other but Father Felix Mulai-Bando. The priest was deeply moved and inspired when he saw the KMC motifs for the first time. That night he woke up at about two in the morning and wrote the KMC hymn that he named "the Three Glories" and it went as follows:

From 3 Glories
From Mezi Mountains Tops
Shines the Guiding Light
Over Your Daughters and Sons
United in Common Hope and Destiny

From 3 Glories
From Mezi Mountains Tops
Eye Effervescent
Beams Over the Land
The Guiding Light of Justice, Fairness and Equality

From 3 Glories
From Mezi Mountains Tops
Eye Effervescent
Guides Its People of Noble Spirit Enlightened

May God of Our Ancestors
Master of Universe
Holds the Shining Light
Over Mezi Forever

In the middle of crowd jammed on the podium, the anonymous author of the hymn, Father Felix repeated the hymn in silence, his heart beating very hard, his eyes heavy with tears. He surveyed the attendance that was enthralled with the hymn reading, and many like Dean Wutugrase deliberately with their eyes filled with tears. Father Felix was now just trembling with joy with the effect and said to himself that some engaging statements or poems like "The Three Glories" are better left anonymous.

When the reading the KMC hymn was over, the marching band took over and with the same lady from the Watu province belted a singing version of the KMC hymn that brought almost to rapture the crowd inside the airport and those outside watching on mounted wide screens. It took another period of thirty minutes before Father Zolani regained the control of the ceremony. He then deferred to Dean Dr. Wutugrase to say the welcoming word.

The old man went to the microphones and wiping his eyes he said, "Brother Kano, it is with a joy I cannot describe that this old tired man is welcoming you in our nation of Mezi. I welcome you to Mandi and Mezi. I welcome you to my dear institution of higher learning, the Polytechnic University where you and I would have some serious talks soon. Now,

Brother Kano, I have said at the beginning it is an old tired man who is welcoming you home. I wish I were the only one to be or look tired. Believe me it has nothing to do with my bones that are also tired and God willing ready to rest.

No, Brother Kano, when I say I am tired, I mean I am terribly tired in spirit and I am no different from many present here today and all over the land. These people are also tired. Brother Kano, we are tired of what this beautiful country is enduring, we are tired of corruption, tired of lack of justice, tired of unfairness, tired of the degradation our sisters, mothers and wives have to endure day in, day out. Brother Kano, we are tired."

A thunderous applaud followed the old man's statement of being tired for about seven minutes with chanting that the marching band accentuated with another local tune for being tired waiting for a better tomorrow.

When the band settled down, the old man continued, "Well Brother Kano, maybe, just maybe it is too soon to call upon you to assist us in this endeavor. But I can tell you this, all these KMC sisters and brothers assembled here, united in one common purpose to stop this old man from getting any more tired in spirit, these KMC sisters and brothers are ready to join together and assist you in that endeavor. Brother Kano, this old man does not want to get any more tired in spirit for long. Brother Kano, welcome home."

This welcome speech went straight to the heart of the matter. The plea that Dr. Wasiri had heard from Father Felix could not be as direct as this one from this old man who was to be his Faculty dean. Dr. Wasiri thought what a welcome, what a pressure.

Next it was again Father Zolani who took the podium, "Brother Kano, again, welcome home. Our elder, Brother Wutugrase has said it all. At this stage we do not want to keep you waiting any longer after this long trip from London. But our sisters and brothers from all over the country, from all our cells in KMC are eager to hear what they need to bring back to their locations from the one they have decided to welcome today without reserve and with much hope and anticipation in our midst. It is with a great pleasure that I am inviting Brother Kano to say a few words to all of us."

Dr. Wasiri approached the bank of microphones, fixed his eyes at the whole gathering in the arrival hall for about a minute, the crowd went silent, and he said in a firm voice and with authority, "Dean Wutugrase,

Father Zolani, distinguished sisters and brothers united in the common bond and purpose of KMC, please accept the most generous greetings from my traveling companion Dr. O'Shea, my mentor, my wife and children back in Kentucky and myself in front of you. It is with a deep sense of humility and grace that we are bowing to the honor that you have extended to us today in this place. There are no words to express how overwhelmed we are at this moment by this magnificent welcome you have shown and given us.

At no time would we have guessed the tremendous celebration KMC has pulled for our arrival. Sisters and Brothers from KMC, again with the utmost humility we want to say to each one of you that we intend to work each day as hard and as long as possible to insure that in the end we are deserving of the honor you have shown us today. This honor would mark each of our days forever. Within the next few days we pledge to touch base with almost all the KMC progressive forces shaping the destiny of this nation to deepen our education and resolve. Sisters and Brothers of KMC, as of this day, let every girl and boy of Mezi know, let every woman and man of Mezi remember that the guiding light of justice, fairness and equality, the guiding light of Mezi people of noble spirit, the guiding light from Nyingaro, Kiese and Kansi mountains, that guiding light of Kany is about to shine as brightly as ever over Mezi, So Help me God. Thank you."

Dr. Kano then bowed his head at the tremendous applause that came back. Dean Wutugrase came over again wiping his tears grabbed the native son and guided him toward his seat. Brother Kano was dripping in sweat and his face was completely transformed. Seated next to the old and beaming Dean Wutugrase, Brother Kano was now besieged and was getting the well wishes from everyone on the podium.

Father Felix came by and embraced the native son and said, "Our wishes are being fulfilled, Glory be to God." Brother Kano did not say a word but smiled and shook his hand. Some members of his family including his two stepsisters with their husbands and young kids then joined him. They embraced in the middle of the tumultuous scene and tried to exchange some family greetings. He simply assured them that he would stop by their residences as soon as his interviews with the university are completed.

He suddenly remembered Dr. O'Shea and turned to the now elated and almost dreaming Dean Wutugrase singing along the various nationalistic songs that the marching bands was playing. He asked about Dr. O'Shea. Dean Wutugrase just pointed toward the left corner where Dr. O'Shea was standing with people who were introduced to them at the VIP section of the airport. He tried to head to that direction but was refrained to do so by Dean Wutugrase who reminded him that he was the guest of honor of the unbelievable first celebration drawn by KMC and it would not look good for him to move about searching or reaching out to people in the middle of all this commotion. Dean Wutugrase added that in this circumstance people would come to him and not the other way around and he better gets used to the new routine. Dr. Wasiri did not like nor appreciate what he heard but he could not move. He managed only to wave in the direction to his mentor who was surrounded by Dr. Umzigwe and Dr. McMillan who was surprised some time earlier to notice that his wife Anna was in the KMC Polytechnic University section, singing and clapping her hands. She was wearing a colorful KMC T-shirt. Dr. McMillan did not remember her leaving their house with the T-shirt. He asked Dr. Umzigwe if he had forced his staff to join KMC and to come to the airport. Dr. McMillan said that Anna had never shown any political inclination all these years they have lived together. Dr. Umzigwe responded, "Not to you maybe when you were too busy climbing the university management ladder. But Anna had lived here all her adult life, and she has seen better times. She does not need a political inclination nor instructions from this old tired paper pusher of manager to know how bad things are. My good friend nowadays everybody has gotten to some kind of political inclination, wake up."

While these old friends from Polytechnic University were exchanging views over Anna, Dr. O'Shea was in cloud nine throughout the entire welcoming celebration. He felt just as much a motor for what was going on around him. At times when the master of ceremony was speaking in Swahili, he was completely lost. But when the speeches and other pronouncements went back in English, Dr. O'Shea had a completely different twist of the event.

He was not oblivious to the launching of the political career of his protégé happening right there in front of his eyes under the guidance of KMC. In the middle of the huge celebration witnessed in the annals of political Mezi, Dr. O'Shea clung to the notion that Emily rules were working overtime and ensuring that the event to welcome Mezi native son leads to the ultimate fulfillment of the grandiose plan let out by Emily. Everything that was happening around him was only process to the same and he was neither impressed nor overwhelmed by the unbelievable noise and the large crowd. They were all working on the account of Emily rules.

When Dr. Wasiri waved in his direction, he responded with a raised fist to Dr. McMillan's amazement. Not only his wife Anna dressed in KMC T-shirt was chanting and clapping with her colleagues in the powerful KMC section of the university, now this old professor from

Kentucky was raising his fist in the typical fashion of long forgotten "Black Power in the United States." Dr. McMillan thought, "What the world was coming to? Was he the only one backward or everybody going crazy?" The only definite thing he knew was that his report to Lady Allistair over this event would take more than ten pages.

The welcoming ceremony was now winding down. Brother Kano walked the all length of the arrival hall thanking every KMC delegation from the country for the overwhelming welcome in company of Father Zolani and Dean Wutugrase. It was when they got out of the airport arrival gate that Dr. Wasiri realized how serious KMC expectation was in regard to his commitment to its leadership. The crowd extended deep miles and miles away.

What started eating Brother Kano inside were the deep worry and the growing ambivalence that, after the big welcome home celebration in the arrival gate hall, he was going to go through this infinite big crowd outside and not feel committed to its main expectation to lead the movement. He decided to block both the worry and the ambivalence when he climbed into the open-air university Jeep rented for the occasion and started waving to the crowd lined up for more than five miles along the highway leading back to the capital. About ten other university limousines including the one carrying his mentor Dr. O'Shea followed the open-air Cheep. The entire cortege ride from the airport to the Tanzire Hilton Hotel took another two hours.

Altogether Dr. Wasiri counted six hours from the time the plane from London to the time the ride reached the hotel. He was now visibly concerned about how his mentor was holding out. When they reached the hotel, Dr. Wasiri jumped from the Cheep and rushed to the next limousine and opened its back door but Dr. O'Shea was not riding in it. When he closed the door and rushed to the next limousine, Dr. O'Shea was standing on the sideline and called him up but he did not hear him. Then he stopped and turned back to look at where the call was coming from. He was relieved to see the old professor standing there and extending his hands as to salute him. Dr. Wasiri run up to his mentor and said, "I am very sorry that it took us six hours to get from the airport to this appointed hotel. It was all unplanned and I am very glad that you put up with all that inconvenience. If I knew this would happen, I would have secured a much quicker ride to the hotel for you. Now let us go refresh and get ready for a nice dinner. I am starving."

He was holding his mentor hand guiding him toward the hotel entrance, happy to finally resume his planned host role. The Polytechnic University and KMC retinue came out from their limousines to witness the engaging relationship between the two scientists. Young KMC assistants were busy retrieving the august visitors luggage from the trunk of the second limousines. Dr. Umzigwe and Dr. Wutugrase led the retinue, exchanged few more pleasantries with the two scientists before wishing them a lot of the rest before the beginning of their official exchanges the next day.

The brain trust then asked a smaller group of KMC militants, still celebrating the arrival of Brother Kano outside the gates of the secluded hotel, to disband. Further it called for an expanded meeting with the main cell representatives who were spending the night in the campus after the KMC successful first political foray. The purpose of this unplanned meeting was to quickly take stock of what had happened that day, build on the momentum that was generated and decide whether, where and when the projected meeting of Traditional Tribe Chiefs was to take place. Dean Wutugrase did not waste a second at this planning meeting. He grabbed its lead and put forth for vote the motion to hold the tribal chiefs meeting the next week on Wednesday at the village of Banfi-Bello. He suggested that the meeting starts at six o'clock in the evening running through midnight when the solemn ceremony would take place starting with the lighting of the bonfire, the retrieval of each burning tree branch by each tribal chief and the throwing of it into the Lake Nyerengi. The meeting was a symbolic repeat of the same meeting held by Sir Banfi Bello to gather in the same village in the northern bank of the Lake Nyerengi.

The small village had taken now the illustrious name of Banfi-Bello. The solemn ceremony will include a lecture of KMC precepts for the country of Mezi and the symbolic casting away of all that was ailing Mezi, corruption, injustice, unfairness, and moral degradation. The solemn ceremony will show the bonfire representing the KMC precepts burning the decaying mores plaguing Mezi, and each tribe chief solemnly casting away these corrupting mores in form of a tree branch in flames.

That was a clever around about way to get almost all the country tribal chiefs to bless KMC precepts and to cast their lots on the promises of the KMC. Dean Wutugrase, in inviting the attendance to vote the motion by acclamation, made it clear that it was high noon for KMC to grab the momentum given to the movement by the extraordinary display of political muscle shown by KMC throughout the day from the airport and throughout the capital of Mandi. The motion was quickly adopted and the meeting adjourned to the relief of the extremely tired brain trust and the festive representatives.

At the same time, the sitting President of Mezi, Mr. Badegou called a small meeting of his own inner circle including his prime minister, Sonjedi, his security advisor, his interior minister, the governor of the capital of Mandi, the army chief, General Gwobazo. Mr. Badegou wanted to get a quick appreciation of what had happened that day almost paralyzing the capital of Mandi. After he opened the meeting, the first to share his opinion was General Gwobazo, who had spent the day monitoring military movements inside and around the capital.

The general explained, "Your excellency, today was nothing more but a bunch of students from Polytechnic University making a lot of noise as usual. In summary, nothing to be politically alarmed about." The interior minister, another retired army colonel, and the governor of the capital seconded the opinion of the general.

The security advisor had another opinion of the event, "Mr. President, I have been warning you about this KMC movement for some time now. I strongly believe that whoever is leading the movement wanted to show how powerful this movement is. I am still puzzled from all I have learned from our people all over the city, why the KMC folks chose the return of that professor teaching at the Kentucky State University, to pull all the stump we saw today. My observers told me that the professor by the name of Dr. Kano Wasiri looked bewildered by the welcome. '

The airport security commandant told me that the professor who came with another older colleague had no idea of what was being thrown for him at the airport. The commandant said that when the plane landed the KMC folks had to take him very quickly to the VIP section of the airport so he could be freshened and changed into what he wore at the welcoming ceremony. The commandant added that he could not believe his own eyes all that were being pulled by KMC in front of what was reported to be a crowd of more than one hundred thousand people. Either it was the biggest con game in the already funny political scene of Mezi or we are in presence of a political Messiah in Mezi. I am utterly confused by KMC intentions. Why should it go the road of deception is behind me? I want to tell you all present here, if I had the opportunity to handle such an outpouring of people confidence, I should have handled a bit different. Mr. President, I have to say not to worry about those KMC political amateurs. Nothing would come out of the so-called political muscle display."

The last person the President Badegou expected to hear from, the Prime Minister Sonjedi remained very quiet and did not show any leaning one way or another toward the first two president advisors. The only thing he would say was that he agreed with both of them and he had nothing else to add. That troubled his Excellency, President Badegou, even more. Mr. Sonjedi kept his own counsel, not willing to show how misguided and short sighted the two previous interlocutors were. From many associates and friends he had come across lately, people generally more knowledgeable of KMC politics, Mr. Sonjedi knew that this professor being ridiculed in the meeting represented a political force to be reckoned with. Among those associates, there was the professor John Awassa who happened to be a friend of a friend of a friend.

He was aware that KMC was in search of a commanding political leader. He was one of few astute political animals in the capital to realize that putting Dr. Wasiri in front of the thousands militants was the biggest coup KMC had realized to date. Mr. Sonjedi was terribly sorry of the small mind posture prevailing in the security meeting President Badegou had called. Unfortunately, he had cast his lot for some time now into what was called the decaying nomenclature of political Mezi, as a young successful economist from the World Bank bureaucracy. From Washington, DC, he had quickly risen to become a confident of Mr. Badegou who appointed him economic advisor, minister of plan, minister of finances, and finally, as prime minister within the last three years.

Mr. Sonjedi still hanged around the Badegou administration in the hope of getting his last administrative appointment of governor of Mezi Central Bank. He hoped to finally hang his economist hat on that nonpolitical and independent function for a minimum of six years. Before receiving the official appointment from President Badegou, Mr. Sonjedi had decided to suffer the fools of the his administration until the next election, he suspected, would bring the overwhelming victory of KMC movement all the way to the presidency.

This was the same general feeling permeating the reporting of the day event by all media in the capital of Mezi. For a change, there was a definite element of freshness about political reporting in the newspapers, radio stations and TV stations. Superlatives abounded in reporting what KMC had pulled the all day. The large number of people who made the trip to the airport was the main item recurring on all reports. Bird views of the traffic and the masses captured most front pages. The endless traffic jams were also shown in the evening news. But the media analysis of the KMC welcoming party fell short of the substance the KMC brain trust expected. There was no account of the speeches made at the airport, nor why KMC went to the trouble of welcoming the obscure professor from an obscure Kentucky State University.

Descriptions of Dr. Kano Wasiri were far and between. Most of the media were advancing the theme of a disappointing trouble free event.

The huge KMC organized welcoming celebration was a letdown for media used to vile political scandals which have become a daily staple of political reporting. The airport event that could be viewed as a call or an appeal to return Mezi to political decency was broached aside by the media eager to return to financial schemes drawn by political appointees or the fights waged by mistresses in front of politicians offices. This was the puzzle that Dr. O'Shea drew when he reached his room and waited in vain for an awesome reporting on the TV of the event he had just witnessed. He got more coverage of the event from a South African channel than all local TV channels.

He was still waiting for the coverage when his protégé, who had been seated in the hotel main dining room, became a bit worried and run up to his mentor's room to find out what was keeping him. He was relieved to find him looking at the large TV set when he entered. Dr. O'Shea did not want to show his disappointment for the complete lack of reporting for such an important event in his protégé life. He shut off the TV very quickly and apologized for making his protégé wait for him that long.

Dr. O'Shea recovered his sense when he noticed how the hotel staff was fussing over his protégé, extending all the VIP regards to honor the man who had shaken the capital of Mandi for a whole day.
They ate quietly, Dr. O'Shea still unable to bring about the awesome welcoming celebration Dr. Wasiri had received.

This lasted until when a very beautiful young lady approached their table and requested Dr. Wasiri's autograph. The lady was at once asked by a nicely dressed man not to disturb the august visitors. This gentleman was part of the hotel staff who was hanging around their table at a very safe distance, apparently appointed to guard Dr. Wasiri's privacy. Dr. Wasiri called upon the gentleman to let the lady collect his autograph. He then signed what looked like a KMC flyer that was distributed at the airport with his mentor looking at the scene with tremendous pride.

When the lady was gone, Dr. Wasiri looked at his mentor, "Please just say what you have been dying to say all this evening to get over it."

Dr. O'Shea laughed, "Son, I would not know where to start or what to say. I just want you to know that I was very proud of you. You might be upset if I repeat this. But all day today, you and I were living Emily's rules. Tell me what you want. She was there."

His protégé smiled, "Dr. O'Shea, believe me when I say that today I would not fight you over that statement. I felt Emily's presence as well at the airport and all day today. Emily's rules were really with us today."

Then Dr. O'Shea turned serious and asked his protégé, "But son, there is one thing you need to help explain or clarify. When you closed your welcome response speech today, I heard you say something you never mention before, and you say it with such gravity of tone it has left me wonder all day and if I remember correctly you said, 'that guiding light of Kany is about to shine as brightly as ever over Mezi, So Help me God.' What did you mean by 'that guiding light of Kany', what is 'Kany' anyway?"

Dr. Wasiri now looked completely bewildered. He asked his mentor to repeat his closing statement and wrote it down. Then he looked at his mentor, "I had no idea that I say all this. I was really struggling there to find the right words to respond to the outpouring of regards we were receiving.

I quickly remembered what the lady read and sang at the beginning of the ceremony. I read the statement very quickly on the paper the lady gave me and decided to adlib along the words in the same statement. You are right there was no 'Kany' in her song or statement. But the word 'Kany' takes many stances in our tribal languages. It usually means the Higher Force, the High Spirit. Don't ask me why I used it. But I knew the effect of that word on an assembled crowd. Given the circumstances, it did not hurt to use that word. It is a tour of eloquence that is commonplace here in Mezi. Do not read too much into this. Besides you notice that it drew a very good response."

Dr. O'Shea a bit mystified responded, "Amazing indeed. Now you see the power of words in every language. Unbelievable for an expatriate like you living abroad all these years. You come home and in one day, you are back using idiosyncrasies imbedded in your mind. All it took was an enchanting crowd of country people. Amazing indeed."

The dinner was almost over and the two scientists continued their conversation. But in the back of his mind, Dr. Wasiri struggled with the reason why he had inserted the word "Kany" in his closing statement. For those who were not aware of this, Kany would sound like what he mentioned to his mentor, a Higher Force or a High Spirit. "Kany" in some parts of Mezi was exactly the name of the mineral Alpha-M that both himself and Dr. O'Shea had been researching all these years. But he had never uttered that word "Kany" to signify Alpha-M. From his own research, he had come to the conclusion that the mineral Alpha-M was to be located in the high plateaus of Mezi. But he had no idea that people in that part of Mezi had a different name for the famous mineral Alpha-M Dr. O'Shea had given his entire academic life and had dragged him into an endless academic battle through his own PhD thesis. When he reached his room, Dr. Wasiri continued to ponder over his insertion of the word "Kany" into his closing statement.

Where had he heard this word and why on earth use it in his first public statement?

CHAPTER 21
Interview

Dr. Wasiri tossed all night over these "Kany" questions without answers. When he finally fell asleep it was almost time to get up and have a late breakfast with his mentor. His interview appointment with Dean Wutugrase was conveniently scheduled late in the afternoon at about three thirty. But his mentor was already out in the field with Dr. McMillan, the foundation managing director for Mezi sites operations. Dr. McMillan came to pick him up and brought him to the office of the University Chief Planning Engineer who was in charge of all the buildings construction that the foundation was carrying out within the Polytechnic University campus. The good news the Chief Engineer shared was that the construction was advancing admirably and with the scant rainy season the construction was now three quarters done. At this rate the Chief Engineer was foreseeing the completion of the Applied Sciences Building by mid April. All the other buildings and landscape should be done by mid May. He was already at the next phase now ordering equipment and furniture for all of these buildings. Another good news was the fact that the well planned and executed construction phase is leaving the university with an excess of construction materials that can be used to build additional residences for the university. At this point Dr. McMillan jumped in and said that he had suggested the building of about fifteen new residences for the university high-level management starting with the chancellor, the provost and all the major Faculty deans.

As a former Chancellor, Dr. McMillan said that he knew very well the difficult and precarious living conditions these high managers shared in the current old university residences. He added that the new residences would be built along the beautiful lake road in the back of the Tanzire Hotel. The university owns all the land tracks adjacent to the hotel going east about six or seven miles. The new residences would build another invaluable goodwill with the university. Dr. O'Shea listened carefully to the request and remembered that his own protégé was going to be interviewed for the deanship of the new expanded Applied Sciences Faculty that afternoon.

With the high probability of gaining this position after the incredible reception of the day before, Dr. O'Shea thought that he would resolve in one shot the housing issue for the Wasiri family if he approved the residences construction.

The beautiful residence will come with the deanship sparing Dr. Wasiri the trouble of finding a new house. He asked the Chief Engineer for the preliminary design of each of the residences. The Chancellor's residence was appropriately the biggest with two story levels, a master bedroom, six other bed rooms, a large living room sitting about thirty people and also a large dining room sitting twenty people. The house had about five bathrooms and a humongous kitchen. It was a going to be a cross between a modern and Venetian mansion with a first story balcony giving into a landscape of two hundred acres on the lakefront. The residences for the provost and the deans were a lesser version of the Chancellor's residence with also a master bedroom, five bedrooms with similar balcony giving into the lakefront. Dr. O'Shea was very satisfied with the designs and asked to see the land tracks where the residences were to be built. Dr. O'Shea went for a ride along the lake road along with the Chief Engineer and Dr. McMillan. The track of land between the road and the lake was the priciest track of land in the capital of Mandi and measured about a mile and half. Luckily enough, an anonymous patron bequeathed the track to Polytechnic University from the beginning of the university construction about sixty years ago. The only section sold to private interests was the Hilton Tanzire Hotel section. After the hotel was built, the general and moneyed public came to revere the lake front area. The university did not budge nor succumb to all attempts to buy additional real estate on that track of land. Dr. O'Shea just loved it. He gave his agreement to use excess building materials to build twenty residences instead of fifteen as it was initially approved. The last five residences will include one where the Emily Thomas O'Shea Foundation offices will be located and the four other residences will be permanently assigned to people attached to the foundation management or board. Dr. McMillan will therefore be assigned his own residence so would Dr. John Awassa, a foundation board member.

In one stroke Dr. O'Shea solved a lot of housing problems for those who would support the foundation endeavors in Mezi. When they drove back to the Chief Engineer office by the way of the construction sites that literally plowed way more than ten miles by five miles of real estate, Dr. O'Shea realized that he had covered almost all he had come to cover this time and this trip in Mezi in about five hours.

He was done with his trip and did not really care to listen to Dr. McMillan additional complaints. He wanted simply to go and relax at the hotel to talk with his protégé.

But it was already three in the afternoon, his protégé's interview appointment time. Dr. Wasiri, who had been relaxing in his room, was picked up on a university minibus and taken to the office of Dean

Wutugrase. There was already a large group of students in front of the office of the old dean to get another glimpse of the professor from the United States and who had made a name for himself the day before. The news of Dr. Wasiri coming to this office spread since the day before when Dean Wutugrase mentioned that the two of them were going to have frank talks. The flurry of activities that took place the morning and afternoon between the chancellor's office and the dean's office betrayed the likelihood that the eminent visitor was coming to the dean's office. When he got out of the mini-bus, the students trying to get autographs mobbed Dr. Wasiri and it took great pain from both Dean Wutugrase and Chancellor Umzigwe to free him from the students. When they were finally in his office, Dean Wutugrase said to the native son that he better gets used to the treatment and it would not get any easier. After Dr. Wasiri regained his composure, he was led to a conference room adjoining Dean Wutugrase office. Dr. Wasiri expected a large gathering of academics going over his credentials. But he was seated across a circular table from Dean Wutugrase who had already shown him so many honors the day before and the University Chancellor, Dr. Umzigwe who was introduced to him very briefly at the airport the day before. There were two large folders in front of each academic.

Dean Wutugrase started the interview solemnly, talking to a small microphone standing on the circular table covered with a dark green fabric, "On this January 15, let it be recorded that Dr. Wasiri, professor of mines engineering sciences at Kentucky State University, Frankfort, Kentucky, USA, has appeared in front of the dean of Applied Sciences Faculty, Dr. Wutugrase and the University Chancellor, Dr. Umzigwe, both of the Polytechnic University, for the purpose of gaining positions with this university. After thorough review of Dr. Wasiri's twenty years teaching credential of the same at Kentucky State University, there was unanimous consent from the Applied Sciences Faculty recruiting committee to offer a tenured professorship of mines engineering sciences to Dr. Wasiri effective immediately. Without objection, I, Dr. Wutugrase, dean of Applied Sciences Faculty, rises to approve and sign the offer of tenured professorship to Dr. Wasiri and request that Dr. Wasiri countersigned the offer to signify that he has agreed to the offer."

Dr. Wutugrase signed the offer and handed the offer to Dr. Wasiri to sign the acceptance portion of the offer. He did sign it. Dr. Wutugrase and Dr. Umzigwe walked on his side and congratulated him for accepting the university offer and rejoined their seats.

Dr. Wutugrase shut off the mike and said, "That was the first part of a two parts interview process. Dr. Wasiri, before you came here today, I pushed my esteemed and learned colleague, Chancellor Umzigwe, so hard to let me go, to give me my long expected retirement, but in one condition, if and only if you replace me as the dean of the Applied Sciences Faculty. I held up that deanship for so long until your mentor came here last time. I begged him to convince you to take up the helm of this august faculty. He declined. He said that he had no sway over you on this matter. Yesterday I came to realize how much respect he has in regard to your intellect and your personality. I envied him for having shared all these years with you. Today I have to rush in five minutes what Dr. O'Shea has been trying to do in twenty years or so, to let your academic prowess shine beyond the cocoon of classroom teaching and research papers review. Mind you, I have nothing against classroom teaching or reviewing research papers. God knows how much I enjoyed it and would have continued doing it if the burden of age has not taken a toll on me. Dr. Wasiri, if you do not want to take the word of this weak and tired old man, tomorrow you would see what your mentor has put in motion to welcome you into this university. He has prepared your way in a manner no other person has done in the archives of this university and I have been here for more than half of century to bear witness to this. I would allow no other person to come and take over this deanship as long as you are teaching here. I would hold up as long as you would resist but look at me, for how long? Please accept this Faculty deanship to honor Dr. O'Shea and your current dean."

Dr. Wasiri looked at the second folder that Dr. Wutugrase had now opened and placed in front of him. The folder had a single paper offering him the deanship of Applied Sciences Faculty. He read it and looked down the dark green table cover for a long time, his eyes swelling with tears. The top of the paper read "Preliminary Offer" with a "Final Offer" to be concurred by the university board of directors. The two old scientists needed his concurrence to the preliminary offer in order to take the matter to the board for a final offer and appointment that will be done solemnly as was the case for the tenured professorship. Chancellor Umzigwe had already signed the "Preliminary Offer."

Dr. Wasiri looked at his new bosses straight in the eyes, "I have resisted most of honor this man, my mentor, Dr. O'Shea has extended to me all these years. I believe I deeply owe him this one. I am proud to accept the preliminary offer for deanship of the Faculty of Applied Sciences of Polytechnic University in his honor and his wife's honor. I sincerely thanked you Dean Wutugrase and Chancellor Umzigwe for the consideration." He also signed his portion of accepting the offer.

Dean Wutugrase let a hooray cry and rushed along with Chancellor Umzigwe to embrace Dr. Wasiri this time. Then they sat back to close the interview. It was Dr. Umzigwe's turn to speak, "Dr. Wasiri, I have seen this day longtime coming. And to arrive right after yesterday's unparalleled event fills my heart with joy I cannot describe. I take pride to welcome you in this university, and I would do everything I can to make your stay with us as pleasant as possible. This calls for a celebration. But before we call on Dr. O'Shea to join us, we would like to invite you tomorrow to a meeting where you would meet the KMC brain trust for the first time. The meeting would take place in my residence at about seven at night. Thank you again for accepting these two offers."

Dr. Umzigwe then called the hotel to locate Dr. O'Shea. When he reached him, he said that he was inviting him to one of the private dining room of the hotel to celebrate a new joyful event. Dr. O'Shea accepted and advised the chancellor that he was going to join them right away. He knew that his protégé had accepted both offers as it was disclosed to him in the previous trip. He went back to his room and said to himself that he should put on his best suit. Figuratively, he felt like he was going to give away another child to a matrimonial condition. He came out dapper as anything else. When he entered the dining room fifteen minutes later, the new dean and the other academics were already seated. Chancellor Umzigwe rose and introduced Dr. Wasiri as the new dean of the Faculty of Applied Sciences of the Polytechnic University. To Dr. O'Shea, the introduction sealed the return of his protégé to his native land. Dr. O'Shea looked at the ceiling and made a slow sign of cross. Dr. Wasiri knew that his mentor was calling on Emily rules again. He smiled and embraced the old man and seated him. He managed to say that he had never seen him so dapper and wondered if his interest had been picked by a beautiful Mezi lady sometime during the day when he was away.
He joked to everybody's delight that he could not trust his adoptive father to be alone for a course of a day without earning himself a new stepmother.

When the laugh subsided, the old man rose and invited the other guests to a solemn toast, "Yes son, I have dressed not to give you a new stepmother. Emily has cornered every spot of that magic feeling and left me well fulfilled. No, I dressed to bear witness to a delightful union you start today with this university when you accepted both the tenured professorship and the deanship at the Faculty of Applied Sciences. Nothing, absolutely nothing fills my heart with joy as much as knowing that you are in your way to tremendous things. I take this occasion to thank both of you Dean Wutugrase and Chancellor Umzigwe for making it happen. I thank you all."

The university managers rose and joined the toast. Then they sat down. Before anyone was about to say anything the old man started speaking again, "Well my job is done here for now. I have made a reservation to leave tomorrow on a flight to London. I am to go there and prepare the board meeting for the foundation. It should start about a week and half from today. Chancellor Umzigwe, you are expected to be there as would be Dr. McMillan and Dr. Awassa. My flight is leaving at about six thirty. Son, now you got so much to do here, I certainly don't want to be on the way. You are in very capable and good hands of these two academics here with us. They have been of tremendous assistance for us all along. You got to lean on them anytime."

At that instant, as if seized by panic, Chancellor Umzigwe excused himself to go make a phone call. Dr. O'Shea asked Dean Wutugrase if he had said or did something disturbing. Dean Wutugrase said that was not the case. At that instant Chancellor came back and apologized for leaving brusquely. He assured everybody that there would be a courier bringing a special gift for the old professor very soon. The reason the Chancellor got up all of the sudden was to insure that the gift was ready to be delivered as soon as possible now that Dr. O'Shea was leaving the next day. A while later when the four scientists were about to have their dessert, a student showed with two small packages and gave them to Chancellor Umzigwe who looked surprised and said, "These students are really working overtime on this."

He then handed one package to Dr. O'Shea and another one to Dr. Wasiri.

"These DVD are holding a small souvenir for each of you. Inside are two DVD copies of the yesterday event. My students were able to put together and edit the entire day of the celebration we had yesterday.

It should last about four hours from the morning jam to your arrival to this hotel. I saw parts of this morning. It is professionally well done. When Dr. O'Shea mentioned that he was leaving Mezi by tomorrow, I had to make the call to get the editing completed. Luckily for all of us, it was done about two hours ago. All it took was to make these four copies. Now, Dr. O'Shea, you have a living memory of the celebration we had in honor of your protégé's return to Mezi."

Dr. O'Shea responded, "Thank you Chancellor Umzigwe. Since last night, I was getting very nervous that I would leave without any visual testimony of what has happened yesterday. I stayed up all night yesterday checking all kinds of local and international TV channels for any reporting of what has happened. Local channels limited themselves to reporting the traffic jam leading to the airport while all that has happened inside the airport was ignored. Not a single shot of the new dean of Applied Sciences Faculty. I was very frustrated by the media here in Mandi. Would you believe it, the only reporting showing my dear Dr. Wasiri was from a South Africa channel? Finally I realized what all of you and your movement are up against in the country. You are the opposition and why on earth would the government give you any TV coverage. It is rough politics indeed. It made sense. Chancellor Umzigwe, I thank you just the same. Dr. Wasiri, you got to be very close to those two veterans of Mezi politics. They know what they are doing."

Dean Wutugrase did not want to miss the opportunity and jumped in, "Dr. O'Shea, we thank you for the astute political observation. We know very well that there will be no free lunch in this endeavor. There will be no pick-nick either. We have opted for the alternate political process through electoral process. We are bidding our time to lawfully take the political helm of this country through the election. We know that the seating government entrenched to the corrupt status quo would never make it easy for political change. And believe it not, we like it that way. Every denial on the government part increases our strength tenfold as you have witnessed yesterday. Do not worry about the TV reporting. We never expected them to provide any coverage of our celebration yesterday. But I can assure that by the end of this week, the DVD copy you are holding would be made a best seller DVD available where possible in every DVD player in every house in Mezi. Our means of propaganda are far superior to those from government TV stations or private commercial TV stations controlled by their friends. Before you know it, this celebration would be shown as by accident and in its entirety in one of these same TV stations over the weekend.

As far as Dr. Wasiri is concerned, I can assure you that he is very familiar of the environment, he should not expect any better. He may need further education to catch up on the latest realities but he is already far gone in the process and would be in good hands here in Mezi."

Dr. O'Shea shook his head in complete agreement. The dinner was finally over. Chancellor Umzigwe and Dean Wutugrase bade farewell to Dr. O'Shea. Chancellor Umzigwe took Dr. Wasiri on the side and advised him to spend as much time with his mentor on the last day of his stay. He added that he did not have to worry if he cannot make it at the meeting scheduled in the evening. Dr. Wasiri answered that he would spend the whole day with his mentor, take him to the airport and get him safely on the flight at six o'clock, and make it back to the campus about an hour later for the meeting if it would not be a problem. Chancellor Umzigwe then said that in that case the meeting would be rescheduled to start at eight thirty.

The next day, Dr. Wasiri rented a car and took his mentor for a brief sightseeing around the capital. He took him for a long ride along the Nyerengi Lake going west of Mandi first to about hundred or so miles outside Mandi. They stopped at a rustic restaurant along the river for a typical Mezi dish for lunch. Then they came back along the same lake road toward Mandi and drove past the hotel and the university campus. Dr. Wasiri then proclaimed that every time he came back to Mezi on vacation, he had taken his family along the Lake Road to spend a whole day camping, having a pick nick, swimming and relaxing. If there was something that attracted Hasbo to Mezi, it was definitely the area. Hasbo and the kids love the place. He said that it had always been his dream if he had to come back in Mezi to live along the lake, hopefully build a retirement home somewhere on that road. He proceeded to talk about the general attraction of the area. He recounted the story of Mandi.

Apparently, Mandi was found by a group of Germans who came around 1897 from Namibia. They crossed the desert of Kalahari and went north with no definite plans about where they were going until they reached the southern coast of Lake Nyerengi. They followed the Eastern side of the lake toward the high mountains. By the time they have started marching westward they saw the beautiful expanse of today Mandi at the same place where we are. If you look closely at that small wall, you would notice the small plaque in German of the founder of Mandi. A German colonel named Hans Mandell signed it. As a matter of fact, Mandi original name was Mandellbourg in memory of that German colonel.

The native population preferred the easier and shortened version of Mandi and that has remained so. But that was then and he was now certain that the area must be a very hot real estate property way past his financial means. The old professor told him that he agreed with him He had also fallen in love with the place the first time he came to Mezi and was taken for a ride with Dr. McMillan. He was told then that the whole area along the lake had not been touched because it belongs to the university. He added that it would not take long before the university starts expanding right there in that area as it is happening on the other side of the road in the campus. From his sources and from Dr. McMillan, Dr. O'Shea said he had learned that about twenty or so residences would be built for the university top board members including the chancellor, the provost, and the Faculty deans.

At the mention of Faculty deans, Dr. Wasiri put on the breaks and stopped the car along the lake road at the edge where the sight of the lake is the most gorgeous. He came out of the car along with the old professor.

He then asked his mentor, "Professor O'Shea, is there anything else I should know about this university, about my hiring, about my coming back in Mezi that would not come out as a surprise after you are gone? Don't you think I deserve to know? What other strings have you pulled for me, for us? Please let me know! Professor O'Shea, believe me I don't want to sound ungrateful for all that you have done for me, for Hasbo, for the kids, for my family, but for God's sake just let me know so I don't look like a fool before these people in this university. They could be assuming things that I have no idea of and would think that I am being disingenuous or worse sly. I simply would appreciate that you tell me, that is all, Professor O'Shea."

The old man went and sat on a bank of rocks on the same edge where they have stopped and looked at the beautiful lake below.

He turned to his protégé, "Son, I learned about the residence's construction yesterday at the same time you were accepting the deanship offer. I was going to tell you about it anyway. I can assure you that the so-called people at the university have also no idea at this time that these residences are about to be built. They would include it as part of the function benefits when they would present you with the final deanship offer. I learned yesterday that the excess building materials at the end of the current construction would be used for the purpose of building the new residences. A gift, so to speak, to the university management. There is nothing wrong or sly about it.

I heard the new residences would replace the old ones dating back to colonial times and increasingly non-operative in the current modern sense of the world. Your family was going to occupy one of the old residences now that you are being appointed as the new dean of the Faculty of Applied Sciences. The fact that you would occupy the new residence is a simple coincidence. By the way before I leave I would appreciate that you show and have the utmost distinctive regards toward the two academics you are dealing with. They are decent people doing the best they can in a rather precarious time and place. Please, promise me that at least. I know I could be devious or whatever you think I am at times. Well that much I have earned dealing with you all these years. But leave these nice gentlemen out of our little misunderstanding. Please, promise me this."

Dr. Wasiri stared at the old man, smiled and said, "I promise. For God's sake, what am I going to do with you, Dr. O'Shea? Now forget all that I have said a while ago. I am sorry if I gave you a wrong impression I have about the chancellor and the dean. I admire them just the same. I have a problem with you as usual. Now it is getting a bit late. Let's go back to the hotel and get you ready to the airport. What am I going to do with you, Professor O'Shea?"

Just as quickly as their odd misunderstanding started, it also dissipated. The two Kentucky scientists resumed their pact and went back to the hotel. Dr. O'Shea was already packed and the university limousine came along to bring them to the airport. Along the ride Dr. O'Shea would not stop talking about the agenda of the board meeting in London. As they came closer to the airport he asked his protégé if he would show the celebration DVD to his family when he would go back to Frankfort.

Dr. Wasiri said that he had not thought about it yet. Dr. O'Shea then advised him to break it a bit slowly and gently to Hasbo. Dr. Wasiri finally concurred that he would have enough time to share what happened with his family once in Frankfort. He bade farewell to his mentor and wished him a wonderful stay in London.

On his ride back to Chancellor Umzigwe residence, he came to the grave realization that he had a lot of explaining to do to his wife and his own family around what the celebration DVD would show. How in the world was he going to explain the unbelievable adulation that he had received when he came back? The chanting, the speeches, the huge unbelievable gathering, the open air convoy from the airport to the hotel, all that was detailed in the DVD.

How would Hasbo take all this? As the limousine was parking in front of the Chancellor residence, Dr. Wasiri decided that he could not resolve his family apparent issue at that instance in Mandi, he would face it when he would be back. Or would he? He heard Chancellor Umzigwe welcoming him in his house. The Chancellor introduced him to his wife and took him to a gathering of KMC brain trust assembled outside on the first floor balcony. Dr. Wasiri recognized Father Zolani, Dean Wutugrase, and Professor Awassa. In addition there was also a middle age lady in a rather plain long blue dress. She introduced herself as Sister Helena Fanzi-Djomba, a lawyer and president of Mezi Human Rights Association and local Representative of Amnesty International. She had short hair with an easy and pleasant smile. Dr. Wasiri tried hard to remember if he had met her the day of his arrival but he could not. Then he asked if they have met before. She said that she missed the big celebration when her plane coming from South Africa could not land in the capital because of the big commotion that was going on at the airport. The plane landed up north in Lusaka, Zambia instead. She came back to Mandi the next day. She then joked that she rather be inconvenienced by that worthwhile celebration than anything else. She added that she was most pleased to meet with Brother Kano and was looking forward to work with him. Brother Kano was certainly pleased to see a woman as part of the KMC brain trust.

The meeting started by Chancellor Umzigwe who reminded everybody of the motion voted the day before to hold what was now being called the "Cast-Away Summit." He reviewed the proposed agenda and purposes of the meeting.

Chancellor Umzigwe emphasized that KMC must take advantage of the incredible momentum generated by the celebration witnessed the day before. He said that holding the Summit became a priority to put every citizen of Mezi on notice that KMC means business and will strive to put in motion everything and anything to bring about profound changes in Mezi political and social landscape. He was also pleased to report that from all KMC sources throughout the country, a great majority of tribal chiefs have responded affirmatively to the invitation issued to attend the Summit. He added that the generous reporting of the celebration of the day before had dramatically increased the interest in the Summit from the tribal chiefs and boosted their number all over the land. The preparations were going very well according to the KMC advance team in place. Chancellor reminded the group that the success of the Summit would not rest in the eloquent pronouncements KMC would put out.

He strongly suggested that the success of the Summit would depend on the effective person to person support and above all the respectful and utmost regards that the entire KMC team would extend to the tribal chiefs who were generally in the sixty-five and beyond of age range. Turning to Brother Kano, Chancellor Umzigwe apologized for expecting him to participate in a meeting that was discussed and planned for some time. He added that the group would welcome his suggestions for the Summit.

Brother Kano told the group that he understood the dynamics of the organization. There were certainly things or instances already put in motion and that he needs to adapt or catch up to. He added that the group should not feel in any obligation to apologize or fall back on issues already settled. It was up to him to find out if he can live with those settled issues or not if he wants to be part of the organization. Brother Kano said that in cases where he would find himself completely in opposite posture on of the settled issues, he would let the group know to talk it over. He was in full agreement with the group about holding the Summit not necessarily to take advantage of the celebration momentum but as a matter of an evolving strategic planning. After listening to the purposes of the meeting as laid out by Chancellor Umzigwe, Brother Kano suggested that KMC would help itself by lining up its pronouncements in terms of major Edicts or communiqués from now on through the election time. Brother Kano thought that the Summit with tribal chiefs is an eloquent wonderful start of putting out these Edicts. There must be a logical sequence in the publication of these Edicts over time. As far as he was concerned the first Edict should cover the theme of casting away all that is corrupt and bad in the current political setting. There could be no important group to do this but the gathering of tribal chiefs who are the guarantors of our traditions.

In his humble opinion, Brother Kano said, "the theme of casting away of corrupt mores has been thoroughly discussed and debated by KMC for a long time. The Summit would be the solemn opportunity to bury these mores and bring about the burning light of KMC precepts. The symbolism of these two acts should be emphasized broadly at the Summit. Then comes the hard part. KMC should be ready not just to state what is bad and wrong and what needs to be cast away. KMC should start putting out Edicts that would spell out what it would do in place of the corrupt mores. The next Edicts would be for instance about how to eradicate corruption in out society, how to promote the respect of woman, how to foster fairness, and how to promote justice. This is where and what each of us should work on diligently from then on.

When we have completed the laying out of these Edicts, we can ask the cells to start selecting KMC election candidates on basis of how close they identify themselves with those edicts. The Edicts would become KMC concrete points of reference for people who would be willing to carry the torch of KMC during the electoral process. I may be ahead of myself here but I am saying that those Edicts if correctly spelled out would leave no doubt whether a candidate is promoting KMC precepts or not. If a cell selects a person to be a candidate based on its own review of the candidate adherence to the precepts, well the cell would have to live with its own selection. If the selection turns out to be bad then the cell has only to blame itself and to pay the consequences of the poor selection. By the way the poor selection can happen at any level of the organization. The idea is that whenever there is grave and detrimental breakdown of KMC precepts on the part of a KMC member, there should be a quick and effective retribution up to expulsion. I am calling on the group on investing a lot of time on spelling out these Edicts. I have been personally challenged to work on the Edict over Women of Mezi, how to promote the respect of our woman. I have invested as much time as I could on this. Believe me, I learned a lot and came to challenge my own deep-seated biases. I hope to publicize it as an Edict. I would like also to take on an Edict about how to eradicate corruption. That would be a tough one. But I realized that you don't need to write an encyclopedia to develop an Edict, simple basic principles should guide you along and the examples are all around us to help. I have talking for some time now. I would welcome any comment from each of you."

Brother Kano did not realize that the minute he was given the floor to give his suggestions, he held the whole brain trust team spellbound.

So, when he requested comments from the group, it took them a while to react. Dean Wutugrase was the first to save the team from the embarrassment.

He continued the logic that Brother Kano was developing, "Indeed, Brother Kano, we could not agree more over the sequence of Edicts you were talking about. From the Summit Cast Away theme to the distinct release of each one of the KMC precepts wrapped in a major Edict, this is a brilliant idea of course. I am sure, Sister Fanzi-Djomba would be happy to provide you with assistance in the development of the Edict for Mezi Women. I should do the same in the areas of corruption by the simple fact that I have seen so much for so long, although I am no lawyer.

Father Zolani would be able to tackle the fairness issue while our esteemed professor Awassa and Sister Fanzi-Djomba, another lawyer, should work together in developing the Edict promoting justice. I have left out the Chancellor for the time being but knowing how resourceful he can be, don't hesitate to call on him over each of these issues, you would be surprised how thorough and erudite he is in almost any subject. However going back to the Summit agenda. I would submit that Brother Kano should be the one to read the Cast Away Summit Edict before the bonfire starts. After the celebration we had, the tribal chiefs are naturally expecting Brother Kano to lead the Summit ceremony. In their minds, this would establish a clear sequence of leadership from the airport celebration to the Cast Away event. Do you agree with this assessment, Brother Kano?"

The team riveted back to Brother Kano who answered affirmatively, "Yes Dean Wutugrase, I would read the Cast Away Summit Edict. But where is it? That should also be developed."

At that instant Father Zolani said that he had some rudiments of the Cast Away Summit Edict. He added that he would be glad to work with Brother Kano for the remaining of days leading to the Summit. Chancellor was terribly happy with the outcome of the meeting he had called. At last they have coaxed Brother Kano to take the leading role in the most important political ceremony that KMC was about to unfold. In order to preserve this unique advance, he decided to close the meeting by repeating various assignments that the brain trust members have given themselves, although Brother Kano took the lion share of them in addition to the leading role in the upcoming Summit meeting. He also requested that each member gives a progress report on the assignment given by Sunday evening. He suggested that Brother Kano uses one of his conference rooms as an office if he wants. At the end, Chancellor Umzigwe invited the group to share native dishes that his wife had labored to prepare all that afternoon. For Brother Kano, the dinner became another occasion to get to know each of the brain trust members on an unrestricted social level. The social gathering lasted very late that night. The next few days, Brother Kano spent countless hours with Father Zolani going over various themes the father had shared throughout the country. They used the MIFF database and slowly together they developed a consistent Cast Away Edict. They worked either in one of the hotel conference rooms or in one of the chancellor conference rooms. They were obviously assisted by a large group of young smart and extremely dedicated students who took turn to summarize the MIFF output and to make it available to the two KMC leaders.

As the Summit Day approached, Brother Kano was attending various meetings reviewing logistics of the meeting and listening to progress reports over the planning of the meeting. He asked a lot of pointed questions during these meetings and conference calls. The meetings kept him awfully occupied the rest of his stay and for some strange reasons he started to enjoy it. When he had a chance to talk to Hasbo, and thanks to the convenience of seven hours difference, he sounded very fresh and full of enthusiasm for every request that his wife mentioned. He had ready-made answers for every request Hasbo made. He started using the appropriate assistance of Dr. McMillan's wife Anna who knew Mandi like the back of her palm and could anticipate every relevant domestic inquiry from Hasbo.

The trip was turning out very important for Hasbo. Questions around housing, children's schools, domestic support, market supplies were never left answered. Her husband, Dr. Wasiri was always ready to give Hasbo good answers at the next call. She was astounded at his diligence. She was relieved that she did not have to insist on the idea of the family returning to Mezi for good. Hasbo was also very pleased with her husband's stay. So were the KMC brain trust members from the time of the huge celebration at the airport to the definite enrollment to KMC leading role. During Brother Kano's stay all had worked as expected. Another person very pleased by Dr. Wasiri's stay was Dr. McMillan. He saw that his rapport with his virtual boss, Dr. O'Shea, was very much improved. The old professor had approved every project he had suggested this time, the most important was the construction of the new university residences including one for himself as Mezi local manager of the foundation. That was a major coup for himself and his wife Anna. He was pestered by his wife to move out the house they bought five years ago when he completed his Chancellor assignment and was heading toward the retirement. In his mind, he bought the house not far the university campus as a parting gift to Anna he did not intend to marry even after she had given him two wonderful children. He was preparing to go back to UK for good. Now that he had changed his mind, returned from UK and married Anna, the house was a testimony of things past both Dr. McMillan and Anna wanted to break off from. The elaborated scheme he pulled with the university chief engineer and planning to come up with excess construction materials really worked. Anticipating that Dr. O'Shea wanted to secure an appropriate and excellent housing for his protégé, he knew that the plan for new residences was a winner. He did not tell Anna about their new residence on the lake road. He wanted to register a bigger effect over Anna when she would learn that they were entitled to the same residence as the Faculty deans including the new and famous Dean of Applied Sciences Faculty.

To further his contacts with Dr. Wasiri, he managed to get him to request as much assistance from his wife Anna every time he made domestic inquiries coming from Hasbo. He knew that he needed to build a strong rapport between Anna and Hasbo. From everything he had learned about Dr. Wasiri since he was contacted in London to take the foundation job, he knew that this rapport would serve both of them well in the future. After what he had personally witnessed at the airport celebration, Dr. McMillan was convinced that getting Anna very closer to Hasbo would bring untold dividends politically and otherwise.

After writing about fifteen pages of the celebration reporting for the attention of Lady Allistair, he abandoned the idea of sending the long e-mail when he bought the hot selling KMC Celebration DVD. An image was worth million words. He intended to send a copy of the celebration DVD to Lady Allistair for a more immediate visual impact and effect. The Celebration DVD answered a lot of questions that Lady Allistair raised at their London meeting including the issue of Dr. Wasiri's political promotion. The answer was obvious Dr. Wasiri's political promotion was nicely being taken care by KMC. He needed to wait a while before sending this DVD as he had this distinct feeling that he had to add something to his reporting of the celebration of Dr. Wasiri's return. He observed that Dr. Wasiri did not stay behind for a vacation after his mentor was gone. More, lately Dr. Wasiri had been seen around the campus in constant company with Father Zolani, they seem to be huddling in endless meetings lasting sometime very late at night. The intensity of these meetings was similar to the one preceding the incredible celebration of the return of Dr. Wasiri. Dr. McMillan had not been able to determine what was being planned. Anna, his wife, pleaded complete ignorance about anything.

All Dr. McMillan had to do was to wait. He was certain that something was going to happen before the return of Dr. Wasiri back to the United States. He was not to be deceived.

CHAPTER 22
Cast Away Summit Meeting

On the Wednesday of planned Cast Away Summit meeting, Dr. McMillan noticed the emptying of the campus after the four o'clock classes. A convoy of buses left the campus at about three in the direction of Lake Road going west along the lake. Unbeknownst to Dr. McMillan, the KMC brain trust, including Father Zolani, Chancellor Umzigwe, Dean Wutugrase, Professor Awassa, Sister Fanzi-Djomba, and Brother Kano left the Tanzire Hilton Hotel in two rented minivans the night before going west along the Lake Nyerengi toward the famous village of Banfi-Bello. This time another illustrious member of KMC, Father Felix Mulai-Bando, joined them for the ride. Brother Kano was much pleased to see his former guest. He did not have the chance to talk to him extensively at the arrival celebration. Given the very busy schedule he had imposed on himself, he wondered when he would have the chance to visit with Father Felix as promised. He was relieved to see him and asked him to join for the ride to the village. Two other members of this ride included Chancellor Umzigwe and Father Zolani.

Father Felix and Brother Kano caught up with their last conversation during the Sunday brunch and the hospitality that Wasiri family extended to Father Felix. Brother Kano joked for a long time about the frantic search of a Catholic Church Sunday service on behalf of Father Felix who joined in describing the morning's endless search by a family of devout Anglican Episcopalians. Father Felix said that the funny part of the search was that Wasiri's children kept mistaking various known protestant churches for Catholic churches and insisted in four instances to go and find out if they were Roman Catholic churches or not. Chancellor Umzigwe also joined in and said that as a Christian of Anglican Episcopalian faith, he knows now that he would not suffer the fate of Father Felix or Father Zolani for that matter, next time he would be visiting Brother Kano in Kentucky.

From the Sunday service joke, Father Felix moved the conversation to a more serious topic. He raised the issue of KMC leadership and asked Brother Kano if he was now comfortable with the idea of leading KMC.

Brother Kano ducked answering the question head-on and said that the current KMC brain trust is working admirably and ably, and each member of the brain trust is providing effective leadership in respective area of expertise as it should be. As far as he was concerned, the leadership issue as raised by Father Felix was a false one. It presupposes that the KMC brain trust would select the KMC leader. He said that he would be more comfortable with the idea of KMC leadership evolving from the bases, the cells as the premises of KMC dictate, anything else would amount to imposing a leader on the cells that make up KMC. He would not be part of such a scheme. At that point, Chancellor Umzigwe intervened and said that he agreed completely with Brother Kano's position. He said that the KMC brain trust had been doing an excellent job to date. It intends to hold a convention at which time the KMC representatives would elect the leader of KMC. That election would resolve once for all the issue of KMC leadership.

To emphasize his point, Chancellor Umzigwe added, "Look to this point, Father Zolani had provided an excellent guidance and diffusion of KMC precepts all over the country. For many people, Father Zolani is the KMC leader. But Father Zolani would be the first to tell you that he is not the KMC leader but the most visible spokesman out there.

It would be the same for Brother Kano. We are extremely pleased to have Brother Kano within our rank. Of course, much would be made of the celebration we had for his return. A lot of questions have been raised about that celebration. Some people suggested that KMC was welcoming back their leader. We, in the brain trust, do not see it that way. We want to grow our pool of current leadership. The celebration of his return was in fact a recruiting of Brother Kano in our midst. We told him in front of thousands of KMC militants that we wanted his involvement in our brain trust leadership. Brother Kano had accepted that role and here we are. As Brother Kano said it, each one of us in the brain trust has a definitive leadership role. When the convention time would come, KMC would look to us to propose a leader. Hopefully, the brain trust would come up with the name of a leader who could be selected either from within the brain trust or without."

Brother Kano was visibly relieved that Chancellor Umzigwe had said loudly what he was having a lot of misgiving, expressing every time the issue was raised since his arrival. At last, he was now given a clear path of his role. He would be part of the brain trust, equal among the members.

He felt very engaged now and without reserve to do the bidding of KMC directives, including what was expected from him at the Cast Away Summit meeting.

In fact, the invitation extended to Father Felix to join the KMC leadership convoy was deliberate. After holding many discussions and reviews around the Cast Away Edict with Brother Kano, Father Zolani decided that there was a need to break the ambivalence that Brother Kano was expressing to him to assume such a prominent role in the summit meeting with tribal chiefs within a week and a half of his return from the United States. Worse, Brother Kano likened his role to a usurpation of the brain trust's previous work no matter what Father Zolani said. The invitation to Father Felix was done after Chancellor Umzigwe, Dean Wutugrase, and Father Zolani met and tried to find the best way to ease Brother Kano's apprehension. Father Felix had given them a thorough assessment of his host when he came back from his US trip. He said that he raised that leadership issue up front and he had noticed a great deal of reluctance from his host. The trio decided that, maybe, including him in the ride and letting him raise the issue again as a continuation of their previous conversation would give Chancellor Umzigwe the opportunity to set the brain trust record straight and to realign Brother Kano's to a positive posture to carry out the task of reading the Cast Away Edict at the Summit. It was obvious that the strategy worked. After listening to Chancellor Umzigwe and Brother Kano, Father Felix said that he had a better reading of the brain trust perspective from the outside. He asked his former host if that was satisfactory to him. Brother Kano answered categorically, "Absolute yes."

Throughout the conversation, Father Zolani kept quiet and took the chance now to give his opinion, "I am very happy that Brother Kano is satisfied with what our esteemed and learned Chancellor Umzigwe has so succinctly said. No to make too much an issue out of this, I agreed also with what Brother Kano said previously when he mentioned that the KMC leadership issue being raised outside the brain trust was a false issue. I have been personally harassed along the same issue by countless people outside the brain trust team. The role I have assumed has put me in front of hundreds of forums throughout the country. Whether you like or not, the more you are out there talking and enlightening people over issues of prime importance to them, the same people would tend to confuse you with the movement and the message. This is where the messenger becomes the message in the mind of the recipients of the message. That tendency always creates problems. I have been personally a victim of that tendency and would probably pay for this the rest of my life.

Believe me when I say that I do not know if I would have survived if I were not a man of the cloth. You see, as my brother here, Father Felix, can testify the cloth has sustained me in my drive to push the message as consistently and effectively as possible without regards of my status of the messenger. This is, I have to tell you, what I admire about Brother Kano. For the few days I had the pleasure to work with him, I have observed that he has already seen and measured the temptation of falling into that trap of being confused with the message. It is a long battle of will within each one of us. To some people, it blossoms very quickly and dies also fast. To others, it grows slowly and surely to become sure-footed and constant as enlightened. That is, in my books, the difference between leadership and enlightened leadership. KMC would always be better served with the latter. Brother Kano, I pray that it is your case. Take your time."

Father Felix noticed the heavy and serious tone that the conversation was taking. Knowing the tendency of Father Zolani to go for the extreme drama to make his point, and fearing that he might bring up again the death of the postulant, Father Felix tried to revert it to its initial joking stance, "Now, be careful with Father Zolani. Before long, he would be asking each of you two of Anglican Episcopalian faith, not only to renounce your faith but to confess every one of your sins from the age of five in order to join the Roman Catholic Church. Worse, in the process, he would have to annul your marriage. I know him very well. He is always recruiting people into Roman Catholic faith. And sometime back, he forgot and tried to enlist me too."

The whole minivan was now shaking of laughter, the driver joined in too. Chancellor Umzigwe was not to be left behind and added, "Father Zolani would have to work a bit harder for him. I remarried after losing my beloved first wife. You got to annul two marriages before I become a Catholic."

The jokes broke the ice of the previous conversation as the convoy was approaching the Banfi-Bello Inn at the entrance of the village. It was about four hours later since they left the hotel in Mandi. Young KMC assistants stood ready to collect their luggage and guide them to the inn's reception desk. The other passengers from the second minivan came along, trying to catch up on the jokes that were shared in the first vehicle and which were still being rehashed by Chancellor Umzigwe.

Before the KMC brain trust members retired to their rooms, they were served a light dinner, and they decided to hold a preparatory breakfast meeting the next day at about nine thirty.

From early morning, buses loaded with students and union members, all KMC militants, started arriving from all over the country. Also convoys were organized so that in each bus, you could count three or four tribal chiefs from the same area and each with a small retinue of younger assistants. The tribal chiefs were quickly guided to huge well-ventilated tents, where they were given appropriate traditional welcome due to their ranks and for those who requested, they were also fed. The sight became solemn with so many tribal chiefs in their colorful dresses and head gears, elaborated canes and arms, and specially designed chairs. They greeted each other profusely, chatted at length, and held different courts under these tents. KMC brain trust members took turns to welcome the tribal chiefs and accompanied them to their respective stations under the tents. Brother Kano Wasiri, Father Zolani, and to some extent, Dean Wutugrase were quickly recognized by some tribal chiefs from the print and visual reporting of the previous week's celebration. Brother Kano was extended a special welcome-home honor by each of the tribal chiefs he greeted or who simply recognized him. By around five in the afternoon, the ten huge tents that were erected for the circumstances were completely full with more than two and a half thousand tribal chiefs. That number surpassed the first Banfi-Bello gathering by more than a thousand. The deafening sounds of various tribal dances, songs, and tam-tam honoring the presence of tribal chiefs gave an air of an unbelievable festival. For an observer not aware of the political nature of the gathering, the summit gave the impression of a very successful cultural celebration of the ethnic diversity of the country of Mezi.

The two and a half thousand tribal chiefs were proportionally representatives of the composition of about six major tribes of the country. The demographic representation of Mezi was no different of the composition of tribes found in many countries of Africa. Most of these countries were cut up at that famous 1919 Berlin conference based only on artificial geographical borders of rivers, lakes, and mountains, irrespective of the disparate tribal composition of people living inside these borders. The tribal composition varied from a four hundred tribal makeup in Congo to a two tribal makeup in Rwanda. In worse cases, the tribal composition was similar in countries separated by rivers. It was not an exaggeration to find the same tribes in three or four adjoining countries.

The six major tribes represented by tribal chiefs at the summit were also found in adjoining countries of Angola, Zambia, Zimbabwe, Botswana, Malawi, and Namibia with one exception, the Bleuh-Nyerengi Tribe that took close to 38 percent of the population.

The remaining tribes represented at the summit included the Nyanza-Chewa with 24 percent of the population, the Lunda-Ganguela with 20 percent, the Tswana with 8 percent, and the Ovambo with 7 percent. The Bleuh-Nyerengi was currently the dominant tribe of Mezi, brought there by the German colonial authorities in consultation with the British from the planes of Tanganyika to work on the railroad track along the Nyerengi Lake's northern side, linking the area of Mandi to the Angola port town of Lobito. The Bleuh-Nyerengi people were brought to Mezi starting around 1905 when the colonial power decided to build the railroad system and the sparse population along the lake would not engage the colonial authorities to participate in building the railroad. At the completion of the railroad system, the Bleuh-Nyerengi stayed along the northern side of lake and settled in a whole series of villages. The Bleuh-Nyerengi, now commonly called the Bleuh, divided themselves into three occupations. Those closer to the lake took up fishing and small farming. Those who settled further away from the lake took up cattle raising and a bit of small farming. The most compelling element of this migration was the imposition of Swahili, spoken by the Bleuh-Nyerengi Tribe, as a second language of Mezi after the German first, then later the English. Swahili became the only language spoken and used by the native population in the army. German first and thereafter English became the main language for the colonial bureaucracy.

The KMC brain trust team had carefully navigated the Mezi ethnic choreography and insisted on the same national tribal composition for the tribal chiefs who came to the Banfi-Bello Village on that day of January 21. The brain trust team also insured that communication among the tribal chiefs was facilitated by young students translating conversations between the six major tribal languages, including the main Swahili and, if needed, the English. Maintaining a relatively harmonious understanding among the tribal chiefs while adhering to both the tribal and age composition of the chiefs was not an easy feat achieved by the brain trust team members.

It was not by accident that the main spokesperson for the assembled tribal chiefs turned out to be Chief Matebele II from the Bleuh Tribe village about twenty miles west of the Banfi-Bello Village. His peers elected him during the afternoon meetings attended only by the traditional chiefs. Chief Matebele II was about eighty-three years old, younger than the oldest tribal chief Sengimo VII, about hundred and four years old from the Tswana tribe from the Eastern high plateaus province of Tongeo. Due to the high respect KMC attached to the age of tribal chief, Chief Sengimo VII was to be seated next to Chief Matebele II.

Brother Kano also chose to sit next to Chief Sengimo VII. Other tribal chiefs within the same age range were also to be prominently placed at the summit dais.

By about ten at night the summit business started. The chiefs were taken to an open-air amphitheater in a two-third semi-closed circle. Journalists from print and visual media occupied the orchestra level. The elevated podium or dais was adorned with a long table covered by bright yellow and black drapes, all in KMC motifs. Beautiful multicolored flowers were placed all over on the long table and on the floor in front of the same table, covering the endless electric lines for lighting, microphones, loud speakers, and the huge video board above. Chief Matebele II, Chief Sengimo VII, and Brother Kano will occupy the three chairs in the middle of the long table. The remaining KMC brain trust members were dispersed on both sides of the table along with the senior tribal chiefs. Father Zolani was again the master of the ceremony. On the open left side of the amphitheater, a bonfire was erected to about ten feet. Next to the bonfire was a stack of more than three thousand small wooden sticks to be used during the Cast Away Ceremony. Before the Cast Away Ceremony, the sight of this organized setting was an eloquent testimony of the effective, remarkable, and extraordinary ability of KMC to pull off in a span of a week, two very significant political gatherings of deep and impressive significance.

Father Zolani got up and went in front of the podium. He called the august assembly to attention. He then asked the eldest tribal chief Sengimo VII to implore God and ancestral spirits to guide the Cast Away Summit. Chief Sengimo VII with the full weight of hundred and four years of age did not move from his special elevated long chair next to Brother Kano, but in a deep and clear voice and in Tswana language rendered his special invocation to God and ancestral spirits to protect all tribal chiefs present, to guide the entire Cast Away Summit to a glorious achievement and to provide to KMC leadership wisdom to adhere strictly to its own professed principles in the future. The invocation was quickly translated and rebroadcast in Swahili and English. Father Zolani then called on the same lady who sang the KMC hymn at the airport to belt it away this time with a solemn rhythm of tam-tams. The young lady did not disappoint. She sang the hymn in English and Swahili to an overwhelming reception by the chiefs. Various tam-tams groups reprised the hymn with their own distinct version for another fifteen minutes. Father Zolani managed again to take control of the Cast Away Summit meeting. He then asked Chief Matebele II, the elected spokesperson of the chiefs to share the message he had been delegated to give at the summit.

Chief Matebele II remained at his seat and gave his address in Swahili, simultaneously translated into five other Mezi languages and English for those chiefs who preferred to follow the speech using available audio-listening phones.

Chief Matebele II said, "Distinguished honorable chiefs of the land of Mezi, brothers and sisters of KMC, we, traditional chiefs of our people in Mezi, keepers of traditions and values of this land, have responded to the call that was issued by our brothers and sisters from KMC for many reasons and, above all, because it is about time. It is about time for those of us trusted by our ancestors to guide the people of Mezi in their traditions to rise as one person and proclaim our very deep disappointment and the unbelievable sense of betray for the current conduct of government business in our beloved country. We need to go back in time to show how we got to this sorry stage. Before the advent of German colonial powers, we, traditional chiefs of people, have quietly exercised our godgiven role on earth, guiding our people as best as we could. The German, and later on the British, brought their mighty war machines and forced us to relinquish our roles and authorities under the pretexts that they knew better in providing better tomorrow for our people. We had no way to resist and let these people from North to do what they wanted to do for about a century. They took whatever they wanted to take for as long as the ancestral spirits allowed them to. But all along, in our own way and with steady support of our people, we, traditional chiefs of the nation, kept our moral leadership over the same people of Mezi. When the wind of freedom started blowing all over the continent, the same people of North came back to us to take over the nation. But we knew better, we did not jump on the bait, we had our sons and daughters ready and able to assume the same authority as the colonial authority. As a nation, we decided that we needed to conduct the business of government in form of institutions, which went beyond what we, traditional chiefs, could not manage nor accomplish. One of our brilliant sons at that time, Sir Banfi-Bello, sought our blessing and gathered us in this same village. He asked us to relinquish our roles and authorities to the institutions, which were taking place to guide us to a better tomorrow. He said at the time that his role would be to insure that these institutions would be strong and efficient enough to provide for the people. He was frank with us and said that the establishment of these institutions would not be easy. It would be long and difficult. He asked us to be patient. Sir Banfi-Bello continued that dialogue all the time he was with us, and I know, brothers and sisters, it was reassuring. We kept our part of our bargain. As long as Sir Banfi-Bello was alive, he insured that those who came after him heard our voices.

Unfortunately, we have to say it loud and clear. Brothers and sisters, dialogue ceased right after Sir Banfi-Bello died. We, the traditional keepers of Mezi, were never to be listened again as a group. We were never to be engaged in a meaningful way from then on. We were never to be invited into an assembly to expose our thought or concerns. The situation worsened during the time of the government by uniformed people. They did not bother with the niceties of the past civil politicians. The uniformed people did not even acknowledge the existence of the traditional chiefs. The same way, they governed the whole country by arbitrary decrees; they held traditional chiefs in contempt, prisoners in their own fiefdoms, unable to communicate with their own people.

"When the uniformed people departed from the seat of government and were replaced by the current batch of civil governments, our political alienation continued unabated. Of course, we were called now and then during election time to deliver votes for this people delegate, that senator, this governor of province, or that presidential candidate. We obliged these politicians knowing full well that their promises were discarded before they reached their offices in the capital of Mandi. We, traditional chiefs, rightly or wrongly but always willfully, played along in the con game of endless deception of 'Give me today your votes, your village will know bountiful and endless prosperity tomorrow.' The prosperity never came. Instead, we have witnessed in a growing and alarming way the pitiful depressing scene of our unemployed sons along with the degradation and the debasing prostitution of our daughters. Brothers and sisters, we did not come here to rehash the painful scenes and sights all over our beloved nation. Brothers and sisters, we came here today to say as one person 'enough.'

"Enough of the bad mores eating away at the fabric of this nation! Enough of the corruption, enough of the injustice, enough of the unfairness, enough of the degradation of our daughters! Enough! Enough! Enough! As we cried enough day in, day out, as we shed tears over the endless abyss where Mezi was plunging, as we implored our ancestral spirits every evening before going to bed to guide our people out of this nightmare, we have also seen a resolute eye growing in critical stature among our brothers and sisters across the land. We have seen the KMC eye lift our spirits and slowly erase the hopelessness that pervaded Mezi's political landscape. We have seen the KMC eye showing the way not only to bury all that is corrupt and backward but also to point out how we need to get out of this morass. Brothers and sisters, we, traditional chiefs of Mezi have come here to answer the KMC call.

"We come here to bury those corrupt mores. We come here to cast away those mores in the mountain of the bonfire about to be illuminated. We come here today the same way we did under the leadership of Sir Banfi-Bello to renew our resolve, to renew our confidence, to renew our expectation and patience in a business of government that put our people first. We come here today to relinquish our roles and authorities to the institutions we sincerely hope to be placed under the shining light and guidance of the KMC powerful eye. We come here today, grateful to KMC for having called on the traditional chiefs to resume their rightful roles of the guardians of Mezi traditions and values.

"We also come here today with the solemn warning to KMC leadership that we, traditional chiefs of Mezi, would not stand by quietly and miss this chance of renewing our stewardship of Mezi traditions and values if KMC leadership does not live up to its professed principles. Distinguished honorable chiefs of Mezi people, sometime later tonight you will be called to cast away the current corrupt mores of Mezi. You would be asked to pick up a wooden stick you see in the pile next to the bonfire and throw it away in the bonfire in a symbolic way to cast away those corrupt mores.

While you do this, we want to ask you to reflect on the act you would perform, the act of casting away the Mezi that we are experiencing today and replacing it with what we want Mezi to be. While you do this, we want also to ask you to reflect on the principles that KMC has provided us, principles that would guide us within this next upcoming electoral process. While you do this, finally we want to ask you to reflect on the fact that this is the last opportunity we are given to effectively guide our people to a better tomorrow under the shining light of KMC. May God and our ancestral spirits bless this solemn day of change in our land. Thank you."

The crowd which was listening in a deafening silence, letting the impact of every word and every sentence in Chief Matebele II's address resonate across the amphitheater, exploded in a thunderous applause and the tam-tams groups reprised the KMC hymn in another fifteen-minute round. Chief Matebele II's address was indeed forthright from each one of the assembled chiefs. It painted in a succinct way the political evolution of Mezi from the arrival of colonial powers through today. It also served notice to KMC leadership that it was not getting a blank check from the chiefs. It would be judged on the merits of its accomplishments.

Brother Kano was reflecting on that part of the message when he was called to deliver the main message that the traditional chiefs have come to hear from the KMC leadership. He advanced to the bank of mikes with the same resolute steps he had shown the week before. Brother Kano picked up his address in English from the chief's warning to KMC leadership.

"Distinguished honorable chiefs of Mezi, sisters and brothers of KMC, it is with deep humility and a great sense of respect that the leadership of KMC comes in front of you to lay the grounds to what would guide this movement from now on. Distinguished honorable chiefs of Mezi, let us proclaim loud and clear on this solemn day that KMC has heard your message, KMC is heading your warning, KMC would stand ready never to take your support for granted, and KMC would work hard to earn your trust every day. At the hour of midnight as the bell tolls seven times for each of the provinces of our beloved nation of Mezi, that is, the province of Chelow, the province of Kansi, the province of Kiesse, the

province of Mandi, the province of Nyerengi, the province of Tongeo, and the province of Wuta, we, in the KMC leadership in consultation with our sisters and brothers throughout the country, proclaim the following first KMC Edict of Banfi-Bello which reads:
The KMC Cast Away Edict of Banfi-Bello

We, daughters and sons of Mezi, assembled on this day of January 21 in this illustrious village of banfi-bello, guided by the shining light of KMC principles, take the solemn pledge before the people of the republic of Mezi, one, unitary and indivisible:

- o *To promote and safeguard at all times Mezi people's inalienable rights to freedom, justice, peace, and prosperity.*
- o *Enjoyment of freedom shall extend to freedom of thought, religion, affiliation, and action as stipulated by the law of the land.*
- o *Firm adherence to the democratic process of alternate political leadership through electoral process.*
- o *Guarantee of the exercise of justice to all, irrespective of gender, race, creed, social status, and ethnic origin—support of all available means to foster peaceful relationships within Mezi society.*
- o *Provision of social and economic environment where every daughter and son of Mezi can realize his or her full potentialities.*
- o *To cast away all the negative values, mores, and tendancies, which are currently eating away at the fabric of Mezi society and pushing the republic lower and lower in the bottomless abyss of corruption, injustice, unfairness, and social degradation.*

Distinguished honorable chiefs of Mezi, sisters and brothers of Mezi, the KMC Cast Away Edict would guide KMC across the land from now on. KMC would stand ready and would welcome to be called and recalled every time it strayed away from this edict. KMC would stand ready to be judged not on what are said in this edict but how KMC would apply the edict every day within and without the business of government. Brothers and Sisters of KMC, as we moved further in time and across this nation, it would not be enough for us to just give references to this edict. KMC would put out concrete guidelines and additional edicts that would amplify on this first edict. KMC would insist that all these guidelines must serve as codes of conduct in your home, your work location, your place of worship so much so that people of Mezi would point out to this day of January 21 as the beginning of shining light in the long dark tunnel Mezi has found itself. Otherwise, all that has happened today would have been in vain. But this KMC leadership would not stand for vain efforts or failure. This KMC leadership pledges to work diligently with you distinguished honorable chiefs of Mezi, sisters and brothers of Mezi to insure that the new dawn of enlightened Mezi takes place as soon as possible in every shape and form. May God and our ancestral spirits grant full speed in the august endeavor KMC is engaging in. Thank you."

As Brother Kano was rejoining his seat next to the elder Chief Sengimo VII on the podium, waving to the crowd under another rousing applause, Father Zolani lined up six young high school students, three girls next to three boys. The youngsters were selected in the six provinces outside Mandi to read the edict of Banfi-Bello translated in the other six major languages spoken in the land. The students acquitted themselves admirably reading the edict slowly to the unanimous approval of the crowd and the assembled traditional chiefs. When the reading of the first KMC edict was completed in all major spoken languages of Mezi, Father Zolani came back and started to describe the logistics for the traditional chiefs to finally participate in the symbolic casting away of the corrupt mores of current Mezi by throwing the wooden stick to the bonfire. At his signal, the bell tolled again for seven times for the seven Mezi provinces. Traditional chiefs started to rise by age order and moved slowly toward the pile of wooden sticks. Then Chief Matebele II was asked to light up the bonfire, and he invited the oldest traditional chief Sengimo VII, assisted by Brother Kano and other people from his court, to throw the first wooden stick to the bonfire. Other chiefs who shared the podium with him followed in this symbolic gesture.

When the elder chiefs were done, the remaining thousands of chiefs from the entire amphitheater followed in the symbolic way of the throwing of the wooden sticks for the next four hours.

When Brother Kano assisted Chief Sengimo VII back to his seat, he was startled by a revelation that the chief made. Through his young translator, Chief Sengimo VII mentioned that about three weeks ago two white men came to his village and claimed to represent Kano Wasiri, a Mezi citizen teaching at a university in the United States. They claimed that this professor had sent them to gather as much information about a mythical mineral that they were certain it was found not far from the village. The two white men wanted to know if Chief Sengimo VII had any specimen of the mineral they would bring back to the professor from Mezi to conduct his own analysis. They gave their names as Dr. Neal Hansberger and Dr. Anthony O'Shea. They claimed to work with Kano Wasiri at that American university. The two men sounded so believable at that time when they heard that a Dr. Kano Wasiri was coming back to Mezi to lead KMC. But after checking with their contacts with Dean Wutugrase who was sitting out there, they could not verify what they were talking about. Dean Wutugrase did not want to be involved in what was apparently a scheme. Chief Sengimo VII told them that they had no idea of what mineral they were talking about, and they left after they had exchanged presents with the village elders and took pictures. Chief Sengimo VII then ordered one of his assistants to show the picture of the presumed scientists. When Brother Kano looked at the picture, he could not identify the two scientists or the one identified to be his very own mentor, Dr. Anthony O'Shea. Taking his breath, Brother Kano said to Chief Sengimo VII that he did not send any one of these scientists to get any information regarding any mythical mineral. He added that he had studied under Dr. Anthony O'Shea and had worked with him for a long time. He said that he knows Dr. O'Shea very well, and he came with him to Mezi a week ago. He was at this time in London. The Dr. O'Shea in the picture was not the Dr. O'Shea he knows, his own mentor for more than twenty years. He concluded by saying that from the entire conversation he heard from Chief Sengimo VII, these two white men were simply impostors. Chief Sengimo VII then asked Brother Kano what kind of mineral analysis he had conducted for his mentor Dr. O'Shea all these years and why the impostor Dr. O'Shea kept mentioning Alpha-M as the subject of the work analysis Brother Kano had done. Brother Kano looked at Chief Sengimo VII straight in the eyes and said that he had conducted a research analysis of Alpha-M for his doctoral thesis under the guidance of Dr. O'Shea, and he had continued to do sporadic researches around the same mineral called Alpha-M.

Chief Sengimo VII then asked the obvious question, "Was Alpha-M the same as Kany?" Brother Kano hesitated and looked up the sky and responded, "Yes, Chief Sengimo VII." Chief Sengimo VII stayed quiet for a time and finally said, "Brother Kano, now I can rest at peace as I have met the one who is about to fulfill the prophecy that my great-grand father has given to the long line of Sengimo family from the eighteenth century. It was a prophecy that talked about 'Kany Rising from the Eastern Starlight.' I have lived and searched this long, hoping and trying to decipher the meaning of that prophecy. After I saw the DVD of your welcome-back celebration, I realized you probably did not know nor had anything to do with those white impostors. Your humility and nobility put you far above such a stupid scheme. You just confirmed that today. Listening to you today reading the first edict of KMC, I finally concluded that you must be the one foretold in the prophecy. You can deny and fight it as much as you can and must, but in my eyes and my mind you are the one. You probably wonder how I came to that conclusion. Now remember what you said in your speech when you came back from the States? At the end of your address, you said, 'that guiding light of Kany is about to shine as brightly as ever over Mezi.' That sentence was a revelation and a trigger for me. Brother Kano, nobody in my long memory has used that sentence in any speech—religious, social, or political. The last person to have used that sentence was my great-grand father. He was the only one who had joined these two sentences at his deathbed when he whispered for the last time to his son, Sengimo II, 'Kany is rising from the eastern starlight and that guiding light of Kany is about to shine as brightly as ever over Mezi.' That prophecy remained in my family since that time. And when I heard you uttering the same sentence at that celebration, my heart almost went. I asked my grandson to replay that passage many times to verify what I was listening to. It was unmistaken that it was the same sentence used by my great-grandfather. I consulted with few other elders in my village and in surrounding communities. They all came to the same conclusion: you must be the one that my ancestor was predicting in his prophecy, you must be 'the guiding light of Kany rising from the eastern starlight and about to shine as brightly as ever over Mezi.' I needed to come here and to see for myself with my old tired eyes. And God always set things straight. You chose to sit next to me during the Cast Away Summit ceremony. I sat here all day observing you from up close. Throughout, you paid me every regard due to my rank and age, not like those pitiful Mezi politicians, but as a respectful and dignified son of Mezi. Your speech at the welcoming celebration was a definite sign for many of us who have been waiting for the signs of that prophecy. Today you have confirmed everything we have been waiting for.

"I am happy to tell you at this moment that I would be sending to you before this weekend what those white impostors were looking for. I know that you would make good use of the power of Kany. Now I am a little bit tired and ready to retire to sleep. Do not trouble yourself to show me off. You got important matters to deal with in this summit. Son, you have the blessings of the entire line of Sengimo family to carry out all that the power and light of Kany would bring your way. I would be providing all you need to make the guiding light of Kany shine brighter."

At his signal, the entire Chief Sengimo VII's retinue got up and removed the chief and his long chair very quietly to the back of the podium. Brother Kano tried to extend his farewell but was gently restrained by the chief's assistants. Dean Wutugrase, who had witnessed the whole scene from a few seats, got up and quickly joined Brother Kano. He tried to entertain Brother Kano who looked now very gloomy after the sermon from the older chief. Dean Wutugrase said, "You got an earful from the old chief, didn't you? Today I must say better you than me. I had my share of listening to Chief Sengimo VII all these years. He is and remains a very wise man. He carries his hundred and four years well. Believe me, he is a wealth of information and wisdom that would serve anybody in the business of government very well. Can you imagine, the Sengimo line of succession has been uninterrupted since 1768 or so, and he can account for all his forebears who came before to date? It is a tragedy that those seating on the helm of power in Mandi have never, I repeat never, availed themselves of such a national treasure. Maybe now you can understand why I tend to be so acerbic and cynical when I talk about our so-called current political leaders. Nullities, that's right, they are a bunch of zeros, nullities with no evident purpose, common or otherwise, except to fill their pockets. I am sorry that I am going again in the tangent here. I sometimes cannot help. But going back to Chief Sengimo VII, I am certain that he mentioned to you that story about two white men paying him a visit in his village and one of them claiming to be Dr. O'Shea. Chief Sengimo VII sent his messenger to me to verify that story. At that time, I dismissed it outright and did not care to look at it any further. We were in the midst of preparing the celebration of your return. I knew that Dr. O'Shea could not be at the same time in that village in Tongeo Province when he was in Kentucky in the United States, getting you ready to come to Mezi. The whole story was so preposterous, it did not merit any time of mine You should know by now that here in Mezi, as well as in many parts of Africa, we are used to all kinds of adventurers from all over the world, whites, people from Middle East, America, Europe, Asia, now Chinese coming here and proposing unbelievable schemes in Mandi and all over the country.

If it was not another Ponzi scheme, it always was the latest incredible investment to return incredible return. Then nothing happened. They disappeared as quickly as they had shown up. I certainly had no time to listen to another sad scheme story. So I dismissed it. Then this morning, when I was in line, welcoming the great chief Sengimo VII, he reminded me of the request he made. I told him again that the two white people were impostors. In addition, Brother Kano, you could not possibly know nor care for them. I also told him that one of the white men must have been misrepresenting himself because Dr. O'Shea just arrived from the United States with you. I did not have to explain to the Honorable Chief Sengimo VII how Honorable Dr. O'Shea is. But Chief Sengimo VII, stubborn as he is, insisted to have a word with you. That is when I revealed to him that you were going to play him host throughout the ceremony. I should have known that the chief would have caused much trouble. Now what did he say, what did he do?"

Brother Kano realizing how far from the real drama Dean Wutugrase was, reassured him, "Dean Wutugrase, there was nothing of concern that Chief Sengimo VII said or did. I am the one being a bit put off by what he was calling prophecy from his great-grandfather. It has something to do with the word 'Kany' that I used in my airport address. Chief Sengimo VII really stretched the whole meaning of Kany to no end. I had no choice but to listen to him. You are right; he exerted a lot of wisdom indeed. And you are right again when you express your disgust with our leaders when they cannot even give the due to somebody like Chief Sengimo VII, what a tragic shame!"

"Tragic shame indeed, but not for long if everything that happened here today can help. Then again, I should say also you must get used to the elders coming up with all kinds of prophecies every time they would meet and talk with you. That is their usual way of inferring and actualizing what they wish to happen. I have seen and heard this before. Nothing special there."

It was getting a bit late at night, the procession to the bonfire continued without a break. The traditional chiefs now owned the Cast Away Summit ceremony, and at every instance they were getting to the bonfire, they released the wooden stick to the fire only after a long and elaborate invocation. Some started singing their invocation, others just belted it away in loud and resounding voice. All took an extreme pride in participating in a ceremony that they presumed would put a lot in motion in body politics of Mezi.

Before long, the traditional chiefs started to circulate a petition to get the KMC leadership to declare the weekend to come a Cast Away Weekend throughout the whole Mezi villages and localities where a bonfire would be raised, and people would throw away small wood sticks in the same manner the chiefs were doing now to signify the break away, the casting away from the corrupt mores debasing the country.

Father Zolani was quick, with the strongest push yet from Brother Kano, to enlist the entire brain trust team that granted the petition under an overwhelming pressure from the elders without debating the political consequences of such meetings throughout the country. Brother Kano reasoned with the team saying that it would be ridiculous for the brain trust team not to approve and to grant the petition. He said that it would amount to trying to put the genie of political awakening back in the bottle after releasing it twice for all the people to see and hear, first, at the airport celebration and now, at this Cast Away Summit meeting. He convinced his teammates to let the natural course of political conscience proceed without reservation. The petition was voted by acclamation by all traditional chiefs still in session. Around four thirty in the morning, the last traditional chief had thrown the small wooden stick in the bonfire, a long musical interlude took place with all attendees embracing each other for the realization of the momentous event. On behalf of KMC, Father Zolani thanked every traditional chief for attending the meeting and asked each one of them to carry forward the message that was shared during the Cast Away Summit meeting. Chief Matebele II, who had struggled to that moment to stay awake, thanked the KMC leadership for the magnificent ceremony and challenged his colleagues to lead and to replicate the Cast

Away ceremony throughout the country during the upcoming Cast Away Weekend. The ceremony closed with the singing of the KMC hymn at about five thirty with the rise of the sun.

It was about seven in the morning when the brain trust team managed to retire for a morning sleep through about three in the afternoon when the team separated into two convoys to return to Mandi.

While the brain trust team was resting and the traditional chiefs finding their ways to their respective villages and localities, a buzz of the third kind was taking place in the print and visual media. Compared to the muted coverage of the airport celebration of the previous week, the Cast Away Summit ceremony was being broadcast as the major political event to hit Mezi since the accession to political independence from the British throne.

Every newspaper in Mandi had the same bonfire cover picture. It showed Chief Sengimo VII raised high in his long chair throwing a wooden stick to the bonfire, and below him, there was Brother Kano applauding. The message was clear, first the traditional chiefs have celebrated the casting away of the present political order by lighting of the bonfire and throwing the wooden stick along with that political order into the bonfire; second, they have done the casting away under the leadership of KMC represented by this new leader named Brother Kano Wasiri whose arrival was celebrated last week. The reporting by various TV channels was more extensive than the week before. For the first time, KMC hymn was broadcast all over Mezi. All the speeches made at the meeting were broadcast unfiltered. Worse, the bonfire lightning and the casting away ceremony were faithfully shown. A new name in Mezi politics was mentioned all over the news, and it was Brother Kano Wasiri. His speech providing the first KMC Edict of Banfi-Bello was replayed and analyzed endlessly in many private channels. Mandi rose that Thursday morning with a completely new political equation. On one hand, you had all representatives of major political parties inside the institutions wondering what to make of the casting away of the current political order; on the other hand, you had those who have written off all that was happening within those institutions as corrupt and not accountable to people aspirations and all the more ready to move on with KMC. Every office of the government, every seat of political power was reverberating with the political shakedown that was clearly profiling in the horizon. The low and high chambers, which have been routinely paralyzed by all kinds of shenanigans, stood still that morning, while its members were estimating how big and violent the popular broom would be to clean the polluted places the next electoral time. Many members of the same chambers, veterans, and champions of the most corrupt practices on the land started exchanging bluntly tips about the best strategy to use to be co-opted by KMC, regardless of their shameful and unspeakable past. Most of the members in these chambers have resigned themselves for some time to the idea of political oblivion awaiting them at the end of this political term.

On the executive branch, the Cast Away Summit ceremony was received with a mix of deep anger and fear. As soon as he received the news of the Cast Away Summit at about seven at night, President Badegou called on the army chief, General Gwobazo, to deploy an infantry along the same Lake Road leading back to Mandi. President Badegou did not want to take a chance just in case these old folks gathered at the Banfi-Bello Village started thinking that they can ride down to Mandi and take over the seat of government.

When confronted with the broad reporting of the night event, President Badegou called another meeting of his own inner circle including his prime minister, Sonjedi, his security advisor, his interior minister, the army chief, General Gwobazo, and his own political party general secretary. The meeting was scheduled for late in the afternoon. When the members of his inner circle gathered at the prescribed time, they found their leader very agitated, as they never have seen him before.

All that he had seen and read all day visibly troubled him.

President Badegou started the meeting by giving a rambling talk: "These old folks want to bury all of us alive. They want to bury these hard-earned institutions that we have built and solidified all these years. And do you know why, well, because we did not want to listen to them or follow their stupid advices. Worse, these other old fools at the Polytechnic University are manipulating them. I tell you, I know exactly what is going on right here. I have never told you this. I always thought that it was a private matter. But now it has gone too far, and I have to say it. It has all got to do with my old nemesis, Chancellor Umzigwe from Polytechnic University. He has this old grudge against me dating back to the time when we were at the University of Makerere in Kampala, Uganda. I was reading law, while he was studying engineering. We were, in fact, friends and both ran to become Student Council president of the university. I won fair and square. From that time to date, Chancellor Umzigwe never talked to me. When I was running to become president of Mezi, he would not give me the courtesy to hold any conference or meeting at the university premises. With time, I simply ignored him. But then, I heard about KMC being organized at the university. I did not say anything. Chancellor Umzigwe has virtually rendered that university a cell of KMC. In other times I would have gone there and closed the entire university and kicked all of them out, including his buddy Dean Wutugrase. The two old fools. Now with the so-called democracy and political alternate process, we cannot do anything. We have to suffer the insults of these old fools day in, day out. I know that there is corruption in our institutions. I am not denying it. But I have worked very hard to stamp it. I may not have been successful as I have wished, but God knows I have tried. Then corruption is not Mezi's only attribute. All over Africa, corruption abounds. Even our friends in the South suffer the same sickness. Still I cried like anybody else, and just the same when I see how our girls are being dragged into prostitution at younger age every day. These fools talked as if they are the only ones suffering the degradation of our society. They talked as if they have the monopoly on the hurt visiting upon our people.

I hurt just the same too, if not more. The difference is that while they talk and sneer, I have to do everything within the law in this era of democracy to prevent the worst excesses of corruption. A lot of people here in Mezi want to make believe that we, in the government, are promoting corruption. I tell you, I can jail every identified corrupt senator, people delegate, and minister, colonel, or general, and I would still not have removed corruption in Mezi society or body politics. Sometimes I tend to believe it got to do with our deep inner psychic. The fact is that each citizen of Mezi wants to be ahead of the next person not because it brings some positive and salutary effect in the order of things or in society in general. No, each citizen of Mezi wants to be ahead of the next person, and whoever that person is, because he wants and needs it that way. That is unfortunately the way it is with all us here in Mezi. It is dog-eat-dog state of mind. That is the start of our corruption state. You see it every day in the small and in the large. Tell me why that person driving his car wants to cut over the next person and for no reason. Tell me why this well-off person wants to beat a two-dollar small traffic ticket by insisting that his powerful friend who happens to be the country attorney general squash the ticket. Tell me why this other person is building this big huge house with eleven large rooms and eleven bathrooms when his wife would be the only person to join him in the house. Tell me why this businessman is giving the import agent ten thousand dollars when the import sticker costs only fifty dollars. Tell me why this colonel wants to walk into this dancing club surrounded by seven bodyguards. I can go on over and over with examples of our corruption state of mind. Now how do you stamp it? Do you stamp it with grandiose proclamations as the ones they did in that village? Are they going to stamp it in the Cast Away ceremonies they are planning to do this weekend as I heard? My friends, we need to stop this nonsense. KMC wants only to stir up troubles and blames the government for suppressing the troubles. Well, KMC will get what it deserves. That is how I see it, and I need your help and input about how we need to react to this nonsense."

President Badegou slumped in his chair, very tired and exhausted. The first to respond was General Gwobazo, fresh from the deployment of infantry on the road to the Banfi-Bello Village, "Your Excellency, I have be waiting for some time for your instruction to bring all these troublemakers back to order. It is about time to get these people to respect the authority of the state. As far as I am concerned, the lack of discipline in our society is just as much the cause of all of this degradation we are witnessing. Just a signal from you, and all will be taken care and very quickly."

Next were the president's security advisor and the interior minister who did no better but second General Gwobazo's harsh evaluation of the current political situation.

Then PM Sonjedi rose to temper the harsh evaluation by his peers, "President Badegou, it would be much easier to respond tic to tac to the so-called Cast Away ceremony that KMC has organized in Banfi-Bello Village. Now we got to be very careful here. Our response must be legal and, above all, constitutional, as you have already said it. When you are at the helm of the nation and when you have sworn to uphold the constitution as you did, you should not and cannot lower yourself to the lever of every rabble-rouser who comes along and wants to disturb the established order. Your task is to govern under the law. That is what the constitution provides for you. The rabble-rousers, KMC included, the traditional chiefs included, have nothing else better to do but to sneer and to talk and to talk. Now let's see if all that has happened violated the law. KMC has received a lawful authorization to hold this meeting from the office of your own minister of interior two weeks prior to this event. Everything that has happened there, including the harsh speeches, the insults, the bonfire, the throwing of small wooden sticks, all that is protected in our constitution under the cover of Freedom of Speech, Freedom of Religion, Freedom of Association, Freedom of Affiliation, Freedom of Action, Freedom of Thought or Thinking, and Freedom of Expression. I would be very happy to know under what cover you would bring these people back to order as the general has put it. President Badegou, it is not a secret to nobody here that I am legalist. I was attracted to your political platform because I know you are also a firm legalist. You have governed to date as such, I would hate to think that you want to change course at this time and place. I have followed and embraced your leadership because you have said and repeated so many times that you will always win anytime in the theater and confrontation of ideas. This is your chance to win in that theater of ideas. You have already challenged those who are screaming out there day and night about corruption, can they show how to stamp it without falling in another abyss of dictatorship?

That should be your course of action. People would take a second look at all these easy answers that KMC is giving out there and would ask them what they are going to do instead. You gave concrete examples of the corruption state of mind; you need to show how to prevent them especially in case of the prevalent condition when each citizen wants to get ahead of everybody else. From the person who likes to speed ahead of everybody else, a stiff fine the first time, a triple fine a second time, a jail term a third time.

For the person who wants to get his traffic ticket squashed by his powerful friend, establish a documented trail of copies registering the offense and the signing up of the squashing of the ticket by the powerful friend. If he has any common sense, the powerful friend would not dare sign the squashing order in the first place when it should be documented. The man building a disproportionately huge house should stand ready to document how he has accumulated so much money to afford the house.

The import agent receiving twenty thousand dollars for issuing a fifty-dollar import sticker would have to prove why he needs to be compensated in the first place by the businessman, he would have to show what the import sticker should be, and if he is not pocketing the difference, the businessman would have to document the true value of the item being appraised for import tariff. As far as the colonel with seven bodyguards in a public dancing place, that is a clear breach of military discipline that need to be appropriately addressed according to military codes of conduct. President Badegou, what I am alluding to is the need for us assembled here to seriously address the issues of documenting violations of our law and rules and reversing all instances of impunity which reinforce the corruption state of mind. That task is not KMC's; it rests solely on the government. If we start it today, we will go a long way to stamp the corruption, we will go a long way to stop the gathering momentum that would clean all of us from this seat of government and give way to the likes of KMC. President Badegou, that is my plea, and I hope you will hear it."

The president who had been listening attentively to the young PM, stayed quiet for a significant amount of time before responding to his protégé, "Comrade Sonjedi, I always respect the insight you bring to our deliberations every time we gather here. This is very helpful for me to ensure that I am getting counsels on both sides of the issue at hand. I understand very well where you are coming from in this matter. But I have to disagree with you. This problem is not a matter of legalism. It is a matter of a bunch of people clearly resolved to take power no matter what. I did not hear these fools talking about winning election. No, my friend, they are talking about lighting bonfires all around the nation this weekend. I certainly understand the symbolism of that. I want also to cast away every form of corruption that is showing up in this country. But in addition to uphold the constitution of this country, I have also sworn to keep Mezi safe from all enemies from within and without. I have sworn to keep Mezi safe from troubles wherever they may come from.

Tell me now where KMC leadership would be if and when these ceremonies degenerate into full riots? Where the KMC leadership would be when the rabble-rousers would take over the bonfire ceremony and start burning everything in sight. That is the dangerous path we need not get to. This is what I am talking about. That needs to be prevented. At this time, I am ordering General Gwobazo to mobilize all military units to a soft general alert around the country. They should stand ready to squash any degeneration observed at these bonfire ceremonies. I thank you all for your input, and I would like to have a restraint preparatory meeting with both General Gwobazo and the security advisor at this time. Thank you."

PM Sonjedi, the minister of interior, and President Badegou's party general secretary left the conference room. President Badegou, still furious from everything he heard about the Cast Away ceremony, turned to General Gwobazo and said, "General, you need to do something about the KMC leadership at the university compound. I believe that going after Chancellor Umzigwe, Dean Wutugrase, or that child molester of Father Zolani would be too easy of a target. I do not want to bother with the figurehead of the young professor Awassa. He does not really matter. I really want to shake down this professor Kano Wasiri from the United States. I heard he is staying in that very luxurious hotel of Hilton Tanzire. A high lieu of Mandi corruption indeed, where, if you remember, one of my infamous interior ministers used to keep a harem of sixteen and below young girls until I got him busted and jailed for a long time, and only to hear that the hotel belonged to Polytechnic University. Well, maybe Chancellor Umzigwe was partaking in that sordid affair, who knows. General, I want you to rent a conference room at the hotel, invite the professor, and make him understand that he does not know what he is getting involved in. Mezi is not US. He would be better off to go back teaching mines engineering in Kentucky, where he belongs. You would do this the day after we have assessed the weekend events. Please do this as professionally as possible. You have already got my order for the soft alert. Proceed at once."

When this meeting ended at around six in the evening, the KMC leadership convoy was reaching the hotel from the Cast Away Summit ceremony. This time the convoy had to fight its way through a large throng of students and well-wishers eager to greet and acknowledge Brother Kano Wasiri as the new KMC leader. It was with great pain that the hotel staff managed to open the minivan door to guide Brother Kano to the entrance of the hotel. He was greeted with a loud KMC hymn song rendition. Brother Kano waved to the crowd and disappeared in the hotel.

The crowd stayed behind and continued to sing various KMC uplifting songs two hours later. The same evening, Dr. McMillan, who finally got his answer to the queries he made regarding the endless meetings which preceded the Cast Away Summit, ran out of tapes to record the Cast Away Summit event broadcast at all TV channels. He had already collected all the newspaper articles that had covered the event. But all along, he was very puzzled by what was happening right in front of his eyes. He could not believe the KMC ascendance that Dr. Kano Wasiri had gained in less than a two weeks' stay in Mezi. He was now less assured that this had happened overnight. It must have been prepared for some time unbeknownst to all people concerned, including Lady Allistair, Dr. O'Shea, and the jailed lawyer Barry Newcomb. Dr. McMillan debated about the real proponents and drivers of this overnight ascendance. Was it really the works of the Emily Thomas O'Shea Foundation with its promoters including Dr. O'Shea, Lady Allistair, and the lawyer Barry, or was it the culmination of the works of the obscure KMC leadership riding along with all that the foundation was doing or wanted to do for the university but knowing very well it was always on behalf of their future leader? Dr. McMillan shook his head. Chancellor Umzigwe and Dean Wutugrase must have really fooled the foundation management pretty good. These two old foxes played their cards and options very well. One has just to look at what they are getting: brand-new big buildings for the Applied Sciences Faculty, the student hall, the hundred town houses for professors, the retirement home for professors, the new residences for the university management. On top of all that, the two old foxes have managed to install very subtly their own man on the leadership position of KMC, which, in everybody's mind and eyes, would be the next governing party of Mezi. And what the foundation was getting in return or exchange, the certainty that Dr. Kano Wasiri was going to work for them. Dr. McMillan thought that this sounded very lame for all that the foundation was providing unless he was missing a very important reason why the foundation was set up in the first place. Even if the theme of Dr. Wasiri coming to Mezi was to work for the foundation or some obscure endeavor not yet revealed, but the question would remain, in what capacity? That also was not clear, unless the prize was always the leadership of KMC and, by consequence, the future political leadership of the country. That thesis would be a bit far-fetched when Dr. McMillan remembered his last conversation with Lady Allistair, who was completely at loss of the current political status of Mezi and also completely unaware of the existence of KMC. At the end, Dr. McMillan concluded that what his successor Chancellor Umzigwe and Dean

Wutugrase have accomplished was extraordinary and all in less than two weeks.

The two old foxes could care less about what the foundation wanted to accomplish in Mezi as long as they saw a convergence of their main objective, raising Dr. Wasiri to KMC leadership, which beautifully met the main objective of the foundation, bringing Dr. Wasiri from the United States back to Mezi in a secure fashion. They knew very well that Dr. O'Shea wanted to move mountains to insure that his protégé would return to Mezi. They were a bit hesitant of all the commitments his foundation made. They gladly went along with all the plans and added more items when they saw that these commitments started becoming a reality. That was the opening they have been waiting for; they did not waste the time in loading the man successively with the tenured professorship and the deanship to satisfy the foundation criteria while they labored endlessly to crown him with KMC political leadership.

And clearly, they succeeded. Dr. McMillan had now a problem. How would he explain all this to Lady Allistair when he would probably be scheduled to meet with her in London in a week? He was invited to make presentations for the board about the foundation works' progress in Mezi. He was also scheduled to meet with his new other boss, this American Patrick Berger. Dr. McMillan resolved that maybe he did not have to go over this intricate web for Lady Allistair. Maybe it was planned all along, and he would be confirming the obvious and looking like a fool. Maybe he did not know enough about the web to provide unsolicited analysis. He decided to leave the web alone. If asked, he would only report about the airport celebration and the Cast Away Summit ceremony. The two events' DVD copies will provide enough visual effect for Lady Allistair to appreciate Dr. Wasiri's new political involvement.

While Dr. McMillan struggled with the analysis over what he believed to be an intricate web, the main actor, Dr. Wasiri, was completely oblivious of the underside disparate courses vying to map his professional and political future. He had accepted his two academic appointments as a matter of fact. He had decided that the tenured professorship was his by the depth and length of his teaching experience at Kentucky State University. The deanship was due to the deep appreciation for all that the couple O'Shea had done for him throughout and to date, including the foundation. He was still struggling a bit with his inclusion in what he believes to be collective leadership of KMC. From his observation, his inclusion comes from the fact that Chancellor Umzigwe and Dean Wutugrase wanted desperately to keep the KMC leadership in the hands of Polytechnic University academics.

These two senior scientists were very fearful to let KMC leadership emerge outside the university compounds and be tainted and corrupted as everything else of honor and value was in Mezi. He agreed with them wholeheartedly. He finally understood why they insisted on his getting the deanship. The academic stature that came with the deanship of the biggest scientific faculty in Mezi would squash any opposition to his inclusion to the collective leadership. Besides, now given four strong academic hands, all from Polytechnic University, in that collective leadership of seven people would always guarantee a definite Polytechnic University stance, in other words, the combined stance of Chancellor Umzigwe and Dean Wutugrase. He went along with this view after all he heard about all other institutions and because he knew that he still had a long learning curve in Mezi politics. The presence of the two old hands would accelerate his learning curve. Now that Dr. Wasiri was in his hotel room after the long night and day of the Cast Away Summit, he was at peace with himself for all that was accomplished.

He thought that the Cast Away Summit was very much appropriate. The feedback he received from the thousands or so chiefs he managed to talk to confirmed the need and the urgency to move Mezi to an entirely new path. Dr. Wasiri had no more qualms about the adulation he was getting. He thought sincerely that after two major political events in less than two weeks, KMC collective leadership will be provided a great deal of regards, which, in some corners, will be turned into some forms of adulation. That would be accentuated more so in an academic environment with so many impressionable young students. It should be expected.

Dr. Wasiri took a day off on Friday. He busied himself with family matters at the United States and in Mezi. He talked at length with Hasbo again, without mentioning the two events and caught up with children's business. He faithfully responded to Hasbo's latest domestic inquiries and introduced Mrs. Anna McMillan in a conference call as the most dependable person to answer any domestic question in Mandi. Hasbo took over the conference call, and Dr. Wasiri was relegated to a bystander while the two ladies exchanged contacts and talked the next two hours and a half about all and nothing. The ladies were interrupted around one in the afternoon when Dr. Wasiri insisted that he needed to have a late lunch. After he was seated alone for a late lunch, two young people he recognized to be Chief Sengimo VII's assistants approached him. They said that they were carrying what the chief had promised to give him.

They gave him an oversized leather attached case and a closed envelope which contained a note from the chief and a number code to open the attached case. They asked him to sign a receipt attesting that he had received the attached case from Chief Sengimo VII. They excused themselves for interrupting his lunch and disappeared in the hall of the hotel. Dr. Wasiri opened the envelope. There was a letter inside signed by Chief Sengimo VII.

It read: "Dear son, I have enclosed in this attached case five pieces of Kany. I am giving them to you at this time as the fulfillment of the prophecy I shared with you that sacred Day of Atonement. Feel free to test the power of Kany. When you are done, please let the people of Mezi know that the light and the power of Kany will raise their nation as far as the starlight of the prophecy which is found in its entirety in the seven pages copies I have included herein. You would need to translate this old Tswana text to find out where Kany is hidden in the high plateaus of Tongeo. May the light and the power be with you, Son of Mezi forever."

A small-attached letter had the number code to open the attached case. Dr. Wasiri smiled and said to himself, "Kany, Alpha-M, will never let up."

He put the two letters inside the envelope and continued his late lunch. When he came back to his room, he opened the attached case and found five most magnificent and shining cuts of a mineral inside equally matching blue velvet pouches. Three pieces were of large size and heavy, configured like the gold bars which are kept in bank vaults. The last two were half size of the gold bar and slightly heavier. Dr. Wasiri's heart started beating very hard. He got an overwhelming, distinct, and strange feeling that he was in possession of something of untold, indescribable value and importance. His hands started shaking violently. He then realized that Chief Sengimo VII had provided him with what amounted to Mezi's national treasury items. He needed to handle them with the utmost confidence. He would faithfully follow the instructions he gave him. First, he had to get them tested, but how? He took one of the pieces out again and almost cried. It suddenly occurred to him that maybe, just maybe, the old professor O'Shea was not crazy after all. Maybe, just maybe, Emily Rules were not to be dismissed so lightly as he had done these last twenty years. Emily Rules were coming back with such vengeance, Dr. Wasiri could not hold out anymore; he went to the bathroom and noticed the cold sweat on his face and the tears streaming from his eyes. He decided on the spot to bring two large pieces to the United States to be tested by nobody else but Dr. O'Shea.

Nobody in this world deserves that honor but his mentor, Dr. O'Shea who had toiled all his academic life to advance the notion that somewhere in this world there was a mineral of outstanding big bang properties. And now possibly and probably Dr. O'Shea was about to turn the table on all these doubters, including his very own protégé, Dr. Wasiri.

The very funny thing was that it took Dr. Wasiri to come back to Mezi, his own country, to be proved wrong about the thesis he reluctantly defended and that Dr. O'Shea had promoted all these years.

No matter what the outcome of the tests, whether Dr. O'Shea's long-held thesis is verified or not, his esteemed mentor would get the first crack to test these extraordinary pieces of mineral. He also decided to bring a small piece to do his own corroborating tests. He would provide remaining pieces, a large and a small one, for safe keeping by his stepbrother. He would put these two items together inside a pack of documents that he was going to leave with his brother. Better yet, he would just put all inside the same attached case given by Chief Sengimo VII. He proceeded to hide the other three pieces inside the large suitcase he would bring back to the States. He called his stepbrother to confirm the dinner appointment he had been trying to hold with his entire family since he came back to Mezi. The brother happily concurred to the dinner. He mentioned that the entire family had been patiently waiting for the time to honor him with a family dinner. Friday night would be the most appropriate time to have such a large and busy dinner. He said finally that he must give him now time to call and alert as many family members as possible for this happy occasion.

Dr. Wasiri closed the end of afternoon, reading newspapers' account of the Cast Away Summit ceremony. As expected, the account showed a narrow range of Mezi political reporting when there were no scandals to write about. While the volume of reporting exceeded the airport celebration reporting, the general tone was, if anything else, extremely discouraging for Dr. Wasiri. It started from the trivial focusing on the size of the bonfire and the colorful headgears worn by the traditional chiefs to the extreme violent doom and gloom foreseen for the current political regime. The whole message of Cast Away Summit was deliberately lost in petty and meaningless editorials of various newspapers. The sad relative reporting of such momentous event in Mezi political reinforced in Dr. Wasiri's mind the strong resolve to push for a definite change in the political life of Mezi. How can the expected political change be promoted in Mezi society when the fourth estate is incapable to raise the level of political reporting and analysis? Dr. Wasiri wrote a note in his diary, "KMC must put in place its own print and visual media."

It was about time to meet his family for a dinner. Dr. Wasiri had lost his mother when he was about seven. His mother passed away after a difficult pregnancy resulting to a stillborn daughter. His father, the village public civil servant registrar, remarried three years later and had three sons and a daughter with his new wife. However, Bleuh society being strongly matriarchate, Kano Wasiri was surrendered to his eldest maternal uncle to be raised. This uncle, detecting his strong inclination and aptitude to sciences, quickly placed the young Kano Wasiri in boarding schools run by the British Episcopalian Church. Kano Wasiri was practically raised in the boarding schools he attended, reinforcing his inclination to pursue his scientific training until he was selected to go to study in the United States.

His contacts with siblings were rather far and in between. It consisted to short Christmas and Easter visitations with his uncle's family. Sometimes, during these short vacation times, he was brought along to see his father at the village. He had trouble recognizing his father as such. His stepbrothers and stepsister were equally strangers. The long summer vacation time was always dedicated to construction works sponsored by the Episcopalian Church to build small schools, infirmaries, social centers, or churches all over Mezi. Students in boarding schools were asked to participate in these construction projects in lieu of tuition payment in schools. This left absolutely no time to enjoy the summer vacation with siblings. Students at boarding schools were what he considered his real brothers.

After his engineering studies and his postgraduate studies, Dr. Kano Wasiri went to teach at the Kentucky State University. All along, he had no specific desire or inclination to go back home where he did not really have what could amount to relative or family attachments. When he married Hasbo, Dr. Kano Wasiri could not bring himself to talk about his own family. With time, he learned about his family more through steady correspondence he kept with his various school "brothers." When Hasbo, herself desperately seeking refuge from her own estranged family, insisted on visiting Mezi, Dr. Wasiri was evidently troubled. He reached out to one of his stepbrothers to arrange a short family visitation to his father's village. He had not seen or talked to this brother for about fifteen years. That was the time he learned about the passing of his own father and his maternal uncle. He also learned about the great economic havoc being brought by the terrible mismanagement of the country by the military. The havoc had displaced most relatives from the countryside to the capital of Mandi. Those with a bit of professional and academic background managed to land on their feet in Mandi's commercial, business, or government works.

Others struggled mightily and saw their families being dislocated right in front of their eyes, with their sons driven to life of drunk, drug addicts or peddlers, various petty or grand larceny crimes, with their daughters invariably drawn to prostitution. But Hasbo insisted, and finally Dr. Wasiri brought his family to Mezi. They stayed alternatively with longtime friends and family members, including the stepbrother. The occasion was the first for Dr. Wasiri to get acquainted with his own father's family. He made for the time lost while Hasbo, unaware what her husband was going through, went about her way to visit many parts of Mezi with her kids and always in company of Dr. Wasiri's younger nieces and nephews. Hasbo had a ball during that first vacation. It left a lasting impression of a family belonging she never shared and wanted so desperately for her own children. It was at the end of that vacation that Dr. Wasiri appreciated the sense of the alienation his wife felt toward her own country when she did not want to pack her suitcases. She stayed locked in their room, unwilling to do anything for a whole day before their return. When her husband asked about what was troubling her, Hasbo said that she did not want to go back to the United States, that she had finally found in Mezi a family she was genuinely part of, and that there was no other place in world she rather be and raise her children but Mezi. Her husband convinced her that he had a few more years to spend in Kentucky State University and would take his family back to Mezi. She agreed to go back to US living for that one hope of returning to Mezi; everything else was irrelevant to Hasbo afterward.

There was a definite festive atmosphere when Dr. Kano Wasiri reached his stepbrother's house, which was in the new relatively wealthy area of Mandi. It was also along the Lake Road but on the other side of Mandi downtown, on the same western road to Banfi-Bello Village. His stepbrother, named James Wasiri, a lawyer by training, had done very well. At the last vacation visit by the Kano Wasiri family, he lived in a decent house not far from downtown Mandi. He was now a general counsel of a growing local business enterprise, which had expanded to include the largest bakery of Mandi, the largest brewery, five supermarkets, and a long-haul truck transportation system. The house was a big villa on the other side of the Lake Road, surrounded by the obligatory high walls. When he got out of the car, his brother, sister-in-law, other family members, and a few longtime friends greeted Dr. Wasiri. He was then led to the veranda in the backside of the house where the big party was already under way. There was a long table on the side where various native Mezi dishes were being warmed. Dr. Wasiri greeted each of the guests while holding small talks with young and old family members.

As usual, he inquired about absent and departed family members and friends, giving a great deal of comfort to all. A pastor said grace for the occasion, thanking Dr. Wasiri for the honor to join the family and friends to celebrate his short stay. Brother James Wasiri followed up and extended family greetings to his brother. When his turn came to speak, Dr. Wasiri said that he was sorry that this was going to be a short stay, but he would have more opportunities to know and to meet each of the guests in the near future when he would come home to stay for good. He thanked everyone present for the welcome extended. Afterward the guests dined and danced around the large veranda for the rest of the night while Dr. Wasiri continued to talk to various guests. The party went on until past midnight. Sometime before leaving, Dr. Wasiri called on his brother James and asked him to hold for safekeeping the attached case that was brought to him by Chief Sengimo VII assistants. He said that the attached case contained very important documents he would need to have when he would come back to Mezi for good, sometime in the month of May. He did not mention the two Kany pieces he placed inside the attached along with KMC documents he had collected during his short stay. He then left the party to return to the hotel. However, on his way back, he noticed that two military jeeps were trailing him. Twice when he slowed down, the two jeeps did the same. He continued his drive to the hotel. When he reached the entrance of the hotel, he saw the two jeeps slowing down first, then continuing to move along the Lake Road. Dr. Wasiri shook his head and thought that this was probably a form of intimidation, the power that had chosen to unsettle him after the two major political events. He thought that this should have been expected anyway in a troubled country like Mezi. He remembered what his good friend Sir Ewas had said, "The real power in Mezi is still in the hands of the military, and behind each current powerful politician, there was a general or a colonel." For an outsider like him, the first real political test must come in simple forms of raw intimidation. That should not be a surprise whatsoever. Dr. Wasiri also decided not to mention the incident to his other brothers and sisters in KMC leadership.

The next day, a Saturday, was dedicated to another series of meetings designed to coordinate and monitor the long Cast Away Weekend ceremonies taking place throughout the country. In the evening, Dr. Wasiri attended a bonfire held within the compound of the university for a Cast Away purposes. Almost all students took part in this ceremony. When this ceremony was over, Dr. Wasiri was approached by a group of students who insisted that he come along to a huge Cast Away ceremony that was going to take place in the Mandi shantytown of Komesah.

Father Zolani did not like the idea of venture late at night outside the university compounds. He thought that Dr. Wasiri could be set up in such environment. Father Zolani said that he would be more than happy to represent him in the shantytown. Dr. Wasiri thought about his proposition and decided to go with the group of students. He said to Father Zolani that he did not join the KMC leadership to be confined in the sheltered compounds of the university.

He added that he was prepared to go wherever KMC leadership asked him to go, be it in the shantytown of Komesah or the Banfi-Bello Village. Father Zolani then insisted to come along to the shantytown.

When they arrived to the bonfire location of Komesah, they were greeted as people leaders. The bonfire was gigantic and was already started by a KMC local leader who was happily surprised to see two of the most senior members of KMC leadership attending Komesah Cast Away ceremony.

He greeted them profusely and asked them to say a few words to the large crowds of more than six thousand.

Brother Kano obliged, "Sisters and Brothers of Komesah, we come to you today to signify our deep felt conviction that Komesah is where KMC light should shine brighter. It is our belief that where Komesah would go, so would Mandi, so would Mezi. Komesah is where KMC must succeed in moving the country. If Komesah is not listened to, if Komesah is not attended to, if the people of Komesah do not see the way out of the mediocrity where the power that be works so hard to keep it, then our work would have been in vain. But I can assure you, KMC work would never be in vain. In our humble design, Komesah would rise because Komesah is ready to cast away all that is rotten, all that is backward, all that brings ruin to our sisters and brothers of Komesah. Thank you for participating in this ceremony of casting away our past and looking toward Komesah's future. Thank you."

When he was done, Brother Kano even surprised himself for all that he said in a brief eloquent way. Father Zolani, a veteran of many KMC gatherings, was also happily surprised. The response from the crowd was just as overwhelming. The young and old people of Komesah have never heard or seen a leader address them in such glowing terms. As a matter of fact, this was the first time in Komesah's memory that a political leader attended a gathering uninvited by surprise. The word went out, and the crowd that started in the six thousands grew to about twenty thousands. The KMC local leader was now beyond deep gratitude.

He was in tears in front of the two leaders. Father Zolani and Dr. Wasiri had no choice but to hang around and greet each of the people who came by on their way to cast away whatever piece of wood or paper they brought along to the bonfire. The session went on peacefully until about three in the morning. The two leaders were then escorted to the waiting student cars that brought them to the location. What started as a wild idea and proposition from hard-nosed students turned into a major event to everybody's surprise. However, on their way back to the university, Father Zolani noticed that three military jeeps were trailing the student cars. He kept looking back but did not say anything to Dr. Wasiri who was engaged in lively discussion with the students. When they reached the university compound, the three jeeps continued their course. Father Zolani took Dr. Wasiri back to the hotel in his own car. When leaving the hotel, he called

Chancellor Umzigwe to mention the trailing of their convoy from Komesah through the university compound. Chancellor Umzigwe was very upset when he heard that the two KMC leadership members went to Komesah without the regular advance notice or protection. He would not appreciate or hear about the overwhelming welcome they received in the shantytown. Chancellor Umzigwe said that as far as he was concerned, the trip was a bit premature, not cleared by the collective KMC leadership. His main concern was the physical protection of Dr. Wasiri. He said bluntly that KMC leadership had invested so much to get Dr. Wasiri to this stage and cannot afford to jeopardize his safety at this time. He added that the trailing at night of their convoy by military jeeps from Komesah to the university compound should be a clear warning to KMC leadership that the holders of Mezi real power would not lie low when it becomes a matter of displacing them from Mezi seat of power. They would fight with all their might to death. He admonished Father Zolani never to forget that. He closed the call by reminding Father Zolani to explain himself at the Sunday meeting when the KMC leadership would hold a meeting to assess the overimpact of the Cast Away Weekend throughout the country. Father Zolani was evidently contrite about the foray to Komesah. He would extend his apology for straying away from the leadership directives.

On Sunday, there were various reports of successful Cast Away ceremonies around the country as well, the largest one taking place in the big village or township of Chief Sengimo VII. That ceremony gathered the largest crowd for Cast Away ceremonies. A Mandi newspaper reported that close to two hundred thousand people took part in this ceremony. To Mandi political leadership, the most disturbing part of that township's Cast Away ceremony was the participation of all units of the nearby military base and the local police contingent in the ceremony.

Chief Sengimo VII cleverly convinced the commanders in both local armed forces to join the Cast Away ceremony as part of their civic duty. These two commanders were quickly relieved of their assignments and sent to supervise remote and smaller units. The Cast Away Weekend was overall very successful. All ceremonies took place in relative peaceful manner with no disturbances, even the hotbeds of violent riots of the past such as the shantytowns of Komesah in Mandi or Zingzong in Ikando, the second largest town of Mezi in the northern province of Kiesse.

The lack of disturbances in all Cast Away ceremonies around the country was also reported in Mandi newspapers with a twist and a major question mark: was this a frightening sign of things to come for the country's political leadership?

The successful Cast Away Weekend was also recognized at the KMC leadership meeting held at about nine that Sunday evening, this time at the conference room of Dean Wutugrase's office. Soon after the KMC leadership hailed the success of the Cast Away Weekend, Brother Kano rose to present his deep regret for bypassing the collective KMC leadership rules and going to Komesah to assist the local KMC cell to hold the Cast Away ceremony. Father Zolani who was preparing the same apology was stunned. Chancellor Umzigwe looked straight at him to correct Brother Kano. When Father Zolani raised his hand to intervene, Brother Kano told the leadership members that Father Zolani was about to take blame for the unauthorized foray that he, Brother Kano, initiated after being urged to go to Komesah by a group of students.

He told the team, "As a matter of fact, Father Zolani did everything in his power to dissuade me from going. But I did not want to lose face in front of these young students. I knew very well that I was taking a bit of liberty when I decided to go to Komesah. But I did not have a choice. What reason could I come up with for these young people always looking up to us? Could I tell them that I did not want to go to Komesah? And for what reason or excuse? KMC leadership knows very well that our ultimate goal is to eliminate every Komesah from the map of Mezi. Not going to Komesah would mean denying that it exists and, in the process, denying that all KMC is fighting for is worthwhile. Not going to Komesah would mean that we don't have to go to a place that does not exist, we don't have to eliminate a place that does not exist. Not going to Komesah would mean that our ultimate goal to eliminate every Komesah was a farce, was in vain.

Not going to Komesah would have made a mockery of all KMC has done and preached all these years and these past two weeks, at the airport and at Banfi-Bello. Leadership team members of KMC, please accept my apology for breaking the internal rules of the team, but I have to tell you right now under similar circumstances, faced with similar challenges, I would still go to Komesah."

Father Zolani was still trying to get the attention to take the blame for what happened the night before. At this point, Dean Wutugrase rose to say what everyone was thinking, "Brother Kano, there is no need for you and Father Zolani to apologize for what I heard was a momentous event ever to happen in Komesah. You did this leadership team so much honor you could ever imagine. The newspaper account, for a change, reproduced your entire speech that was baptized 'The Call from Komesah.' That was the best speech heard anywhere to date in Komesah. I don't have to tell you that you moved that place to no end. We are all extremely grateful for your address. However, something must also be said about our internal rules. Those rules have kept us as one functioning unit all these years. You may not realize but KMC was not born yesterday nor the day before yesterday. KMC has been built slowly for years from the toils and sweats of many, some of those were cut down by bullets or thrown in jail for their work or involvement with this movement. It was so bad that the movement had to survive underground for a long long time.

That is where and when it grew larger and bigger. You have, sometimes, to put up with our underground behavior, including our internal rules that were painstakingly laid out during our long march in the political desert of Mezi. These rules have served us very well. None of us believe that we are out of the long march in the desert. Now and then, we can come out and tell the world that KMC must be counted on and dealt with as we did at the airport celebration, Banfi-Bello Village Cast Away Summit, and yes, Komesah Cast Away ceremony. But whether we like it or not, we are still on our long march in the desert and those internal rules will remain our only protection. We need to abide by those internal rules as long as we are still on our long march. Brother Kano, you must agree with me when I say that our long march in the political desert of Mezi has still a long way to go."

Brother Kano responded, "Dean Wutugrase, I understood perfectly well what you are telling me. And as I said, please accept my apology. And this would never happen again."

The exchange closed the issue of Komesah sortie to the great relief of Chancellor Umzigwe who was torn over the entire episode of Komesah, especially the military jeeps chasing after the student cars carrying Father Zolani and Brother Kano back to the campus. He did not want to raise the scare all that evening and was afraid that Father Zolani might bring it about. He was very happy with the intervention of his old friend Dean Wutugrase who always finds the right words to make a collective point as directly and subtly as possible. The meeting ended in a rather pleasant parting.

CHAPTER 23
H5 Exchange

However, if Chancellor Umzigwe had winds of what was being planned in a similar meeting at the office of President Badegou, he would have shared his concern about the military jeeps chasing after student cars. President Badegou had invited General Gwobazo to give him an early report regarding the so-called Cast Away Weekend promoted by KMC. He could not wait for the reporting until Monday morning as it was preliminarily planned. General Gwobazo showed up at the office of the president at about ten thirty at night. General Gwobazo gave the same report of what had happened during the weekend as the one KMC leadership received but with a different appreciation. He stated that there was no disturbance, to speak of, anywhere in the country after the Cast Away ceremonies and the bonfires.

But he also reminded the president of the need to teach the KMC folks some discipline lessons, especially that professor from the United States, a perfect target to shake down. President Badegou agreed but insisted that the general proceeds in a professional manner. For the general, this would not be different from what used to happen in times of colonels when a little shakedown of stupid civilians was in order every night of patrolling in the capital of Mandi. This was to remind everybody who was in charge of the country. He was then a captain navigating and climbing the officer ranks of the army. He did not mention to President Badegou that he had already posted a few military people to watch Dr. Wasiri's movements since he heard of the instructions from President Badegou at that meeting when his boss was clearly enraged. The unit broke into five military jeeps following Dr. Wasiri from and to the hotel without making any overt move. These were the military jeeps that Dr. Wasiri saw after the dinner with his family on Friday and that Father Zolani saw that late Saturday night. When General Gwobazo was leaving President Badegou, he told him not to worry a bit about what he would do. President Badegou did not think much about it and ended the meeting.

When the general reached his headquarters, he called a meeting with a few trusted officers. He informed them that he would need to raise a large body of military troops of about a thousand and half people.

He needed so many troops to encircle the Tanzire Hilton Hotel and prevent students from invading the hotel periphery and preventing his shakedown operation. Some of his officers were surprised by the scope of the operation and wondered whether it was really justified. They proposed to simply arrest Dr. Wasiri and bring him to the headquarters for interrogation. They were overruled. General Gwobazo informed his officers that his advance team had observed a permanent group of students who literally keep a watch over Dr. Wasiri at the hotel. He was more worried about these students alerting the whole university body of thirty thousand people to come to the rescue of Dr. Wasiri. That can degenerate to an unforeseen calamity he might not be able to control. The large contingent of armed forces would present a strong dissuasion force to those students according to the general. But he made a mistake of calling the hotel reservation staff to book a conference room overnight for a conference over military strategies. The lady who received the call was a part-time worker, a student from Polytechnic University, a dedicated KMC militant. She passed on the news of the request to a KMC coordinator who relayed the information to Chancellor Umzigwe at about one in the morning. The chancellor became very agitated and saw the occurrence of the worst he had warned Father Zolani against on Saturday night. Chancellor Umzigwe, who had already authorized the permanent group of students to watch over Dr. Wasiri at the hotel, requested that the permanent group be increased to a number of five hundred students. He sent a quiet alert to a few key student leaders saying that some people wanted to do harm to Dr. Wasiri, and he needed a lot of protection. Increasing the number of students in the permanent group would be a good precautionary measure. Chancellor Umzigwe went back to sleep. He rose at about five thirty in the morning and alerted his old friend Dean Wutugrase who decided to go and hang around at the hotel without disturbing Dr. Wasiri. Dean Wutugrase would wait for the general at the hotel premises. When he arrived at the hotel, more than six hundred students had already taken posts around the hotel perimeter mixing with the hotel staff. Dean Wutugrase was taken to an observation post at the top of the hotel with a walkie-talkie in permanent communication with selected student leaders around the hotel.

At about nine in the morning, Dean Wutugrase saw the first contingent of military people coming from the west of Lake Road avoiding completely the northern university compound. They entered the hotel perimeter from the lakeside. Dean Wutugrase gave the signal to all students to encircle the hotel for general observation. Next another large contingent entered the hotel compound from the east and marched straight to the hotel entrance.

That is when they were met with the throng of students, about three hundred, who stood silently in front of the hotel entrance. General Gwobazo came out of one of the jeeps surrounded by armed guards on all sides. The general had close to thirty armed people with him. He was dressed in battle fatigue uniform. He went straight through the students' throng and directly to the lobby. He asked where was the conference room he made the reservation for. It was indicated to be Conference Room H5. He then asked to speak to the hotel manager. When the manager showed up, the general ordered him to go fetch a Dr. Wasiri and bring him over to the Conference Room H5. The manager declined to do anything, as he was not in the business of fetching people without their consent. He said that if the general wanted to arrest Dr. Wasiri, he should do that by himself; he did not need the hotel staff to do his job. This got the general very upset and enraged. He screamed obscenities at the manager and said that if he did not do as told, he will be arrested at once. The manager ignored him and went back to his office. The general then ordered the manager's arrest and got him handcuffed, a bit roughed up, and taken to one of the jeeps parked outside. He then sent an officer with five military people to go look for Dr. Wasiri and bring him over to the Conference Room H5. When this officer reached Dr. Wasiri's room, there was another group of about twenty students standing outside the professor's room with Dean Wutugrase leaning at the door, talking to Dr. Wasiri. The officer asked to see Dr. Wasiri. The students asked him for what purposes he wanted to see Dr. Wasiri. He then said to the students that it was none of their business and he did not come to cause any trouble but to get Dr. Wasiri to go and talk with the general to Conference Room H5. At that instant, Dean Wutugrase introduced himself and said that he would be glad to go and talk with the general, but he did not see why the general is so interested in talking to Dr. Wasiri, who is a visiting professor from the United States. The officer said that he had strict orders to bring Dr. Wasiri to the general and that he intended to carry the order whether Dean Wutugrase liked it or not. He ordered the military men to clear his way to the room.

A scuffle with the students ensued as they progressed toward Dr. Wasiri's door. With people pushing back and forth, Dean Wutugrase was caught in the middle and fell on the floor. Witnessing the imminent danger Dean Wutugrase had placed himself in, Dr. Wasiri came forth and screamed loud enough for the students to stop barricading the hall, and he said to the officer, "Officer, I am Dr. Wasiri. Am I under arrest? If that is the case, I would go talk to this general if you do not cause harm to the esteemed Dean Wutugrase or any of the students present here."

Dean Wutugrase rose with a bloody nose and a few other bruises. Dr. Wasiri rushed him inside his room to the bathroom to wash him. The officer and the other five military people barged in the bathroom, and before he knew it and while he was trying to clean and assist the old Dean, the officer put handcuffs on Dr. Wasiri and dragged him outside the room. Another scuffle took place with students keeping guard outside Dr. Wasiri's room when the officer came out pushing the handcuffed Dr.

Wasiri ahead of him. Dr. Wasiri kept screaming and ordering the students who were now fighting with the military people and trying to snatch him from the officer's escort to go and assist the helpless Dean Wutugrase in his room. The officer took advantage of the distraction to drag the scientist very quickly to the Conference Room H5.

The general was very surprised to see the handcuffed Dr. Wasiri with a shirt covered with blood as if he was beaten. Things were not going as instructed by his boss, President Badegou. The professional shakedown was not going to take place as expected. General Gwobozo screamed at the officer to remove the handcuffs off Dr. Wasiri. He told the officer to get out of the conference room and wait for further instructions in the parking lot. The general asked the scientist to sit down and apologized for the inconvenience that had happened.

He then smiled and said, "Dr. Wasiri, I came here today to have a civil talk with you. You know, with us military people, we live and die by receiving and executing orders. There is no two way about it, otherwise, there will be no army. Now I notice your friends at the university went to so much trouble to mobilize all these troublemakers of students outside. I don't know what they were thinking. They forgot that we carry arms for one and only thing, to maintain order. We stand ready to use these arms against all enemies of this country, all troublemakers, and all enemies of order. You came in this beautiful country, and in less than two weeks, you have decided to join all the troublemakers, all enemies of Mezi, and above all, the enemies of order. Look at what they are doing in this hotel and outside. You must agree with me that it is all against order and against Mezi. Dr. Wasiri, I know you are a sensible and wise man. I am calling on you to stop this agitation nonsense. It would go nowhere as long as you have an army in Mezi, ready to put people in their place. It is about time for you to realize this KMC nonsense would only lead to suppression and more suppression until it is completely annihilated and buried forever. That is our plan. I am not talking about the weakling, worthless dressed-up civilian authorities.

I am not talking about the president, the PM, the government, the Supreme Court justices, the presidents of Lower and Higher chambers of Mezi, all of them worthless as usual, one after another. No, sir. I am talking about the plan of the real power behind the throne, behind all these useless civilian comedians trying to play in men games, I am talking about us officers and members of the Mezi armed forces, the keepers and holders of the order. If you think that we would ever answer to stupid civilians like you or all the jokers we have in place today, you really got it coming. Now do yourself a big service, go back to your safe teaching job in the States and spare us the stupid noises you have been making these last two weeks. We have heard enough of it. We heard it before from the likes of you. As usual then nothing, zero, but trouble and trouble making. Take this as a friendly warning. Because I, general of army, Gwobazo, would not repeat myself again and would not be any nicer as today. Next time, you would get a good night session at the barracks, and when it will be finished, you will be only good to be fed to alligators of the southern coast of Lake Nyerengi. Take this as a warning."

When the general was talking, Dr. Wasiri noticed the red and green lights flashing next to an electric marker high above the large LCD board. When he was in the same room, the flashing had indicated that the entire conversation was being videotaped from the hotel communications room. That gave the scientist a jolt in his confidence knowing that the general had just shared with the whole wide world his own troubling misguided concept of power.

Dr. Wasiri responded, "I could not believe hearing what you just said, General Gwobazo. All these years I have heard secondhand all that you have just said and from people who were eager to attribute these quotations to you. I did not believe it, I thought that they were pure fabrications and at best slanderous. Today, I sit here in front of you, it pains me greatly to hear from the current leader of armed forces that this institution does not believe in the rule of law. You have just said that the army marches according to its own tune, and it will continue to march to its own tune forever. And to hell with the constitution and the laws of this beautiful land of Mezi. I wonder what all these worthless civilian authorities, as you put it, would say when they would hear your frightening view of constitutional power. I wonder what these same worthless authorities including President Badegou, your titular boss, the PM, the Supreme Court justices, the presidents of both chambers think, what would they make of the pledge of allegiance to the constitution you have taken when you were made chief of staff of Mezi armed forces? What is just a joke for you, General Gwobazo, do you remember saying that you pledged allegiance to nothing else but the constitution that is the rule of law? I sit here and listen to you thinking with great trepidation that all women and men enrolled in our armed forces share your view of power. But I know for fact that they don't. General Gwobazo, let me clarify something for you, you are alone in your outdated view. If you were not, you are about to be anyway. It is not I who will insure that you are to be thrown out to the past oblivion. It is the underestimated light of KMC, the underestimated ideas behind KMC that you are ridiculing. These ideas are about to cast away all that you have just said and that you represent. You have more to fear from those younger ones outside than this lowly professor in this room. Believe me, those outside would never give you an excuse or a time of the day. As far as they are concerned, you do not exist and have ceased to exist long long time ago. As far as I am concerned, I am here to stay. I am not about to run to anywhere or no other place, I would not go back to the States, I will be right here teaching at Polytechnic University. Mezi is my country, and I intend to stay right here unless you and your likes force me into exile for a time. Then again, I would be back. Because I know that those outside would not let it happen anyway. Now if you do not need me anymore, if you do not have any more to say, I want to go and help my senior colleague, Dean Wutugrase, who has been brutalized by your people and is in need of medical attention. By the way, you should know that all this conversation has been fully taped and about to be broadcast all over Mezi. Good day, General."

The last sentence threw the general in a violent rage. While Dr. Wasiri was quietly exiting the conference room, the general ordered his troops to ransack the entire conference room, to cut all visible wires coming or going from the room. Before long, the conference room was completely dark. Still not satisfied, the general came out of the Conference Room H5 on his way to the hotel concierge. But he was confronted with a much large group of students who have literally taken over the entire hotel premises. The large throng of students overwhelmed this time the general's contingent of about twenty armed military people. Unless the general was to give orders to open fire on the students to fight their way to the hotel exit, the contingent was completely surrounded and immobilized.

The general was faced with an urgent choice, and he was not ready to assume the responsibility to any bloodshed. Besides, he realized that the students vastly outnumbered the contingent. A few would certainly die if force was used, but with this mob of students, anything was possible, the military people could be disarmed; then the general and the remained soldiers would certainly pay for their life the use of deadly force on the students.

The general ordered a retreat to another Conference Room H3 that was closer. General Gwobazo was now prisoner of the students. In addition, the general could not understand why he could not reach through walkie-talkie any of his commanders dispersed around the hotel perimeter. He had lost all communication the minute Dr. Wasiri was brought into the Conference Room H5, and he did not know this. In fact, his command and control center had been taken over by the students for about two hours ago. All have been switched off now by orders of Chancellor Umzigwe, who was now in full control of the Tanzire Hotel premises and was literally holding the entire military expedition at bay, thanks to more than thirty thousand students and other curious civilians who have taken over the hotel as soon as the news of the expedition was broadcast through the university and relayed by a local radio station. The thousand or so soldiers who came for the expedition to the takeover of the Tanzire Hilton Hotel were now in deep conversation with the students and exchanged political views not found in their daily military training exercise manuals. The commanding officers were kept in their respective command jeeps, unable to communicate with neither one another nor the general, now held prisoner.

The hotel manager who was led handcuffed outside was already freed two hours ago. After receiving medical attention, he changed his bloodstained suit and was standing now at the concierge, overseeing the siege. Dean Wutugrase was quickly brought to the University Medical Center after the scuffle around Dr. Wasiri's room. He was now stable, receiving more medical care. A few students were guarding his room. When Dr. Wasiri went back to his room, he was relieved to meet with Chancellor Umzigwe, who assured him of better whereabouts of Dean Wutugrase. He advised Dr. Wasiri to change the room right away before the next stage of the confrontation he could not foresee. He apologized for the commotion Dr. Wasiri had to endure during his stay. Dr. Wasiri dismissed the apology by saying that he understood when he signed up with KMC that he was bound to go through such commotion one way or another, sooner or later. He was then helped by a few student volunteers to move to one of the hotel suites on the tenth floor. Chancellor Umzigwe did not explain to Dr. Wasiri that he was in the midst of delicate negotiations about how to end the stalemate. He also knew that he had the complete upper hand for the time being. He intended to play it to the till.

He had already ordered to get the hotel video feeds sent to a local TV station, a KMC sympathizer, to broadcast, first, the enraged General Gwobazo ordering the arrest, handcuffing, and roughing of the hotel manager.

The second video feed was broadcast to show the first scuffle around Dr. Wasiri with Dean Wutugrase's bloody head and the arrest of Dr. Wasiri with bloody shirt and in handcuffs, being led by an officer toward Conference Room H5. These two video feeds brought the entire capital of Mandi to a standstill, anticipating every second the next stages of the military expedition to Tanzire Hotel led by General Gwobazo. At that instant, every TV station of the capital joined the fray, sent their teams to broadcast live what was going on at the hotel. It was a terrific sight of the students mixed with military people waiting to see how the event was going to unfold. The TV and radio stations gave all kinds of wild theories over what was happening. The real protagonists kept very quiet, letting the event speak for itself. General Gwobazo, held prisoner by the students, could not explain his mission.

At about four in the afternoon, the same TV station that started the broadcast commotion announced that it was about to broadcast a special bulletin giving the real reason of the Tanzire Hotel event. It broadcast the exchange between General Gwobazo and Dr. Wasiri. The entire population of Mandi and Mezi, including the students, soldiers, and people gathered in the Tanzire Hotel, saw and heard the exchange and appreciated to its full extent the messages that the general and Dr. Wasiri wanted to convey.

By four thirty in the afternoon, the PM, the presidents of both chambers, the president of the Supreme Court came one after another to see President Badegou. An impromptu meeting was held.

President Badegou said to his visitors, "I am above all a legalist. I have sworn allegiance to the constitution when I became president of Mezi. I would faithfully follow the constitution. General Gwobazo will be removed from his duties effective immediately. To preserve the military code of conduct and code of honor, I would get him retired immediately while I have to find a new competent chief of staff for our armed forces. I am asking PM Sonjedi to carry out negotiations with all parties to bring this dreadful situation at Tanzire Hotel to a peaceful end. I will start the negotiations by calling on a longtime friend Chancellor Umzigwe to do everything possible to hold the students calm while PM Sonjedi would get the military out of the location. Colonel Namweli, my military advisor, will assist you, PM Sonjedi, in these negotiations. I thank you all for coming to assist me in this perilous time."

The visitors left the office of the deceived and very distraught President Badegou who then called Chancellor Umzigwe and conveyed the same message he had shared with his visitors.

In the presence of his PM, he cursed General Gwobazo and called him a fool. He reached below his desk and reached for a Scotch whiskey bottle that was already half empty and asked the PM to leave him alone for a while. The PM went to another office and asked for Colonel Namweli to join him. He called Professor Awassa and requested to meet with him at the hotel. He had known Professor Awassa for more than ten years and had crossed paths with the professor many times in Mandi's various elite circles. They respected each other's political views and governing choices. He drove with the colonel to the hotel in an unmarked car. Professor Awassa greeted him and Colonel Namweli, now in civilian clothes, at the entrance of Tanzire Hotel and led them to the office of the hotel manager. Chancellor Umzigwe was waiting for them.

PM Sonjedi started speaking, "Chancellor Umzigwe, I am the bearer of a message signed by President Badegou, the presidents of both chambers, the president of Supreme Court, and myself, apologizing for all that has happened here today. All people who have been wrongly affected or impacted shall be compensated duly. The same would be for Tanzire Hotel. The message also conveys the need to severely punish immediately those who have transgressed the laws of the land and disturbed peace. It is the serious intent to get all military people removed from Tanzire Hotel premises immediately. I am asking you to allow me to get General Gwobazo and his men released to the custody of Colonel Namweli here in my company in order to close this sorry episode of our republic. It is the solemn hope of both President Badegou and myself to never see such a stupid incident occur again."

Chancellor Umzigwe rose and addressed PM Sonjedi, "I am sorry that you feel the need to address the message to me. This message should have been addressed to those younger ones outside and especially to my esteemed colleague Dean Wutugrase, who is presently at the hospital and to whom I need to convey this message. He needs to know that this happened for a reason. Son, I keep asking myself all day why! Why did this general see the need to mobilize a whole battalion of soldiers to disturb one unarmed person? Was this part of strategy of your government? Who in God's name saw the need or urgency to do such things? I know we were far apart to handle our political affairs decently, but this went too far. Son, I am not going to hold you too long. You are free to do what you were delegated to do. Get the general out of this hotel premises quickly.

I need to go out and address my students who have kept their side of bargain to act as peacefully as possible. I guess you would not explain to me why. Good luck and good day."

Chancellor Umzigwe then called on all key student leaders to let the delegation led by Professor Awassa safe passage throughout the hotel. Chancellor Umzigwe also ordered the student team holding the military command control van parked about a mile from the hotel to vacate it and return it to its commanding officer. By the time the PM and Professor Awassa reached Conference Room H3, all students who were keeping guard were gone. When the door opened, the General Gwobozo was busy now giving orders to the officer at the command and control center that had just regained control of his own unit. At that instant, the general recognized PM Sonjedi and Colonel Namweli. He then said that he was planning for a breakout from the Conference Room H3 and get hold of the hotel manager for another trashing. This was definitely too much for Colonel Namweli who gathered the exhausted soldiers still in the conference room and who were visibly confused by the evolution of the siege. He explained to them what had happened while the general was still barking his orders.

Colonel Namweli then put General Gwobazo under arrest for grave insubordination and fragrant indiscipline. He managed to guide him to the back door of the hotel where a military vehicle was waiting for him and whisked the general under guards to the office of President Badegou along with PM Sonjedi. At the same time, another colonel took over the military retreat from Tanzire Hotel.

Chancellor Umzigwe also managed to address the thousands of students who came to maintain a siege of the hotel to go back to the campus, assuring them that Dr. Wasiri was safe in his room, and Dean Wutugrase and other injured students were all stable and being taken care at the University Medical Center. At the end, he asked them to remain vigilant as the long fight and the long march would continue. Chancellor Umzigwe then collected Dr. Wasiri and Professor Awassa. Together, they went to pay a visit to Dean Wutugrase, who was now surrounded by hundreds of followers and a long line of well-wishers. Chancellor Umzigwe and his cohorts had to fight their way to see the old dean who had recuperated somehow by now. Father Zolani and Sister Helena Fanzi-Djomba were already there in his room, paying their respects. Dean Wutugrase was much relieved to see Dr. Wasiri with no marks of hurt on his face or anywhere.

He then said, "I assumed that you were going to get some trashing from the general's thugs. That was why I wanted to block these fools and I fell. Believe me, I would do the same next time they tried."

Chancellor Umzigwe was not amused. "There would be no next time. I am terribly sorry that I delegated you to go there today. I trusted that a little bit of respect to elders would go a long way to negotiate our way. I should have known what people we have to deal with in this country. I should also have known how much you love to engage them anytime you can, fistfight, if possible. That was my mistake, and now you are here lying in bed. I hate to see you in this condition. Dean Wutugrase, please, you are not what you used to be, you are no longer who used to move mountains. Dean Wutugrase, we need you, and we do not want to lose you at this time, at no time, so help us God." All around people responded, "Amen."

With one exception, Dean Wutugrase, who responded, "Not so fast, Brother Umzigwe, you seem to be holding a bit prematurely my funerals. I am not dead yet. I can still have a few rounds in equal footing

with that thug of General Gwobazo. Give three, just three, rounds of boxing ring, and I would send him to the floor, just three."
The assembled well-wishers broke out in an endless laughter, including Chancellor Umzigwe who then told KMC leadership team members that the planned meeting for that evening was obviously cancelled, but they must try to meet sometime before the Wednesday's scheduled departure of Brother Kano to the United States and Professor Awassa and himself to London.

While still in Dean Wutugrase's room, the KMC leadership team busied itself to watch and analyze the rendition of the now famous exchange between General Gwobazo and Dr. Wasiri. It was now called throughout Mandi the "H5 Exchange." The episode was being rebroadcast endlessly throughout Mezi. In less than two weeks, Dr. Wasiri had graced the TV screens of Mezi three times: first, there was the airport arrival celebration, then the Cast Away Summit, and now the H5 Exchange. No other politician in Mezi had gotten so much publicity in such short time as Dr. Wasiri did. While the first two sequences were rehearsed, the last one was under duress in front of the hostile general. And Brother Kano came out in flying colors in an outstanding lesson given in matters of democracy and rules of law. Nobody could do any better. In one address, Brother Kano was able to salute and to give honor to established institutions, including the presidency, the PM, the Lower and Higher Chambers, all elected, the Supreme Court, and the Military High Command, all sworn to one thing, the constitution and the rule of laws. In the same address, he highlighted the ideas of KMC that the general wanted to trash, dismiss, and bury, and above all, the supremacy of youth ready to embrace KMC ideas and to cast away the outdated view of General Gwobazo. From now on and after seeing the exchange, Dr. Wasiri was clearly established as one of the future Mezi political leaders.

It was one of political imprints that make for not only political dramas but also the advent of a leader. No other but KMC leadership understood this. Chancellor Umzigwe and Dean Wutugrase exchanged that devious eye contact at the end of the visit to signify that, if anything, Brother Kano's commitment to KMC leadership was sealed after the H5 Exchange.

It was also the same appreciation that came to Dr. McMillan, who followed all the episodes on TV and radio stations at home after the entire university was closed, and all students were summoned to Tanzire Hilton Hotel. Dr. McMillan chose to gather his wife, Anna, and to go home to follow the event in the safety of their house. Dr. McMillan was completely surprised by the stupidity of the general to amount an expedition so close to the visibly hostile campus and in the premises of a hotel belonging to the university. It was obvious that Chancellor Umzigwe would have an upper hand on this episode, being able to mobilize the entire university body next door. Dr. McMillan told his very frightened wife, Anna, that it would be a matter of time when the government would give in, and if they came to arrest Dr. Wasiri, he would be freed in no time. He was vindicated when the TV station started broadcasting the video feeds from the hotel.

He was aware of these feeds installed for security precaution from the time of the unfortunate rape and killing of two ladies engaged in a prostitute ring about the hotel. This had happened when he was still a chancellor. The feeds have been greatly and digitally enhanced now to produce live superb videos on demand from a centrally controlled room next to the hotel manager's office. The feeds were put everywhere except in client rooms for privacy. Dr. McMillan was not surprised by the quality of the last feed providing the famous H5 Exchange. Conference Room H5 got all the best electronic support in the hotel. The hotel staff knew this when they directed the general to have his talk with Dr. Wasiri in that room. Again, he thought that Chancellor Umzigwe and Dean Wutugrase played their cards very well. Dr. McMillan taped the episode for additional reporting for Lady Allistair.

When Colonel Namweli's escort arrived at the office of President Badegou, he asked the PM and the colonel to leave him alone with General Gwobazo. Already drunk, President Badegou, now completely humiliated by the unforeseen Tanzire event and the famous H5 Exchange, castigated the general in no uncertain terms, "What got to you to almost get this presidency impeached? I told you to proceed as professionally as possible. I did not ask you to lead a battalion to shake down an unarmed professor in a hotel next to the university.

This was the most stupid and last thing you have done for me. I have covered a lot of your stupid mistakes. But this is the last one. Today you have disgraced and humiliated the armed forces of Mezi and all the men and women placed under your command. You have caused the gravest dishonor to these forces, and I do not know how long it would take to undo. I have here the drawn papers for your retirement effective today. You have no choice but to sign them, otherwise, I would be only glad to hand over your head to all these people you have graciously insulted in your famous speech. They are waiting for your head to be hanged in the lower and higher chambers, in the government, and the Supreme Court. General Gwobazo, this is the only chance for you to get out of this town alive and back in some far-away barracks for retirement. Sign these papers, and you can get your forty-two years of honorable discharge and all nicely paid retirement for the rest of your life after serving the nation. That should serve a lesson for you and those who would not heed this lesson that you should never stomp on, trash, slap, or insult the very hand that is feeding you."

General Gwobazo signed the papers on the spot and gave his boss a final salute and said, "I am sorry, sir." He left the office unescorted and went to take a seat at the office waiting room. The president called on the PM and the colonel and said, "All is done. The general signed the papers and retired today, and Colonel Namweli would escort him to his retirement home in the military barracks at the northern province of Kiesse tonight. A government communiqué would be released tomorrow morning announcing the retirement of General Gwobazo and the name of the new chief of staff I would designate. I want to thank you for resolving this nightmare peacefully. Goodnight."

The next day, Dr. Wasiri spent it packing his suitcases including the three pieces of Kany that were given by Chief Sengimo VII. When he was done, he went to see Mrs. Anna McMillan to go over various remaining items that Hasbo had sent inquiries about. Dr. Wasiri had faithfully transcribed most of Anna's responses into a notebook that was now about 85 percent full.

Late in the evening, he took another ride to his stepbrother's house to say good-bye. He was now going around under a police escort of three people given by express order of President Badegou as a good faith gesture to KMC leadership to let all know that Dr. Wasiri would no longer be threatened by anybody during his stay in Mandi.

He did not listen nor care to listen to a government communiqué that was issued about nine in that morning advising everyone that "Effective immediately, General of Army Godefroid Gwobazo has requested and was granted his retirement after forty-two years of service in the armed forces of Mezi. He would be replaced in his function of Chief of Staff of Mezi Armed Forces by Major General John Djanzali."

So, when he reached his brother's villa, he was surprised to hear him talking about the slayer of the big one. His brother added that it takes a great man to accomplish in two weeks what all the people outside the military have attempted to do these past forty-two years as they saw the steady rise of Godefroid Gwobazo from enlisted soldier to becoming general of army along all of unspeakable dreads and crimes he left behind. He was visibly feared by all, and it took a very stupid move on his part to be undone overnight, and worse, his antagonist was now given police protection.

Dr. Wasiri told his brother not to trust the appearances. What is given today can be taken tomorrow as long as Mezi is not governed completely under the rules of law and according to what is enshrined in the constitution. All the rest is simply a series of sad stances of political drama Mezi cannot afford. He told his brother that he was counting on him to assist him in the preparation of his definite return. He would be sending a lot of housing items and goods by air and maritime freight, and he would be charged to receive them and to place in warehousing until he would come back. They went over some housekeeping routines, and Dr. Wasiri departed from his brother's home once more.

By the time he reached his hotel room, he received a message from Chancellor Umzigwe calling for a KMC leadership meeting at his conference room at about ten in the morning on the day of his departure scheduled at about eight in the evening. Chancellor Umzigwe also announced that Professor Awassa, Dr. McMillan, and the chancellor, all going to London on his first leg of his long trip back to the States would join Dr. Wasiri. Dr. Wasiri decided to finish his packing before attending this meeting the next day. When he arrived for the meeting the next day, he learned that Dean Wutugrase's medical condition had turned to an expected sad condition.

He needed to be operated to remove fluid that had accumulated on his left lung after his fall at the hotel. He was in intensive care now. A very saddened Chancellor Umzigwe opened the meeting with a prayer for his longtime companion of long political struggle.

He also admonished the team from paying his old friend anymore visit and to allow him as much rest as possible. Then Dr. Wasiri learned that the meeting was being held to set up an active protocol of exchange of information between the team in Mandi and himself, far away in Kentucky. Most correspondences would be handled using a secured data service provided by this unknown South African company. Hard printed confidential documentation will be exchanged using the good services and diplomatic pouches of Sir Ewas at the UN Mission in New York. Chancellor Umzigwe asked the team members to adhere strictly to the delivery schedule of their assignments for the KMC Edicts. Brother Kano was told that he needed, if possible, to meet the delivery of his assigned edicts to two upcoming conferences. The first conference, to be held at the Catholic University in Washington, DC, and organized by Mezi college students throughout the States, would take place during the first weekend of April. Dr. Wasiri was invited to give a presentation about KMC Edict over corruption. Father Zolani would attend this conference as well. The second conference would be held in the second part of the month of May at the Free University of Mezi in the second largest town of Ikando. Various Mezi women associations would be holding a huge congress at the time. Dr. Wasiri was also invited to give a presentation about KMC Edict over women of Mezi along with Sister Fanzi-Djomba. Chancellor Umzigwe closed the meeting by reminding all to apply excellency and due diligence in the drafting and delivery of their assigned edicts. On his way to the airport, the news of Dean Wutugrase in intensive care left Dr. Wasiri very quiet, morose, and wondering if it was really worthwhile the price this old man was paying now. The sight of Mandi capital bustling about its evening business was all the more unnerving to Dr. Wasiri, who asked whether the people knew or cared about that old man in the intensive care at the hospital. When they approached the airport, he could not help but say a prayer in silence, "Lord makes this price worthwhile for Dean Wutugrase and for Mezi. Lord heals Dean Wutugrase to recover to a happy warrior. Amen."

CHAPTER 24
Professor Awassa

When they were making preparation to board the plane, Dr. Wasiri decided to sit next to Professor Awassa. He had not engaged the young professor as much as he had wished during his two weeks' stay in Mandi. He wanted to make up for time lost. An hour after the plane was airborne, professor was busy correcting students' papers while Dr. Wasiri was reading a stack of Mandi newspapers he had brought along. When the stewardess interrupted them to get their refreshment orders, Dr. Wasiri took the opportunity to engage Professor Awassa by asking him how the elite in Mandi managed to sustain themselves intellectually with empty news and empty editorials in every column of Mandi newspapers.

Professor Awassa closed his stack of students' essay papers and said, "We don't rely on newspapers to sustain ourselves intellectually, if you want to know. We have formed many Internet networks of news concerning Mezi. The same journalists, from whom you read empty news and editorials and who are paid to write in newspapers, turn around and provide the real news accounts in the Internet networks using various nicknames. These Internet articles are as thoroughly written as anything you can find in Financial Times of London, New York Times, or Le Monde of Paris. You might think that due to the fact nicknames are used to sign off these articles that they may lack in quality. But every article is critiqued and challenged by knowledgeable readers for its authenticity, its facts, and references. At the end, the journalists always and nicely bear their facts and references. Only some diligent readers know exactly who they are. As you can see, when you read these articles, and what I can call forum discussions which follow, you get the gist of the event covered and much more than you would find in the so-called newspapers. These forums have been the lifeblood of our information, and we are very satisfied with these important Internet links. I should provide many of those web sites you can access anytime you want on daily basis. But I must warn you, sometimes it can get tedious and you got to be very patient with these forums."

"That is very genial of these journalists. I would appreciate to get these web sites. Now I understand why the leadership never bothers with the newspaper's news account.

When I got so frustrated by all that I read after the Cast Away Summit, I was ready to suggest that KMC comes up with its own newspapers in Mandi. I can see now that this newspaper would be closed someday, either for lack of sustained readership or for offending this politician or that colonel. But I must come back and counter this notion of information easily circulating among the elite through Internet networks or whatever you call it. I am very uncomfortable that this information is never accessible to a large population out there. This population needs to be informed just the same if KMC wants its ideas to be broadly publicized on daily basis and, most importantly, receive the needed feedback from the population to know if KMC is consistently on the right track. Otherwise, how will KMC leadership know when everything is delivered from top down? I am sorry I am diverging here a little bit when I asked you a question about how does the elite rely on local newspapers, and you answered me to the point. But I am sure you see where I am going here, Professor Awassa."

"I would also prefer to be called Brother Awassa, if you don't mind. Frankly, do not think for an instant that I would be offended for describing how crucial information circulated in my working and living environment. And let us face, we are talking about Polytechnic University, currently the top echelon of learning in Mezi, in other words, the top seat of the country elite. I know very well that the way the information circulates is terribly constrained and less than 1 percent of Mezi population gets to that level of unfiltered information available to us. Should there be striving to broaden the information reaches, definitely! Have they been tried, yes, and more than often with negative results! The question is why? Why we, in the elite, are not able to reach out to the general population when it comes to convey what we call crucial information? KMC leadership had discussed this question time and again to no clear answers. I have, in my opinion, a disturbing answer. It comes down to the level of interest people attach to the information. You see, we have spent about an hour in this flight talking about the need to spread important news to the general population. How many people discuss such matters but the elite?

The current level of interest in the general population is more basic, how to feed the kids tonight, how to meet the monthly rent payment at the end of this month, how to keep this low-paying job as long as possible when people are being laid off every day at the shop, how to insure that the doctor's bill payment is met when taking this daughter to the clinic to check the endless bad coughing that is keeping everybody up all night, and more.

When a Mezi citizen of average means gets up in the morning, he is not worried about what President Badegou would scheme that day or how many people General Gwobazo would get beat up at the barracks or if the Lower Chamber would finally vote on the workable code of investment. All these issues, however closely impacting on his well being, are far from his mind and appreciation. That Mezi citizen is worried about making it that day and starting all over the next day, so help him, God! Now and then he runs into these grave matters. But he does not want them stated the way you and I relate to them: issue, analysis, propositions to correct, selection of the best solution and implementation, and so on. That Mezi citizen wants the statement of the issue as lightly as possible and preferably with a lot of humor. It is not by chance that the newspapers are full of scandals, political and otherwise. Scandals sell, political analysis does not. When issues reach crisis proportion, the attention of that Mezi citizen would be raised a little bit but usually not for far long until it dies, and the citizen is back to scandals reading. Now why scandals are more interesting? Brother Kano, scandals sell because for a change, they elevate the citizen's self-esteem to a level where he or she knows not to fall below. Scandals give the citizen a chance to look down on the powerful ones who happen most of the times to come from . . . the elite. This is where the circle closes. Again, that is my opinion gained after a long time of diligent observation. I said disturbing opinion for a reason."

Dr. Wasiri, who was listening intently, came back, "Brother Awassa, what you just shared is very refreshing and insightful, thank you. I knew you were going to enlighten me about a lot of topics. I am glad that we are together in this plane ride. I hope to hold you prisoner here next to me for the next six or seven hours of this flight. Now I have heard all that you say about critical information and critical information sharing. I would not say I agree with your opinion, but I cannot deny its strong merits. Just the same, you heard Chancellor Umzigwe getting me into a tight delivery schedule over the two edicts I volunteered to draft. Well, that would teach me a lot, my big mouth and me. Any way, you know I have taken over the drafting of the edict over corruption. As you remember, in one of the meetings, I mentioned that it was good for KMC leadership to state the obvious about corruption. Nobody I know, unless you can come up with a name, has ever run for any political seat on the program to promote corruption.

"Everyone runs against corruption; everyone promises to get rid of corruption. It is the norm, and KMC, I am afraid, is and will not be different in this area. As a matter of fact, from all I have seen and observed today that has been KMC's biggest trump card.

KMC has done an extraordinary job in that field. My only problem has been that after a while, it is bound to become a bit stale. What I mean is that, after a while, KMC has not only to run against corruption but has to show the way out of corruption. That is where the leadership team must come with good and convincing ideas to sustain KMC's prominent seat in Mezi politics. That is why I have chosen to tackle that topic of corruption. But I have to confess it has not been easy. I have been struggling to come up with a significant way to differentiate our stance against the next political movement or party. I have been struggling to come up with a strong difference in the drafting of KMC Edict on corruption. I want to sincerely address what breeds corruption in our society and come up with ways to stop or limit the corruption breeding. I am not an eminent economist like yourself, but I want your honest input in my logic. Let me tell you, during this last episode with General Gwobazo, I was not struck by the level of vindictive and ignorance that the general was sputtering against KMC or the level of commitment to KMC shown by all these students. I was and I am very much aware of these stances from which KMC has drawn a good deal of benefits to date. However, when I was quickly moved to the safety of the upper-floor suite during this event, I saw from the bedroom window the mass of people assembled outside the hotel walls, the majority of these people were not students. The sight of so many unemployed people witnessing another sad political situation that, at the end, did not change their unemployment status then struck me. And to rejoin your previous analysis, these people woke up the next day as unemployed as ever but frightening so ready to offer their toil, sweat, or service to whoever would give them a job or an occupation to take care of whatever was waiting for them at the end of the day. Believe me, they would have done so right there during that event if General Gwobazo had the devious sense of coming out and telling them that they would each receive two hundred dollars for every student that they can remove from the hotel perimeter. The majority of these unemployed would have jumped on this opportunity. That would have certainly changed the outcome of another battle that KMC had handily won. Thank God, KMC has to face the likes of General Gwobazo with their rough and unimaginative concepts of governing.

"Brother Awassa, it will not always be the same in the future. Sooner or later, the opposition, born from these bowls of corruption, would match KMC in the arena of ideas. We got to be ready to stand these challenges. As I was saying, getting to the bowls of corruption, identifying clearly what breeds it would put KMC ahead of the curve. I searched and came up with one fundamental observation and let me know if you concur.

The main cause of corruption in our society is the lack of enough financial capital to grow and expand our economic base where more and more citizens of Mezi would find their ways and opportunity in order to meet their obligations, financial and otherwise, on consistent basis.

"In my view, everything else, every other instance of corruption flows from that lack of abundant financial capital. Name it and sooner or later, it comes down to the fact that there is lack of capital, financial to be sure. There is lack of this or lack of that because people have no money, there is no money because there is no job, there is no job because nobody is willing to employ anybody, nobody is willing to employ anybody because there is no intent to produce anything, there is no intent to produce anything because there is this lack of enough capital invested in means of production to create jobs to employ people to have money to meet payment of this or provision of that. I hear a lot about lack of transparency breeding corruption. That is a very good observation, but transparency without job is like a chained sheep left in a starving lion's garden. If the intent was to prevent the sheep from wandering during the night, it would be hopeless to recover the chained sheep in the morning; sooner or later, the starving lion would devour the sheep.

Much is also made of power corrupting and absolute power corruptingabsolutely. Closer examination reveals that access to power is always made possible and always enabled by those who control capital, the flow of capital, and the concentration of capital in any society. Capital begets power, not the other way around. Brother Awassa, that is, in an otherwise crude form, my analysis of what fundamentally breeds corruption in our society. That could be also the case in most of African societies, and I ventured to say in most less developed economic societies around the world. Of course, we have corruption in developed economic societies too, but what breeds it there is quite different compared to our societies. What do you think?"

Brother Awassa who had been following with great interest Dr. Wasiri's analysis was quick to respond, "Brother Kano, you called me eminent economist when you started this analysis. I would not agree with that qualification. I am at this stage learning from eminent and wise people like Chancellor Umzigwe up front, our very dear, and God protect him, Dean Wutugrase, and now from yourself, Dr. Kano Wasiri. All of you have been tested in age, experience, knowledge, and wisdom. A rare combination not easily matched in many academic circles in Mezi. I have to tell you I am blessed to be among you, the best educators in Mezi.

Now I do not believe that I have heard as concrete and complete economic analysis as the one you just laid on me regarding what is ailing our society, our institutions, and our country every day.

"You nailed an observation that I have been testing myself when carefully reading and analyzing what has happened in People's Republic of China, where in less than thirty years, a country has been literally catapulted from a backward agrarian society to a semi-developed country already matching and surpassing the big Western countries in terms of economic production capacity. Mind you, I am not proposing that Mezi copies the China model, not at all. But the evidence is all there for all to see and all points to one thing you have alluded to—what abundant financial capital can accomplish when properly applied on other factors of production. In my view, PRC did not innovate in the areas. The same process has happened before throughout the history of mankind.

When an objective analysis is made over the rise and fall of every civilization or empire throughout the world, it always comes back to an application over time of an abundant form of capital over existing forms of production, that application invariably increased what is called the wealth of the society or nation. This in turn enabled the society or nation to expand its control over a large expanse of territory. The expansion is either done through military means or commercial exchanges. The expansion goes on until a new form of capital starts taking shape somewhere and challenging the old form of capital and the process starts all over again. This does not mean that the process is continuous and readily observable for all to see and appreciate. In some instances, this took thousands of years. In other instances, the process was simply stomped as in Middle Age. But we have heard of Inca Civilization, Chinese Civilization, Egyptian Civilization, and many other known and unknown civilizations in Asia, America, and Africa, dating back twenty thousand years BC. All these ancient civilizations have risen and fallen behind one form of capital or another. From the beginning of the twentieth century through now, we have witnessed the advent of all kinds of forms of capital in such accelerated rate that we are in awe of what we have seen yesterday against what will come tomorrow. All in all, it has been and remains fascinating. To go back to our society, it always amazes me to see and hear fear and contempt when the notion of capital is brought to bear in any conversation, learned or otherwise. The first inclination is that of exploitation of people by those providing capital. Well, I am not here to sing the praises of capitalism. When I am talking of capital, I am talking about any human-made resource used to create goods or services.

That is an honest economist definition of capital. Those who provide such resource would not do so for nothing. They expect compensation.

"I mentioned above the remarkable history of PRC, the Communist China, indeed. I believe that there is no other important date in the twenty-first century as the February 27, 1972. That is the date when the famous Shangai Communiqué was issued between the United States and PRC at the end of President Nixon's first visit to PRC. There were four important pledges in that Communiqué: Normalization of US-PRC relations, the two countries declining to seek hegemony in the Asia-

Pacific region, US acknowledging One-China policy, expansion of economic and cultural contacts between nations. A thorough review of current PRC economic standing should tell any observer today that the first three pledges were necessary to provide the country enough time and assurance to enable the most important of all pledges, the last pledge, which, over time, brought an unprecedented transfer of capital from one country, the USA, to another, PRC. And for all those ideological doubters, this has happened between a country led by a dogmatic communist party and another, bastion of unfettered capitalism. This should also serve as a defining reminder to those in underdeveloped parts of this world who love to cling to unworkable political and economic dogmas that nations have only interests when it comes to international relations and everything else is pure theater. It was obvious that after the failure of the great leap-forward policy engineered by Mao, the PRC leadership has started to look for something workable for the great masses. The soul searching was long and difficult with the intermittent Cultural Revolution. At the end, even Mao, the staunch communist, will reluctantly acquiesce to accrued economic contacts with USA at the peak of the Sino-Soviet split.

"These economic contacts and the resulting massif capital transfer would be accelerated after Mao's death at the urging of Deng Xiaoping marking China's transition from a planned economy to a mixed economy. This new economic system has evolved rapidly the last twenty years into an increasingly open market economic system. The bottom line was that PRC leadership had concluded and accepted the proposition that for a decent shared return, the holders of capital should be able to transfer capital to PRC, apply it over a low-cost labor, produce and sell goods at lower price, conversely allowing PRC new enterprises to grab entire market shares of these goods and literally control and dominate the entire chain of production and marketing of these goods.

PRC leadership was then able to replicate the process over a whole series of industries from the most manual intensive to the most automated. This had brought not just unprecedented wealth to PRC, it had also enabled PRC to consolidate its military prowess in the region. The most remarkable consequence of this economic transformation had been the dramatic reduction of poverty rate in China from 53 percent in 1981 to less than 8 percent today.

"This is a drastic reduction in the level of lack we were talking about as far as corruption is concerned. This reduction was definitely brought about by that influx of capital into China and its judicious careful application over time. It should also be said that while China has not yet written the last page of this dramatic rise, it is now confronted with a widening rural-urban income gap, a definite source of corruption in present China. Brother Kano, this is a long-winded illustration of my agreement with your proposition that all goes back to capital or lack of it. I also agree with what you said about transparency.

"However, when it comes to power, I want to beg to take exception here. I may be doing this because of all that I have seen all these years I have lived in this country. I certainly agree that capital begets power and not the other way around. But when you look at this a bit further, you see that once capital has begotten power, power may not necessarily respond to its first impulse. What I am saying is this, when power becomes absolute, it has, in my opinion, already ceased to abide by capital. Power then takes on its own quirky lives. Examples abound in this area: Stalin, Hitler, Mussolini, Nero, Caligula, Mao, Pol Pot, Idi Amin, Bokassa, Mobutu, and all those who have exercised sheer dictatorship for a long time. They all have one thing in common, they all love power for the sake of power.

"This is the ultimate indication of corruption when those in power start believing or are obsessed with their own version of facts. It does not have to get there. Every mean must be exerted to prevent this to happen from the beginning. Human being human, this tendency, in my opinion, should never be left to chance in a group or in a person. This should also be true for KMC when you are devising ways to prevent any descent to the bowls of corruption. What I am saying here is that you don't have necessarily to have a lack of capital to start having corruption. An obsession in own belief or set of own beliefs would invariably leads to a vast array of corruption. This has happened in a lot of countries where a single party or ideology had found ways to accede to political power, usually through a form of revolutionary process rather than electoral process.

What started as truly idealistic and popular wounded up being grabbed by one person or few people, who, under the guise of popular dictatorship, are quick to implement their own cruel ways of governing. USSR, Albania, North Korea, Paraguay, Nicaragua, Cuba, Cambodia, China, and many others are all sad reflections of that tendency. We may think and believe that it may never happen in Mezi. But then again, there is no assurance about this. Therefore, what you need to include in the KMC Edict over corruption are ways to guard Mezi citizens against its guardians in whatever institution they reside: presidency, government, the two chambers, the Supreme Court, or the army. A clear and distinct statement around protecting citizens against its protectors would go a long way to reassure people that KMC would never trample on their hard-gained rights."

As this exchange evolved, Chancellor Umzigwe joined and sat next to Brother Awassa; he listened all along, very proud of his protégé Professor Awassa, and at the end, he ventured to say, "Sorry for disturbing you, gentlemen. Sorry for eavesdropping. But then I could not help. How about that, Brother Kano, how about that analysis, I am glad that you two finally are engaged in a meaningful conversation. I knew that sooner or later, you were to exchange very productive ideas. Brother Awassa can be a great resource for the drafting of those edicts. Consult with him whenever you like. Now I came here just to thank you again, Brother Kano, for all these very productive two weeks you shared with us. Besides joining Polytechnic University, your elevation to membership of the KMC leadership has given us much hope and much joy. I do not have to argue the merits of all that has been accomplished the past two weeks, thanks to your contribution. I want also to let you know that I broke my own rules about disturbing my old good friend before boarding this plane. I could not leave Mandi without a strong assurance that I would come back and have a few shots of local beer with my old buddy. I saw his doctor, and he assured me that Dean Wutugrase would come out of it very soon. They have removed all that fluid that was causing him much pain in his lung. He would continue to be sedated for a day or two and should be much stable by Friday. I noticed how glooming and silent you were when we were boarding the plane. I did not want to intrude until you regained your composure in this animated exchange. Now I do not know what kinds of arrangement your mentor has for us in London. I really wished that you joined us in London even for a day. But I understand you would be on another flight to Chicago, two hours after this plane has landed in London. I guess that leaves you no time to hang out with us in London. But rest assured that KMC leadership is extremely grateful all the same. Now you two can go back to earth-shaking exchange."

On that note, Chancellor Umzigwe went back to his seat next to Dr. McMillan. Dr. Wasiri turned to his younger colleague, "Chancellor Umzigwe has a lot riding on your star. What is the secret, what is the attraction?"

Brother Awassa smiled and responded, "Chancellor Umzigwe is a longtime friend of my family. He grew up with my father right here in Mandi, attended the same schools, and went to Kampala, Uganda, for college studies. They separated when he went to London for his graduate and postgraduate studies, and my father went to Los Angeles at UCLA for his graduate degree in construction engineering. My father came back to Mandi and built a good civil engineering practice for about thirty-two years. Then they reunited and continued their strong friendship until my father passed away about ten years ago after a long cancer bout. Chancellor Umzigwe has been watching over me since. No star ride, thank you. Chancellor Umzigwe simply insured that I collected a bunch of postgraduate degrees from major world universities, thanks to his broad academic contacts. Every time I expressed an interest in a particular field, there I was in my way to a graduate school for a specialization. It started with Sorbonne in Paris, then McGill University in Montreal, then Harvard University and MIT, then Oxford and Cambridge in England, and finally, University of Osaka in Japan. In the process, I got three master's, two PhDs and five Advanced Graduate Studies Certificates. What you can call a walking academic zombie. All that went on within about twelve years. At the end, he got me a tenured professorship in less than two years. And here I am. Luckily for me, I was not involved in any matrimonial situation. I am still looking. I have a sister who practices law, representing and defending people mainly in the Supreme Court. She is married with two beautiful kids."

Dr. Wasiri continued his probing, "Well, I accept your version of riding the star. On the serious note, I like your comment around guarding Mezi against its guardians, are you also talking about KMC here? Can you help me?"

"Be glad to. Look, with everything KMC is putting in place, chances are that during the next electoral KMC runs away with the presidency, the government, overwhelming majority in both chambers, the ability to replace all Supreme Court justices within two years and, of course, the ability to retire all the General Gwobazo look-alikes and replace them with officers of KMC mode. In other words, after the next election, KMC would have the whole government to itself in an equivalent of almost one-party system.

What assurances are we giving to all those who would trust us with the entire government? What assurances are there that we would not act as in those famous and funny one-party systems of the past? At least today, in spite of the cacophony emanating from the government, the chambers, and the presidency, there is no clear majority party; there has been no mention of monolithic way of governing. I would be concerned if KMC comes to power with 80 percent of vote and the dissenting voice is suppressed. That worries me a lot, and that is what KMC needs to guard against, that is why we need to clearly spell out in that edict, KMC's desire never to effect laws that go against freedom of speech, thought, association, affiliation, action, or any other form of freedom."

Dr. Wasiri was now a bit dejected. "I see your point, and it would be graciously noted. This is very strange indeed. Here we are working so hard to win the hearts and minds of people of Mezi. At the end, when they have listened to us and placed us where we wanted, we have to turn around and tell them to beware of us, their saviors. The burden of governing is always many times greater than the burden of opposition. It does not get any easier. Well, Brother Awassa, you have advanced this edict farther, I would not have been able by myself. I beg you to share any idea or thinking that comes across and send it to me. By the way, before you forget, I would appreciate to receive those web sites you talked about at the beginning. Thank you."

Brother Awassa told his senior partner that he was a bit tired by now and trying to hold out as long as possible before passing out. They still had about four hours and a half before reaching London. Every passenger was asleep by now. They all awakened as the flight captain announced the descent toward London. The Polytechnic University passengers said good-bye to Dr. Wasiri who literally ran to catch his next flight to Chicago.

CHAPTER 25
Return to Frankfort

Eight hours later, when he reached home in Frankfort, Kentucky, Dr. Wasiri was simply a ghost of himself. He could barely open his eyes to greet his wife and the kids. It was about five in the afternoon when he climbed into his bedroom. He crashed to sleep to Hasbo's terrible disappointment. The two weeks and a half separation seemed like two months and a half. She received her husband with a great deal of anticipation. Now she could do nothing but listen to his profound snore, and it was only about five in the afternoon. The only concern her husband expressed when she started emptying his two suitcases was to make sure to put in secured place the three metal-looking pieces inside packages covered by heavy dark blue velvet material. He did not express any concern about the clothes, shoes, portable PC in the attached cases, and bunch of documents that Hasbo moved to his office. Dr. Wasiri did not awaken until the next day around noon, a Friday. He was still tired with no plan to go out or move around. He finally realized that Hasbo had not been cuddled as she had expected and told him the day he was leaving Mandi. With the kids still out in school, Dr. Wasiri made up quickly for the time lost. It was around three in the afternoon when the Wasiri couple woke up, and Hasbo was finally relieved. It was about time to share all that had happened in Mandi. Dr. Wasiri had no problem to share the successive appointment of tenured professorship and the deanship. When it came to three political events, which shook Mandi, Dr. Wasiri told his wife that he had three DVD to show to the entire family at an appropriate time.

That really piqued Hasbo's interest. She wanted to know how bad the DVD was. Was she going to be upset or happy to see it? And why did Dr. Wasiri want to bring the kids into this? Dr. Wasiri calmed his wife and assured her it was all for good, and he really needed to get his kids to witness what he had experienced in Mandi. Hasbo did not tell him that she had an inkling that something momentous had happened when she received a call from New York from Mrs. Mbow who had not kept in touch for some time and suddenly called to announce that Dr. Wasiri, her husband, had shaken Mezi upside down. She did not elaborate when, in fact, she had just finished watching the two DVDs reporting the arrival celebration and the Cast Away Summit meeting.

After Dr. Wasiri's last trip to New York, Hasbo had noticed a complete decline in exchange of calls between Dr. Wasiri and Mr. Mbow. Mrs. Mbow also cut down on regular calls they used to have. She asked her husband the reasons of the change; he had no clue and advised his wife not to worry about it. Hasbo was really surprised of the call from Mrs. Mbow and was a bit worried if something had happened to her husband in Mandi. But the daily telephone call exchanges she had with him from Mandi did not reveal anything. She discounted Mrs. Mbow's call until now. She was ready to ask about Mrs. Mbow's call, then she thought better not to, maybe this mystery concerned only the immediate family. She did not see the need to involve Mrs. Mbow at this time. She would wait for the viewing of the DVDs as proposed by her husband. Before long, the children were home and were happy to finally grill their father about the trip after they had their dinner.

The first thing he joked about was the fact that he saw Father Felix again at least twice while he was in Mezi. He mentioned that he had dinner with Father Felix and other university members. He said that Father Felix gave a jokes-filled version of that Sunday search of a Roman Catholic Mass in Frankfort Protestant churches. He added that people laughed for a long time. He got out a few gifts he brought for the kids, mainly small Mezi local designs and carvings.

The children asked him if he had visited locations where they loved to go swimming and hacking while in Mezi. That is when he pulled the first surprise for Hasbo. On his portable Apple PC very screen he showed pictures of the area along Mandi Lake Road where they had a long pick-nick day. He then indicated for all to see the spot not far to the location of the house where the family would live in about five months. He indicated the house design, the proposed landscape, and the extraordinary view over the lake. He informed his family that the construction for the house had already started. He was informed that it should be completely done before he returned a month ahead of everybody at the end of April. Hasbo was now in tears and covered his eyes. He showed more pictures he had taken along the lake with Dr. O'Shea, the day before his departure. The children were a bit confused to see their mother in tears, looking at the pictures. Dr. Wasiri begged her to reassure the kids that all was OK. Hasbo wiped her eyes and told the kids not to mind her tears of joy. She said that she was overwhelmed to see her long-held dream to live on that very spot along the lake realized. She added, holding her little girl, that she could no longer wait to leave and to go to Mezi. She still had tears flowing from her eyes. She got up and went upstairs to her bedroom.

At that point, the elder son told his dad that it would not be easy having his mom around in Frankfort the next four months. Dr. Wasiri smiled and said that as a family, they would manage. Then he also informed the children not to make any plan for the Saturday evening, as he would show them another DVD surprise right after dinner. He dismissed the kids and then went to check on Hasbo, who was already deep in sleep. He went in his office and closed the door. He then called Sir Ewas who had been anxiously expecting his call.

He screamed as hard as never before, "Geffadi, Geffadi, I received all the DVDs from Mezi, including the H5 Exchange. Man, Beni Mbow and I have reviewed these DVDs so many times and could still not believe what we were watching. It was a triumph of a visit. From the arrival celebration to the exchange with the general, just excuse my French, fucking unbelievable. Yes, sir. How are you? How are you holding after so much in such short time? My only question is this, how is your wife dealing with all these events? I got a call from Chancellor Umzigwe from London. He mentioned what the leadership had decided around confidential document. Do not worry a bit about this. We are beautifully covered. Geffadi, Geffadi, do you realize where all this is leading you? We were overjoyed, all of us, when we saw these sequences. Mrs. Mbow cried a lot looking at you giving that other speech at Komesah. Do you know that she grew up in Komesah? It was serious, Geffadi, very serious all that you said throughout that trip. Forgive me, I sound so disjointed, I have been talking a bit too much. Give the news from home."

"I was surprised myself of the rapid succession of events during these last two weeks. No wonder when I came back yesterday, I slept from five in the afternoon until today at three in the afternoon. I was terribly exhausted, mentally and physically. The trip was very successful indeed. It was only on my way back when I got off the plane at Chicago that I was finally back to being Kano Wasiri, professor of, you know what, Kentucky State University. It was only when I reached Chicago that I recovered my cherished anonymity. Because when we reached Mandi, it was pure chock to Dr. O'Shea and me. On that DVD, you saw the celebration at the airport, and can you imagine what it was like at the airport? It was like a surprise birthday party but ten thousand times bigger. You know I really need to read people's mind sometimes. The conversations I had with Father Felix and you before going to Mandi should have alerted me that something was up. When you look at the airport DVD, it was obvious that I did not know what to say nor act, so overwhelmed and I believe comatose I was. That speech came out basically by adlibbing Dean Wutugrase and Father Zolani. That is when my nightmare throughout the rest of my stay started. It did not end until I reached Chicago.

I wondered all along if this was true what I was living. You asked me if I have told Hasbo. Not yet. I was relieved when I heard that Dr. O'Shea was stopping in London for more than three weeks before coming back. You know that he would not have resisted showing the copy of DVD of the airport celebration to Hasbo while I was still in Mezi. Would that not be a disaster? No, I am trying to figure out how to break all these events to Hasbo and the kids. Well, I have decided to show the first two DVDs tomorrow, Saturday evening. After the airport event, I said a prayer and really begged the Lord to guide me and to do to me as he pleases. I knew then that a lot of things would come my way I could not possibly control.

Then it was the double appointment to tenured professorship and the deanship. Next we had to prepare and chair the Cast Away Summit. That was out of sight and the real coming out for KMC. It was so dignified with all these two thousand and a half traditional chiefs. Out of sight. That led to the Cast Away Weekend, which I believe was the top of insults and aggravations for General Gwobazo and probably President Badegou. That also gave me a lot of confidence to go to Komesah, the shantytown I never heard of, and I did not even know that it existed all these years I have been living in the United States. The exchange with the General Gwobazo was very comic. Of course, I was afraid for my life after I saw what they did to Dean Wutugrase. But inside that Conference Room H5 when I noticed that our conversation was being tapped, I got a lot of confidence. I spoke as dignified and indignant as I did because I knew no matter what, that was the end of the general who had nicely fallen in the trap that KMC had set for him. As I said, I am still trying to recover from all these events. The only sad note is about Dean Wutugrase, his condition turned a bit critical when we left Mandi. I hope you have good update for me at this time."

"Yes, indeed, he came out of the intensive care and is nicely recovering. He should be all right in a day or two. Well, Geffadi, I got to let you rest now. I will tell Beni that we talked. Have a well deserved good rest."

The next day, Dr. Wasiri spent most of his time either catching up on his electronic and print mail or resting a little more. The family had a nice dinner and settled to watch the much-anticipated DVDs he had brought from Mezi. Before playing the first DVD, the one showing the airport celebration, Dr. Wasiri warned his family that they would see him in a light totally different from the one they have been used to.

He added that his last trip to Mezi had been and will be, for better or worse, life defining for himself and probably for the entire family. He also begged his wife and the children to reserve judgment about all that they will see. He then started the DVD of the arrival celebration. When the DVD playing ended, his younger daughter Fazi asked her father, matter-of-factly, if he was an actor. That broke the tense moment that was running through the living room during the entire viewing of the first tape. The whole family was laughing now.

That helped the father to denying that it was acting, "My dear Fazi, what you saw was not acting at all. The welcoming we received at the airport surprised Dr. O'Shea and me. As you saw at the beginning, I was requested to change into a ceremonial suit when we landed. The large number of people who showed up at the airport shocked me. There was an estimation of between two to three hundred thousand people at the airport. That was only part of the story. The enthusiasm was electric. I don't know if you saw members of my family at the podium. All my brothers and sisters with their families were there. If you look closely, I was really in daze by the surprise and the overwhelming support. When it came time for me to respond to such an unbelievable level of enthusiasm, I was out of place, sweating profusely, and I had no choice but to repeat in my own words what previous speakers have said. However, all the time I was seated in front of these people chanting, dancing, and screaming, I thought about all you back here in Frankfort. I asked myself whether you would be ready for this kind of change. I have to warn you that as a family, we will be confronting this kind of regards most of the time in Mezi. It is up to you to decide whether you do or do not want to put up with this. I would go along with what the entire family would decide. Whether to go back to Mezi or to stay here? It was obvious as soon as I landed in Mezi that I could not separate my teaching assignment from what must be my involvement in shaping what Mezi should be in the future. As long as we stay here, I would happily stick to my teaching assignment only. There would be no involvement in Mezi politics. That would not be the case if we go to Mezi. The surprised celebration I received at that airport was a way for all these people to tell me that I must be involved. I do not believe that they would take no for an answer as long I am in Mezi. It was clear that a lot of people in Mezi have decided that I should not separate my teaching assignments from my political activities in that university. For your information, the university is actually the bastion of great opposition to the current regime. A movement called KMC, which stands in Swahili for Cells in support of New Directions, is solidly implanted in the university. As a matter of fact, that movement organized the airport celebration and had a deep and diverse following throughout the nation of Mezi.

The KMC leadership actually resides at the university starting with the chancellor of the university who is strongly supportive of my appointment to become dean of Applied Sciences Faculty, the top elite faculty in Mezi. To tell you all the truth, I have been solicited for a long time to join in. I resisted for a long time to follow suit because I thought that my family would not want to go to Mezi, let alone approve of my political involvement in Mezi. Then we went to Mezi on vacation twice. I saw how much you loved it there. Still I resisted the thought of going back to Mezi. Your mother can tell how many times we fought over this. My final decision came after the last trip I took to New York.

When I came back, I told your mother that we would go back to Mezi. When the folks at the university heard of my final decision to come back, they intensified their request for me to become part of KMC leadership. A lot of emissaries were sent to the United States, including Father Felix. I told them that I want my political involvement to grow as much as possible when I would be in Mezi. As you can see, I was not given the time to find out. I was given a great welcoming celebration party to let me know that I did not to have time to get my involvement evolved but that I was already part of the movement. I accepted. I am now part of KMC leadership team. So much so that a week later, a major summit was held in a village called Banfi-Bello. The summit gathered close to two thousand and a half traditional chiefs of Mezi. These chiefs were invited by KMC to hold a Cast Away Summit around a bonfire with the intent to exactly and symbolically cast away all the bad mores, which are eating away at the fabric of the nation of Mezi. I may be getting a little too deep for the children now. But the second DVD would show that ceremony and a speech I made for the occasion."

Hasbo rose and told her husband and children that she had already decided to go to Mezi no matter what. She would not go back on her decision. She added that she would be supportive of whatever course her husband had followed and will be following in Mezi, because she knew that her husband would not lead his family astray. She then asked her husband to start the next DVD showing the Cast Away Summit. She then cuddled next to her husband. The children were mesmerized by the extraordinary display that the traditional chiefs were showing in this segment. The bonfire and the cast away filing was another source of entertainment for the kids, some of it comical. The length of the filing made for a monotonous showing which started to put the kids to sleep. Their father asked them if they wanted to continue watching the DVD. They declined.

He stopped the player and repeated what he said before, "I heard what your mother said. I concurred with what she said. But I want this to be a family decision. If you have any reservation or anything you want to talk about over what you saw today, your mother and I are here available anytime to talk."

Hasbo got up and started going up to their bedroom. Dr. Wasiri followed her, as he knew that was a signal that she wanted to talk but not in front of the kids. When he closed their bedroom door, Hasbo said, "Kano, if you were struggling with all that political involvement, why did you not talk about it and share your doubts? I was always there for you. True, I did not want you to back out of going back. I did not realize what kind of pressure I have put you in. I am sorry if I looked like I was not supportive. But my God, three hundred thousand people throwing a surprise party for you! I am very sorry for you. What about poor old Dr. O'Shea, how did he take this all commotion? I can just see what went in his head. He must have invoked Emily's rules ten thousands of time at the podium. But three hundred thousand people just for you! Only now I understand why everybody was so considerate and forthcoming every time I asked for something on the phone. I did not realize that they were dealing with the KMC leadership team member. I see now that you were treated as a very big shot all that time you were there. Tell me, darling, what are you going to do with all that power, dear Kano, are you going to seduce the poor girl from Frankfort?"

Hasbo slipped inside the bed sheets and was looking at her husband with inviting gestures. Dr. Wasiri responded, "Now it is easy for you to say all this. But you did not put any pressure on me at all. The pressure was from myself. I did not know if I was ready to respond to their appeal. The airport celebration did it. It was overwhelming, indeed, and frightening at the same time to see so many people desperately hoping for some kind of leadership in the movement. That was electrifying, yet frightening at the same time. Hasbo, I pray and hope that with you at my side, I would be up to the challenge. Just one thing, as long as you would stand by me in this endeavor, I would be OK, remember that always. Well, you are right about Dr. O'Shea. You see, as soon that celebration started we were separated. I kept looking his way throughout the ceremony, I could see him waving at me and giving me thumbs up and a lot of signs of cross as he loves to do when he is invoking Emily's rules. When we got back to the hotel, he simply held my hand and told me God speed! You know I managed to accept and agree with anything he said to me the rest of his stay. I did not want to disturb his balance as he was also in daze all the time we were there.

I cannot wait to see him when he would come back from London. I got to find out when I need to go pick him at the airport. Now as far as the power I got from Mezi, you have been already entertained by that power, it has not changed. If you hold, I would come back to prove it after I check with the kids and get good old Dr. O'Shea's return schedule." Dr. Wasiri left the room and realized how easy he got off with Hasbo and the kids about the past events in Mezi.

CHAPTER 26
The First Foundation Board Meeting

The same events practically dominated the stay in London of Dr. O'Shea and the crew from Polytechnic University, including Dr. McMillan, Professor Awassa, and Chancellor Umzigwe. During the Emily Thomas O'Shea Foundation board meeting, the only person who was not aware of the events was Patrick Berger. No attempt was made to bring him up to speed by the other board members. Dr. O'Shea had always jealously protected the privacy of his protégé. He would not talk about him but to Lady Allistair. Chancellor Umzigwe and Professor Awassa felt the same for KMC leadership strategic reasons. Dr. McMillan had been specifically instructed by Lady Allistair to forward any confidential notes regarding Dr. Wasiri personally and directly to her. Dr. McMillan was not about to upset his assignment for the account of his new young manager.

The board meeting took two long days with basically endless presentations by Dr. McMillan and Patrick Berger. Dr. McMillan gave the evolution of Mezi operations, which entirely consisted of the huge construction deployments taking place at the Polytechnic University. Patrick provided the financial side of the execution of the construction operations in Mezi. He congratulated Dr. McMillan for bringing the overall cost expenditures on budget and on time. New York and Lexington administrative expenditures were also covered by Patrick to complete satisfaction of the board members. It was learned that the three remaining board seats should be filled by the next board meeting in September, and Dr. McMillan was slated to become a board member by then. At the end of the first day of board meeting, the members were invited to a sumptuous dinner, and Lady Allistair, chairwoman of AMX, joined them as a major fundraiser for the foundation, so read the invitation. Lady Allistair was very gracious with each board member and held small talks as if she was meeting them all for the first time. She held a much longer small talk with Patrick, who was said to report to her directly.

Chancellor Umzigwe and Professor Awassa had no idea of the closer relationship the Lady maintained with Dr. O'Shea nor that she was the main source of all the bounties presently coming to Polytechnic University. They did not know that Dr. O'Shea had met with her more than three times since he came to London preparing for the board meeting. When Lady Allistair got to hold the same small talk with Dr. McMillan, Lady Allistair maintained the same distant appearance and cut him short when he tried to get an appointment to update her over Mezi politics. Lady Allistair said that it won't be necessary this time and wished him good luck on his Mezi assignment. When Dr. McMillan insisted, she repeated the same thing and told him that she had already been properly updated about Mezi politics. Dr. McMillan was very discouraged. First, he thought that she might have found him less reliable after the Barry Newcomb's episode. But after another conversation with his new American boss, he learned that Lady Allistair had cut the Mezi politics channel, and Dr. McMillan would continue to be properly compensated as agreed, but he would have to channel all his findings through Patrick Berger. What the young American manager did not know was that in one of his private meetings with Lady Allistair, Dr. O'Shea had shown her the airport welcoming celebration party DVD. After a long discussion, both of them concluded that Dr. Wasiri was slated for higher offices in Mezi in the very near future. That literally cut off the need to rely on Dr. McMillan's works to inform over the political promotion of Dr. Wasiri in Mezi. It was clear that it had been taking place for some time, thanks to the movement called KMC. Dr. McMillan became dejected the second day of the board meeting. He did not quite pay attention of what was going on at the meeting. His board membership slated for the following September board meeting did nothing to excite him. He spent the rest of the board meeting counting the time to go back to Mezi. While Dr. McMillan regretted putting so much useless preparation to update Lady Allistair over Dr. Wasiri's political promotion, Dr. O'Shea and Chancellor Umzigwe decided to have a very private lunch the second day to discuss the same.

Dr. O'Shea opened the discussion by going straight to the point, "Chancellor Umzigwe, as you know, I have done everything in my power to insure that Dr. Wasiri returns to Mezi under the best circumstances. I laid this foundation and got the necessary funding for it so that my protégé and his family's return would be as secure as possible. I was hoping that he continues the work we have together dedicated our lives in the study of some particular minerals in Africa. I trust nobody else but Dr. Wasiri to conduct those researches. This foundation is sparring nothing to get Dr. Wasiri to that stage.

But after all I saw at the airport celebration, I am no longer certain that it will be possible for him to dedicate himself to his teaching and research assignment and at the same time be involved politically in advancing the works of KMC leadership. Can you reassure me that he can attend to both? You know that we have already invested so much now in your university, can you reassure me that we are working toward the same goals?"

Chancellor Umzigwe sat quietly for a while to collect his thought as he knew that from the time he arrived, he was going to have this conversation sooner or later during his London stay. "Dr. O'Shea, let me first thank you for all that you have done for our university. We are immensely grateful. When it comes to Dr. Wasiri, I can assure you that we are all working toward the same goals. At the university, we have quickly approved his tenured professorship and deanship so that he can stay with us and start working for us by May when he will come back. True, he is now part of KMC leadership. But our KMC goals are a long, long, long-term. You see, Dr. O'Shea, some of us in Mezi have been marching in the political desert for a long time. We will probably walk in that political desert for a longer time. Dr. O'Shea, for your information, our selection of Dr. Wasiri in to KMC leadership is to guarantee that there is continuity in that long march in the desert. It is not evident that those who have started the march will be around much longer. We need credible fellows like Dr. Wasiri to maintain the steady march. At the same time, we also want to maintain a strong Polytechnic University's presence in the KMC leadership. It is our sincere hope to keep that leadership in the confines of that university. As you will see and learn, anything outside that university falls prey quickly to the dangerous corruption that is eating the elite of Mezi. So by choosing to come to this university, Dr. Wasiri had chosen an academic environment that not only will grow his academic and research standard and activities but also will keep him away from the nonsense and nullities that permeated the social abyss outside the walls of our proud university. Sooner or later, you would recognize that bringing him into KMC leadership while he is at Polytechnic University very much fulfills your goals of pursuing those minerals scientific analysis works you have shared all these years while at the same time holding up very high the torch of our march. I would appreciate that you remove all second-guessing about our goals and all that you have accomplished and hope to accomplish with the man you call son. Dr. O'Shea, I do not need to remind you that in spite of my involvement in KMC leadership, I am still chancellor of that university. My primary function is academic, to see to an ever growing and expanding scholarship of the university. Bringing in your protégé in to our university was intended to further that goal.

Appointing him as dean of the premier scientific faculty of the country should confirm the same. Believe me, we are not about to destroy your goals or to separate you two in any way. Dr. Wasiri had made it abundantly clear that you are more than his father. He had told us and repeated many times that he would not tolerate any disrespect or slight toward you or what that you represent. All of us in this university management team and KMC leadership team were properly warned and would be better served by refraining from jeopardizing our standing with Dr. Wasiri or yourself. We have so much respect for the relationship you two have. Rest assured that we would do nothing to disturb it."

Dr. O'Shea had heard all he needed to hear and concluded, "I appreciate all you have said and all the regards you have shown me in Mezi. I thank you again. Let us eat. This lunch is getting cold."

When the foundation board meeting ended, there was a unanimous observation that all was going satisfactorily. Chancellor Umzigwe and Professor Awassa took additional three more days to touch basis with friends and family members residing in UK and held two meetings with UK KMC contacts. Dr. McMillan had two more management review meetings with his new boss, Patrick Berger. He resigned himself to provide him with the three DVDs of last KMC events involving Dr. Wasiri and a summary of articles that appeared the last two weeks and a half while Dr. Wasiri was in Mezi. Patrick Berger had never heard of Dr. Wasiri and told Dr. McMillan in a typical American manager way that he would look into all these materials and learn a bit more about this Dr. Wasiri who, for some strange reasons, had dominated the background noises throughout the two days' board meeting. Dr. McMillan was ready to scream to let him know that all that had happened in London the last two days revolved around and concerned with only one person, Dr. Wasiri. But he did not press the case. He calmly declined to have another dinner with his boss. He also excused himself to meet with family members he did not have in London. In fact, he touched base with old M16 friends to acquaint himself of the Barry Newcomb intricate final episode. He spent the last two days buying gifts for Anna and Mezi contacts while waiting for the flight back to Mezi with the other academics. He could not wait to tell Chancellor Umzigwe that Patrick Berger, vice president of AMX Strategic Initiatives, direct report to Lady Allistair, did not know who Dr. Wasiri was and what he represents to the Emily Thomas O'Shea Foundation. On that basis alone, he would order and drink an entire bottle of twenty-four-year old blended whiskey.

He decided to continue doing what he was doing, being handsomely paid and taking good care of the love of his life, Anna, while slowly earning back the affection of his children. Patrick Berger had a short meeting with Lady Allistair on his way to catch his flight back to New York, very happy and gratefully satisfied for a very well-run meeting. He did not dare raise the issue of Dr. Wasiri that had dominated the two days' board meeting with his boss, Lady Allistair, under the primary management principle of not talking about people or things you have no idea of.

However, Dr. O'Shea did not have that reservation. In his two hours' meeting with Lady Allistair that same evening, he shared the conversation he had with Chancellor Umzigwe about Dr. Wasiri. To his surprise, Lady Allistair shared entirely Chancellor Umzigwe's point that there was congruence of interests with Dr. Wasiri going back to Mezi becoming dean of Applied Sciences Faculty while rapidly rising in KMC leadership team. As far as she was concerned, Dr. O'Shea had to think about what bigger and greater opportunities Dr. Wasiri would open for him, his Alpha-M researches, the Foundation, AMX, BI, and Uncle Kiri if Dr. Wasiri leads KMC all the way to the highest office in the land of Mezi. Lady Allistair smiled and said that was what they wanted in the first place, anyway. And it was happening at a much faster and cheaper rate than expected. She begged him not to worry about Dr. Wasiri's KMC involvement. From that DVD he had shown her, the involvement had shown the tremendous standing the good professor had in Mezi. She added that you couldn't buy that kind of support. She concluded that this involvement was bound to bring a lot of good news and very soon to everyone, Dr. O'Shea included. Dr. O'Shea left the meeting in higher and better spirits than he started.

The last statement that Lady Allistair made about getting a lot of good news from Dr. Wasiri was most endearing for Dr. O'Shea. He was now ready to go home after about four weeks on the road.

Lady Allistair was in better spirits now that she had closed the Barry Newcomb episode. She had gradually and effectively taken control of the AMX CEO function. She had gone and closed most of the pending issues that her uncle had left unresolved when she ascended to the position of AMX CEO. The board of directors and the management committee members were all coming in line to follow her leadership. The top priorities directives from Uncle Kiri were on track or about to be on track. The board of foundation meeting scheduled in London had brought a lot of comforting news around the strategic Mezi initiative.

The direction of Uncle Kiri's African initiatives was entirely positive, so she noted.

Dr. Wasiri had come to her in the best footing now that he was taking over the helm of a major political movement. ABDI was moving along pretty nicely. She thought that as soon as the East Africa Water Project advances further into the implementation phase, ABDI leadership would need to change. Its chairman, His Honorable State Senator Jeremy Massay would have to take on new political challenges as she promised him at the beginning. He would be groomed now to become the next senator of the state of Georgia. The exposure he would get when all these heads of state and big shots will visit Atlanta and ABDI for the signing of the East Africa Water Project would project him to do for Georgia what he had been able to do for more than six countries in Africa. In addition, AMX would be able to quietly stir the pot on his favor by dangling new oil-drilling projects off the coast of Georgia and His Honorable Massay would lead the political fight to win favorable popular support for these projects. His honorable would be ready for the big time then. His able vice chair, the fine, good-looking Dr. James F. Stringer, who literally dazzled the AMX evaluation team with his thorough presentation of ABDI projects, including the vastly complicated Eastern Africa Water Project, is more than ready to assume the leadership of ABDI. But the main reason of moving His Honorable Massay to DC will be to afford a stronger advocate for the various and important Africa initiatives than what was in place at this time. Major General Richard "Bull" Fadden had been as effective as possible for the very minimal expectation we had for his lobbying effort in DC. He was never cut out for the hard driving heavy political lifting that would be required now that the African initiatives are about to blossom. An African American senator from Georgia would be a formidable spokesperson to guard against attacks that BI Africa initiatives would generate soon or later in many Western capitals around the world, including Washington, DC. These initiatives would expand exponentially as soon as Uncle Kiri migrates to Varonne-Sur-Baie in the next two years or so and hopefully with the ascension of Dr. Wasiri to whatever high political position he is aspiring to in Mezi.

CHAPTER 27
BBC Play

A similar evaluation of political events entered the mind of Max Watson, BBC Nairobi chief correspondent, vacationing on the most beautiful Indian beach in a secluded compound south of Durban along the east southern coast of South Africa. On Sunday morning, he happened to watch a South African cable channel specialized in analyzing news coming from many parts of Africa. The segment Max was watching was titled "The Political Awakening in Mezi." The segment provided captions of the three events that shook Mezi during Dr. Wasiri's stay: The celebration of his arrival at Mandi International Airport, The Cast Away Summit ceremony at Banfi-Bello and the Mandi shantytown of Komesah, and finally, the H5 Exchange with the near-riot event preceding it.

To date, reporting over Mezi by international visual and print media had been next to zero. Mezi had always been considered as a boring stopover of international assignment reporting, an impoverished land-locked nation endlessly mired in a state of corruption not different from most other African countries. Compared to other countries, Mezi was considered rather a politically peaceful country with a moribund democratic system, after the sad succession of military regimes. Mezi was not known for radical upheavals or ethnic or regional wars seen in Chad, Congo-Zaire, Rwanda, Somalia, or Sudan. Mezi did not capture the attention of major news organizations when it came time to report major social, economic, and political dislocations visiting upon vast swaths of African continent and brought about by the new intruding giant industrial and financial behemoths from China-PRC, India, major Western countries, Russia, Japan, and South Africa.

However, one of Max's freelancing correspondents residing in Mandi by the name of Mhlabi Zenzi, a full-fledged KMC militant, had been sending him a lot of reports around the political awakening taking hold in Mezi. Max dutifully paid the lady journalist for her reports but refrained from undertaking a major reporting initiative. The viewing of that segment prompted Max to call Mhlabi Zenzi right away, and he informed her that he was about to come to Mezi and follow up on the Mezi political awakening she had pressed upon him the last two years.

Mhlabi Zenzi was happily surprised and told Max that she should be able to align most of the current protagonists of Mezi political scene to assist Max to create an original segment over the political awakening of

Mezi. Mhlabi Zenzi did not mention that most of protagonists she had in mind were KMC militants or leaning toward KMC ideology. Mhlabi Zenzi was not interested in an unbiased reporting about Mezi. If BBC can now be used to advance KMC political aims, so much the better. She reached her dear friend, Sister Fanzi-Djomba, a member of KMC leadership team, who in turn quietly talked with her peers. KMC leadership reached a strategic consensus to refer all major KMC salient strategic pronouncements to their leader, Dr. Kano Wasiri, presently completing his last teaching assignment contract at Kentucky State University in Frankfort, Kentucky, and about to return to Mezi for good in May. A delicately coded message was sent to Dr. Wasiri to that effect with explicit follow-up instructions forwarded through diplomatic pouch to Sir Ewas.

When Max Watson showed up three days later in Mandi, he was paraded first in front of the entire KMC leadership team members, who emphasized in different various degrees the leadership role of Dr. Wasiri while reviewing the three DVD sequences. Max was taken to each one of locations where Dr. Wasiri made his marks: the airport, the Tanzire Hotel, the Banfi-Bello Village, the shantytown of Komesah. Max also interviewed students and various faculty members who turned out to be ardent supporters of KMC. He went back to Komesah to talk to bystanders. The message collected was the same and, again, with strong KMC input. When she felt that Max had received as much KMC input as possible, Mhlabi Zenzi took Max to the leaders of the country institutions. Max visited with the two presidents of legislative chambers of the country and a few key parliament commissions leaders. He added two Supreme Court justices, the premier minister, the interior and finance ministers, the army Chief of Staff. President Badegou declined to be interviewed. To each of these leaders, he asked the same questions: what was the biggest political challenge facing the country? What are these leaders doing to address the challenge? How do their actions compare to what KMC is doing to change the directions of the country? The leaders agreed that corruption was the biggest political challenge facing the country. They gave very different approaches to stem corruption from outright jailing of every political leader caught in a corruption case to major awareness campaigns addressed to the general population identifying patterns of corruption.

When it came time to evaluate how their actions compared to what KMC was doing, the leaders declared that KMC had preferred the underground route of never assuming any concrete responsibility in the institutions of government, remaining outside and shouting useless slogans and always ducking when it came time to help people or to lead. Together they shared the opinion that it was very easy for KMC to shout slogans from the outside while they have opted for the hard daily fight and the cumbersome ability to pick and choose limited ways to lead and govern a country.

When he had received what he thought a good balance of opinions, Max decided to pursue his collection of information further by visiting with the main character portrayed in the South African cable news analysis segment. He was away from Mezi. Dr. Wasiri was currently in Frankfort, Kentucky, in the United States. But Max Watson did not realize that he had completely missed surveying the massive construction operations taking place in the larger compounds of Polytechnic University. He could have widened his information segment to include the investigation of the mysterious foundation that was footing the construction bill, and for what purposes. That would have led to Dr. O'Shea and the foundation, to Lady Allistair and AMX, and eventually to Nadov Kiriyan and BI. But as usual, in case of such reporting investigation, easy access to ready-made protagonists becomes the main story. The so-called heavy journalistic investigation lifting is thwarted to the much-vaunted discovery of the manipulated obvious.

When Max Watson came to Frankfort to interview the famous Dr. Wasiri, he found an almost reclusive scientist so intent to protect his family privacy that he would not allow any camera into his house. The initial interview took place at his own chosen time in his small crumpled office of professor of mines engineering. When the dean of the School of Engineering Sciences witnessed the commotion at this faculty member office, he allowed the interview to proceed in the conference room next to his office. It was very difficult for Max Watson to realize that he was in presence of the leader KMC had selected to guide it to next political phase Mezi would undergo in about two years.

Dr. Wasiri as usual was the most reluctant leader one can find. He answered all questions regarding KMC pronouncements forwardly but at every turn insisting on the concept of KMC collective leadership, giving contribution credit at every instance to each leadership team member even in a case where he had done or worked on an entire pronouncement.

When Max asked the same questions he had asked the institutions leaders in Mezi, Dr. Wasiri answered it differently. He said, borrowing from the long conversation he had with Professor Awassa, that the main challenge confronting Mezi was lack of abundant capital investment, which had produced the vast cycle of corruption permeating the country. Only an equal infusion of capital investment would cure that malaise in more than 60 percent range as it did in China-PRC, Dr. Wasiri added. He concluded that KMC elevation to lead and govern the country of Mezi would be premature if it is not ready to initiate and operate that infusion of capital investment, the rest will be pure demagogy. When Max shared with Dr. Wasiri the view of KMC advanced by the Mezi current political leaders, he concurred with the view saying it is harder and more difficult to govern than to issue pronouncements.

But he added, KMC would advance to lead and govern Mezi not on the strength of its pronouncements, but on the realization of everything contained in its pronouncements, including the orderly infusion of capital investment and above all, on the gracious integrity and humility of those entrusted to carry those pronouncements so that the citizens are duly protected not against their accomplishments, but against the excesses these accomplishments might generate in the minds of KMC leaders, their new protectors.

Max was perplexed by the original view of power that Dr. Wasiri was projecting for KMC leadership. He asked him if he had discussed it with his peers and what was their reaction. Dr. Wasiri said that he had discussed it with one or two members but not the entire leadership yet. But that would be his strong preference of governance. He wanted also to know if he would allow that part of interview to be made public since it was a bit unprecedented. Dr. Wasiri smiled and said that would be the first time that a journalist was asking him for permission to pick and choose what to publish. He added that he was free to edit the interview as he saw fit. Max then asked him if he had anybody else in mind to help him get a more personal assessment of him besides his wife. Dr. Wasiri said that Dr. O'Shea, his retired professor of mines engineering, was the only person he knew who can talk about him at that level. Max ended his interview and thanked him for the time. But on his way to his hotel, he discounted talking to Dr. O'Shea, a key person in the formative years of Dr. Wasiri, in fact, a key person in this whole episode of returning to Mezi.

Max Watson caught his flight back to Nairobi the next day to edit his BBC segment of "Mezi at Political Crossroad, Political Awakening, or Political Stalemate."

The segment was promoted worldwide as a new penetrating view of a popular movement shaking up Mezi out of its doldrums. It was released two weeks later on a Sunday. KMC leadership in Mezi congratulated itself for another excellent propaganda coup. The members took special note over the issue of the new protectors. They planned to debate it at length. They decided to send a collective congratulatory note to Brother Kano Wasiri. To add a powerful effect, the note was going to be drafted and signed on behalf of the entire KMC collective leadership by no other but Dean Wutugrase, now fully recovered and in full exercise of his impressive mind and what he loved to call his cut-throat big mouth. There was also an intriguing segment in the note. Below the names of the KMC collective leadership, there was a caption reading "And The Most Reverend Monsignor Felix Mulai-Bando," a typical Dean Wutugrase way to announce the much expected elevation of Father Felix to the rank of monsignor. For the time being and before the definite promotion to the position of auxiliary bishop of Mandi, Monsignor Felix would remain the most reverend rector of St. Charles Seminary.

The Mezi current political leadership dismissed the segment as another biased BBC news episode. It was used to BBC already chasing after anything that was not current. Lady Allistair was gratified that there was no mention of Dr. O'Shea, the Emily Thomas O'Shea Foundation, AMX, herself, BI, or Uncle Kiri in the segment. When Patrick Berger saw the segment, he was mortified to realize that Dr. McMillan had given him all the captions referenced in the segment. He was to review the DVD and articles and provide Lady Allistair with a management summary of what he saw and read. That was about a month and a half later. When he had a weekly conference call review with his boss, he confessed that he had all these materials but did not get around to summarize and share them with her. Lady Allistair erupted in an anger he had never seen or heard her display. She made him understand that he had completely failed his first great strategic mission. She requested that he catches the first flight to London with all the DVD and articles he was supposed to review for her. She hung the phone on the spot. In fact, it was all theater. She was already happy that nothing from her side had transpired or made it to the segment. But as the protégé confessed, she realized that she had trusted Patrick to supervise Dr. McMillan without telling him what that supervision consisted of. She had not told Patrick about the other task Dr. McMillan carried, literally reporting on Dr. Wasiri's political promotion in Mezi. When Dr. McMillan was trying to set up the appointment during the foundation board dinner, Lady Allistair declined, thinking that she had transferred all of that reporting duty to Patrick. In fact, she had not done so.

Now she pulled the superb upset act to confuse her protégé about her real motives, an old management trick. By the time she would see him again in London, she would apologize for the outburst, and all would be forgotten. But Patrick certainly needed a one-to-one talk over this additional supervision of Dr. McMillan's Mezi political monitoring activities. She did not want to talk over telephone or to have a conference call about this important sensitive topic. Bringing Patrick to London would close a lot of loose ends all at once. Uncle Kiri was not a BBC fan, so he missed watching the segment about Mezi political awakening. Lady Allistair would update him about this anyway. Dr. McMillan saw the episode with his wife and wished Patrick good luck whether or not he had shared DVD with Lady Allistair. He rightly guessed that if he had not, he was going to be in the rough house. Dr. O'Shea did not see the BBC episode. He had other priorities to sort out since he came back. Dr. Wasiri gathered his family to watch the segment that Sunday afternoon, and the family was amazed that BBC was broadcasting the same episodes they have seen the Saturday after Dr. Wasiri came back. They were more fascinated now that in the segment, background people were making glowing comments about him. He also received countless congratulatory notes from friends and KMC contacts throughout the world. The most heartfelt note was from the KMC leadership team with two wonderful news, the full recovery of Dean Wutugrase and the promotion of now Monsignor Felix. He quickly shared the news of Monsignor Felix to his family. When he called his mentor to find why he was not mentioned in the interview, Dr. O'Shea was completely surprised by what he was talking about. He said that he had received no request from any Max Watson from BBC to talk about anything. When Dr. Wasiri explained to him that the BBC interview segment was broadcast that afternoon, his mentor said that he was going to get to it sometime later and that he was very busy verifying the properties of the stuff he brought to him. He would not dare mention Alpha-M on the phone. In fact, on the day Dr. O'Shea returned from the London foundation board meeting, he almost had a heart attack when Dr. Wasiri gave the gift he had wished to get all his life.

CHAPTER 28
Gift of Kany

When the plane carrying Dr. O'Shea from London, with Chicago stopover, landed, Dr. Wasiri was already at hand to pick up his mentor, gravely anticipating what the old man would say at the sight of what he had brought back for him from Mezi. But the old professor looked very tired, indeed, after the combined long trip to Mezi and the three weeks' stay in London. Dr. Wasiri decided to take it easy with his mentor, maybe postpone the whole business of presenting him with the gift from his country. When Dr. Wasiri left the Louisville International Airport for the fifty minutes ride to Lexington, a light rain started falling, slowing the traffic to Lexington. For about twenty minutes of the slow ride, Dr. O'Shea was already at sleep and did not say a word. As soon as the traffic picked up, Dr. O'Shea woke up and looked at his protégé for a long time and then asked him whether he had shared the Mandi airport episode with Hasbo and the children.

Dr. Wasiri responded rather quickly, "I did, of course, and more. It was very hard to do it at first as you can imagine. But what I feared most was to find out that a member of my family, Hasbo or one of the kids, has seen one of the many events I lived through in Mezi before I had a chance to give my side of the story. I had no choice but reserve this past Saturday evening to show them two DVDs with ample explanation. The kids were rather entertained by the viewing, and as expected, they did not quite grasp what their father has become. Hasbo was another story. Up front, she stood by the plan to go back to Mezi, to my great relief. She was surprised by the scenes at the airport, but she could not get over of the fact that three hundred thousand people came to celebrate our arrival. At the end, I believed I came out pretty good, much much better than I expected. One thing is certain, nothing would stop Hasbo now, and you better come up with that residence along the Lake Road before we reached Mandi in May. Otherwise, my head would be chopped."

Dr. Wasiri was now laughing loud along with his mentor who was now fully awake. Dr. O'Shea added, "A woman in love is a woman determined. Hasbo would always stand by you, her husband. And I tell you, before long, she would come up with those rules similar to Emily's, and you can mark my words on that.

While I was in London, I worried sick about you and how Hasbo would react to the viewing of your newfound political star. I am relieved that Hasbo took it all in stride. When I was in that hotel in London, I spent time reviewing that celebration segment, and I saw things that are not paid attention to the first time around. I saw adulation. That worried me somewhat. Son, always remember that nothing disturbs a woman more than the sight of her mate's celebrity, political or otherwise. That goes for a man too. If you don't believe me, next time you play that DVD, observe carefully how Hasbo is looking at the people in the attendance, especially the women who were throwing the confetti and singing your praise, their faces literally transformed as in complete adulation, as in trance. That is what celebrity does to people. Observe how Hasbo would be checking their eyes. Never neglect that side of the women, no matter what."

Dr. Wasiri could not believe what he was hearing from his mentor, "Thank you very much, Doctor Love. I never knew that side of you, Doctor Love. Thank you so much. You have known me for some time to believe that I would fall for anything like that. In fact, you know to date I really thank God that the whole celebration was a surprise. Otherwise, if I was not who I am, I would have passed judgment as to whether it met my expectation. That is the fact when you know that something would happen. For the arrival celebration, if I was not who I am, I would have been thinking and asking, were there enough people here, enough flowers, was the podium large enough for me, were the costumes glamorous enough with my effigy all over, etc. Since I was who I am, let me tell you, I took all in stride. Do not get me wrong. I enjoyed the celebration, the acclamation, and the regards. No doubt about it. Only a conceited person would say otherwise. But the question is, your question is, did I buy into the celebrity stuff? Absolutely and categorically not! The reason was simply, I did not do anything at that time to deserve it. And I said it plainly so. In my book, you would come to deserve anything when you have done something. As far as I know, I have not done anything for Mezi yet to deserve the celebrity status. In my mind, all that has happened there was celebrating hope, no more and no less. Again, I could be wrong, and Hasbo could be worried about the so-called celebrity status. I would do what I have done before, I would tell her to look ahead and to stand by me and all would be all right."

Dr. O'Shea, sensing a tone of anger in Dr. Wasiri's speech, tried to calm his protégé, "I am certainly not worried about you and Hasbo. I know your relationship is strong. But give me the chance to warn you, as your beloved father, about the deceptions of celebrity and power.

They have a way to creep in one's conscience and slowly they take hold. Not that it would happen to you, no. But as long as I live, and as long as you allow me, I would speak my mind and guide you and scold you and keep you from the vagaries of human failings. I have seen it so many times. I have suffered it so many times. I would not be your father, your guide, and your mentor if I cannot speak about it, if I would let those vagaries of human failings destroy you, not on my watch. Now speaking about mentorship, I want to tell you that I had a frank talk with the one I am presuming would be your mentor in Mezi.

Chancellor Umzigwe and I talked extensively in London. I can see that he is taking on the same role I have enjoyed here in Kentucky of guiding you and mentoring you. You may be surprised about this. I am not appointing him as such, but I have observed your relationship. Anyway, we talked and came to a mutual understanding. He realized that I have done as much as I could in mentoring you in the field of sciences and a bit of life, thanks to Emily. He is coming in, taking over the mentoring on the political aspects of it. From what I have seen, he would do a wonderful job. I have no idea why he is hell bound to stick by you, why he has selected you of all people. He must have seen what many have missed or disregarded.

He has made his choice, in my books, a wonderful choice, and he would live with it. Just as I made mine and I have been living with it happily ever since. When we talked, we reassured one another that our goals, if anything, are complementary. And he confided to me that you have insisted on the complete respect and utmost regard of our scientific works and goals. That endeared me to you to no end. I knew that when you would be faced with difficult choices, you would abide by Emily's rules. That removed all concerns I had about what you would be doing in Mezi in addition to your scholarship works. You have at this time my sincere blessings."

Dr. Wasiri looked at his mentor with complete surprise. He was a bit taken aback that these two senior fellows have met over his whereabouts. He took it in stride that they had to agree about his future. He knew how possessive Dr. O'Shea was of his protégé. He understood that his mentor was not really happy about or keen to all the political initiatives surrounding his stay in Mezi. Dr. O'Shea's priority was Alpha-M. Anything else was secondary. In light of that condition, he took the opportunity to surprise his mentor and bring his stay back to his cherished perspective.

"It is rather interesting that my senior guardians have met and have agreed about the course I need to take in the future. This is amazing. I wish Chancellor Umzigwe were here. I would have said to both of you that I respect you so much that I would not do anything to go against your wishes or goals. And as far as I am concerned, I would never let my scientific goals be trumped by any political goal I may entertain and vice versa. Now seriously speaking, Dr. O'Shea, we have known each other for over thirty years or so. You have guided me to a scientific path that in times I resented. But thanks to the kindness of Emily, I stood by you and followed you in the studies of exotic minerals. I am glad, and I have the honor to say that it has carried me this far. And I am thankful and grateful for all. All these years I have searched for ways to show my appreciation for all you have done. Because you have been relentless, Emily's rules besides. Maybe this was due to happen sooner or later; maybe it is luck of the draw. But you have kept your eyes on the ball, you have kept the faith, and you never doubted the righteousness of your cause in finding what you were searching.

Anyway, when I stayed behind, some people from the high plateaus of the province of Tongeo brought five specimen of what they claimed to be Alpha-M. I have carried two of them with me for you to test and verify if they are what you have been looking for all these years. I took extreme risk to do this, to carry them across three borders, Mezi, UK, and USA. Now think about this, if these specs are from Alpha-M, at last, they will mark the fulfillment of all your academic professional life as you have wished all these years. They would mark the true and definite fulfillment of Emily's rules. I could not be happier for you. That will be the least I could have done. That would be the token of ultimate appreciation I have been aiming to extend to you all the time I have been here in the States."

Dr. O'Shea had been listening with amazement to what his protégé was saying. He held his right hand closer to his heart as if he wanted to control its beat. Then he stood up, spread his arms, and looked up the ceiling.

He shook his head violently; he closed his eyes and cried, "Glory to God in the highest, glory to his daughter Emily, praise him forever! Amen. Whatever these specs show, whether they verify what we have been looking for or not, son, you kept your bargain. The Lady was right when she said that sooner or later, I should receive some good news from Mezi. I certainly did not expect it so soon. Here we are. You got it much sooner than planned. Let us rejoice."

They were already entering Lexington, and in less than ten more minutes, Dr. Wasiri was parking in front of his mentor's house. After discharging all his suitcases and bags into the house, he went in car's back seat to retrieve the dark green package with the largest specs. Dr. O'Shea was already seated on the long sofa in the living room. Dr. Wasiri opened the green package and showed the shining dark specs. Dr. O'Shea approached the specs with trembling hands and literally caressed them and told his protégé that he needed a secured location to hide the specs. He would buy a special vault for the task. Then it occurred to him that he had lost all privileges to conduct tests as he used to do at the university. The thought of going and begging his way back to what he called devil's run, another name for the University of Kentucky he had come up the last five years of his tenure, gave him the coldest sweat along his spine. Dr. Wasiri reminded him that he was still a full-fledged tenured professor at the School of Mines Engineering at Kentucky State University, with full privileges to conduct whatever scientific tests he wanted. Dr. O'Shea did not want to drive to Frankfort every day. He would put a few calls to recover his privileges and find his way back to the School of Mines Engineering lab of the university. To avoid undue exposure, Dr. O'Shea asked his protégé to use the special electric saw in the basement to cut the first spec to get small lab-size specs for himself and his protégé. He was not to go about the validation of Alpha-M by himself. Dr. Wasiri would conduct similar tests at his university, and they would compare notes to buttress and certify their findings among themselves before going any further. When Dr. Wasiri was done, he joined his mentor in toasting the tests they were to conduct separately to prove once for all the properties of Alpha-M. It was like old time all over again. With the exception being that the schedule Dr. Wasiri had imposed on himself for the remaining three months in Frankfort was getting tighter and tighter every day, including all the current academic works he needed to scale down, the KMC Edicts he scheduled to complete, and now Alpha-M tests. He decided that he should manage. But before leaving, he wanted to warn his mentor about the intrusion of people he was working for.

"Dr. O'Shea, just as much I was pleased and eager to share these specs with you, I have to tell you that people you are working with are bound to cause a lot of problems with native Mezi people. As usual, they show no respect to anything sacred or traditional. Worse, they showed up misrepresenting themselves as you, of all people. Well, about the week before we got to Mezi, two scientists or whatever they called themselves by the names of Dr. Neal Hansberger and Dr. Anthony O'Shea showed up at the village of a very old tribal chief in the high plateaus of Mezi.

This Dr. Anthony O'Shea was described as short and a bit rumpled, completely unlike you. In fact, this happened in the same region I have forecasted to find Alpha-M. They claimed to have been sent there by yours truly to touch base with the tribal chief and to be directed to the mountainous caves where the legend had it that the tribal chief's great-grandfather had hidden the Alpha-M specs when the German soldiers came to the village to check various stories of miraculous healing and gold and diamond reproduction. The tribal chief ignored their request but asked to give him time to verify whether I sent them. You should know that this was happening as KMC was preparing the airport celebration. The word was out that we were coming, and I learned later that KMC was making preparations throughout the country to make the celebration a huge successful event with representatives from each corner of the country. The KMC representative in the village was asked to check those scientists' story with Dean Wutugrase, who thankfully denied it categorically. Now thanks to the fast reproduction of the DVD showing the airport celebration, the tribal chief established that these two scientists were a bunch of fraudulent hustlers. It was not a surprise that these scientists never came back. I don't know if these people work with you. But what they did tells me that they were more than thoroughly aware of our relationship. It was one thing to use my name to try to hustle the tribal chief. Nothing new there, that is a common trick widely used in Mezi or anywhere in this world to get something, drop so and so name and hope that you would impress people with the reference to get ahead. At that time, my name must have been widely circulated in many circles. I can understand that it has been used or is being used for more than charitable purposes. That goes with the territory. But the gall of these scientists, using your name and misrepresenting themselves and posing as Dr. Anthony O'Shea, I believe that was an elaborated scheme. You should agree with me that it smells something of an inside job from people you may have been in contact or people who are following your work very closely from the outside. Whatever it is, I have to tell you that it shows how dangerous things can get when you deal with unscrupulous people outside our academic scientific world. Believe me, where we see the lifting of basic human conditions; these people see monetary profit, huge monetary profit, and only monetary profit. They would stop at nothing to get at it. Dr. O'Shea, I trust that we are not putting our lives in danger in this business. We just have to be a little careful who we are dealing with."

Dr. O'Shea, who had just been built up to heaven with the sight of the Alpha-M specs, or whatever his protégé had brought from Mezi, was taken and shot back to earth with the story Dr. Wasiri was telling.

He knew a Dr. Neal Hansberger who showed up at Emily's funerals. He never met the man before until that day. He remembered that he was teaching somewhere in Minnesota and was somewhat linked to the university CIA contact, General Richard "Bull" Fadden. By the way, the same Dr. Neal Hansberger was the one who referred him to Lady Allistair. Then he disappeared, never to hear about until now. Dr. O'Shea resolved to get to the bottom of this new aggravation by talking to Lady Allistair as soon as possible. But he stayed very quiet and stoic. He did not want to get his protégé involved with these people connected with intelligence services.

He looked at Dr. Wasiri and said, "I would never guess that somebody would go to the trouble of misrepresenting himself as me and being short and a bit rumpled. Emily must be having a heck of a laugh from where she is. Son, I have no idea who these people are and why they were in Mezi hustling the poor old tribal chief. And thanks to Dean Wutugrase and that airport celebration, all has been dispelled and the tribal chief has trusted you with these specs. I believe that the tribal chief got rid of these specs to your custody in case these pseudo scientists were to come back. The chief would then say the specs were already sent to you and trap them in their scheme. Either way, I believe that they would not come back to the chief. Now if these gangsters believe that they have provoked the chief to get rid of the specs and give to you, then we are all in danger. But if that was the case, you should have been approached or attacked while you were in Mezi. I don't think that was the case. It was not the case when you came back and waited until today to deliver these specs to me. There has been no burglary at your house I should have known of to date. Son, I am going by process of elimination to reassure you that these people who troubled the tribal chief have decided that they were not going to get the specs that we have and have no idea that you have brought them back to Kentucky for validation. That is why I wanted nobody else but you and I to validate these specs and do it in the most transparent way, as if we were testing basic drinking water. That should eliminate any misgiving or suspicion. I am more concerned about the time when we will be in possession of the definite validation of Alpha-M. We should leave this worry to that time."

Dr. Wasiri saw the logic in his mentor's response and was reassured about the course of action to take. He was shocked that he did not think of the dangers he might have put himself and his family, carrying these specs from Mezi to Frankfort and keeping the specs at home. He dismissed all these frightening thoughts on the basis that nothing had happened and nothing will happen, so helps us God!

When he left his mentor, his mind was bulging with crazy scenarios of chase and shots. He was glad that he did not mention the H5 Exchange event to his mentor when he was talking of being attacked at his hotel. This attack was of completely different intent. He also realized that as long as there will be talk of Alpha-M or Kany, his life would always be in danger. He wondered how to explain this to Hasbo. He decided not to.

Back in his home, Dr. O'Shea was completely upset now. He got ready three times to call and scream at Lady Allistair for disturbing the mind of Dr. Wasiri. But three times he refrained to make the call. He was convinced that somehow Lady Allistair or her cabal up to Chairman

Kiriyan was involved in this sordid cover in Mezi. Now he started to recollect.

This Dr. Neal Hansberger with a strong German accent was very mysterious to him from the start. He never understood how a man would come from Minnesota and goes to the funerals of the wife of an academic all the way in Kentucky. This Dr. Hansberger did not know him. He did not remember him from countless conferences he had attended in the United States and throughout the world. But he came and paid his respects to Emily and gave him his card and Lady Allistair's contact numbers. It was completely out of the blue at the time. He did not dwell on it at the time when he was in the middle of funerals and completely lost in memory of his best friend, confidant, guardian of the rules, tower of strength, and wife, Emily Thomas O'Shea. Dr. Hansberger must have been following up on something he knew very well. Dr. O'Shea, back then, thought that he was a mutual colleague in the pursuit of eclectic minerals that CIA was funding all over through the good old General Richard "Bull" Fadden.

Then nothing, he disappeared. He heard now and then from the general. He was not quite sure what the general was doing. But he knew that he was still in DC, providing some CIA covert activities. He never asked the general if he had heard of that Dr. Hansberger or what was his current activity according to the unwritten rule of their past involvement, a sort of "Don't Ask and Don't tell" predicament. Dr. O'Shea did not know that the same person, Lady Allistair, was funding both their activities and compensation. Dr. O'Shea did not know that the general had never heard of a Dr. Neal Hansberger. The more he thought about all that Dr. Wasiri said and the past encounter with Dr. Hansberger, he realized that calling Lady Allistair might initiate a chain of events he might not be able to control.

He would be breaking Emily's rules at the very moment that victory was almost at end. He decided to complete the validation of Alpha-M before confronting Lady Allistair. He was not about to deny his troop the taste of victory about to be gained. He couldn't care less what Lady Allistair had expended to date with the Russian's money. All was going according to Emily's rules. The Alpha-M specs were now resident in his home where they belong. They got to be validated. He also remembered very well what Lady Allistair said at their last meeting. She said something to that effect, "This Dr. Wasiri's political involvement was bound to bring a lot of good news and very soon to everyone, Dr. O'Shea included." Maybe, just maybe, Lady Allistair was fully aware of what had happened in that Mezi village. Maybe she had sent Dr. Hansberger and that pseudo Dr. O'Shea to provoke the tribal chief to give the specs to Dr. Wasiri. Maybe she knew that eventually Dr. O'Shea would get the specs and test them. That is why she said that there will be good news and very soon to everyone. She must have been in the know of all this. That is why it would be pointless to contact her and ask the obvious. She would deny it and probably send a commando to take the specs away. That would not happen.

Dr. O'Shea decided that he would keep one spec with him for research purposes while renting a safe in a local bank, where the second spec would be hidden. The bank safe would be bequeathed to Hasbo Wasiri and his children if he was to be murdered or something harsh was to happen to him.

It was about two in the morning that Dr. O'Shea, exhausted by the trip from London and worked over by the gift from Mezi and the Dr. Hansberger story, went to a deep sleep. He woke up the next day at about eleven in the morning. He checked the whole house for any sign of intrusion, but there was none. He got ready and placed the cut-up spec in the safe behind a bunch of college material books. He put the second spec back in the same dark green velvet box that came with it. The small lab specs were nicely arranged in small plastic bags and thrown in his attached case. He went to a small local bank he had never used, opened an account, and asked to rent a bank safe. Before getting there, he went to a jeweler and bought an amount of ten thousand dollars of women's and men's elaborate gold and diamond chains and watches. They were also put in a dark maroon velvet long package. While the bank officer was processing his request, he busied himself in reviewing the content of the jewelry package. When he was left alone in the bank vault, he retrieved the Alpha-M green box from his attached case and placed it inside the safe box.

He then put the jewelry box on top of the green box and about five thousand dollars he had removed from his main bank account on the other side of the town. This was the balance of about twenty thousand he wanted to use to open an account and rent for five years the bank safe.

The bank officer, a lady, treated Dr. O'Shea with the utmost curtsy extended to the bank's big clients. She expedited the process with Dr. O'Shea looking at his watch every two minutes. When he left this bank, Dr. O'Shea went straight to the office of the dean of School of Mines Engineering. There was a new dean in place according to the same secretary who welcomed the old professor. The new dean was very happy to see Dr. O'Shea and quickly granted his request to conduct test using the new very advanced and sophisticated instruments to date. The new dean said that he had attended Dr. O'Shea's seminary over exotic minerals once at the University of California in Berkeley, where he came from. The dean said that with most of known minerals being depleted around the world at unprecedented rate, universities were mounting a drive to look very carefully into these exotic minerals for new applications. He then joked by saying that it was never too late for Dr. O'Shea to reconsider his retirement to come back and share his extensive background in exotic minerals. The dean surprised him by showing a letter that he had drafted three months ago after he learned about Dr. O'Shea's whereabouts. He wanted to send the letter only after he had talked to him. Unfortunately, nobody was home. He called for three days in a row. He learned that Dr. O'Shea was in an extended trip to Europe when his secretary managed to track one of his contacts, a Dr. Wasiri in Kentucky State University.

The letter was inviting him back, not to teach but to organize seminars around exotic minerals once or twice a month and to assist the dean to build a strong scholarship around the same. The new dean told Dr. O'Shea how honored and surprised he was to see him back. He would quickly grant all privileges he requested, he needed and wanted, and more. He asked him to consider his request. When Dr. O'Shea asked him how sophisticated were the new lab instruments, the dean said that they can provide all known DNA of material analyzed back to time they were formed with a precise time stamp. Dr. O'Shea told the new dean that he was honored by his request, and he would certainly consider it, but after he had completed the analysis that a mines company in Brazil had asked him to conduct over some iron, copper, and tin specs they have found in the jungle of Amazon. Dr. O'Shea added that with his advanced age, he had been limiting his professional involvement.

He said that he came to the university to conduct the tests very reluctantly, only to help out a son of a close friend who had taken a nice job with that mines company in Brazil. The test results should assist the young man to strengthen his ties with this company. The kid wants to make a strong impression on his management and thinks, as his father, that this would help. As you can see, I am in a serious bind here. The new dean said that he understood and told him that he should be free to come and go as he pleases and if he needs a student assistant for his lab works, one would be made available. Dr. O'Shea thanked the new dean and said that he would need a bit of training over the new instruments. He was then given the proper credentials and went to see the new instruments and to get a bit of training to use them.

He reflected over how different things have changed in less than a year at this same university where he left almost in shame and humiliation. He could not believe it when the new dean asked him to come out his retirement and to give lectures over the very subject that gave him so much grief for forty years. He could not wait to share this new rapport with Dr. Wasiri. The student assistant who gave him the training over the new instruments was just as deferential. After about two hours of training using both manual and guided instruments, all controlled by a PC-based program, the student assistant of about twenty-four years old confessed that he had hoped to attend Dr. O'Shea's famous lectures when he started his main engineering degree courses. He was very upset to learn that Dr. O'Shea had since retired. The student added that he was looking forward to his lectures, not necessarily to accumulate mines engineering knowledge, but to be intellectually challenged and stimulated by his lectures as he was told around the campus he would be. He was disappointed not to have benefited of Dr. O'Shea's tremendous scholarship. Dr. O'Shea looked at the young student and said that nothing was lost; he would be around as much as possible the next few months. He would be happy to review any subject of interest with him. He also added that the so-called tremendous scholarship he heard about was not for the rote crowd.

And with a grave voice and as if he was back in front of his beloved students, Dr. O'Shea went on, "This scholarship can sometimes strip bare fundamental tenets of our comfortable order of knowledge, dismissing all accepted and known principles, transporting and pushing the uninitiated to the ultimate corners of what, when, where, and why. This is where tremendous scholarship can either set you apart elevating you above the peers or drop you and leave you in the dungeon of knowledge. You could stay in that dungeon for a long time, or worse, you could die there.

However, if you are lucky, the next cycle of knowledge sparks can free you, and the web would start all over again. And this would be possible only if you are willing to accept the unbelievable price to be paid while waiting for that elusive next cycle. Are you willing to pay that price?"

When he stopped talking, Dr. O'Shea realized he was talking about himself and all that had happened to him within the walls of this university while the student assistant stood there looking at him with amazement and wondering what to say and how to respond. The old professor helped him by saying, "I am sorry, son, this was a rhetorical question addressed to no one in particular. As I said, I would be around, and we would talk. Thank you for the training." He left the building. When he reached home, he called his protégé and told him about the new dean, his request, and the new instruments. Dr. Wasiri was happy to hear about the wonderful atmosphere his mentor had encountered at his old school. He told Dr. O'Shea to think twice about taking on new assignments with everything he had on his plate as chairman of foundation, trustee of ABDI, now tester of Alpha-M, father of three, grandfather of many, all-around guide of Wasiri family, part-time retired, always traveling for some people in London and more and more. Dr. Wasiri said that he forgot to mention the new instruments that should cut down on time he would have dedicated on the same validation before. He was also going to use them. However, he warned him that he was sometimes concerned when the results from these instruments show unknown properties or unknown elements. That could be the case for these new specs. Then they would have to decide what to do. Dr. O'Shea accepted his protégé's approach. He was not worried about unknown properties and elements. That had been his condition for forty years. That is where he strives.

CHAPTER 29
Dr. Neal Hansberger

The precautions for testing that the two scientists in Kentucky have taken to keep the specs from falling in wrong hands were not necessary. It turned out Chairman Kiriyan took a few liberties to verify how far his Africa Initiatives have progressed under the guidance of his trusted aide, Lady Allistair, AMX CEO. Uncle Kiri was a bit disappointed about the Barry Newcomb episode. He would have wished tighter control. With the Varonne-Sur-Baie move growing in stature and the noticeable suspicion and resentment he was detecting from Moscow, he did not want to leave the Africa initiatives to chance. To start with, he wanted to get an appreciation of Mezi initiative from an independent observer. He called on his old reliable all around agent, Dr. Neal Hansberger. This man had assumed so many names and personalities; it was very difficult to determine exactly his true identity. From the archives of various intelligence services, he was born in the Eastern section of Germany at the end of Second World War when the Soviet troops were entering Nazi Germany. He was abandoned in a maternity ward in the town of Fürstenwalde.

When the Russian army took over the town, there were about twelve newborn babies nicely bundled up in the small hospital building that had escaped the ferocious bombing the town had received from the advancing troops. Sometime later, a Soviet nurse, a Major, by the name of Magida Solenskova gathered about these infants found alive in the nursery and in relatively decent health, processed them and started the arduous task of shipping them along with adult captured German soldiers to Soviet Union penal camps per strict orders from Stalin. She also made arrangements to have one of the found children she named Alexiev Kramokov to be retrieved and to be taken care by her sister who had remained in Moscow and was a high level KGB officer in the general staff command of the army. Major Solenskova created false documents showing that the infant was born out of wedlock from a romance between an unknown Soviet soldier with another Soviet nurse. While the unknown soldier was gone and disappeared with the advancing Soviet army in the southern fronts to Czech-Slovakia and Hungary, the Russian nurse revealed to the Major that she was pregnant and about to have a child. She gave birth some time later but died from lack of basic rudimentary maternity care in the front.

According to the documents she filed, Major Solenskova decided then to adopt the child for the time being and to sort out the child proper maternity and paternity at the end of the war. However, having divorced her husband two years ago, with no plans of future marriage, Major Solenskova knew that there was not going to be any sorting out of this child's maternity or paternity after the war. Most likely she would keep and raise this child. But Major Solenskova was also killed in action soon after Soviet army entered Berlin. Her sister, the KGB Officer in Moscow, who did what her sister instructed her to do, had no choice but to officially adopt Alexiev Kramokov as her own son. She enjoyed a rather stable family life at the time. Her husband was a mid-level official in the Foreign Affairs Ministry. They had already two daughters. After the war, they raised their three children as decently as possible while both, committed communists, were rising in the respective management ranks of KGB and Foreign Affairs Ministry. The wife reached the rank of major general in KGB while the husband became successively Soviet Union Ambassador in Mongolia, North Korea, and Bulgaria during the tumultuous succession in the Communist Party general secretary position from Stalin to Kroutchev. Alexiev Kramokov was afforded the education reserved to the children of Soviet elite at the time. Alexiev went as far as getting a PhD in Nuclear Technology Sciences at Moscow University while attending every KGB and Communist Party training classes. Alexiev was accepted into KGB and started climbing the ranks of KGB. His nuclear expertise opened a lot of international venues. He was to be stationed with his adopted father in Mongolia and Hungary. He also did a long stint in East Germany.

Through family members, he was shocked to learn one day that he was an adopted child. He started the odyssey to learn who he was and where he came from. With the help of well-positioned acquaintances in KGB, he got hold of the first documents establishing his adoption by Major Solenskova. Alexiev confronted both his adopted parents with these documents. They agreed that he was adopted, but they could not help him any further. Alexiev persisted in his search in East Germany to no end. There was no trace of the Russian nurse his first adoptive mother was talking about. But he found in the Fürstenwalde city archives the list of twelve children abandoned in the maternity ward at the time but never to hear from. Everybody believed that they were shipped to various penal camps in Soviet Union. Again, examining the KGB archives, he came across the list of infants coming from Fursten-Walde two weeks later, trans-shipped through Moscow to a Siberia penal colony. The list had only eleven infants.

That was proof enough that he was of German descent. He did not try to confront his adoptive parents with all these evidence items. By this time, his adoptive parents were old and not ready to part with whatever dirty family laundry they have carried all along. He decided to do all he could to trace his own German family. That is the time he came across Nadia Kirelenko, a longtime KGB contact and colleague. He told her about how despondent he was on learning that he was adopted and the fact that he was not getting the right answers no matter whom he turned to. Alexiev said that he needed to stay far away from Moscow, from family, friends, and other contacts in order to sort things out for himself. At the same time, Nadia was recruiting mainly committed KGB agents for the expanding and booming enterprise under the leadership of Nadov Kiriyan, director of Fourth Mining Region in the Eastern Siberia Region. Nadia encouraged Alexiev to join the enterprise in Amovir. This was almost seven hours from Moscow and ideally suited for Alexiev to recharge his batteries. When he came to Amovir, he was quickly adopted by Nadov Kiriyan, who saw a remarkable opportunity to grow Alexiev Kramokov into a full-fledged representative of the enterprise interests in various economic regions of Soviet Union and its satellites. This was also the time Kiriyan instructed Alexiev to mold into different names and personalities depending on circumstances to advance the business interests of the expanding industrial concern of the Fourth Mining Region. Using multiple aliases, Alexiev visited all regions of Soviet Union, its satellites, Mongolia, and China. He even kept a permanent residence in East Germany for the sole purpose of tracking his natural family. With the breakup of Soviet Union and the reunion of Germany, he managed to finally locate his natural family and to recover his original name of Neal Hansberger. He learned that running from the advancing army and knowing the acerbic Nazi reputation that his grandfather built around town, his entire family fled from Fursten-Walde as far west as possible to rejoin a distant family in a small village outside Munich.

The sad story was that her mother had just given birth to him the night before the Soviet army took over the town. The manager of the hospital that had been so far spared from bombing advised all the new mothers to leave the building while a small staff of nurses was going to take care of their new infants. The manager warned the new mothers that he did not want to be responsible of their survival, and most likely, if they remained in their bed at the maternity ward, they would be easy targets of advancing Soviet soldiers, risking rape or death or both. He convinced them that the new infants would be spared. After the town had been taken over, the mothers would have a chance to recuperate their infants.

However, as soon the bombing intensified, panic took care of dispersing the small staff of nurses. The manager of the hospital was killed in the crossfire. The new mothers fled with their families to whatever directions they thought would spare their lives. When the fight subsided, the hospital was the only building in town still standing and became the temporary headquarters for the advancing Soviet army.

The new infants were evacuated to the care of Major Solenskova's unit of Soviet nurses. When three surviving mothers came back to claim their new infants, they were arrested, raped, and killed. After listening to his past sad episode, Alexiev Kramokov or Neal Hansberger was now questioning whether it was really worthwhile to unearth his past of a German born into a family led by a reputed Nazi grandfather. He realized that he was a product of a difficult and troubled time. He could not decide what was worse, the fake adoption that his Russian adoptive parents have concocted for more than thirty-five years or the Nazi past of his natural family. He resolved that he could not do worse working for Nadov Kiriyan, another mysterious adoptive manager. He severed all links to his natural and adoptive families. When Chairman Kiriyan started to put in place CIB in Liechtenstein, Dr. Neal Hansberger decided to settle in Vaduz. This location would afford him complete freedom of action and movement anywhere in the world and any time Chairman Kiriyan needed an independent agent involvement. After Dr. O'Shea made a remarkable lecture in the St. Petersburg conference and was identified as somebody to nurture for his insightful but neglected advanced researches over exotic minerals, Dr. Neal Hansberger, prompted by Chairman Kiriyan, showed up at the funerals of Emily to make his first contact with Dr. O'Shea. This contact had borne unexpected results to date, including the much-expected return of Dr. Wasiri to Mezi.

To verify if Dr. Wasiri's return was definite, Dr. Neal Hansberger again came to Mezi with another freelance agent from South Africa, the pseudo Dr. O'Shea. That freelance agent, a former South African mercenary with military campaigns in Angola and Congo, was knowledgeable of Mezi terrain and politics. He easily guided Dr. Hansberger through Mezi political and social labyrinth to gauge the impact of Dr. Wasiri's return. Then they learned how deep and serious KMC was committed to have Dr. Wasiri as part of their leadership. To verify this commitment further, both agents took the side trip to that village in the high plateaus of eastern Tongeo Province to test the tribal chief Sengimo VII's allegiance to Dr. Wasiri.

The allegiance was readily verified when the tribal chief would not provide any information about the so-called caves hiding the famous pieces of extraordinary minerals that German missionaries have heard of at the beginning of this century. The two agents went to South Africa right after this visit knowing very well that their presence in Mezi while Dr. Wasiri was in the country was not welcome.

CHAPTER 30
Ludmilla's Revenge

Chairman Kiriyan knew that his plan for the Varonne-Sur-Baie move must now be accelerated. But he needed to do so at the same time he was disposed to teach his Russian managing director, Karlov Yelgin, a good civic lesson. Dr. Hansberger, assisted by Ludmilla Borensky, was going to lead the dance with his assorted team of new and old KGB now FSS hands. Karlov and Ludmilla have decided to come to Moscow the first week of March right after the last snow that obliterated the circulation in the town. They have elected to arrive in town over the weekend after the eight to ten hours flight from Amovir with stops over Novosibirsk and Yekaterinburg. Ludmilla did not spare a thing to hook the poor Karlov from the time they boarded the plane. First, Ludmilla royally ignored him at the airport, where he was dropped and attended by his matron of wife. She knew that he was in trouble with his wife who gave her disdainful regards every time she moved about the Amovir Airport's huge waiting room fixing her blonde hair, her tight jeans or her bust overflowing the tight open and low-cut shirt she was wearing. She can hear Karlov's wife pestering him with questions whether he knew the young sexy lady about to take the same trip. Was she the latest in the long series of mistresses Karlov had maintained all their married life? Every time Karlov denied something, she raised another question on the topic.

It was a much-relieved Karlov who quickly boarded the plane to be rejoined at the last minute by Ludmilla who took about ten minutes to take her seat next to Karlov after giving him an eye full of her bust, her thighs, and her behinds. They were conveniently seated in the first class row, and Ludmilla took the window seat after loosening up her jean belt and lowering the pants zipper two inches below. When she sat down, she could not help but notice the already growing member of Karlov, who was trying to find a proper position to undo the visible damage.

Ludmilla chose that instant to whisper in his ears while extending her hand over and caressing the hardened part, "Brace yourself, this is going to be a long trip."

Karlov looked at her straight and responded in kind, "A long trip indeed, and I am now at your disposal. Anytime and anywhere in this plane you want the hard part, I am yours."

Ludmilla hushed him, "Not so loud, your wife would hear us. You would have to wait until we get out of here. We got plenty of time."

Karlov laughed loud while the captain was announcing that the plane was about to take off. The plane was a very comfortable Airbus plane from one of the numerous airlines companies that were established and survived the big shakeout following the collapse of the state-owned Aeroflot.

As soon they were airborne, Ludmilla requested a large woolen cover and covered herself from the neck down. Karlov took the request as the sign of things to come, a heavy mutual petting below. His lower part grew even larger. Ludmilla, seeing the additional effect on Karlov, carefully covered his pants and whispered that he needed to control his hard part, otherwise, at that rate she would have to request a cup to collect the blow out that would inevitably come out. Karlov was now beside himself. With his right hand, he reached below Ludmilla's side of the cover, only to find that she had unzipped her jeans completely and her very small yellow tong slip was showing barely covering her shaved lower part. Karlov stood up all of a sudden and rushed to the bathroom that was three seats away and closed it. As soon as he secured the door closed, he unzipped his pants and relieved himself. He was lucky he did not stain himself or his pants. He cleaned himself and the toilet bowl and came out releasing a strong sexual stench along. He was confronted with curious stares when he returned to his seat. The stares dimmed the urge he held bent up when he boarded the plane. Ludmilla was now covering her head now and did not budge a bit.

Karlov kept his distance for the next forty-five minutes. But he kept being aroused by the scent that Ludmilla was exhaling, which gave away deliberately her sensuous smell. It got worse every time when she lowered the cover and the low cut revealed her huge breasts. Karlov was ready to exchange his seat with the lady on the side who looked more than aggravated by the goings-on next seats. Ludmilla lowered the whole woolen cover again to her thigh. Now she was cleverly exposing her naked shaved lower part beneath zipper split of her jeans, and there was no more yellow slip, as if she had managed to remove it when Karlov was in the bathroom. As quickly as she exposed her body, she pulled the cover over her head. Karlov sat back, closed his eyes, and thought about what was going on. He realized that Ludmilla was teasing him, running high speed. He then asked the stewardess if there were empty seats in the coach. She answered affirmatively.

Ten minutes later, Karlov got up and headed back to find an empty seat at the end of the plane and went to sleep until the plane landed at

Novosibirsk Airport. He got up and went back to his original first class seat. Ludmilla sounded surprised that he left her alone. She asked him if she was not well behaved. Karlov said that she would be if she kept her clothes on. She then apologized and said that she thought he would enjoy her naked during the entire flight. She assured him that she would not be showing any of her diamonds. She begged him to keep his seat because the lady sitting on the other side looked very displeased with his coming and going and probably was thinking that she was a terrible wife. When Karlov was finally settled down and the plane took off for the second leg of the flight, Ludmilla lowered the woolen cover. She was wearing a multicolored scarf that covered nicely and adequately the open low-cut shirt. The zipper of her jeans was not open, and the belt was also decently secured.

She turned the conversation to the company business they were going to handle in Moscow. She led the conversation with her thought about the promotion of Lady Allistair to become AMX CEO.

"I do not believe that I know any other smart and dynamic woman like Lady Allistair. She really deserved that promotion after all that she had been through. She was literally exiled from the management of that company from London to New York. I tell you, in terms of sales, she was the most productive of all these executives in AMX, bringing in on an average, year after year close to 65 percent of AMX's total revenue. It was not by accident that Chairman Kiriyan promoted her to be the CEO. I am very proud of her."

Karlov's face turned red all at once at the mention of Lady Allistair and he blurted, "A whore and a bitch, if I may say so. Nonsense. What are you talking about? Ludmilla, please do not get me upset at this time. Did you verify those sales figures you are talking about, or are you repeating what she told you while you were between her legs? Let's be serious, Ludmilla. Foreigners are eating our lunch, and you are clapping. What do you make of your Russian identity? Ludmilla, I could care less who you go to bed with. But do not, I beg you, do not turn your lover into a saint or a magnificent business leader. Lady Allistair got there because Mr. Kiriyan wants to have somebody he can control in that position. The one who was there before, her uncle, Robert Mendham, did not pay Mr. Kiriyan any mind. He got fed up and got rid of him and placed your very smart lover Lady Allistair. My dear, I have been in this company longtime enough to know what was going and what is going on and I want to help you to see the truth.

Lady Allistair is not the magnificent business leader you are making her to be. I saw her when she was a simple research analyst when she came in Amovir, bedding every plant manager on the sight. You certainly would remember that. You lived with her during that time. Oh, I am sorry. I forgot that you were lovers. Too bad I did not have the chance to know her myself. You see, I was too busy with the best of them all. My lovely Nadia, your old boss. What a lady!"

Ludmilla stayed quiet for a while, collecting her thought, making sure she did not get sidetracked and that the big surprise she had in mind in Moscow goes on schedule. She tried to lower his temper, "Comrade Karlov, you are literally shouting at me. I do not appreciate it. I don't understand with you men. Every time a woman moves up, it is the end of the world. You are ready to tear down everything that the lady had done by treating either a whore or a bitch. I told you what made her successful, the AMX sales figures. They are there to be seen and reviewed on the Internet if you want to. AMX publishes on quarterly basis their operations data. Check them for yourselves you would see if I were lying. Instead, you are jumping all over the place, being disrespectful to your traveling companion and calling us names. I don't know what you have with women being lovers. But it never bothered you when you were annoying that young plant manager, and it was very well known all over Amovir that you were madly in love with him, above your wife and my old boss Nadia. Nobody called you name then, a whore or a bitch or whatever they called man preferences. I tell you something, I am very proud of my relationship with Lady Allistair. We love each other to death. If you cannot deal with it, well, though. I am sure deep down, you dream to see us one time just one time doing it to death. You would probably jerk off as you just did a while ago over nothing. What is the matter with you? It is very sad that we cannot have a simple intelligent conversation without tipping the scale violently one way or another. Is that the mark of the Russian managing director? Then I am so sorry for the Russian identity. You got to be a little bit careful about your attitude and behavior. It would drag you down the drain. Now you cannot talk!"

Karlov had turned his head as if going to sleep, then turned again and said, "Ludmilla, the rumor about that plant manager and me remains a rumor. I have never confessed, as you just did, to have any male lover. Listen. Let me repeat. Lady Allistair, your lover, should not be put high up there on any high chair, with or without AMX sales data. For your information, any executive vice president can claim sales data generated below her or below him. Lady Allistair had North America territory for AMX.

Sales generated in North America AMX territory automatically were accounted and accumulated to her position whether she worked for it or not. It was all predisposed by Mr. Kiriyan from the start to make her look good, so after so many years of looking good, he could justify to elevate her at the CEO level. It was that simple as long as she did not screw it up. My dear Ludmilla, that is how the game is played. Nothing more, nothing less. You can be made chairperson of EXXON by playing along similarly. By the way, you are missing the point. I could care less to know what Lady Allistair does or does not. I could care less to know whether Lady Allistair plays the male or you play the female when you are together. I don't care. It is none of my business. You mentioned my Russian identity. That is my burning concern as we travel to Moscow, the center of Mother Russia. There is one thing I am concerned about above all. I remember that AMX was bought with BI's Russian money, but Mr. Kiriyan had managed to date to insulate all AMX operations from BI financials. There is absolutely no consolidated financial reporting of AMX into BI. Tell me why! I wonder why! Every time BI buys a new foreign company with our hard-earned Russian money or sets up a new foreign company with our hard-earned Russian money, BI financials are fretted away, and BI is completely reduced in size as a parent company. That is not rational. How can a company disappear in front of our own eyes every time it is supposed to grow? The only part that does not change is the representation of our Russian operations. The rest is gone. I believe it is managed away into all these new centers of excellence Mr. Kiriyan is now fond of talking about. Maybe I am the last idiot in the house of Russian BI. But nobody had been able to explain all that BI international empire to me. It seems the BI Empire had evaporated or resides only in Mr. Kiriyan's head. You may say what you want. I am no Russian xenophobic here. But let us make something clear. When you use hard-earned Russian money to do something, then reflect or compensate the Russian owners of that capital. This is what I don't see Mr. Kiriyan doing, and that is wrong."

Ludmilla became a bit lost and could not quite follow Karlov, "If you are accusing Chairman Kiriyan of stealing money, I don't think he would have lasted this long doing it. All I know is that he took a backward Russian regional company and slowly made it into a premier international minerals company of the world. I cannot explain all the financial intricacies he has used to grow BI, but you must admit that it is today the jewel of Russian enterprise. I would advise you to understand those financial intricacies before throwing stones to the enterprise. Maybe this whole trip is useless.

Maybe you just need to go and have fun, instead of going all over Moscow and making a fool of yourself in front of people who have already been briefed by Chairman Kiriyan and have supported his strategy all along. Maybe I should prepare a good session for you with two ladies in Moscow. You may come back more appreciative of two female lovers. I would not have the honor to indulge you since you have decided I have seen too much of Lady Allistair's inner tight. I am, how you put, a damaged commodity. That is fine with me. I can take a rejection."

Karlov became now sentimental. He held Ludmilla's hand and said, "Sorry. I would never reject you. Look what you did to me when we left Amovir. If you can bring a female friend when we get to the hotel, that would be fine. A male friend would be OK too. As long as you are there, you would make my day. I am suffering all this flight for one and one thing only, to have you. Ten hours to get you. That is worthwhile. You would not deny me this. Look at my left pant. It is going up again. Enough of those company politics. I have said all I needed to say. Let me go to sleep and dream that I am inside you. I wish I could get a woolen cover for myself not to disturb the lady next to me. I am afraid when she would notice the effect on my left pant while I am dreaming, she would attack me."

Ludmilla smiled and gave him the woolen cover. Karlov went to sleep. Two hours later, the captain announced the descent toward Moscow, and the plane landed at Domededovo International Airport, the largest in terms of traffic out of the three Moscow airports. It was seven in the evening. Ludmilla and Karlov were both very tired. They were met at the airport by a distinguished dour gentleman who said that he was BI's new representative in Moscow by the name of Alexiev Kramokov. He was to drop them at their hotel. Karlov thought to have heard about him long time ago through Nadia Kirilenko. He agreed and reminded Karlov that poor Nadia was instrumental in bringing him to into what used to be named the Fourth Directorate back then, and now it had this capitalist name of BI. Alexiev and Karlov briefly lamented about how things have changed.

Karlov even quoted one of the new Russian Republic leaders celebrated "No Soul, No Brain" ambivalent comment about the end of Soviet Union, "Anyone who does not miss the Soviet Union has no soul, and anyone who wants to bring it back has no brain." Alexiev told the BI guests that he would be at their disposal all weekend until Monday. He took Karlov on the side for a few seconds, and in a hushed tone, he said that he would be glad to take him out sometime during the weekend for a manlike party, if he is inclined to come.

Then noticing how they have left Ludmilla standing by herself not quite knowing what to do, he apologized to Ludmilla that he did not mean to embarrass her. Karlov said that Ludmilla was a very strong girl and that she had seen and heard worse. Both of these new buddies erupted in a laugh. Karlov added that for the time being, the voyagers from Amovir were very tired and in need of rest, but he should fully recuperate by Saturday. Alexiev Kramokov alias Neal Hansberger dropped them at the plush hotel reserved for BI managers. The hotel named Baltschug Kempinski Moscow was on Balchug Street, located across the Moskva River from Kremlin in the Russia's main historic and cultural center. The hotel was overlooking Moscow's historic center, offering spectacular view of Kremlin, Red Square, and St. Basil's Cathedral. While they waited for the concierge to ready their rooms, Ludmilla was seated far in the lobby busy on her cell phone, making arrangements for the night escapade promised to Karlov. Karlov retrieved four room passes from the concierge, two for each of their respective rooms. But he handed only one room pass to Ludmilla and kept all the other remaining three. They finally got clearance to go to their separate rooms, which turned out to be on opposite sides of the seventh floor. Karlov asked about the night escapade. Ludmilla said that it would come right after the dinner when the entertainers would join them below at the dinner salon. She warned him again to brace himself, to stay strong, as the night would be long. When Ludmilla got to her room, she received another phone call, this time from Alexiev Kramokov who asked if the bait was done. Ludmilla answered affirmatively and that Karlov had great anticipation of the action. He should be started with two mature ones that night, some kind of confidence building. Saturday night would be the night of the big compromise. Ludmilla added that she trusted Alexiev to do all in his power to insure that the bastard does not come near her during their entire Moscow stay.

She then went to the bathroom and took her shower, and when she came out half naked, with only her towel around her thigh, she was shocked to see Karlov waiting for her in her bed, naked. She raised her arms to her head in shock; her towel fell and she froze and she would not dare run. She was standing there naked and trapped in her own game. She asked him what he wanted to do and how he managed to enter her room. He lied, saying that he had bribed the hotel boy into duplicating her room pass. She protested and said that she was not ready to indulge at this time without the stimulation of another female companion as she had initially suggested. Karlov said he was ready now, and he had been waiting for this opportunity the whole day. He did not need another person but her. She resigned herself to the game she thought she was going to control.

Not to arouse his suspicion over the trap she was leading Karlov to during this Moscow visit, Ludmilla, still naked, came to bed along the overexcited Karlov and let him enjoy himself. But after relieving himself the first time, Karlov became very indignant. He told her that she was about to pay for all the homosexual rumors spread about him in Amovir. He then sodomized her by force. He left the room with a grunt and called Ludmilla a whore and a bitch.

Ludmilla, hurt and paralyzed, stayed in bed for a long time, crying and wondering what had happened to her. When she had garnered enough strength, she removed the bloodstained bed sheet, got up, and helped herself to the bathroom. She filled the bath tub with hot water, sat in the tub for a while, cleaning herself. She also cursed herself for allowing a lowlife like Karlov to trap, play, and abuse her so easily. She then called the concierge to bring cleaner bed sheets and to change the room pass. When two hotel assistant ladies showed up with new room passes and clean bed sheets, more so to investigate what had happened, she did not report the incident but claimed she was having female problems. She cancelled all the other appointments and went to sleep. The next day in the morning, Alexiev called to find out why she had cancelled the appointments. She said that she was falling at sleep and did not want to have a boring party. She added that from all the conversations she had with Karlov in the flight from Amovir, he was dangerously bent on destroying Chairman Kiriyan during the following stay in Moscow, and he needed to be taught a very good lesson before he gets to that. She also said that she was not going to join their party through the entire weekend. She would be visiting with old-time friends.

She collected all her strength and called Karlov to advise him to have a good day and not to wait on her because she was going to be away, probably all weekend, visiting friends. Karlov, now ashamed of himself, said that he hoped he had not hurt her and he was sorry if he did. He would do everything to make it up to her. She said that that was quite all right and those kind of things happened among consenting or nonconsenting adults. She closed by saying that she would survive this one. She hung up and spat on the phone. Karlov still in his room received a call from Alexiev who was very upset that he was still home, attending to one thousand chores his wife and kids had lined up for him that Saturday morning. He assured his new buddy that he would be by the hotel around twelve to have their lunch. In fact, Alexiev was putting all the dots on the new weekend strategy since Ludmilla had cancelled the Friday appointments.

A new set of borrowed FSS hands were needed to mount an effective and convincing operation for Karlov. Alexiev made it on time to have lunch with Karlov.

As soon they were seated in the hotel, Café Kranzler, Alexiev raised the favorable Karlov topic about where the Russian BI operations were headed. Alexiev again lamented about the Fourth Directorate and the time when Nadia could get any KGB operative job with the Fourth as it had happened with Alexiev. He pointedly asked Karlov where this Russia Republic was heading.

Karlov then took over, "To hell, my friend, to endless hell pit, I can tell with the likes of Mr. Kiriyan reducing BI to nothing else but the shadow of the Fourth. Can you imagine? Year in, year out, our Russian operations that yours truly never missed the beat, 6 to 7 percent sales volume growth annually, and what happened with our money, sometime it is AMX in London or that tanker company in Dubai or the port facilities management company in Australia or a chain of secluded hotels along the beaches in south Thailand, let's just call them properly, a chain of brothels in Thailand, on and on. Let us not forget that mysterious bank in Vaduz in Liechtenstein. What is BI becoming? I sit in my office in Amovir and I see all these crazy deals happening and I cannot say a thing. That burns me up, and I feel like I am going to explode."

Alexiev asked Karlov whether as the managing director of Russian operations he had raised any concern with Mr. Kiriyan.

Karlov laughed, "My dear man Alexiev, please be happy to keep your position here in Moscow where you can breathe, and nobody is bothering you except some out-of-town jokes like myself you need to entertain now and then. Amovir, I have to tell you, still lives in the era of Stalin. No glasnost there. Mr. Kiriyan is Stalin in Amovir. Everything starts and ends with Mr. Kiriyan. There is none of the give-and-take that you see here in Moscow. And if you are a managing director like myself, surrounded by KGB/FSS agents all over like that whore of Ludmilla, ready to do what she calls Chairman Kiriyan bidding every second, you shut your mouth, you confide to nobody but your wife. Back then, when Nadia was around, I had ways to channel my frustration. Nadia had solid Kremlin channels. Mr. Kiriyan was afraid of her. By the way, I have to tell you that I was literally and figuratively very tight with Nadia, if you see what I mean. She was a terrific broad insight out. A body to kill, and she used it like no woman I can remember. And would you know that this whore of Ludmilla slowly replaced Nadia.

And now she is the main FSS leader in the shop. Is that a joke or what? How can a bitch in service of that English AMX CEO be the main FSS leader in the shop? No Russian identity whatsoever? Serve her well! Yesterday I mounted the bitch and hard on both sides after you were gone. And today she said that I raped and sodomized her. How can you rape a whore? Mind you, did she report the rape? Hell no! Am I arrested for rape? Hell no! I am here talking to you. She teased me all the way from Amovir in the plane for ten hours. I am not kidding, showing me her shaved stuff all the time. What was I supposed to do? Well, after you were gone, she asked me to her room to have a dinner. I got there, she is walking around naked. When the food came, she ran in to the bathroom. We were naked eating in her room, looking across the lights bathing Kremlin. What an awesome view! And then she would not let me finish the real dinner. My God, nobody should be allowed to provoke a man to that point. You don't invite a man to your room when you are naked and eat with him when you two are naked and deny him a little bit of closure. Well, I did it and that is that. My dear Alexiev, I am sorry to tell you all these sordid stories. She probably would tell you a different story sometime later."

As Karlov was rambling and going about his encounter with Ludmilla, a hotel assistant was pointing out two well-dressed ladies to their table. The ladies came and introduced themselves as Katherina and Helena, friends of Ludmilla. Katherina was a copy of Ludmilla in size, body, hair, face, and looks. She could pass for her twin sister.

She said that she was Ludmilla's distant cousin, and she was supposed to meet with her yesterday night until she called and cancelled the date. She came in at this time with her friend Helena to meet with Ludmilla, but she learned that she was not at her room and left for the day. She said to Karlov, "When I wanted to leave, one hotel assistant remembered that you came together with Ludmilla last night, and you were in the Café Kransler. We just wanted to ask you if you know how we can reach Ludmilla now, as her cellular phone is no longer reachable." While Katherina was talking, she moved about places the same way Ludmilla did. Alexiev said that he did not have Ludmilla's whereabouts, maybe Karlov did. He did not, but he said that he was sorry about last night. They were supposed to have dinner together. But he suggested canceling it because they were very tired after the ten hours flight from Amovir. He asked the ladies how he could make it up with them. Katherina was not sure if that was going to be possible without Ludmilla. Then they left and went to the lobby. After speaking a while with the staff at the concierge again, they decided to talk to Karlov again.

This time, Helena, a vixen bomb in her own right, said that they did not want go back home at this hour and probably come back to the hotel if Ludmilla were to call and renew the date. They would join the two men for the next two to three hours while waiting for Ludmilla if that did not cause any problem.

Alexiev protested and said that this could upset their evening plan. Karlov, always on the flesh attack, dismissed his buddy's concern. He reassured the ladies that they could stick around as long as they liked. If Ludmilla was still not around, they were welcome to wait for her in his room upstairs. Alexiev started getting nervous and showing it. He pulled Karlov on the side and warned him about the ladies in Moscow.

"You got to be in your guards in Moscow. You never know who is going to knock you off." Karlov was still sure that he could manage two beautiful ladies if need be. Alexiev then decided to leave and said that he would check him up later that evening for a night out. He also gave him a stack of traveler checks in Euro totaling about five thousand euros for his extra expenses. Karlov was all set now. After he offered the ladies some drinks and exchanged small talk with the ladies for about thirty minutes, he said he wanted to rest in his room and the two ladies were welcome to come upstairs and continue to wait for Ludmilla. They hesitated, then they agreed to join him in his room.

Karlov did exactly what he promised to do. He went inside the bathroom, removed his clothes, and put on his pajamas. He asked the ladies to take a seat on the long sofa in the room and watch anything they wanted on TV while he was sleeping. They took the seat and ordered an adult movie and watched it while Karlov now excited by the sound of the skin movie pretended to sleep. After about ten minutes watching explicit sex scenarios, Katherina went to the bathroom and came out in her newborn baby suit and climbed inside the bed covers on Karlov's left side. Helena followed suit minutes later on the right side. Katherina then asked Karlov if all this was what was planned the night before when Ludmilla was setting the date. Karlov, who had already removed his pajamas underneath, agreed.

Together they continued to watch the adult movie and started petting each other. The three lovers indulged each other sexually for the next two hours until they were completely exhausted and fell asleep. Alexiev called at about six thirty as expected. The ladies quietly and strongly suggested to Karlov not to invite this boring Alexiev into their next escapade.

Karlov obliged and told Alexiev that he had his hands full for the night and would prefer to hang tight in his room. Alexiev said that he was a bit relieved not to come, given the hassle he was getting from his wife and kids at home. He told Karlov he was making arrangements to get him transportation if he needed it during the night. He gave him the transportation contact number and bid him goodnight. The girls were excited. They said whether Ludmilla showed up or not, they were ready to show Karlov the night of his life. Karlov was now on the hook as beautifully as planned by Alexiev and Ludmilla, who monitored all these happenings across the street on the tenth floor of an office now transformed into a live-in headquarters for the purpose. What Karlov did not realize was that every time he was drinking or eating something, he received a good dose of narcotics from the ladies' long fingernails. When he fell deeply asleep, a dozen of explicit pictures were taken, showing him in the worst possible compromising positions with the two ladies. These pictures were quickly e-mailed to the headquarters' PC in the next building for Ludmilla's safekeeping. All of their conversations were also being taped for accuracy. Nothing was being left to chance. Worse, while Katherina was well beyond consenting age, Helena had fake papers showing that she was barely fourteen.

At around seven, Karlov told the ladies that he was now ready for a big Moscow night out. He asked them if they had any spot suggestion. They had plenty, but they needed to go home and change into more comfortable nightdresses.

Karlov responded that with all the money he was carrying, they could afford better dresses in the huge mall shops around the corner. He gave each of the ladies five hundred euros to shop for the night. They came back an hour and a half later, full of bags. Karlov called the transportation contact number that Alexiev gave, and he was promised to have a limousine in less than twenty minutes. Karlov came down with his two fantastic escorts for a night out. They went first to Doug & Marty Boar House for a late dinner. When they were done, it was off to Piramida, then Nightflight. The ladies finally suggested Hungry Duck, which Karlov knew from experience, having gone there during previous stays. The ladies knew that serious hanky-panky business usually took place there at about two in the morning after the male strippers' show was completed and the female patrons, drunk and overexcited, were ready for anything. They were not disappointed. As soon as they entered the joint, two middle-aged ladies kidnapped Karlov. Twenty minutes later, Karlov, now over-intoxicated, came back with his pants undone and tie on his head.

While the ladies dragged him to a comfortable corner, a well-dressed man started screaming Karlov's name, claiming to have gone to St. Petersburg Mines Engineering School with him. The man had Karlov's biography down pat from his younger age outside St. Petersburg to the time he went to work for the Fourth Directorate. He knew his entire family and friends. But Karlov, drunk, struggled to recognize him and his name of Stanilas Shostov. The man talked and talked about old time to Katherina and Helena's complete indifference. At about four in the morning, the ladies wanted to extract Karlov from the loquacious man to go back to another escapade at the hotel. But this Shostov had a better idea. He convinced Karlov to go to one of those underworld dachas outside Moscow, where they have a casino and plenty of titillating sex à la carte. Katherina and Helena did not like the idea and would prefer to go back to the hotel.

Then they reached a compromise. The girls would be brought back to the hotel using Karlov's limousine and wait for Karlov who would go with this Shostov using his limousine to do some gambling in the famous dacha and, of course, get more sex time à la carte. The girls were dropped at the hotel in Karlov's limousine while Karlov and his new lost-and-found friend continued the night out in Shostov's limousine. The ride to the dacha took more than an hour along Shchelkovskoye Shosse to A103 going east toward the small town of Balashikha. The dacha named La Boheme was three miles right after crossing Moscow outer ring highway MKAD 103 but before the town of Balashikha. The entrance to the dacha was by appointment and was manned by heavily armed guards behind the huge metal door. It took another five minutes of driving through a narrow road along a range of tall trees to arrive to the dacha. Inside the castle-looking house, the scene was very serene with young female and male attendants shuttling middle-aged or older patrons to different game corners. Video slot machines, blackjack tables, poker tables, roulette, and various casino equipment were lined up along what seemed to be an endless hall. From far, Karlov could also distinguish entrances to open and closed huge rooms. In some open doors, people sat looking at nude young people copulating. Other rooms were marked with private sign where Karlov was informed patrons were indulging in à la carte scenes. Karlov knowing how drunk he was requested to first win some money gambling. He bought slots for two thousand euros. In no time, he had string of unbelievable wins. First, he made sixty-four thousand dollars on the roulette corners with barely naked vixens urging to go for more. Next, he placed ten thousand dollars on the blackjack table and won seventy thousand. He was now ahead with close to hundred forty thousand dollars. His good friend Shostov had long disappeared. He couldn't care less about him.

He took a break and was guided to see a nude young couple in action. After about twenty minutes, he went back to the roulette table, and he won eighty thousand dollars. He could not believe his streak. He then requested à la carte private session. He was led to a room where there was a very young couple waiting. He asked to stay with the young man. He remained in the room for the next hour or so he thought. When he was awakened, he was in the back seat of Shostov's limousine in front of the hotel Baltschug Kempinski Moscow. He checked his watch; it was already ten in the morning. He noticed that his winning moneybag was next to him. He checked it; it was still full of money. He thanked his luck and his new lost-and-found friend Shostov for being so gracious to bring him back to the hotel alive with all his winning dough after the big party at the Boheme dacha. He graciously tipped the limousine driver for putting up with him so late. He also asked him to extend his regards to Mr. Shostov. He struggled to get out of the car and back to his hotel room. The ladies were no longer there. He thought that was fine, given his sorry condition he could no longer indulge the ladies. He took off his clothes, took a hot shower, went to bed, and fell asleep. If he knew the extent to which Alexiev and team have gone to mount the charade he went through all night, he would have been better off to go home right away: the middle-aged women who grabbed him at Hungry Duck, Stanilas Shostov, the dacha La Boheme, the casino, the fake sex scenes he saw, the room with the young boy available for à la carte request. All were acts nicely rehearsed by Alexiev; all captured in photos as evidences to put him away for twenty years at minimum, especially the sodomy scenes with the young man of thirteen. The worse part, he was now in possession of two hundred thousand dollars, all fake money he won and that he was proudly distributing. He had already tipped two hotel employees who assisted him to regain his room with the equivalent of fifty dollars. Karlov woke up at about five in the afternoon. The moneybag was still there. He caressed the moneybag. He realized that all that he went through was no dream. He won and got the money at the dacha casino. He counted all his winning. The total was two hundred one thousand and thirty-nine dollars with some other currency bills he could not quite figure out. He reflected that the trip was turning up very good after all. He can now call it quit with BI and Amovir and return to his native city of St. Petersburg to retire quietly. Enough of kissing the ring of Czar Kiriyan. Freedom at last! He felt still very tired again and went back to sleep. Two hours later, he woke up and tried to reach Ludmilla, but she was not answering her phone. He went down to have his late dinner alone. He tipped the waiter and people who got the dinner ready with three fifty-dollar bills. He was back to sleep again at around eleven. Next thing he knew, it was already Monday morning.

Their first meeting was starting at ten in the morning. He called Ludmilla again, but there was no answer. He got ready to go to the meeting. But he still had the sinking feeling of being very tired and indisposed. He went down to have his breakfast at eight thirty. Ludmilla was downstairs in the cafeteria with Alexiev. He joined them. Alexiev asked him how was Saturday night. Karlov answered "Unbelievable." At the same time, two undercover policemen approached their table with the hotel assistant manager. The manager pointed Karlov as the person who had been distributing fake dollar bills since the night before. Karlov tried to protest, but he was handcuffed and led upstairs in his room. Fifteen minutes later, he was led down still handcuffed through the big lobby of the hotel with his suitcases and the moneybag now nicely wrapped in police evidence plastic bag. It was a humiliating scene for the high executive of BI. Ludmilla rushed to the head detective asking what he had done to be arrested. The detective turned around and showed the moneybag inside the plastic bag with dollar bills overflowing. Ludmilla told Karlov that they will come to the police station to find out what had happened and if they can help. Thirty minutes later, Alexiev and Ludmilla came to the station and asked to talk to the station commander.

When the commander received them, he said, "Your colleague was in deep trouble. He could not explain how he came in possession of about two hundred thousand counterfeit dollars. He is either drunk or intoxicated. Everything he is saying does not make sense. He talked about a dacha that does not exist, a casino nobody ever heard of. He is just crazy. He is leaving me no choice. I am about to release him into FSS custody to get to the bottom of this counterfeit money. I have seen a lot of things in my career but nothing like this. This has definitely major financial security implication. He certainly got into very bad company last Saturday night. He has a lot of explaining to do."

When Alexiev and Ludmilla saw him briefly, Karlov had aged suddenly. He was still under the influence and was having trouble speaking. He kept repeating, "I am sorry Ludmilla, I am so sorry." He was in a pitiful state. Ludmilla went back to the hotel and collected her stuff after sending a coded message to Chairman Kiriyan saying mission accomplished. She also changed the hotel and joined her friends Katherina and Helena at the modest Holiday Inn hotel for two days of fun before returning to Amovir. The same Monday night, Alexiev Kramokov recovered his Austrian passport and went back to Vienna from Moscow as Dr. Neal Hansberger.

When Chairman Kiriyan got the full report of the trip and weekend events, he got very worried of the tone of opposition that his last managing director of BI Russian operations revealed to the international expansion of BI. Kiriyan wondered how widespread that opposition was right there in Amovir. He realized that after the intoxication effect had subsided, Karlov would start blabbing the same acerbic xenophobic opposition to his plan of making BI a major international player. He knew that sooner or later; he would get sympathetic hearing with someone within FSS. And no matter how much help he would provide to help him legally and financially, his objective would remain to stop the internationalization of BI. The move to Varonne-Sur-Baie would be the tipping point for all those opposed to his plan. He had no choice but accelerate his Varonne-Sur-Baie move. He would also assist the now much-exposed Ludmilla to rejoin her friend Lady Allistair in London for good.

The humiliation of Karlov Yelgin was turning out to be a Pyrrhic victory for Chairman Kiriyan.

CHAPTER 31
KMC Edict over Corruption

About the same time, a concern of different level visited Patrick Berger in New York. After the trashing he received from his boss for missing out on sharing, revealing important facts regarding Dr. Wasiri's stay in Mezi, he went the next day and had the most cordial meeting with his boss, Lady Allistair. She filled, for his benefit, most of the gaps concerning the underside business of the entire Africa initiatives, including Mezi. She certainly left out the critical factors such as Alpha-M. But Patrick left London with the strong commitment to closely follow the whereabouts of these two main players, Dr. O'Shea and Dr. Wasiri. So Patrick was a bit disturbed when Dr. O'Shea started missing, for no apparent reason, regular staff meetings related to the foundation's important business issues. He was not as much available as he was on regular basis before going to Mezi and London. Dr. O'Shea was also very distant, as if he was preoccupied about some other issues. One evening, after he had missed another staff meeting, Patrick caught up with him late at about ten o'clock. He was not home but eating alone at his favorite steak house restaurant. Patrick reminded him that he had already missed four staff meetings in a row. He wanted to know if there was anything that was bothering him. Dr. O'Shea, who had spent a whole day and evening at the labs of university, testing the Mezi specs, was quiet first, then came with a story about being worried about the health of his granddaughter in Arizona.

He was not about to reveal the specs testing episode. Not to this young wannabe. However, Patrick, showing his sympathy, suggested that he was ready to get a local part-time manager to assist him on important ongoing business issues of the foundation while he was away, paying a visit to his granddaughter and his family in Arizona. That was the last thing he wanted to hear. He cut Patrick short and told him that he would get back to him on this, and if he needed, somebody local he reserves the right to select the help he needs. When he hung up his phone, he realized what an error he made and that he needed to plug it very quickly before Patrick reports his distraction to Lady Allistair who would surely suspect that there was a need to check on his whereabouts. That can blow the cover over the tests he was conducting.

He decided to hire a very reliable local administrative assistant able to provide the cover he would need the next two to three months. He called old academic friends to get good references. He settled on a retired lady who had worked for the School of Mines Engineering and was a very close friend to Emily. The next day, he introduced the lady named Sandy Goshen to Patrick Berger.

All went well from then on. While his mentor was resolving one pressure point, Dr. Wasiri was facing multiple pressure points. The household preparations to return to Mezi took an accelerated rhythm. The house was emptying at a frenetic pace of all unnecessary items which were finding their way either into the rented dustbin or the large freight storages parked outside or the rented storage spaces at the outskirts of the town. Hasbo imposed selection criteria which at times were plain hilarious for the whole family. This particular furniture found its way in the freight storage because it reminded her of a distant stop at a store in Missouri. While this collection of jazz albums was going to go to the storage for the time being until she decides what to do with them although Dr. Wasiri had the same albums in CD format. Dr. Wasiri spared himself all arguments by emptying from his office all his books and academic documents into the freight storage the first time it arrived. As he warned his family when the packing started, "My books or no Mezi." The bare office became now his favorite location when discussions started about to throw or keep an item. As far as he was concerned, they did not need to bring any furniture to Mezi. They will have enough time to pick and choose far less expensive and authentic furniture when they will get there.

They needed to concentrate in buying labor-saving appliances, essential and needed electrical equipment. Hasbo had decided that she wanted to do this last, after a complete inventory of what she would need. She was spending hours on the phone with Anna McMillan about that inventory list. It was very exhausting for Dr. Wasiri. On top of all this, Dr. Wasiri had to help out on conducting tests over the Mezi specs. He decided to concentrate on those as early as possible every morning. He started leaving home at the most unusual hour of five thirty or six in the morning. That afforded him at least two hours of undisturbed test and analysis with complete access to the limited PC necessary to monitor those tests. He increased these hours to about four or five on Saturday and Sunday. He insisted on assisting the old man the last time he expected to work with him. The first weeks of those tests were trying, and he neglected to work on the drafting of the KMC Edict over corruption he was expected to present at that rapidly approaching students conference in April.

When Father Zolani called over the weekend and started sharing the complete agenda of the conference and his own travel plans to come to Washington, DC, Dr. Wasiri got a sense of panic. He pulled all the notes he had taken in Mezi, KMC's various documents, notes taken in the long plane conversation with Professor Awassa, and his own previous notes about the subject. The corruption topic was all over the map with no obvious plan of presentation and redress. He felt a bit defeated, and he had less than fifteen days to come up with a coherent presentation. He literally needed time out of the house to concentrate. He started leaving home at six in the morning to get back after ten at night spending the rest of evening researching materials over corruption at the university main library. Hasbo became concerned seeing how exhausted her husband returned home every day, only to crash in bed, sometimes without eating.

When his wife raised her concern, Dr. Wasiri knew that he probably was going about the development of his draft the worst way possible. Through his lengthy research, he kept going back to the same four major themes around corruption, including lack of abundant financial capital, lack of documentation, lack of positive values, and abuse of power. After a week and a half of looking at the same draft, he decided that the problem was not in the draft. The main issue was the presentation format he was using. No matter how he would go about it, if he would stand there in front of two to three thousand students and give a long lecture about corruption, he would not be able to keep half of these students after thirty minutes, no matter how many examples he comes up with to hold their attention.

The key in such presentation is holding and keeping the students' attention. In fact, in that type of forum, each person had his or her own valid idea of why corruption exists, and each of these ideas would have its own merits. The fact that he would stand there in front of the student body does not make him expert or authority on corruption. That is well known by the students and the speaker. Dr. Wasiri decided to change the format. He would not give a lecture on corruption. He would engage the entire audience to develop the triggers of corruption, summarize them in major categories, and lead a debate about how to address and eliminate those instances of corruption condition. He would need the collaboration of the student organization to change and support the new format. He called Father Zolani and shared with him his new plan and requested that he engaged his contacts in the student movement to support the new format. He added that the success of the new format would strongly depend on maintaining orderly surprises in the execution and guidance of the entire conference.

Surprise in the presentation of the topic, surprise in rearranging the podium, surprise in selection of the audience spokespeople, surprise in collecting the audience inputs, surprise in summarizing of inputs, surprise in finding ways to eliminate instances of corruption, surprise in concluding the conference. Father Zolani agreed readily and shared his concern about the old format.

Father Zolani also apologized that he would not be able to come to Frankfort to visit with him before the conference as they have agreed in Mezi, now that he needs to provide a strong presence among the students to guide the format of the conference a few days before it happens. Dr. Wasiri also decided to show up in Washington, DC, Thursday night before the conference. Father Zolani came to meet with him at the hotel where he was staying, not far from the American University where the Mezi student conference was scheduled to take place. One of the main lectures was the presentation by Dr. Kano Wasiri of KMC Edict over corruption. The reunion of the two KMC leadership members started very warm at the lobby of the hotel. However, he noticed that Father Zolani had already built a following of young assistants around him for the conference, and they came along at this reunion. They stood ready to give him any help he needed. They were surprised to see Dr. Wasiri showing up by himself at this conference.

Dr. Wasiri joked and asked Father Zolani how he had managed to build an entourage in less than two days of his stay. He was surprised and shocked to learn that Father Zolani had traveled with three young assistants, two female and one male, all expenses paid by KMC, as he was proud to state it. Dr. Wasiri then asked the assistants to excuse them for a while, as they were to discuss a very important issue. He took Father Zolani to a far corner of the lobby. He asked him if that was routine to travel using KMC funds. Father Zolani answered that it was the case in Mezi, but this was his first foreign travel under KMC auspices.

He also added that the Mezi student organization had volunteered to pick up a good proportion of these expenses. Dr. Wasiri told Father Zolani that he wished that he knew about those expenses. He would have volunteered paying for his travel expenses alone. He added that he would advise KMC leadership at the end of the reunion on the same night that he would reimburse KMC for all the expenses incurred on behalf of Father Zolani and his assistants. He insisted in an unmistakable tone that as far as the student organization picking up a proportion of Father Zolani's trip expenses, that would not happen.

Dr. Wasiri said that he would appreciate to communicate as quickly as possible to the student organization contacts that there was no need for it to pick up a portion of Father Zolani's and assistants' expenses. Father Zolani was now contrite about the reaction of Dr. Wasiri regarding his travel. He apologized to Dr. Wasiri and told him that he did not think he was going to react so negatively about his trip. Dr. Wasiri stayed firm and said that KMC leadership must show and give the right examples at all the times; otherwise, there would be no purpose giving lessons to anybody anywhere in Mezi. Dr. Wasiri told Father Zolani that his position was not necessarily directed to him personally. He said that he would have reacted as such toward any member of the leadership team if similar expenses under similar conditions were being brought to his attention, and he would have no choice but to show his displeasure around such expenses and to address the issue right away. He would not hide and talk behind his back. He would, without hesitation, let him know right away how displeased he was. He took Father Zolani alone upstairs to his room to continue their private talk and told him that Father Zolani had to pay a lot of attention to perceptions he created around him.

He added, "How can he travel from Mezi to Washington, DC, to a conference about corruption and make KMC spend its little financial resources on him and three other young assistants, while at the same time requesting that the organization holding the conference to pitch in for a portion of the same expense? My dear Father, that is mad and maddening! It is one thing to engage KMC into spending money over yourself and three companions, another to ask the student organization to contribute somehow.

Please think hard about the perception in this matter. Is it not the same thing we in KMC are preaching against? The same wasteful spending KMC speaks about and that goes on daily basis in various institutions of our country. Tell me, does it make it right if it happens within KMC? Should KMC not uphold the same principles it is promoting on daily basis? If you want to tell me that this was discussed and agreed to at a KMC leadership team meeting, well, I have to tell you that I strongly disagree with that decision, and I would let the team know my position."

Father Zolani protested, "Brother Kano, I did not say that this was decided by KMC leadership. I told the leadership that I was coming here, and I would advise them about the total expenses of my trip when I would be back. That is when they would reimburse me for all expenses incurred. The student organization had volunteered to pick up some expenses and that is perfectly normal.

If you are upset about me bringing three assistants, I understand your outrage, but you do not know how much work and commitment it is needed to deliver a well-run conference or lecture. Brother Kano, I did not come here to undermine KMC message. Far from it, I came here to support your work on behalf of KMC. I am so sorry that my support is not being appreciated at this time."

Dr. Wasiri would not back down. "Father Zolani, maybe, just maybe all that you are doing are with the best intentions. Maybe, just maybe, you never intended to destroy KMC image. Why would you do it? You live and breathe KMC promotion, day in, day out. But this is exactly what we have to guard ourselves. When we live and breathe KMC activities, we may start doing things in the name of living and breathing KMC, whether doing so supports or does not support KMC cause. That, my brother Father Zolani, is what we have to guard against. I am raising this today here and in our own privacy, and as you can see, there is nobody else but two of us. I am not screaming at the ceiling. I am addressing this to you at this time, at this instant so you can appreciate what I am driving at."

Father Zolani went and sank on the room sofa and reflected at what his colleague dropped on him. He sat there for about five minutes and had tears coming down his eyes. Then he looked at Brother Wasiri and said, "I had a lot of reservation about you coming to KMC leadership. I never understood why my friend Father, now Monsignor Felix, Chancellor Umzigwe, and Dean Wutugrase insisted so much to bring you on board. I went along with the move anyway, hoping that somewhere I should be able to grasp and join their position. Brother Kano, today, I realize and appreciate what they were looking for and why they have done everything, I mean, everything to bring you aboard KMC leadership. It is clear to me at this moment why you could not have come soon enough. I thank you for the counsel. Now what do you want me to do about these three assistants?"

Dr. Wasiri came and held Father Zolani's hands and pulled him to stand up and told him, "Father Zolani, believe me, it is not my fight that is being waged here. It is KMC's fight. It is Mezi's fight. Let us wage it in a positive, distinguished, and transparent way for all to honor and follow. We got a lot to do. You will talk to the young assistants and request that they lie very very low throughout the conference as good guests. And this is between only the two of us here. I would take care of all expenses of the young assistants from Mezi to DC and back. Please, not a word of this to them or KMC leadership team."

After Father Zolani had freshened up his face, the two KMC leadership team members went downstairs in the lobby where the young assistants were patiently waiting. Dr. Wasiri announced that he was inviting everybody to come and eat at this terrific Chinese restaurant he knows somewhere in downtown DC. The Mezi folks joined him in the SUV he was renting for the conference stay. They spent the rest of the evening reminiscing about news from Mezi. The young assistants were amazed to be in company of the man who led the famous H5 Exchange.

When asked if he feared for his life in the presence of General Gwobozo, Brother Kano answered, "Who would not be, my dear, in the presence of heavily armed men, aggravated and fearing for their own life! I gained more confidence only when I realized that the whole episode was being taped. Still, all that time I kept thinking, great it is being taped but what if the general was to give orders to shoot me, then what purpose will that taping serve? You see, it is easy to do today what it is called here in the United States "Monday Morning Quarterbacking," in other words, replay the game and find all the right moves to win on Monday morning the game that had been played on Sunday. When you are faced with the danger or death, it is completely a different situation. You act and pray for one and one thing only—survival. I did not do any extraordinary thing but what any person in similar conditions would do, that is to survive. With the grace of God, it worked, and I am sharing these delicious dishes with you."

Dr. Wasiri proceeded to ask and to engage the young assistants in all kinds of questions regarding Mezi, its institutions, the future electoral process, and its future with or without KMC leadership. The very high level of political maturity and their strong commitment to KMC ideals struck him. He got close to apologize to Father Zolani for insinuating bad perceptions for bringing along on this trip young assistants of such outstanding caliber. But he would not revise nor change his mind about the bigger picture that KMC must support to avoid bad perceptions. They left the restaurant very late and went back to their respective hotels in the American University vicinity.

The next day was dedicated to meeting again with the conference organizers. The new format will require remote wireless audiovisual equipment with very high performance standard. They were not available at the university. Dr. Wasiri chose to pay for a highly recommended dedicated service company ready to project, monitor, and tape on remote wireless audio and visual format everything that was going to happen during the conference.

The session was even tested for about twenty minutes from the podium to the last row in the auditorium of close to three thousand people. Satisfied with the session performance, Dr. Wasiri called it a day at about eight at night and again invited Father Zolani, the Mezi folks, and some student organization leaders to a seafood restaurant in Washington, DC. On Saturday, the Mezi student organization was happy and proud to have invited two of the illustrious KMC leadership team members to its conference. When the scheduled lecture about corruption was about to start, more than three thousand students jammed the auditorium; the overflowing crowd was guided to an adjoining smaller auditorium, which filled as quickly as the first one. This auditorium also had large monitors needed to follow the proceedings from the first main auditorium. There were also students from other African countries in attendance, at least those who have been following what had recently taken place in Mezi. The main auditorium erupted in ovations when the Mezi Student Organization leader introduced the KMC invited guests. First, Father Zolani was introduced and whose notoriety needed not to be established among students back home and abroad. When Dr. Wasiri was introduced, he received a long outstanding welcome, with students singing the KMC lead song, the same that was sung the first time during the airport celebration. The monitor projected both the airport celebration as well as the Cast Away Summit captions while the KMC lead song was being played. This introduction took about ten minutes. Father Zolani stood up and invited Dr. Wasiri to start the lecture.

"Brothers and Sisters, I come to you today with warm greetings from our brothers and sisters back home in Mezi under the shining light and banner of KMC. I thank you for the warm welcome you addressed to our Brother Father Zolani who took time from his tremendous work to advance the cause of KMC in the trenches of Mezi to be with us today here in this splendid establishment of the American University in Washington, DC. Please join me in extending our warm and loud thank-you to Father Zolani. I want also to equally extend the same warm and loud thank-you note to the Mezi Student Organization and its leadership for having the forthright notion to hold this conference and gathering the future of Mezi in this location. Our special thank-you note goes to this organization for never stopping to engage you, the students, in the building of Mezi today and tomorrow. Talking about engaging you students, I hope the Mezi Student Organization would allow me at this time to borrow and use its engaging methods and steps. You see when I came here, I was thinking about standing here and talking about corruption for the next two or so hours.

At the end of this, you were going to ask me questions, and I was going to, to the best of my ability, answer them. And we would call it quit and go home to your studies for most of you students in this auditorium, our teaching for me, well, I am after all a professor at Kentucky State University, our promotion of KMC principles for Father Zolani back in Mezi, or back to whatever we were doing before coming here today. And guess what, all that I would have said or spit out here the next two hours would be what, now do not hesitate to say it, and my pride or whatever is left of it would not be shot. Now repeat after me, all that I would have said or spit out here for the next two hours would be . . ." And the attendees shot back what the big monitor was flashing, "Lost and Forgotten." Dr. Wasiri yielded, "Repeat" and the audience said, "Lost and Forgotten." Dr.

Wasiri continued, "I don't think we want that kind of outcome when we come here today. Not Father Zolani from Mezi, certainly not me from Frankfort, Kentucky, not that young man who told me yesterday he came from Birmingham, Alabama, not these two beautiful young women who told me that they drove from Toronto, Canada, nor this group of students who pulled their savings together to rent the minibus to come from Bloomington, Indiana, or the other group of students who drove from Tallahassee, Florida, and more. I know and I would say this because I was of your age too and a student as well. I know that when we found ourselves in such gatherings, our minds can sometimes go wild. It is time to touch basis with this one or that one. It is time to touch basis with this girlfriend or that boyfriend. It is, let us be honest, well, also party time later on. I know that and I understand it. But as I say all that would come up later. So in the meantime, we got to make our meeting count and count in the way that it would not be lost and forgotten. That is why as I say there would be no lecture today. There would be no me standing in front of you and telling about things you probably know more or better than I do. I am about to change the format of this conference.

"I want each one of you to be engaged and to build the KMC Edit over corruption. Now tell me if you agree or not with the change." The audience responded loud, "We do." Dr. Wasiri walked the long of the podium to get the audience to repeat, "We do," four or five times. Dr. Wasiri took over the lectern again and started to give guidance over how the engagement would proceed. "You would be engaged in whichever way you would feel comfortable with, through mike by going to people walking around with remote wireless mikes and giving you input, through hand-held electronic tables distributed in the auditorium by entering manually your input. You would be engaged in one of two languages you feel comfortable to communicate with, English or Swahili.

And finally, do not feel that you need to give or sign your name when you are talking or entering your input. Your privacy is definitely assured. You would entertain every one of your input and as long as it would take. The first series of input we need to gather from you would be this "What do you think are the triggers of corruption in Mezi, what do you think breeds corruption in Mezi?" Feel free to either write your answer on the electronic table or approach the remote wireless mike when you are ready to give your input orally. The selection of speakers is done randomly any time you press the yellow button in front of you. The selection of those willing to write their answer will be done when you press the blue button in front of you. Believe me when I say that everyone willing to say or write will be given the chance to do so. I am now giving you about ten minutes to think through your answers. By the way, people in the next auditorium have exactly the same opportunity to be engaged as those here in this auditorium." When the ten minutes delay was up, Dr. Wasiri learned that there were already about three hundred twenty-four entries through the electronic tables while about fifty-six people were lined to give their input. The large monitor started displaying the electronic input while the speakers were called one after another in both auditoriums to give their input. Every time the speaker provided their input orally, it was entered electronically until the speaker was satisfied with the interpretation or translation of the input. At times, the speakers were plainly hilarious; in other cases, specific examples were provided to the general consternation of the audiences. Female student speakers provided most of specific incidents around the moral and financial corruption they faced back home and, in some cases, still continued to face within the same Mezi student community right here in the States or Canada.

One female student took the opportunity to give her own testimony of living the life of prostitute in Mandi to raise enough money to come to Canada to continue her academic career. She shocked the audience by revealing that she was about to complete her PhD degree in molecular biology and to go back to teach at the same university in Mandi which had denied her college entrance on the grounds that she was too poor and did not have enough references from the very big shots and elite who were abusing her days and nights. She was ready to go back and walk into each one of these big shots to show her hard-earned PhD degree. The lady was carrying her bearings high and proud. She did not shed a single tear while the whole audience was listening in silence and the younger female students were sobbing quietly. She concluded by advising her sisters to never give in to nay trumpeters who always get their account in time of dreams differed.

She added that her sisters should wait to confront these worthless abusers in time for dreams realized the way she would very soon. The lady was warmly applauded and embraced by a long range of students before getting back to her seat.

Another illustrated case came from a young man who told about the process whereby a well-known general managed to loot his family's large farm in the province of Chelow during a period of fifteen years with impunity to the point that the entire family had no other choice but to abandon the farm and flee from Mezi. The family is currently dispersed around South Africa, England, and the United States. Both of his parents have died as penniless heartbroken refugees in Zambia. The student wondered aloud what he had to come back to in Mezi now.

The speeches got more personal and tragic one after another until the last one. By the time Dr. Wasiri took the lectern again, the audience was physically drained. A fifteen minutes break was taken while the inputs were grouped along major categories.

Dr. Wasiri took back his lecture seat, "Brothers and sisters, now you see why I could not have done justice to each of you who contributed your input if I had given you a straight-line lecture on corruption. I would not have been able to bring the same eloquence and authenticity to your poignant stories as you did even if I have tried to stand here and relate your stories. As I say, in this context of corruption, each one of us has her or his own story, only each one of us can bring in a manner that is sometimes very personal, and believe me, all the times very painful. As I sit here, nowhere and at no time did I hear a happy story. It is always hurtful and painful because at the end, we all come out very much diminished and nullified. At this time I want to ask each one of you to stand up and give a resounding thank-you applause to all who were kind enough and brave enough to share their story and to give their input. When you are done, I also want each one to turn to the person next to you to extend your thank-you for sharing his or her story. Now we can continue our meeting.

When we look at the monitor above and or the one close to you, you will see how your colleagues have summarized all the inputs you have shared with us into various categories. We see about ten main different categories, where they grouped about five hundred or so inputs. This is an awesome listing that was raised here, and KMC leadership must be very thankful for this. Let us review it together and see if we are in the same wavelength. In fact, this is the time when I start pushing back and pretending to know something about this topic.

Brothers and sisters, do not feel compelled to agree with me. Please, push s back whenever you think those of us up here in the podium are way off the target. I have first to warn that as we go over the listing, we would notice that sometimes the triggers are listed as causes of corruption, and some other times, the triggers are listed as effects of corruption. For instance, without negating the impact of this particular trigger, let us take the case of lack of job.

Lack of job becomes a trigger for corruption when one talks of lack of compensation or salary that must compensate the job. If you work for nothing, that is charity, and you should not become liable to be corrupted. If you work, and you are not compensated duly, then your employer is stealing your rightful compensation for job. This is another case to deal with later, an abomination of corruption. But when you do not have job, then you are not receiving any salary, and then you become fully open to corruption. So in this case, lack of job leading to lack of salary leads to a trigger for corruption. I hope you are all following where this is going.

On the other side, when you look very closely at lack of job, it works to lack of employment, to lack of means of employment, to lack what the experts want to identify as a major trigger of corruption, and which is lack of abundant financial capital. I am certain that it was mentioned somewhere here. Yes, it was and probably by one learned student of economics. Lack of abundant financial capital, as you would see, is a major trigger of corruption.

A lot of cases you mentioned go back to that lack of abundant financial capital. Lack of job, prostitution, corruption of minors, money in the hands of a few, lack of good infrastructures, and so on, anytime you link corruption to money or lack of it, you are basically talking about one major trigger of corruption: the fact that there is no abundant source of financial capital to fund and pay for means of production of goods and services. I would also submit that the lack of abundant financial capital is very close to another major category that was mentioned, that is the lack of documentation.

Let us think about this a little bit. We know that without financial capital, corruption is king. But when you have financial capital and start funding all kinds of means of production, the next roadblock to do it right is basically good documentation. The lack of thereof is a trigger of corruption, because the lack of documentation triggers another source of corruption, which is lack of accountability.

Documentation supports accountability. But that does not mean that corruption is eliminated. Let's go back to the framework, you got abundant financial capital that funds means of production within an environment of documentation that supports both transparency and accountability. However, you still have predominant bad practices born out of poor values system. That is in my view a third layer of corruption trigger. When a society is mired in a system of values that are twisted, then corruption would take hold no matter what. I am talking here about our own values system. I am talking here about the so-called traditions, which dominate our lives in Mezi. Now let us be careful and clear here. There are good and bad traditions. I rather say there are good and very bad traditions in our society. Some of these traditions create a system of values, which promote corruption. You know those traditions.

One that comes to my mind is to see how when a founder of a growing enterprise dies in our society. The relatives come to the funeral not to honor his growing enterprise, but to dispossess the inheriting family of the capital that had made the enterprise flourish in the first place. It does not take long for the enterprise to go bankrupt after a few months, putting the employees out of work and insuring that the whole chain of productive capacity is broken. We cry as much as we want about the people of North not willing to invest in our country and so on. But what if the now bankrupt enterprise was supposed to support a chain of production in Berlin in Germany, Toulouse in France, or Leeds in UK? Would the people in North come back to such negative industrial terrain? Absolutely not! You see in this framework I have designed so far, we went from the first main category, lack of financial capital, which in most cases in our country, is exogenous, that is it must come from outside most of the time. The next category, lack of documentation, must come from both outside and from inside our own environment. The value system category is purely endogenous. This comes and depends on our own traditions and us. This category is looking at us right here in this auditorium. The lack of a good value system is nobody's fault but our own. I like to summarize the framework now at ten thousand feet categories.

We talked about three major categories: lack of financial capital, lack of documentation, and lack of good value systems I want to ask this question to all of you listening to me at this time in these two auditoriums: do you think we would have eliminated corruption in Mezi if we had brought definite remedy to these three categories? Those who think yes, please hit the yellow button; those who think no, please hit the red button; maybe please hit the blue button.

Now the yes had about 78 percent, the no had 16 percent, the maybe had 6 percent. Brothers and sisters, I would go with the 6 percent, maybe.

When I survey the five hundred or so input, I did not see any item or input related to the last category, I believe you must always insist on the fight against corruption. As a matter a fact, you must insist on this category anytime you push for any reform, economic, political, and social or otherwise, anywhere including Mezi. This category establishes the right to recall against all put in place and trust of doing any public service.

Let us go back again in our framework: corruption is eliminated, or so we think, when abundant financial capital is made available under orderly documentation environment of a wonderful value system. Everybody is happy. However, sometime later, as it is always the case in any human system, there appear some cracks in the system because those entrusted to carry the society's torch, those entrusted to lead start showing . . . some chips on their shoulders. This is the last category of corruption when power starts corrupting the leaders and where absolute power corrupts absolutely.

Brothers and sisters, this last category pertains not to the audience but to the podium. When those in the podium have changed the last social order of things, they have established more positive and progressive ways of governing, they have managed the country's means of production in an excellent fashion, the results from their management of public goods are outstanding, they are bringing the most positive élans throughout the society, but they start also believing in their own tune and self-rightness. That is the last category all of us need to guard against in the audience and in the podium, in Washington, DC, or Mandi, in Komesah or Mezi, in KMC or without. That is the time we have to request to be guarded against our own guardians whether they are from the army or from KMC. Human history is full of those instances of corruption, do not think in one instance that we in Mezi would somewhat be exempted unless we insist that our leaders are accountable, not just to those in KMC but also to the whole population of Mezi. That is the framework of corruption I wanted to share with you.

"Now the question is how KMC intends to address these failings. I would submit at a very high level that KMC must, above all, be devising an economic policy that attracts financial capital abundant enough to fund a lot of means of production in the country, giving jobs, jobs, jobs.

Without this first endeavor, KMC does not need to be in place or running candidates for any political position anywhere in the country. Providing jobs must be the first and paramount objective of KMC. It would not serve any purpose for KMC to make a lot of noises, only to fall in the same quagmire as all those who preceded it in power. If there were no financial capital, there would be no job. Of course, with time and with financial capital, the lack of documentation should be remedied. The lack of good value system will not be easy to address as this would call for upsetting a lot of longtime-held bad behavior. However, leaving those bad traditions in place would eventually lead to reverse the gains made in accessing abundant financial capital and commanding outstanding documentation practices. We will have no choice but engage the traditional chiefs in reversing bad traditions and keeping the good ones while insuring that their power has remained uncontested. This is as much I wanted to share with you today, and I would now entertain any question you have for me. Thank you."

The first question was the following, "How much internally versus externally Mezi needs to raise the financial capital?"

Dr. Wasiri answered, "Let us be clear about what I said. There is a definite lack of abundant financial capital in Mezi. If there was a way to raise it internally, we should have done so long time ago. The fact is that we cannot raise internally as much financial capital as we need to jump-start our economy. Now we certainly have resources such as minerals, vast agricultural spaces, and people ready to be employed. What are missing are equipment to be funded by financial capital, money. When you have equipment, then you can extract minerals to export and irrigate large farms for agricultural production for export. While you use these equipment, you need people to work on these equipment and to move the mining and agricultural products to different markets and exportation. One thing is clear is that you attract financial capital when you promised a certain compensation to the capital to be used. This is what you hear all the time, and it is called return on the capital. This is not nuclear science here. A lot of mystification has been created around this concept of return on capital. There is no question that there has been abuse on the part of holders of financial capital requesting exorbitant return on financial capital deployed in Mezi. But a closer review of documentations around the so-called exorbitant return on capital has clearly revealed time and again the following: 'the exorbitant return on capital included a risk rate summarizing corruption clauses designed to enrich the local elite in charge of signing the exorbitant rate return contracts.' What has happened the past thirty years in Red China has confirmed this.

If financial capital deployed in China included exorbitant return on capital as the one decried in our country, I don't think PRC would have made as rapid and deep economic advance as anybody can see today. PRC, as red and communist as anybody knows, made terrific use of the abundant financial capital that was provided for about twenty-five years. It is ironic that PRC was able to do this, thanks to the strict discipline in the execution of a strategy initiated by the very Communist Party leadership so detested and vilified for more many years by the holders of financial capital.

"What has changed was the meeting of a common purpose from both the PRC leadership and the holders of financial capital. The common purpose was the agreement to compensate the holders of financial capital for an accepted rate of return. What was telling was the consistent and determined unity of purpose that PRC leadership has shown through and through. The rest is history. It is obvious now that those who have deployed that financial capital have received a profitable return on their capital all along, so much so that today PRC enterprises are ready to play the same 'capitalist rate on return game' in Mezi and throughout Africa as any French, British, American, Italian, and Japanese capitalist company. Still the mystification over return on capital has continued here in Mezi and in Africa.

"The issue has nothing to do with the rate of return on capital. It has all to do with our own elite always eager to sell out and take out personal gain or profit on business projects of national interest. The same elite is quick to manipulate the native population with misguided lies about foreign exploitation of our natural resources any time they were prevented to pass those corruption clauses in contracts with American, French, or other Western companies. The greedy elite did not care much about the collapsing of their country's economy as long as it maintained their power and their share of ever-meager profit. And after ten or twenty years of leaving their resources unexploited, we have not heard the same elite scream about the foreign exploitation when in desperation they start giving away the same natural resources to PRC enterprises at less than the going rate of return on capital.

As I say, we have to decide how and when we should play the rate of return on capital games as astutely as anybody else. That is your charge, I believe, you are learning the steps and methods. Do not hesitate to use them when you are trusted to do so for Mezi but always and only in the national interest. PRC has shown us what other nations have been telling us all along: 'In international business exchanges, there is nothing more sacred but national business interest.'

We have also learned for a long time now that every time there is an international crisis, major powers do not deploy their might for the benefits of people of Mezi, Chad, Bangladesh, Morocco, Congo, Thailand, Vietnam, Paraguay, Ecuador, Nigeria, or Haiti. Absolutely Not! When USA deploys its forces it is for USA, France for France, Russia for Mother Russia, PRC for PRC, and every time for their national interest. Anything else is beautiful speech good to amuse the UN halls. As long we are not ready to internalize that concept, we will continue to swim endlessly in our underdevelopment quagmire. Brothers and sisters, we need to wake up and bury these mystifications, these zombies, and all of these useless myths, which have kept us in development limbo for so long. We need to wake up to a consistent and determined unity of purpose to break the cycle of underdevelopment forever."

The next question came to ask when is Dr. Wasiri going home? He answered, "Not soon enough."

Another question alluded to changing our traditions, how far we need to go? Dr. Wasiri said, "As far as our daily lives would allow it. It is obvious that change would come faster in urban centers than in villages. In some respects, we would have to enter those changes in the form of laws. This would prevent uneven and unequal application of reforms we want to see implemented. But as I have said it, it would not be easy. We need to seriously engage those whom the traditions impact the most, the traditional chiefs. Believe me, from what I have noticed lately, at least in my interaction with some of them, they want to see Mezi gets rid of bad traditions as quickly as possible. For your information, tribal chiefs get their authority out of consensus of people. If anyone of you in this auditorium is nourishing the ambition to become a traditional chief, please come and talk to me after this meeting. It is not a task earned after a class of Advanced Mathematics or Philosophy. It is earned by judicial and consistent delivery of pronouncements concerning very complicated human transactions and without the benefit of written laws, but excellent judgment and oral traditions. And this is done with the assistance of a council of elders. It is not dictatorship there. The fact that the chief has to gain the approval of the council on every pronouncement gives the overall process a system of checks and balances that is the envy of our own political institutions. Anyway, I saw how they were deliberating during the Cast Away Summit ceremony; it was admirable how they reached their consensus, of course after many gives-and-takes. But consensus was reached nevertheless. If they can come to the Cast Away Summit, I do not see why they would not be disposed to come to any other meeting where they would get rid of bad traditions.

The key again is to engage them seriously. Now I need also to clarify something here. When I have mentioned a good value system, I am also talking of good values that emasculate and put to rest one of the terrifying scourges in Africa. You know what I am talking about here. It is tribalism, sectarianism, ethnocentrism, or whenever we start believing in the superiority of our ethnic group over another. I am sorry to say it, but it is being displayed right here in this auditorium, maybe not overtly but it is there. Anytime you frown your face when hearing another person's ethnic dialect you don't understand, it is there. Anytime and for apparent no reason you ask for the village of origin to a school colleague, it is there. Anytime, when a friend drops by, you lower your voice to talk to your cousin in your dialect, it is there. Anytime you start displaying some strange attitudes when you have just learned that your girlfriend or your boyfriend is from a different tribe, it is there. Anytime you start playing hide-and-seek when a parent is visiting from home and you don't want to introduce your longtime friend to this parent, it is there. I can go on forever. And you also need to add to tribalism, the scourges of racism and xenophobia. All these negative values work to strengthen corruption because they foster impunity. When we are motivated by tribalism, racism, or xenophobia, we are quick to overlook small and big awful deeds perpetrated by those, we believe, who belong to our privileged circle. I am always amazed, and I found it utterly tragic when I hear folks from Mezi or Africa complain about and decry murder, beating, and other alike criminal acts against blacks in the United States by white racists, but they would not raise one finger about or decry massacres that their own ethnic people have perpetrated against other ethnic people. The same folks, who would scream at the white racists, are completely silent about atrocities reported in their country or region. Brothers and sisters, murder is murder. Whether it is committed in the back alley of Louisville, Kentucky, in the shantytown of Komesah, Mandi, in the long ravine of Kiribati, Nairobi, or in the bar of Matonge, Kinshasa. Murder is murder and needs to be punished equally. Giving comfort to criminals because they belong to own tribe is worse than the crime itself. That is why I said that when it comes to good value system, we have a lot to do."

The meeting had progressed past closing time and the Student Organization leader was sending signals to Father Zolani to close the presentation. It was about eight thirty when Father Zolani approached the lectern and advised Brother Kano to pull back. He told the still eager young audience that the meeting was over and thanked them for their active participation. He assured them that their input would find their way into the KMC Edict over corruption that is being drafted and would be published soon.

He thanked the Student Organization for the wonderful conference and thanked Brother Kano for guiding the meeting through difficult and memorable sequences.

KMC hymn was sung for the closing ceremony. Brother Kano and Father Zolani were mobbed by the students asking additional questions or simply convey their sincere thanks for the excellent presentation. When they were able to do so, the two KMC leadership members retired to an Ethiopian restaurant with the Student Organization leadership team for further exchange of opinions. The owner of the restaurant greeted them warmly and guided them to a private eating room. He surprised them by offering free meals. He told Brother Kano that he was at the conference and was so impressed by his presentation that he cried. He told him to keep it up. The eating party shared the dinner until about two in the morning discussing again various Mezi national and international topics.

The next day, Dr. Wasiri joined the Mezi folks for a late breakfast. He had another private meeting with Father Zolani who had already collected the entire taped audiovisual conference and the presentation text files. The Student Organization and the audiovisual company hired for the event had done an excellent job in capturing all the conference events and downloading them into CD and DVD formats. Dr. Wasiri was given a stack of about six DVDs and three CDs. He was able to leave the American University area at around three, saying good-bye to Father Zolani and his cohort. He reached home at around seven thirty after about two hours flight from DC. When he got home, he was a bit overwhelmed by all that needed to be done before his flight back to Mezi at the beginning of May and ahead of his entire family expected to reach Mandi by the end of May. He was expected to be in Mandi by middle of May for the retirement of Dean Wutugrase and his investiture as new dean of Applied Sciences Faculty at Polytechnic University. Chancellor Umzigwe had carefully coordinated his return to coincide with the big Mezi Women's Congress to take place the third week of May at the Free University of Mezi in the country's second largest town of Ikando in the northern province of Kiesse. Hasbo had postponed most freight shipping until May. So Dr. Wasiri thought that Hasbo would find herself without proper guidance or control of all that needed to be shipped to Mandi.

At this stage, he was reassured that his main documents and books were already in the largest freight storage in the parking lot. He would pray that all he would need in Mandi would be made available.

As far as his tests of Alpha-M went, he had completed all the required tests, and they pointed to Alpha-M in the 99.99999 percentage range from the DNA and time range analysis. As expected, the DNA map of close to twenty pages showed a lot of unknown or undefined components. He was going to turn all these results to his mentor. He won't be able, however, to conduct the applications tests Dr. O'Shea requested. He would not have the time or the facilities to do these tests. He had scaled back as much as he could of his tenured professorship function at Kentucky State University. His boss, the school dean, was more than supportive of the transition to a young professor from the University of Oklahoma. They had exchanged materials and schedule and list of supporting PhD students' works. He had also already graded all the student papers for the June graduating students. His concern was the packing and the shipping of the household stuff. He worried that Hasbo may not be up to the task. He raised the concern with Hasbo who was expecting it and was ready for the argument. She stopped him cold by suggesting that all he had to do from that day on was to take care of himself before taking the plane for Mandi and leaving her to worry about the rest. The next day he went to the University of Kentucky to meet with his mentor at the labs. He gave him all of the results from his tests, and they matched perfectly with his results. Dr. O'Shea told him not to worry about the remaining tests. He had not planned to complete them by the end of May anyway. Dr. O'Shea said that he would keep him informed about the results he would get, and he believed that so far they were in the right path.

He urged his protégé to spend the rest of his remaining days to pack and cuddle his wife before his final departure. She would need it. Before leaving, Dr. Wasiri surprised his mentor with another spec of Alpha-M gift. He said that he had kept it hoping to complete the rest of his tests with it. Now that he was about to leave, he did not think that he would need the spec anymore.

Besides, he joked, "We got plenty of those in the high plateaus of Mezi." Dr. O'Shea was shocked that his protégé was treating the spec so casually. He quickly hid it in his worn attached case.
He then said, "You don't know how many people could get killed by some very bad people to get this spec." Dr. Wasiri laughed, "Well, it is now in your hands, the all three specs. This way, the very bad people would not bother my family. Just the same I would see you soon."

CHAPTER 32
Back to Mezi

As soon as his protégé departed, Dr. O'Shea jumped in his car and was driving toward the bank where he was renting a safe. But on his way, he thought better and changed his mind. He went to another bank not far from the one he had used. He opened another account and rented a new bank safe where he deposited the new spec. He knew that two bank safes would increase the likelihood that one of them would not fall into the wrong hands. For some strange reasons, Dr. O'Shea had the feeling that a treasure hunt of frenetic murderous kind would take place the minute that his possession of Alpha-M specs is known. Each day, he became more than obsessive of that feeling, he became outright paranoid. He stopped doing all his routines. He became more reclusive and unwilling to talk on phone except with his family and the Wasiri family. Even Sandy Goshen, the lady he hired to put Patrick Berger at bay, became the object of deep suspicion. When she started working in the house, he advised her to use the kitchen and other facilities anytime she wanted.

One day when he returned home before her quitting time and found her looking for a water bottle opener in the kitchen, Dr. O'Shea erupted and accused her of snooping all over his house. The lady was shocked and told him that she was not going to take any verbal abuse from him or anyone and that she was going to resign her job on the spot. Soon after Dr. O'Shea realized how stupid he had acted and begged her to forgive him. Ms. Goshen got very confused by his behavior and advised him to have a medical check for signs of amnesia or worse. Dr. O'Shea begged her not to mention the incident to anybody. He claimed that he had been working a little bit too much on this particular research at the university, and he probably was upset that the research results were not coming out as expected. Sandy Goshen told him, as a very good friend of his late wife, she was not going to denounce him in one and only condition that he submitted to a medical checkup and she was willing to take him to have as many medical tests as possible to make sure that he was not coming up with a dangerous medical case of amnesia or Alzheimer's. Dr. O'Shea submitted to the checkup and all the tests came out negative. Sandy Goshen was reassured and dropped the matter altogether.

Sandy Goshen decided that the good old professor was probably suffering from being alone all the time, and she was going to be more than an administrative assistant but a devoted life companion without any intimacy intent. Dr. O'Shea went along with the intrusion for a while until he was able to impose a great deal of limits to preserve Emily rules and the sanctity of his love for Emily. At the same time, Dr. O'Shea was making great progress in the phase of his validation tests. The application tests he had devised in the computer models before his retirement, the probable application tests that his protégé summarized in his PhD thesis, all these tests were being equally validated one after another. The euphoria from the results and the resulting paranoid condition were probably the reason he was set off that day when he got angry with Sandy Goshen. He constantly reminded himself that victory was getting so close at hand; he had to keep everything to himself. He made Sandy's attempt so difficult that she pulled back from the life companion trial. She kept to her daily job. She was paid more than generously, more than she was ever paid throughout her life. She enjoyed the salary and did not want to lose it. The daily routine was very light except when Patrick had scheduled his weekly staff meeting. When Dr. O'Shea was home, he led the meeting. When he was away to whatever he was doing at the university, Sandy was around just to listen and take notes over all kinds of topics that Patrick was talking about. The meeting lasted no more than two hours. Lately, there were a lot of questions around the new residences at that university in Africa. Dr. O'Shea wanted to get them completed by May for some reasons.

The new residences were progressing nicely. But Dr. O'Shea was still not happy of the work evolution of the new residences. He put a lot of pressure on Patrick and his right-hand man in Africa, a Dr. McMillan. This is the same environment that Dr. Wasiri would find out when he would reach Mandi. But before that, he spent a very busy two weeks period before his departure. There were two or three farewell parties from the university staff, close friends, and neighbors he had to attend. Dr. O'Shea was not to be left out. He took the entire family for a whole Sunday recreation party from breakfast to a late dinner. The kids loved it, Hasbo was tearful most of time and tried to hide it, and Dr. Wasiri was silent as usual and reflecting with pride all that the old man, his adoptive father, had done for him and his family and would continue to do in the future. He told the whole family that they need to keep a promise to Uncle Tony, as he loved to be referred to by the Wasiri kids. The promise was to welcome him in less than a year in Mandi and take him on a tourist tour around the Nyerengi Lake. Dr. O'Shea was teary throughout until when he was dropped off home.

The day of departure, a Saturday, Hasbo made arrangement to have Dr. O'Shea come with the entire family to Louisville International Airport; that gave the two scientists time to iron out some last-minute deals. There was none. Dr. O'Shea avoided talking to his protégé. He spent the whole ride telling jokes to the kids about school works, sport, movies, or TV shows.

The only thing he managed to say in whispers to Dr. Wasiri when they were separating was, "Son, Keep Emily rules shining like Kany."

That shook Dr. Wasiri to the core, and he finally released the tears he had been holding up all that time during the long ride to the airport. He held the old man very tightly to his own family's admiration and kissed each child and his wife so tenderly. His eyes were so red that he needed to refresh himself two times before boarding the plane to Chicago, then the flight to London, and finally to Mandi. The long flight to Mandi was smooth and a nonevent. The plane landed very late at night, and the arrival was very quiet, nothing like the last one.

Still the whole KMC leadership team was at hand at the VIP section to welcome him, and he was brought to the same Tanzire Hotel complex. This time, he was going to occupy a huge townhouse. There were further, in the back of the hotel, a series of townhouses leading to the Tanzire Hotel lake embankment. The townhouses were for rent to people with long-term residency requirements in Mandi, mainly business people and sometimes university professors.

The townhouse was set for a medium-sized family like Dr. Wasiri's. It was very functional and extremely convenient, so Dr. Wasiri thought. As soon as he was done with the guided tour of the townhouse and he was finally left alone, Dr. Wasiri called his family to advise them that he made OK to Mandi and already missed them and could not stop from thinking so much about them and Dr. O'Shea. He closed by blowing a lovely kiss to each one of the family members. It was about four in the evening in Frankfort, Kentucky.

The next day was used to recuperate from the long flight, and Dr. Wasiri was invited per Hasbo's instruction to Dr. McMillan's house for a dinner and to get a preliminary review of Hasbo's household inquiries. When they were settled in the living room, Dr. Wasiri told the old chancellor that he was lucky not to worry about the intricacies of household like he was to be.

He asked if the McMillans were willing to exchange their household with the beautiful townhouse he was renting; this way, Hasbo would have a ready-made house with every item she had argued about with Anna during their long international telephone calls. He also joked saying that the board of his Frankfort local telephone company would be sending a note to Chancellor Umzigwe requesting that he (Wasiri) remain in Frankfort until year-end to keep their profitable telephone line because of the international calls Hasbo had been making. During the dinner, Dr.

McMillan gave him the good news: he said that his family's new residence would be the first to be completely done—building, landscape, color, and everything else by the middle of the month. He assured him that he would receive his family directly into the new house. Of course, Anna would be around to monitor the painting per Hasbo's instructions.

Dr. McMillan advised Dr. Wasiri to keep away from these aggravations on top of all he was to undertake. Dr. Wasiri raised his glass of wine, "I second your motion, Dr. McMillan, and sincerely appreciate your sympathy."

Anna was not amused and intervened, "Well, if it was up to men, a cave would do anytime. You need to thank us for making the house livable. I would have a word or two about this with Mrs. Wasiri."

Dr. Wasiri tried the smooth approach, "I am sorry, Mrs. McMillan. I never intended to belittle your amazing contribution. By the way, a cave would do for a man as long as there is a soft big bed. All we ask is a chance to go to sleep and maybe watch the late news, and maybe watch the sports, and maybe and maybe and maybe. That is where you come in. But when Hasbo asked me to review the entire household inquiries with you, Anna, I was completely defeated. Don't worry, we would do it. I just hope that Dr. McMillan here had stashed away his good McDs so that by the time I have reviewed the last-page twenty of the household inquiries, I would still be standing as I should."

They all laughed aloud. Dr. Wasiri gave the long list of household inquiries from Hasbo to Anna McMillan who promised to look into it. Then they talked about Mezi politics and other university news. It was about ten when Dr. Wasiri left after getting all assurances from Anna that she would answer each one of Hasbo's inquiries.

The next day, Dr. Wasiri started getting ready for the transition to deanship. He was to pay a visit to Dean Wutugrase and to hold meetings with Sister Fanzi-Djomba in preparation for the Mezi Women's Congress. Dean Wutugrase looked better than the last time he was recuperating from the commotion of Tanzire Hotel event. He had slimmed down and lost his slow walk. He was in the midst of packing the last belongings from the office he had occupied for more than twenty-five years. He still had mementos he was struggling to throw away or keep. When Dr. Wasiri entered the office, Dean Wutugrase was captivated by a collection of photos from a time bygone. He did not hear his new protégé come in. He was shaking his head, reviewing people on the photos, probably retired or deceased or both. Then he turned around to notice Dr. Wasiri. He got up and embraced the younger dean calling him this time "the slayer of Gwobazo."

He went on with his usual monologue, "Finally, you have come to reclaim what has been waiting for you for some time. These old bones were not to take one more day in this office, if I could help it. It is all yours, son. And I know you would take care of it better than I did. I was looking at some old pictures circa 1987, a few years when they made a mistake of appointing me dean of Faculty of Sciences. You see at that time, the British still controlled the university. Their idea of Polytechnic University was more tutelage if any. The university was lined up behind the University of Kent from every aspect of management and ownership. As British faculty members were leaving and vanishing, it was a big struggle for the board of directors to keep the tight tutelage with that University of Kent. My appointment was a turning point.

First of all, I did not ask or want it. I was begged into it. On that picture, you see the chancellor at that time. I forgot his name and right behind, you see Dr. McMillan still young looking but slowly rising in the university management. He had a different take on the tutelage. He knew that it needed to change, but he was bidding his time. He also had his personal reasons for hanging around. He fell in love with Africa and his people to date. Dr. McMillan can always be counted on when it came time to move Polytechnic University from the tutelage ownership to its current Mezi no-profit incorporation. The current administration and the current legal framework and status of incorporation of the university were all the working of Dr. McMillan when he became chancellor. He literally severed the links that legally bound this university with the University of Kent.

One board meeting, he showed up and said there was no more legal reason to keep the tutelage and said that after a lengthy review of the status of Polytechnic University by an international legal team in Mezi and in London, he was advised, starting that day, he was to answer only to the board that was present in front of him here in Mezi. And just like that, it was done. Chancellor McMillan paved the way to Chancellor Umzigwe. Those two are very close too. The first chance Dr. McMillan got to come back, he did not hesitate to jump on it and here he is, here he would remain. My good man, never hesitate to take advantage of his help and general good disposition. Here I go again babbling to no end.

"I should have asked you what else you needed to start. I have all the documents lined up by categories, super confidential, confidential, very urgent, urgent, regular, and not so regular or important. I have to tell you I was not much involved in personnel issues, you know, discipline, firing, feedback, performance appraisal, and all the other management junk business directives. My slate was clean. I told my boss that I did not believe in it. On top of grading students, I did not have time to grade professors, tenured or nontenured.

As far as I was concerned, professors gained their tenure not from my evaluation; I left it to a tenure-management committee of outstanding professors. My job was to select people to join that committee, who in fact, did the real job. I always went along with the committee recommendations with one exception of course, your selection. I took personal interest in that one and closed it without that committee input. Not bad for a change. Now you don't have to follow my procedure or lack of thereof. You should do what you feel comfortable and stick with it. At the end, I believe my team and my boss did not care much what procedure I used or did not use, but what they expected from me was consistency. As I leave this place, I came to one important management lesson, consistency—that is the key."

Dr. Wasiri was not convinced, "Dean Wutugrase, I hear all that you are saying, but all I heard is that you were extremely appreciated, that is not the right word, you were very much loved by your staff and students alike. How do you explain that? There must have been a system, a procedure that you followed and people appreciated and loved you for that system or procedure and for this long. I believe that you are being modest about it. I do not expect to get you today to reveal the secret. I am in no hurry or rush anyway. All I know is that you would be with us after today and the day after and the day after if you see where I am going with this.

In fact, I would make sure that you would be available for a long time so that I would be able to slowly gain a better grasp of your famous system. I intend to continue my education as long as I can get in touch with you."

Dean Wutugrase smiled, "My dear son, for your information, the Lord, the Higher One has already given me as much time to be around you and enjoy the so-called system. I sincerely believe that he has been calling me lately to go back to Him and to give account of the terrible mess I have left behind."

Dr. Wasiri was now irritated. "Nonsense, Dean Wutugrase, nonsense! I would appreciate that you spare me that kind of talk. Nonsense. You just came out of an aggravated assault from those bandits who call themselves nation soldiers. What was that from, if not from the hands of God? And tell me at what age? Nonsense. You are and will be with us for a long time, so help us God! Please, Dean Wutugrase, promise not to use that language again. Now what about your family, don't they count somehow? You hardly talk about them, why? Somewhere in that sacred brain of yours, they must count somehow. As I am certain, along with all of us, they also pray daily to God to preserve and protect you among us. Because you are very dear to them as you are to all of us. Now I feel ashamed coming here and taking your valuable sacred position. I would not have accepted this deanship if it was a matter of making you take a long chair to wait for his call. No, I don't want to be part of that kind of succession. As far as I was concerned, I was only taking a relieve stand so that you would be able, with all your energy, wisdom, and why not, your big mouth to guide KMC toward the promised shining Mezi, land of peace and prosperity. Dean Wutugrase, we all need you ever so much now that we are entering the crucial testing phase of separating us from what you call worthless class. Tell me how else would we do it without you. I say nonsense."

Dean Wutugrase got the message. "It is very hard for most of you to share in any humor when I talk. You take things too seriously, and it starts getting very depressing. I am going nowhere, Dean Wasiri. Thank you very much. As far as my family is concerned, you have a point. It is true that I don't talk about my family since my lifetime partner, Miss Ivy Wutugrase, preceded me in the mighty Lamb domain. That was about eleven years ago. In the meantime, I have waged a hopeless battle to get just one of my three children to come back home from those splendid sunny corners of America that you call California and Florida. They don't want to come home.

Why would they with every stupidity that goes on here, who in his or her right mind would think of coming back? Two daughters, both with very advanced and settled medical practices, one an expansive anesthesiologist, another a brilliant surgeon. They have both married African-American men. They both have two children each. They both have settled into a very comfortable, as you call it, upper-middle-class life in the Berkeley area of the San Francisco Bay. Their younger brother has followed my footsteps in construction engineering. He is building those big mansions on the western coast of Florida. A confirmed bachelor, he is not about to leave his well-paying job in Florida for the hustle of Mandi or Mezi. My dear, I tried and tried everything to get them back here. They would not budge. It has gotten even worse now their mother is gone. They want me to come and retire among them in California or Florida. Do you see me taking it easy in California or fishing the blue fish along the coast of Florida? I don't want to forfeit the present and future fights against all of the Gwobazo's of this world, not for any California sun or the white sand of western Florida. When you see me out there, throwing punches, it is not only for Komesah or Zingzong of Mezi, I am also battling all these attempts to get me across the Atlantic. And for what? I have decided for some time that they have made their choice in the United States just like I have made mine in Mezi. I asked them to respect mine as I have resigned to respect theirs. But you know how the kids are. They are getting to their reverse-age appreciation. They believe that I have now become senile and in grave danger to myself. And now and then, they forget the agreement we reached and try to reverse the deal. Funny, I did not hear from them after the last fight at Tanzire Hilton Hotel. I am afraid, this time, if they heard what happened, they would file a suit to try to get me committed. But now that you are here, I know that they would find their match as I have adopted you as my son as of today."

Dr. Wasiri smiled and added, "Maybe I need to work on the younger one from then on. Nothing is lost yet as long as he remains a confirmed bachelor. There is always an outside chance that he would come round back to Mezi."

Dean Wutugrase wanted to change the subject now. "Thank you and good luck. By the way, I saw the tape of Washington conference. Just out of sight. You blew the kids out the water. Far out. Father Zolani was elated. He kept us going from six in the evening until four in the morning with the entire session. God, does he know the purpose of tape editing? It was fabulous. Love it. I would love to go to the Women's Conference for the same reason.

But I have medical appointment during that week to recharge my batteries, you know for the next fight. I hope you got the speech ready for tomorrow's investiture. Mine would be brief: 'Here he came, here he is, salute Dean Wasiri.' I have to take my walk exercise now, doctor's orders. Will see you soon, son."

Dr. Wasiri stayed behind in the dean's office looking at the pile of personnel documents Dean Wutugrase had refused to deal with. He would have to make a decision very early, either to trash the pile or review each case separately. He was not sure if the old man would care to talk about those cases again. After rearranging and refilling the documents, Dr. Wasiri was ready to receive Sister Fanzi-Djomba, who was right on time to go over the draft of the edict for Mezi women. Taking the cue from Dean Wutugrase, Dr. Wasiri asked Sister Fanzi-Djomba whether it would be appropriate to use the format that they used in Washington, DC, to drag the audience to provide input to the draft. Sister Fanzi-Djomba said that if the conference lasted two weeks, then that would be possible. But in this case, they would try their best to effectively control the format within the limits of time allocated; otherwise, they would not be able to complete the draft. Lecture format would be appropriate with an allowance of few lengthy external interventions.

The two KMC leadership members proceeded to edit the first draft that Dr. Wasiri wrote during Christmas time. The one-page listing was now approaching close to ten pages of insertions, all thanks to Sister Fanzi-Djomba. They worked until about eight in the evening and separated for dinner.

Chapter 33
Badegou/Sonjedi Split

While Dr. Wasiri was getting ready for his deanship investiture and the Women's Conference week, the PM, Sonjedi, was preparing his own coup against his political mentor, President Badegou. From the episode of H5 Exchange, President Badegou became suspicious of his PM. His inner circle convinced him that the young PM, Sonjedi, was a little bit too eager to humiliate the general whom he disliked intensely and had let it be known in many occasions and in many government circles that he was a relic of the past his government could no longer afford. The sooner he was retired or relieved of his functions, the better off the army would be. He had also added that General Gwobozo was kept for two reasons: he was a good reliable drinking partner for President Badegou during their Friday-evening endless blackjack and poker games, and he came from the same tribe as his mentor. President Badegou was now suggesting that the PM had deliberately tilted the negotiations to release the General Gwobozo in favor of his many friends in the KMC circle, including Professor Awassa and his nemesis, Chancellor Umzigwe. In two occasions, he confronted his PM over the H5 Exchange episode, and the two government officials had a violent exchange. At the last one, President Badegou withdrew his promise to appoint the young PM to the position he coveted to become Mezi Central Bank governor for a period of six years. When the young Sonjedi tendered his resignation, President Badegou refused to accept it. The PM, Sonjedi, took a two-week vacation time in South Africa and came back to patch up with his boss.

About two weeks later, he requested a private meeting with his mentor to talk about political courses to take in light of the rapidly approaching electoral process. He then suggested a rather positive and sensible political course of action. PM Sonjedi advised his mentor to work very hard to rally around him all existing political parties into a major political coalition to face KMC. That would insure an equal distribution of political forces in Mezi. He said that KMC would rather come in alone the electoral process with zero support from existing political parties it had already rejected in block. PM Sonjedi added that he took the liberty of testing the waters by talking to the presidents of the Lower and Higher Chambers of Parliament.

Both agreed that this was the proper political course of action for all those parties outside KMC. Both said that they were willing to set aside their petty political rivalries in order to save their necks during the next political campaign battles in front of the mighty KMC. However, when

PM Sonjedi mentioned the name of the president of the Lower Chamber, he apparently set off his mentor. He had forgotten the ugly budget fight that the president of the Lower Chamber had waged against the government's latest very tight budget and pushing it to the humiliating defeat. He had earned the irreconcilable enmity of President Badegou from that day. The President had decided from that mishap to see him removed from the Lower Chamber presidency. The fact that PM Sonjedi was holding meeting with this man and promoting his future political future was sheer betray as far as President Badegou was concerned on top, of course, of the H5 Exchange selling out.

President Badegou cursed the PM and accused him of betraying him every step of the way and sabotaging every one of his political initiatives by going behind his back and negotiating political unions with his worse enemies. That was definitely too much for a consternated PM Sonjedi. He went straight to his office and released to the press a one-sentence line reading "Effective immediately PM Sonjedi has resigned his position of premier minister, and President Badegou has accepted his resignation." Again, he packed his suitcase and by the end of the day, he was resting at a hotel along Cape Town beach in South Africa. It turned out later on that day, President Badegou had been drinking since that morning, a dangerous habit he had formed since the H5 Exchange fiasco and the increasing financial and budgetary shortfalls the country was facing. The pressures of the office were no longer sitting well on this relatively pleasant man of about sixty-five of age. The firing of General Gwobozo had also started to affect him as he literally missed his preferred drinking companion of long date. With the general around, he was able to control his own intake in spite of warnings from his doctor, who had detected early signs of untreated ulcer on President Badegou. When the general took a forced retirement to that remote northern province camp, President Badegou lost a devoted friend and drinking companion. He accelerated his drinking habits, ignoring his wife and family members' pleas. It was now twice in less than a month and in curiously similar circumstances that President Badegou had a falling out with his young PM. This time, he ignored the PM's resignation for five days until he was prompted by his minister of interior to find a replacement in the person of another young PM, Blair Kensoy, the minister of finances and Sonjedi's very close friend.

In the meantime, the press was completely at loss of the sudden resignation of Sonjedi from the PM post. Speculations went so wild and as far as accusing Sonjedi of having fathered a child out of wedlock at the expense of one of President Badegou's granddaughters, a frequent guest of Mandi's high society night life.

KMC Leadership, in disdain, completely ignored the resignation as a nonevent and not different from many other daily scandals which visited the political institutions in place, including the government of the young able PM Sonjedi. But KMC leadership underestimated the split between President Badegou and his protégé at its own cost. Another keen observer from South Africa, the same mercenary companion to Dr. Neal Hansberger, was in town to take his monthly political temperature as strongly advised by his boss from Vaduz. When he reported Mandi's latest political dance to his boss, he was surprised to hear him advising to urgently fly back home, to find out where Sonjedi was residing, and to wait for him in Cape Town. The pseudo Dr. O'Shea was not amused. He was no longer up to assassination plots. He was now geared to soft plots like political bribing and the likes. Yet he did what he was told and waited for Dr. Neal Hansberger. But a completely transformed boss showed up; he was no longer Dr. Neal Hansberger. He was now a tanned Mr. Jan VanCourtens, vice president, Global Marketing Enterprise of CXM, Canadian eXchange Minings, based in Toronto, looking for mining opportunities in Mezi. Mr. Jan VanCourtens showed up with a young beautiful assistant from Calgary, Miss Angela Beefount, a wholesome brunette, thirty-two years of age. Mr. VanCourtens and Miss Beefount managed to stay in the same first-class hotel as Mr. Sonjedi. The mercenary was sent back to Mandi to keep a sharp eye on the political evolution in Mandi and to report it as quickly as possible. The Canadian guests worked hard in befriending the now completely despondent Sonjedi wondering how to rebuild his political fortune in Mandi. After three days of chance encounters, Mr. VanCourtens asked Mr. Sonjedi to join them for a drink in a very remote corner of the hotel outdoor café on the beach while Miss Beefount provided Mr. Sonjedi a more-than-adult show of her assets from head to toe, including a bare bottom. At one point, when Miss Beefount excused herself to a nearby bathroom, Mr. VanCourtens suggested that Miss Beefount was literally beside herself and would not mind to partake in the bathroom. Mr. Sonjedi did not bite. He told Mr. VanCourtens that he was not there to be entertained in the bathroom or otherwise. He said that he came to that hotel on the beach to collect his thoughts over important business issues back home in Mezi. And he had no use for pimps and their ladies.

Mr. VanCourtens apologized and introduced himself properly and told Mr. Sonjedi that he was also coming from Mandi after two weeks of fruitless pursuit of mining contracts in the provinces of Chelow and Tongeo. He asked Sonjedi what were the proper conduits to gain mining contracts in Mezi. Sonjedi laughed and said to Mr. VanCourtens that he was looking at one of the proper conduits to get mining contracts in Mezi, unfortunately a week later. He then explained that he had just resigned the position of premier minister of Mezi. Mr. VanCourtens rushed to the nearby bathroom, where Miss Beefount was still waiting for action, and asked her to come hear the wonderful story. Miss Beefount came out, still adjusting her skimping undergarments to Mr. Sonjedi's complete indifference. Mr. VanCourtens admonished his companion, telling her that Mr. Sonjedi, the former premier minister of Mezi was not interested in casual sex as the two lying governors of the provinces of Chelow and Tongeo did. Mr. VanCourtens asked Mr. Sonjedi how he could manage to work in the middle of so much corruption. He told him how the two governors managed to go to bed with Miss Beefount and would still not sign a single contract paper. Mr. Sonjedi laughed and asked Mr. VanCourtens what he was doing when the governors were busy with his lady companion. He said he faithfully waited for her at the hotel for the signed contracts in vain. Mr. Sonjedi told the Canadian that money talks faster than sex in Mezi. Those two governors would have had three younger virgins after Miss Beefount on that same day. Going to bed with Miss Beefount did not mean much to them. He added to Mr. VanCourtens's attention, if you believed that you were gaining some kind of premium by bringing in a white woman for the governors, you could be so grossly mistaken. That does no longer work there in Mezi. People who fancy color or white women can jump in a plane and indulge over any beach from Mombassa in Kenya to Cape Town in South Africa.

He got up and said, "The fact is I do not believe your story anyway, and this Miss Beefount does not look or sound as bold enough to take the plunge in Chelow, Tongeo, or in that bathroom. Mr. VanCourtens and Miss Beefount, thank you for the drink, and as a word of advice, you need better pimping practices. In Cape Town, the vice squad police is very effective and do not play around here."

Mr. Sonjedi left the two Canadians and went to sleep. The next day, Mr. Sonjedi saw the Canadians around lunch and waved at them; they looked gloomy. He told them that he apologized for treating them as a pimp team and was ready to offer them a lunch to make up. They accepted.

He took them to his favorite seafood restaurant along the beach, and the Canadians were impressed by the attention Mr. Sonjedi was getting at the restaurant. At the end, Mr. VanCourtens said that he had been in touch with his headquarters in Toronto, and he was strongly reminded that his trip objectives were not being met to date, and he needed to either change his strategies or resign his executive position. He asked Mr. Sonjedi for advice. He repeated the same things he said before that money talks faster than sex in Mezi. Mr. VanCourtens told him that a man in his positions, a former PM, must have a lot of entries and sorties around town he can use to help him secure a signed mining contract. Mr. Sonjedi finally said he could definitely act as his company consultant to secure all kinds of contracts for a fee. When Mr. VanCourtens asked how much, he said that all depended on the size of the contract. But Mr. Sonjedi confessed that all that was small potatoes. He was now more interested in one thing and one thing only—to kick President Badegou out of his presidential chair. The sooner, the better. If his company can help him achieve that, then his company would have access to any open mining contract it wishes to get anywhere in Mezi.

Mr. VanCourtens was acting confused now and did not know what to make out of kicking President Badegou out of his position. He told Mr. Sonjedi if he was talking of a coup d'etat, that would be out of question, as his company was not interested in military coups or assassination plots. His company wants all legit. Mr. Sonjedi laughed again and said, "Military coup, absolutely not. We are going to simply play a tough legal political game. The game is simply this: you allocate so much funds to allow me to form a huge political party coalition and get as many of President Badegou's current political people as possible to my side to a point where he is deserted and would give up running for presidency during the next electoral process. That is what I meant by kicking President Badegou out of his presidential chair.

"You see, this is exactly what I was proposing to him when, drunk, he forced me to resign because he became so stupid, cursing me, calling me all kinds of names because he did not like one person I mentioned and who had agreed to join us in this great political coalition. I tell you, he acted like a complete fool he is, I have decided to cut him under and clean his slate of all his support before he knows it. You are wondering why would I do that. It is also that simple. There is this huge political movement that had operated and would operate outside all the other existing political parties.

This movement is gathering steam and needs to be stopped before the next electoral process; otherwise, all of us in the institutions would be out on the street and all the institutions would be in the hands of these renegades called KMC.

"I have been sounding the alarm for the last two years, and nobody would listen. All of a sudden, the past three months, everybody from every end of our political spectrum has suddenly awakened to the realization that if KMC triumphs, all of us would be out of work. It is simple as that. And this stupid sitting president sacked me for sounding the alarm a little bit too loud for his eardrum. Just stupid. Now this would also go for your mining contracts. You see you have all the chance to get those contracts now, to work with our side in the political landscape.

But a year or so from now, if KMC comes to power, you would not have the same political cover you have been enjoying all along with us. It could well be bye, bye, no more contract, and this is very much possible. Mr. VanCourtens, you can get your contracts signed anytime, that is not the issue. In a country like Mezi, as we say it, a contract, a dozen. The most important thing is how your contracts are being executed and most importantly under what political climate. If the political climate is unfriendly, such as under KMC, you may as well tear that contract away, because it would be worthless. If the political climate is ours, under that great political coalition I want to establish, then you would be OK. I hope now you understand what I am talking about."

Mr. VanCourtens started grasping part of the story, and Miss Beefount woke up and asked, "What about the United States in this business?" Mr. Sonjedi answered, "Mezi is too small for the United States to bother. It has no vested interest there that I know of. The United States would probably go along with KMC's take over under the stupid democratic umbrella. You see, I am talking to you because I know that a lot of companies in Toronto Exchange have mining contracts in Mezi, and they do not want to lose them. It would be up to you to wake them up to help us protect those contracts. I know, deep down, that they have sent you to check me up. That is my message to them. Too bad you have wasted your valuable time for three days with the silly pimping game. Now that we have come to a grown-up understanding, you can send Miss Beefount to my room for a serious partaking. No offense, but you still had a lot of effects on me, Miss Beefount, would you indulge me now?"

Miss Beefount looked embarrassed and looked at Mr. VanCourtens for direction. Mr. VanCourtens said, "Miss Beefount as you wish!" Miss Beefount got up and followed Mr. Sonjedi. They took the taxi back to the hotel while Mr. VanCourtens was still finishing his seafood lunch. By the time he reached the hotel about two hours later, he saw around the huge hotel pool, first, Miss Beefount in the sexiest bathing suit, lying next to the sleeping and tired Mr. Sonjedi. The latter was having his well-deserved repos du guerrier. Mr. VanCourtens went up to his room and had a long talk with the mercenary emissary in Mandi to verify all that Mr. Sonjedi had said, and when satisfied, he reached out to his main Amovir correspondent to raise the down payment for political activities for Mr. Sonjedi's great coalition party in opposition to KMC. He came down and told Mr. Sonjedi that the Canadian side had agreed to the bargain, and an initial sum of ten million dollars will be made available. Mr. Sonjedi, who had not opened his eyes, smiled. He said that was OK for a start and that Miss Beefount was most satisfying. Two days later, with Miss Beefount having now taken permanent residency in Mr. Sonjedi's room, the new partners agreed on contacts and follow-ups. They parted company. Mr. VanCourtens took his flight back to Vienna via Paris as Dr. Neal Hansberger. Miss Beefount stayed until the day when Mr. Sonjedi returned to Mezi. She washed her brunette hair and took the plane back to London as the blonde Ludmilla Borensky.

It was Chairman Kiriyan who applied himself again this time so hard to orchestrate the montage involving Mr. Sonjedi, Miss Angela Beefount, and the bumbling Mr. VanCourtens. It was a very well-designed act. After the Karlov Yelgin coup, Chairman Kiriyan was convinced that with African initiatives rapidly evolving in multiple venues, he could not afford to let anything slip for no reasons and for lack of trying. Chairman Kiriyan decided that as far as Mezi initiative was concerned, he could not live with putting all of his eggs in one KMC basket, no matter how promising it looked and no matter how Lady Allistair was confident about the eventual outcome of the Mezi initiative. For added assurance, Chairman Kiriyan decided to wire any political opposition to KMC from the get-go. At this stage of his master plan, he was convinced that he had overshot a bit in the Karlov episode. Sooner or later, he would have to pay some consequences from the Karlov's episode. His best course of action was to accelerate the Varonne-Sur-Baie move. But the Varonne-Sur-Baie move would not make much sense if the Mezi initiative were not in the bag, no matter who would be manning Mezi ship of state in the near future, whether it is KMC or any political movement opposed to KMC.

Chairman Kiriyan did not want to suffer any surprise in Mezi; his best insurance was to support incentives to both KMC and any KMC opposition. Either way, Chairman Kiriyan would come out a winner. A simple matter of gaming the game. Through the effective network of political surveillance that Dr. Neal Hansberger had set up in Mezi under the tutelage of that former South African mercenary, Chairman Kiriyan had learned of the panic that was seizing and paralyzing the current political leadership in Mezi. It was not clear which way that panic would favor the fortunes that KMC was obviously enjoying at that time. The split between President Badegou and his young PM Sonjedi confirmed how desperate the moribund political leadership was becoming. The chairman had made an astute political analysis of the current situation. He decided to fund and support Mr. Sonjedi's drive to form a huge political coalition to counter the growing KMC movement. That would be the most effective way to control both ends of Mezi political spectrum and to avoid unpleasant surprises while Lady Allistair was assuring him to have gained the complete allegiance of KMC leadership through the largesse currently dispensed by the Emily Thomas O'Shea Foundation.

Along the same order of initiatives, Chairman Kiriyan had touched base with Lady Allistair to take Ludmilla back into AMX London staff. Ludmilla was becoming highly exposed in Amovir with thousands of questions being asked about Karlov Yelgin's whereabouts. Worse, Mrs. Yelgin, in spite of all the bribing that Chairman Kiriyan had poured her way since the disappearance of her husband, showed up one day at the office, attacked and accused a horrified Ludmilla of having her husband kidnapped by some underworld people in Moscow because her husband had declined her sexual advances during that famous trip. Before long, Karlov Yelgin's sex pictures with Katherina, Helena, and the young man at the dacha started circulating in Amovir, more speculations about his whereabouts abounded. The underworld kidnapping gained strength until the day a Moscow FSS prosecutor showed up to interview Ludmilla Borensky only to learn that she had taken an overseas assignment because of the harassment suffered at the hands of Yelgin's wife. The Moscow prosecutor was surprised and rectified the prosecution records for everybody. That was also the first time that Karlov's wife learned the truth about her husband's counterfeit transactions, which had landed him in a Siberia FSS jail for twenty-five years. She talked to Chairman Kiriyan and accused him of the downfall of her husband and swore to get to the bottom of that grim story.

She told the prosecutor that her husband was probably compromised by both that whore of Ludmilla Borensky and Chairman Kiriyan and most likely because her husband knew too much of stealing that Chairman Kiriyan had done against the national interests of BI. The prosecutor assured her that he would get to the bottom of what she was talking about. However, the prosecutor never asked to see or talk to the chairman except to give him a copy of what he had collected during his stay, including the accusations from Mrs. Yelgin. Chairman Kiriyan took the notes to mean to watch out that he would be the target of higher up investigation before long. Varonne-Sur-Baie move was now becoming a matter of urgency for Chairman Kiriyan.

CHAPTER 34
KMC Edict for Women

It was with a different degree of urgency that Dr. Wasiri, expecting an imminent reunion with his family in Mandi, faced two important events in both his academic career and his fast-growing political career.

For his investiture as dean of the Faculty of Applied Sciences of the Polytechnic University, his new boss, Chancellor Umzigwe, did not spare any pomp. He lined up the entire academic and management body of the university for the ceremony. He associated also the heads of Mandi Catholic and Protestant Churches. The minister of education and his entire central and provincial staff people were included in the ceremony. The current PM, Blair Kensoy, and the former PM, Sonjedi, showed up. The entire retinue of Polytechnic University alumnae showed up. The audience was there for two reasons, to thank Dean Wutugrase for his long-serving services and retirement and, at the same time, to welcome this much-talked about new dean, Dr. Kano Wasiri, who had shaken Mandi political scenes in less than two weeks of his political sortie. Dr. Kano Wasiri was already established as a political icon in Mezi. He had yet to prove his academic credential after the long scholarship of Dean Wutugrase. But during the ceremony, it was a little bit difficult to tell who was coming into from who was leaving the deanship position. To hear the long and eloquent speech that Dean Wutugrase gave to welcome Dr. Kano Wasiri in the short line of deans of Applied Sciences Faculty, you would think that Dr. Wutugrase had worked forever under the guidance of the eminent younger Dr. Wasiri. When the latter came around thanking his new mentor, he detailed his long consistent winning tradition in all battles, the scientific, the social, the judicial, the political, the familial, and, the most important, the battle of life. At that instant, Dean Wutugrase was all tears and embraced his younger protégé and called on the audience to extend to this man the same accolades and regards they have mistakenly shown to a less than deserving gruffly old man not yet ready to bend. Chancellor closed the investiture with another resounding speech, lauding the works of his two distinguished scientists and placing the extraordinary redesigned dean sash with the bright and shining yellow and black colors of KMC.

That new design subtly served notice to all that the new dean, Kano Wasiri, would be carrying, both the scientific academic torch of the premier Faculty of Mezi as well as the KMC torch.

The next event took place a week later at the location of Free University of Mezi in Ikando, the capital of the Northern Province of Kiesse. The occasion was the Mezi Women's Annual Congress.
The president of Free University, Dr. Injewi Ingoma, had already extended the day before a warm welcome to KMC leadership team members from Mandi. A rather discreet gentleman, Dr. Ingoma, was a worldwide authority in Advanced Research Studies in Numerical Analysis after receiving his PhD in Mathematics at the prestigious South African University of Witwatersrand and another PhD in Philosophic Logic Concepts from the University of California at Berkeley.

He had also the distinguished honor of being the only Mezi academician being knighted by England Queen Elisabeth for his major contribution in the foundation of the British Commonwealth Institute of Advanced Studies at Kuala Lumpur, Malaysia. To date, he has remained the emeritus chancellor of that prestigious international institute. What was most remarkable was that a man of such notoriety had still chosen to remain in Mezi to take up the arduous task of building a nondenominational university at the distant place like Ikando, the second largest city in Mezi. Through various contacts and worldwide support, the Free University had grown to its present fully accredited university status and matching the Polytechnic University in many scholarship fields.

Dr. Ingoma had been fiercely instrumental to that university's expansion and status. Dr. Ingoma, although very sympathetic to KMC ideals, was not what you would call a political animal like Chancellor Umzigwe. Before this trip, Chancellor Umzigwe had strongly advised Dr. Wasiri to touch basis with Dr. Ingoma. Chancellor Umzigwe said that if KMC could bring Dr. Ingoma into its inner circle, it would have half won the next electoral process. Chancellor Umzigwe had an enormous respect and regards for Dr. Ingoma. He said that Dr. Ingoma was the first in the short list of Mezi academics for whom he would readily leave his current chancellor position at Polytechnic University. Dr. Wasiri looked with great anticipation to meet Dr. Ingoma. The meeting over dinner the day before the Edict for Women present was very cordial.

But throughout the meeting, Dr. Ingoma kept referring ironically to the "Polytechnic U. Polit. Bureau" of KMC leadership team. It was a clear jab to the monopolization of KMC leadership into the Polytechnic University crowd. At the end of the dinner, he took Dr. Wasiri on the side and pointedly elaborated on the theme of enlarging KMC leadership team first outside the university compound of Polytechnic University and then outside Mandi. He added that a serious complaint he had registered around the country and a major feedback Dr. Wasiri needed to bring back to his colleagues in Mandi was that KMC leadership team is in serious need to open its ranks to all progressive forces outside Mandi and which are more than ready to carry its banner higher and higher all over Mezi. This was a very urgent imperative; otherwise, he was afraid these progressive forces outside Mandi would find their way in many splintered groups that would sap the strong unity that KMC had built these past ten or so years. Dr. Wasiri listened very attentively at the message and assured Dr. Ingoma that it would get a priority hearing when he would be back to Mandi.

That sad observation permeated Brother Kano throughout the Women's Congress Meeting weekend. The routine for these meetings was to give first to the current sitting government its due and opportunity to present its program and accomplishments in promoting women causes and agenda. However, due to the commotion that had followed the split between President Badegou and PM Sonjedi, the government went almost standstill for a while, and the invitation to the government from the Mezi Women's Congress went unanswered for two weeks before the congress meeting. It was also rumored that the invitation was simply withheld by KMC operatives inside the Women's Congress. When the new PM, Blair Kensoy, was finally reached with a request to send a government representative two days before the meeting, he could not identify a good reference or the documents from the previous year's presentation. The PM had no choice but to decline the invitation. That breach opened a huge opportunity for KMC to make its mark over the Women's Congress meeting. Various KMC contacts inside the Women's Congress governing body saw to it that KMC presentation took precedent over anything taking place inside the meeting's proceedings.

When Dr. Kano Wasiri, Sister Fanzi-Djomba, and Father Zolani took their prominent seats at the podium to give KMC Edict for Women presentation in lieu of the previously scheduled and now cancelled government presentation at the PM's request, the deck was more than titled in favor KMC, the political deck was huge and all KMC's.

Sister Fanzi-Djomba, well known for her flaming intervention in many political symposiums, took the podium and electrified the audience with her introduction of Dr. Kano Wasiri, who was called Brother Kano throughout the presentation. She also set up the format they have elected to use for the presentation. The format was going to be a forthright presentation of the Edict for Women that KMC had been working on for some time. The audience would have plenty of time to intervene during and after the presentation when it was being done. The presentation would be shared between the three representatives sent by KMC leadership, including Brother Kano, Father Zolani, and Sister Fanzi-Djomba. She begged the indulgence of the audience to listen to a man promoting the causes and agenda of women.

"Sisters of Mezi, you have heard me in many locations, you know where I am coming from, and where I am going when I stand in front of many of you, expounding over the issues dear to us. I don't have to tell you, and you know that I take no prisoners. I spare no one when it comes to our issues. But I have to tell that the one who is coming after me on this podium has shattered my own understanding of these issues. The beauty of what I have heard sits in the framework that this man has brought to bear on the subject matter on hand. I am honored to introduce to you Brother Kano Wasiri from Polytechnic University in Mandi."

Brother Kano, slowly and with decisive steps, came to the podium. "Sisters of Mezi, I come to you, thanks to the collective wisdom of our movement KMC. I come to you, thanks to the presence of all those women who have preceded me and given me the notion of life: my mother, my grandmother, my great-grandmother, and all the women before her. I come to you also thanks to the presence of that little one that I called my daughter and for whom along with all these little ones you have left at home we are proud to dedicate this "Edict for Women." Sisters of Mezi, I would be amiss if I do not give a whole lot of thanks to the one who has kept me still all these years, to the one who has given me the support I need and has sustained that small unit that I called my family day in and day out. I would be amiss if I do not give a whole lot of thanks to that lady called mother of my little daughter. I would be amiss if I do not give a whole lot of thanks to my lifetime partner, my wife.

"At the end of the day, it comes down to how that daughter, that wife, that lifetime partner, that mother, that grandmother, that great-grandmother, that sister is, yes loved, yes adored, yes treated at all times to make sense of what we are going to propose today.

Our first proposition is to set forth and proclaim unequivocally that the respect for women is fundamental and nothing, absolutely nothing should be added or retracted when it comes to the notion of the fundamental respect for women. What we are saying here is equivalent to the instance when some people gathered sometime ago and demanded that Mezi exists as and becomes an independent state.

Irrespective of what the colonial power thought about the request, the thought of an independent Mezi took shape and form. It grew to its logical conclusion of an independent state of Mezi. We believe that the respect for women is just as fundamental and must be brought irrevocably to its logical conclusion or outcome. Otherwise, all that we value in life, as we know it, would lose value and face.

We have to make the proposition of respect for women as fundamental as when we scream about fundamental liberties or notions of freedom such as freedom of thought, freedom of expression, freedom of press, freedom of association, or freedom of action. We do not argue or debate these notions of freedom.

They are, so we say, fundamental to the well-functioning democracy. What we argue about most of times are instances whether these notions of freedom are in place or not. We accuse each other of suppression of these notions of freedom. We spend a great deal of time, energy, and resources over these long debates. Well, we are here making the same proposition for the respect for women. We have to raise that proposition to the same fundamental truths of freedom, and when we say that we are all born equal, we do not say that we are born men or women and equal. The preface is direct, universal, and logical. If it is not accepted and internalized, then all these so-called notions of freedom and equality would not mean anything. It would be simply a farce.

"Sisters of Mezi, I would submit that all the problems we experience to date at all levels of our national political landscape must probably come from the basic fact when the respect for women is completely discarded. Remember that every time we have disrespected a woman, a sister, a mother, and a daughter, somewhere somehow, we have discarded a whole half of the nation. How can you function as a nation when you are discarding a whole half of your body? The answer is clear and unequivocal, you won't.

"Sisters of Mezi, we wish we were saying all this to gain your approbation or your agreement. That would be too easy, and believe me, you won't go for it because you don't need it, not at this time, not at this location. But we come here and make all these propositions because we have seen the waste and the devastation that are all around us in the cries of a raped sister, in the degradation of prostitution, in the discrimination of employment, in the homelessness of widows, in the whisper of battered wives, and in the silence of murdered spouses."

The last sentence shook the auditorium to its core. Brother Kano had been building the tempo of his delivery as eloquently as ever before. In the auditorium, there were hands raised in the air to affirm and to confirm the same witnessing that Brother Kano was alluding to. There was also quiet sobbing heard from those women in attendance and who either have suffered one of the tragic fates mentioned or have seen beforehand their sisters, mothers, aunts, daughters, friends, or neighbors suffered the same fate. Somewhere in the middle range of the auditorium, a middle-aged woman was overwhelmed by the emotion in the crowd, stood up shaking her fist. With teary eyes and all her last strength, she shouted to the direction of the podium, "Leave no stone unturned, Brother Kano, leave no stone unturned!" For the next two minutes, the entire auditorium reprised her statement, "Brother Kano, leave no stone unturned," while another group of women, young and old, not far from the middle-aged woman, came around, formed a circle around her to give support, to tell her that they knew exactly where she was coming from. Brother Kano looked up in the direction of the middle-aged woman and said, "Sister of Shining Light, I heard your pain, and I want to assure you that no stone would be left unturned before I am done here and nothing, absolutely nothing would stop me." The auditorium erupted again in approval.

Brother Kano continued, "The waste and devastation we have seen time and again ought not to be. The waste and devastation must be done with, eliminated for our sisters to support this nation in its great pursuit of peace and prosperity. Now we should talk about how we need to tackle these insidious attacks on the respect and dignity of Mezi women.

"Sisters of Mezi, on top of proposing that respect for women becomes a fundamental precept of our national life, we also say that the respect for women must proceed from five distinct values. We would go over these very important distinct values.

I urge you to stop or to intervene any time you believe that you need to discuss what you hear or to challenge anything KMC is proposing here.

"The first distinct value is defined as the equality of woman and man in every organ and precept of the law. That distinct value has already been touched upon when we were talking about the notions of freedom and equality which we say need no longer be debated or argued during any public discourse. But, Sisters of Mezi, are these notions fully implemented in our society?" Brother Kano did not have to wait for the big shout back, "No." He repeated what the audience said, "The answer unfortunately is a big no. Now remember each one of the distinct values is a building block to the overall framework of respect for women. So it goes without saying that we would not get to the logical conclusion of the respect for women if the equality of woman and man is not completely enshrined in every organ and precept of the law in Mezi. Without this building block, this framework would be no different from the sand castle built on the beach and washed away when everybody is gone, when nobody is looking, and the next tidal wave of ignorance carried it to the sea. There is no denying that here in Mezi, we have copied a lot of laws from other countries and which attempt to enshrine that concept in the matter of law. But in this male-dominated environment, we have also blocked every attempt to follow through the basic application of these laws.

"Sisters of Mezi, here I have to take a major exception too as I would do sometime later. Unfortunately, it has been observed in many instances that the roadblocks, which are erected in this male-dominated society to thwart the application of these laws, are reinforced by many of our sisters in this very hall." Another woman, not far from the previous middle-aged woman, stood up and yelled, "Yes, sir, Brother Kano, You tell them." The auditorium was now laughing.

Brother Kano also smiled and continued his presentation, "The prevention is done either in the name of undefined and obscure allegiance to religion or tradition. We would come back to this later.

"The second distinct value KMC has identified is that the majority of women are established from the age of eighteen. Have you ever asked yourself why a young man fifteen years of age cannot marry, but the young girl of fifteen can be literally kidnapped or sold into a matrimonial arrangement, with parents' authorization, only and only to satisfy the vile sexual appetites of that old man of eighteen or more.

Now this is one of many grave contradictions of what we have just stated, equality of woman and man in every organ or precept of law. Nobody would be able to explain to me that grave contradiction. At the end of the day, it comes down to another undefined and obscure allegiance to tradition of vile exploitation of women in every shape and form. Raising the legal maturity of consent for women would put them at par with the men at least. Here also we have a lot of work to do. I can already hear a lot of justifications for that unfair rule—child-bearing ability, rapid growth, rapid maturation, and so on. Sisters of Mezi, I stand here in complete and total rejection of each one of these justifications. As far as I am concerned, I would submit that what is good for the fifteen-year-old girl must be also valid for the fifteen-year-old boy." A resounding applause followed in the auditorium. "If it is not, then it should not be applied. We were talking of building blocks in our design of the framework for the respect for women.

"The next distinct value should reinforce the preceding distinct value, and it is stated as the integrity of woman in her body and spirit. You cannot respect women without valuing the integrity of woman in her body and spirit. Here we are simply raising the stakes and calling on the total rejection of physical and mental abuse perpetrated on our sisters. Abuse of any form, physical or mental, must be rejected on the basic premises that it is against the laws as far as assault on any physical person is concerned. I stand here in full apology. It is sad to bring this up as a distinct value at this stage only because like most laws in our book, they are not unanimously enforced to the full extent of the law. Otherwise, we would not have so many cases of battered women and, worse, murdered women. Our courts are called daily to adjudicate awful cases of barbaric abuse on our sisters.

"Sometime before, I said that I took a major exception in agreeing with our sisters in Mezi. The next distinct value stated that the respect for women must transcend Mezi women's negative values. What we are saying here is crucial. The proposition is simple. The respect for women can rest on the equality of man and woman, supported by every organ and precept of the law, the legal maturity of woman at the age of eighteen, the integrity of woman in her body and spirit. However, if women do not do their part in supporting these distinct values, the whole exercise would be meaningless. We have already shown that in many instances, women are willfully supporting negative values that keep them in the bind of refuting all respect for women. I don't know if I am in a good position to list or to mention those negative values that many of our sisters' support.

To start with, in this hall, during all the time I have stood in front of you, how many of you have already made a displaced comment about this lady's dress or that lady's hairdo. Now I am not about to start any fight out there, but this is where negative values start." A big murmur traveled throughout the vast auditorium. It was not clear if it was for approval or rejection. Nevertheless, there was a vast murmur.

"Then when we go to the society at large, those negative values abound. When a sister spends so much energy to take over another sister's matrimonial position, that is a display of negative value. When a mother encourages her teenage daughter to become a fourth wife of this seventy-year-old rich man, that is a display of negative value. When a sister enters a gentleman's office in a see-through garment, that is a display of negative value. When a married lady spends all her waking hours visiting her husband's friends' offices, that is a display of negative value. When a sister accepts to be financially kept by a man without a firm commitment to a matrimonial situation, that is a display of negative value.

When a woman, young or old, abandons a fetus or abandons a newborn baby in a box in a bush, along a railroad track, in the public or private bathroom, that is also a display of negative value. I can go on and on. But you know these negative values. I don't need to elaborate any further. As I said, these cases of negative values are popping up all over Mezi in our society, and they act as major blocks to our main proposition of respect for women. There could not be lasting respect for women at the same time women are promoting negative values.

"To close out the series of distinct values supporting the respect for women, it would only be logical to call up in the same perspective the last two distinct values that simultaneously address the valuing of family from woman consideration and the emancipation of woman in every productive aspect of the society. The center of respect for women should be not just the woman as a person, but above all, the very unit that she holds together at good time or bad time or all the time, and which is the family. On daily basis, our Mezi society is showing signs of how far the family unit has gone when the woman is disrespected. It has gone downhill. Behind every child abandoned in the street, there is a disrespected woman who has given up. Behind every child pregnant of another child, there is a disrespected woman who has called quit. Behind a scattered and disoriented family, there is a disrespected woman abandoned by her husband. The list is long, painful, and worrisome.

But the minute the family is valued, the minute the family is honored around a center called woman, our main proposition predicts that last distinctive value, the emancipation of woman, in every productive aspect of the society. That, in fact, Sisters of Mezi, is the logical conclusion of the respect for women.

That is the fundamental value that KMC wants to see implemented and anchored in the Mezi society as long as it is centered around the respect for women, the respect of all, and each one of you sisters in this auditorium and all around us in this beautiful nation of ours, Mezi. Thank you very much."

Women in the audience rose to their feet to give a thunderous applause to the presentation given by Brother Kano. The applause was later amplified and sometime drowned by KMC hymn that was being blared out. The raised hands or fists were bandied throughout the auditorium along with large head, neck, and shoulder scarves in shining yellow and black colors, KMC colors. The commotion went on for a long time directed by Sister Fanzi-Djomba at the podium and selected KMC operatives dispersed in the auditorium. The KMC hymn was accentuated by well-rehearsed and pointed KMC political slogans to a point it became difficult to tell whether the meeting was for Mezi Women's Congress or for KMC. The resounding endorsement of the Edict for Women by all delegates that followed surprised KMC leadership team members who were there, including Brother Kano, who was expecting to have a spirited and dynamic debate of the entire Edict after his presentation. When Father Zolani was approaching the podium to initiate the discussion phase of the presentation, the president of Mezi Woman's Congress, another cover KMC operative, ran to the bank of mikes and requested that the audience voted by show of hands whether to adopt or not the recently presented Edict for Women as Women's Congress Edict. It was voted by show of hands by all delegates. The vote removed the need to debate various points of the presentation.

Brother Kano was not amused. He held an impromptu meeting with the congress president and Sister Fanzi-Djomba. The compromise was to have an additional seminar among many others to take place during the congress and where the Edict for Women was going to be analyzed and debated by Brother Kano and Sister Fanzi-Djomba. The seminar turned out to be well attended but very academic. But Brother Kano missed the common touch that was widely present in the auditorium, and he had hoped to elicit through the question-and-answer session.

He resigned himself to the notion that the Edict for Women as presented at the congress would not need to be improved again. The best and powerful redeeming factor KMC leadership could fall back on was the fact that KMC Edict for Women had been adopted as a matter of fact as Mezi Edict for Women. Nobody can ask any better than this. This is also what the press reports reflected in summary for all that had happened in Ikando that weekend.

The big title in one popular Mandi journal was "Brother Kano is back, Electrified Women's Congress." Another read "KMC Edict for Women = Mezi Edict for Women."

However, overall, Brother Kano considered Ikando meeting as a missed opportunity to argue the Edict for Women on KMC merits. Later on, Brother Kano confided to Dean Wutugrase that he would have preferred to have that debate to trash out the Edict for Women in any shape the audience would have wanted, the same way he did in Washington, DC, over the Edict over Corruption. It was not perfect, but at least, it was dedicated to KMC ideals thoroughly discussed in that edict. He also said that KMC leadership should beware of quick and easy public approval of its pronouncements without thorough review as the one that had happened at Ikando.

He added, "I suspected that the president of Mezi Women's Congress, an already avid KMC sympathizer, has deliberately rushed the vote of the KMC Edict for Women. She probably thought that she was doing KMC a favor, a very bad favor because there were certainly in the audience people not necessarily won over to KMC side. The rushed vote probably froze their attempt to argue and clarify any ambiguity they may have about KMC. These people may not have another chance to evaluate KMC intents in an open forum."

On his return, Brother Kano reported to Chancellor Umzigwe and Dean Wutugrase the feedback Dr. Ingoma had given him and how urgently KMC leadership team was expected to show its willingness to make the team more inclusive. The two old leaders assured Dr. Wasiri that the broadening of the leadership team was in the works plan as they approached the mapping of the first KMC political convention. KMC leadership team would be announcing very shortly a new governing body called KMC Provisional Leadership Committee of about fifteen or so members. This committee would replace the current KMC leadership team in every function. Very strong leaders, already identified in KMC cells around the country, including Dr. Ingoma, would be invited to join that committee.

Chancellor Umzigwe added, "We will make sure to let them know that this committee's main charge would be to guide KMC toward the political convention where members of a permanent KMC Standing Leadership Committee would be elected along with a secretary general and specific high delegate with specific KMC major commission responsibility such as economy, women, security, corruption drive, and so on."

Dr. Wasiri was relieved to hear that a plan was in motion to address a very troubling note that bothered him at the weekend meeting. In addition, he shared his displeasure over the lack of appropriate debate to review the Edit for Women. He said to the two senior leaders that KMC leadership should always strive to win people to its side by the strength of its ideas and ideals, thoroughly debated or reviewed.

CHAPTER 35
Emissaries' Visit

In addition to Dr. Ingoma's feedback and the reservation Brother Kano had about the outcome of KMC presentation of the Edict for Women in Ikando, the upcoming arrival of his family to Mezi was upsetting him for different reasons. He worried that Hasbo, his wife, was being overwhelmed by the incredible arrangement she had to put up to get so many stuff bought, rearranged, and shipped to Mezi. After he delivered a more or less complete list of appliances, tools, and other things to buy according to Anna, Dr. Wasiri wondered how Hasbo was going to pay for all these things. Before his return, he had moved a sizable sum of money from his London account to his Frankfort bank account for the only purpose to fund the entire transition from Frankfort to Mandi. When he checked his account online in Frankfort and in London, no money had been withdrawn or spent from his account. That troubled him even more and confirmed his worry about Hasbo being well behind her ability to manage this big transfer. When he called his wife, she said not to worry, that all had been taken care, and that there was no need to use his Frankfort bank funds. The whole process just did not add up. Hasbo maintained that all was being paid and all was in order for the departure from Frankfort and arrival to Mandi for the rest of his family.

Hasbo could not bring herself to reveal that as soon Dr. Wasiri had made plans to go back to Mezi a month before his family, Dr. O'Shea had convinced her to hold off all preparations to go back until after Dr. Wasiri was gone. The adoptive father then busied himself to buy and pack everything for the definite departure of his adoptive family. He paid for a packing service company to come to his protégé's house and rearrange into big freight storages all that the family would need in Mandi. Of course, he counseled Hasbo not to say a word about this to Dr. Wasiri, already in Mandi. This would be another surprise to him when the family would land in Mandi. The list that Anna McMillan sent was similarly taken care of. Hasbo gave it to Dr. O'Shea, who faithfully bought and inventoried each item on the list and got them delivered to the packing company. A week before Hasbo and children's departure for Mezi, all had been packed and shipped to Mezi at Dr. O'Shea's expenses.

The old professor had then completed all the tests he needed to do regarding the Alpha-M specs. He was paying all the expenses for Wasiri's transfer as a thank-you note to Dr. Wasiri for coming through with the Alpha-M specs, the real thing.

Now that he validated all he had expected from Alpha-M, Professor O'Shea was close to euphoria. The problem was that he could not bring himself to reveal anything to anybody except to Dr. Wasiri according to Emily rules. He was not going to call any huge press conference and announce to the world that he had in his possession the ultimate mineral ready to increase world industrial capacity exponentially. That was not part of Emily rules. Besides, Dr. O'Shea had no time to spend his precious diminishing energy to convince the same unbelievers who had fought him all his academic life. That was going to be useless. Emily rules hierarchy had not changed and would remain the same: Emily, first, high up there, taking care of all, then Dr. O'Shea followed by Dr. Wasiri, Hasbo, and Wasiri's family. His own children were always excluded. Inside the many items that found their way to Mandi, Dr. O'Shea had also included all the results from the tests he had done. He had downloaded and included them in more than fifty CDs and packed in a special box. He got rid of any other references to the tests after that. He also took care to place the remaining Alpha-M specs from the tests inside the box at the rented bank safe.

When Hasbo struggled to come up with a decent explanation to her husband about the payment of all the expenditures, Dr. O'Shea told her that Dr. Wasiri would clearly understand if she told him that the results from the tests paid for everything. Dr. O'Shea assured Hasbo that is all his protégé would need to know, and he would understand. Hasbo did not want to argue about what the old man was saying. She was used to the often cryptic, obscure, and vague communication that went on between her husband and Dr. O'Shea. She went along with the plan. As soon as the entire Wasiri family was gone to Mezi, Dr. O'Shea realized that his Alpha-M odyssey was about to reach its final conclusion. He was going to finally retire now that all had been delivered to his adoptive son. According to Emily rules, it was now up to Dr. Wasiri to do as he pleases and when he pleases with the Alpha-M. From then on, that decision would firmly rest on his protégé's shoulders.

The next days, weeks, and month, Dr. O'Shea struggled about how to deliver the retirement news to Lady Allistair without jeopardizing Emily rules confidence.

He decided that Lady Allistair and Chairman Kiriyan have been the enablers of Alpha-M odyssey after all. He had used them as much as they thought they were using him. Thankfully, so far he had been able to control the Alpha-M agenda up to receiving those specs and validating all past theories around the exotic mineral. He had also managed to ship all important tests results to Dr. Wasiri's home in Mezi, establishing his protégé as the sole keeper of the Alpha-M jewel. And looking at the way things were evolving in Mezi, it was becoming evident that BI and Chairman Kiriyan would be the beneficiary of Alpha-M before long, depending on how Dr. Wasiri handled his inheritance of Emily rules. He reflected deeply over a clever and ironclad strategy to talk about Alpha-M to Lady Allistair without implicating his beloved protégé.

After about two more days, on a quiet Saturday evening, Dr. O'Shea reached the phone to talk to Lady Allistair. After trying three different numbers in vain, Lady Allistair answered him back using the first reach number. It was about past midnight in London; Ludmilla was indulging Lady Allistair in her own townhouse. Ludmilla's return to London gave Lady Allistair a perspective of trust and confidence in her private affairs she was unable to steer when she came back from New York City. Ludmilla removed all the tentative steps she took to establish a high-society single lady life in the complicated after-work night scenes of London. She was extremely concerned of the appearances she carried as CEO of AMX. She watched every step she took at work and outside work for any connotation to her prior well-publicized bisexual life. She restrained herself from going to the various joints she used to favor when she came from New York to London for a short stay or on vacation. She steered herself away from all the casual acquaintances from the past. No more one-night stand she indulged every other week in New York. Before Ludmilla's return, Lady Allistair was settling to an unhappy frustrated life of a high-society single boss. Now Ludmilla provided her with every cover she needed to recover in her own privacy the New York life she missed dearly. It was during one of those Ludmilla nights that Dr. O'Shea made his calls. The persistence of calls at her most discreet private numbers told her that there must be an urgent important call. When, still naked and in an overwhelming heat, she verified where the call was coming, she realized that she needed to take the call right away and excused herself from Ludmilla.

She rushed to the bathroom to take a quick cold shower to douse her senses. Then she put on a robe and went downstairs in the basement to her office away from office. She called the old professor.

Dr. O'Shea went straight to the meat of his call. He said that he was going to share three things: a stern protest, a very good news, and a very sad news.

As far as the protest went, Dr. O'Shea said, "I believed that we have agreed from the beginning of our business undertaking that I and I alone was going to handle Dr. Wasiri for the fundamental reasons I have shared with you. I thought that I have made it clear that Dr. Wasiri should not be disturbed one way or another as long as I am dealing with him. You told me the last time that we were in London that everything was going our way now that he is evolving in that political mix I was not crazy about. You said that at the end, it was going to be profitable for all of us. But I also remember the way it came out from your mouth when you said, and I quote, 'Whatever was going profitable for all of us was going to happen very soon enough.' You see I did not understand that part soon enough while I was in London. But when I came home, I learned through contacts I left in Mezi that some people connected with your business were going around Mezi and requesting pieces of Alpha-M using my name and Dr. Wasiri's name. In fact, you remember Dr. Neal Hansberger, he was the man who introduced me to you way back. Now I learned through my contacts in Mezi that this Doctor Neal Hansberger and another short guy calling himself Dr. Anthony O'Shea went to the Tongeo Region and checking village after village for information about Alpha-M. Worse, they went to see this old tribal chief and frightened the hell out of him to provide them with pieces of Alpha-M. Lady Allistair, let me make something perfectly clear: I don't care what you do in search of Alpha-M in Mezi, or how you have to conduct your business there. It is your money and your own business imperative and I understand that. But I would never forgive you or any of your business partners for using my good name and misrepresenting me at the same time. That was a low blow to all the trust I have placed on you. What is very strange is that all these crazy events happened about a week before Dr. Wasiri and I arrived in Mezi last time, you remember, the big airport celebration and the like. You can just wonder how these people from Tongeo felt when they saw me on TV or in person, and I was being introduced as Professor O'Shea who went around bothering people about the pieces of Alpha-M and pretending to be close to Dr. Kano Wasiri. Thank God, I was not approached by anybody while I was in Mezi to verify what the hell I was doing, going around Mezi threatening poor old tribal chiefs. Lady Allistair, I beg you to tell me the truth and to come clean on this one. Otherwise, I am going to stop all cooperation with everything you're hoping to do in Mezi. My question to you is this, is Dr. McMillan involved in this sordid affair? If that is the case, then he should be fired and dismissed immediately."

Lady Allistair was now sweating bullets when she heard the story. All libidinous pretenses she was carrying around in the office hoping to return to with Ludmilla upstairs evaporated. She thought that the story sounded like one of forays Chairman Kiriyan loves to engage Dr. Neal Hansberger. She had seen and heard about those forays before. She needed to keep Dr. O'Shea on her side very quickly.

"Dr. O'Shea, I have absolutely no idea what you are talking about. But believe me, I should know exactly what happened here before the end of this night. When I mentioned that things would be favorable to all of us very soon last time, it was a simple matter of rhetorical speech to reassure you about the political engagement of Dr. Wasiri. I had no idea that this Dr. Hansberger was threatening up our plan at the same time as you are saying it. In addition, I could be wrong, but I am certain that Dr. McMillan would not be involved in anything like this. He has been around the country for so long, and he is easily recognizable to play any game pretending to be you a week before you get to Mezi. It sounds very far-fetched. After listening to you, I have formed my own theory about how this story has developed: someone in Amovir wants to accelerate things in Mezi for BI. But why when everything is going so well, especially in the envious position where Dr. Wasiri has found himself in now. I am simply speculating and asking myself why Chairman Kiriyan would do something like this when he has given me full authority to guide all that Mezi business. I have made it clear to him that you are the sole man when it comes to Dr. Wasiri. Nobody else but you. Believe me, it is not like Uncle Kiriyan to sabotage his own design and plan. As you can see, so much is being invested around Dr. Wasiri to mess it up with stupidities. I still believe that somebody up there in Amovir got his or her directions screwed up. Yes, I know Dr. Neal Hansberger. But I have not seen him or heard from him for more than two years since I asked him to get in touch with you, I believe, at the passing of your beloved wife. Dr. O'Shea, I assure you that by tomorrow, I would have all the answers you want and need. Now what is the good news you wanted to share?"

Dr. O'Shea stayed quiet for a while, insuring that the flow of the call was following his initial strategy. "The sooner you get back to me with a plausible explanation the better, because this good news would require a strong building of trust and confidence between you and me. Because, as soon as Dr. Wasiri departed, I received a phone call from a man who said he was a pastor from the province of Tongeo, in fact, a pastor. He was in Dallas, Texas, attending a religious conference. He told me that he was going to send me a gift from a tribal chief residing in the adjoining province of Chelow.

He knew this chief from many of his preaching sessions in the Chelow Province. This pastor said that the chief had sent a special gift box containing three specs of Alpha-M. But he did not call it Alpha-M. I believe he was calling it Kansaye or Konseye. Anyway, he assured me that he was sending the special gift box by mail. I thought that after the Dr. Hansberger episode, somebody wanted to play me for a fool and that this was going to be a sad joke. I did not want to alert the so-called pastor to send the precious package by FEDEX. So I thanked him on phone, and I waited for the package. To my big surprise, the box was nicely made, and it effectively contained Alpha-M. I have been conducting all kinds of tests on these specs to validate all that I know about Alpha-M. To my surprise, everything so far is checking up to the penny. I sincerely believe that I have Alpha-M with me. Do your folks in Amovir would like to take a look at it?"

Lady Allistair had almost a seizure. Since she was sitting reclining on the huge leather chair with her feet crossed, resting on the large wooden desk, and because of whatever move she made when she heard that Dr. O'Shea was in possession of Alpha-M, Lady Allistair fell off the reclining chair and found herself naked on the floor, with her robe hanging on the reclining chair. Her shock over this outstanding news was so big that she wetted herself profusely lying on the office carpet. Dr. O'Shea thought that he had lost her and kept yelling, "Are you there, Lady Allistair, are you there?" Lady Allistair slowly regained her composure, staggered to the bathroom to get a towel, covered the reclining chair with the towel, and took her seat back on the chair while adjusting her night robe and said, "Yes, I am here. I was a bit shocked beyond my sense when you said that you had Alpha-M. That is a very good news. I tell you what, I would need to get in touch with Uncle Kiri right away to give him the very good news he has been waiting to hear all his life. You certainly have made my day and Uncle Kiri's too. Now that you almost killed me with your very good news, what else can top this as a very sad news?"

Dr. O'Shea now realized that he had reached the objectives of his delivery and said, "Well, now that I have delivered Dr. Wasiri, and I am about to provide you with a sample of Alpha-M, I thought that you won't need me anymore. I should take my retirement now from this business."

Lady Allistair cut him short, "I am sorry, Dr. O'Shea, how can you talk about retirement when you are just starting to work with us? My only question to you at this time is this, who else knows about Alpha-M in the United States at this time besides yourself and that intermediary pastor?"

Dr. O'Shea knew exactly where she was going with this line of questions. "Nobody else but myself. The pastor is long gone back to Mezi. He probably had no idea what he was carrying in his suitcase. Lady Allistair, this has been a personal odyssey I have engaged, nobody else besides Dr. Wasiri from the start. I have not yet shared this finding with him. I would probably share the results of my tests with him sometime later. I have to. Dr. Wasiri is the only person in this world I trust as far as Alpha-M is concerned. I told you this because as you have said it, you have already invested so much to support the Alpha-M endeavors. When I called you today, I started protesting the undue process that was taken to get to this. All along, my objective had been to keep Dr. Wasiri protected and at arm's length. You have respected that objective except for that episode with Dr. Hansberger. Dr. Wasiri, at the end, will remain the big prize in this endeavor. He is where Alpha-M is found and will be extracted. I have tried to let you understand that if he is not properly engaged in the Alpha-M endeavor, then there will be no Alpha-M, and all will be lost. Look at me. Old and feeble. You would not build the Alpha-M future around me. We all know that. We have already dropped all the pretenses about me. So at this time, I am a bit saddened when you asked if I have shared this wonderful news with anybody else.

"Even if I have wanted, I would not do it because, and for your information, I have wasted my entire academic and professional life trying. I was never listened to, so why would I try it again? That would be sheer lunacy and stupidity. But Dr. Wasiri, that is another story. I hope I have made myself clear. I simply want to see some kind of end game where I fit. That was why I brought the whole story of retirement."

Lady Allistair now smelled the strong scent of her release on the office carpet and was inclined to get rid of it when she said, "True, you have been a man of trust throughout. You have proved this without a doubt. I don't think we have kept our bargain as this Dr. Hansberger episode demonstrated. As I said, I must get to the bottom of this right away. We will keep our bargain as far as Dr. Wasiri is concerned. I have to go and share the very good news with Uncle Kiri. I want also to beg you to stick around for a while with us. We need you now more than ever. Dr. O'Shea, I hope to talk to you tomorrow and very soon."

She rushed to the bathroom next door and retrieved everything to clean the room. When she came out of the bathroom, Ludmilla was standing there in the middle of the office away from office, naked. Lady Allistair realized that the huge release she had was as a result of both the Apha-M story shock and the libidinous expectation of returning to Ludmilla waiting in vain, upstairs.

The ladies rushed to each other's arms, climbed on the reclining office chair to finish their postmidnight affair in spite of the strong scent on the office carpet. They abandoned the reclining chair for the huge bed on the townhouse first floor. Two hours later, Lady Allistair was back to her office in the basement. After cleaning the place, she sat down and called Chairman Kiriyan. She gave the very good news first before checking about Dr. Hansberger's adventure in Mezi. Uncle Kiri quickly concurred with her theory of a poorly received and executed instruction given to Dr. Hansberger. Chairman Kiriyan denied that he would put himself in a position to sabotage his own master plan. He mentioned to Lady Allistair that he was going to send emissaries to verify Dr. O'Shea's story. Dr. Hansberger would definitely not be part of the delegation. He insisted that Lady Allistair does not get in touch with Dr. O'Shea until after the delegation had made contact with Dr. O'Shea. As a matter of fact, he suggested that Lady Allistair refrained herself from getting in touch with Dr. O'Shea until such time when he would call and let her know that it was OK to call.

In his exalted voice, Chairman Kiriyan instructed Lady Allistair to note the following: "if the Alpha-M story checked out, the Emily Thomas O'Shea Foundation funding would be increased to three billion, the ABDI to six billion, and Dr. O'Shea and Dr. Wasiri's finder fees would amount to one hundred million dollar each, to be promptly deposited in their respective London accounts." Lady Allistair did not mind the compensation that Uncle Kiri would throw away if the story were verified. She became more concerned when Uncle Kiri mentioned emissaries to touch base with Dr. O'Shea. Why not use her? After all, she was in charge of Dr. O'Shea dossier. She became even more alarmed when Uncle Kiri insisted that she stayed out of touch and out of sight while the emissaries were going to deal with Dr. O'Shea. She prayed that no harm would come to the old man. She also remembered that the old professor was about to be compensated to the tune of big one hundred million dollars.

Not bad. Still Lady Allistair was concerned. It was the same for Dr. O'Shea. After he had talked to Lady Allistair, he knew that he had opened some unknown doors. He assumed that Lady Allistair would not wish him any harm. But Chairman Kiriyan with his two stooges of couple Dudarev was another story altogether when it comes to the exotic minerals. Although he had clearly requested it, he did not know how Chairman Kiriyan was going to go about verifying the story of Alpha-M. Dr. O'Shea had resigned himself to face whatever violence Alpha-M episode would bring.

He strongly believed that after fighting for the merits of exotic minerals for forty years of academic professional life, he was ready to face anything, including death now that he had seen a clear path to victory for one of these exotic minerals, Apha-M. The more he strengthened his resolve to face anything including death, the less worried Dr. O'Shea became about the outcome of the Alpha-M episode. By midnight, Dr. O'Shea was sound asleep. He woke up the next day at about eleven when he heard noise downstairs. That was quite unusual since this was Sunday, and he was not expecting to have Sandy Goshen working. Besides, she usually starts her daily commotion around nine in the morning when she busies herself making her coffee and using the coffee machine that Emily left in the kitchen.

But the commotion coming from the kitchen spoke a big meal preparation. When he was coming down, Dr. O'Shea asked himself who in the world had decided to wake him up on a Sunday and to occupy his kitchen. He was not ready for the surprise as he saw a man in the living comfortably reading his Sunday paper. He had never met the man. At the same time a middle-aged woman was coming from his kitchen with a cup of coffee to offer to the man who appeared to be her husband. What shocked Dr. O'Shea was the casual attitude this couple was displaying in his own household.

Before the lady got to give the cup of coffee to the man reading the paper, Dr. O'Shea took the cup away and stood between the two strangers and said, "As I am about to call the police in the next two minutes, would you tell me who the hell are you, who gave you the authorization to enter my house, and what are you doing in my house this Sunday morning?"

The woman calmly took the seat next to the man who was reading the paper. He closed the paper, got up, and said, "Dr. O'Shea, we were hoping to come and pay you a surprise visit this Sunday after the conversation you had with Chairman Kiriyan about some very important items in your possession. We were also hoping that you would be happy to see us again. I guess we were wrong, because you don't seem to recognize us. We are the Dudarev couple from Amovir. We talked about first and second tiers people and the regeneration process. Do you remember that? Does that ring a bell in your confused mind now? Talking about rings, do you remember the K ring we were wearing back then? It looks like you also earned one. Not bad! Now we need to update you about something.

"You see, right after we talked, our regeneration process in our unit kicked in. So much so that we moved to first tier level and Chairman Kiriyan moved down to second tier level, meaning that Chairman Kiriyan has been working for us at this time. We understand now why you could not remember us today. We were second tier back then attending to people's needs as Chairman Kiriyan butlers. We have remained his butlers in the eyes of people in Amovir, but the fact is that in our hierarchy, he takes all his orders from us. Our main purpose in Amovir has not changed. It is and remains the same to get hold of as much kabislovoskry as possible and bring it to our domain. Last time when we talked, we were not able to reach a common understanding of our ways. We are not certain that we are going to be able to establish any common ground today. We came here as soon as we learned from Chairman Kiriyan that you have been in possession of kabislovoskry. We want to look at it and verify that they have the properties we are looking for. Are we making ourselves clear?"

Dr. O'Shea looked at them and sat down opposite the Dudarev couple and said, "How do I know that you are the ones to verify the mineral as I requested. I remembered the ring, but anybody can show up with a fake K ring. I would need something else, a reference, a call, a letter; anything that tells me that Chairman Kiriyan sent you after I made the request. I am a bit surprised that I could not remember you by your face, have you also regenerated your appearance? I am definitely confused at this time."

Mr. Dudarev responded, "You are probably right about appearance and other signs. Since we moved to first tier level, we needed to take on an advance appearance to keep up with the human being perception of higher form of existence. You see, in our domain, the status first, second, or third tier level has nothing to do with the function that the domain has reserved for you at that point and at that time. Function is strictly time bound, but tier level can last the equivalent of eternity. For instance, take Chairman Kiriyan, he reached here sometime around 1792 as tier three level but acted as a prince in many European courts until he reached tier two regeneration during the Russian Revolution. He acted as managing director of that Fourth Director, and we came into his unit as tier two too. Chairman Kiriyan was automatically moved to first tier level to handle our unit. Unfortunately, his regeneration phase is entering a judgment phase. Chairman Kiriyan has not delivered in his most important assignment from the domain. He could be recalled anytime. Anytime could mean now or within one, two, or three hundred years, depending on the domain council judgment. His assignment is the same as ours around kabislovoskry.

And he is entering a third-regeneration phase, and he may not make it. You cannot imagine how many brakes you are giving Chairman Kiriyan with your pieces of kabislovoskry. We are ready to take up other domain assignments if we can bring back those pieces and leave the chairman vouch for other bigger domain projects. You asked for signs, well, I believe you spoke with Chairman Kiriyan, or somebody made it known to Chairman Kiriyan that you had pieces of kabislovoskry at about one o'clock Monday morning in Amovir, and that is the time we learned about our delegation to come here and to negotiate something about kabislovoskry. Tell me how long does it take to get from Amovir to Lexington in Kentucky? I believe it took you somewhere around twenty-seven hours of flight alone. And here we are in Lexington, Kentucky, less than eleven hours after you have communicated your message.

"Do you want to know how we got here so fast? You know this reminds me the story about two astronomers on earth who were excited to see for the first time, using their telescope, the explosion of a distant star. They celebrated the occasion with all kinds of festivities and pomp. When a young lady curiously asked one of the astronomers when did that explosion happen, the astronomer proudly said that it happened three hundred thousand light years ago. The lady persisted and wanted to know the exact date. The astronomer explained that the explosion happened probably before the existence of the planet Earth, the solar planetary system, the Milky Way Galaxy, and all adjoining galaxies. The lady left the party in disgust and told an arriving friend that she should not bother to go to the stupid party as she was going to celebrate an event that happened before she was born as well as her parents and great-grandparents and that there was nothing real in human terms about what was being celebrated. It is the same for our domain and us. You would never understand our signs. Do you want some other signs? Do you want some other references? You see our domain council has been relentless in the pursuit of this mineral from the time one of our major scientists established its direct source at the fourth phase of the big bang process. In our domain we believe in the basic process or generation and regeneration of the matter. We believe that all that was created at the beginning will go sooner or later to the steady state of the beginning. From the beginning of time, the process has been endless: generation, regeneration, combination, and recombination. At every stage, some form of energy is always released, sometimes very small, sometimes billions of times of what you call nuclear energy, and no matter how small, how big the energy is expending, no matter how small or how big the generation or regeneration takes place, at the end, something is created.

And the process goes on and on into creation of what you call planets or stars or galaxies, but we also call domains. And finally, the life form takes place within the generation and regeneration process. Our quest has always been to get to what enables the generation and the regeneration. The proposition was that it must be dispersed along the expansion of the universe. The domain council has decided to chase it all over countless galaxies, planetary systems, planets, and stars. We have located it in some distant domains including here on earth. It is amazing how backward this place called earth is. All the time we have been here chasing after the biggest enabler in the universe, we have witnessed countless wars and conflicts of unimaginable waste and devastation. Every day I go around, I want to grab people and show them how small earth is in the great scheme of universe, how earth is one small dot in the trillion upon trillion of stars, planets, galaxies, which make up the universe, how earth is one grain of sand in the gigantic constitution of universe. Only when those who inhabit earth would come to realize how much they need each other and how much all these stupid conflicts are wasteful, then the whole earth would move up in science and knowledge to use the enabler like kabislovoskry to reach a steady state of generation and regeneration as found in our domain.

"Dr. O'Shea, now you probably can understand why we keep to ourselves to observe our hosts and send all kinds of information to our domain about you. Dr. O'Shea, I don't know if I am making sense or I am boring you with my endless talk. Do you still want more signs, references, or letters from us?"

Dr. O'Shea who had been literally dozing, as if hypnotized by the glare of Mr. Dudarev's glasses, now woke up and said that he did not need any more signs or references. He just ventured to say that he did not have the pieces of Alpha-M or kabislovoskry with him in the house but he had them in . . . Mr. Dudarev completed, "In the bank safe box. That is the first true statement you gave today. The pieces that you tested are in the bank safe box we are going to retrieve tomorrow morning. Now for our protection and yours too, can you call the lady who works with you, Sandy Goshen, and tell her that she can take a day off tomorrow because you have unexpected visitors from out of town? This way, we can spend the day verifying whether these pieces were genuine."

The details with which Mr. Dudarev was making his request struck Dr. O'Shea as remarkable and removed all attempts on his part to check or challenge the couple's references.

He called Sandy Goshen and left her with the request to take a day off. From the tone of her voice, he knew that she would show up to check on him anyway.

Yet he felt very tired and wondered about it. He felt exactly the same way when he was last time in Amovir. At least he traveled a long way to get to Amovir back then. But here he woke up in his own house and did not go anywhere except he was in company of these people talking about tier level, generation, regeneration, domain, and so on, and getting him very dizzy. He went to sleep again. He was awakened at about seven in the evening to come down and partake a nice dinner prepared by Mrs. Dudarev. He declined to join the couple but checked his refrigerator and picked few fruits he could find and a glass of water. He was speechless looking at them eating like any other normal human beings.

He finished his fruits, drank the glass of water, and went back again to sleep, very tired. A ring at the main door awakened him at ten in the morning. As expected, it was Sandy Goshen who came to check on him. She came in, verified that Dr. O'Shea had two very tanned visitors who introduced themselves as Dr. and Mrs. Julius P. Nottinghem from

Canberra, Australia. Dr. Nottinghem was a longtime scientific acquaintance of Dr. O'Shea. The couple said that they had stopped over to pay Dr. O'Shea a surprise visit on their way to visit a daughter who is married and resided in Overland Park, Missouri. Sandy Goshen was satisfied and relieved and wished Dr. O'Shea and guests a wonderful day. She left promptly. It was about time to retrieve the specs from the bank vault. Dr. O'Shea asked Mr. Dudarev if he was going to come along. He declined and said he trusted the professor to do the right thing. Dr. O'Shea then left and went to the first bank to retrieve the large spec and the remains of the spec used for testing purposes. When he came back home, Mr. Dudarev told him that he must have forgotten something else. Dr. O'Shea looked surprised. Mr. Dudarev said that according to his automatic mapping guidance, there was another piece left in another bank safe box he needed to retrieve also. Dr. O'Shea jumped in the car to pick up the last spec that Dr. Wasiri had given to him. When he came back to his house, he found the couple Dudarev all packed and ready to leave. Mr. Dudarev took the last spec and gave Dr. O'Shea the remaining small specs used for testing. Mr. Dudarev told him that he had done wonders. He was in possession of the real kabislovoskry. However, he was not to talk about them or whatever happened that weekend to anyone for about two months.

The couple also said that for whatever reason it was worth, and for all the trouble he had gone through, they had provided him with programs and videos of directions for countless applications of kabislovoskry as a thank-you note.

The Dudarev couple left by the front door, turned left, and went to the house driveway parking lot, as if they were going to take their car. When Dr. O'Shea followed them and quickly opened the front door to offer them directions to where they wanted to go, there was no sign of the couple, and they had completely vanished. Dr. O'Shea also remembered that there was no other car on the driveway but his. He looked all around his house and his neighborhood for the couple but in vain.

Then he went back in the house, reflecting over what Mr. Dudarev said that they were already in Lexington on Sunday morning when they were supposed to leave Amovir.

Dr. O'Shea felt very tired again. He also felt that his mouth was very heavy, as if wired. He went to sleep again.

He woke up the next day by the usual commotion that Sandy Goshen made. He was in definite need of coffee. He came down, and as soon as Sandy saw him, she screamed and told that his face was very puffy as if he was beaten and needed to see a doctor.

Dr. O'Shea did not feel any pain or anything but could not speak. Sandy thought that something was wrong and took Dr. O'Shea to the hospital. After a whole series of tests for two days, the doctor wrote on a piece of paper what was wrong with him. His vocal cords were severed, and he would be operated on. He won't be able to talk for the next two months. He asked him whatever happened to him over the weekend. The doctor said nothing of special, and he knew that he was not beaten. The doctor concluded that it must have been a shock he encountered that weekend that had caused that rupture.

A few days later, Dr. Wasiri read the following e-mail message: "Dear son, I am alerting you to receive a very important courier arriving very shortly by FEDEX. There in is an important message you have to read carefully. Greetings to Hasbo and my grandkids. Yours, Tony." While Dr. Wasiri was scratching his head about the latest mystery e-mail message from his mentor, Hasbo came in with a large envelope just delivered by FEDEX. The strange thing about the box was the originating address. It was not Lexington, Kentucky, but Tempe, Arizona.

That prompted Dr. Wasiri to open the envelope very quickly. He was taken aback by the content of the large envelope. He found about twenty or so CDs and DVDs inside and a letter written by hand by the old professor.

Hasbo was looking at her husband for a particular reaction. He said that maybe the letter was not that important, probably giving him more instructions or results about research studies they were conducting before he departed. He did not mention his apprehension about a new originating address from his mentor. Hasbo left the room to give her husband more privacy to go over the letter from his strange adoptive father.

This letter read, "Dear son, I am writing this letter to ease any concern you might have if you receive a call from my son, Anthony Jr. from Tempe, Arizona, where I am currently recuperating from an extensive surgery to stitch back my vocal cords which were severed last week. The good doctor assured me that age has probably contributed to this unfortunate demise. Do not believe anytime that this had anything to do with our endeavor.

I assure you, absolutely not! As expected, I had a visit from some emissaries who wanted to know more about the test results of the item. The emissaries were very polite and revealed future applications of the item far-reaching and far advanced than anything you and I would have imagined. They left videos and other instructions I have sent to you in this package. I reviewed some of those videos. They are outstanding and for this old and feeble scientist, just a bit frightening for the future of the earth as we know it. I am also sorry to tell you that I had no choice but to provide the emissaries with the specs of the item you gave me. I have learned through other contacts that they have paid dearly for the specs.

First, the foundation funding has been increased to a budget of three billion dollars, next the Atlanta ABDI budget also increased to six billion dollars. You and I would be thanked for the contribution increase at the next ABDI board meeting in November. The emissaries have not forgotten you and me. You would be surprised the next time you check your London account summary. I was, for mine was to the tune of additional one hundred million dollar. The emissaries have a better appreciation of the item in question than most people in this world. Otherwise, why would they expand so much for so little? If you can answer that question, then you don't need to be associated with the endeavor. But I know that you are part of the team selected and appointed by Emily according to Emily's rules.

The fact that you are about to carry the lead role in the endeavor has been sanctioned by Emily's rules because you have been entrusted to do the right thing, you are going to do the right thing and you are going to do it by righteousness. There is no other way about it. Think about it, I could have chosen the profitable selfish way and retire very rich and famous with all that I have discovered about the item. But you know very well such insidious act would have enriched the very ones who have not merited the endeavor benefits. Those are the same people who have trampled on our work for the past forty or fifty years. I would have broken the strict Emily's rules. That would have been sheer lunacy. Instead, I have chosen to transfer all to you to carry the lead role of the endeavor in that remote corner of the world of Mezi, where I am convinced the next glorious chapters of the item would be written. Son, as long we stand by Emily's rules, we would accomplish as much as what the emissaries believe we should. In the meantime, I would urge you to continue doing the right thing where you are. I am prepared to direct the foundation budget increase to do ever-great things on your behalf. Just identify the public services you believe are most needed now, and the foundation would support them through whatever channels. For instance, I remember what your friend, Father Felix, said about the children abandoned in the street of Mandi. Providing decent shelter and education to those kids would be a tremendous public usage of the foundation funding on top of expanding the university academic services. Father Felix can manage it while the university and the foundation would point to an excellent public endeavor. Just think about it. I pray that Hasbo and my grandkids are adjusting very well to life in Mandi. I think about them all the time. Please reassure my son that I should be OK within two or three months when I should recover my big mouth and be able to talk and to talk and to talk. That would be just about time a month or two before the Atlanta ABDI meeting when and where I am expecting to see you again. Maybe it is all Emily's rules to keep me quiet for the next two months for only better purposes.

"Kiss Hasbo and my grandkids warmly. Best regards and greetings to Chancellor Umzigwe and Dean Wutugrase. Say hello to our man in Mandi, Dr. McMillan. Many thanks to him and his wife for all the help they have provided to get you settled. Your father, O'Shea."

Dr. Wasiri had been surprised by many instances the old man had pulled in their many years of interaction. This letter topped them all. It had all included herein, reality, fantasy, premonition, speculation, science fiction, and future political condition. First, he had a surgery for ruptured vocal cords.

Then he was visited by some emissaries who have nothing to do with his unfortunate medical condition. He gave the emissaries all the specs of Alpha-M and in exchange the emissaries increased the budget for the foundation and ABDI by the billions and pay him hundred million. That was an attention grabber. And there was something there for him to check later. Then he got back to Emily's rules. It is always Emily's rules. Dr. Wasiri was confused about how to take or to respond to the letter. He also noticed that if he wanted to keep any electronic or letter correspondence with the old man, he had to adopt his spylike, vague, and mysterious ways to communicate. Never say directly what you have in mind without expansive circumlocutions. That was a bit too much to ask of Dr. Wasiri. In a way, he was happy that he would not have to talk to his mentor for the next two months until they meet in Atlanta.

He was very interested in his last comment about children of the street. That was a very important public service that was beyond need. Dr. Wasiri confided once to Hasbo that if he would go to politics one day, it would be on the account of the children of the street. That sight troubled him to no end and a lot whenever he drove in Mandi. He did not want to understand or to analyze the decision made by those who abandoned their children, some at the age of one. He certainly did not want to pass judgment. All he wanted to do was to help out the children of the street. So when Dr. O'Shea suggested that he was prepared to provide help in that direction, Dr. Wasiri literally forgave his mentor all the other indiscretions contained in the letter. He intended to approach now Monsignor Felix very soon about the process to launch such an important service through Catholic charities. Dr. Wasiri was still tempted to verify what the good old professor said about his London account. He was shocked to see that it had increased by 120 million dollars. Since the last time he had checked the account, it looks like every time he withdrew an amount, the amount was reinstated two times over. And all that he had spent for the overall transfer to Mezi had been reinstated twice. Only Dr. O'Shea can explain this, and he would have his chance to get to the bottom of the mystery when he would see him in Atlanta in November. There was no point troubling him at this time when he was recuperating from that surgery. Besides, he could not talk, and Dr. Wasiri was not about to leave any electronic tracking imprint by sending him an e-mail message. In spite of all was said about electronic security, Dr. Wasiri would trust nobody about keeping such a secret around his ownership of 125 million dollars in a London account. How would he explain it? He would remain as quiet as possible, handling whatever life is providing at this time.

In fact, when he received the news from Dr. O'Shea, Dr. Wasiri was adjusting pretty good to his new life in Mezi as dean of Applied Sciences Faculty of Polytechnic University, along with his family recently arrived from the United States and in the just completed beautiful residence along the Lake Road. Hasbo was very busy handling the final landscape touches of the house and the interior design of the house going back and forth between the rented freight storage and the stunning mansion on the lake. Anna McMillan became a steady companion to Hasbo as her husband Dr. McMillan predicted and expected. Brother Kano also kept to his KMC leadership team assignments attending all meetings and events without reserve. He was the first to complete and present his assigned edicts. He was now looking forward to the KMC first political convention where the definite political leadership of KMC would be elected and would guide the movement to the next electoral process projected now in less than two years. It was generally assumed that Brother Kano would be elected to the top position of KMC general secretary. To date, no effective opponent had emerged to challenge Brother Kano, thanks to the skillful steering of KMC leadership team led by its two wise, old leaders, Chancellor Umzigwe and Dean Wutugrase.

To show how jealously the two men guarded the proceedings of KMC leadership, during one leadership team meeting there was a motion brought by young John Awassa and seconded by Father Zolani. The motion was to determine under what conditions KMC should ally the movement with any other existing political party which would express the desire to merge with KMC for the purpose of running together under one political coalition banner during the upcoming electoral process. Brother Kano, not quite sure of the merits of uniting KMC with any existing political party, stayed quiet throughout the discussion. But Chancellor Umzigwe, Dean Wutugrase, and Sister Fanzi-Djomba were categorical in their total rejection to form any union or coalition with any existing political party. Chancellor Umzigwe was very vehement in his rejection. He said that KMC had spent the last ten years rejecting all those who have joined the corrupt political fray. It would be a complete sell-out for KMC militants if for the purpose of election KMC had to start playing the political game of joining this political front versus this other one. Chancellor Umzigwe said that in doing so, KMC would alienate all those who had stood by it during its long march in the political desert. He concluded that KMC would be better off to march alone to electoral defeat instead of wasting its true political ideals and shining colors with unnecessary search of political coalition. Besides, he added, political coalition usually means political compromise.

He asked the leadership team what would KMC compromise? Would it be its Edict over Corruption or its Edict for Women? Chancellor Umzigwe said he would favor a coalition if the leadership points clearly for him the areas of compromise with other political parties. That position sealed the fate of KMC to continue its long march in the political desert alone as a sole and unique movement or party. Chancellor Umzigwe, Dean Wutugrase, and Sister Fanzi-Djomba were completely adamant and would not be swayed one inch by the argument that this position may open the way for the making of a bigger coalition of all the other Mezi political parties against KMC. Dean Wutugrase responded, saying that had been the case all along for the past ten years or so. That would be the case for the next electoral process. Besides, he commented Mezi is in the dire state at this time because of thousands of compromises among the existing political parties for the past ten years. These political compromises have been quickly made and quickly undone for the same reasons most of these compromises failed. There always comes a time when one party would feel that it was no longer getting the full benefits of the compromise or the other party wants to get out of the perceived worthless or bad compromise.

That time always comes when this political leader believes that he or she is getting less money from the deal or that other leader wants to keep the whole bag of money from the compromise for herself or himself. Any way you look at it, these political compromises have done one and one thing only for the country—they have deepened the bottomless abyss of corruption in Mezi. That was definitely not the way to go for KMC. The leadership team then approved the resolution stating that KMC would not form or join any other political party or any coalition of parties for the purpose of the next electoral process; KMC would march alone to achieve the hard and long fought electoral process victory. People from other parties who want to join the great cause of KMC would do so on individual basis, not as members of an existing party.

Beneath their uncompromising stand, Chancellor Umzigwe and Dean Wutugrase were in fact loath to bring in a more astute politician ready to challenge Brother Kano leadership. They would not allow that even at the risk of losing the election. In the same line of strategy, the two old leaders were also working very hard to control the proceedings of the proposed enlarged KMC Provisional Leadership Committee to insure that Brother Kano's leadership went uncontested all the way to the upcoming first KMC political convention. Young Awassa had brought the motion as a result of the rumors that had reached him and Father Zolani.

It was becoming more and more apparent that the split between former PM Sonjedi and President Badegou was definite and that each one of these two politicians was lining up leaders of existing political parties to join into their respective new political coalitions for the purpose of winning the upcoming electoral battle. Younger Sonjedi was amassing a much larger coalition of parties than his former boss who was becoming more and more despondent over the rapid desertion he was witnessing from his old political allies. There was also a persistent rumor that Sonjedi had lined up sizable funds from South African industrial connections and with very deep pockets. The story went that these South African contacts combined with various Canadian mining interests were sworn to support him to become president of Mezi in the next election using funds alleged to the tune of unheard-of fifty million dollars to start. Nowadays any political leader who approached, saw, or met Mr. Sonjedi in his brand-new office across from the parliament building always came out with a bundle of green notes. If there was something Sonjedi did not seem to lack, it was a bundle of green notes available at all time and all around. Young Awassa got wind of all these political chicaneries from many of his political friends. When he raised the motion of political coalition, he was just following the political rumor du jour. When his own mentor, Chancellor Umzigwe, attacked mercilessly his motion and brought it down with his powerful arguments, he was rather chastened to have raised it in the first place and to have convinced Father Zolani to second it.

CHAPTER 36
Kiriyan's Escape

Compared to the political problems Chairman Kiriyan started encountering in Amovir, what was taking place in Mezi was rather tame. Right after his so-called delegation left Lexington Kentucky, Chairman Kiriyan had a very brief time to celebrate what he had worked for his entire cycle of time on earth as Mr. Dudarev had nicely explained to Dr. O'Shea.

Chairman Kiriyan contacted Lady Allistair to release the funds he had promised to the foundation, ABDI, Dr. O'Shea, and Dr. Wasiri. Lady Allistair tried in vain to reach the hospitalized Dr. O'Shea to give the news. She finally sent an e-mail message that was promptly answered by Dr. O'Shea a day before being released from the hospital after the surgery to stitch back his vocal cords. He told Lady Allistair of the surgery but also insisted that the severed vocal cords were all natural due to old age and nothing to do with the visit from the emissaries from Amovir. He also wrote in e-mail that he would be recuperating for two months. He made a request to Lady Allistair to get the foundation to allocate and to release shortly very discreetly about one hundred to two hundred million dollars to establish a charity foundation to shelter and educate children of the street of Mezi. The funds would come from the recent increase in foundation funding. He said that this charity foundation would go a long way to assist Dr. Wasiri in his various political endeavors. He would give sometime soon the discreet modalities or channels how the funds would be released. He also asked Lady Allistair to keep Patrick Berger away from him while his sit-in, Sandy Goshen, would attend all meetings and would forward all staff meeting accounts to him when he is on vacation visiting family in Arizona. She assured Dr. O'Shea that she would keep all he said in confidence and would execute his charity request accordingly.

She insisted to meet with the good old professor at the Atlanta ABDI November meeting that promised to be an awesome meeting. She did not give any more detail. She also contacted His Honorable Jeremy Massay to let him know that thanks to persistent lobbying efforts from Dr. O'Shea and Dr. Wasiri, ABDI funding budget was increased to six billion dollars.

This funding amount should allow ABDI to increase its share of the Easter Africa Water Project and to add broad coverage of thirty other additional projects that were waiting for final funding. The more than doubling of ABDI funding shocked His Honorable Massay. He mentioned that the new funding would insure that November board meeting would mark a major milestone to celebrate the completion of two-thirds of the Eastern Africa Water Project and the completion of already started projects. The November meeting can now change into a gathering of a lot of heads of African States, which are recipient of and have benefited from all of these projects. He was also expecting to welcome Lady Allistair as a major VIP guest. He would also send a big thank-you note to the two Kentucky scientists who have been working behind the scenes to make things happen. When Lady Allistair had completed her reporting, she called her boss in Amovir to check why Dr. O'Shea had suffered the vocal cords disruption right after his delegation's visit. Chairman Kiriyan was shocked to hear this news. He repeated what his emissaries had said when they left the good old professor, "They said to the professor to keep his silence around their visit for the next two months and they left." Chairman Kiriyan added, "Other things along with the visit must have shocked the poor old professor. The emissaries left with him videos to see. Whatever Dr. O'Shea saw in those videos must have been a little bit shocking for a man of his age. I am talking about advanced applications of Alpha-M you would be amazed of. In any case, my emissaries are gone now and have been replaced by a new crew of about fifteen people from our domain. I forgot to tell you that as a result of the last Kentucky visit over Alpha-M, I have no choice but to have Varonne-Sur-Baie move not only accelerated as I speak but to have it moved to grade one or super-priority One. The Kentucky visit was extremely positive, no question about it. I was very excited and elated by the visit but at the same time Amovir is now in complete jeopardy. I would keep you posted soon enough."

This conversation left Lady Allistair with more interrogations than she needed. She would have to wait to get more information about what was going on in Amovir.

She tried her good friend and lover Ludmilla Borensky, but she was completely out of sync and out of touch. She was more remorseful for having triggered something with that trip to Moscow with Karlov Yelgin. She had no idea what Chairman Kiriyan was referring to when he said Amovir is now in complete jeopardy. She called a few confident contacts, but they were also in the dark about the goings-on at Chairman Kiriyan level.

She apologized to her friend Lady Allistair she could not help her. In fact, Chairman Kiriyan had a whole set of issues that were making his stay in Amovir less and less hospitable. Since the incarceration of his Russian operations managing director, Mr. Karlov Yelgin, Chairman Kiriyan was monitoring the events in Moscow to find out if the acerbic Russian denunciation of his BI international expansion by Karlov was getting any track. The many faces of Mr. Alexiev Kramokov/Dr. Neal Hansberger went full blast. What Alexiev collected increasingly did not please his boss in Amovir. It showed that as soon as Karlov was out of the drug treatment he received in the FSS penal system, he became a big mouthpiece railing against the demons and catastrophes that all current big business oligarchs were perpetrating against the Russian national wealth.

He used his full grasp of business enterprise to establish how they have operated to amass unbelievable amount of resources and means of production by deception and corruption of various levels of government. In the remote FSS jail in Siberia, Karlov started holding lengthy seminars and lectures for the benefit of high-level FSS officers who, in general, looked with great suspicion the advent of these oligarchs they associated with the growth of the current powerful underworld. In each of their analysis about maintaining a crime free Russia, FSS generals have never stopped to point out that only oligarchs were responsible for the growth of the underworld activities in Russia. Getting rid of Russian oligarchs was equivalent to stopping underworld crimes in Russia and making Mother Russia crime-free.

That simplistic crime concept was gaining a lot of ground and believers in security circles of Russia, which was KGB/FSS based. In the same context, Alexiev warned his boss that he should not be surprised to learn that Karlov had been released after about a year of incarceration and after FSS had investigated and established that he was drugged and had no idea where the two hundred thousand counterfeit dollars came from. Before FSS got to that eventual release, it had to establish that Karlov was a victim of a conspiracy in . . . Amovir where he had been protesting the theft of Russian patrimony invested in BI for the past seventy years. Alexiev concluded that, according to his contacts, FSS was about to start investigating all that Karlov had been saying about Chairman Kiriyan for the past two years. Major FSS audits of BI were about to be launched unless Chairman Kiriyan comes to Moscow and stop all these shenanigans; otherwise, he would have to leave Amovir soon.

Alexiev also noted that Karlov's wife had been spending a lot of time staying with her husband at that FSS facility. When she came back to Amovir from that FSS location, she proudly told a few confident people that her husband was not in jail; he was in a very good and outstanding Russian protection while all is put in motion to arrest Chairman Kiriyan and his cohorts. She was very clear that her husband was spending most of his time in this beautiful dacha with a protection of a full FSS armed detachment. He spends time writing paper exposes around business enterprise in time of oligarchs and was being shuttling around the country giving lectures to big Russian former true comrades all expenses paid by FSS. Karlov's wife had been using quite a few people in Amovir to provide her with financial evidence to show how Chairman Kiriyan had completely destroyed BI enterprise and had moved all that wealth outside Russian in far-away companies that Chairman Kiriyan had acquired with BI Russian money. Mrs. Yelgin did not look as remorseful as she was before she went to see her husband in that location in Siberia. She said to her confident people that it was only a matter of time when her husband would be back to Amovir, not as managing director of BI Russian operations, but as the first real Russian Chairman of BI. The most striking observation was that when she was not visiting her husband in Siberia, Mrs. Yelgin had been going around all the republics, oblasts, and krais that made up what used to be called in the Soviet Union time, the Eastern Siberian Region and political entities around Lake Baikhal.

The political entities included Irkutsk Oblast, Tyva Republic, Khakasia Oblast, Buryatia Republic, Tajmyr Oblast, Evenkia Oblast, Krasnoryarsk Krai, and Ust-Ordynsk Autonomous Oblast. She went around paying visit to each governor of these political entities to lobby them about how they can reclaim their entity share of BI income as it was at the time of the Fourth Region Mining Directorate at the time of Soviet Union. That lobbying was turning out more politically troublesome to Chairman Kiriyan than anything that FSS would do in terms of audits. FSS audits could be nicely controlled as far as their distribution or release, thanks to the political channels that Chairman Kiriyan had infiltrated and controlled. However, anytime each one of the governors would start giving speeches about not getting a fair share of income from BI for more than twelve years, it would become very difficult to control. Kremlin would be no match against those rabble-rousers of politicians. After the economic debacle that followed two political administrations from the time of Yeltsin, it was obvious that real political center was moving away from Kremlin toward the most prosperous and powerful entities of Siberia and southeast, including those around Baikhal Lake.

Three months later, it was with no surprise that, in the course of two weeks, three different FSS prosecutors came to Amovir to inquire again about the departed Ludmilla Borensky and the never-heard-of Alexiev Kramokov. While Ludmilla was clearly localized in an overseas assignment in AMX London Staff of undetermined time length, Mr. Kramokov was another story altogether. His last physical presence in Amovir dated back to about fifteen years ago. His whereabouts became a whole mystery afterward although he was clearly identified by Karlov as being the BI's international marketing representative in Moscow with a family of three at the time of the famous Moscow trip. He could not be identified in BI Human Resources files. That was a big puzzle that the three prosecutors suspected to amount to a conspiracy that was either cleverly devised by the missing Ludmilla Borensky or the sitting chairman of BI, Mr. Nadov Kiriyan for the very reasons that Mr. Karlov Yelgin had given all along, the reaping and stealing of BI financial assets. The three FSS prosecutors returned again three weeks later to announce that a major financial audit of BI from 1993 to present would be launched. The period covered was exactly the time when the Fourth Mining Directorate was incorporated by Chairman Kiriyan into Baikhal Industries which would be metamorphosed into Baikhal International of present days. The next day, and for the first time since the death of President Yeltsin, Chairman Kiriyan went to Moscow to pay visit to his major contacts, including the president of Russia Republic, the premier minister, major government economic policy ministers, the president of Duma, and five presidents of its economic and finance commissions, and some remaining FSS sympathetic generals.

Chairman Kiriyan spent four days of inconclusive meetings. He was repeatedly told that the issue was not in Kremlin that had faithfully supported and understood BI international expansion, without mentioning the big and generous BI financial retainers that various groups of people in Kremlin and legislative branches had seen landing in their overseas bank accounts for the past ten years. The issue was coming from the six or seven governors of republics, oblasts, and krais around Lake Baikhal. Theses governors insisted on accounting for the tax income due their provinces since 1993. Kremlin was unable to squash this request during the difficult economic times that the entire republic was going through. The PM even suggested to Chairman Kiriyan to go abroad and lie low somewhere in Europe until the political storm is taken care of. There was absolutely no point fighting these basically new warlords of the Russian political entities. Kremlin, and other Moscow power centers would not join him in the looming legal fight.

In fact, they would be ready to sacrifice him high and dry. It was an unmistaken warning that Chairman Kiriyan had received from the Moscow trip. The bottom line was that he was being given a rope to run away from Amovir as quickly as he could. Amovir was therefore in complete jeopardy. Chairman Kiriyan started putting all preparations for his escape from Amovir while FSS prosecutors multiplied their audits.

His first order of actions was to secure the heart of his international empire, the Liechtenstein Central Investment Bank or CIB. Chairman Kiriyan had already given Lady Allistair high-priority instructions to secure this money center when she was appointed AMX CEO in her last visit to Amovir. This time he wanted Lady Allistair to take effective control of CIB by linking it directly under her management.

Chairman Kiriyan suggested to Lady Allistair to set up an effective authority presence in Vaduz. Lady Allistair clearly understood this instruction and appointed her friend, Mrs. Evelyn Bottown, current AMX CFO as chairperson of CIB for the duration. Evelyn agreed to move to Vaduz to take over that position while her trusted deputy, Mr. Sydney Whitehall, was temporarily appointed as AMX CFO. The second action was to designate his most faithful lieutenant, Dr. Neal Hansberger, as his main contact with the French Intelligence Services in Paris. Chairman Kiriyan was only collecting at this time his due for all that he had done in connection to moving his enterprise's headquarters to Varonne-Sur-Baie.

To date, the move had cost BI more than four billion and counting. The move started slowly with the arrival of small investment banking operations of CIB, which have now mushroomed to sizable international money center operations grouped under the deceptive and very French company named La Maison d'Investissements—Boissy International borrowing the reputed initial of BI. On top of banking investment operations, Boissy International became in no time a major real estate owner controlling about two-fifths of Varonne-Sur-Baie land. The real estate included the most forbidding areas of the island where the sea waves were the roughest and where there was no ready access to road or navigable water. This was to keep up with the extreme privacy and reclusion requirements of the future owner of mansions built in unlikely places on the island littoral. The mansions were being built using the most elaborate architecture known on earth to sustain the extreme harshness of the unbelievable landscape of that part of the difficult littoral terrain. In some instances, the mansions were to be linked to roads or embankments through underground passages dug only to enhance the need for privacy of the owner, Chairman Kiriyan.

The BI move to Varonne-Sur-Baie had also generated a rapid growth of the island to become a big international money center starting to rival the like of Dubai and Abu Dhabi. American, German, British, French, and Middle East major financial establishments flocked to the island being rapidly followed by Chinese, Japanese, and Asia-Pac major banking interests. Between tourism and banking, Varonne-Sur-Baie's political authorities were at a loss to choose which of the two interests to promote.

French authorities, from the president to various government economic leaders, who have diligently pursued and encouraged Chairman Kiriyan's initial move, were more than ready to assist Chairman Kiriyan in his last step to close the move of BI to Varonne-Sur-Baie. All along, from the start they were very wary of Russian susceptibility. They helped Chairman Kiriyan to hide all forms of BI headquarters move to Varonne-

Sur-Baie. They even suggested that very original French name of Boissy International to cover entire BI operations in Varonne-Sur-Baie and to deceive Russian authorities. When Chairman Kiriyan indicated that the final chapter of the move was not going to go down smoothly, the president of France himself put in motion a full package of worldwide intelligence services to assist Chairman Kiriyan escape from Amovir to Varonne-Sur-Baie. As one of the president's close advisers put it, "At the end, it would be a zero sum game with a total Russian loss against a total French gain."

There could be no other person fit in representing Chairman Kiriyan and directing his ultimate escape operation as much as Dr. Neal Hansberger, always dedicated to Chairman Kiriyan's various causes. The above actions were enablers taking place outside Russia and Amovir scenes. For the purpose of the escape, Chairman Kiriyan would depend on a small crew of about twenty people from his own far-away domain when the couple Dudarev suddenly disappeared from Amovir.

This young-looking bunch showed up for one reason only—to plan and execute all the escape routes and channels to get Chairman Kiriyan out of Amovir. They were the ones putting together a complete submarine at the lake's landing set connected to Chairman Kiriyan's another huge mansion on the lake. The landing set had two parts: a visible one that showed the huge boat that Chairman Kiriyan used to cruise the Baikhal Lake in better times; the invisible one in the huge basement of the mansion that was used to build the elaborate super high technology submarine.

The last three months of his stay in Amovir, Chairman Kiriyan stopped going to his Amovir main office at the other side of the mountain in the direction of his own private airstrip. Two Dassault Falcon 9X private jet planes were permanently kept in that airstrip hangar. Chairman Kiriyan stopped going to his office after being harassed by the now intrusive FSS prosecutors from Moscow. He would not give them any satisfaction answering their probing questions. To get even with those in Kremlin and legislative branches and who have launched the annoying probes, Chairman Kiriyan deliberately released documents from the 1993 period when he handily incorporated all the Fourth Industrial and Mining Directorate operations into Baikal Industries. These documents were not intended to show any act compromising the Chairman Kiriyan's integrity. The documents laid bare the mountain of legal authorizations that Chairman Kiriyan was able to draw from those in power at the time to form the new private BI conglomerate out of the blue. What was telling was that each authorization signature was gained through a fee payment that sometime was the equivalent of 10 percent of the net worth being transferred to BI. There were so many prominent names in these documents with clearly identifiable fees received to authorize the requested transactions that the young FSS prosecutors from Moscow had begun to fear for their own function and life. In some cases, the same authorization was being revisited and requested year after year for the sole purpose to maintain the fee payment into foreign bank accounts in Helsinki, Finland. When Chairman Kiriyan started the company's international expansion, the authorizations along with the fees went on unabated through present. The FSS prosecutors from Moscow consulted with their boss, a FSS major general who saw clearly what Chairman Kiriyan was doing, he was not going to be implicated in anything without bringing down the huge house of corrupted cards starting right there in Kremlin. The major general collected all the documents submitted by his prosecutors and brought the matter to proper authorities in Kremlin and legislative branches.

All of the sudden, the FSS audits were stopped for a while and Chairman Kiriyan was asked one afternoon to go to his private airstrip to meet with an important traveler from Moscow. The important traveler turned out to be his former main economic legislative contact in Moscow. He told him that he was carrying an important message from the office of the premier minister of Russia Republic. The PM was renewing his advice for Chairman Kiriyan to go quietly to Europe or any other place and to lie low until the business at hand would be taken care of at the level of recalcitrant governors in Baikal Region.

In addition, Chairman Kiriyan was strongly advised to stop releasing documents that may cause a serious embarrassment to a lot of powerful people. Chairman Kiriyan listened attentively and asked his main contact what would be the alternative if he did not follow the advice. The emissary was direct and said that the alternative could be fatal to Chairman Kiriyan. It was clear by now that in addition to the rabid governors, Kremlin had decided to eliminate Chairman Kiriyan once and for all. In the Chairman Kiriyan's mind, that was the outcome he most desired in order to cut all his links with Russia and start anew in Varonne-Sur-Baie. In his plan, he intended to lure his adversaries to eliminate him while he was designing a different escape routes. The escape route should take him south of Lake Baikal to the Irkutsk Oblast that bordered the Republic of Mongolia where French Intelligence Services would manage a way out to Varonne-Sur-Baie.

It also turned out that Chairman Kiriyan had cultivated a long outstanding relationship with the high political official of the territory south of Baikhal Lake in the area of Vydrino, a border town between

Irkutsk Oblast and Zabaykalsky Krai. This political official, named Shimzast Ziamian couldn't care less what the governor of Irkutsk, in the far-away capital of Irkust, thought of the Chairman. Chairman Kiriyan had often collected this official in his huge boat to cruise the lake in better long weekend party times in the past. BI had no mining or industrial in the territory. Chairman Kiriyan saw an opening in this situation. His emissaries started working on Mr. Ziamian to authorize the transfer of BI headquarters from Amovir to a new city to be built along its Lake Baikal coast on his side of territory. The official bought the argument of the move along a very generous retainer fee. He was overwhelmed when Chairman Kiriyan provided him free usage of one of his private jet planes that he stationed at a small military airstrip under his administrative preview and very close to the town of Vydrino. He also took care to provide the small military airbase commander with a lot of financial incentives, including ladies from Moscow nightlife. When the building of the submarine was complete, the young bunch did three dry run tests from Amovir to the southern territory coast and back. The ride was very fast, under forty-five minutes, and timely back. Some days before the decisive escape-planned weekend, Chairman Kiriyan literally and plainly advertised his imminent departure by closing BI international staff and sending all non-Russian staff members to their country of origin to await further instructions. The Friday before the departure, Chairman Kiriyan took a ride with mechanics to the private airstrip hangar apparently to check and to prepare his remaining Dassault Falcon 9X private jet for the escape flight. The visit lasted more than an hour.

The next day, the same convoy took the ride to the airstrip, and the private jet plane took off shortly after. The flight took a strange path. It went north at low altitude along the huge lake on the eastern coast, then when it reached the northernmost post, it turned south flying along the western coast. When it was about to reach the southern tip of the Lake Baikal, the plane turned right along the Selenga delta and maintained the low altitude flight path. As the plane approached the Baikhal Mountains, it started rising higher. But before reaching the cruising altitude of twenty-five thousand miles, the plane started picking up speed in the direction of Kazakhstan. Just about the time it was to cross the rising Baikhal Mountains, the plane exploded. The entire flight had taken about two hours and forty-five minutes.

The next day, Sunday, at noon Moscow time, a military communiqué announced, "A private jet plane which left Amovir on Saturday morning has crashed in the Baikal Mountains far from the borders of Kazakhstan. The jet was believed to be carrying BI Chairman Nadov Kiriyan, two staff employees, and a plane crew of four. There was no crash survivor as the jet plane exploded before the crash. The military was combing the whole area for further investigations." The brief flash was quickly distributed around the world at the same time that a tanned French citizen by the name of Norbert Krimotte, President-Directeur-General de La Maison D'Investissements—Boissy International, was relaxing along the deserted pool at a Southern Thailand private resort in the island of Phuket with another man named Dr. Neal Hansberger. They laughed at the CNN flash announcing the demise of Chairman Nadov Kiriyan. Dr. Neal Hansberger quickly placed a call to London and reached Lady Allistair who was just waking up from a busy Saturday night and had not yet seen the CNN or BBC flash.

Lady Allistair talked with Mr. Krimotte for about fifteen minutes and shook her head. She then saw the CNN flash and laughed. But later, when she called Ludmilla and warned her not to pay too much attention to all that was going to be said about Chairman Kiriyan, she found her lover and friend in complete disarray, almost in a wake. She rushed to console her friend in her apartment. Ludmilla was crying since she saw the CNN flash. She said she knew that Chairman Kiriyan must have taken all necessary precautions not to be assassinated by people in Kremlin. She was not concerned about Chairman Kiriyan, who would be fine although she was not sure how. She was concerned about herself and her family. Now that Chairman Kiriyan is out of picture in Russia, Ludmilla strongly believed that she would have hard time to go back home. She would be in virtual exile in London now, unable to see her parents for a long long time.

She told her friend that she was certain that all this shooting down of Chairman Kiriyan's plane came about after and because of her trip to Moscow with Karlov Yelgin. She kept saying that all started because of that trip. She did not want to go over the details of the trip, only to say that a lot of things happened during that trip and led to the current debacle. She was very remorseful to have failed Chairman Kiriyan. Lady Allistair was at a loss with her lack of specificity and completely dismissed her claim to be at the center of a struggle between Kremlin people and Chairman Kiriyan. She was a bit aggravated at her friend for suggesting that it was all about sex or lack of sex.

In her own devious way, Lady Allistair would not reveal what she personally believed was the reason of the debacle, the precipitous flight to Varonne-Sur-Baie by Uncle Kiri. The move to Varonne-Sur-Baie was probably and secretly revealed to Kremlin folks and they decided to eliminate Chairman Kiriyan. She maintained her silence later that Sunday when a close adviser of the British PM came to pay her visit at her official residence and inquired about AMX status in light of the tumult around Chairman Kiriyan. Lady Allistair kept a stiff upper lip and stated that AMX status was fine. She also claimed not to know much what was going on in Russia. The advisor was trying to improve the PM's understanding of the latest Russian disaster. The day before, a CIA emissary and M16 specialists had already briefed the PM about the episode using the spy satellite video that had captured Kiriyan's jet plane explosion. But the British PM, along with the American president, did not appreciate what they were hearing from the French government that seemed to add more confusing statements about the episode than was necessary. To understand what had happened, the British and the American needed more soft intelligence on top the satellite video. They suspected that the French government was somehow involved in this explosive episode. Lady Allistair was of no help and less so after the visit to the remorseful Ludmilla.

Everything Chairman Kiriyan had planned for his escape from Amovir worked as expected to precision. First, the flight of the Dassault Falcon 9X jet plane was entirely autopiloted from Amovir to the crash site, thanks to the fly-by-wire system digitally enhanced by the recently arrived young bunch. Chairman Kiriyan assumed that his private jet plane would be shot down as soon as it was airborne. The plane was retrofitted not just with very advanced state-of-the-art autopilot system; it was also rigged with dynamite to get it blown at that very site where it was estimated it would be taken out by military-guided missile if the chairman's adversaries wanted to.

The crash location was so remote to allow any possibility of any witnessing of either explosion or shooting down of the plane. And if the crash were seen by anybody, the explosion of the plane would have raised the likelihood that it was shot down. Chairman Kiriyan did not want to leave his demise to any chance. Either the plane he was supposed to be flying was going to be shot down or it would be blown up. The result was going to be the same. He would be reported dead after the reported crash and all recourses initiated in Russia against him will cease. The low-altitude flying over Lake Baikal for about two hours was also programmed to advertise to whomever that Chairman Kiriyan was leaving but using the evasive low-altitude flying techniques to avoid flight detection. The roundabout low-altitude flight over the lake, starting from the east coast going north, then going south on the west coast was also needed to allow Chairman Kiriyan enough time to manage his alternative escape route. As soon as the fake convoy with the chairman's limousine left the mansion toward the private airstrip, Chairman Kiriyan went down to the basement and boarded the submarine while at the same time, another crew was boarding a medium-sized boat, not far from the mansion. This boat looked like a regular dirty sturgeon fishing boat commonly seen along Lake Baikal. As the submarine was speeding below toward the southern destination, the above medium-sized boat made a steady and equal trip to southward with one purpose—to survey any military or police activity above and to protect the submarine below. When the two vessels approached the town of Vydrino, the submarine was raised inside a special compartment cut up within the fishing boat. Chairman Kiriyan was now in an army uniform of a major. The young bunch was also in military outfit with machine guns. Afterward the submarine was lowered and autopiloted to the deepest point of the lake. The plan was to program it to be blown up at midnight. The entire fishing boat crew left the boat at a specially designated landing set. The major got into an equivalent military jeep with three other younger subordinates. The rest of the crew jumped into an open truck. The military convoy then took the direction of the small military airbase at the time when its base commander and Mr. Ziamian were in the middle of Lake Baikal on the western side of the lake, fishing sturgeons with four other friends using a large pleasure boat rented by Chairman Kiriyan for a long weekend of partying. When the major reached the base entrance, he was welcomed by one of the young bunch, who had infiltrated the base military regiment. On the weekend, the majority of the three hundred or so military recruits took a leave of absence. When the skeleton of recruits who remained in the base learned that the base commander was going to be far away from the base, less than twenty recruits were going to be in the base.

The captain who welcomed the convoy was at the time the commanding officer. He led the military convoy to the Dassault Falcon 9X hangar. He was executing the commander-falsified instruction to move the plane back to Amovir airstrip. This had happened before in two separate occasions and always on weekends. The private jet plane was readied for a flight toward the Mongolia borders.

The only major issue was crossing the borders without being shot down. Here again, the president of France took the matter in a particular intelligence service fashion.

While Chairman Kiriyan was preparing his escape route, a French government and business delegation was visiting Yakutsk, the capital of the Republic of Sakha, the largest in Siberia to prospect gas and oil explorations in remote northern oil deposits of the republic. The delegation was to head down to Ulaan Batar, Mongolia, after the visit. But the French delegation would take two private jet planes for the flight. The idea was to time the crossing of the two planes into Mongolia along with Chairman Kiriyan's flight that at this time had already converted to the French flight clearances, including the flight number from Yakutsk. This deception eluded the Russian air surveillance team in the border area. In addition, there was no particular military alert to raise the border surveillance status during a relatively quiet weekend. Chairman Kiriyan's flight was beautifully squeezed between the two flights from Yakutsk, and at about five on that Saturday evening, three French jet planes landed in a Mongolian military base outside the town of Nalayh, east of Ulaan Batar. The French ambassador to Mongolia had cleared the flight of three jet planes from Yakutsk, instead of two, to the Mongolian foreign ministry, extremely eager to start high-level international exchange talks with the large French government and business delegation, so much so that the Mongolian foreign ministry provided a special military hangar for the French ambassador to welcome the entire delegation from Russia in total privacy. In the process, the ambassador gained the authorization to allow the refueling and departure of one of the jet planes toward Thailand. While the ambassador was busy to welcome the delegation from Yakutsk, the French president's advisor, who came along, went to the mysterious third plane to verify that Chairman Kiriyan had a safe flight. Dr. Neal Hansberger accompanied the advisor inside the plane. He met briefly with the chairman. He simply said that his boss had kept his word. Chairman Kiriyan responded that he was most grateful and hoped to see him in the island of Varonne-Sur-Baie very soon.

Six hours later, the Dassault Falcon 9X, with complete French flight credentials, landed on the small airstrip on the south tip of Thailand.

The following Monday of the audacious escape started what was going to be called the Kiriyan sighting around the world. An article was published in Houston Chronicle stating that according to the intelligence sources, the Russian military had shot down the private jet plane of the financier Nadov Kiriyan because he was becoming very annoying toward a lot people in power over the international management of BI. The Russian government protested energetically the article at the State Department. Another article came out of a major publication in Kuala-Lumpur, stating that Chairman Kiriyan was sighted in Dubai where he was in hiding.

He was helped to leave Russia by a particular group of Kremlin insiders indebted to his past services while he was building BI internationally. An Italian magazine went even further and reported that Chairman Kiriyan was not killed; in fact, he had taken the political leadership of the underground political secession of the newly formed Republic of Buryatia along the Mongolian border. The report of his plane crash was all a diversion by Moscow to hide the mounting discontent in the new republic. All these articles were carefully dispatched and funded by the newly funded propaganda cell that Dr. Neal Hansberger had mounted outside Vaduz. The three articles threw the Kremlin men in total disarray. They did not anticipate such an international outcry over a matter they had considered to be strictly Russian.

With a stroke of a pen, the office of premier minister issued a sweeping decree which accomplished the following: it reversed all government documents authorizing the incorporation of the Fourth Mining and Industrial Region into Baikal Industries, recapitalized the Fourth into a company called East Siberia Mining and Industrial company, added enough state capital to make it operational and viable for the next five to six years, distributed the resulting equity to the republics, oblasts, and krais which were reclaiming the tax income lost since 1993.

As soon as the decree was approved by the Duma as part of an ongoing budget resolution, the new East Siberia Mining company, in existence for less than two weeks, was quickly merged into another mammoth state and private owned industrial conglomerate based in Yakutsk, in the Republic of Sakha, the company was named Transiberia International Exchange or TSIX.

This company was the exact duplicate of BI in terms of operations in the entire Siberia region and growing rapidly with every new gas and oil deposit it discovered every other month in the endless Siberian territory in addition to all other minerals mines the company already owned. The company was the jewel of Moscow Stock Exchange. The governors initially concerned about the tax income shortfall from BI were very pleased by the federal government's action and dropped all legal or political pursuits they were hatching. Mr. Karlov Yelgin, who had triggered the aggravating episode, was thanked for his efforts by having his twenty years counterfeit money sentence reconfirmed by a higher appeal court and was sentenced for additional ten years for sexual abuse of minor and sodomy rape of the thirteen-year-old boy. He was promptly shipped to a further remote and harsher penal system in Eastern Siberia. When his wife protested against another monstrous state conspiracy, she was accused of becoming a major security risk against the state and was forced to join her husband with their young children. The couple Yelgin died of chronic bouts of pneumonia three years later, and their children were dispersed in to orphanages in Siberia.

The real objective of all these government actions was not to protect the Russian patrimony. The real objective was to squash away the dissemination of the compromising documents revealing the widespread craft that ruled the day and push the advent of most of the big conglomerates in the hand of the Russian nouveaux riches. The release of those documents was bound to upset and put at risk the new political order taking hold in Russia. For better or worse, the Russia's current leadership owed its political rise and allegiance to most of the people whose names were found on the bottom of official authorizations which either created or expanded the mammoth industrial companies of nowadays Russian oligarchs.

Chairman Kiriyan, or Norbert Krimotte, intended to spend the next two or three months finally lying low at a place of his own choosing in this secluded hotel in the island of Phuket in the southern tip of Thailand, while the young bunch crew and Dr. Neal Hansberger would be preparing his final move to Varonne-Sur-Baie.

CHAPTER 37
KMC Convention

Sometime before the political downfall of Chairman Kiriyan in Russia, Dr. Wasiri went to see Monsignor Felix to follow up on the advice his mentor gave him to look for ways to help the children of the street in the capital of Mandi. That was the first chance Dr. Wasiri ventured to the St. Charles Seminary where Monsignor Felix was the rector. As soon as Dr. Wasiri raised the issue of the children of the street, Monsignor Felix asked him how the Mezi Women's Congress in Ikando was. Dr. Wasiri was puzzled to see the relationship between the congress and the children of the street. Monsignor Felix went on to ask if while at the Free University location Dr. Wasiri had managed to see Dr. Injewi Ingoma. Dr. Wasiri answered affirmatively and added that they added a long and very positive exchange regarding the KMC leadership team. Monsignor Felix then asked him if there was no other issue raised. There was none said Dr. Wasiri.

At that point, Monsignor Felix told his visitor that he came to the wrong place for counsel, although he appreciated the visit. Monsignor Felix said that Dr. Ingoma had already built a shelter for children of the street in Zingzong slum of Ikando. If there was someone as dedicated to the cause, Dr. Ingoma was the person to learn from all the intricacies of setting a shelter of children of the street. Monsignor Felix strongly advised Dr. Wasiri to go back to Ikando to talk with the president of Free University in Ikando if he was serious to launch such a needed public service. At that instant, Dr. Wasiri invited Monsignor Felix to accompany him the weekend after to talk to Dr. Ingoma.

Monsignor Felix gave his visitor the background of the illustrious Dr. Ingoma. "It turned out as soon as he was born in seven months, premature, his mother died of birth complications. She was about seventeen years old and suddenly showed up at this convent location belonging to the Catholic order of Sisters of Charity. The convent had a small maternity. It was never determined where the young lady came from. She was definitely not from Ikando or the surrounding villages or localities. She probably arrived there by bus or some difficult transportation means of the time. As soon she arrived at the convent by foot, she started bleeding. She was admitted into the maternity and gave birth soon after to the premature boy.

She died during the night as a result of acute internal hemorrhage. She never had the chance to give her name or her background. The Sisters of Charity sheltered the child from infancy to the age of six. When it came time to place him in one of the state-run orphanages, a sister named Genevieve Ingoma decided to keep the boy under her tutelage. That put her in collision course with the order.

"She could not part away the boy she had raised from infancy. She decided to adopt the boy against her superior's wishes. The bishop of Ikando finally reached a compromise with the Catholic order. Sister Ingoma was going to leave the order, adopt the boy, and continue to work in the maternity as a prenatal and natal nurse. The compromise suited Miss Ingoma very much. She rented and finally bought a house not far from the convent, went to work to the maternity daily, and attended to all sisterhood tasks in the convent as well as all motherly tasks of raising the boy she named Injewi Ingoma. Injewi meant 'from the street.' The young Ingoma progressed nicely in his studies while being provided a strict religious upbringing by Miss Ingoma. It was not a surprise when young Ingoma entered St. Charles Seminary at the end of his high school. After about three years of priest formation, Mr. Ingoma stated that he was not cut out to be a priest. His adoptive mother, who continued to be addressed as Sister Ingoma until she passed away, was a bit disappointed but did not show it. Mr. Ingoma went on to the famous academic scholarship achievement we know today to rise to the presidency of Free University of Ikando and that prestigious deanship in Kuala Lumpur. The question had always been why that attachment to Ikando for a man who could have made it anywhere in the world. Well, from what Monsignor heard, Dr. Ingoma, who never married, had made a pact with his adoptive mother; since he did not become a priest, he would establish a shelter for children of the street in Ikando, he was one of them.

By the way, when he came back to Ikando, the first thing he tried to do was to build the shelter. Of course, he ran against a myriad of problems. But he never gave up. While he was more successful building an entire university, he never forgot his first call. He persevered. He told me that the proudest moment of his life came when his adoptive mother, Sister Ingoma, at the advanced age of eighty-three came to cut the ribbons of the first building to house the shelter for children of the street of Ikando. He gave the original name of 'Circle Bongani' to the place. Bongani means, depending on the situation, either 'where are you going to' or 'where are you coming from.' There was no better way to describe the place where the children of the street would come to but through that word, 'Bongani.'"

In his ride back from the seminary to his home, Dr. Wasiri decided that Dr. Ingoma was a man to depend on at all cost, all the time.

During the next meeting of KMC leadership team, when the list of the new members of KMC Provisional Leadership Committee was being made, each current leadership member was asked to introduce a name. Brother Kano suggested the name of Dr. Injewi Ingoma, to the great delight of Chancellor Umzigwe, who protested comically of being robbed of his trump card name. Two other names which were proposed by his colleagues intrigued Dr. Wasiri. They were Mr. Mengi Sakoto and Mr. Komasi Bello. The first suggested by Sister Fanzi-Djomba was an inspector at the Ministry of Finances; the second, suggested by Dean Wutugrase, was a retired army colonel, presently managing large farm complexes in the Tongeo Province. Dr. Wasiri was surprised and delighted to hear Chancellor Umzigwe proposing his very good friend Sir Ewas as one of the new members representing KMC in overseas matters. The list was reviewed two more times before being publicly released.

The new KMC Provisional Leadership Committee was as politically, professionally, ethnically diverse and balanced for Mezi with the exception of women representation. Out of sixteen members, only four women were chosen. Dr. Wasiri raised that issue and told his colleagues that they should do better by the end of the political convention. Ironically, the list was very well received by all of the progressive forces and associations allied to KMC. All proposed new members also accepted to be invited into the committee including Dr. Ingoma, who was delighted to receive Dr. Wasiri and Monsignor Felix when they came over to talk about the shelter for the children of the street. No matter how Dr. Ingoma tried to change the subject to the list of the KMC new governing committee, Dr. Wasiri was focused to learn as much as possible about the launching of the shelter on a national level. Dr. Ingoma finally left the political matter aside and gave the visitors a long lecture around his pet prospect.

At the end, having taken as many notes as possible, Dr. Wasiri told Dr. Ingoma that his vision was quite feasible and should be in place and functioning in less than six months. To start, there would be two major installations to be completed within two to three months in Ikando and Mandi to house the first batch of children of the street in Komesah and Zingzong slums of Mandi and Ikando. The next phase would include the building of self-supporting huge resorts in the outskirts of Mandi and Ikando.

All these endeavors would come under a new foundation called Bongani that would fall under the leadership of Monsignor Felix. Dedicated administrators would be chosen in the Catholic, Protestant, and secular hierarchies, people with demonstrable dedication to the causes of children of the street. Dr. Ingoma would be the chairman of board of the foundation Bongani. He assured Dr. Ingoma that the funding of the foundation is on track, thanks to his preliminary contacts with major foundations dedicated to such works in Sweden, Austria, and Canada.

Dr. Ingoma was literally in heaven after Dr. Wasiri had finished describing how his vision was going to be implemented. Dr. Ingoma, looking at Monsignor Felix, repeated what he told the congregation at the end of the Mass celebrated during the funerals of his adoptive mother, "Sister Ingoma's spirits have not done with us children of street yet. She would come through someday somehow."

Dr. Ingoma had tears in his eyes. Dr. Wasiri consoled his new colleague, and trying to change the conversation to the political talk he initiated before, he told him, "Let it be known, Brother Ingoma, you have not done with us politically yet, you would come through someday somehow. We are all children of the street. We dearly need you. Mezi needs you."

Dr. Wasiri was able to meet Dr. Ingoma's vision half way, thanks to intense e-mail correspondence he had exchanged with his mentor regarding this issue the previous week. Dr. O'Shea, in turn, pestered Lady Allistair and Patrick Berger in New York to line up all the resources to make each of the initiatives required to render the Foundation Bongani an effective organization as quickly as possible. What Dr. Wasiri presented as future steps were already in the pipe, close to realization, including the setting of the legal status of the new foundation, the complicated overseas foundations support he alluded to, the preliminary works to start the new installation in Komesah, and to enlarge and enhance the current building of Circle Bongani. The modesty and the beauty of all his efforts was that nowhere in the bylaws, status, or other documents bringing about the Foundation Bongani, his name was mentioned. So much so that when Dr. Ingoma asked if Dr. Wasiri was going to be part of the foundation board of directors, he answered that would be the case if the new board would invite him to join. Dr. Ingoma smiled. To date, there were only two board members: Monsignor Felix, the purported president of the foundation, and Dr. Ingoma, the chairman of the board of the foundation.

While riding back to Mandi with Monsignor Felix, Dr. Wasiri wondered when his appointment to become bishop of Mandi would become effective, Monsignor Felix was surprised to hear the question and said that he was very happy serving the Lord in the formation of new priests at the seminary, and he was honored to take on the challenge he gave him to lead the organization that would provide shelter to the unfortunate children of the street. He added, the position of bishop of Mandi so meshed in the church bureaucracy would keep him far removed from the children of the street, the children of God. Monsignor Felix then asked his companion if KMC had specific designs for Dr. Ingoma. Dr. Wasiri answered that as far as he was concerned, KMC must include major plans to use such a man of outstanding destiny like Dr. Ingoma. It would be foolish and outright stupid not to.

Less than a week later, Dr. Ingoma and the entire old KMC leadership team were present at the first Mass celebrated at the Cathedral of Sacred Heart by the newly appointed bishop of Mandi, none other but Monsignor Felix Mulai-Bando. He finally replaced, as it was expected, the retiring and very sick, his Excellency Kodeye Henry Nzerima, archbishop of Mandi.

Father Zolani, who had sworn never to come close to the cathedral after all that happened between him and the retiring archbishop, was also present, very much relieved to see his own friend take over a seat that had caused him much grief. After the Mass, at a reception given by the archdiocese to greet the new bishop, Dr. Wasiri, along with Dr. Ingoma, chided the new bishop about the new administrative duties that would keep him away from the children of the street, the children of God. Now Bishop Felix said, to his friends' laughter, that it was obvious that he had spoken a bit prematurely. No task would keep him away from the children of the street, appropriately called the children of God. He was going to keep his function of president of the Foundation Bongani until such time he would be overwhelmed to be forced to give it up. But before that would happen, he would continue to do the will of God. He also announced to Dr. Wasiri's surprise that the foundation board had elected to formally invite him to join the board.

That was also the time for great preparations for the upcoming KMC first political convention scheduled in the last week of October in Vabiseo, the capital of the Tongeo Province, by a special request made by the tribal chief Sengimo VII, who insisted to have the first political convention of the true political party predicted by his ancestor on his soil.

The chief village was about five miles from the capital of Tongeo. Vabiseo appeared to have all amenities to house the important convention. A dedicated college named appropriately Sengimo Institute, specialized in mines and agricultural engineering from bachelor to PhD degrees. It had the largest auditorium in town to gather the expected four thousand and a half, the estimated total number of combined delegates, guests, and journalists. The college campus dormitories and few hotels in town and surrounding communities were also enough convenient to welcome the same number of visitors. Chief Sengimo VII had also readied his extensive real estate properties outside the town for all other festivities to honor the delegates from all corners of Mezi.

With lodging accommodations taken care of, Dr. Wasiri decided to raise money to fund the services of the same American company which covered the KMC presentation of Edict over Corruption at the American University at Washington, DC. At first contact, the company thought that the scale of the political convention was well beyond their technical capacity. After further probing by many KMC operatives in DC area and its own review, the company accepted the challenge to provide advanced state-of-the-art digital video and audio resources for the entire convention. The challenge to accomplish this was obvious for this young and small company, being far away from its major provision sources and somewhere in the middle of Africa. The only redeeming factor was that most of its provisions would be now about two hours of flight from South Africa. When Dr. Wasiri presented the dilemma to his mentor, he quickly relayed it to Lady Allistair. The DC Company suddenly found itself in company with a major respected UK firm that had worked in equivalent tasks in South Africa and was very much aware of technical challenges, which would come in similar circumstances. This company was going to assist the DC firm in the coverage of KMC convention. Its fees have already been taken care of by some other third parties. Dr. Wasiri was going to raise the total fee to DC firm, initially estimated to around two million dollars.

Chancellor Umzigwe reminded Dr. Wasiri that the entire political convention was being held with the help of thousands of volunteers ready to help when required. KMC was also helped to fund the printing of various documents, the designing and production of thousands of variety of KMC fliers, gadgets, mementos, memorabilia, balloons, and so on. Chief Sengimo VII took care of food provisioning by mobilizing people from his village and surrounding communities.

Nothing, absolutely nothing, was left to chance as the main coordinator of the convention in Vabiseo, Mr. Komasi Bello, the recently appointed KMC Provisional Leadership Committee member, said.

When the political convention started at 3:00 p.m. on that Thursday, on that last week of October, everything went clockwork, with military precision, from the beginning invocation to the closing speech given by the newly elected KMC general secretary, Brother Kano Wasiri. Of course, it should be noted that behind the scene, eight major players in addition to Brother Kano worked relentlessly to ensure that all went accordingly to plan: Chancellor Umzigwe, Dean Wutugrase, Chief Sengimo VII, Dr. Ingoma, Father Zolani, Sister Fanzi-Djomba, Mr. Komasi Bello, and Professor John Awassa. They either lined up and introduced the various speakers, they led the introduction of the six or seven important KMC Edicts to the general assembly, they monitored the voting of the permanent KMC Standing Leadership Committee, they saw to it that everyone was fed and properly housed, or they stood one step ahead with technical issues around the digital video and audio coverage of the convention.

Mr. Komasi Bello was very efficient in insuring that the overall flow of the convention was kept orderly and timely. Chief Sengimo VII, in spite of his very advanced age, also maintained a strong presence throughout the convention. The best memorable event was probably the KMC celebration he gave close to his village in the middle of a beautiful field, where close to thirty huge tents were raised, and the delegates were fed and serenaded through three or four in the morning. The range of dishes and drinks was outstanding.

The voting for the proposed new members of the permanent KMC Standing Leadership Committee went all right except for a new member, who withdrew his name after learning that his medical condition would not allow him to be effectively involved in the upcoming electoral process. He proposed a new female member in his caucus. She was unanimously elected. This raised the ratio of female to male leadership members from four to five against eleven now. This was a better surprise for Fanzi-Djomba and Brother Kano. The vote to elect the general secretary was a nonevent, well orchestrated by Chancellor Umzigwe, Dean Wutugrase, and seconded by the august Chief Sengimo VII. The old man solemnly entered the auditorium for the first and last time in his elevated chair for the sole purpose to read his brief speech to second the candidature of Brother Kano Wasiri. There was no other candidate. Brother Kano Wasiri was elected by acclamation KMC secretary general.

The following were also elected as heads of KMC commissions: Professor Awassa, Economic Commission; Komasi Bello, Security Commission; Father Zolani, Propaganda Commission; Sister Fanzi-Djomba, Women and Social Commission; Dr. Ingoma, Commission over Corruption; and Sir Ewas, Overseas Commission. These people would be the main public translators of KMC Edicts and pronouncements relative to their topic or area of interest. Along the way, the two wise old men of KMC, Chancellor Umzigwe and Dean Wutugrase, were also elected to the nebulous but powerful positions of senior political advisors to KMC Standing Leadership Committee.

The closing speech by Brother Kano Wasiri in his new function of KMC general secretary was as dynamic and electrifying as ever. He held the audience at their feet the same way he did in Washington, DC, and in Ikando. He challenged the delegates not just to denounce the lacking of mores among people in Mezi but also to be the real representatives and implementers of solutions to most problems Mezi was facing.

At the end, he added, "As we move forward and get closer to the judgment day of election, KMC should not expect a plate of goodies handed to it. Like everything in politics," he said, "KMC has to earn it. There are many ways to earn victory in politics." He continued, "You can go out and bribe everybody under the sun as our opponents would certainly do. That has been their norm election in, election out for the past ten or twenty years. Let me tell you what I would advise the people of Mezi faced with such despicable outrage—take it. Yes, I am telling you, take it, because it is yours. Now the fact that you are taking what is yours does not make you bribed or whatever the students of politics would like to call. When you take what is yours, please let the crooked politician know that your soul at this time and place of our republic is not for sale. Let him know that you know exactly where that bribe has come from. Let him know that the bribe has come from your sweat, let him know that the bribe has come from the lack of foods to many starving kids, the lack of jobs to many unemployed, the lack of mechanisms to stop this young thirteen-year-old girl who is entering today the trade of her body, the trade of prostitution. Let him know how you feel about him trying to bribe you. Let him know that you are going to make sure at this time and this place of our republic that there will be no more doing public business in the remote corners of the parliament or behind closed doors of government cabinets, there will be no more made-up complicated budgets, which never tell what is being spent and how it is being spent and from what funds, there will be no more abuse of power from the guardians of this nation, there will be no more trampling of our citizens rights, there will be no more holding down our heads in constant shame in international circles, no more, no more. There will be no more of all these negative values we talked about at Banfi-Bello because you would let him know that you, the people, have already cast them away, you have cast them at the oblivion of the past where that politician belongs and where together we will leave behind the bottomless abyss of corruption, injustice, unfairness, and social degradation the same politician has relentlessly tried to enchain Mezi.

"And as we move this beloved country of ours ahead, we would again take the same solemn pledge we took at Banfi-Bello to promote and safeguard at all times Mezi people's inalienable rights to freedom, justice, peace, and prosperity. That is not only our pledge, but that is our goal for a better and proud future Republic of Mezi.

Brothers and sisters in the shining light of KMC, the only way we would be able to keep this solemn pledge is if we follow the instructions we have laid out in all of the KMC Edicts we reviewed and debated throughout this weekend. If anything, the KMC leadership wants you to keep dear from this gathering is the set of the edicts you have discussed and, we hope, internalized.

If we stay close to those edicts then, as I was saying at the beginning of this expose, KMC and all of us here in this auditorium would earn the trust of Mezi people. But if we don't, then we would be harshly judged and rightly so by the same people who would see and read these edicts and would use them as frame of reference to evaluate our governance. For a people abused, trampled, and ridiculed for so long, that would be cataclysmic.

"Brothers and sisters in the shining light of KMC, that would not pass under this leadership, I would not allow it, not on my watch. Brothers and sisters, I have to tell you in all clear confidence that I have accepted at this time and this place the election to KMC general secretary in one and only condition that we do not go back to those sad times when the trust of Mezi people was completely disabused.

I pledge to you today that I would hold myself and each of us in the leadership committee and on this podium accountable to the respect of all that the edicts have prescribed. That is what KMC wants, that is what New Directions mean and is all about. Brothers and sisters, if I sound as if I am repeating myself, please indulge me. If what I am saying sounds like a broken record, I am sorry.

But as long as I have the last breath in my lung, as long as I have the last drop of blood in my veins, I would never stop saying this, we will not go back to those failed times of entrenched corruption, unmitigated injustice, runaway unfairness, abject poverty, denied freedom, and denied prosperity. Those times would be gone under the shining light of KMC, so help me, God. Thank you."

The KMC first political convention was very successful. The organization was superb. What was very noticeable was the overall digital video-audio support that the convention received. The overall support was beyond excellent. The simultaneous remote and wireless production and diffusion of multiple sessions taking place all over Vabiseo were executed flawlessly. There was not a station in the convention that was left without an advanced video screen where any convention session cannot be retrieved. People have never witnessed such a thorough coverage of an event in Mezi.

Chancellor Umzigwe was so impressed, during the convention he suggested to Brother Kano to attempt to keep the rented equipment to mount a similar KMC TV station in Mandi. That was an idea the chancellor refused to entertain every time it was raised in any meeting. Brother Kano reached out to Sister Fanzi-Djomba to touch base with the freelance journalist, Miss Mhlabi Zenzi, from the famous BBC extraordinary propaganda piece. She was very conversant and knowledgeable about this advanced technology.

She could help estimate what would be needed to set up a TV station with such an advanced technology. She was somewhere around covering the convention, and she can start the conversation with the technicians and managers from UK and the United States. They helped her to come up with a blue print of such a TV station. At the end of the convention, Miss Mhlabi Zenzi had enough information to present to the next KMC leadership meeting.

The print and video coverage outside the convention was a bit tame. It was definitely not to the satisfaction and expectation of KMC leadership. That was probably the real Chancellor Umzigwe's motivation to finally set up a proper TV and Radio station for KMC. One evening when he asked whether his wife, still back in Mandi, had seen this wonderful presentation that Dr. Ingoma gave around the Edict over Corruption at the convention. He was beside himself to hear that there was absolutely no coverage of the convention in all Mandi TV stations. Radio stations provided more coverage than usual, but it was still constrained and limited.

His wife yelled at her husband and said that KMC must stop expecting other people and organizations to do its propaganda job. She said that KMC must do its own propaganda with its own means. Then she hung up the phone on her husband.

CHAPTER 38
Sonjedi's Coming-Out Party

The lack of broad diffusion of a very successful first KMC political convention was welcome news in one particular quarter, Mr. Sonjedi's. The former PM had succeeded, at this time, to drain all the political allies from his former boss, President Badegou, to his new political coalition party he had chosen to call Party for United Mezi, or PUM.

The new coalition had gathered in addition to the President Badegou allies, the Mezi Socialist Congress (MSC) of the president of the Lower Chamber and the People for Change Party (PCP) of the president of the Higher Chamber.

Other smaller parties, generally called the pigsty or pigpen parties for their gluttonous habit to join in any corruption scheme hatched in both chambers, were quick to follow suit to enlarge the number of political entities to be swallowed by PUM. The desertion that President Badegou suffered was driving him deeper to despair and insobriety. The coup de grace came when the latest young PM, Blair Kensoy, decided to resign his post after only three months to become deputy general secretary of PUM, under his childhood friend, Mr. Sonjedi.

In a desperate attempt to show that he was still in control, President Badegou appointed his old drinking buddy, the now retired General Gwobozo as minister of defense before even naming a new premier minister. The move was met with such an outcry from all institutions of the nation, even from the new Chief of Staff, the Major General John Djanzali, who said that the army was not going to follow any order issued by the new Minister of Defense.

That sealed the fate of President Badegou. Both chambers passed resolutions to bar General Gwobozo from taking any position in the upcoming government. President Badegou relented and rescinded his strange appointment. General Gwobozo never returned to the capital to take his new job. He told the press he thought that the president was joking.

A few days later, President Badegou turned to an old college friend, Mr. John Menmeki, presently Mezi ambassador to UK, to form another government. After swearing in this last government, President

Badegou literally retired from the business of governing the country. He took refuge in the many bottles that adorned the bar in his bedroom. He would hardly come out of the presidential palace family quarters. It was a steep decline from then on, prematurely force-retired by his own protégé, Mr. Sonjedi.

The week after the KMC Convention, on a Saturday morning, Mr. Sonjedi decided that it was about time to show the world how politically powerful and connected he had become. He would hold a mini summit of all those people who have joined PUM in the great cause of uniting and moving Mezi forward according to his original brand of economic reconstruction. Mr. Sonjedi was now flushed with additional twenty million dollars promised by his mysterious Canadian financial backers if the political coalition he predicted to form became a reality.

To stage his big political re-entry, he chose the latest newly built luxury hotel complex called MeziStar on the northern part of Lake Nyerengi. The hotel built by a South African Resorts and Entertainment Group copied the design and architecture of Tanzire Hilton Hotel down south, but triple its size. It started from the lake embankment where there was a huge outdoor restaurant and dancing club to the hotel compound along the Lake Road. The hotel had built also a golf field going north of the complex. Luxurious villas for rent stood every half mile on the lake along the ten-mile golf course. MeziStar was a symbol of luxurious life and life achievement less than a tenth of 1 percent of Mezi population would currently attain. It was generally being promoted as a strong tourist attraction for South African, American, Canadian, and European travelers.

This was a prime attraction for Mr. Sonjedi and most of his new political backers who came from the business community and each of Mezi governing institutions including the armed forces heavily represented by a strong contingent of retired colonels and generals who, in reality, stood behind each significant and visible face of the government and both lower and higher Mezi chambers.

By ten thirty, the political, military, and business VIP of Mandi packed the main ballroom of the hotel located at the south end of the vast complex. The attendance was near seven hundred people. Mr. Sonjedi made his grand entrance with his childhood friend Mr. Blair Kensoy and the two legislative chambers presidents.

A longtime-behind-the-scene retired General Zegelino Gambu, who broke the reign of military regimes and handed over power to the first elected president, was prominently seated next to Mr. Sonjedi. The podium display wanted to signify to the world that Mezi elite had broken with President Badegou and was investing all its resources on the relative young brilliant economist, Mr. Sonjedi, whose mission was clear: to safeguard its hard-gained interests against the dark and unreliable assault of KMC in the upcoming electoral process. The elite had decided to start the process sooner rather than later after the shakedown President Badegou had received at the hands of KMC, first at the Cast Away ceremony of Banfi-Bello Village and later during the H5 Exchange at the Tanzire Hotel. Mr. Sonjedi was not going to disappoint this crowd.

After he had introduced the leaders of political parties which were joining his coalition, now about thirty-three of them, he rose quickly and came to the task, "Distinguished ladies and gentlemen, there always comes time in any republic when it becomes imperative and necessary for those entrusted with guiding the ship of state to seize the moment. Today, we are seizing the moment. I am not going to go over how we got here, but we all know how it happened and regrettably so. But I would tell you that I have been sounding the alarm to anybody who was willing to listen, and I have done so for the past two years. I knew that the time would come when our voice would be heard, and I am more than happy to see that it has been and here we are. The alarm I was sounding came to reality the last six months or so. We saw the despicable and disingenuous display of arrogance that was propagandized at Banfi-Bello where our beloved tribal chiefs were lied to. Worse, we saw how our sober and valiant military men, keepers of law and order of our republic were ridiculed, spit at, and attacked by the renegades of a bloodthirsty mob. Last week we heard their endless lies, insults, calumnies, vituperations, and exaggerations about our beloved country and institutions. In their eyes, nothing, absolutely nothing, works in this country, even the democratic environment where they are allowed to say anything and wish anything under the sky. That very democratic environment, our beloved valiant man of the moment, General Zegelino Gambu, here among us has seen to bring about.

"Ladies and gentlemen, General Zegelino Gambu also seized the moment when he opted for democratic reform. He did not go about it by lying, insulting, or exaggerating. He went about by doing something. This is the real difference between those who met last week somewhere there in the country and those of us here in this magnificent place. The difference is this: they talk, we do.

I would make no bone about it. I may not have the experience of many of you who are here in this room, but the twenty or so years I have worked and traveled the world and met people of different background, political, economic and race, I have observed one thing: you can be in Egypt, Mongolia, Japan, Indonesia, Australia, Ecuador, Chili, Brazil, Jamaica, the United States, Canada, Ireland, UK, Lithuania, Italy, Sweden, Russia, Mali, South Africa, Burundi, Senegal, or Mezi, you always find people who do and people who talk. When I came back from my assignment in World Bank, I purposely chose to join you, people who do.

The choice was deliberate because I knew where Mezi stood in the rank of development in the world. But I wanted to invest my time in doing something at whatever capacity the institutions in place wanted me to operate. I did not have any illusion about the difficult tasks at end. But I have invested myself in doing something. I do not regret the time I have spent doing something for my country instead of screaming from the outside.

"This is the difference between those who have screamed last week and you, who every day wake up and try to find solutions to problems facing the country. And you do this quietly day in, day out. In the process, you provide jobs to the unemployed, you finance charities, you attract foreign financing for this agricultural project or that mining project, you fund financial institutions, and above all, you maintain law and order in the country for the proper functioning of the institutions of Mezi. I have seen all these endeavors from far and from close, and I have much respect for them while those outside have the audacity to scream that you are doing nothing.

"I guess that is all they have to offer, nothing. Ladies and gentlemen, you may be asking yourselves why they have chosen to do nothing. Well, it is much easier to do nothing than to do something. It is even much easier to do nothing when you have loaded your heads with confusing ideas as most of them have in those universities where they have taken refuge. Have you noticed that the leaders of the other side always have their name preceded by a Dr. and I am not talking of medical doctor? It is always Dr. this, Dr. that.

I know one of them who has gone to so many universities around the world, grabbed so many PhDs and Masters' that when he wakes up in the morning, he is confused, he cannot tell which classroom he is supposed to go to teach and what course. Mind you, he has this super PC in the world with his schedule properly set. But every morning, I heard it is the same routine.

It is getting so bad that he has requested to be awakened at five in the morning to give him two hours to get some orientation. For your information, and I am not kidding, I heard that he would be in charge of economic issues for the other side. Can you imagine what it will be like if we let them manage the economic ship of the state?

"Ladies and gentlemen, this is what we call elitism. The other side wants to impose their brand of elitism on the country. We cannot let that happen. Mezi would not be their laboratory to try out junk ideas they dream about days and nights in the safe and acclimated confines of seminaries, convents, colleges, and universities. We cannot let that happen. That is why I am asking you bankers, entrepreneurs, businesspeople, doers, or keepers of law and order to join me in our endeavor of moving Mezi ahead surely. I am asking you to stand ready to raise as much funds as possible to match the other side and to clobber the other side every step of the way in the upcoming electoral process. If they believe that we will leave the electoral terrain without a fight, they would be very well surprised. We would fight them all the way; if they raise one million, we would match them with ten million, if they raise five million, we would go fifty million, and so on.

"Because we have the way, because we have the resources, because we have been wisely entrusted to steer the ship of state for this long. Thank you for coming. May God bless Mezi."

The crowd loved every word from this speech. It had been a long time or never somebody spoke their language as plainly as Mr. Sonjedi did. He said in loud voice what each person in that ballroom was thinking about the current political situation. And they knew exactly what he meant when he mentioned the other side. While they stuffed the large bags that were being circulated in the ballroom with checks and large sums of money, they thanked themselves for retiring the old, drunk President Badegou as quickly as possible. It was obvious that President Badegou was no match with what the other side was putting upfront. They needed a dynamic young leader to wage the next electoral battle. They found that person in Mr. Sonjedi, now a huge political star, walking around the huge ballroom to thank those who came to join his political coalition. The ladies did not mind to fuss suggestively all over him in front of their tired old rich men. Some of the ladies managed to drop in his suit pockets explicit invitation cards to partake sexually in time and place of his choosing. Later that night, when he was home and removing his clothes, he found about twenty of these cards with names and private cellular phone numbers.

However, if Mr. Sonjedi thought that he had a monopoly of political discourse or propaganda that Saturday, he was sadly mistaken. When Brother Kano heard through many of his KMC operatives that Mr. Sonjedi had planned a coming-out party at that luxurious MeziStar hotel that Saturday morning, he called on Dr. Ingoma and Bishop Felix to move to Saturday afternoon from Sunday morning the inauguration of the new already completed huge buildings to house the children of the street under the auspices of the Foundation Bongani in the shanty towns of Komesah in Mandi and Zingzong in Ikando. The idea was to present a stark contrast between the politician preoccupation of Mr. Sonjedi against the humanitarian preoccupation of KMC leaders.

Brother Kano was going to be with Dr. Ingoma to chair and celebrate the inauguration of the Zingzong facility while Bishop Felix assisted with Sister Fanzi-Djomba, Father Zolani and Komesah KMC leaders would conduct the inauguration of the Komesah building.

When he went home, and after reading with delighted pleasure the twenty or so salacious invitation cards from spouses or mistresses of his financial backers, Mr. Sonjedi almost broke his big screen TV when the first news item of the day from his preferred TV station was not his coming-out party and the speech he gave. Instead, the speaker lady was trembling with tears when she recounted the surprising news of the inauguration of this new huge building to house about six hundred children of street in Komesah. While she spoke, there was the video feed showing the inauguration celebration presided by none other but Bishop Felix that Mr. Sonjedi had always suspected to be a cover for many KMC deeds. Bishop was on the stage with Father Zolani and the sinister viper-mouth of Sister Fanzi-Djomba.

The lady speaker made matters worse when, still in tears, she added that similar celebration took place the same day at Zingzong in the city of Ikando to inaugurate the expanded building to house about three hundred children of the street of that town. Mr. Sonjedi was infuriated to see Dr. Ingoma next to Dr. Wasiri, leading the inauguration celebration of this building inauguration.

While going back and forth between the two buildings, the lady speaker, now sobbing, editorialized that she came up as a child of the street, and she apologized to the audience for not being able to control her temper when she saw that so many of her own would finally leave the street. She closed the segment by saying that in any decent society, there should never be children of the street.
She went on to thank the auspices of the Foundation Bongani for the extraordinary realization. Mr. Sonjedi observed that this segment took almost the entire Mezi news session of the day in most TV channels. His coming-out party was barely mentioned in two out of seven TV stations that night.

The reporting of Saturday events got worse in the print journals. One major publication captured in one title what Brother Kano was expecting and what Mr. Sonjedi went mad about. The title said: "Sonjedi to Raise Fifty Million Dollars for Political Fame, Dr. Wasiri Raised Two Million Dollars for Children of the Street in Komesah and Zingzong." The title was a distortion of facts, a fabrication by the publication. But that did not matter. Mr. Sonjedi's coming-out party was soundly defeated in the public opinion by the perception that KMC had struggled and helped to build a much needed shelter for thousands of poor children of the street in two important locations Komesah and Zingzong, poverty barometers of Mezi, while at the very same time Mr. Sonjedi was wining and dining the country fat cats, in the process raising fifty million dollars for one and one purpose only—to keep Mezi's political power.

This was not the political debut that Mr. Sonjedi had intended to have. KMC was teaching him the first political lesson in the hard scrabble of Mezi politics. Mr. Sonjedi took it in stride. KMC leadership did not sit on its victory either. Very quickly, the KMC TV station became a reality with the assistance of the same US and UK firms which provided the digital video and audio coverage of the last convention. The same freelance journalist of BBC broadcast fame, Miss Mhlabi Zenzi, became its first managing director. The station had twenty-four hours coverage with KMC slant of news, political analysis, culture, and sports. The TV could be viewed anywhere in Mezi, thanks to satellite retransmission. Its studio facilities were within the Polytechnic University compound in one of the new huge buildings erected during the last university building expansion at the far southern end of the compound.

CHAPTER 39
Geffadi's Return

It was under this quiet and resolute KMC climate in the middle of the month of November that Dr. Wasiri, KMC general secretary, took his first flight back to the United States to attend the second board meeting of ABDI in Atlanta, Georgia. He stopped briefly in New York to pay visit to his old friends Sir William Ewas, now KMC overseas commission leader, and Mr. Beni Mbow, still at PNUD. For a change and per a longtime request by the lady of the house, he elected to spend his New York stay-over at Sir Ewas's home. Both Mr. Ewas and Mr. Mbow took two days off for a nonstop entertainment of their august visitor. It was so telling of the status Dr. Wasiri had achieved at home that the Mezi UN ambassador, Sir Ewas's boss, made time to come to pay him a visit. No matter how Brother Kano looked embarrassed and no matter how he tried to distance himself from the honor his hosts were bestowing on him, he was no longer viewed as a friend but as a distinguished honorable above peers. Ewas's family and Mbow's family outdid themselves in their treatment of the most likely to be elected as the next president of Mezi.

Every conversation became an exercise of circumspection to a point Brother Kano had to excuse himself, go back to the guest room, and retrieve the copy of the speech that Mr. Sonjedi gave at his coming-out party. He then asked Mr. Mbow's eldest son, who had come with his parents, to read the entire speech and asked the parents to listen to it very carefully. And they did. Somewhere along, they became very uneasy. They waited in vain until the end of the speech and would not dare look up at the host. Then Brother Kano asked them if they knew who made such a speech. They were not aware of the author of the speech. He revealed to them that Mr. Sonjedi made that speech less than a month ago and explained the circumstances of the speech and how KMC outmaneuvered him in the diffusion of the speech. Finally he said that he would very much appreciate that his very old friends treated him the same way Mr. Sonjedi did and the people who attended the coming-out party would certainly. Everyone remained quiet for a while and burst out into a big laugh. At the end, he thought he finally got his hosts to act the way he wanted them to.

The conversation became less tense, and they went on reviewing in a relaxed environment a lot of events that went on in Mezi lately. When Mr. Mbow asked Brother Kano if he knew whom Mr. Sonjedi was referring to in the speech when he mentioned the so-called mad professor, Brother Kano answered that he knew that person very well. He also said that the man, Professor Awassa, is very well balanced person. He told them that this was the problem in politics. Somebody comes and tells a plain lie in front of seven hundred people and they believe him and there is absolutely no retraction, no repair. He also reminded them that Professor Awassa had previously said that he was a very good friend of Mr. Sonjedi. Brother Kano didn't know if that was still the case.

He went on, "By the way, during the H5 Exchange episode, Mr. Sonjedi, before he was fired by his former mentor, President Badegou, called on the same Professor Awassa to mediate between the government and Chancellor Umzigwe, who was holding General Gwobozo virtual prisoner at the hotel. Why Mr. Sonjedi had to reach out to a crazy person to negotiate such a delicate situation? In addition, just for your information, it was again Professor Awassa who got the then premier minister Sonjedi, and at great personal risks to himself, to get through the columns of angry students who had cordoned off the entire Tanzire Hilton Hotel. Now why did Mr. Premier Minister Sonjedi trust his life at the hands of a very good friend he was calling now crazy? Anyway, that is unfortunately what it is called harsh politics Mezi style. Say anything you want whenever you please. We in KMC would not practice it, if I can help. I have instructed our team not to go in the gutter every time you want to make a point. It had gotten now senseless. It is just plain unbelievable. I am sorry I am again back in Mezi. As you can see, Mrs. Mbow, I have learned pretty fast. All you need to do is, just go into the heart of Komesah, you would then learn pretty fast."

Brother Kano almost slurred when he mentioned Komesah and stopped talking and brought his hands to cover his eyes that were now wet with tears. He got up, went to the window giving a view to the street, looked at the traffic, and then wiped his eyes. He repeated again "Komesah" and shook his head. He went back to his seat, and the entire room remained very quiet again.

After a few minutes, he apologized to his hosts for getting so emotional. He begged them to think of Komesah anytime they want to talk about Mezi. He assured his hosts that everything he had been involved since he reached Mezi was intended to get rid of everything that Komesah represented in Mezi.

Realizing how depressing the conversation was leading, Brother Kano tried to change the conversation and went back to General Gwobozo.

"When I saw General Gwobozo at the hotel, I did not know what to make out what he was telling me. I did not know whether I was supposed to laugh or not. Do you know what he was doing when we had that famous exchange? Do you know why he sounded like he was slurring? Well, he was very calmly eating a large piece of mango cutting with this big knife and talking at the same time without any concern for the world. Now you know when I came in to that Conference Room H5, I realized right away that the whole scene was being taped. But he did not know until I revealed it to him at the end when I was leaving. But before that, he was very calm and eating and talking as straightforward as we are here. The whole scene was very comical. I could have ruined the taping if I had laughed. I held up cracking up until when I left the conference room and those students rushed me to the safety of the upper floor. But while we were running, the students thought that I was a little bit delirious. They thought that I was poisoned or something worse until I reassured them how comical the whole episode was. Can you imagine? You come to the Tanzire Hotel, commanding close to a thousand or so military people and you sit there eating your mango. Just plain unbelievable! I guess these folks have been in power for so long, it has become almost second nature to act the way they do on daily basis." His hosts had also recovered their composure and were laughing accordingly.

The he turned to Mr. Mbow and said, "Beni, now I got plenty of materials to keep you cracking up all Saturday morning. Who do you call now on Saturday morning?" Mr. Mbow responded, "Well, I don't call anybody. Sir Ewas wakes me up every Saturday morning to go shopping. Then he would share the latest from Mandi. The last one was the 'nonappointment of General Gwobozo to become Minister of Defense' and to have the general to say that it was a joke. Man, you must have steel nerves to get up every morning in Mandi. How are you managing?"

"Managing is a strong word. You just get up and follow the schedule you have set at the beginning of the week, or we made it up as you went. In fact, it is not that bad when you have as much support as I have when everybody is rooting for you to succeed. It becomes less a matter of your success but everybody's success that is what makes it worthwhile. Now I am speaking for myself now, different people have different sets of circumstances. Now that Hasbo is there, it is really a pleasure to wake up to the sound of a distant roost.

I never realized that I have missed that sound until I came back. That sound carries so far, it is unbelievable. I was saying, Hasbo is gone all the time with this other lady who used to work at the administrative building of the university. She is so tight with Hasbo, I heard she would be resigning and retiring soon to keep up with Hasbo. They are doing all kind of decorating and redecorating. I got to be very careful, now that I am venturing in restricted domains of the ladies of the houses. To make a long story short, it is endless, and Hasbo is very very busy. The kids are very relaxed too, now that they are outside all the time.

"The one missing in action is yours truly. And I am paying it dearly lately with Hasbo and the kids. The cold shoulder, the cold dinner, and the rest! What do you know, between the new deanship of that Faculty and now the big title of general secretary of KMC, I am tight on everything? But if you ask, would I want this otherwise? Yes, I want it and love it. I was not sure before. But every day, it rises to me as imperative. And I do not want to go there again, but frankly, after all is said and done, there is Komesah. Komesah is what keeps me going."

Sir Ewas, who had not said a word since the beginning of the conversation, jumped in, "What about that new KMC TV station, would it help?"

"It must help. We did not have a marketing support to speak of. I raised this when I arrived. I was told that word of mouth would suffice. But as you know, our very successful first political convention went unreported. Can you imagine? All that work that went on at Vabiseo was not reported. It took that grave lapse for the leadership to wake up to twenty-first century. The TV station is operative twenty-four hours a day and can be seen in every corner of Mezi. What a jump! From zero to one hundred percent. That is Mezi and Africa. Well, it is all worthwhile. That young lady who helped us enormously with the BBC episode is now managing director of the station. So far so good.

"What I liked a lot about the convention is the permanent leadership team that emerged out of there. You know when I read that speech of Mr. Sonjedi, I was relieved that he raised a true criticism of KMC leadership team that was there before the convention. He was right that it was full of PhD folks. It was not as well balanced as it is now. I was very sensitive about that aspect of KMC before. No more, when we have added Komasi Bello and Mengi Sakoto and other members.

I do not remember their names, including our very own, the host of this house. I am always confused when it comes to lawyers, are they Doctoris honoris causae or something to that effect? Anyway, the good news is that the ratio now is about ten to six PhD folks. Not bad. But before it was strictly PhD folks and that always made us feel as if we were looking down on people. You know I used not to pay much attention to perception in public opinion. But in politics that is all that is there: perception, perception, perception. When you read Mr. Sonjedi's speech, it was all about perception or what he believed was public perception.

"I told the leadership team that KMC would not cede one iota of public perception to our adversaries. KMC would hit them as hard as possible with facts in the great court of public opinion. That business of children of the street was the first lesson in public perception battle we taught our good friend Mr. Sonjedi. I heard he was shocked. He has seen nothing yet."

At that instant, the ladies who had labored all the day in kitchen interrupted the talk and invited everybody to dinner. While the dinner was going on, Sir Ewas had to welcome more visitors, Mezi country men, who came to pay their respects to the man the Mezi entire Diaspora was talking about and supporting to carry the torch of KMC in the upcoming election. More people showed up during the course of the evening, and the entire party moved to the basement for better accommodating space. As usual in similar gathering, Brother Kano sat and listened to coming guests more than he was willing to share his ideas or what he had in mind. He always asked a lot of questions to allow people to talk more about themselves than himself. The procedure never failed; when given a chance, people always wanted to talk about themselves more, good or bad. Brother Kano did not mind the exchanges. He believed that you never know when you would encounter a very bright person with very useful ideas.

The next day, as the word spread that Brother Kano was in town, a larger contingent of country people showed up by Sir Ewas's home. The small avenue along the house became a huge parking lot. A quick decision was taken about three in the afternoon. Brother Kano was going to say hello to the Mezi New York community sometime around seven in the evening at an auditorium of a parish church about three miles from Sir Ewas's home. That prevented the police commotion that started developing near Sir Ewas's home. In fact, two cops were stationed near his house, now directing the growing number of visitors to the parish. At seven, the church auditorium was packed with close to two thousand people.

The number of people who came through word of mouth only dumbfounded Mr. Mbow and Sir Ewas. They thanked their stars for quickly suggesting this meeting; otherwise, there was going to be a big disaster at Sir Ewas's home. When Brother Kano arrived, the people with the cries of "Geffadi, Geffadi" mobbed him. He was also very surprised to see so many people from Mezi in one place abroad. He would learn later that they came from the whole east coast from Boston, Massachusetts, down to Richmond, Virginia, with the arc going as far west as Pittsburgh, PA. That was from about one to five or six hours driving one way. He thanked them for the unbelievable welcome, shared a little bit of news about home and their common fight to repair what was ailing the country, and shook the auditorium with the same speech he used to close the last KMC convention. He sent the people home with the thought of Komesah and Zingzong so that wherever they lived and worked, their prayers would rest to eradicate the abject poverty and the untold sufferings that crush the humanity in those places. He closed by saying that whatever was KMC's fight, and no matter where they were, that was their fight.

His hosts were amazed and were now having trouble to recognize the same person who, less than a year ago, was so reluctant to go back home and, even less, to enter Mezi politics. When they reached home around eleven, they were completely exhausted and went to sleep very quickly.

CHAPTER 40
His Honorable Massay's Triumph

The next day, Sir Ewas took his guest to LaGuardia Airport to catch the flight to Atlanta, GA. He told his friend that he hoped to be very very quiet when he would return on his way back home. Brother Kano smiled and said, "Don't worry, that is the way it is daily back home. As Chancellor Umzigwe warned me, you got to get used to it."

He took the flight to Atlanta and was greeted at the airport by three people: his mentor, Dr. O'Shea, who had become visibly aged and had recovered his loud mouth, His Honorable State Senator Jeremy Massay, and Dr. James Stringer. They all came out from this long-stretch limousine. He embraced his mentor for a long time, then greeted the executive of ABDI. He was a bit surprised to see them at the airport. The last time he sent his mentor his itinerary, the schedule was for him to rent a car, wait for his mentor, and drive to the hotel. He asked the direction to go get his rented car. He was then told that it was canceled. The limousine was going to be their only mode of transportation as long as they were in Atlanta at the expenses of ABDI. It will take a while for Dr. Wasiri to realize what was going on. As usual, he kept very quiet, trying to figure out what he had done to merit this honor or what had his good old mentor done again. When they arrived at a very luxurious hotel, it was not next to ABDI offices as in the time of the first board meeting. He inquired why they did not go to the old nice hotel. His Honorable said it was for security reasons. That was another puzzle he needed to get an explanation about.

Now he was very much in a hurry to be alone with his mentor to get to the bottom of all these changes. While the bellman was retrieving his luggage, Dr. Wasiri excused himself from the ABDI executives and pulled his mentor on the side to find out what was going on. To refresh his memory, first Dr. O'Shea started to roll his eyes, a signal to let his protégé know that he was about to establish a series of events that had led to what was going on. Then he reminded him that they were the ones who had successfully argued for ABDI budget increase to six billion dollars and second the board meeting had been moved to this luxury hotel where ABDI would receive heads of states and a lot of bigwigs to celebrate the completion of the major projects they had reviewed the last time they were here. His mentor also added that he should not feel that bad. He was in the same boat as the old professor; he did not read the ABDI invitation program that was sent. When Dr. Wasiri wanted to know a little bit more about the mysterious budget increase to six billion funding, His Honorable State Senator Massay joined them to invite the two scientists from Kentucky to come and quickly toast their successful intervention to get ABDI budget to the six billion funding level.

He was holding Dr. O'Shea's hand and guiding him to a remote table adorned with four glasses and a champagne bottle. At the same time, Dr. Stringer was talking to Dr. Wasiri thanking him effusively also for the great help ABDI had received. When they were seated, His Honorable said, "I should have waited for the entire board of directors to toast your intervention, but then, the question would be raised how to know how did you do it? I would not be in your shoes to share any misplaced confidence. I understand that you are very closely connected to the management of corporations that are funding our work, including AMX. You can help us now to share a little bit, if not all, of the process you went about to achieve the more than doubling of our funding."

Dr. O'Shea, who had already been approached to answer the same question and had told his hosts to hold on to the toast until his good friend, Dr. Wasiri, arrived had now clearly formulated the response. "OK, after the wonderful presentation you made about the projects in those African countries and especially the East Africa Water project, Dr. Wasiri and I have talked extensively about the need to increase the amount of funding you needed to be effective. Now thanks to a lot of friends that Dr. Wasiri had at the UN and World Bank, we established a must priority list of African projects that have been languishing on the shelves of those institutions. After totaling them, we came up with the funding needs that rose to close to twenty-one billion dollars. Of course, we were not going to get that amount, but we submitted it anyway to AMX contacts, insisting that if the donors were serious about making an impact in African continent, this was where to start. In addition, as you know, Dr. Wasiri and I went to a conference in Mezi at the Polytechnic University last January. We met quite a lot of ABDI major contributors, mainly South African business interests. We were surprised that you did not show up. Anyway, we lobbied these people intensely. The only thing we got was a promise to look into our list. You can only imagine that the list went through a lot of gyrations among these donors. I am not sure why they came up with three billion or so increase.

We learned from our AMX contact that the donors were willing to raise that amount and here we are. The bottom line is that you got it. Of course, as you can appreciate it, we have done this under the strict rules of confidentiality from these donors. And we intend to abide by those rules. It could have gone the way of 'well, no, thank you, ABDI has enough funding to work with for the time being and will talk later.' It did not, and we can only say that we are very grateful, and we were very lucky this time. But we have to stick to the rules of confidentiality imposed on us. We are a little embarrassed to talk about what you are calling our contribution.

We are even surprised that you are asking us questions about this. As board members with specific goals in mind, we wanted to take ABDI goals a step further and fulfill our obligations by intervening whenever and wherever we can. When we got there, our deal was going to be, well, wonderful donors, well done, but what about the difference, the other eighteen billion initially requested. That was going to be the case if and only if we maintain our strict rules of confidentiality. We do not want to be in a position to trumpet our intervention when we know that we got only a seventh of the total funding needs. We do not want to be ungrateful, but for anybody who has been in Africa, you know that development needs are gigantic, and they dwarf the three-billion-dollar funding increase. We are asking you to indulge us in these confidentiality rules and not to mention our intervention."

His Honorable Massay raised his glass and said, "Excellent, Excellent. Dr. Stringer and I thought along the same line. We have gone to so many countries in Africa. Obviously the needs always exceed the resources. We understand better now the nature of your intervention, and we are most grateful. We would certainly abide by your rules of confidentiality, and we would not mention why and how we got the increase except to mention that it was as a result of ABDI's request, if you do not mind.

For your information, when our AMX contact informed us of the increase, we were told it was as a result of your intervention. Maybe we should have left it at that unless you have brought it up. I really have to ask you to excuse me. I have underestimated the level of your academic modesty. I wish I were a university professor like the three of you. You also have to indulge the immodest flairs of a politician that I am. Still I have to toast what you have done for ABDI, and thankfully, this would be the last time and the last occasion we have talked about ABDI funding increase. Cheers, friends of ABDI."

The four ABDI board members toasted quickly, and the champagne bottle disappeared quickly to his honorable suite upstairs. When the Kentucky scientists were finally together in their suite, Dr. Wasiri left out a big laughter. He looked at his mentor and said, "My good professor O'Shea, you were very good indeed. If you were not at such advanced age and weak of body, I would have engaged you as a special advisor in charge of making up stories for our political party in Mezi. Man, you were flawlessly very good. Where in the world you got that story? Now I cannot even make sense of it. Where it started and where it ended. You have to repeat it for me in case I am confronted to explain it sometime later. I did not keep up. Please repeat the story again. Man, you went above everything this time. I am certain that it was for a very good cause. Indulge me, Professor O'Shea."

The old man was smiling now, looking from their tenth-floor suite window at the imposing arrival of an African head of state. He turned to his protégé and said, "That was nothing compared to the true reason why ABDI got the increase. And there is nothing on earth that would force me to reveal the true reason ABDI got the increase. I know you are not naïve enough to forget that it all started when you came back from Mezi with those specs of Alpha-M. If you were not busy running that political party in Mezi and check the results of tests that I sent to you, you would have noticed that the test results validated that the specs were indeed from Alpha-M and all subsequent validation application tests concurred. As I told you in the letter I sent to you via FEDEX, the so-called donors were going to increase the foundation money to three billion, which was done, ABDI funding was also increased to six billion, which we were toasting, for the same reason I was paid one hundred million dollars, and you got about the same amount of money. Tell me, was I supposed to tell the ABDI chairman how his organization funding was increased, thanks to the test validation results? Hell no, hell no, hell no.

"My very dear Dr. Wasiri, you got to wake up to the hard facts of this world. You and I live by certain principles and rules. Yes whether you like it or not, I would continue to scream it inside your deaf ears, they are Emily's rules. They have gotten us this far. I would not invite a stranger into our rules, our sacred domain, whether you like it or not. You do not have to worry about His Honorable Massay checking further about our story. He has already got the story from his so-called AMX contact. I was only repeating the same story he already heard. He was being slick to try to find discrepancies in the story. Not from me. I may be old but not feeble minded. If his honorable wants to play con games with me, I would be twice as con than he is.

I was more afraid that you would be trapped telling something about our intervention. His honorable wanted to go pick you up and ask you a lot of questions about our intervention. Well, I stopped that nonsense. I had to be there and that really stopped the entire shenanigan he tried to pull. You know, it is all about money. I have seen his game last time we were here in Atlanta. He has been trying to figure out what was our station in the larger scheme of things with the donors. He knows that I am very tight with the primary ABDI donors.

"Remember last time we were here in Atlanta, and Dr. Stringer was let out to question your background and your relationship with Lady Allistair. It was again the same thing this time. Where were we coming from and what was our relationship to ABDI pot of money? When he was explicitly told that we were the reason of ABDI funding increase, the all three billion, that probably set him off. I knew that things would be a bit tense this time around. I also learned that I did not have to get all uptight and mad about his slick moves. That was why I had to tell them up front and as calmly as possible to leave us alone using that confidentiality rules bogus story. And it worked, didn't it? I am sorry, son, I have to tell you this, I would let nobody, absolutely nobody, disturb Emily's rules and that would be the same for the so-called donors. I repeat, nobody."

Dr. Wasiri was brought back to the same story he had heard for the past twenty or so years he knew this man.

By time, the story was extremely trying. At the same time, in spite of all in the past year, the story was becoming more and more a reality. Dr. Wasiri struggled intensely with the story, dismissing it outright only to be confronted with it again as in the present situation.

He reviewed all that had happened lately: the Foundation Emily O'Shea funding had been increased; yes, did he use the funding increase to establish the Foundation Bongani for Mezi Children of the Street? Yes, ABDI funding had been increased, yes, his bank account had been increased, yes, did all these increases occur after the test validation results? Yes. There was nothing in the sequence of those events to stop him from making the leap of faith about Emily's rules. He was still struggling with it.

He looked at his mentor and said, "Professor O'Shea, I hope I am not giving you the appearance of doubting anything you are saying. I am old enough to still question Emily's rules. I have seen the rules operating here and in Mezi. I am just grateful that I have somebody to see to it that we are accomplishing so much and for the good.

You have to bear with me and indulge me if I sometimes come out as the eternal St. Thomas in this Emily's rules business. Maybe that is my role. You, a fervent faithful, and I, an eternal doubter. Maybe Emily intended her rules to survive that way. If we were all on the same wave, there could be a danger of exaggerations and possible breakdowns in support of Emily's rules. I am becoming more and more convinced that

Emily intended the rules to be tested that way. Every time something happens, I am only interested in the obvious logic of things when you bring the intent of Emily's rules, and every time you come ahead. I should know by now. Yet I resist, and we go through the process all over again. Today is no different from previous episodes. And here we are, you are totally proven correct in your twisted logic. Now, please, I beg you to indulge me again."

Dr. O'Shea came to his son and embraced him. "Of course, I would always indulge you. It has been a lifetime battle, I would attest to that. But you are certainly right. Emily's rules were intended to be as contradictory as we are. She probably set them for that very reason. To make life easier for yourself, I would ask you to indulge Emily's rules. Now I feel like such a fool. All these times we have spent arguing about nonsense, I did not have the chance to ask you about Mezi, Hasbo, my grandkids, and your new boss, Chancellor Umzigwe, and the other one, Dean Wutugrase. How is everybody? How they are treating you? What about that huge political party? My son, I read somewhere that you have become the general secretary of KMC. Is that true? And when are you going to the election? Give me the news from Mezi and spare nothing good or bad, your adjustment and the family's, everything."

The next three to four hours, Dr. Wasiri covered all these topics. And from his mentor, every story led to thousand questions. They were interrupted at the end by a phone call. At the other end, there was Lady Allistair who announced that she was at the eleventh floor and requested to come down to meet the man she has been dying to see for the past two years, Dr. Wasiri. The old man responded affirmatively and told her to come down. He looked at his protégé and started adjusting his tie and shirts. He said that an ABDI donor was coming down to see them.

About ten minutes later, Lady Allistair came in the suite, with her all AMX CEO profile and very sexy presence. As usual, she was dressed to kill, less showy as before, but the light brown double breast suit she wore on top of a satin gray blouse were not to be found in your regular high-end boutique, most likely in the by-appointment-only preserves of the British nobility.

She was alone and was welcomed by Dr. O'Shea, who quickly introduced her to Dr. Wasiri. She almost bowed to the man from Mezi and said, "Dr. Wasiri, we keep hearing wonderful news about your academic and political rise in Mezi, we hope you would find your final happy anchor somewhere along."

Dr. Wasiri realized that he was dealing with an astute reader of events back home and replied, "I notice Lady Allistair is well informed of the events in Mezi. As far as I am concerned, it is more a relentless search of that anchor, as you put it, rather than a rise in either academic or political setting of Mezi. I sincerely hope it should not take much longer."

Dr. O'Shea beamed at the exchange, as he knew that given any setting, his protégé would rather introduce his perennial brand of modesty than his accomplishments. He was not disappointed. Lady Allistair, on the other hand, was startled by what Dr. Wasiri said after all that she heard the man had accomplished in less than six months of his return back to Mezi. Indeed, a man to be reckoned with.

Lady Allistair tried another question, "Indeed, but how do you see the political evolution in Mezi? I heard you are facing a despondent opposition on the other side?"

Dr. Wasiri noticed the trap. "Far from it, the sitting government and its allies have been entrenched in Mezi body politics a long time with tentacles reaching every venue of national scene. Our political movement has been on a long march in the political desert, singing the praise of good governance, integrity, justice, fairness, economic development, and all these principles you are very familiar with in your respective countries. People are slowly responding, but I would still say it is a long shot. Corruption is an insidious thing, everybody hates it, but everybody abides by it. This is where we are in Mezi. It is hard to predict if the demons of corruption would triumph over the forces of progress. The only betting chance for us and Mezi is that the sad dance has lasted way too long. It is now stinking and people are clamoring to get out of the dance and to put an end to it. Of course, that is my very biased perception. I hope it stands."

Lady Allistair heard the hopeful politician's message and replied, "It is not just your biased perception, believe me, it is an opinion generally shared in the international business community ready to do business in Mezi on basis of good governance. Well, I certainly wish you good luck, and it was a great pleasure meeting you in person.
I heard so much about you, and I was dying to meet with you. One thing I have to say listening to you, you have undeniably revealed all the great characters attributed to you, the inner strength, the integrity, and the passion to move Mezi beyond the pettiness it is ensnarled in. Mezi would, without a doubt, have a great future under your leadership. There are a lot more people outside Mezi routing for your cause you would not know. I hope to talk to you again during the ABDI meetings."

She turned to Dr. O'Shea who was now swimming in Lady Allistair's adulation of his son and woke him up. "Dr. O'Shea, thank you for the pleasant introduction. I believe we have to close on that important issue we started talking about a month ago. I am looking forward to meet with you sometime tomorrow in the afternoon right after the big ceremony. Gentlemen, thank you very much for the pleasant time. I will see you some other time."

She left the suite and was gone. The exchange took less than fifteen minutes. Dr. Wasiri asked his mentor who actually was the lady. Dr. O'Shea responded that she was the CEO of AMX based in London, UK, and one of the major contributors to the foundation Emily Thomas O'Shea as well as ABDI. A very powerful lady. He also revealed that most of time he works with her. Dr. Wasiri then timidly asked him if she was part of the emissaries who retrieved the specs. Dr. O'Shea was surprised by the question.

"She was not. I do not think that the emissaries would show up in the ABDI meeting. Lady Allistair is a very sweet lady. She used to work out of AMX New York offices. She was recently promoted to become AMX CEO. She had no idea about those emissaries. I have never been able to determine if she works for the emissaries. That is another story. But she has helped us a lot. You see, this business of emissaries is very complicated. In my view, they probably represent a super conglomerate of business interests around the world, trying to control the access and exploitation of Alpha-M. Is AMX part of it, I don't know, and if it were, Lady Allistair would never tell. As far as I am concerned, the super conglomerate is actively supporting our cause at this time. They are providing a lot of resources in the process. Are we working for them, I don't think so. Are we getting more than we have bargained for? Definitely yes. My very dear son, stay with me on this one, do not trouble yourself about whether we are working for them or not. If our purpose is noble and higher, it does not matter. If in the process, we come to realize or accomplish great things for those who count for us, so much the better.

Think about it, in your case, if in the process, you come to accomplish unbelievable things for Mezi, would it not be so much the better? Look at what has happened recently. You brought these specs no more than twenty pounds. We tested them, and we certified them to be Alpha-M. The emissaries came and retrieved the specs in exchange they gave two billion to the foundation and about four billion to ABDI. Tell me who is ahead in this case? I don't know what they are doing with the specs. Are they killing people with the specs, I don't know, and I did not hear of any killing so far. But much good has gone around for the Children of Street in Mezi and for the expansion of African projects. This is the time and the occasion when people would say, 'Keep your eyes on the prize.' That is why I am saying to you, stay close to Emily's rules, you would not be burned. I know that you are not about to blow the money that you received to do stupid things or buy fancy stuff. Absolutely not. Because you are of the noble heart predisposed to do good, Emily chose you for that goal, and when the emissaries would come to you one day for a bargain, I know that you would choose to do good, not for you but hopefully at that time it would be for Mezi. That is what you have signed up for. Do you agree with me?"

Dr. Wasiri, who was enlightened a while ago before the lady showed up, was again defeated by what his mentor was saying. He resigned to say in spite of himself, "I do, Professor O'Shea. I really don't know where all this is leading to. I don't know what you got me into. I guess I am already so far in the dungeon, I would never be able to get out. I pray for you, and I pray that everything would be OK. You know you are getting me very tired with all this talk. I need to take a nap before the dinner."

Visibly dejected, Dr. Wasiri got up and went to sleep in his suite room. He did not get up until about nine thirty. He was not going to go downstairs, he ordered his dinner. His mentor was not in the room. While he was waiting for his dinner, he caught up with his overseas calls to Mezi, student papers, and other deanship papers, KMC papers, and Mezi news articles. He called Sir Ewas to thank him for the hospitality and to apologize for the mess he put him through. Sir Ewas told him that what went on the day before was nothing compared to the active search that was going on to find out where Brother Kano went. He said luckily he was reached at his cell phone. He took his wife and family away from their house, and they are spending the night at a hotel. They run away from countless phone calls and untimely knock at their door. Two policemen are protecting their house at this time. Sir Ewas asked him if there would be any TV coverage of that ABDI ceremony tomorrow in Atlanta.

Brother Kano thought that there would be, given about eleven heads of African states came for the ceremony in addition to the American VIPs. Sir Ewas advised him to stay far away from the TV lens to avoid any assault from Mezi countrymen down south. Then he remembered that ABDI board members would occupy prominent seats during the ceremony. He prayed that there is not going to be any reading request from the ABDI executives.

When the dinner came, there was another knock at the door, and there was a gentleman with three bodyguards. Dr. Wasiri did not recognize the man who asked to come at the same time that Dr. O'Shea materialized.

The bodyguards stayed at the door. Dr. O'Shea then introduced the gentleman to Dr. Wasiri who was still very perplexed of the man. At the end, Dr. O'Shea said that was his Excellency, the president of Zambia.

Dr. Wasiri's heart sank. He apologized to the president and wondered how he can help him. He jokingly said that a good glass of Scotch would do. In turn, he apologized for disturbing him while he was about to have his dinner.

Yet he sat down. "I am your great fanatic. I have been closely following what was going on in Mezi and was extremely delighted that at last KMC was rising from its torpor." He also revealed, "I was a classmate of your boss, Chancellor Umzigwe, while we were pursuing engineering studies in London. I did not go to PhD level like my smart colleague, but we have kept in touch all that time. Of course, given the African political sensibilities, when I come to Mezi, I do not see Chancellor Umzigwe. But whenever the chancellor wants to rest from his academic and management occupations, he is always welcome at the palace at Lusaka."

He went on saying that Chancellor Umzigwe was very very high about Dr. Wasiri's return to Mezi. Chancellor Umzigwe kept telling him that Dr. Wasiri was definitely the one. He added, "From all that we have seen to date, my good friend has been proven to be right so far. Chancellor Umzigwe also alerted me that you were attending ABDI meeting to my greatest surprise. You know, ABDI funded this wonderful copper mining project in Zambia. I came to extend our thanks and appreciation. I promised that I would touch base with you the first chance I get. And here I am, thanks to Dr. O'Shea who was sharing the dinner with us. When I heard he was sharing the suite with you, I troubled him to come up and introduce myself to you. You would not believe how happy I am to meet with you personally.

I am convinced that you would bring a new dawn of prosperity to your country." Dr. Wasiri moved closer to the guest seat and said, "I really appreciate the regards. I certainly look up to Chancellor Umzigwe who has done so much to get me back home. I would let him know that we met. As far as Mezi is concerned, I don't think I would not have accelerated my learning phase, and I am still learning, without the strong support of wonderful people like Chancellor Umzigwe, a great asset to Mezi. We still have a long way to go even if we came out of the closet, so to speak. But everything is pointing to a broader appeal and wider acceptance of our message, and we are certainly hopeful that will carry us to the people and victory very soon."

At that instant, the president got up and thanked Dr. O'Shea for the introduction, and turning to Dr. Wasiri, he said, "Please, do not forget to invite me to your inauguration. I cannot wait." The president of Zambia left the room. Dr. O'Shea then proceeded to talk about what went on downstairs when he was still sleeping.

"All members of the board had arrived, and they joined the dinner with a few heads of states who came down. We were led to this private dining room. I sat next to Lady Allistair. Too bad you slept that much. I made some silly excuses for you. You need to heat this food that has gotten cold. There is a microwave machine in the back there. Now what is going on TV? My God, that is two in a row people wishing you the best in the next election. You got it going. Talking about the election, I don't know much about Mezi, but here in the United States, it is money, money, and again money that run elections. Tell me the truth, do you have enough funds to run your elections next time around?"

Dr. Wasiri, who was heating his meal, came back.

"I was going to plug the hundred million you got us lately into the campaign. I don't need that money."

"Very good, and how were you going to do this? How are you going, as you said it, to plug hundred million into your campaign without raising any political impropriety about being bribed by some sinister foreign business interests? Son, leave that campaign funding business to the pro, and you would never get you and your political folks into any trouble. Look at how this whole funding of the university expansion has gone. Did you hear any political clam or scandal about this? Well, absolutely not.

To tell you the truth, I came to this conference to resolve that serious question of your political campaign funding, and I see that you did not think that through. I rather just shut my mouth now so you would not know how and when this would go about. All you would notice is that it is done as legally as possible. You should continue doing what you do best, politicking and stay above the fray as you should while other folks would be actively oiling your elections by all means necessary. Again do not play around transferring any money from London. Just too risky! Did you hear me? I hope you realize that this is no time to play anymore. It is now the time of big risk and big reward. Don't screw it up with your 'too good to be true' face off. I am sorry, son, I don't want to upset you again. But I need to tell you all these things for your own sake. By the way, you did not finish your dinner. You did not even start it. Come on. Eat your dinner."

The old man left the suite living room and went to his room. In fifteen minutes he came back in pajama. He helped himself with a good size glass of red wine. His protégé was still eating. While watching the news on TV, he shared a few family stories out in Arizona where he was still staying. He said that he did not really want to go back to Kentucky.

While in Arizona, he seriously considers selling his house. He was still contemplating moving to South Carolina for retirement, but he did not want to impose on his kids who are making too much of that house they want to buy for him.

With all that money he got, he wanted to just go down there and buy the house. But after all the planning they have put into this, the children would be very upset to hear that. So Dr. O'Shea felt that he is left with no decision and indecision.

His protégé said that he would strongly advise him to let the children make their entire plan as long as possible and not to interfere. He said that it was their project and let them bring it to its natural end. He added that Dr. O'Shea should let them spoil their father for a change, they deserve that. The old man changed the subject, and looking at his protégé, he said that he should help him write his last will, he was not getting any younger. He said that it was obvious he would not be able to spend all that money that was flowing to him this late in his life. He did not think that he should leave it to his children who have not participated in their great endeavor. His protégé stopped him on the course and said that no matter what he was thinking, his children or grandchildren must inherit his financial assets unless he wanted to give it all to charity.

He also added that he would not be part of any writing, designing, or developing of his last will. If he wanted to get one, a lot of lawyers in Arizona or Kentucky will be happy to help him. Dr. O'Shea was asleep now, and his protégé dragged him to his room. When Dr. Wasiri put him to bed, Dr. O'Shea murmured something to mean, "Just like old time."

The next day was the day of the biggest pump in the life of His Honorable State Senator Jeremy Massay. All that he had planned regarding what he called the ABDI gig had come to unbelievable fruition. He was going to play host to not one but eleven heads of African States, the US Secretary of States and lesser US federal bigwigs, the French foreign minister, about thirty congressmen and nine senators, UN and World Bank senior representatives, the Georgia State governor, and a slew of State Legislature leaders, the Atlanta mayor, hundreds of CEOs of local and foreign corporations, not mentioning the stunning Lady Allistair, his part-time lover, the Atlanta business and city government elite, and other curious people.

This was the day he had envisioned from the day he accepted the chair of ABDI board of directors. It was the biggest luck of the draw as he kept repeating to himself and to his faithful friend and vice chair, Dr. James Stringer. This was the day he would show all these Atlanta mean elite minions what the Gullah son of the island of Sapelo had accomplished, how he had made very good and risen above their little pettiness to be able to play host to eleven heads of States, of all people. That was a feat that none of them would ever accomplish in spite of their empty million-dollar mansions and the silly showy expensive cars, including Mercedes Benz, Lexus, Lamborghini, Rolls-Royce, or Bentley. These Atlanta sob-elite minions never missed a chance to remind the Gullah son of Sapelo that he would never fit in their gentry set. But not today, today the whole Atlanta would honor him.

When he woke up that day, his wife found him crying of joy in the bathroom. He told his wife that the only thing he regretted on that momentous day was the fact that his grandmother, who raised him and wished that he became priest, was not around. She was not going to witness that, though he did not become a healer of spirit as she had wished, he had become, in ABDI, a healer of hunger, thirst, poverty, disease in distant lands back home where the ancestors of very proud Gullah people came from. That was a testimony his grandmother would have enjoyed. That was an achievement his grandmother would have been the most proud. And for all that was worth, with the steady growth of ABDI, his wife had quietly abolished Vanessa rules.

Unbeknownst to his honorable, the end of the harsh restraining rules came subtly after one of the big dance parties that ABDI gave. From afar, Vanessa noticed how the wild ones were deliberately and suggestively fussing over the ABDI chairman of the board, who was simply standing there waiting for his wife still in bathroom. She was shocked to see how one of her married friends she had invited to the affair, stuffed the most salacious note in her husband's tuxedo pocket, inviting him to evade to some remote corners along the Highway 85 in direction of Charlotte. Her husband did not notice that the note was in his pocket. The next day, his honorable asked his wife to drop the tuxedo for cleaning on her way to work. Vanessa retrieved the note and sometime in the afternoon she called her husband to verify his whereabouts.

His honorable was very busy at work and excused himself for not being able to talk. He called her back later when she was on the way to the hotel where her good friend was waiting for his honorable. She went up to the designated room where her friend was waiting in bed, lying naked exactly as she had described in the note how his honorable was going to find her. She confronted her with the note and advised her that her innocent husband never saw the incriminating note and was too busy at work to come. In no uncertain terms she told her that in the future she must remain as far away from her as possible and that was the end of whatever relationship they had enjoyed in the past. What burned Vanessa to no end was the fact that she was the same married friend Vanessa had confided to about her rules not less than a week ago. His honorable never found out about the breach. He simply noticed that the access to the house master bedroom was no longer restricted. He was just happy to resume his sacred matrimonial duty after about two years of lapse. His honorable was too busy growing ABDI, and this was his biggest reward day.

The big ceremony started at about ten thirty in the morning in the hotel's biggest ballroom designed as stately as possible for the occasion. The agenda of the entire ceremony was arranged in such manner that all local, state, international, and foreign dignitaries came ahead singing the praise of the extraordinary accomplishments made by ABDI in those distant places in Africa, thanks to the unparalleled leadership of its chairman of the board, the Honorable Georgia State Senator Jeremy Massay and its staff. The president of Senegal, main country beneficiary of the Eastern Africa Water, led the way representing the other presidents from adjacent or direct beneficiary countries of Mauritania, Mali, Niger, Burkina Fasso, and Chad. Next came the president of Zambia representing the presidents from countries that were beneficiaries of other ABDI projects.

The Secretary of State and the French foreigner minister joined in to congratulate ABDI and His Honorable Massay for pulling off the extraordinary management coordination of the Water Project, with the participation of the United States, France, UN, World Bank, and other private partners' financial resources and technical expertise.

No mention was made of AMX/BI major crucial financial funding, and this was keeping with the deliberate low-key approach that Lady Allistair wanted to impart to her own boss' involvement. Federal, Georgia State, and Atlanta public and business dignitaries closed the round of praising ABDI and its chairman in varying degrees of extrapolation that kept the son of Gullah in near tears. During the ceremony, Mrs. Vanessa Massay whispered to her husband in more than one occasion that she wanted to drag him to the next bathroom to kill the burning sensation that was building underneath her every time one of dignitaries sang his praise. His honorable smiled and told her that he was still following Vanessa's restraining rules. Near the close of the ceremony, the ABDI vice chair, Dr. James F. Stringer, introduced the man of the hour, the Honorable Georgia State Senator Jeremy Massay.

His honorable took the long acknowledgement applause in stride and gave a very short and very modest speech. "Misters Presidents, very distinguished guests, fellow members of ABDI. The members of the board of ABDI thank you, distinguished guests, for all the regards you have extended today to this organization and its staff. It has been exactly two years since ABDI has been put in place. It should be said that much has been accomplished in that record time. Much has been accomplished indeed, and all thanks to the arduous and extraordinary dedication of ABDI staff that has spared no energy, time, and effort to realize the feats we are celebrating today.

For the same reason, at this time, I want to ask you to extend an outstanding note of appreciation to the unequaled, extraordinary, and tireless power behind ABDI engine, distinguished guests, I am proud to present Dr. James F. Stringer, the vice chair of ABDI. The accomplishments and feats realized by ABDI are extraordinary for an organization of its size and scope. When you work in an organization like ABDI, your best reward remains in the hope that the projects you are implementing would alleviate the terrible scourges of hunger, thirst, unemployment, poverty, or disease in those distant lands. I do not want to repeat at this time what were the impacts of these projects. Each of the previous dignitaries has detailed those impacts in eloquent and commanding terms.

But as we recognize and applaud the impacts of these projects, we should always bear in mind that every one of these accomplishments and feats calls for more of the same in many other parts of the continent. The call is so resounding that it becomes almost premature for us in ABDI to accept the honors you were kind enough to bestow today upon this organization for the accomplishments and feats being celebrated at this time. We certainly thank you from the bottom of our heart for the kind regards. However, for some us who have traveled and seen those distant lands, the accomplishments and feats celebrated today pale in comparison with what remains to be done. We know that as much as we are proud to have somewhat alleviated one or two of the scourges we mentioned above in some locations, other scourges have remained unabated or worsened in other locations. That is the difficult and long-term task assigned to ABDI to see to it that those scourges are eradicated once and for all, not just in locations we covered today, but in the large continent of Africa. We hope that next time when ABDI would be celebrating other accomplishments and feats, we would have moved along that long arduous path of eradicating the terrible scourges that are visiting daily upon the people in those distant lands of Africa. Misters Presidents, very distinguished guests, thank you for coming. Thank you for your generosity and support. Thank you for ABDI staff and board. Thank you so much."

The speech was completely unexpected from His Honorable Jeremy Massay. It was certainly not the long speech he had worked on with his friend Dr. Stringer the night before. Dr. Stringer sat there completely surprised to hear his boss challenging the audience to go beyond the celebration of current accomplishments, to raise their sight to the overall goal of attacking the continent scourges of poverty. There was no iota of self-congratulatory note for himself. As a matter of fact, the gracious honorable extended his main congratulation to no other people but ABDI staff and his vice chair. That was not the cunning politician Honorable Jeremy Massay that Dr. Stringer knew. He would ask him later whatever happened to their speech. His honorable wanted, probably, to show a side of his character that Dr. Stringer needed to discover.

But the speech was extremely well received by the heads of African States who surrounded his honorable as one of them at this time. The American audience, the African American in particular, was very moved by the open display of adulation that these presidents were extending to one of them. Mrs. Vanessa Massay, who had not been quite acquainted with the work that her husband was doing, moved from the libidinous urge she could not contain a while ago to a religious epiphany of pious kind revealed in her eyes full of tears.

The reception that followed was a sensation, gathering the entire Atlanta elite under one roof in honor of His Honorable Massay. His honorable made the round of the ballroom in endless exchange of congratulations for having moved in two days the international diplomatic center of the United States from New York to Atlanta. When he reached the table where the members of the board were seated, he was surprised not to see Dr. Wasiri. When he inquired about Dr. Wasiri, Dr. O'Shea told him that Dr. Wasiri had received urgent calls from home at the end of the ceremony, and he was trying to answer the calls in the suite upstairs.

The ABDI chairman jokingly reminded the board members to be ready for the long board meeting starting at nine the next day. By the time he saw Lady Allistair, she was in deep conversation with the US Secretary of State. She excused herself and dragged his honorable to a quiet corner where she issued an invitation for him to come to her suite by the next day late afternoon. When she was done, she noticed that Vanessa was fast approaching the quiet corner, probably to check what was being transacted there.

As astute as ever, Lady Allistair turned to Vanessa's direction and reached out to Mrs. Massay to say, "At last I have the pleasure to meet the beautiful Mrs. Massay." She extended her hand and looked at Vanessa straight in her eyes. Vanessa stopped cold and returned the gaze for a few seconds but blinked. The two ladies telegraphed to each other in invisible signals only women relate to. The signals revealed to each of them that the battle for his honorable's soul and body is yet to be over. At that instant, His Honorable Massay was standing between his two ladies and said, "Honey, this is Lady Allistair, the CEO of Anglo Minerals Exchange in London, England. She has been the prime financial fundraiser of ABDI. We would not have come to this day and this occasion without her tireless involvement. Lady Allistair was the person who recruited me to chair ABDI as I told you at the beginning. ABDI owes so much to Lady Allistair."

Vanessa still fixated over the tall beautiful and radiant lady with a British accent absently said, "Of course, I remember." Lady Allistair, satisfied to have made her strong impression on Mrs. Massay, started returning to her seat yet she sent another salvo at Vanessa. She said very loudly to the man of the hour, "His honorable has a very beautiful wife." While his honorable was thanking Lady Allistair, Vanessa suddenly felt a shiver on her spine. She firmly grabbed her husband's right hand and moved him away from the quiet corner.

They both returned to the huge honor table where Dr. Stringer had been waiting to ask his friend the important question about the speech. Before Dr. Stringer would say a word, his honorable turned to his friend and said that his grandmother confided the speech to him. When Dr. Stringer looked puzzled, his honorable revealed that in time as memorable as this day, he needed to give a speech from his soul. Then he added that his grandmother's spirit came upon him the night before and told him that "respect and honor are given to those who do not look at the miles traveled but rather at the horizon to reach." That inspiration, he said, forced him to change his speech from dwelling over about to be celebrated accomplishments, but instead, to refocus the audience's attention over the long difficult tasks to come. He concluded that his puzzled friend had only to judge the effect and impact of the short speech he gave. Dr. Stringer concurred that the effect and the impact of the speech had been far greater than what he had anticipated. They toasted each other to the amusements of their wives.

While the big ABDI party was taking place in the ballroom, Dr. Wasiri was being inundated with frantic calls from Mezi in the suite. The news, which was now being flashed on CNN flash, was ominous. President Badegou had passed away as a result of a heart attack in his presidential palace. The frantic calls were coming from the KMC leadership senior advisors, Chancellor Umzigwe, and Dean Wutugrase. There was a constitutional crisis at hand in Mezi. The Constitution has determined the line of succession in case of death or incapacity of the sitting elected president with the following people and in that order: the elected president or Speaker of the Lower Chamber, the elected president of the Senate or Higher Chamber, the premier minister, the president of Supreme Court, the vice president of Supreme Court.

However, the current Speaker was not the elected Speaker, he was an acting Speaker automatically designated according to the Lower Chamber rules which picked the leader of the party with the highest number of elected members when the old Speaker was incapacitated after the Mrs. Monica Kello Ngoma debacle. There was never enough quorum or votes to elect a new Speaker by a simple majority of 51 percent as required by the Constitution. After many trials, the matter was postponed sine die until the next electoral process. The incapacitated Speaker was still in the hospital recovering and was not about to reclaim his elected position. The horse trading, among the political parties in the Lower Chamber to elect a new Speaker, became so vile and corrupted that for a change good conscience prevailed to leave that selection to the next elected Lower Chamber.

The elected president of the Senate, accused of provoking the health demise of the old Speaker during Mrs. Ngoma affair, refused to succeed President Badegou. He firmly and surprisingly invoked his good conscience not to profit from his colleague's disability. The prime minister, an old friend of President Badegou and near retirement, who had reluctantly accepted the position of PM less than three months ago and returned from his peaceful ambassadorship in UK, did not want any more aggravation with the presidential appointment. The Supreme Court justices flatly refused the position on unspecified grounds.

The compromise solution, put forward by the Supreme Court justices, was to install the acting Speaker as president on condition that he would not run for the office, he would call for new elections in six months, and most importantly, the Lower House would vote on this appointment and the opposition would not object to it. By opposition, the Supreme Court meant any organized opposition within and without the legislative chambers. This generally meant KMC. The two senior advisors were already contacted to issue on behalf of KMC a statement to acquiesce to the compromise solution.

As expected, the two foxes saw another opportunity to put forward the face of KMC leader and to show to the people of Mezi how far the country had fallen to pay so dearly for corrupt practices entrenched in country institutions. They advised the government and Supreme Court contacts that they needed time to decide which way they would go on this grave issue. They quickly called an urgent meeting of the entire KMC Standing Leadership Committee less Dr. Wasiri, the general secretary, on a trip to the United States. The meeting lasted all day with all kinds of media journalists camping around the Polytechnic University conference room where the KMC leadership was gathered.

The length of the meeting was purely for a show. The decision was made in the first hour of the meeting to agree with the compromise solution offered by the Supreme Court. The rest of the all-day meeting was purely tactical, to insure that the KMC agreement would be read in front of the world by nobody else but the KMC general secretary, Dr. Wasiri still in the United States. At about nine in the evening, the KMC leadership senior advisor, Dean Wutugrase, read a statement from the KMC Leadership Committee, and it said, "In this grave hour of our republic, in memory of the passing of President Leon Masefo Badegou, the KMC Standing Leadership Committee extends its deep condolences to Mrs. Badegou and his entire family.

Regarding the presidential succession compromise solution proposed by the Supreme Court, the KMC Standing Leadership Committee will issue its definitive statement pending the return from an oversea trip of the KMC general secretary, Dr. Wasiri. Our general secretary is expected to arrive tomorrow." The statement intent was to hold the entire country's leadership succession for another day, waiting on the good grace of Dr. Wasiri. It went without saying that the statement deeply infuriated the government, the legislative branch members, the Supreme Court justices, and the Sonjedi coalition party members. For the first time, KMC was holding them hostage as a result of their lack of unified standing.

Mr. Sonjedi took a very good note of the issue. He wrote down in his diary that this statement would be a strong point to rally anyone in the political arena, who was still standing on the fringes waiting for KMC manes. Dr. Wasiri took his last call with all the seriousness he needed to show, given the circumstances. He must be home within twenty-four hours. He went downstairs in the ballroom where the party was still going strong and went to see his mentor. He explained to Dr. O'Shea what he had learned and the need to get home quickly. Dr. O'Shea calmed his protégé and assured him that he would be home in about ten hours. He then asked him to go back upstairs and start packing. Dr. O'Shea raced through the ballroom and caught Lady Allistair who was just getting up and leaving the party. They took the elevator while Dr. O'Shea was explaining the urgency his protégé was facing. When they reached Lady Allistair's suite, there was already another gorgeous young vixen Dr. O'Shea had seen with Lady Allistair in a very animated conversation before in the ballroom. She was lying on the sofa. When she saw Dr. O'Shea, she looked surprised and mumbled something, saying that she did not know the job interview was going to take place with two people. Dr. O'Shea joked that he would make sure that she would fail the interview. Lady Allistair intervened and said that the interview would take place after she had taken care of a very important issue. She made three calls, and at the end, she told Dr. O'Shea that there would be a private jet plane in about two hours to take his mentor from Atlanta to Johannesburg, South Africa, including two stopovers. There would be a regular commercial flight from Johannesburg to Mandi the following day and Dr. Wasiri should be home at Mandi at about noon. That was all right for Dr. O'Shea, and he called his protégé to come down to go to the airport.

Dr. O'Shea left Lady Allistair with the young lady to continue what would turn out a serious interview in bed. When the old professor reached his suite, Dr. Wasiri had already finished his packing.

They went downstairs and took the twenty-four hours limousine to the private jet section of the International Airport of Atlanta. In no time, Dr. Wasiri was airborne back to Mezi.

Later on that same night, while in their hotel suite, Vanessa Massay kept asking her husband a lot of questions about Lady Allistair and their relationship. At the end, her exasperated husband said, "If you want to accuse me of having any sexual relationship with the lady, just go ahead and say it. But I would hate to disappoint you. Just as beautiful and sexy as she looks, men do not apply. Let me tell you something, at this very moment you want to act jealous about her, she is probably in a tight embrace in her suite with you know who, your good friend, Miss Eleanor Kensington. Yes, the beautiful young vixen Eleanor, the recently appointed vice president, treasury operations of the Peachtree Golden Trust Investment Bank. Lady Allistair had preferences that completely exclude men and including yours truly, if you want to know. Vanessa, I don't understand anything with you anymore. I would appreciate if you accuse me with trying to go to bed with every woman who was downstairs in the ballroom. But now you are going too far when you accuse me of trying to convert a full-fledged lesbian. You should know by now that I have learned my lesson and paid the price long enough to screw it up again. You can believe me on that one."

Vanessa now in her most revealing negligee approached her husband and put her hand over his mouth and asked him if he would love to join the two ladies. His honorable said he never thought about it before and would not know what to do. Vanessa was now lying down on her back on the huge bed. While her hand was slowly rubbing her husband's hardening member, she said that he just confirmed what she had suspected in the ballroom. She could tell right away that Lady Allistair was coming on her by the way she looked at her straight in the eyes. She added that Lady Allistair's manners reminded her of an incident that happened long time ago in Washington, DC, when she just became a postulant to become a Catholic nun. One of her colleagues, a tall, very beautiful Irish girl came into her room and wanted to help her tie a very complicated blouse they used to wear as postulant. This girl, instead, reached below the blouse and started to caress Vanessa's breast, looking at her straight in her eyes. Vanessa said she felt paralyzed and she did not know what to make out of the scene, but at the same time that she fell strongly and sexually connected with her. The scene went on for a minute or two, and Vanessa also reached at her breast and caressed it too. But when she tried to lean down and kiss the tip of her breast, she pushed her back. The lady left the room abruptly.

Vanessa retied the blouse by herself. They avoided each other for a long time until she just disappeared from the convent forever. Vanessa added that she knew from that time if she wanted to become a nun, she needed to overcome her sinful urges every time she undressed and saw the tip of her breast. She wondered every time why the tip of her breast attracted the young woman that much. Vanessa said that finally when her future husband kissed her breast for the first time in one of their early escapades, she understood what the girl was aiming at. And that marked the end of her nun vocation. By that time, his honorable reached out for her breast and kissed its tip.

The next day as early as nine in the morning, the board members reconvened in a smaller conference room. Dr. Wasiri was not present. By this time, Dr. O'Shea excused his absence by stating that a very urgent and unfortunate family event rushed him back home the night before. He added that Dr. Wasiri was very upset to miss the board proceedings and sent his regards. The board members went through another grueling session of reviewing about twenty new projects that Dr. Stringer covered in detail. By lunch time, the board had covered about seven projects. When they came back from lunch, they covered about four more by which time his honorable excused himself for an important meeting with two major donors.

When His Honorable Georgia State Senator Jeremy Massay reached her suite, Lady Allistair was still wearing her red silk pajama ensemble, a top shirt open through the last two buttons, and a pair of short culottes that left nothing to imagination every time she moved her legs.

When his honorable came in, Lady Allistair directed him to the seat across the sofa chair where she sat, with one leg on the sofa extension and pretending to polish her toes nails while reading memos scattered about the floor and the sofa.

The awesome sight of her near nakedness started acting on poor Honorable Massay. After about two minutes of letting the man absorb and lose himself in the picturesque tableau in front of him, Lady Allistair opened up.

"What a very beautiful wife you have, Honorable Massay. To tell you the truth, I was very jealous of you yesterday. She could be a very attractive companion for me. I mean it. You know my preferences, and she fit the bill. Don't you think so?"

"Lady Allistair, I do not think you invited me here to tell me that you wanted to go to bed with my wife. I would not approve of that. And she would not approve of that.

But she said that you are a very attractive woman yourself, and she would not trust you with me in the same room for a hundredth of a second. And, for a change, she was right. You left us a bit early yesterday. Were you tired? Was everything all right?"

Lady Allistair looked at his honorable straight in the eyes, and knowing how sarcastic his comment was, she said, "Remember, your were expected yesterday in the afternoon after the big party. Yet you would not come to my humble suite yesterday, too busy entertaining your attractive wife who must have been completely drenched throughout the whole day in the anticipation of what she would offer you last night. I cannot blame her. If my partner had received the same adulation you received yesterday, I would have been walking like those beer-drinking soccer fans who pee on themselves after their team victory. She certainly was a lucky woman last night. I don't know what she got left for poor me today. Forget it."

Lady Allistair got up and went inside the suite bedroom. She came back five minutes later, dressed up with a pair of black pants and with none of voluptuous tramp scene about her. She pulled her hair back and had a turtleneck pullover nicely tucked inside the black pants. Lady Allistair had all of business demeanor back. She took back her seat on the sofa. She resumed her conversation, "I want to ask you something and take your time before answering it. What did you take out of yesterday's ceremony?"

His Honorable Massay answered right away, "There is still much to be done."

Lady Allistair jumped from her seat and walked toward the big window and turned back to say, "Exactly, there is much to be done. You did not have to think about it. I was saying a while ago that I was very jealous of you. Point of correction, I was very jealous of your wife because yesterday she was with the most powerful person in Atlanta. Not in the sense of money or power. No. Yesterday, I saw a different Honorable Massay. In your memorable speech, you went beyond the politician Honorable Massay. You went beyond the accomplishments everybody was clamoring about. You were not satisfied of the accomplishments that quickly became for you a thing of the past. You were there planning for the next accomplishments. That is what I saw yesterday. And I love it for you and, yes, for your wife too. I saw yesterday a man at peace with himself and ready to take on more challenges. Very few people, in similar circumstances, reach those stages, and that is where you are at this time. Congratulations.

Now I want to take you back to our first conversation. I have suggested to you that this endeavor ABDI may become a stepping stone to something bigger.

"Do you remember what we said? Well, let me refresh your memory. I remember I asked you 'What political station would you like to advance to in the next five years?' I remember also that you laughed at the question but replied that you would like to represent Georgia as senator in Washington, DC. I took good note back then. It was about two years ago and the clock is ticking. Today I am ready to say that you do not need five years. You are ready now to go for that seat. From what I saw yesterday, that seat is yours for asking. Remember you did not know ABDI from anything back then, you did not plan for anything remotely resembling ABDI, and yet you have accomplished so much beyond your own dream. Can you imagine what you can do for a political office you have already thought about and probably planned for it? I believe without a doubt that is completely feasible. Remember, yesterday you were praised by not one but eleven sitting presidents, two foreign affairs ministers, thirty congressmen, nine senators, A governor, a mayor, and countless political officials. How many of these senators who came yesterday have traveled that road with similar adulation unless they were counting on some political fundraising or some people of the same background? Yours is, Honorable Massay, natural. You have already cornered the political goodwill and the extensive I-owe-you politicians dream about. They are both there, and all you have to do is to shake them down. If you are concerned about ABDI succession, I believe you have convinced everybody already that Dr. James Stringer, your able friend, can succeed you anytime. I am sure he is doing a great job downstairs as we speak here. That should not be an issue. When it comes to political backing, I have to tell you at this time the same people who did everything to ensure the successful ABDI would move mountains to insure that your political goal is realized.

"There is one big project we are going to back, and you can start promoting as a launching pad of your campaign. It is the offshore gas and oil drilling along the Sapelo Island on the Atlantic Georgia coast. We are ready to associate your good name with that project. As I remember, you are the senator from the region. What a splendid way to start your campaign! On the east coast, you would have sown the new gas and oil projects. In Atlanta, you have ABDI and all the business community with you. It is a winning combination. What do you think?" His honorable got up and went to the window and gazed at Atlanta skyline and turned back to face Lady Allistair.

"I appreciate the confidence you have shown in me today. I appreciate that you are ready to support me in my next political venture. I believe it is a long road I always wanted to travel. I would need a lot of time to think about it and to size it. You were right that I was looking forward to a five-year plan. I hope your encouraging analysis is right. But I want you to give me about four to five months to conduct my own analysis and to reach a level of comfort that I did not have when I walked in. I am certain that you would help me along the way so much so that when I would announce, there would be no backing out."

Lady Allistair responded affirmatively, "Four to six months would be sufficient for anybody to come to a definitive decision. I realize that it would be a momentous decision that would test a lot of your comfort zone. It would not be easy. But I am convinced that this is the time and the moment for you, Honorable Massay, to take that plunge. That is all I wanted to talk to you about, and unless you do not have anything else to add or say, I want to let you know that I would leave tonight at about ten to go back to London."

She got up, walked up to His Honorable Massay, and gave him a deep wet kiss. Forty-five minutes later, when they took their shower together, Lady Allistair and His Honorable Massay did not have anything more to say to each other. They were mentally and physically spent.

It was about five in the afternoon when the chairman of ABDI board walked in the conference room where Dr. Stringer was closing on the project number seventeen. Thirty minutes later, a tired Dr. Stringer called it quit for the day, and the meeting was adjourned until the following day.

Dr. O'Shea remembered that he forgot to meet with Lady Allistair and wanted to catch up with her before she left to go back to London. He called her in her suite, and she was still there. She said that she also wanted to talk to him and to know if he would not mind to keep her company on her way to the airport. They would make a stop at this restaurant she loves on their way to the airport. Dr. O'Shea agreed and requested a little time to freshen up. The old professor always enjoyed the company of Lady Allistair he compared to his own two daughters he hardly saw. The ride to the restaurant was bumper-to-bumper Atlanta style, on Highway 285. They were very happy to reach the exit to get to the restaurant. As soon they were seated, the old professor, in his irreverent way, started talking about what he read about Chairman Kiriyan's plane being blown away in Russia.

"Lady Allistair," he said, "you would agree with me if I said that this all business of private jet plane being blown was a complete fabrication by the Russian government. In my estimation, Chairman Kiriyan cannot be blown up in any plane. He receives a lot of briefing on Russian intelligence service, so he would know when and how the Russian military would attempt to blow his plane away. First, I know for fact that there are always two private jet planes in Amovir. If one was blown out, there has been no mention in Russian communiqué about the other jet plane. Yet they show that there were no more airplanes in Amovir. Whatever happened to the second one jet plane? Second, the entire BI business empire is running as if nothing has happened. I was not expecting to see you here in Atlanta, if there was a complete collapse of BI or if Chairman Kiriyan has been blown away. Yet you are here as beautiful as ever and going about your business with ABDI as if nothing has happened unless I am speaking to the master of the universe, the Chairperson of BI. Lady Allistair, you can discount the first two points I am trying to make. But the business I saw with those two emissaries when they came to retrieve the specs, convinced me that the emissaries and Chairman Kiriyan are from a higher form than you and I. They do not respond to the same laws of physics like you and I do. Case in point, when I called you to provide you with the good news, less than six hours later, the emissaries were in my house or maybe sooner I could not tell because I went to sleep very early that Saturday. They were very relaxed inside my house. I am talking about the couple you know very well. The Ds. I may be getting old, but I still know my physics. How could they get in my house in less than three hours if I add the time it took you to reach Amovir? I would always remember what the husband D told me: 'The emissaries have the ability to get there before they leave here.'

"Do you know what that means, my dear? Fascinating, just plain fascinating. I am telling you all this to let you know that all of us, including yourself, Dr. Wasiri, and I have chosen a path of no return with these emissaries. We would rise or fall with their designs. I have no doubt about it. I have to warn you to do like I have done, and I am sure you have done the same when you left Amovir the last—we have to resign to our fate. I am now working on Dr. Wasiri to reach that basic conclusion. Take as much as you can, do good, and resign to your fate. I have no illusion about that."

Lady Allistair, who was following the conversation with a bemused face at the beginning, became more serene as a sphinx with the progress of Dr. O'Shea's talk. She sat quietly for a moment and finally said, "Dr. O'Shea, what if all you just said has no bearing in reality, it is all pure fabrication.

To tell you the truth, I have no way to disprove everything you say. But at the same time I cannot take it for reality. I live in the realm of reality. I have worked with Chairman Kiriyan the past twenty-five or more years. I have yet to encounter anything you say. Yes, I have met the couple D. But you are saying that they were in your house the minute Chairman Kiriyan learned that you got the specs. Are you certain that they were the couple D I have seen in Amovir? Dr. O'Shea, I have great respect for you and your scientific achievement. Sometimes I just cannot follow you where you are going."

Dr. O'Shea was smiling now and retorted, "Lady Allistair, I am not asking you to follow me where I am going. Besides, you won't. But I am simply telling you that each one of us has to decide for himself and herself what fate to resign to. As far the reality or realm of reality, I have two sets of examples. The last case again was when the couple D came to the house. As soon as they got the specs, they disappeared right there in front of my eyes. Next thing I know you were confirming the wiring of money and so on. How in the world did you know that they got the specs and were back in Amovir? Somebody must have confirmed this and probably Chairman Kiriyan. How soon did he learn that the specs were real? I am talking now to quote you about the realm of reality. The other case was in Amovir when I was there for the International Conference. I went to see Chairman Kiriyan, and it took me into what he called galactic jump. That was the most frightening tour of universe I have ever seen. It took me two weeks to recover from that galactic jump. To date, I could not tell if I was drugged or it was real. All I have is this badge of honor, this K ring that you are also wearing. Well, you must have taken the trip, did you? Well, we would never convince each other about those things.

"Lady Allistair, I love you as my daughter. I am just sharing things that I know we have shared and would continue to share. Talking about something we are sharing, I very much appreciated the speed to fund the shelter for the Children of the Street. Dr. Wasiri got a lot of mileage on that one. Now talking of political mileage, it is opportune to talk about how we are going to help Dr. Wasiri in the upcoming electoral process. We got this far, we got to go all the way now, don't we? I told him that I would raise the election funding issue with you. This is a complete different animal for me. I hope you would take care of this appropriately as long our protégé is not involved from near or from afar."

Lady Allistair intervened, "You should not concern yourself about this. We got the request, and it would be done. I was very upset about that surgical operation about your vocal cords.

I am so relieved to see you talking. That was my primary motive to come to Atlanta. The second was to see Dr. Wasiri in person. The third was ABDI, of course. Well, it went pretty good, that big ceremony. His honorable was very good too. He is going place if you ask me. Well, it is about time for us to go back to the airport. Come and keep me company and drop your missing daughter at the airport."

Lady Allistair gave him a kiss on his forehead. As the limousine sped toward the airport, Lady Allistair told the senior advisor, "Dr. O'Shea, let me tell how I survive in this environment: things I can change, I address them; things I cannot change, I leave them to those who can address; and things in between, I don't worry much about them. This way when I go to sleep, I have a deep sleep until the next day. And it starts all over. You should follow the same process. You would be OK."

The limousine dropped Lady Allistair at the private jet hall and took Dr. O'Shea back to the hotel for the remaining sessions of the board of directors last day of meeting. When she boarded the AMX private plane to go back to London, Lady Allistair took note of the entire conversation that Dr. O'Shea shared at the restaurant. Deep down, she knew that Dr. O'Shea was right. They both have resigned to whatever fate had reserved for them. In some instances, where she was more accessible to certain realities than Dr. O'Shea was, there was obviously a different perception of that fate. Compared to the incertitude and ignorance of Dr. O'Shea, she knew that Chairman Kiriyan was resting in Thailand after the incredible escape from Amovir. And that was a story she did not have to share with anybody. However, she drew a blank when she asked herself where were the couple Dudarev at that moment. The whereabouts of the Dudarev couple fell under the category of things she could not possibly know or change. And when she started thinking about her own galactic jump in

Amovir, she felt even more uneasy and at loss. The galactic jump fell under the category of things in between, she had stopped worrying about that trip long time ago. She called on the flight attendant and requested a generous glass of Scotch. Lady Allistair was deep in sleep as soon as her private jet was airborne toward London.

That same night, when his honorable came home after the closing of the ABDI second board meeting, he thought about sharing with his wife Lady Allistair's latest request that his honorable considers running for the State of Georgia Senate Seat. He was not in a mood to start a long discussion about their future matrimonial situation in the midst of a huge difficult political campaign.

Besides, their past marital problem came as a result of his first campaign to represent the Sapelo area in the Georgia State Senate. He was not about to dig out the painful memory at this time; instead, he could not resist chiding his wife over Lady Allistair,

"Honey, this is just to confirm what you thought, Lady Allistair did not get over the very beautiful and attractive Mrs. Massay, and so she said. She bluntly told me that she was very jealous of yours truly. And here comes the kicker, and I am not kidding, she added that while Eleanor was giving her whatever treat the ladies give to each other in those conditions, Lady Allistair kept fantasizing about Mrs. Massay. At one point, she stopped poor Eleanor and asked her if she knew you. Eleanor was very cold the rest of their evening. My dear Vanessa, you don't know how furious I was to hear such a nonsense. I told her that if she were not a lady I knew, I would have smacked her right there in that restaurant where we were eating. Now I am afraid that Eleanor would no longer be in speaking terms with you. You know she ignored my outrage and said that Mrs. Massay did not have to be so beautiful and so attractive. That remark calmed and mellowed me down a great deal to get me in the warming stage you are putting me in now."

Mrs. Massay threw the pillow in her husband's direction and went inside the bed's big cover. By the time his honorable finished taking his shower and came back in bed, Mrs. Massay was naked underneath the big cover. Vanessa rules were history, hopefully for good.

CHAPTER 41
In Memory of Father Zolani

Dr. Wasiri reached Mandi International Airport much faster than he expected. The private jet plane did not have to make any stopover, and it reached Johannesburg in less than seven hours from Atlanta. The funny thing was that it zipped by Mandi. But a big scandal would have ensued if Dr. Wasiri of proletarian KMC had come back from an unspecified trip in a private luxurious jet plane. The South African Airways regular flight fits better into KMC budget, and Dr. Wasiri would not have to explain where he was coming from. The media mob at the airport was grotesque. The entire somber KMC Standing Leadership Committee members under the guidance of Senior Adviser Dean Wutugrase welcomed KMC general secretary.

However, the lecture of the KMC statement would take place at the Polytechnic University campus. There was another convoy of KMC cars trailed by the media buses led back to the new imposing building of Applied Sciences Faculty. It was not clear why KMC had chosen the new building except to say that this was where the general secretary had his dean's office. Somewhere along the ride from the airport, Brother Kano thought KMC was overplaying its hand and decided he would read the statement as soon as he would get off from this amazing convoy. When the convoy arrived in front of the building, and the entire KMC Leadership team lined up behind its leader, Brother Kano read the following statement: "The KMC Standing Leadership Committee, on this day of November 18, decided the following: it concurred with the President Succession transition plan which appoints the current acting Speaker of Lower Chamber as acting president of the republic, The President Succession Plan would be voted by the Lower Chamber unanimously, The acting president would call legislative and presidential general elections within four months of his appointment, The new elected president and the new elected Lower and Higher Chambers would be installed within a week of the proclamation of the elections. Signed for the KMC Standing Leadership Committee by Dr. Kano Wasiri, KMC general secretary."

Brother Kano declined taking any question and went home. Within an hour later, the Lower Chamber voted on the President Succession plan unanimously. The acting Speaker was sworn in as acting president.

The Lower Chamber also voted on the entire process for the funerals of President Badegou. They were scheduled to take place in about four days. It was learned through gossip that President Badegou literally killed himself by excessive drinking of hard liquor in spite of the fact that his untreated ulcer was aggravated daily. He had a massive heart attack when he went to the master bedroom bar to retrieve another Scotch bottle. The government buildings were cleaned up for a change for the funeral occasion. The protocol insisted to have the undeclared presidential candidates from the government and the opposition next to the acting president followed by the premier minister, the new acting Speaker, the president of senate, and the Supreme Court justices. That was the first time that Dr. Wasiri's face was so prominently presaged in public in a semi-public function. That was also the first time he met all the country VIP continually denigrated by KMC. Dr. Wasiri was the most generous to Mrs. Badegou who confided to him to watch out for the gang of vipers around him. She would not accept the salutation from what she called her husband's assassin, Mr. Sonjedi. Otherwise, the country gave a rather pompous farewell to a forgotten politician. The only former high official to openly weep for his drinking buddy was none other but General Gwobozo, who stood next to Mrs. Badegou most of the difficult ceremony at church.

The next day, Mandi quickly recovered its political pace for the accelerated electoral process. Mr. Sonjedi quickly released the composition of the office of his national campaign, including names of people he did not bother to consult whether they have declared their support for his candidacy. Mr. Sonjedi wanted to show his deep broad support nationwide. But within two hours of the release of that communiqué, no less than twenty-seven people in the national campaign disavowed their support of his candidacy. That was another unfortunate slap in the face of Mr. Sonjedi.

A major newspaper wondered "Are Dead People Next in Mr. Sonjedi's National Campaign List?" Another major publication counseled Mr. Sonjedi to keep a long list of people out of his national campaign. This was going to be a rather rude campaign for the young former PM. By the end of the same week, the KMC Standing Leadership Committee requested that each cell provided the headquarters with three names of potential candidates to the Lower Chamber and Higher Chamber. The names were promptly entered in a computerized system and showed the leading candidates by each Lower Chamber territory and Higher Chamber higher territory. The lists were totally transparent and were sent back for concurrence and change. The lists for the most part were confirmed.

Where there were major points of tension or conflict, an independent KMC leadership member was dispatched to resolve the issue. Within a month, a complete list of candidates was released to the electoral board for the purpose of campaigning for the territory seat. The process gave KMC an unbelievable advantage over other party candidates. These parties were very slow to find a consensus candidate for each party or for Mr. Sonjedi's coalition of parties. Each party vouches for its own candidate. Mr. Sonjedi spent a great deal of his time resolving these intra-party squabbles. By time, he simply paid them off to determine a single coalition candidate to go against a KMC candidate wherever possible.

Mr. Sonjedi also noticed that his urgent request for the growing election fund needs went unanswered from abroad for two months at great dissatisfaction of various coalition partners. When the funds materialized, there were already splintered parties' candidates at every elective position, including the presidency. Worse, about thirty-seven former members of the Lower Chamber and fourteen former members of the Higher Chamber begged their way to join KMC as party candidates. The responsible cells vetted these candidates for three weeks. Twenty-eight former Lower Chamber members passed the test while only eight senate candidates were accepted. By the end of February, before the closing of lists of candidates, there were about seven presidential candidates, including Mr. Sonjedi and Dr. Wasiri.

KMC had also been able to file candidates in every territory and higher territory. The funding for KMC electoral process was kept at minimum with the KMC TV and Radio Stations doing around the clock candidates' propaganda. The KMC campaign funding process that Lady Allistair initiated after ABDI meeting was a big mystery. It was left as such by the very few people who knew the process. Brother Kano was left completely in the dark about the process.

Dr. O'Shea never talked about it again and never raised it in the e-mail messages he routinely exchanged with his protégé. But of all the potential troubles or scandals capable to test KMC during the election time, none was as virulent as the one resting on the shoulders of Father Zolani. During the proceedings of the first political convention of KMC, Father Zolani was already called on by Chancellor Umzigwe who approached him very discreetly in one of the Free University classrooms where delegates to the convention met in smaller groups. Chancellor Umzigwe wanted to talk about persistent rumors that have reached him and put a recently divorced woman in the Father's inner circle of aides.

Chancellor told Father Zolani that he was the last person to manage the conduct of his life, but he would not tolerate rumor mongering about a member of KMC Provisional Leadership Committee and more so when the member happens to be a member of clergy. Father Zolani was shocked to hear what Chancellor Umzigwe was saying and wanted to check the facts before responding to the rumors. What Father Zolani found out alarmed him even more.

There was a woman by the name of Belinda Batwan Dangello, recently divorced from an army major named Guytan Dangello. Mrs. Dangello claimed to have suffered a state of permanent abusive relationship from the time she met the obsessively jealous major seven years ago through the four years of marriage. She bore a boy from the marriage. There was a lingering child custody dispute between the Dangellos. When she decided to call it quit, she enrolled in an Advanced Accounting Certificate program at Polytechnic University in order to improve her chance of re-entering the professional career life when her divorce would become final. She recently completed the program and was working as a senior accountant at a huge gas distribution company. The tour at Polytechnic University had earned her a lot of acquaintances in KMC circles and among Father Zolani aides. When the convention was being planned, Mrs. Dangello volunteered to be among Father Zolani's aides. Father Zolani had absolutely no idea that Mrs. Dangello came to Vabiseo as a member of his inner circle. Unfortunately, Father Zolani's aides were always noticeable in any gathering. They wore prominent specially designed badges. Mrs. Dangello was remarkable as much as she was very beautiful and much older lady among the young aides. She gained the aura of being the instant beautiful leader of the pack of Father Zolani. She busied herself giving orders left and right to the aides when Father Zolani was not around. She probably knew better, but the younger aides, the female aides in particular, did not take it kindly to be ordered by this new lady. These aides started spreading rumors about Mrs. Dangello during the first two days of the convention. Chancellor Umzigwe was the early recipient of those rumors when he talked to Father Zolani.

On the third day of the convention, when Mrs. Dangello finally talked to Father Zolani, that was the first time they met. The Father thanked her for volunteering but asked her to refrain from giving orders to his aides. Mrs. Dangello assured Father Zolani that she did not intend to usurp any authority. She said that she came in as a volunteer to help out at whatever capacity Father Zolani expected her to work at.

It was not clear what really transpired from that private meeting, but Mrs. Dangello became a constant companion of Father Zolani after the convention. Mrs. Dangello became de facto secretary of the KMC Propaganda Services, now renamed Communication Services, which

Father Zolani was asked to lead. When Chancellor approached Father Zolani to inquire about the presence of Mrs. Dangello at the office of KMC Communication Services, Father Zolani first explained away the convention issue; he also added that Mrs. Dangello was also volunteering her time at what should be a paid function. Chancellor Umzigwe was not convinced. He insisted that the paid function be filled not by a volunteer but a qualified person. Mrs. Dangello was excused for about two weeks. But she came back replacing the recently hired and paid secretary of KMC Communication Services. Father Zolani justified the hiring on the basis of Mrs. Dangello's experience and superb training.

Father Zolani did not add that he was virtually becoming party in a violent legal custody battle that the Dangello couple was waging over their four-year-old boy. The fact of the matter was that the obsessively jealous major was trying to prevent his former wife to gain custody of the child on the ground of lacking substantial means of support. He had already got Mrs. Dangello dismissed from her last job by his repeated harassment of her on the job premises. He resolved that as long as he succeeded in keeping Mrs. Dangello unemployed, her custody chances will be eliminated, and she would eventually resign to come back to him and live with him. Father Zolani was very revolted by this major's behavior. He vowed to put an end to the abuse. He figured that the only place where Mrs. Dangello would never be abused would be within the Polytechnic University compound that was generally off limit to uniformed military people.

At the same time, Father Zolani would not bring such a straightforward issue to the leadership meetings to gain support from other KMC leadership colleagues. He was probably afraid to raise old memories of differences that have opposed him with the ailing former archbishop over the death of his beautiful niece. Although the issue was totally different, Father Zolani was still afraid that the passing of that girl, his perennial guilt and calvary, would be back no matter what. Father decided to manage Mrs. Dangello's business by himself. Worse, it became a dangerous habit of Father Zolani to get Mrs. Dangello to travel with him along with his younger aides in his various visits around the country. Father Zolani claimed now to Chancellor Umzigwe that he wanted to protect Mrs. Dangello from her husband's daily harassment when she reached home.

Chancellor Umzigwe told him that he certainly sympathized with Mrs. Dangello, but he also warned the Father telling him that he was going way beyond the call literally injecting himself in the couple's matter.

Chancellor Umzigwe was visibly embarrassed to see that he had let his colleague's involvement to reach that impasse. He was at loss how to help him. At the same time, the rumor mill about their relationship amplified. They were regarded according to the young aides as c-i-l or common-in-law.

Forty-five days before the election, Chancellor Umzigwe received a call at three in the Sunday morning from Dr. Ingoma, president of Free University and a KMC Standing Leadership Committee member. Chancellor Umzigwe was informed of the passing of Father Zolani as a result of gunshot wound received on his head and heart. Not far from his room, a lady by the name of Mrs. Belinda Batwan Dangello was also found dead in her room, killed in similar fashion. Dr. Ingoma also said that the double murders were quickly resolved when a major by the name of Guytan Dangello was found and arrested in a hotel room close to the university campus. The major called the campus police station, revealing that he had just shot Mrs. Dangello and, I quote, her lover, Father Zolani. Dr. Ingoma asked Chancellor Umzigwe to alert Brother Kano to come to Ikando right away to state the matter as forthrightly as possible before rumors take this horrified news in the middle of elections to unnecessary and frightening level and extent.

Chancellor Umzigwe rose from the bed, shaken. He placed the call to Brother Kano who did not ask for any details but said he would be ready to go to Ikando right away. Dean Wutugrase was also advised of the catastrophe that had happened but was excused to take the road for health reasons. Mr. Komasi Bello, Professor Awassa, and Sister Fanzi-Djomba were the other members of KMC Standing Leadership Committee asked to come to Ikando as soon as possible. The Mandi KMC members came together. Mr. Bello took the road from Vabiseo to Ikando by himself. The KMC people reached Ikando around noon on Sunday. Chancellor Umzigwe had the good inclination to invite the prime minister, the chief of army, and Mr. Sonjedi to come.

Chancellor Umzigwe wanted the entire Mezi population to see the faces of the government, the army and current leading presidential candidates, all present deploring the horrifying murder of two people by a deranged military man. He wanted to remove any suspicion on anybody's mind that the double murder was politically connected.

At two in the afternoon, it was left to Ikando chief of police the opportunity to read the macabre murder information. The prime minister not only regretted the double murder but also assured the people that justice would quickly take its course followed him. The army chief also was sorry that a double murder had taken place. He was extremely troubled that this had happened at the hand of an army officer. He also assured the people of Mezi that both civilian and military justice would take their course very swiftly.

Brother Kano Wasiri, general secretary, stood next to Mr. Sonjedi and appealed to the people of Mezi not to listen to any rumor that would go from this place. He said that the issue is sad and that simple: two people have been killed by a third person who happens to be a military man, because of a civil legal suit of a child's custody. He continued to say that Mr. Sonjedi is fully in accord with me to state that the issue had absolutely nothing to do with politics no matter what would be said.

He added, "As the chief of police, the prime minister and the chief of army have said, justice would be rendered and swiftly. At this time, we want to lead our two KMC people, who passed away, to their place of eternal rest."

The appeal was very effective. Dr. Ingoma congratulated his peers for the intelligent mobilization of the government, the army; the presidential candidates to deliver one message that the double murder was a civil case, not a political one. The car trip home for the KMC folks was the longest quiet trip. Before leaving Ikando, the KMC general secretary requested that the KMC TV and Radio stations provide only somber music and testimonies in memory of Father Zolani and Mrs. Dangello. When they reached the Polytechnic campus, Chancellor Umzigwe requested to talk further with Brother Kano at his house.

He then provided Brother Kano with his confidential details of what went on between the three people. He sincerely apologized for not stopping a calamity that was developing in front of him.

He said, "I sincerely believe Father Zolani has not developed any personal or displaced feeling toward the lady. He was sorely motivated by the abuse she was suffering and how to stop it. He was so afraid to be construed to be her lover that he made sure that every time they met or talked, there was always somebody in place. Now I am afraid all that Father Zolani has done or said, risk to be put asunder.

He has sacrificed so much and his life at the end. That needs to be said."Brother Kano told Chancellor Umzigwe that he should say exactly those words in his eulogy for Father Zolani. He also remembered without mentioning what then Father Felix said about Father Zolani and his demons. As soon as Chancellor Umzigwe departed, a tired Dr. Wasiri called Bishop Felix and exchanged deep condolences. They reminisced what he told him at Frankfort about Father Zolani. Dr. Wasiri asked the bishop not to neglect to mention that he fought through the end to pay for his demons as you predicted. Bishop Felix assured his friend that he would do just that and more. The days, which followed, got KMC in quandary. The KMC leadership had a major problem finding a successor to the legendary Father Zolani. Its seat was to remain vacant for the remaining election time. Sister Fanzi-Djomba would be acting propaganda services manager as far as presiding over the KMC TV and Radio stations programs, operations and direction. But Father Zolani's scheduled visits around the country were simply canceled.

The bishop of Mandi took charge of Father Zolani's funerals. It was as if Father Zolani was never banned, never left, but came back to the church with all of his priestly functions when he died. Bishop Felix saw to it that the elite had to realize on which side the church was at this time. He emptied all Mezi seminaries and convents and brought to the cathedral all these Catholic religious students, about three thousands of them to make all the funeral arrangements for Father Zolani. He dressed them up in obvious gleaming black and gold color of KMC. The cathedral was also dressed in black and gold colors. Bishop emptied all Catholic schools in Mandi. The students were also given a modified black and gold uniform to attend the televised mass at the stadium of the small Catholic College. Inside the cathedral where KMC leadership had the premier seat arrangement after the clergy, each available seat became a premium for the Mandi VIP set. Most stood erected during the three hours service.

Visibly shaken and in tears, Bishop Felix blessed Father Zolani's coffin covered in a KMC flag outside the church. In a loud voice, he welcomed Father Zolani into the cathedral as a friend he would dearly miss. He led the prayer and the Mass as nothing he had done all his life. First, he called on testimonies for his friend from the little ones, the poor, the children of street, the old ladies from Komesah and Zingzong, the sisters of Pamzelo convent in the Kalahari Desert, the friars at the tip of Lake Nyerengi, and at last, Chancellor Umzigwe who gave a tearful rendition of the same eulogy he had already shared with Brother Kano. Bishop Felix showed to what extent Father Zolani had touched so many lives.

Bishop Felix also revealed a lot of confidences he had shared with the illustrious departed son of Mezi. One confidence was about how he would be gone. He said that Father Zolani told him he hoped to die serving God and his people. He revealed the story of Mrs. Dangello that Chancellor Umzigwe did not share with anybody but Dr. Wasiri. Bishop Felix said that he got it from the horse's mouth. He revealed how Father Zolani was troubled by what people would say and think. In a rhetorical question, Bishop Felix asked how many in the congregation would have stepped up in face of so much jeopardy to help a woman facing deadly harassment and threat.

Bishop Felix added, "When my friend, Father Zolani, asked me for direction, what to do in this apparent deadly matrimonial conflict, I did what most of the congregation would have said and done, I counseled him with extreme caution in a matter that concerned two people. I advised him not to inject himself in that marital issue. I warned him to beware of what people would say. Brothers and sisters in Christ, I am sorry to confess to you, my congregation, that I did the cowardly thing. I did not assist my friend in time of crisis. I did not appreciate the gravity of his predicament. Brothers and sisters, the passing of Father Zolani must remain a serious and troubling reminder to all of us to stand up and be counted when we hear the voice of distress however small the tone and especially when that voice is muffled by fear of what people would say. At the end, if we fail to listen to that voice in distress, we would be opening avenues to worse as in this case, not one but two lives ended. This is a reminder for all of us, this is a lesson that Father Zolani leaves with us never to wait when help is needed and asked, to be always engaged when there is a distress call, and to stand ready to assist those in danger or in jeopardy no matter what people would say."

The funeral mass was carefully and visibly colored by KMC politics. In this grandiose funeral Mass, Bishop Felix made it plain throughout he was not at all concerned that the passing of a politician rather than a priest was being commemorated.

What mattered to Bishop Felix above all was protecting the memory of a friend who happened to be a priest and a brilliant politician not afraid to take on ideals that challenged the clergy hierarchy at the core of its teaching. Bishop Felix envied his colleague in a way he took enormous risk to live the gospel fully and in a more significant reality than other priests, including then Father Felix, safely confined in the church schools, parish houses, and other properties.

Father Zolani's lifestyle gained him the increasing enmity of the Catholic hierarchy torn between the ready and profitable access to the Mezi political elite and the deepening of suffering and misery endured by the general population of Mezi. The amplified and bereft corruption of the elite aggravated the gulf between Father Zolani and the clergy hierarchy. The death of the Archbishop Nzerima's niece cemented the split and threw Father Zolani on the side of vigorously promoting KMC precepts that have been diligently nurtured in the cells of the same Catholic Church. From the beginning, Father Felix supported unequivocally these precepts more than any other priest. He went to the same seminary as Father Zolani.

He struck an enduring friendship with Father Zolani that would last through that day of his assassination.

In the funeral Mass of Father Zolani, Bishop Felix gave back to his old friend his deserved due long time denied by the previous clergy hierarchy.

CHAPTER 42
Geffadi's Triumph

Father Zolani's KMC precepts came back with unmitigated triumph throughout the election campaign. KMC Standing Leadership Committee completed the list of candidates in every challenged political slot and more than two months before the Election Day. These foot soldiers enjoyed a decisive advantage in engaging the electoral in a way that was more primitive than original. They associated their political adversaries with every political corruption or scandal moment that had happened in Mezi from the time of independence.

The association came down in the form of propaganda expression of two slogan questions: "Where Were You?" and "What Did You Do to Stop It?"

The first question asked a political opponent simply where he or she was when a particular scandal erupted. If the opponent denies any knowledge of the scandal, an indirect association is established anyway through political mentors, friends, associates, family members, and so on. When the association was firmly established, the next question, "What did the political opponent do to stop the scandal?" was intended to doom the candidacy of the opponent to probable repetition of the scandal in the future. For every candidate, KMC TV and Radio stations took over asking and answering the above questions repeatedly, sometimes for a whole day. It was a little bit difficult to know if every answer provided by the stations was factual or imagined. But that was not the KMC leadership's concern as long as a strong push was made to secure a significant majority in both chambers and at the presidential level. Where there was no visible opponent to a KMC candidate, there was no letup, the propaganda machine worked equally hard to secure the seat.

While the campaigning for the Lower Chamber was on the solid ground, there was a definite serious issue to secure a significant majority in the Higher Chamber. The election in this chamber had never been political party based; seniority and extensive professional experience were valued in this electoral category. KMC was having a serious problem to line up convincing candidates with substantial seniority and a broad range of professional experience.

As expected, KMC political base was considerably younger and short on professional experience. To compensate for this shortage, KMC relied exclusively on the counsel of three thousands or so tribal chiefs who attended the Cast Away ceremony at Banfi-Bello to designate potential candidates. The process paid off generally in most locations, but it also brought forth candidates of unreliable repute. These candidates invariably scored very low during the vetting process given by the KMC local cell. In some instances, KMC was left out with no credible candidate and simply abstained from visibly supporting its own candidate. When a sponsoring tribal chief protested the lack of support of the proposed candidate, a member of KMC Standing Leadership Committee was dispatched to have a serious talk with the tribal chief showing the results from the KMC cell vetting process. In worst cases where there was a deliberate and evident show of cronyism, KMC leadership did not respond to the tribal chief's protests and literally abandoned the candidate.

The opposition to KMC took time to organize and to put in place a credible campaign in spite of the overwhelming and apparent advantage KMC enjoyed the first three to two months before the election. The opponents used the whole reliable card in the election, the I-Owe-You indices, built over time by giving various favors, small or big, to a lot of people, even those of KMC obedience. The next potent card used by the opposition was the old reliable ethnic card. That card worked to the extent that it was still useful in less urbanized areas of the country that had gone about 65 percent urban in the last thirty years. In the urban centers, KMC operatives effectively ridiculed the ethnic card with the common push back, "Where were you?" or WWY; Where were you when I was out of work? Where were you when my mother lacked medical help and passed away? Where were you when my family was kicked out of this apartment when I could not pay the rent? Where were you? The same question used to tag opponent with corruption sins was being used to ridicule the ethnic card. The last potent card used by the opposition to KMC was the perceived KMC elitism that Mr. Sonjedi laid out during his coming-out party. KMC was unfortunately easily liable on that ground. The perception was that KMC leadership was PhD top heavy. The opposition claimed that if you did not have a PhD, you could not have a hearing with the KMC leadership.

To illustrate its contention, the opposition came up a sketch story about a fishing village along the Nyerengi Lake. At a village meeting, a debate about the length of the fishing nets took place. The tribal chief told the village that there would be no decision about the length of fishing nets until the issue was studied and reviewed by a PhD that KMC had promised to send to the village.

The PhD fishing specialist never came to the village; he was too busy resolving the grave political problems of Mandi. Fishing stopped, and people starved and left the village. The village is still waiting for the PhD fishing specialist. The sketch under the title of "Fishing PhD" became very popular and was turned into a big hit by a famous troubadour from the town of Ikando. The sketch became a rallying song in many opposition political meetings. KMC had no credible answer to the elitism charge, except to show time and again through statistics how deep and varied was the list of candidates.

During one of the two presidential candidates' debates, Brother Kano answered the critique head-on. He asked his main opponent Mr. Sonjedi whether he was ready to park and not use everything he had learned while acquiring his two masters' in Economics and in International Management if ever he became president. Mr. Sonjedi assured him that he would not. Brother Kano went on to say that he would not apologize to make use of his PhD in mines engineering as long as he could help Mezi find and extract new mineral deposits. He then addressed Mezi people by warning them to beware of false debates that do not advance the pressing economic and social agenda of the country. He concluded by remarking that it was all distraction from addressing the real issues facing the country, and it was all distraction good to amuse the gallery.

The much-expected presidential debates were a big disappointment for those expecting a lively exchange between the main contenders of the day, Mr. Sonjedi and Dr. Wasiri. Mr. Sonjedi effectively diluted the importance of these debates by insisting on the participation of all seven candidates in the three hours televised debate. Worse, the moderator insisted on receiving answers from each of the seven candidates. It took about thirty minutes to cover each question. By the close of each televised debate, no more than six questions were asked. Each time, the lesser-known candidates went about the longest circumlocutions to answer the question to everyone's exasperation but Mr. Sonjedi. KMC made the most of its TV and Radio stations to wage the campaign for all of its candidates.

The results from the peaceful electoral process did not surprise. Dr. Wasiri was elected Mezi President with 68 percent. KMC won the majority in both chambers, gaining 71 percent of seats in the Lower Chamber and 59 percent of seats in the Higher Chamber. All KMC Standing Leadership Committee members won the seats they campaigned for, including Dean Wutugrase, KMC senior advisor who became a member of the Higher Chamber.

Chancellor Umzigwe had chosen not to run and to remain the Polytechnic University Chancellor. Dr. Ingoma, elected senator, was quickly asked by Dr. Wasiri to form a new government. Sister Fanzi-Djomba became the Speaker of the Lower Chamber and Senator Wutugrase took over the presidency of Higher Chamber or Senate. Dr. Wasiri reached out to Professor Awassa, elected as a member of the new Lower Chamber, to become his scientific advisor and to lead a new Higher Education Commission that Dr. Wasiri would use to expand the academic education in Mezi. In reality, Dr. Wasiri wanted to have Professor Awassa available to take on higher government assignment when needed.

The new president also decided to bring in two high-level advisors, Mr. Komasi Bello, elected senator, to the security advisor position, and Mr. Mengi Sakoto, a finance ministry inspector elected in the Lower Chamber, to the economy advisor position surprisingly bypassing Professor Awassa, KMC's economic guru.

One of the biggest surprises of all appointments made by the new president was without a doubt when Mr. Sonjedi was appointed governor of Mezi Central Bank, a position he had aspired to before trying to become president of Mezi. When he met the new president, he was surprised to hear that he was highly recommended by the crazy professor Awassa from way back.

When President Wasiri was sworn in, Mezi economic indices started pointing downward. There was the endless monsoon-like rain that had flooded many parts of Mezi for the past two months and was still on the horizon. Huge expanses of lower and high plateaus were inundated. People from these areas abandoned these areas for high ground or other agglomerations.

Mezi was almost cut in three parts when major East-West and South-North highways were blocked. Before adding one revenue cent in the treasury, the new government was already thinking about to spend about a third of the country's savings to help the farmers and the distressed areas. This sudden turn of events was not foreseen in KMC scripts of governing. Because of the monsoon-like rain, the big political event of President Wasiri's swearing-in was moved from the huge 120,000 seats Mandi municipal stadium to the Hall of Zeweli, the biggest auditorium in the capital. The large overflow crowd stood soaked in the rain and the new president was so moved by the sight to shorten the proceedings of the swearing-in.

Given the somber and difficult environment Mezi was confronting, President Wasiri annulled all the festivities planned for the advent of KMC to power except for the scheduled visit to the Children of the Street new shelter in Komesah. The children had planned a thank-you celebration for the new president, and he had promised to be among them when elected. President Wasiri could not, in good conscience, decline after having stated in so many words and in so many circumstances that the first priority of his presidency would be Komesah and all that is associated with Komesah.

It was very funny to see how Mandi VIP struggled to reach the shelter in the area of town they never knew it existed and would never have venture to if this new president had not brought his motorcade to the shelter. His Excellency, the High British Commissioner's limousine was lost three times in Komesah streets without names before accidentally reaching the shelter. One of the Supreme Court justices, curious enough to see for himself the dire Komesah conditions heralded in many court cases he had to adjudicate, was compelled to forgo the visit to the shelter. His car was stuck in the unforgiving mud when he made a wrong turn into another no-name street of Komesah. It took two hours to extract his car from there.

The only foreign president to show up at the swearing-in was the same Zambia president who met Dr. Wasiri in Atlanta. He was also surprised to be the only sitting president of Mezi's neighboring countries to come to Mandi. He assured Dr. Wasiri not to be concerned of the cold shoulder that his colleagues were giving him so early. He added that most were afraid that KMC-like movement was fast spreading in their respective countries and before long would take over power in the similar fashion. He advised Dr. Wasiri that in this business you are better off feared for the righteousness of your cause than the shame of your deeds. He stayed another day as a guest of his longtime friend, Chancellor Umzigwe.

The advent of KMC to power, with Dr. Wasiri elected president, was quietly celebrated in Mandi and was the toast of many world places. Chairman Kiriyan was now firmly in place in Varonne-Sur-Baie after about three months of rest in that reclusive hide-away hotel in the island of Phuket in Thailand. He stayed there long enough to get his new hide-away location up to the strict reclusive requirements he had made. When the famous escape from Amovir took place, the private jet airstrip was about 65 percent completed. The airstrip started inland but extended about three miles in a man-made island on the roughest side of Varonne-Sur-Baie, far from the main island's huge and busy international airport.

When the airstrip was completed and tested, Chairman Kiriyan was ready to move to Varonne-Sur-Baie. He already had a huge corporate campus about twenty miles from his main housing location. The corporate campus contained now a good chunk of investment banking and treasury operations that used to be in Vaduz. In fact, the way Chairman Kiriyan directed it, both locations would become exact copy of each other's operations. The corporate campus with the name of "La Maison d'Investissements—Boissy International" was to grow to employ more than fifteen thousand employees by the time the entire expansion is completed.

Chairman Kiriyan's private plane landed on the private airstrip one early morning at about four. He was whisked away to the nearby palace of about five stories built against a huge rock by the littoral while its last two basement stories were built partly inland but also extended for about thirty yards under the sea water. The huge basement windows gave into the bottom of the sea. In that outstanding palace, Chairman Kiriyan received the news that his African Initiatives have reached their crossroad with the election of Dr. Wasiri. Chairman Kiriyan placed one call to his faithful aide, Lady Allistair, congratulated her on the outstanding achievement and advised her that the Mezi Initiative must enter the next phase within six months. He said that he was ready to enter in direct negotiations with President Wasiri when appropriate.

Lady Allistair was equally elated. When her lover, Ludmilla Borensky, was surprised that she opened a bottle of champagne to celebrate the election of an unknown Dr. Wasiri of never-heard-country-of Mezi, Lady Allistair told her that before long, all of them would be working for Dr. Wasiri. Ludmilla thought that her friend must be indulging in more than the champagne she had already served twice. Lady Allistair went down in the private office of her basement and called Dr. O'Shea who was now making plans to finally move from Lexington to the retirement house his children bought for him in South Carolina. Dr. O'Shea was also having his own celebration at the fulfillment of a major milestone of Emily's rules. Mrs. Sandy Goshen joined him but did not fully comprehend the meaning of Emily's rules. Dr. O'Shea listened carefully to Lady Allistair and told her that he was prepared to move the Mezi episode to the next level according to the resurfaced Chairman Kiriyan. He did not elaborate to say that Chairman Kiriyan's next level was perfectly fitting Emily's rules. He personally called his protégé, now President Wasiri, to congratulate him on the great event. He also talked to Hasbo who was beyond ecstatic, trembling with joy.

Among the major players of the African Initiatives, His Honorable Massay, who was not following the events in the Republic of Mezi, was the most surprised and sent very quickly a perfunctory congratulatory note to a board member of ABDI for becoming the president of the Republic of Mezi. The evening after the day of his elevation to the presidency of Mezi, Dr. Wasiri had a quiet moment at the campus residence he elected to use as his temporary official residence while Hasbo was sorting out how to redecorate the official government palace. He was reading a stack of congratulatory notes in his office. He noticed one striking similarity between the congratulatory note that Dr. O'Shea talking about a major step in Emily Rules and the first surprising congratulatory note that Chairman Kiriyan sent where he also talked about a major step in African Initiatives. Both notes boldly alluded to his ascendancy to Mezi Presidency as a major milestone in their respective endeavor. Dr. Wasiri put these two notes side by side and wondered aloud if they were talking about the same endeavor he had in mind for Mezi. Dr. Wasiri leaned back and gazed at the sundown over the Nyerengi Lake. The rays of sun were glistening over the lake water strangely giving a reflection of radiant gold over the water that was getting dark. KMC colors were shining over Nyerengi Lake. Dr. Wasiri got up and moved closer to the window opening to the splendid balcony. He smiled at the obvious reflection. He then looked back at the two congratulatory notes on his desk and thought, "What about Mezi and its people? What is it there for Mezi and its people?"

CHAPTER 42

Land Locked

The rain was falling timidly on the yellowing grass outside the main house of the government palace compound. It was very early morning on the last Saturday of the last month of the dry season. The sparse rain was a welcome sign at the end of the dry season, which had brought havoc on the already meager harvest all over the country. The harvest for maize, soybean, cotton, and manioc was catastrophic, thanks to the endless deluge of rain, monsoon-like, which hung over every patch of land, valley, or plateau in the landlocked Republic of Mezi. This was followed by the dry season lasting from the end of May through the beginning of September, producing huge hot dust winds that blew north from the desert of Kalahari on the southern tip of the country. The dust winds blanketed mercilessly every area of the country dedicated to agricultural producing. Food stocks started dwindling rapidly, running well below the republic's twenty-year lowest average. The country was facing a famine of dire proportion.

To make matters worse, the July 15 volcanic eruption from the Mount Tingaro in the western province of Watu had left a lingering thick dust cloud over the entire Nyanga National Wild Life Reserve. The same dust cloud also invaded the entire Nyerengi Lake territory, depleting the country's main source of commercial fishing. It also forced the closing of vast tourist compounds around the largest lake in Africa. For the same reason, the government was left with no choice but to close all tourist areas in Mezi for health risk reasons.

Deprived of foreign tourists' spending, with no significant raw mineral to extract and sell in the world market, and with low cash crops from aggravated food shortages, the Republic of Mezi's future looks beyond bleak, indeed. Restless population in the southwestern part of the country, much closer to the ever-expanding Kalahari Desert, started agitating. A few riots, ignited spontaneously in many parts of the country, were suppressed a week ago.

Mr. Mengi Sakoto, economic adviser to the president, was carrying in his worn out black leather attaché case all the bad news that his excellence, Dr. Kano Wasiri, recently elected president of the Republic of Mezi, was hardly eager to hear or digest.

At the president's urgent request, Mr. Sakoto had spent three sleepless days and nights with his staff and various government economic leaders, compiling all the most recent data to show the economic conditions of the young republic. From whichever spin he tried to give to these data, he came back to the same constant realization; the Republic of Mezi will go through severe calamities in the months to come. These calamities would severely test the fabrics of the young democratic process that started at the dawn of endless military regimes. The country went through a long series of coups fomented by unscrupulous generals. What followed was also a long tentative democratic phase that led, about thirty years later, to the truly democratic and representative election when Dr. Kano Wasiri was brought to the highest office of the republic. As Mr. Sakoto entered his office, Dr. Wasiri, already up since five thirty that morning and fortified by two cups of coffee grown from his native eastern province of Nyerengi, was whistling the latest tune of the local troubadour, while reading the morning newspapers of the capital of Mandi. Dr. Wasiri noticed the long face that Mr. Sakoto was giving and inquired, "Mr. Sakoto, is there something I should know, given the sad and long face you have on this beautiful rainy Saturday morning? Mr. Sakoto, you should appreciate sometime the beautiful things nature had reserved for us. What is the matter?"

"Mr. President, the economic condition of the country is, to put bluntly, no good. I have but bad news to give no matter how you look at it. You have only to look outside at the state of the yellowing grass surrounding the government palace to realize what the country will face in the next few months: drought, famine, and riots. I am not your security advisor, but you need to declare a state of emergency right now before things get worse in a few weeks."

Putting aside the stack of papers in front of him, Dr. Wasiri looked up and using his grave baritone voice said, "Mr. Sakoto, I appreciate your blunt assessment. In good or hard times, a president is better served with the direct unadulterated reading of the nation's economic condition in order to properly steer the ship of state. If you have given me a middle-of-road reading full of confusing charts about times as difficult as the ones we are confronting, I would have stopped you and demanded that you stated clearly whether Mezi economic condition was good or bad. Thankfully, you just did. I know how difficult your position of bearer of very bad news is. I certainly appreciate your honest input. At the end, it is not about you or me. It is about those who are doing on daily basis without food, without job, without basic necessities out there.

That being the case, what does it take to say that the economic condition of the country, as you Mr. Sakoto saw it, is no good? Simple and straight forward. No more no less. If people starve in a few weeks as you are foreseeing, nobody needs to doubt that the economic condition is no good. It should also be stated, Mr. Sakoto, that we signed up not just to state the economic condition of the country but also to provide solutions to economic issues we are confronting. We also signed up to govern no matter how good or how bad was the economic condition we found in the country. People, who trusted the government of this country into our hands, assumed that we signed up to correct bad economic conditions or to improve on good or better economic conditions. Mr. Sakoto, from here on, this government's overriding priority would be to do exactly that, to correct current Mezi's dismal economic conditions very quickly. Now you were right also saying that you are not my security advisor. As you have noticed my security advisor, Mr. Komasi Ballo, is not here. At this hour, he must be sound sleeping after our long all night conversation with some very interesting foreign visitors last night. You have also noticed that I have not declared a state of emergency following your counsel. And that is for a good reason you will understand in days to come."

President Wasiri got up from his large chair, walked up toward the large window giving to the beautiful patio of the presidential palace, still addressing his economic advisor, "In our last government executive council meeting, I was debating the need for our nation to embark on the course of new horizons and new politics. I do not think that many attendees at that meeting understood what I meant. I am afraid that you did not understand either. Let me explain. Yes, we have acceded to the political leadership of this nation through the election process and under the guiding light of KMC, our forward-looking political party. I remember that the notion of KMC was to move the nation to new directions. Let us be honest here for a moment. The claim of new directions has been part of almost all political parties' slogans during the election process the last time around. We have survived and led the pack because of the work that has taken place for a long long time by our various cells throughout the country. That work has identified KMC as the true political party leader in moving the country toward new directions. I strongly believe that it is about time to concretize the notion of new directions we want to move the country to. We need to effectively communicate what are the tenets of the new directions. In my humble opinion, new directions must include new horizons and new politics for Mezi. I need to awaken our people to this realization that we are at the dawn of new horizons, new politics. If I can accomplish about 5 percent of that awakening, I will be very happy.

Believe me; we are not going back to the times of empty slogans of political generations gone by. No, I am not talking slogans here; I am talking about positioning our people to things to come, to new horizons and new politics way beyond everything you have described to me a while ago. The dire economic conditions you described will be negated and repaired by the time we start engaging ourselves in the circle of new horizons and new politics. I am a bit ahead of myself now, and I believe that I have taken much of your time. I sincerely thank you for your economic assessment, and I need to ask you to review something very important for all of us. I want you to get your hands over anything that has been published about Alpha-M from every angle you can get: economic, politic, mining, etc. And please report back to me at the same time next week. Mr. Komasi Ballo will also join us then."

"Gentlemen, in years to come, you will remember today's meeting as the dawn of the era that will make our dear Republic of Mezi shine above all in this world."

This is how Dr. Wasiri started addressing people he referred to as his main brain trust, comprising Sir Injewi Ingoma, the prime minister, Mr. Komasi Ballo, his security advisor, Mr. Mengi Sakoto, his economic advisor, and Professor John Awassa, the chancellor of State University Corporation, his scientific and political advisor.

"I called this meeting to share with you what will drive the successful economic, political, financial, social, and cultural unprecedented expansion of Mezi. Let me give a background first. A week ago, Komasi Ballo and I had the pleasure and the surprise of meeting an important foreign delegation from the company called BI or Baikhal Industries. The delegation was led by BI's chairman called Nadov Kiriyan, The presentation made by this delegation was exceptional in that it placed Mezi's economic resources in the center of BI's in particular, and believe or not, the world's business expansion for next twenty to fifty years. Yes, Gentlemen, if the presentation made by this delegation comes to be materialized, the republic of Mezi will become extremely rich and will meet head-on not just his current citizens basic needs but also his citizens' needs two or three generations to come. The BI's delegation was convinced that Mezi had the unique known deposits of a mineral called Alpha-M in the world. BI is dedicated in bringing about a variety of business applications of Alpha-M in medical, agricultural, and security fields amounting to the equivalent of seven to nine trillion dollars of income to Mezi in the next five years starting this year.

Gentlemen, listen to me now carefully. I would have dismissed Mr. Kiriyan's and his delegation's presentation offhand right then and there as it had happened many times before when we have met with countless of foreign schemers who show up now then in our midst and in every other African chancellery, peddling the latest miracle investment process and God only knows other get-rich-quick schemes. Fortunately, I am thoroughly knowledgeable about what Chairman Kiriyan was talking about and proposing. I have seen and verified the scientific merits of Alpha-M since I, myself, wrote a PhD thesis around the proprieties and deposits location of this mineral. This is something I have been intimately involved for a long long time. I have waited all my life to test and attest to Alpha-M merits. I have prayed that, as we ascended to the political leadership of the Republic of Mezi, we become capable of getting Mezi's people to partake in the riches of its mineral deposits including Alpha-M. I did not know how and when this was going to happen. I am happily relieved that it is about to happen now. I am inviting each one of you now to react to what you have heard, starting with Mr. Sakoto. I have asked him without much elaboration to gather as much information around Alpha-M."

After the president spoke, there was a long moment of silence among his four senior advisors. It was the same and a bit startling for Mr. Komasi Ballo. Although he had assisted in the previous week's meeting, including the presentation from BI's delegation, he did not quite appreciate the significant impact that meeting had left with his boss, Dr. Wasiri. He had already dismissed and was ready to dismiss the meeting as one of endless schemes presentations he had been regularly invited by Dr. Wasiri to witness. Yet, he should have sensed that that meeting was a bit different. For once, he was not invited back by the president to review and laugh about the latest schemes as Dr. Wasiri had done many times in the past. When the meeting with BI concluded very late that Friday, Mr. Komasi Ballo was happy to be excused by the president to leave and get some needed sleep. He was to be flown about noon Saturday to Mombassa, Kenya, to attend a regional conference on Eastern African States security. He was not aware that Dr. Wasiri continued conversing alone with Mr. Kiriyan, the chairman of BI, until about three thirty in the morning. When he came back from Kenya the following week on Wednesday, he did not get the chance to review the BI meeting with the president as other pressing security matters came forward, and he was trusted to deal with them. He saw the president briefly on two or three other occasions during the rest of the week and at each occasion, Dr. Wasiri reminded him about the present scheduled Saturday morning meeting. He had no inclination of what will be discussed.

He had always considered these Saturday morning meetings as Dr. Wasiri's ways to review most of current issues of the day in a more relaxed atmosphere with his most trusted advisors. These meetings were held without a fixed agenda. The president raised an issue, and this was kicked around until some consensus was reached on ways to resolve it and time permitting, another issue was tabled, and on and on until about noon when the meeting was usually called off and the president invited to lunch whoever wanted to come. The fact that Mr. Sakoto and Dr. Awassa were to take part in this meeting convinced him of more of the same. Today's meeting was a bit different. It took an air of solemnity about it. The president's tone of delivery was grave and very intense.

At this point, having fully digested the meaning of the meeting, Komasi directed his remarks to the assembled brain trust and President Wasiri:

"Mr. President, I absolutely had no idea that the last week meeting was so important and crucial to the future of our republic. I sat there thinking that BI's presentation amounted to a brilliant scheme by a group of Russian businessmen. I disregarded the entire meeting from the time there was a talk of trillion-dollar income to the Republic of Mezi. Frankly, it was and is still too good to believe. I did not know that you wrote a PhD thesis around Alpha-M. I failed completely in my task to listen and provide important counsel to you in matter of such high importance. I will . . ."

Dr. Wasiri raised his hand to cut his security advisor, "Mr. Komasi, I appreciate your candor, and I would not allow you to add any more to what you had in mind at this time. You are my security advisor and a very good one. Thank you. I never expected you to know every bit detail of my life prior to my political involvement in Mezi. I expect you to assist me in the matters of Mezi's security for a long time, because I trust you. I have consistently depended on these Saturday meetings to call on each of you, my trusted senior advisors, to allow you to provide me counsel away from the daily professional and informal atmosphere of the government, surrounded by a multitude of officials. There is nothing wrong with these official channels of government, they serve their purpose. But I always need more than the formal discourse, and I need your counsel in informal settings. This is my main conduit, and I would not let this meeting to degenerate into an appraisal conference. By the way, I have asked Mr. Sakoto to gather as much information as he could about Alpha-M for our benefit.

When I made the request, I anticipated that Mr. Sakoto was going to consult with Dr. John Awassa for his important scientific input. It is not by accident that Professor Awassa was invited to this meeting. Now let us hear from Mengi and John to share what they had dug up about Alpha-M."

Mengi and John nodded. And Mr. Sakoto started talking:

"Mr. President, with John's help, I have assembled a great deal of information about Alpha-M. From the onset, I was completely surprised and baffled by your request. Only when I came upon a brief description of your PhD thesis, my attention was piqued. John alerted me about your thesis to tell you the truth. The University of Kentucky for obvious reasons could not release the full text of your thesis. But your thesis advisor, a professor Anthony O'Shea, retired and residing in South Carolina, provided us with a copy after we solicited your wife's assistance in securing it. She knew exactly how to get it. We are sorry having troubled the first Lady but our curiosity took the best of us. Your thesis advisor was delighted to hear from us and took the liberty to visit with us at the office of the Cultural and Scientific Counselor at the Republic of Mezi's embassy in Washington, DC. He personally delivered this copy of your thesis and many more related papers and articles, including his own. Professor Anthony O'Shea also provided us with hundreds of references around the world to deepen our understanding of Alpha-M mineral.

This enabled us to follow up and expand our data gathering using our Cultural and Scientific Counselors stationed in our embassies in London, Paris, Moscow, Berlin, Tokyo, and Beijing. I have to warn you that in all of these documents, we did not find any that addresses the current state of business applications for Alpha-M. Most of these papers including your own thesis describe outstanding potential Alpha-M applications in very general terms. There was no mention of BI Company or any other business enterprises in these references. Some of these potential applications are so far ahead of the current state of technology, frankly to tell you the truth; they appear to be science fiction like. Until you talked today, the process of gathering all these documents by which I went through made me wonder what you really had in mind. I asked myself whether you were shooting for the stars. The more I got engaged in this, the more I became baffled and worried. I said to myself, Here we are in the middle of dire crises the country has ever experienced, and I am collecting data about science fiction applications.

Mr. President, this was not a pleasant week for my deputies and me. All along, I tried as hard as I could to reserve judgment about your motives. It was not easy. Since I am not versed in the mining engineering science, I called upon John Awassa to digest these documents. John was extremely useful. I will also confess that he was more generous and much closer to your assessment than I was in his review of the documents we had assembled. Being a scientist, John was excited by the possibilities that Alpha-M presented. He kept repeating to me that if your thesis was right on target, the Republic of Mezi was in for the most exciting periods of the whole planet Earth. The only thing John questioned was the source of investment to harness Alpha-M potentials. Who will be willing to plug billions and billions of dollars, close to fifty billion in his preliminary estimation, to mine Alpha-M in those high plateaus in the eastern region of Mezi? He probably can speak for himself now that he came to realize that he was much closer to your version."

It was Dr. John Awassa's turn to speak but he deferred back to Dr. Wasiri by saying that Mr. Sakoto had provided a correct and appropriate summary of their work the past week. He added that he was more excited to hear what Dr. Wasiri wanted them to do in order to accomplish the goals of making Alpha-M the main driver of Mezi's economic progress for years to come. He concluded by revealing that among the documents they had gathered, there was an interesting story dating back to 1903 when Germany established Mezi as a colony. The story captured his imagination since he read it, and he felt compelled to share it. The story related that a German missionary went by foot to the high plateaus area to convert the indigenous population to Christianity. This missionary was generally unsuccessful in reaching the plateaus people. Apparently, there was a powerful indigenous sorcerer with tremendous following among the plateaus people. This high priest and sorcerer will cure any sickness with the imposition of a luminous rock he had in his possession. He called the rock Kany. The high plateaus people held him in very high regards and considered him as their rightful chief. They had no use for the Germany missionary conversion. They literally got whatever they wanted from their chief with his magic luminous rock. The harvest season always started with dedication from the chief rolling the luminous rock along each village field, then the hunting season will kick off with the chief capturing the largest sport, again thanks to the rock; the fishing will not start without the chief plunging in the river with the luminous rock. The harvest, hunting, and fishing always brought more than enough to the people from the high plateaus. They revered the chief with the luminous rock. The German colonial authority sought in vain to get the chief to reveal how and where he got the luminous rock.

One day, the German authority decided to put an end to this indigenous chief power and attempted to wrestle the rock from him. Before the chief was arrested and killed, he managed to hand the luminous rock to one of his trusted aides for safekeeping. The aide took the rock to one of the highest mountain in the area and dropped it in the deepest cave he could find. A German scientist passing through Mezi at the time heard the story and speculated that the luminous rock seemed to have all the properties of Alpha-M mineral. With the departed chief and the missing rock, the people of high plateaus were left at the mercy of the German authority. The story went on to speculate that, apparently, having lost the Republic of Mezi to England after World War I for war reparations, one of the Nazi Germany's major ambitions in Africa was to retake Mezi as a colony in order to mine Alpha-M in the Tongeo eastern province high plateaus.

John asked Dr. Wasiri if he heard about this story before or when he was working on his thesis. Dr. Wasiri said that he never heard of the tribal chief, his luminous rock, or the help he provided to the plateaus people, although he had visited the region many times in the past. Dr. Wasiri was intrigued by the story as Dr. John Awassa was giving it. He decided that from then on, they would call Alpha-M by its indigenous name of Kany.

ABOUT THE AUTHOR

Born in 1949 in Kinshasa, Democratic Republic of Congo/Zaire with high school concentration over Latin and major international literary works, Zephirin Ebonzo, "Xebo", pursued university studies successively in Dakar Senegal, Louvain Belgium and NYU in New York where he received an MBA in International Finance. After more than thirty years of professional growth and accomplishments in various assignments in the US Corporate world in areas of System Analysis, Internal Auditing and International Finance, and no matter what dispositions and predilections which visited or directed him one way or another, he kept being drawn back to the endless shocking and regressing conditions of political and economic despair in parts of Africa he came from. "Kany Rising" is an attempt to set a record straight for a completely different and better horizon if and only if different objective propositions and criteria were to be applied and followed.

Family

"On the Party Cruise around Manhattan, New York with Lovely Wife, Jessy Ebonzo, Grand-Children, Mayelle Guillaume & Mateo Guillaume."